SPACE-AGE ADVENTURE!

The Legion of Space. Her name was Aladoree Anthar, and her safety was critical to the System because she was the only person alive who knew the secret of AKKA—the most awesome weapon humanity possessed.

The Cometeers. While stargazing one night, Bob Star, heir to AKKA, noted something odd in the constellation Virgo—a greenish fleck which, unknown to Bob, had been under the scrutiny of the System's top astronomers for weeks. In their opinion, it was a comet of monstrous proportions . . . a grave threat to the System. It had to be removed—using AKKA.

One Against the Legion. Hoping to clear his name after being convicted of a murder he didn't commit, Legionnaire Chan Derron escapes from prison—and so becomes the prime suspect when a mysterious being, known only as the Basilisk, launches a terrifying crusade . . . aimed right at the heart of the System.

LEGIONNAIRES TO THE RESCUE!

Books by Jack Williamson

The Cometeers
The Starchild Trilogy (with Frederick Pohl)
Three from the Legion

Published by POCKET BOOKS

THREE FROM THE LEGION

THE LEGION

Jack Williamson

PUBLISHED BY POCKET BOOKS NEW YORK

POCKET BOOKS, a Simon & Schuster division of
GULF & WESTERN CORPORATION
1230 Avenue of the Americas, New York, N.Y. 10020

CONTENTS

THE LEGION OF SPACE

THE COMETEERS

ONE AGAINST THE LEGION

ONE AGAINST THE LEGION

NOWHERE NEAR

THE LEGION
OF SPACE

DEDICATION

To all the readers and the writers of that new litera-
ture called science-fiction, who find mystery, wonder,
and high adventure in the expanding universe of
knowledge, and who sometimes seek to observe and
to forecast the vast impact of science upon the lives
and minds of men.

PROLOGUE

The Man Who Remembered Tomorrow

"Well, Doctor, what's your verdict?"

He sat up on the examination table, with the sheet wrapped around his bent and stringy frame, and firmly commanded my nurse to bring back his clothes. He looked at me, his bright blue eyes sharply curious and yet oddly unafraid—for I knew he expected a sentence of death.

"Acquittal, John," I told him honestly. "You're really indestructible. Remarkable shape, for a man of your age —except for that knee. You'll make me a good patient and a better chess opponent for the next twenty years."

But old John Delmar shook his weatherbeaten head, very seriously.

"No, Doctor." In that same tone of quiet and unexcited certainty, he might have said today was Tuesday. "No, Doctor, I've less than three weeks. I've known for several years that I'm going to die at eleven-seven on the morning of March 23, 1945."

"Nonsense," I told him. "Not likely—unless you jump in front of a truck. That knee may always be a little stiff, but there's certainly nothing else—"

"I know the date." His thin, old voice had a flat, impersonal conviction. "You see, I read it on a tombstone." He didn't seem to regard that statement as remarkable. "I came in this morning just to see if you can tell me what it is that I'm to die of."

He looked entirely too sane and cool to fall victim to any superstitious notion.

"You can forget the idea of that," I assured him heartily. "Physically, you're sounder than most men twenty years younger. Except for that knee, and a few assorted scars—"

"Please don't think I want to question your diagnosis,

3

but I'm really quite positive." He seemed apologetic, and oddly hesitant. "You see, Doctor, I've an unusual—well, call it a gift. I've meant, sometime, to tell you about it. That is, if you'd care to hear—"

He paused, diffidently.

I had wondered a long time, about old John Delmar. A faded, stiff little man, with thin gray hair and blue eyes that were curiously bright, strangely *young*. Still erect and agile, for all the years he owned to, he walked with a slight, quick limp from that old bullet wound in his knee.

We had first met when he came home from the war in Spain—he looked me up to bring me word of a friend of mine, not a third his age, who had died beside him, fighting with the Loyalists. I liked him. A lonely old soldier, he didn't talk too much about his campaigns. We discovered a mutual interest in chess, and he made a pleasant companion. He had a youth of heart, an eager and unquenchable vitality, rare in a man so old. My medical interest, besides, was aroused by his durable physique.

For he had endured many things.

He had always been reticent. I was, I believe, his most intimate friend through those last, unwontedly peaceful years, yet he had given me no more than the barest hints of his long and remarkable life. He grew up, he told me, in the frontier West; he rode with a gun in a cattle war when he was only a boy, and somehow he got into the Texas Rangers a little short of the legal age. Later he served in the Rough Riders, and in the Boer War, and under Porfirio Díaz. In 1914 he joined the British Army —to make up, he said, for fighting the British in South Africa. Later he was in China and in the Rif, in the Gran Chaco and in Spain. It was a Spanish prison camp that stiffened his bad knee. His hard-seasoned body began to fail him at last, and he finally came home, too old to fight again. That was when we met.

I knew, too, that he was busy with some literary project—dropping in at his rather shabby rooms for a pipe and a game of chess, I had noticed his desk piled with closely written pages. Until he came to the office that morning in the spring of 1945, however, I had supposed that he was merely writing the memoirs of his colorful past. I had no inkling that his manuscripts dealt with recollections of the more wonderful future.

Fortunately, no patient was waiting that morning, and his quiet air of matter-of-fact certainty about the moment

4

of his death piqued my curiosity. When he was dressed again, I made him fill his pipe and told him that I'd be glad to hear.

"It's a good thing that most fighting men are killed before they get too old to fight," he began a little awkwardly, settling back in his chair and easing his knee with thin, quivering hands. "That's what I was thinking, one cold morning, the year this war began.

"You remember when I came home to New York—or I called it coming home. But I found myself a stranger. Most people don't have the time that you do, Doctor, for old fighting men. There was nothing for me to do. I was useless as a worn-out gun. That wet, gusty morning—it was April thirteenth, I remember—I sat down on a bench in Central Park, to think things over. I got cold. And I decided—well, that I'd already lived too long.

"I was just getting up from the bench, to go back to the room and get my old automatic, when I—remembered!

"That's the only word I know. Memory. It seems a little strange, though, to speak of remembering things that haven't happened yet. That won't happen, some of them, for a thousand years and more. But there's no other word.

"I've talked to scientists about it, Doctor. A psychologist, first. A behaviorist. He laughed. It didn't fit in, he said, with the concepts of behaviorism. A man, he said, is just a machine. Everything a man does is just mechanical reaction to stimulus.

"But, if that's so, there are stimuli that the behaviorists have never found.

"There was another man who didn't laugh. A physicist from Oxford, a lecturer on Einstein—relativity. He didn't laugh. He seemed to believe what I told him. He asked questions about my—memories. But there wasn't much I could tell him, then.

"What he told me helped to ease my mind—the thing had had me worried. I wanted to talk about it to you, Doctor. But we were just getting to be good chess companions, and I didn't want you to think me too odd.

"Anyhow, this Oxford man told me that Space and Time aren't real, apart. And they aren't really different. They fade one into the other all around us. He spoke of the *continuum* and *two-way time* and a theory of the *serial universe*. I didn't understand it all. But there's no real reason, he said, why we shouldn't remember the future—all of us. In theory, he said, our minds ought

5

to be able to trace *world-lines* into the future, just as easily as into the past.

"Hunches and premonitions and dreams, he believed, are sometimes real memories of things yet to come. I didn't understand all he said, but he did convince me that the thing wasn't—well, insanity. I had been afraid, Doctor.

"He wanted to know more about what I—remembered. But that was years ago. It was just scattered impressions, then, most of them vague and confused. It's a power, I think, that most people have to some degree—it simply happens to be better developed in me. I've always had hunches, some vague sense to warn me of danger—which is probably why I'm still alive. But the first clear memory of the future came that day in the park. And it was many months before I could call them up at will.

"You don't understand it, I suppose. I'll try to describe that first experience, in the park. I slipped on the wet pavement, and fell back on the bench—I had got cold, sitting there, and I wasn't so long back from Spain then, you know.

"And suddenly I wasn't in the park at all.

"I was still falling, all right. I was in the same position—but no longer on the Earth. All around me was a weird plain. It was blazing with a glare of light, pitted with thousands of craters, ringed with mountains higher than any I had ever seen. The Sun was burning down out of a blue sky dark as midnight, and full of stars. There was another body in the heavens, huge and greenish.

"A fantastic black machine was gliding down over those terrible mountains. It was larger than you'd think a flying machine could be, and utterly strange. It had just hit me with some weapon, and I was reeling back under the agony of the wound. Beside me was a great explosion of red gas. The cloud of it poured over me, and burned my lungs, and blotted out everything.

"It was some time before I realized that I had been on the Moon—or rather that I had picked up the last thoughts of a man dying there. I had never had time for astronomy, but one day I happened to see a photograph of the lunar craters—and recognized them, and knew that the greenish crescent had been the Earth itself.

"And the shock of that discovery only increased my bewilderment. It was nearly a year before I understood that I was developing an ability to recall the future. But that first incident happened in the thirtieth century, in the

6

conquest of the Moon by the Medusæ—the man whose last moments I shared was one of the human colonists they murdered.

"The faculty improved with practice, like any other. It's simply telepathy, I'm convinced, carrying thought across Time and not merely through Space. Just remember that neither Space nor Time is real; they are both just aspects of one reality.

"At first I got contact only with minds under great stress, like that of the dying colonist. Even yet, there are difficulties—or I shouldn't have asked you to examine me this morning, Doctor. But I've managed to follow human history, pretty well, through the next thousand years. That's what I've been writing.

"The history of the future!

"The conquest of space is what thrills me most. Partly because it's the most difficult achievement of human engineering, the most daring and the most dangerous. And partly, I suppose, because my own descendants played a big part in it."

An eager ring of enthusiasm had risen in his voice, and now he paused awkwardly, as if suddenly self-conscious because of it. His sharp blue eyes searched my face. I kept silent until he went on, sure that the least show of doubt would stop him.

"Yes, Doctor, I've a son." His thin brown face showed a wistful pride. "I don't see much of him, because he's a very busy young man. I failed to make a soldier out of him, and I used to think he'd never amount to much. I tried to get him to join up, long before Pearl Harbor, but he wouldn't hear of it.

"No, Don never took to fighting. He's something you call a nuclear physicist, and he's got himself a nice, safe deferment. Now he's on a war job, somewhere out in New Mexico. I'm not even supposed to know where he is, and I can't tell you what he's doing—but the thesis he wrote, at Tech, was something about the metal uranium."

Old John Delmar gave me a proud and wistful smile.

"No, I used to think that Don would never accomplish much, but now I know that he designed the first atomic reaction motor. I used to think he had no guts—but he was man enough to pilot the first manned atomic rocket ever launched."

I must have goggled, for he explained:

"That was 1956, Doctor—the past tense just seems

7

more convenient. With this—this capacity of mine, you see, I shared that flight with Don, until his rocket exploded, outside the stratosphere. He died, of. course. But he left a son, to carry on the Delmar name.

"And that grandson of mine reached the Moon, Doctor, in a military rocket. After uranium was discovered there, he went back to take command of the American outpost —a little camp of air-tight domes, over the mines. But the ghastly atomic wars, in the 1990's, isolated the Moon. My grandson died there, with the rest of his little garrison, and it was nearly two hundred years before human civilization was far enough recovered from the wars to build another space rocket.

"But it was a Miles Delmar, late in the twenty-second century, who finally went back to the dead mining camps on the Moon, and then set out for Mars. He left too much shielding off his atomic reaction motor, to lighten his ship for that voyage, and the leaking radiation killed him and all his crew. The dead ship carried the bodies on, and crashed in the Syrtis Major.

"Miles's son, Zane Delmar, patented the geodyne— which was a vast advance over the heavy, dangerous atomic reactors. He found the wreck of his father's ship on Mars, and survived an attack from the native Martian beings, and later died of a Venusian jungle-fever. The victory of men over space wasn't easy—quite! But Zane's three sons carried on the war. And they made a huge fortune out of the geodyne.

"In the next century, all the solar system was pretty well explored, as far out as the moon of Neptune. It was fifty years more before a John Ulnar reached Pluto—our family name was changed, about that time, from Delmar to Ulnar, to fit a new universal identification system.

"His fuel exhausted, so that he couldn't return, John managed to keep himself alive for four years, alone on the Black Planet. He left a diary that his nephew found, twenty years later. A strange document, the diary!

"It was Mary Ulnar—a peculiar Amazon she must have been—who began the conquest of the silica-armored desert life of Mars. And Arthur Ulnar, her brother, who led the first fleet to attack the cold, half-metallic beings which had extended their own rule over the four great moons of Jupiter—he died on Io.

"More battles, however, were fought in the laboratory than in space. Explorers and colonists met terrific, endless difficulties with bacteria, atmospheres, gravitations, chemical dangers. As planetary engineers, the Ulnars contributed a full share to that new science, which, with gravity generators, synthetic atmospheres, and climate-controls, could finally transform a frozen, stony asteroid into a tiny paradise.

"And the Ulnars took a generous reward.

"For a dark chapter of the family history begins with the twenty-sixth century. By then, the conquest of the solar system was finished. The Ulnar family had been the leaders, and they seized the spoils. They had controlled interplanetary commerce since the time of Zane and his geodyne, and they finally dominated the whole System.

"One bold tycoon had himself crowned Eric the First, Emperor of the Sun. For two hundred years his descendants ruled all the planets as absolute despots. Their reign, I'm sorry to say, was savagely oppressive. There were endless outbreaks for liberty, cruelly put down.

"Adam the Third, however, was at last forced to abdicate—his great mistake was an effort to suppress the freedom of scientific research. The scientists overthrew him, and the Green Hall Council launched the first real democracy of history. For the next two centuries, a genuine civilization existed in the System, defended by a small body of picked and well-trained fighting men, the Legion of Space."

Wistfully again, old John Delmar shook his lean gray head.

"If I could have lived a thousand years later!" he whispered. "I might have fought with that Legion. For that golden age of peace was broken. Another Eric Ulnar ventured away into space, the first man to circle another star. He reached that strange dwarf sun that astronomers know as Barnard's Runaway Star—the few nearer stars having proved to possess no planets. And he brought back terror and suffering and the shadow of doom to the human planets.

"The mad ambition of that remote descendant of mine brought war between our System and another," that slow old voice said sadly. "War and invasion, treason and terror. Even the Legion was betrayed.

"And then there was an epic achievement by a few loyal men of the Legion of Space—perhaps the most heroic thing that men ever did. One of those few was

9

another Ulnar. John Ulnar. I like to think that his name came down from me."

My office nurse chose that unfortunate moment to announce another patient. And little John Delmar hastily knocked out his pipe, apologetic for having taken so much of my time. He came to his feet, unsteady on his bad knee, and a vision seemed to fade from his oddly bright, *live* blue eyes.

"I must be going, Doctor." And he added, quietly, "Now you see how I know that I'm due to die on the morning of March twenty-third."

"You're sound as a bell," I insisted again. "And much too sane to let any such notion— But this is a very remarkable thing you've told me, John. I wish you had mentioned it before; and now I'd like very much to see those manuscripts. Why don't you publish them?"

"Perhaps," he promised vaguely. "But so few would believe, and I don't like to expose myself to any charge of fraud."

I let him go, reluctantly. I meant to call at his rooms, to hear the rest of his story and read his manuscripts. But the urgencies of wartime practice kept me busy all that week—until his landlady phoned me, to say that poor old Mr. Delmar had been down sick with a cold, for the last two days, alone in his rooms.

In two hours, in spite of his feeble protests, he was in the hospital. If I had only made the time to call, a few days before—but yet, perhaps, as he quietly believed, it may be that the future is really already determined, as firmly unchangeable as the past.

Influenza, with pulmonary complications. The outlook seemed good enough, the first few days, and I knew that old John Delmar's fighting heart had pulled him through a hundred more desperate situations. But sulfa and penicillin failed. His old heart surrendered. He knew he was going to die, and he did—quite peacefully, under an oxygen tent, on the morning of March 23. I was standing by his bed, and I looked at my watch.

The time was eleven-seven.

Whatever others may decide, I was well enough convinced, even before the proof of death. John Delmar at first wished to have his manuscripts destroyed, because his splendid scheme of a full history of the next thousand years was far from complete, but I persuaded him to leave the finished sections in my hands. As mere fiction, they would be enormously entertaining. As a real prevision of future history, they are more than fascinating.

The selection which follows deals with the adventures of John Star—born John Ulnar—who was a young soldier in the Legion of Space, in the thirtieth century, when human treason sought an alliance with the unearthly Medusæ, and so brought alien horror and black disaster to the unwarned worlds of men.

1

A Fort on Mars

"I'm reporting, Major Stell, for orders."

John Star, lean and trim in his new Legion uniform, stood at attention before the desk where the stern, white-haired officer sat toying with the silver model of a space cruiser. He felt the major's merciless eyes come up from the tiny ship to search out every detail of his small-boned, hard physique. Taut and almost quivering, he endured that probing gaze, burningly anxious to know his first assignment.

"Are you ready, John Ulnar, to accept your first order in the Legion as it should be accepted, to put duty above everything else?"

"I hope so, sir. I believe so."

What would it be?

"I hope so too, John Ulnar."

John Star was then called John Ulnar; the "Star" is a title of distinction given him later by the Green Hall. John Star we shall call him, according to the Green Hall's edict.

This day, one of the first in the thirtieth century, had been the supreme, the most thrilling day of his twenty-one years. It marked the end of his five arduous years in the Legion Academy, on Catalina Island. Now the ceremonies were finished. His life in the Legion was about to begin.

Where, he wondered eagerly, would his first tour of duty be? On some cruiser of the Legion Patrol, in the cold wastes of space? At some isolated outpost in the exotic, terrible jungles of Venus? Or perhaps in the Guard of the Green Hall itself? He strove to conceal his consuming impatience.

"John Ulnar," old Major Stell spoke at last, with maddening deliberation. "I hope you realize the meaning of duty."

"I think I do, sir."

"Because," the officer continued, as slowly, "you are being assigned to a duty that is peculiarly important."

13

"What is it, sir?"

He could not resist the desire to hasten the satisfaction of his anxious curiosity, but Major Stell refused to hurry. His keen eyes still scanned John Star pitilessly, while his thin fingers continued to turn the silver toy on his desk.

"John Ulnar, you are being given a duty that has previously been entrusted only to seasoned, chosen veterans of the Legion. It surprised me, I may say, that you were selected for it. Your lack of experience will be a disadvantage to you."

"Not too much of one, I hope, sir."

Why didn't he come to the point?

"The orders for your assignment, John Ulnar, came directly from Commander Ulnar himself. Does it happen that you are related to the Commander of the Legion, and his nephew, Eric Ulnar, the explorer?"

"Yes, sir. Distantly."

"That must explain your orders. But if you fail in this duty, John Ulnar, don't expect any favor of the Commander to save you from the consequences."

"No, sir. Of course not!"

How long could he endure this anxiety?

"The service to which you are assigned, John Ulnar, is not well known. It is in fact secret. But it is the most important that can be entrusted to a soldier of the Legion. Your responsibility will be to the Green Hall itself. Any failure, I warn you, even if due only to negligence, will mean disgrace and very severe punishment."

"Yes, sir."

What could it be?

"John Ulnar, did you ever hear of AKKA?"

"Akka? Why, I think not, sir."

"It isn't 'akka.' AKKA. It's a symbol."

"Yes, sir. What does it mean?"

At last, was he coming to it?

"Men have given their lives to learn that, John Ulnar. And men have died for knowing. Only one person in the System knows precisely what those four letters stand for. That person is a young woman. The most important single duty of the Legion is to guard her."

"Yes, sir." A breathless whisper.

"Because, John Ulnar, AKKA is the most precious thing that humanity possesses. I need not tell you what it is. But the loss of it, I may say—the loss of the young woman

14

who knows it—would mean unprecedented disaster to humanity."

"Yes, sir." He waited, painfully.

"I could assign you to no duty more important than to join the few trusted men who guard the young woman. And to no duty more perilous! For desperate men know that AKKA exists, know that possession of it would enable them to dictate to the Green Hall—or to destroy it.

"No risk, nor any difficulty, will deter them from attempting to get possession of the young woman, to force the secret from her. You must be unceasingly alert against attempts by stealth or violence. The girl—and AKKA—must be protected at any cost."

"Yes, sir. Where is the girl?"

"That information cannot be given you, until you are out in space. The danger that you might pass it on, unwittingly or otherwise, is too great. The girl's safety depends on her whereabouts being kept secret. If they become known—the whole Legion fleet might be inadequate to defend her.

"You are assigned, John Ulnar, to join the guard of AKKA. You will report at once, at the Green Hall, to Captain Eric Ulnar, and place yourself under his orders."

"Under Eric Ulnar!"

He was astonished and overjoyed to know that he was to serve under his famous kinsman, the great explorer of space, just returned from his daring voyage beyond the limits of the System, to the far, strange planet of Barnard's Runaway Star.

"Yes. John Ulnar, I hope you never forget the overwhelming importance of the duty before you. . . . That is all."

Queerly, John Star's heart ached at leaving the old campus of the Academy, at parting from his classmates. Queerly, for he was a-thrill with eagerness. Mystery lay ahead, the promise of peril, the adventure of meeting his famous kinsman. With native optimism, he ignored Major Stell's grim hints of the possibility of disastrous failure.

From the ports of the descending strato-flier, that afternoon, he first saw the Green Hall—seat of the Supreme Council of the united planets.

Like a great emerald, it shimmered darkly cool in a waste of sunbaked New Mexico mesa—a colossal marvel of green, translucent glass. Three thousand feet the square

15

central tower leaped up, crowned with the landing stage to which the strato-plane was dropping. The four great colonnaded wings spread over a full mile of luxuriantly verdant parkland—a solitary jewel in the desert, under the rugged, mile-high wall of the Sandias.

John Star was a-throb with eagerness to see Eric Ulnar, then in the full radiance of his fame for commanding the first successful expedition beyond the System—if an expedition could be called successful when but a fourth of its members returned, and most of those dying of a fearful malady involving insanity and hideous bodily disfigurement.

Dark chapters, and silent ones, were in the story of the voyage. But the public, like John Star, had ignored them. Honors had been showered on Eric Ulnar, while most of his companions lay forgotten in hospital cells, gibbering of the horrors of that remote solitary planet, while their bodies rotted away unspeakably, beyond the aid or the understanding of medical science.

John Star found Eric Ulnar waiting for him in a private room in the vast Green Hall. Long golden hair and slender figure made the young officer almost femininely handsome. Burning eyes and haughty airs proclaimed his passion and his insolent pride. Retreating chin and irresolute mouth betrayed the man's fatal weakness.

"John Ulnar, I believe you are a relative of mine."

"I believe I am, sir," and John Star, concealing the stab of disappointment that pierced even through his admiration. He stood at attention, while the arrogant eyes of Eric Ulnar boldly scanned his lean body, hard and capable from the five grinding years of Academy training.

"You are under some obligation, I believe, to Adam Ulnar?"

"I am, sir. I am an orphan. It was the Commander of the Legion who got me the Academy appointment. But for that, I might never have been able to enter the Legion."

"Adam Ulnar is my uncle. He had me select you for the duty ahead. I hope you will serve me loyally."

"Of course, sir. Aside from the obligation, you are my superior in the Legion."

Eric Ulnar smiled; for a moment his face was almost attractive, in spite of its weakness and its pride.

"I'm sure we shall get on," he said. "But I may require services of you as a kinsman that I couldn't ask of you as my subordinate in the Legion."

John Star wondered what such services might be. He could not hide the fact that Eric Ulnar was not all he had hoped of the heroic explorer of space. Something about him roused a vague distrust, though the man had been his idol.

"You're ready to start for our post?"

"Of course."

"We shall go aboard the cruiser, then, at once."

"We're leaving the Earth?"

"You'll serve yourself best, John," Eric Ulnar said with an air of cutting superiority, "by obeying orders and asking no questions."

An elevator lifted them to the glittering confusion of the landing stage on the green glass tower. The *Scorpion* was waiting for them there, a swift new space cruiser, taperingly cylindrical, a bare hundred feet long, all silver-white save for black projecting rockets.

Two Legionnaires met them at the air-lock, and came with them aboard. Vors, lean, stringy, rat-faced; Kimplen, tall, haggard-eyed, wolfish. Both years older than John Star, both, he soon learned, veterans of the interstellar expedition—among the few who had escaped that mysterious malady—they displayed for his inexperience a patronizing contempt that annoyed him. It was strange, he thought, that men of their type should have been chosen to guard the infinitely precious AKKA. He would not, he thought, care to trust either of them with the price of a meal.

The *Scorpion* was provisioned, fueled, her crew of ten aboard and at their posts. Her air-lock quickly sealed, her multiple rockets vomiting blue flame, she flashed through the atmosphere into the freedom of the void.

A thousand miles off, safe in the frozen, star-domed vacuum of space, the pilot cut out the rockets. At an order from Eric Ulnar, he set the cruiser's nose for the far red spark of Mars and started the geodyne generators. Quietly humming, their powerful fields reacting against, altering, the curvature of space itself, the geodynes—more technically, electro-magnetic geodesic deflectors—drove the *Scorpion* across the hundred million miles to Mars, with an acceleration and a final velocity that science had once declared impossible.

Forgetting his uneasy mistrust of Vors and Kimplen, John Star enjoyed the voyage. The eternal miracles of space fascinated him through long hours. Ebon sky;

frozen pinpoints of stars, many-colored, motionless; silver clouds of nebulae; the supernal Sun, blue, winged with red coronal fire.

Three meals were served in the narrow galley. After twenty hours, the geodynes—too powerful for a safe maneuver in the close vicinity of a planet—were stopped. The *Scorpion* fell, checked by rocket blasts, toward the night side of the planet Mars.

Standing by the navigator, Eric Ulnar gave him directions from some private memorandum. About the whole proceeding was an air of mystery, of secret haste, of daring unknown dangers, that mightily intrigued John Star. Yet he had the sense of something irregular; he was troubled by a little haunting fear that all was not as it ought to be.

On a stony Martian desert they landed, far, apparently, from any city or inhabited, fertile "canal." Low, dark hills loomed near in the starlight. John Star, with Eric Ulnar and rat-faced Vors and wolfish Kimplen, disembarked; beside them was lowered their meager baggage and a little pile of freight.

Four Legionnaires came up presently through the darkness, the part of the guard, John Star understood, that they had come to relieve. The four went aboard, after their leader had exchanged some documents with Eric Ulnar; the valve clanged behind them. Blue flames jetted from the rockets; the *Scorpion* roared away, a dwindling blue comet, soon lost amid the blazing Martian stars.

John Star and the others waited in the desert for daylight. The Sun burst up suddenly, shrunken and blue, after the briefest yellow dawn, flooding the red landscape abruptly with harsh radiance.

Under violet zenith and lemon-green horizons, the ancient planet lay weirdly and grimly desolate. Lonely wastes of ocher drift-sand, rippled with low crescent dunes. Cruel, jutting ridges of red volcanic rock, projecting from yellow sand like broken fangs. Solitary boulders, carved by pitiless, wind-driven sand into grotesque scarlet monsters.

Crouching above the plain were the hills. Low, ancient, worn down by erosion of ages immemorial, like all the mountains of dying Mars. Tumbled masses of red stone; broken palisades of red-black, columnar rock; ragged, wind-carved precipices.

Sprawling across the hill-top was an ancient, half-ruined

18

fort. Massive walls rambled along the rim of the precipices, studded here and there with square, heavy towers. It was all of the red volcanic stone characteristic of the Martian desert, all crumbling to slow ruin.

The fortress must date, John Star knew, from the conquest of the weird, silica-armored Martians. It must have been abandoned a full three centuries ago. But it was not now deserted.

A sentry met them when they climbed to the gate, a very fat, short, blue-nosed man in Legion uniform, who had been dozing lazily on a bench in the warm sunlight. He examined Eric Ulnar's documents with a fishy eye.

"Ah, so you're the relief guard?" he wheezed. " 'Tis mortal seldom we see a living being here. Pass on, inside. Captain Otan is in his quarters beyond the court."

Within the crumbling red walls they found a large, open court, surrounded with a gallery, many doors and windows opening upon it. A tiny fountain played in a little garden of vivid flowers. Beyond was a tennis court, from which a man and a slender girl vanished hastily as they entered.

John Star's heart leaped with excitement at sight of the girl. She must be, he felt immediately certain, keeper of the mysterious AKKA. She was the girl he had been ordered to guard! Recalling Major Stell's warning of desperate, unknown enemies anxious to seize her, John Star had a pang of apprehension. The old fort was no real defense; it was no more than a dwelling. There were, he soon found, only eight men to guard her, all told. They were armed only with hand proton-blast needles. Truly, secrecy was their only defense. Secrecy, and the girl's secret weapon. If those enemies discovered she was here, and sent a modern, armed ship—

During the day he learned no more. Eric Ulnar, Vors, and Kimplen remained insolently uncommunicative; the four men left of the old guard were oddly distant, cautious in their talk, unmistakably apprehensive. They were busy bringing up the supplies from where the *Scorpion* had landed—provisions, apparently, to last many months.

An hour after dark, John Star was in the individual room he had been assigned, which opened on an ancient court, when he heard a shouted alarm.

"Rockets! Rockets! A strange ship is landing!"

Running into the yard, he saw a greenish flare descending athwart the stars; he heard a thin whistling that increased to a screaming bellow, deafeningly loud. The

19

flame, grown enormous, dropped beyond the east wall; the bellow abruptly ceased. He felt a sharp tremor underfoot.

"A great ship!" cried the sentry. "It landed so near it shook the hill. Its rockets burned green, a thing I never saw before."

Could it be, John Star wondered, with an odd little pause of his heart, that the girl's mysterious enemies had learned where she was? That this ship had come to take her?

Captain Otan, the commander of the tiny garrison, evidently had some such apprehension. An elderly, thin man, very much agitated, he called out all the Legionnaires to station them about the old walls and towers with hand proton guns. For three hours John Star lay on his stomach, watching a crumbling redoubt. But nothing happened; at midnight he was dismissed.

The old officer, however, must still have been alarmed over the strange ship's arrival. He ordered the three others of his own relief—Jay Kalam, Hal Samdu, and Giles Habibula—to remain on guard. From him, John Star caught a sense of terror and impending doom which he was not to escape for many dark and dreadful years.

2

An Eye and a Murder

John Star found himself abruptly sitting bolt upright in his bunk, staring at his open window, beyond which lay the great courtyard. It was no alarm that he could name which had aroused him; rather, a sudden chill of instinctive fear, an intuition of terror.

An eye! It must be, he thought, an eye, staring in at him. But it was fully a foot long, ovoid, all pupil. Thin, ragged black membranes edged it. It was purple, shining in the darkness like a great well of luminescence, somehow infinitely malignant. Mere sight of it shook him with an icy, elemental dread.

20

For only the briefest instant it gazed at him, unutterably evil, and then it was gone. Trembling, he scrambled out of bed to give the alarm. But the shock of it had left him doubtful of his senses. When he heard one sentry hail another in the court, as if nothing were amiss, he decided that the frightful eye had been no more than nightmare.

He wasn't given to nightmares. But after all, he had heard nothing; and the thing had vanished the very instant he glimpsed it. It was sheer impossibility; no creature in the System had eyes a foot long, not even the sea-lizards of Venus. He went back to bed and tried to sleep—unsuccessfully, for the image of that fearful eye kept haunting him.

He was up before dawn, anxious to know more of the strange ship. Passing the weary sentries in the court, he climbed the spiral stair in the old north tower, and looked out across the crimson landscape just as the sun rose abruptly above the horizon.

Dunes of yellow sand, shattered, weirdly eroded rock —he saw nothing else. But crumbling walls, eastward, shut off his view; the vessel, he thought, might lie beyond them. His curiosity increased. If it were a friendly, Legion ship, why had the rocket-blasts been green? If it carried enemies, why had they not already struck?

The girl was behind him when he turned: she whom he had glimpsed on the tennis court and guessed to be keeper of AKKA. He saw again that she was very lovely. Slim and straight and cleanly formed; eyes cool gray, sober and honest; hair a lustrous brown that made magic of flame and color in the new sunlight. She wore a simple white tunic; her breast was heaving from the run behind him up the stairs.

It surprised him that the keeper of AKKA should be so young and lovely.

"Why—why, good morning." He felt confused—for Legion cadets have little time for the social graces—yet very delighted and eager to please her.

"It must be very near!" she cried, breathless. Her voice, he perceived, was adorable—and alarmed.

"Beyond the walls, perhaps."

"I think so." Her gray eyes studied him frankly, weighed him—warming, he thought, with approval. She said abruptly, voice lower: "I want to talk to you."

"I'm quite willing." He smiled.

"Please be serious," she appealed, urgently. "You are loyal? Loyal to the Legion? To the Green Hall? To mankind?"

"Why, of course I am. What——"

"I believe you are," she whispered, gray eyes still very intent on his face. "I believe you really are."

"Why should you doubt me?"

"I'll tell you," she said swiftly. "But you must keep this to yourself. Every word. Even from your officer, Captain Ulnar."

Her face, when she spoke the name, tensed with a dislike that was almost hate.

"If you say. Though I don't see——"

"I shall trust you. First, do you know why you're here?"

"I've orders to guard a girl who knows some mysterious secret."

"I'm the girl." Her voice was more deliberate, more confident. "I don't matter. But the secret, AKKA, is the most valuable and the most dangerous thing in the System. I must tell you a little more about it than you seem to know. For AKKA is in terrible danger. You must help us to save it!"

Quietly, then, she asked a question that seemed odd:

"You know the history, I suppose, of the old wars between the Purples and the Greens?"

"Why, I think so. Purple was the color of the Emperors. The Greens were the faction led by the research scientists that revolted and set up the democratic Green Hall. The last Emperor, Adam the Third, abdicated two hundred years ago."

"Do you know why he abdicated?"

"No. No, the books didn't say. I used to wonder."

"I must tell you. It's important. The Emperors, you know, enjoyed despotic power. They were vastly wealthy; they commanded private space fleets and owned whole planets, outright. They ruled with an iron cruelty. The enemies they didn't liquidate were deported to Pluto.

"An ancestor of mine, Charles Anthar, was shipped out—because of a chance remark in favor of free speech and free research, made to a man he thought a friend! The finest physicist in the System. He spent fourteen years in the cold dungeons of the Black Planet.

"On Pluto, he made a scientific discovery. The theory he worked out in his dungeon by pure mathematics. That took him nine years. Then his fellow prisoners smuggled

22

materials to him, to build the apparatus he had planned. It was very simple, but he was five years finding the parts.

"When it was finished, he destroyed the prison guard. Sitting in his cell, he forced Adam the Third to obey his orders. If the Emperor had refused, Charles Anthar could have wrecked the solar system.

"Since, his discovery has defended the peace of the Green Hall. It is so very dangerous that only one person at a time is permitted to know it. Only this much of it has ever been put in writing—an abbreviation."

She showed him, tattooed on a white palm, the letters AKKA.

"And now you are in danger?" John Star whispered.

"I am. The Purples didn't lose their wealth and influence, you see, and they've always plotted to restore the Empire. The terrible power of AKKA is all that restrains their schemes. They want the secret, but it has always been safely kept for the Green Hall, by the descendants of Charles Anthar.

"My name is Aladoree Anthar. I had the secret from my father, six years ago, before he died. I had to give up the life that I had planned, and make a very solemn promise.

"The Purples, of course, have known about AKKA from the first. Endlessly they have conspired and bribed and murdered to get possession of it for themselves. With it, they'd be supreme, forever. Now I think Eric Ulnar has come to take it!"

"You must trust Eric!" protested John Star. "Why, he's the famous explorer—and the nephew of the Commander of the Legion!"

"That's why I think we're betrayed."

"Why, I don't see——"

"Ulnar," she said, "was the family name of the Emperors. Eric Ulnar, I believe, is the direct heir, the pretender to the throne. I don't trust him, or his scheming, plotting uncle——"

"Adam Ulnar, scheming, plotting!" John Star was outraged. "You call the Commander that?"

"I do! I think he used his wealth and influence to become Commander, so he could find where I am hidden. He sent Eric here! That ship, last night, brought the traitor reinforcements, and a way to escape with me!"

"Impossible!" gasped John Star. "Vors, perhaps, and Kimplen. But not Eric!"

"He's the leader." Her voice was cold with certainty. "Eric Ulnar slipped out of the fort last night. He was gone two hours. I think he went to communicate with his allies on the ship."

"Eric Ulnar is a hero and an officer of the Legion."

"I would trust no man named Ulnar!"

"My name is Ulnar."

"Your name—Ulnar," she whispered, shocked. "You're kin——"

"I am. I owe my commission to the Commander's generosity."

"Then I see," she said bitterly, "why you are here!"

"You are mistaken about Eric," he insisted.

"Just remember," she whipped out furiously, "that you are a traitor to the Green Hall! That you are destroying all liberty and happiness!"

With that she whirled and ran back down the old stone stairs. He stared after her, breathless and disconcerted. Even though he had defended Eric, he was left with a haunting doubt. Vors and Kimplen he mistrusted deeply. The proximity of the strange ship had alarmed him. And he was very sorry, just now, that he had lost the confidence of Aladoree Anthar. It would make her harder to protect —and, besides, he liked her!

Eric Ulnar met him when he came back to the court, and told him with a grim, sardonic smile:

"It appears, John, that Captain Otan was murdered during the night. We've just found his body in his room."

3

Three Men of the Legion

"Strangled, apparently," said Eric Ulnar, pointing to a swollen purple mark. In the soldierly bareness of his quarters, the dead commander lay face upward on his narrow cot, limbs rigid in agony, thin face contorted, eyes protruding, mouth set in an appalling grin of terror and pain.

Bending over the corpse, John Star discovered other strange marks, where the skin was dry, hardened into little greenish scales.

"Look at this," he said. "Like the burn of some chemical. And that bruise—it wasn't made by a human hand. A rope—perhaps—"

"So you're turning detective?" cut in Eric Ulnar, with his thin, superior smile. "I must warn you that curiosity is a very dangerous trait, John. But what's your theory?"

"Last night," he began slowly, "I saw something rather —dreadful. I thought afterwards it was just a nightmare, until now. A huge, purple eye, staring into my window from the court. It must have been a loot fong! It was evil —pure evil.

"Something must have come into the court, sir. It looked in my window. And murdered him. And left those stains. That mark about the throat—no human hand could have made that."

"You aren't going space-happy, are you, John?" There was a little, sharp, angry edge to the amused scorn in Eric Ulnar's voice. "Anyhow, this thing happened while the old guards were on duty. I'm going to hold them for questioning." His narrow face set coldly. "John, you will arrest Kalam and Samdu and Habibula, and lock them in the old cell block under the north tower."

"Arrest them? Don't you think that's extreme, sir, before they've had a chance to speak—"

"You are presuming on our kinship, John. Please remember that I am still your officer—now in sole authority here, since Captain Otan is dead."

"Yes, sir." He subdued his haunting doubt. Aladoree *must* be wrong.

"Here are the keys to the old prison."

Each of the men he must arrest occupied a single room opening upon the court. John Star tapped on the first door, and it was opened by the rather handsome, dark-haired Legionnaire whom he had seen on the tennis court with Aladoree Anthar.

Jay Kalam was in dressing gown and slippers. His gravely thoughtful face showed weariness; yet he smiled at John Star, courteously but silently invited him in, motioned him to a seat.

It was the room of a cultured man, quietly luxurious, reserved in taste. Old-fashioned books. A few select pictures. A case of shining laboratory apparatus. An *opti-*

25

phone, now filling the room with soft music, its stereo-scopic vision panel aglow with the color and motion of a play.

Jay Kalam returned to his own chair, his attention back on the drama. John Star did not like to arrest such a man for murder, but he took his duty very seriously. He must obey his officer.

"I'm sorry——" he began.

Jay Kalam stopped him with a little gesture.

"Please wait. It will soon be done."

Unable to refuse such a request, John Star sat quietly until the act was ended, and Jay Kalam turned to him with a slow dark smile, reserved and yet attentive.

"Thank you for waiting. A new record that came on the *Scorpion*. I could not resist the temptation to see it before I went to bed. But what do you wish?"

"I'm very sorry——" began John Star. He paused, stammered, and then, seeing that the thing had to be done, went on swiftly: "Sorry, but I am ordered by Captain Ulnar to place you under arrest."

The dark eyes met his in quick surprise; there was pain in them, as if they saw some dreaded thing.

"May I ask why?" The voice was low and courteous, unsurprised.

"Captain Otan was murdered last night."

Jay Kalam stood up quickly, but did not lose self-possession.

"Murdered?" he repeated quietly, after a time. "I see. So you are taking me to Ulnar?"

"To the cells. I am sorry."

For an instant John Star thought the unarmed man was going to attack him; he stepped back, a hand going to his proton gun. But Jay Kalam smiled a hard brown smile, without amusement, and told him quietly:

"I shall go with you. A moment, to pick up a few articles of clothing. The old dungeons are not famous for comfort."

John Star nodded, and kept his hand near the needle.

Crossing the court, they descended the spiral stair to a hall cut through red volcanic rock. With his pocket light-tube, John Star found the corroded metal door; he tried it with keys Eric Ulnar had given him, and failed to open it.

"I can turn it," offered his prisoner.

John Star gave him the key; he opened the door after

26

a little effort, gravely returned the key, and stepped through into dank darkness.

"I'm very sorry about all this," apologized John Star. "An unpleasant place, I see. But my orders——"

"Never mind that," said Jay Kalam quickly. "But remember one thing, please!" His tone was urgent. "You are a soldier of the Legion."

John Star locked the door and went after Hal Samdu.

To his astonishment, this man met him in the dress uniform of a general of the Legion, complete with every decoration ever awarded for heroism or distinction in service. White silk, gold braid, scarlet plume—his splendor was blinding.

"It came on the *Scorpion*," Hal Samdu informed him. "Very good, don't you think? Though the shoulders are not quite——"

"I'm surprised to see you in a general's uniform."

"Of course," Hal Samdu said seriously, "I don't wear it in public—not yet. I had it made, to be ready for promotion."

"I regret it," said John Star, "but I've been ordered to place you under arrest."

"To arrest *me?*" The broad, red face showed ludicrous amusement. "What for?"

"Captain Otan has been killed."

"The Captain—dead?" He stared in blank incredulity that changed to slow anger. "You think I——"

His great fists knotted. John Star stepped aside, whipped out his proton gun.

"Stop! I'm just obeying orders."

"Well——" The big hands opened and closed convulsively. Hal Samdu looked at the menacing needle, and John Star saw simple contempt of danger in his eyes. But he stopped.

"Well——" he repeated. "If it isn't your fault—I'll go."

The third man, Giles Habibula, did not open the door when John Star knocked, but merely called out for him to enter. The massive, blue-nosed sentry of the day before, he was now sitting, comfortably unbuttoned, before a table burdened with dishes and bottles.

"Ah, come in, lad, come in," he wheezed again. "I was just eating a mortal taste of lunch before I go to bed. A blessed hard night we had, waiting for trouble in the cold.

"But draw up, lad, and have a bite with me. We got new supplies on the *Scorpion*. An agreeable change from

27

these mortal synthetic rations. Baked him, and preserved candied yams, and some ripe old Dutch cheese—but look it over for yourself, lad."

He nodded at the table, which, John Star thought, bore food enough for six hungry men.

"No, thank you. I've come——"

"If you won't eat, you'll surely drink. We're mortal fortunate, lad, in the matter of drink. A wine cellar left full when the fort was abandoned in the old days. Aged precious well—the best wine, I dare say, in the System. A full cellar—when I found it. Ah——"

"I must tell you that I've orders to place you under arrest."

"Arrest? Why, lad, old Giles Habibula has done no mortal harm to anybody. Not here on Mars, anyhow."

"Captain Otan has been murdered. You are to be questioned."

"You aren't jesting with poor old Giles, lad?"

"Of course not."

"Murdered!" He shook his head. "I told him he should drink with me. He lived a Spartan life, lad. Ah, it must be terrible to be cut off so! But you don't think I did it, lad?"

"Not I, surely. But my orders are to lock you in the cells."

"Those old dungeons are mortal cold and musty, lad."

"My orders——"

"I'll go with you, lad. Keep your hand away from that proton gun. Old Giles Habibula wouldn't make trouble for anybody."

"Come."

"May I eat a bite first, lad? And finish my wine?"

John Star somehow liked old Giles Habibula, for all his grossness. So he sat and watched until the dishes were clean and the three bottles empty. And then they went together to the dungeons.

Aladoree Anthar met him as he returned to the court, her face shadowed with worry and alarm.

"John Ulnar," she greeted him, and winced at the name, "where are my three loyal men?"

"I have locked Samdu and Kalam and Habibula in the old prison."

Her face was white with scorn.

"Do you think they are murderers?"

"No, I really doubt their guilt."

28

"Then why lock them up?"

"I must obey orders."

"Don't you see what you have done? All my loyal guard are murdered or locked up. I'm at the mercy of Ulnar —and he's your real murderer! AKKA is betrayed!"

"Eric Ulnar a murderer! You misjudge——"

"Come! I'll show him to you, a murderer and worse. He has just slipped out again. He's going back to that ship that landed last night—to his fellow traitors."

"You're mistaken. Surely——"

"Come!" she cried urgently. "Don't be blind to him."

She led him swiftly along ramps and parapets to the eastern flank of the old fortress, up to a tower platform.

"Look! The ship—where it came from, I don't understand. And Eric Ulnar, your hero of the Legion!"

Age-worn precipices and tumbled red boulder-fields fell away from the foot of the wall to the lurid plain. There, not a mile from them, lay the strange ship.

John Star had seen nothing like it. Colossal, so vast it stunned his mind. Intricate and strange. All shining, jet-black metal.

The familiar space-craft of the System were all spindle-shaped, trimly tapering; all of them silvered mirror-like to reduce heat radiation and absorption in space; all comparatively small, the largest liners not four hundred feet long.

This machine had a spidery confusion of projecting sive, jointed metal levers—all jutting from the hull, which parts—beams, braced surfaces, vast, wing-like vanes, mas-was a gigantic black globe. It was incredibly huge; the metal skids on which it rested lay along the red desert for a full half mile, the sphere was a thousand feet thick.

"The ship!" whispered the girl. "And Eric Ulnar, the traitor!"

She pointed, and John Star saw the man's tiny figure, scrambling down the slope—dwarfed to the merest insect in the shadow of that machine, so huge and strange and queerly black.

"Now do you believe?"

"Something is wrong," he admitted reluctantly. "Something . . . I'm going after him! I can overtake him, make him tell me what's going on. Even if he is my officer."

He plunged recklessly down the stairway from the old tower.

4

"Well, John, I Am a Traitor!"

The black mass of strange flier filled the eastern sky, the central globe looming like a dark moon fallen in the red desert. The black skids, lying for half a mile upon the debris of boulders they had crushed, were like tall metal walls. In the shadow of that incredible machine, the toiling man ahead was shrunken to the merest human atom.

Midway to the black hull—almost under the top of the dark wing that covered an eighth of the sky—he still had not looked back. John Star was within forty yards of him, breathing so hard he feared the other would hear. He gripped his proton gun, shouting:

"Halt! I want to talk to you."

Eric Ulnar stopped, looking back in astonishment. He made a slight movement as if to draw the weapon in his own belt, but stopped when he saw John Star's face.

"Come here," John Star ordered. He waited, getting his breath, and trying to control the nervous tremor of his weapon, while his famous kinsman walked slowly back, with sharp annoyance on that narrow, weak, and handsome face.

"Well, John." Eric Ulnar gave him a tolerant, superior smile. "You're exceeding your duty again. I'm afraid you're too zealous to make a successful Legionnaire. My uncle will be sorry to hear of your failure."

"Eric," said John Star, surprised a little at his own deadly calm, "I'm going to ask you some questions. If I don't like the answers, I'm afraid I'll have to kill you."

White fury mounted to Eric Ulnar's girlish, passionate face.

"John, you'll be court-martialed for this!"

"Probably I shall. But now I want to know where this ship came from. And why you are slipping out here."

"How should I know where it's from? Nothing like it was ever seen in the System before. Simple curiosity was enough, John, to bring me out here."

Eric Ulnar tossed his bare, golden head, and smiled mockingly.

"I'm afraid, Eric, that you are planning treason to the Green Hall," said John Star quietly. "I think you know why this flier came, and why Captain Otan was killed. Unless you can convince me that I am wrong, I'm going to kill you, release the three men I locked up, and defend the girl. What have you to say?"

Eric Ulnar looked up at the great black vane above them, and smiled again, insolently bold.

"Well, John," he said deliberately, "I am a traitor."

"Eric!" John Star was dazed with shock and anger. "You admit it!"

"Of course, John. I've never planned to be anything else —if you call it treason to take what is mine by right. I suppose you don't know you have imperial blood in your veins, John—your education seems to have been neglected. But you have.

"I am the rightful Emperor of the Sun, John. In a very short time I shall take possession of my throne. As a prince of the blood, I had hoped that you might claim a high place under me. But I doubt, John, that you will live to enjoy the rewards of the revolution. You are too independent."

"Just what have you done?" demanded John Star. "And where did this flier come from?"

He kept his eyes, and his menacing weapon, fixed on the other.

"That ship came from the planet of Barnard's Star, John. You've heard, I suppose, of the dying men we brought back from the expedition? Heard what they babble of? They aren't as insane as men think they are, John. Most of the things they talk about are real. Those things are going to help me crush the Green Hall, John."

"You brought back—allies?"

Eric Ulnar smiled mockingly at the horror in his tone.

"I did, John. You see, the masters of the planet we found—they are as intelligent as men, though not at all human—the things we found need iron. It doesn't occur on their world—and it's priceless to them—for magnetic instruments, electrical equipment, alloys, a thousand things.

"So I made an alliance with them, John . . .

"They sent this ship, with some of their weapons—they have fighting machines that would surprise you, John;

31

their scientific achievements are really remarkable. They sent this ship to help crush the Green Hall and restore the Empire. In return, we agreed to load the ship with iron.

"Iron is cheap. We may do it. But I rather think we'll wipe them out, after we have AKKA, and the Purple Hall is safely in power again. They're not too pleasant to have about. Worse than you might imagine. Those insane men— yes, John, I'm sure we should destroy them, after we get the secret weapon.

"The girl must have told you about AKKA, John?"

"She did! And I thought—I trusted you, Eric!"

"So she suspects, already! Then we must get the chains on her, before she has a chance to use AKKA. But I suppose Vors and Kimplen have her safe, by now."

"You . . . traitor!" whispered John Star.

"Of course, John. We're taking her away. I suppose we'll have to kill her, after she's told us about her little secret gadget. Too bad she's such a luscious beauty."

John Star stood paralyzed with unbelieving shock, and Eric Ulnar smiled.

"I'm a traitor, John—by your definition. But you're something worse. You are a fool, John. I brought you along because I had to have a fourth man, to complete the guard. And because my uncle insisted that you must have a chance in life. He appears to have an exaggerated idea of your ability."

A sudden, high-pitched, girlish giggle burst from Eric Ulnar.

"You've been a fool, John. If you want to know how big a fool, just look up above you." And the handsome golden head made a mocking little bow.

John Star kept his eyes on the other, expecting some ruse to distract him. Glancing warily upward now, he saw his danger. Some fifty feet above him swung a sort of gondola, a car of bright black metal suspended on cables from a great jointed boom that reached out of the flier's confusion of titanic ebon mechanisms.

Inside it, he glimpsed—*something!*

Beyond the black sides of the gondola he could not see it clearly. But the little he did see made the short hair rise on his neck. It sent up his spine the cold, electric tingle of involuntary horror. His breath was checked, his heart pounded, his whole body tensed and quivered. The merest glimpse of the thing set off all his danger-instincts —the very presence of it roused primeval horror.

Yet, in the shadows of the queer black car, he could see little enough. A bulging, glistening surface, translucently greenish, wet, slimy, palpitating with sluggish life—the body surface of something gross and vast and utterly strange.

Staring malignly from behind the shielding plates, he met—an eye! Long, ovoid, shining. A well of cold purple flame, veiled with ancient wisdom, baleful with pure evil.

And that was all. That bulging, torpidly heaving green surface. And that monstrous eye. He could see no more. But that was enough to set off in him every reaction of primal fear.

Fear held him frozen. It stopped his breath and squeezed his heart. It poured the choking dust of terror down his throat. It washed his rigid limbs with icy sweat. He broke free at last and threw up his weapon.

But the half-seen thing in the gondola struck first. Reddish vapor puffed down from the side of the swinging car. Something brushed his shoulder, a mere cold breath. And then a red avalanche of unendurable pain hurled him to the sand. Black oblivion brought mercy.

When consciousness came back, he contrived to sit up. He was miserably sick, his body trembling and wet with perspiration, his arm and shoulder still paralyzed and aflame with scarlet agony. Dizzy, still half-blinded, he looked anxiously about.

Eric Ulnar had vanished, and at first he couldn't find that black gondola. But the Cyclopean ship still loomed monstrous against the greenish Martian sky. He searched its maze of vanes and struts and levers, until at last he saw the swinging car.

The titanic boom had reached out over the fort. The car was just rising above the red walls when he found it. Swiftly the cables were drawn in. The mile-long lever telescoped itself, and the gondola was swallowed through a huge valve in that black, spherical hull.

It must have picked up Eric Ulnar, he thought, and then swung over the fort to take aboard Vors and Kimplen, with Aladoree. The girl, he realized, heart utterly sick, was already taken inside the enemy machine.

Very soon it rose. Cataracts of green flame thundered from cavernous jets. Endless ebon wings tilted and spread to catch the tenuous air of Mars. The ground trembled under him as those vast black skids lifted their burden from the yellow desert. A monstrous, evil bird, the black machine lifted obliquely across the greenish sky, into the violet zenith.

The noise of it beat about him, mauled him with raging seas of sound. A furnace-hot wind whipped up curtains of yellow sand, dried his sweat, stung his eyes and burned his skin.

He watched it shrink to a grotesque black insect. The green flame faded; the thunder died. It dwindled, grew dim with distance, at last was lost.

He lay in the sand, ill, agonized, and bitter with self-reproach. It was late afternoon before he could rise, still weak and faint. His shoulder and upper arm, he found, were strangely burned, as if some mordant fluid had been squirted on them. The skin was stiff, lifeless, covered with hard, greenish scales.

The corpse of Captain Otan had been marked like that. And the eye of that greenish, heaving monster in the black gondola—it was like the nightmare eye that had stared through his window! Yes, *something* from the ship had killed Otan.

Driven by a faint spark of irrational hope, he staggered back up the hill to the old fort, to search the inhabited section. It was silent, utterly deserted. Aladoree was really gone, and AKKA lost. Aladoree, so freshly lovely, was in the hands of Eric Ulnar and those monstrous beings from the dark planet of Barnard's Star.

Only black self-accusation remained to haunt him. Admiration of his famous kinsman had blinded him too long. A misplaced sense of a Legionnaire's duty had driven him to actual treason. However unwittingly, he had helped betray the Green Hall and the Legion.

5

The "Purple Dream"

"Ah, lad, it's time you thought of us!" wheezed Giles
Habibula plaintively from the gloom behind the bars of
the old prison. "Here we've been, life knows how long,
locked up in the cold and dark of a mortal tomb! My old
bones will ache with this wicked damp, lad.

"Ah, but I'm famishing, lad. Faint with mortal hunger.
How could you leave us so long, lad, without a blessed bite
to eat? Mortal me, lad, have you never known the gnawing agony of starvation?"

John Star was unlocking the rusty door. Here was one
thing that he could do to repair the traitorous work of
his kinsman—though the greater deed, the rescue of
Aladoree and her mighty secret, was all but hopeless.

"Can you bring us some broth, lad?" whined the old
Legionnaire. "And a bottle of old wine from the cellar?
Something to revive us and give us strength for stronger
victuals?"

"I'm going to turn you out," said John Star, adding
bitterly: "That much I can do, to make up for the fool
I've been!"

"You must help us creep out, lad, and up to the blessed
sun. Don't forget we're mortal weak. Ah, me, we're starv-
ing, lad. Not a bite to eat since the day you locked us up.
Not a morsel, lad, for all that mortal time. Though I cut
off the uppers of my boots, and chewed them, for the bit
of precious nourishment in the leather."

"Ate your boots? Why, it was just this morning that I
brought you here!"

"Don't jest with poor old Giles Habibula, lad! Don't
be so heartless, when he's had nothing but his blessed boots
to eat, rotting in a dungeon for mortal weeks. Ah, and
wasting his precious skill trying to pick a lock that's
ruined with wicked rust!"

"Weeks? It wasn't ten hours ago! And I let you eat all

that breakfast in your room, just before—enough to provision a fleet!"

"Don't torture me with your jokes, lad! I'm starved to a blessed bag of bones! For life's sake, lad, help old Giles Habibula out into the sunshine, and find him a drop of wine, to warm his poor old blood again."

The rusty bolt at last shot back, the door creaked open. Giles Habibula waddled out, Hal Samdu stalked behind him, and Jay Kalam walked deliberately.

"We are free?" asked the latter.

"Yes. The least I can do. I've been a total idiot! I'll never be able to undo the crime I helped Eric Ulnar carry out—though I'm going to spend the rest of my life trying to!"

"What has happened?" Taut anxiety edged Jay Kalam's voice.

"Eric Ulnar was a traitor, as Aladoree thought. After I had locked up you three, he had the way clear. The ship—the one that landed last night—came from that planet of Barnard's Star. Monstrous creatures aboard, allies of Eric's—it was one of them that murdered Captain Otan. He's promised them a ship-load of iron, to pay for their part. Iron is precious to them. The ship took Eric away, and Aladoree. I was—hit. Can just now walk again."

"It's the Purples?"

"Yes. As Aladoree thought. The plot is to restore the Empire, with Eric on the throne."

They entered the courtyard, bright with the afternoon sun. Giles Habibula stood with his thick hands stretched out in front of him, staring in amazement. He fingered his heavy-jowled face, slapping his bulging paunch.

"For life's sake, lad!" he gasped. "Tell me, was that no joke? Is this the same mortal day? . . . All that suffering! . . . My blessed boots!"

"Forget your belly, Giles!" shouted Hal Samdu, the slow and homely giant; and he turned to John Star with helpless anger on his broad red face.

"That Eric Ulnar——" He was panting, incoherent in his rage. "Aladoree—he has taken her, you say?"

"Yes. I don't know where."

"We'll find out where!" he promised savagely. "And bring her back! And Eric Ulnar——"

"Of course." It was the low, calm voice of Jay Kalam. "Of course we shall attempt her rescue, at any risk. The safety of the System demands it, if it were not our simple duty to Aladoree. The first thing, I suppose, is to find where she is—which won't be easy."

"We must get away from here," added John Star. "Is there a radio?"

"A little ultra-wave transmitter. We must report to Legion headquarters, at once."

John Star winced, and added bitterly:

"Yes, of course. Report what a fool Eric Ulnar made of me!"

"Don't blame yourself," Jay Kalam urged him. "Others, higher up, were deceived, too, or he wouldn't have been sent here. You could have done little alone. Your only guilt was obedience to your officer. Forget your regrets, and let's undo the harm!"

"But I can't help feeling——"

"Come on. We'll send a message to the base—if they didn't smash the transmitter before they left!"

But the little transmitter, located in a small tower room, had been systematically and utterly destroyed. Tubes were smashed, condensers hammered to shapeless metal, wires cut to bits, battery jars emptied and broken.

"Ruined!" he said.

"We must repair it!" cried John Star.

But with all his optimistic determination, he soon had to admit the impossibility of the task.

"Can't be done. But there must be something. The supply ship?"

"Won't be back for a year," said Jay Kalam. "They come seldom, to avoid attracting attention."

"But when the station here remains silent, won't they know something is wrong?"

"It was only for emergencies. We had never used it. The signals might have been picked up and located. We depended on absolute secrecy—together with the power of AKKA itself. And of course Aladoree didn't keep her weapon set up, for fear it would be stolen—that was what gave the traitors time to take her. We weren't prepared for treason."

"Could a man walk out?"

"Impossible. No water in the desert. This is the most isolated spot on Mars. We wanted no accidental visitors."

"But there must be *something*——"

"We must eat, lad," insisted Giles Habibula. "Even if it is the same mortal day. Nothing like good food to quicken the mind. A good supper, lad, with a bottle of the old

37

wine to wash it down, and you'll have us away from here this blessed night!"

And, indeed, it was while he sipped a glass from the old man's precious cellar that inspiration came.

"We've light-tubes!" he cried. "We can step up the output—it doesn't matter if they soon burn out. Flash a distress signal. Against the dark background of the desert, somebody would see it from space!"

"We'll try that," agreed Jay Kalam. "Might not be a Legion cruiser, but it would have a transmitter to call one."

"Ah, lad, what did I tell you? What did poor old Giles Habibula tell you? Didn't a drop of wine sharpen your brain?"

When the green afterglow was gone, and the cold, clear dark of the Martian night crashed down on the red landscape, John Star was ready on the platform of the north tower, his pocket light-tube in hand, its coils rewound to increase its brilliance a thousand-fold.

Into the purple, star-shot night he flashed it, forming again and again the code letters of the Legion signal of distress. The tube burned his hand, as the electrodes fused and the overloaded coils went dead. But Jay Kalam was ready with another, its potential stepped up in the same way; he kept flashing the silent appeal for aid.

It seemed incredible to him, as he stood there, that Aladoree had been with him that morning on the same platform. Incredible, when now she was lost somewhere in the black gulf of space, perhaps ten million miles away. With a little ache in his heart, he pictured her as she had stood—slender and straight and cleanly molded; eyes candid and cool and gray; sunlit hair a splendor of brown and red and gold.

His determination to restore her to safety could hardly be less, he knew, were she just an ordinary bit of humanity, not the keeper of the System's priceless treasure.

It was long after midnight when the last light-tube went out.

Then, until the lemon-green dawn, they waited on the platform, scanning the star-sifted purple, anxious for the blue rocket-exhausts that would brake the descending ship. But they saw no moving thing, save the faint tiny spark of Phobos, rising in the west and creeping swiftly eastward.

Giles Habibula was with them, lying on his back, peacefully snoring. He woke with the dawn, and went down to the kitchen. Presently he called up that breakfast was ready. The others were about to leave the tower in despair, when they heard the roaring rockets of a ship landing.

A long silver craft, an arrow of white flame in the morning sun, it dropped across the fort, pushing ahead the blue flare of its rockets.

"A Legion cruiser!" John Star exulted. "The latest, fastest type."

His blue eyes keener than they appeared, Hal Samdu read the name on its side:

"Purple—something—she's the *Purple Dream!*"

"*Purple Dream?*" echoed Jay Kalam. "That's the flagship of the Legion fleet. The ship of the Commander himself!"

"If it's the Commander's ship," John Star said slowly, his high spirits falling, "I'm afraid it won't bring us much good. Commander Adam Ulnar is Eric Ulnar's uncle. The real leader of the Purples.

"It was Adam Ulnar who sent Eric on that interstellar expedition and Adam Ulnar who found that Aladoree was hidden here and sent Eric to be commanding officer of her guard. I'm afraid we can't expect much but trouble from the Commander of the Legion."

6

The Empty Throne

The four of them went out of the old gate—Giles Habibula still eating morsels he had stuffed into his pockets—and down the red boulder slope to the *Purple Dream,* lying amid the yellow dunes of the sand desert.

Her officer, a man too old for his rank, thin and stern, with a jaw like a trap, appeared in the open air-lock.

"You flashed a signal of distress?"

"We did," said John Star.

"What's your difficulty?"

"We must leave here. We have an urgent matter to report to the Green Hall."

"What's that?"

"It's confidential."

"Confidential?" the officer repeated, looking down with frosty eyes.

"Very."

"Come aboard, then, to my stateroom."

They climbed the accommodation ladder to the great valves, and followed him down the narrow deck into his cabin. Closing the door, he turned on them with sharp impatience.

"You need keep nothing back from me. I'm Captain Madlok of the *Purple Dream*. I enjoy Commander Ulnar's full confidence. I know that you men were stationed here to guard a priceless treasure. What account have you to make of it?"

All his companions hesitated, Jay Kalam habitually taciturn, Hal Samdu, slow with words, Giles Habibula overly cautious. John Star spoke out bitterly:

"That treasure is lost!"

"Lost!" snapped Madlok. "You've lost AKKA?"

John Star nodded, sick at heart. "A traitor was sent here——"

"I don't care for alibis!" rapped Madlock. "You admit that you have betrayed your trust."

"Aladoree Anthar has been kidnapped," John Star said stiffly, Madlok's stern face recalling his lectures in military courtesy. "I suggest, sir, that she must be rescued. And I believe, sir, that the news should be communicated to the Green Hall."

Madlok's voice had a brittle snap: "I shall take care of any reports necessary."

"Sir, the search must begin at once," said John Star, urgently.

"I'm accepting no orders from you, if you please. And I shall take the four of you at once to Commander Ulnar, at his estate on Phobos. You can report your failure to him."

"May I go back, sir, just a few minutes?" appealed Giles Habibula. "Some things I must bring——"

"What things?"

"Just a few mortal cases of old wine, sir."

"What! Wine! We're taking off at once."

"If you will pardon me, sir," gravely offered Jay Kalam,

40

"our mission gives us a peculiar position in the Legion, regardless of military rank. We are not under your command."

"Your signals were seen from Commander Ulnar's private observatory on Phobos," snapped Madlok. "Inferring—and rightly—that you had betrayed your trust and lost AKKA, he sent me to bring you to the Purple Hall. I trust that you will condescend to obey the Commander of the Legion. We take off in twenty seconds!"

John Star had heard of the Ulnar estate on Phobos, for the magnificent splendor of the Purple Hall was famous throughout the System.

The tiny inner moon of Mars, a bit of rock not twenty miles in diameter, had always been held by the Ulnars, by right of reclamation. Equipping the barren, stony mass with an artificial gravity system, synthetic atmosphere, and "seas" of man-made water, planting forests and gardens in soil manufactured from chemicals and disintegrated stone, the planetary engineers had transformed it into a splendid private estate.

For his residence, Adam Ulnar had obtained the architects' plans for the Green Hall, the System's colossal capitol building, and had duplicated it room for room. But he had built on a scale an inch larger to the foot, using, not green glass, but purple, the color of the Empire.

The *Purple Dream* dropped upon the landing stage atop the square, titanic tower. Beyond the edge of the platform, when they disembarked, John Star could see the roofs of the building's great wings, glistening expanses of purple stretching out across the vivid green of lawn and garden. Beyond, the woods and hills of the tiny world appeared to drop with an increasing, breath-taking abruptness, so that he felt as if he were perched insecurely on the top of a great green ball, afloat in a chasm of starry purple-blue.

They dropped in an elevator three thousand feet, escorted by Madlok and half a dozen alert armed men from the cruiser, and entered an amazing room.

Corresponding to the Green Hall's Council Chamber, it was five hundred feet square, arched with a tremendous dome. The lofty vault and columned walls were illuminated with colored lights to secure effects of ineffable vastness and splendor.

In the center of the floor, all grouped in a tiny-seeming space, were a thousand seats, corresponding to the seats of the Council of the Green Hall—empty. Above them, on a high dais, stood a magnificent gem-canopied throne of purple crystal—vacant. On its seat lay the old crown and sceptre of the Emperors—waiting.

They marched, astonished and awed, across the vast floor, under the whispering vault, and around the dais. Behind the throne they entered a small room, beyond a guarded door. There Adam Ulnar, Commander of the Legion of Space, master of all this splendor and the immense wealth and power it represented, was sitting at a simple table.

Though twice Eric Ulnar's age and almost twice his weight, Adam Ulnar was as handsome as his nephew. Square-shouldered, erect, he wore a plain Legion uniform, without insignia to show his rank. The calm strength of his face—nose prominent; mouth firm; blue eyes deep-set, wide apart, steady—contrasted with the reckless girlish weakness of Eric's narrow face. His long hair, nearly white, lent him the same distinction that Eric had from his flowing yellow locks.

John Star, to his surprise, felt an immediate instinctive admiration for this man of his own blood, so generous to an unknown relative—but now, it seemed, a traitor to the Legion he commanded.

"The men, Commander," Madlok reported, briefly, "who lost AKKA."

Adam Ulnar looked at them, without surprise, a faint smile on his distinguished face.

"So you were the guard of Aladoree Anthar?" he said, his voice well-modulated, pleasant. "Your names?"

John Star named his companions. "And I am John Ulnar."

Smiling again, the Commander stood up behind the table.

"John Ulnar? A kinsman of mine, I believe?"

"So I understand."

He stood still, coldly unsmiling; Adam Ulnar came around the table to greet him, warmly courteous.

"I'll see you alone, John," he said, and nodded to Madlok, who withdrew with the others.

Then he turned to John Star, urged cordially:

"Sit down, John. I wish now that we had met sooner, and under less awkward circumstances. You made a brilliant record at the Academy, John. I've a career planned for you, equally brilliant."

42

John Star, remaining on his feet, his face taut, said stiffly:

"I suppose I should thank you, Commander Ulnar, for my education and my commission in the Legion. A few days ago I should have done so very gratefully. Now it seems that I was intended merely for a dupe and a tool!"

"I wouldn't say that, John," Adam Ulnar protested softly. "It's true that events did not take place just as I had planned—Eric is taking affairs too much into his own hands. But I had you placed under his direct command. I was planning——"

"Under Eric!" John Star burst out hotly. "A traitor! Much as I once admired him, that's what he is. Obeying his orders, I helped betray the Legion and the Green Hall."

"Traitor is a harsh word to use, John, just because of a political difference."

"Political difference!" Shocked outrage shook John Star's voice. "Do you admit to me openly that you are false to your own trust as an officer of the Legion? You, the Commander himself!"

Adam Ulnar smiled at him, warmly, kindly, and a little bit amused.

"Do you realize, John, that I am by far the most wealthy man in the System? That I am easily the most powerful and influential? Doesn't it occur to you that loyalty to the Purple Hall might be more to your advantage than support of the democracy?"

"Are you trying, sir, to make a traitor out of *me?*"

"Please, John, don't use that word. The form of government I stand for has a historic sanction far older than your silly ideas of equality and democracy. And, after all, John, you are an Ulnar. If you will consider just your own personal advantage, I can give you wealth, position, and power, which your present impractical democratic attitude will never earn for you."

"I will not consider it."

John Star was still standing stiffly in front of the table. Adam Ulnar came around beside him to take his arm persuasively.

"John," he said, "I like you. Even when you were very small—I suppose you don't remember when we were ever together—you displayed qualities I approve. Your courage, and that stubborn determination which is about to keep us apart now, was one of them—something left out of my nephew's disposition.

43

"I've been interested in your career, John—I've followed it more closely than you ever knew. Your progress at the Academy—everything you have done—was reported to me in detail.

"I had no son of my own, John. And the family of Ulnar isn't very large—just Eric, the son of my unfortunate elder brother, and you and I. Eric is twelve years older than you are, John. He was pampered in his youth. He was always told that one day he would be Emperor of the Sun; he was spoiled.

"And I don't quite like the results, John. Eric is weak; he's headstrong, and yet a coward. This alliance with the creatures from the planet of the Runaway Star was a coward's device—he made it without my knowledge, because he feared my own plans for the revolution would fail.

"Anyhow, with you, I tried a different way. I put you in the Academy and left you ignorant of your high destiny. I wanted you to learn to depend on yourself, to develop some character and resource and courage of your own.

"This last experience has been a sort of test, John. And it has proved, I think, that you have everything I had hoped for. Besides, I like you, John."

"Yes?" said John Star, coldly, and he waited.

"The Empire is going to be restored. Nothing can halt our plans, now, John. The Green Hall is doomed. But I don't want to set a weakling back on the throne. Ulnar is an old name, a proud name, John. Our ancestors paid for the Empire, with blood and toil and brains. I don't want our name disgraced, as such a man as Eric might disgrace it."

"You mean——" cried John Star, astounded. "By all this, you mean that I——"

"That's it, my boy!" Adam Ulnar was smiling at him with pleasure on his proud, distinguished face, and a fond hope. "That's it. I don't want Eric to be Emperor of the Sun when the Green Hall surrenders.

"The new Emperor shall be you!"

John Star stood motionless, staring dumbfounded into that fine strong face, with its crown of snowy hair.

"Yes, you shall be Emperor, John," Adam Ulnar repeated softly, warmly smiling. "Your claim is really better than Eric's. You are in the direct line of descent. I have proof."

44

John Star shook off his hand then, and moved back a step, laughing incredulously.

"What's the matter, John?" The tall Commander seemed deeply concerned. "You don't——"

"No!" John Star caught his breath, and spoke decisively. "I don't want to be Emperor. If I were ever Emperor, I'd abdicate. I'd restore the Green Hall."

Adam Ulnar went slowly back behind the table, and sat down heavily, wearily. A long time he sat silently, watching John Star's tense, determined figure with a frown of painful thought.

"I see," he said at last. "I see you're in earnest. An unfortunate result of your training, which I had not anticipated. I suppose it's too late to change you, now."

"I'm sure it is."

Again Adam Ulnar mused awhile, and then he stood up suddenly, his lean face imperious with decision.

"I hope you understand the situation, John. Our plans are going ahead. If you won't be Emperor, Eric will. Perhaps, with my advice, he won't do too badly. Anyhow, the Green Hall is doomed. I suppose, with your foolish attitude, you'll be against us?"

"I will!" John Star promised warmly. "I hope for nothing more than a chance to smash your crooked schemes."

Adam Ulnar nodded; for an instant he almost smiled.

"I knew you would." The family pride rang briefly in his sad, slow voice. "And that means, John—I'll be as honest with you as you have been with me—that means that you must spend your life in prison. Unless it becomes necessary to kill you. I have far too much confidence in your ability and your determination to set you at liberty."

"Thank you," said John Star, his tone more friendly than he intended.

Something softened the proud authority of the old Commander's face.

"Good-bye, John. I'm sorry we must part this way."

He laid his hand a moment on John Star's shoulder, and showed a sudden concern at his involuntary shudder of pain.

"You've been hurt, John?"

"Some weapon from the black ship. It made a greenish burn."

"Oh, the red gas!" The Commander was suddenly very grave. "Open your tunic, and let me see. The stuff is

45

believed to be an airborne virus, really, though the biochemical reports brought back by the expedition are incomplete and extremely confusing. The effects of it are
rather distressing, but my experts in planetary medicine
have worked out a treatment. Turn, and let me see. . . .
You must go right to the hospital, John, but I think we can
catch it in time."

"Thank you," said John Star, less stiffly—for he remembered terrifying rumors of men insane and rotting
alive from that red gas.

"I'm sorry, my boy, that I'll never be able to do more
for you. I'm really sorry that you choose to go to prison
from the hospital—not to the empty throne in the Purple
Hall."

7

Giles Habibula's Higher Calling

In a hospital room in the south wing of the colossal
Purple Hall, a gruffly capable, tight-mouthed doctor
washed John Star's injury with a blue, palely luminescent
solution, covered it with a thick salve, bound it and made
him go to bed. Two days later the old skin began to peel
off in hard, greenish flakes, leaving new healthy flesh
beneath it.

"Good," said the laconic physician, bending to examine
him. "Not even a scar. You're lucky."

John Star practiced one of the wrestling holds he had
learned in the Academy. He walked out of the room in
the doctor's clothing, leaving him gagged and bound,
furious but unharmed.

Four men in Legion uniform met him at the door,
armed, unsurprised, and warily courteous.

"This way, please, John Ulnar, if you are ready now
to go to the prison."

With a taut little smile, John Star nodded silently.

The prison was a huge space, square and lofty, beneath
the north wing of the Purple Hall. Its walls were white

metal, shining and impregnable. The triple doors were massive, sliding slabs of armor plate, with guards in the short halls between. The mechanism permitted only one door to open at a time, so two always sealed the way to freedom.

The cell block stood in the center of that great room, a double tier of big, barred cages, partitioned with sheet metal. Each cell had a hard, narrow bunk, and the barest necessary facilities for a single occupant. One guard was always on watch, pacing endlessly around the block of cells.

John Star, locked in alone, threw himself hopelessly on the bunk. His heart was set on escape. For the Legion, under Adam Ulnar, would get no orders to attempt the rescue of Aladoree. The Green Hall, he realized bitterly, wouldn't even be informed that AKKA was lost.

But how escape? How leave the locked cell? How evade the sentry outside—who carried only a club, lest some prisoner snatch his weapon? How pass the triple doors, with guards between? How get through the endless labyrinthine corridors of the Purple Hall, a veritable fortress? How finally get away from the tiny planet, which was virtually a private empire of Adam Ulnar, policed by his loyal retainers? How accomplish the sheer impossible?

He heard a wheedling voice from the next cell:

"Ah, have you no heart, man? We've been locked in this evil place a blessed time, on bread and water, or precious little more. Is your heart of stone, man? Surely you can bring us something more for supper. Just an extra morsel, to edge our appetite for the regular prison fare. A thick steak with mushroom sauce, say; and a hot mince pie for each one of us. Just to give us an appetite."

"An appetite, you bag of tallow?" retorted the sentry, good-naturedly, walking past. "You eat more now than seven men."

"Of course I eat," came the whining plaint. "What else can a man do, a devoted old soldier of the Legion, rotting in this black dungeon, accused of murder and betrayal of duty and life knows what other crimes he didn't do?

"Ah, come, man, and bring me a bottle of wine. Just one blessed bottle. It'll bring a bit of warmth into a poor old soldier, against the cold of these iron walls. It'll help me forget the court-martial that's coming, and the lethal chamber beyond it—life knows they mean to kill the three of us!

47

"How can you be so heartless, man? How can you refuse one little drop of happiness to a man already doomed and as good as dead? Come, for life's sake? Ah, just one bottle, man, for poor, starved, beaten, condemned old Giles Habibula——"

"Enough! Keep quiet! I bring you all I can. Six bottles you've already had today! No more, the warden said. At that, I never knew such generosity! It's only by the special order of the Commander himself that you get a drop. And no more talking, now! That's regulations."

John Star was glad to hear again of his companions, though it was no good news that they were waiting trial. Adam Ulnar would be ruthless with these loyal men, whose real crime was only the knowledge of his treason.

He still lay hopeless on the narrow cot, when a low, cautious tapping on the metal partition by his head abruptly recalled him from his apathy of despair. For the muted rappings formed letters, in the Legion code:

"W-H-O?"

Quickly, cautiously, he replied: "J U-L-N-A-R."

"J K-A-L-A-M."

He waited for the sentry to pass again, and tapped: "E-S-C-A-P-E?"

"C-H-A-N-C-E."

"H-O-W?"

"G-U-A-R-D-S C-L-U-B."

For the most of a day and a night John Star watched that club, as it passed at regular intervals outside the bars. A simple, eighteen-inch stick of wood, the grip taped, the slender part above wrapped with green-enameled wire, for reinforcement. He did not see how it could be very useful, but evidently it was part of some plan for escape conceived by Jay Kalam's deliberate, analytic mind.

Each guard was locked in the great room with them four hours at a time, pacing around the cell block, reporting through a speaking tube at fifteen-minute intervals.

Their habits differed. The first, a good-natured man, carried the club safely in his farther hand. The next walked a precise, cautious beat, well out of reach. The third was not so careful, swinging the club by a leather thong, sometimes from one wrist, sometimes the other. He would swing it sometime, John Star thought, within a foot of the bars. He waited, unobtrusively alert, until the guard was changed again. And his chance had not yet come.

Again the good-natured man. And the precise, cautious man.

Then, again, the one who swung the club. John Star waited an hour, sprawled on the cot with gloom on his face, aimlessly picking the lint from his blanket—and the chance did come.

Every minutest motion of it he had planned, rehearsed in his mind. He was keyed up, ready; his trained body reacted with lightning quickness. He sprang, soundlessly, when the club began its swing. His arm slipped through the bars. His straining fingers snapped around the wood. He braced knee and shoulder against the bars. His arm came back.

It was all done before the guard could turn his head.

The leathern thong on his wrist jerked him against the cell; his skull struck the bars; he went down silently.

John Star slipped the thong over his limp hand, whispering:

"Jay! I have the club!"

"I hoped you might," spoke Jay Kalam, quietly, quickly, from the cell to his right. "If you will please hold it out to Giles——"

"Outside here, lad!" The fearful, wheezing gasp came from his left. "Quick, for life's sake!"

He thrust the club back through the bars, felt Giles Habibula's fingers grasp it.

"Shall I search him?" he whispered. "For keys?"

"He had none," said Jay Kalam. "They knew this might happen. We must depend on Giles."

"My father was an inventor of locks," came the absent nasal whine from the cell on the left. "I learned a higher calling. Giles Habibula was not always a crippled old soldier in the Legion. In his nimble days . . ."

The voice drifted away. John Star restrained his curiosity, waiting silently. There was nothing else to do. In the next cell, Giles Habibula was busy. His breath became audible, panting. John Star could sometimes hear a fearful muttering:

"Mortal minutes! . . . This wicked wire! . . . Life's precious sake! . . . Ah, poor old Giles . . ."

"Hurry, Giles!" implored Hal Samdu, from the cell beyond. "Hurry!"

There were tiny, metallic sounds.

"We've another five minutes." Jay Kalam's voice was calm and low. "Then the guard's report is due."

The sentry groaned. John Star silently restored him to unconsciousness with a trick he had learned at the Academy—one quick blow with the edge of his open hand.

His door swung open. He stepped out to join Giles Habibula. The short and massive body of the old Legionnaire seemed to quake with apprehension, but his thick hands were oddly sure and steady. Already he was feverishly busy at the door of Jay Kalam's cell, with a bit of twisted green wire—the winding which had reinforced the club.

"Poor old Giles wasn't always a lame and useless soldier in the Legion, lad," he wheezed abstractedly. "Things were different when he was young and bold— before mortal disaster overtook him, back on Venus, and he had to join the blessed Legion——"

That door let out Jay Kalam; the next gave freedom to Hal Samdu.

Breathless, John Star whispered, "Now what?"

They had four minutes before the guard would fail to report. The great room that housed the cell-block was massively metal-walled, windowless. It had one opening —with armed men waiting between the three locked doors across the single passage.

"Up!" said Jay Kalam, as urgently as he ever spoke. "On top of the cells."

John Star swarmed up the bars. The others swiftly followed, Giles Habibula puffing, hauled by John Star from above, pushed by Hal Samdu beneath. They reached the metal net that covered the second tier of cells, the white-painted metal ceiling still fifteen feet above.

"Now!" whispered Jay Kalam. "The ventilator."

He pointed to the heavy metal grating in the ceiling above, from which a cool draft struck them.

"Your part, Hal! If your strength was ever needed, it is now."

"Lift me!" cried the giant, great hands ready.

They lifted him.

Puffing Giles Habibula and Jay Kalam stood on the netting, John Star, lightest of the four, on their shoulders, while huge Hal Samdu stood upon his.

The ventilator grille was strong, though it had been placed where men were not likely to reach it. Hal Samdu's immense hands closed about its bars; he strained; John Star heard mighty muscles cracking. His breath came in short, laboring gasps.

"I can't——" he sobbed. "Not this way!"

"We've one minute longer, perhaps," Jay Kalam told him softly.

The giant lifted himself from John Star's shoulders, and doubled his body, planting one foot on each side of the grating, hanging by his arms.

"Catch him!" cried John Star.

Hal Samdu straightened, with his feet on the ceiling. Strained metal snapped. He fell down, head foremost, fifteen feet, the grate torn out in his hands. The tube yawned black, above, a cold stream of air pouring down from it.

The three caught him in their arms.

A whirring from the door of the great room. The lock mechanism was opening the inner valve. In seconds, the guardsmen would come, to find why the speaking tube was silent.

"You first, John," said Jay Kalam. "The lightest. Help us."

They lifted him to the opening. He hung his knees over the edge, and swung down his body, hands reaching.

Giles Habibula came first, wheezing, hoisted from beneath. Then Hal Samdu, who lowered John Star, a living rope, so that Jay Kalam could catch his hands.

"Halt!" rang the order from the opening door. "As you are! Or we fire to kill!"

They scrambled upward into the narrow black mouth of the ventilator tube. Another rapped command. The blast of a proton gun lit the dark tube with brief, intense violet, and spattered fused metal behind them. It reached all with rumbling electric shocks.

They tumbled ahead into cramped black spaces.

8

With Death Behind

The horizontal passage they followed was formed of heavy sheet metal, square, not three feet high, and as Giles Habibula put it, "black as the gut of a mortal whale."

They scrambled along on all fours, bruising limbs and heads upon rivets and interior braces. Giles Habibula was ahead, then Jay Kalam, and Hal Samdu, with John Star behind.

The guards must have delayed to get a ladder—escape into the ventilation system must have found them unprepared—for at first there was no sound of pursuit. The four dragged themselves through the narrow dark, the strong wind from the fans rushing about them, Giles Habibula puffing like an engine.

"If it branches," gasped Jay Kalam, "we must turn against the air current. That will guide us toward the fans, away from the small dividing passages. We must get past the fans, and out through the intake. If we lose the way, they'll have us trapped like rats——"

He stopped. The wind against their faces had abruptly ceased.

"They've shut off the fans," he whispered bitterly. "Now we haven't the air to guide us."

"I hear voices," John Star breathed. "Behind us. Following."

"Sweet life's sake!" wheezed Giles Habibula a little later. "A mortal wall! I bumped my old head into it."

"Go on," said Jay Kalam, behind him, quietly urgent. "Feel about. There must be a way."

"My blessed head! Ah, yes, there is a way. Two ways. 'Tis another passage we're entering. Right or left?"

"A blind chance, since they stopped the fans. Say, right!"

They hastened on for another while, on hands and bruised knees.

A gasp from Giles Habibula. "My mortal life! A fearful pit! I half fell into it. For life's sake, don't push so! I'm sprawling on the edge!"

"The shaft turning down, it must be," said Jay Kalam. "We turned wrong, I'm afraid—the intake must be above. But it's too late to turn back. Feel about. There should be rungs, a ladder—in case the shafts should need to be cleaned, or repaired."

"Ah, yes, right you are, Jay. I've found them—and precious flimsy they are, for such a man as I. Ah, Jay, I should have stayed back in the cells, to let them torture me and starve me and use my poor old body as they would, court-martial me and seal me in their ghastly lethal chamber. Old Giles Habibula is too old, Jay, too ill and lame, to be running through black and filthy rat-holes on his knees, and dancing up and down flimsy little ladders in the dark. He's no mortal monkey!"

Yet he had slipped over the edge in a moment; he was already tumbling down the dark ladder, the others behind him, punctuating his phrases with the gasps of his panting breath.

"A floor!" he wheezed presently. "Ah, it's all up now, I'm afraid. I've struck bottom. No way out but tiny pipes a rat himself couldn't creep through."

They explored with anxious, bleeding fingers, but found no branching passage large enough for a man to enter.

"We should have turned left," Jay Kalam said.

"We must go back," John Star cried. "If we hurry, perhaps we can beat them."

Now ahead, he rushed back up the ladder. He reached the horizontal shaft, and plunged down it, reckless of bumps and bruises. Hal Samdu kept close at his heels, Jay Kalam not far behind. Giles Habibula, heaving and gasping frantically, called out from far in the rear:

"For dear life's sake, you can't abandon poor old Giles! Wait for me, lad! Jay, Hal, you can't leave an old comrade alone, to be starved and tortured and done to his death! Wait just a second, for poor, lame and suffering old Giles Habibula to snatch a breath of blessed air."

John Star saw the white flicker of a pocket light-tube on the wall ahead; again he heard voices. The pursuing guards, then, were just approaching the intersection. He scrambled desperately to reach it first.

The light flashed briefly, out of the intersecting tube, to strike the wall. He oriented himself by it, and waited,

53

crouched behind the angle, breathing quietly as he could. Hal Samdu came up behind, and he cautioned the giant to silence with a pressure of his foot.

Far back, he heard Giles Habibula's plaintive appeal:

"Just one blessed second! For life's own sweet sake! Ah, a poor old soldier, sick and crippled, imprisoned and unjustly sentenced to a wicked traitor's death, deserted by his comrades and caught like a dying rat in this stinking hole——"

The light flashed again, close now. The leading man came out of the side tunnel. John Star caught his groping arm, and hauled him around the metal corner, into deadly combat.

A fight in utter darkness, for the dropped light-tube went out. A savage battle; the unknown guard fought for his life, John Star for more than his. And brief; it was over before the next man in line could reach the cross-passage.

The Legion Academy had trained John Star. He knew every weak point of the human machine. He knew the twist that snaps a bone, the jab that pulps a nerve, the shift that kills an opponent with his own fighting strength. He was light, but the Legion training had made him hard and quick and sure enough to fight the Legion, now.

The other man tried first to use the heavy little proton gun in his right hand, and found that his wrist was broken. With his left hand, then, he struck into the darkness, and his own blow hurled him against the wall of the shaft. He twisted back, tried to butt, and broke his neck.

That was all.

When the next man flashed his light, to see how the battle went, John Star had the proton gun the first had dropped, pointed ready down the tube.

A thin, searing jet of pure electricity, the proton blast fused metal, ignited combustibles, electrocuted flesh. It was a narrow, killing sword of intense violet incandescence —not quite a toy!

A matter of split seconds.

The other men had similar weapons, also ready. But they must have held themselves a moment, must have waited to aim. John Star did not delay.

And five men died in the shaft, the three foremost by direct, searing contact with the ray, the two others electrocuted by current conducted through ionized air—the proton gun was not a toy; and John Star pulled hard on the lever, to exhaust all the energy of the cell on one terrific blast.

The blinding violet flame went out. There was darkness in the shaft again. Stygian, complete. Silence. The pungence of ozone in the air, from the action of the ray. The acrid smell of seared flesh and smoldering cloth.

Such swift spilling of life sickened John Star. This was the first test of the deadly arts he had learned; he had never killed a man before. He was abruptly trembling, faint.

"John?" whispered Hal Samdu, uncertainly.

"I'm—I'm all right," he stammered, and tried to get possession of himself. There had been no choice. He had had to kill as he would surely have to kill again. A few lives, he told himself sternly, were nothing against the safety of the Green Hall. Or—whispered another part of him—the safety of Aladoree!

He fumbled weakly for the dropped light-tube.

"The guards——"

"They're all dead." he whispered dully. "I killed them —all."

"You've a proton gun?" Hal Samdu did not sense his horror.

"Dead!" But the question brought him back to the needs of the moment. "Yes. Useless, though, until I find an extra cell. Burned out."

Forcing himself to it, he searched the body by him, found no extra, and moved on to those the ray had slain.

Jay Kalam came up.

"You used the proton blast? Full power? No use, then, to look for weapons, or light-tubes either. Anything electrical. Burned out."

He found another proton gun; half fused, reeking with burned insulation, it was still so hot it seared his fingers.

Far down the shaft, toward the prison, he heard a command; he saw a flicker of warning light.

"They're coming again. We must get on. To the left this time."

Giles Habibula came noisily up; he blundered into Jay Kalam, wheezing:

"Time we rested! I've lost ten mortal pounds, already, scampering through these foul and endless rat-holes. Ah, but I'm hot as——"

"Come on!" retorted Hal Samdu. "You'll be hotter when a proton blast catches you in the rear!"

On they tumbled, desperate, bruised, gasping for breath,

again without a weapon—save for the useless proton gun —still without light. Running on all fours. Colliding painfully with rivets and flanges. "Playing an evil game of rat-and-ferret," sobbed Giles Habibula.

John Star, now ahead, reported suddenly:

"Another shaft! Larger. Runs both up and down."

"Up, then!" said Jay Kalam. "The intake must be above us. Probably on the roof."

They ascended flimsy metal rungs, in close-walled, smothering dark.

"The roof!" John Star whispered suddenly. "Can we get to the landing stage, above the tower? There are ships on it."

"Possibly," said Jay Kalam. "But we must pass the fans —easy to do if they keep them stopped. But there are guards on the landing stage, and we've no weapon."

They climbed rungs without end, up through rayless gloom. Breath came with painful effort. Muscles screamed and quivered with the agony of fatigue. Worn, blistered hands left blood on the metal.

Giles Habibula, lagging a little behind, puffing noisily, yet found breath for complaint.

"Ah, poor old Giles is dying for a drink. Perishing for one blessed sip of wine! His precious throat is dry as leather. Poor old Giles; lame, feeble, sick old Giles Habibula—he can't stand this any longer. Climbing till he feels like he's turned into a mortal mechanical monkey!"

"I've been counting the rungs," Jay Kalam said calmly, at last, breaking the silence of endless, tortured effort. "We must be in the tower."

A current of air presently struck them, blowing down the shaft.

"The fans, again!" muttered John Star. "I wonder why——?"

He soon knew. The downward wind increased. It became a tempest, a howling hurricane. It yelled in their ears with demoniac voices. It ripped garments from their bodies. It snatched at them with prankish hands, hammered them with savage blows.

"Trying——" screamed Jay Kalam above the roar of it, "to blow us—off the ladder! Climb on—stop—fans—"

The wind whipped his voice away.

John Star climbed on, against the relentless pressure of howling air, fighting the tearing demon talons. The flimsy

56

metal rungs quivered, bent beneath the strain. Steadily, painfully, he won his way against the narrow storm.

Another sound was at last in his ears, above the shrieking air—a whine of gears, a whirring of great rushing vanes. The purring of the over-driven fans, deadly in the dark.

Upward he battled, inch by hard-won inch, to the top of the trembling ladder, to a wide platform of vibrating metal bars. There he paused to play a game with death. Somewhere in the dark above, those great blades were racing, and he knew they would never pause as they split his skull and splashed his brain.

Cautiously he moved, feeling his way. He was out of the main air-current, now; he could move more easily. Yet sudden, freakish blasts still drove at him savagely; they were demon hands jerking him toward the racing unseen vanes.

Toward the whine of gears he moved. With cautious fingers he explored the frame of the vibrating machine. He tried to shape a mental image of it. At last he found the end of a rotating shaft; and he thrust, slowly, carefully, with the heavy little gun, three times in vain.

Then metal teeth snapped it from his hand. The purring changed to anger. The gears snarled and screamed. They chewed metal, and spit the fragments savagely. And they broke. The unloaded motor whined briefly with rage.

Silence, then. Peace. The whirring, invisible vanes slowed, and stopped. The demoniac air was stilled. John Star waited in the quiet dark, panting, resting his trembling muscles, while the others climbed up to his side.

"Now, the intake," softly urged Jay Kalam. "Before they come!"

"Wait a mortal moment," wheezed Giles Habibula, sobbing for air. "For sweet life's sake, can't you wait for a lame old soldier, climbing like a dog in a treadmill, with his hair blown out by the roots!"

They climbed again, up a huge, still blade, and out along the massive, motionless axle. They ran upright into the vast, horizontal intake tube and came to the bottom of another vertical pit.

"Light!" exulted John Star. "The sky!"

A square bright patch, at the top of the shaft, shone like a beacon of welcome. It was not the sky, however, but only the undersurface of the great landing stage.

Up the last short ladder, and over a low metal wall, and

57

they stood at last upon the tower's roof. Flat, and tiled with purple glass, the enormous roof was spaced with the opening of other ventilator shafts, and crowded with the forest of gigantic piers that supported the immense platform of the flying stage, yet another hundred feet above.

"They will know we're up here," Jay Kalam reminded them gently. "From the fan. No time to waste."

They ran to the edge of the roof, and climbed again, up the diagonal lattice-work of an enormous vertical member. The last five feet, around the edge of the gigantic, metal platform, John Star climbed alone. Clinging like a human fly, he peered cautiously over the edge of the immense flat table.

A mere hundred feet away lay the nose of the *Purple Dream*. A slender bright arrow, the flagship was ashimmer under the small sun which burned hot through the thin air of Phobos.

The *Purple Dream!* Only thirty yards away, it was freedom and safety and the means to search for Aladoree. Slender, beautiful; the newest, finest, swiftest cruiser of the Legion fleet. A splendid hope, and hopeless.

Her air-lock was sealed, her bright armor impregnable. Twelve Legionnaires, armed, stood in line beneath her valves, wearily alert.

What madness, for the four to think of taking her! Four tattered fugitives, bruised, exhausted, with not one weapon save their bodies, and a thousand hunting them. What madness, when the cruiser was the System's most powerful fighting machine!

John Star knew it was madness, yet he dared to plan.

9

"To the Runaway Star!"

He climbed back to the others, mutely eager Hal Samdu, cool, composed Jay Kalam, wheezing, groaning Giles Habibula.

"The *Purple Dream* is there. Her valve toward us,

sealed. A dozen men guarding her. But I think I see a way—a chance."

"How?"

He explained, and Jay Kalam nodded, offering quiet suggestions.

"We'll try it. We can do no better."

They climbed down the pier to the roof again, Giles Habibula complaining bitterly at the new effort. They ran diagonally across the purple tiles among the maze of beams, and clambered wearily up again to the platform, to the edge behind the *Purple Dream*.

Again John Star looked above the surface.

No sentry, no searcher, was now in view. That herculean climb up the shaft, three thousand feet, the last thousand against a hurricane, the escape through the blades of the fan—all that must not have been comprehended in the plans of their pursuers.

The flat platform. The side of the *Purple Dream*, fifty feet away, a shimmering curve of armor. Purple-blue sky above and beyond.

"Now," he whispered. "All clear!"

In seconds, he was over the edge, although even for his trained body it was an awkward scramble. Hal Samdu, with his help, came more easily. Giles Habibula, hauled limp and green-faced over the edge, looked once three thousand feet down, to the purple roofs of the wings and the green convexity of the tiny planet, and grew suddenly and amazingly ill.

"Sick!" he groaned. "Mortal sick and dying. Hold me, lad! For poor Giles is faint and dying—and he feels he's falling off the whole blessed moon!"

For all her fleetness and her fighting power, the *Purple Dream* was not large; one hundred twenty feet long, twenty feet her greatest diameter. Yet it was not easy to get silently and unobserved on top of her, as John Star's plan demanded.

They ran beneath the black, projecting muzzle of her port stern rockets, and lifted John Star to it. And he, again, helped the others up. From the rocket, over the glistening smoothness of her silvery hull, they inched a slow and perilous way up and forward.

Once Giles Habibula fell. He started to slide down her polished shell, croaking in mute terror; John Star and Hal Samdu caught him, drew him back. At last they were safely amidships.

There they lay, waiting, atop her flattened hull.

At first they were glad enough to rest from that super-human climb. But the sun beat down on them, through the thin artificial atmosphere of Phobos, blinding, intense, and terrible. It drove back upon them from the mirror of the hull. They were blistered, gasping with heat, and thirst came to torture them.

They dared not move; they could only wait. And their position held a mounting peril.

True, they were invisible from near the ship. But the bright metal platform, at a distance, was visible, shimmering and dancing in the heat—and any chance searcher there could easily see them on the cruiser.

Two hours, perhaps, they had been broiling on that flat silver grille when they heard a bell below, and taut, excited voices:

"From the Commander. He's going aboard in five minutes. The cruiser will be ready to take off at once."

"Have the valve unsealed. Inform Captain Madlok."

"Wonder where he's bound?"

"Wants to get away, I guess, until these escaped prisoners are captured."

"Legion men, they say. One an old criminal. All desperate fellows, dangerous."

"Hiding in the ventilation shafts, they say."

"Don't blame the Commander, if he's going away. Men clever enough to break out of that prison——"

"They've already killed six, in the tubes."

"Twelve, I heard it—with their own guns!"

The sound of hurried feet on the stair from the elevator. A ringing clang of metal, as the great outer valve dropped to form a tiny deck under the air-lock. Feet on the accommodation ladder, entering the vessel. At last the crisp order:

"All clear! Close the valves!"

"Now!" whispered John Star.

He rolled swiftly off the hull, and slid down feet first, to the little platform of the lowered valve. The jar shook him, but he caught his breath and darted inside the air-lock. Hal Samdu was a second behind him, then Jay Kalam; Giles Habibula, for all his bulk, was very little later.

In the struggle that followed, they had the advantage of complete surprise. The first man, at the control mechanism of the valves, was not even armed. He gasped at

60

sight of John Star, his face abruptly white with panic—for the new reputation of the four had preceded them aboard. And he tried to run.

John Star caught him. A sharp jab to a vital plexus, a flat-handed blow near the ear. He slumped, limp and silent.

Giles Habibula stumbled wheezing over the flanges, and John Star shot at him:

"Close the valves!"

Once the air-lock was sealed and secured from within, he knew, the *Purple Dream* was armored well against outside danger.

With the gigantic Hal Samdu close behind him, and Jay Kalam, he burst upon the narrow deck.

Two uniformed men appeared before them, gasped, started, and tried to reach their weapons. The first of them met Hal Samdu's fist, rebounded against a bulkhead, and crumpled slowly to the deck. A proton gun fell spinning, and Jay Kalam scooped it up in time to meet a third attacker in the Legion green.

John Star met his own opponent, briefly. They both had Legion combat training, but John Star fought for AKKA—and Aladoree herself. The other snatched for his gun, and staggered back screaming, arm snapped, back broken. Seizing his weapon, John Star turned in time to meet Captain Madlok, just emerging from his cabin.

Madlok came out crouched and snarling, a proton needle ready in his hand. But once again John Star was first—merely the hundredth of a second, perhaps, but enough. A white blade of electric fire stabbed out, and the *Purple Dream* had a new commander.

They divided, then. Giles Habibula remained to guard the airlock. Hal Samdu ran toward the crew's quarters, in the stern. Jay Kalam plunged down into the generator rooms, below the deck. John Star darted forward, toward the Commander's cabin and the navigation bridge.

The four were still outnumbered two to one—the full complement of the *Purple Dream* had been twelve; and such a crew was ample, since the cruiser was handled almost completely by automatic mechanisms, needing men chiefly for inspection and navigation. But they had not completely lost the advantage of surprise.

John Star found two men forward. The navigator came out of the bridge-room with a proton gun in his hands. He saw John Star and tried to fire. But he lacked the peril of

AKKA and its keeper to nerve his urgency. By a few fatal thousandths of a second, he was too late.

John Star flung open the door marked COMMANDER, and found Adam Ulnar in his cabin, hanging up the coat that he had worn aboard.

For a long second, the tall, white-haired master of the Legion and the Purple Hall stood quite motionless, breathless, staring at the menacing needle of the proton gun, his handsome face frozen into absolute lack of expression. He breathed suddenly. The coat fell out of his hands. He sat down heavily in the single chair.

"Well, John, you surprised me," he said with a short, husky little laugh. "I had learned you were too dangerous to keep alive. I was going away until you had been disposed of. But I was hardly expecting this."

"I'm glad you value your life," John Star snapped harshly. "Because I want to trade it to you."

Adam Ulnar smiled, defensively, recovering his suave self-possession. Again he was the shrewd elder statesman of the Purple Hall.

"You have the advantage, John. Your men, I suppose, have control of the cruiser?"

"I imagine so, by now."

"You know, this adds piracy to your long list of crimes. All the Legion fleets will be hunting you, now."

"I know. But that doesn't save your life. Shall we trade?"

"What do you want, John?"

"Information. I want to know where you have Aladoree Anthar."

Adam Ulnar smiled in faint relief, and spoke more easily:

"Fair enough, John. Promise me my life, and I'll tell you—though I don't think the information will give you any satisfaction."

"Well?"

"I didn't approve the thing, John. I wanted her brought here, to the Purple Hall. I think Eric is trusting his strange allies too far. . . . She wasn't disposed to talk, you see. It was difficult to persuade her, without the danger that she would die, and her secret with her. And we still have to deal with a few stubborn fools in the Legion—men like you, John—still loyal to the Green Hall."

"But where is she?"

62

"They took her on the Medusæ flier, John, back to the Runaway Star."

"Not there!" he gasped. "Even Eric wouldn't——"

"Yes, John," his famous kinsman told him soberly. "I didn't think you'd find much comfort in the fact."

"We'll go after her!"

"Yes, John, I believe you would do that." There was a note, almost, of admiration in Adam Ulnar's voice. "I believe you would. But you couldn't possibly hope to succeed."

"No?"

"Our allies, John, are a pretty efficient race. They've had a longer existence than the human race. I don't like them, myself—I've had contact enough with them. I don't approve the alliance. And I didn't approve taking the girl there. I don't trust them so far as Eric does.

"They aren't human at all, you understand—not like any form in the System, though Eric called them Medusæ. They have a queer psychology. Unpleasant. Frankly, I'm afraid of them.

"But they're scientific, able, advanced. They have the accumulated knowledge of ages I can't estimate. Weird as they are, they've splendid brains. Cold, emotionless intelligence. They're more like machines than men. They get what they want, quite efficiently, with no human scruples.

"So I think, John, that they will be able to guard the girl, on their own planet—and make her tell the secret. They have set up very effective defenses, to guard their own strange world. That Belt of Peril, that the insane survivors of Eric's expedition keep babbling about.

"And even if you keep me helpless, John, our plans will go ahead. The Medusæ will come back. The Legion will go over to them—our Purple organization controls it now. The Green Hall will be wiped out—the Medusæ have amazing weapons, John. And Eric will take the throne.

"The throne you might have had yourself, John."

10

Farewell to the Sun

Giles Habibula made queer noises. He gasped, strangled, sputtered. Fragments of food flew out of his mouth. His face—save for the ample purple protuberance of his nose—had faded to a greenish, sickly pallor. His fat hands trembled as he tilted up the big flagon of wine, and cleared his vocal organs sufficiently to permit articulate speech.

"My dear life!" he sputtered, rolling a fishy eye about the little bridge-room. "My mortal life! We can't go there!"

"Probably we can't," John Star agreed soberly. "The chances are against us—a hundred to one, I suppose. But we can try."

"Bless my bones! We can't go there, lad. 'Tis beyond the System—six light years, and more. That's a frightful distance, when it takes a precious ray of light six long and lonely years to cross it!

"Ah, there are ten thousand mortal dangers, life knows! I'm a brave man—you all know poor old Giles is brave enough to deal with any common peril. But we can't do that. Of all the doomed and dismal expeditions that ever dared to fly outside the precious System, only one ever came back!"

A tiny red light glowed suddenly on the geodesic telltale screen; a warning gong rang out.

"Another Legion cruiser," observed Jay Kalam, tautly quiet. "Scouring space for the *Purple Dream*. That makes five in the range of the telltale. Hunting pirates was always a popular sport with the Legion."

"And the nearest within ten thousand miles," added John Star, with a glance at the dials. "Though they probably won't discover us until we contrive to get the generators repaired, and start moving."

"And to the Runaway Star!" Giles Habibula wheezed on, dolefully. "Sweet life's sake, to the green Medusæ's dark and evil world! The expedition the Legion sent there had five fine fighting ships. The best the System could build. Full, trained crews. And look what came back, after a whole eternal year!

"One crippled ship! The men on her, most of them, blessed babbling lunatics, chattering to freeze your blood about the horrors they had found on the dark and hideous planet of that evil star. And rotting away, all the fearful while, of some frightful virus the doctors never saw before —the flesh of their mortal bodies turning green and flaking off.

"Mortal terrors! And you want us to go there, in one poor and lonely little ship, with her geodynes already wrecked. Just four men of us, against a whole planet full of green and cunning monsters!

"You can't ask old Giles Habibula to go out there, lad. Poor old Giles, half dead from scampering like a hunted rat through the ventilator tubes in the Purple Hall. Old Giles is too feeble for that. If you three idiots want to go out to your death of madness and howling horror, why then you must let poor old Giles off the ship on Mars."

"To be tried and put to death for a pirate?" asked John Star, smiling grimly.

"Don't joke so with old Giles, lad! He's no swaggering, red-handed pirate, lad. Old Giles is just a poor——"

"The whole Legion is hunting us, Giles," Jay Kalam broke in quietly. "Ever since we took the *Purple Dream*. The agents of the Legion would soon have you—you'd never disguise that nose!"

"Good life's sake, Jay, don't talk so! I hadn't thought of that. But we *are* blessed pirates now, with the hand of every honest fighting man against us. Ah, every man looks on us with trembling and horror, and seeks to strike us down to death!"

His fishy eyes glistened with tears; his wheezing voice broke.

"Poor Giles Habibula, aged and crippled in the loyal service of the Legion, now without a place on any planet to rest his mortal head. Hunted through the black and frozen deep of space, driven out of the System he has given his years and his strength to defend. Driven out to face a planet full of green inhuman monsters. Ah, me! The ingrate System will regret this injustice to a mortal hero!"

He wiped the tears away, then, with the back of a great fat hand, and tilted up the flagon.

He had found opportunity for a raid on the galley since they took the ship. His capacious pockets were stuffed with slabs of synthetic Legion rations, sweet-cakes, and fragments of baked ham, which now flowed again toward his mouth in a stream of traffic interrupted only by the trips of the wine-flagon to the same destination.

The *Purple Dream* was adrift in space, a hundred thousand miles off the huge, tawny, ocher globe of Mars. Tiny Phobos had long been lost among the million, many-hued points that pierced the black sphere of vacant night. They lay with lights and signals dead, helpless; and the avid fleets of the Legion hunted them.

Commander Adam Ulnar safely locked in the brig, their other prisoners released through the air-lock, they had driven the cruiser away from the landing stage on the Purple Hall under rocket power. John Star had felt freedom in their grasp.

But then a dying engineer—true to the Legion traditions—had thrown a switch, burned out a geodyne unit. With generators useless and rockets inadequate to move the vessel fast or far through these hostile immensities, the four gathered for a council of desperation.

"She's in the hands of those monsters?" huge Hal Samdu asked again, his big hands knotting. "The monsters that Eric Ulnar's crazy veterans kept talking about?"

"Yes. Except that I doubt that those things are enough like men to have hands."

"With care," began Jay Kalam, "organization——"

"Ah, that's the word," broke in Giles Habibula. "Organization. Regularity. Four good meals, hot on the moment; twelve hours of good sound sleep. Organization—though a blessed man might still take a cat-nap now and then, or a cold bite and a sip of wine between meals."

"There's the matter of navigation," Jay Kalam went on. "I know the rudiments, of course, but——"

He looked doubtfully about at the walls of the bridge-room, bewilderingly crowded with all the shining, intricate mechanism of telescopic periscopes, geodesic telltales, meteor deflectors, rocket firing keys, geodyne controls, gyroscope space-compasses, radar, thermal and magnetic detector screens, star-charts, planetary maps, position-, velocity-, and gravitation-calculators, atmosphere and temperature gauges—all the apparatus for the not quite simple business of taking the cruiser safely from planet to planet.

"I can handle her," offered John Star quietly.

"Good. Then we must have an engineer. To repair the geodynes—we *must* somehow get them repaired—and then to run them."

Giles Habibula grunted, sputtered crumbs, failed to speak.

"That's right, Giles. I'd forgotten that you were a qualified technician."

He swallowed, tilted the flagon, found his voice.

"Sweet life, yes, I can run the precious geodynes. Giles Habibula can fight, when fighting has to be done, old and lame and feeble as he is. Ah, me, no man is braver than old Giles—all of you know that. When fighting must be done. But, as a matter of choice, he'll always stick to his blessed generators. It's safer—and there's nothing else but wisdom in a blessed bit of caution."

"You can fix the burned-out unit?"

"Ah, yes, I can re-wind it," promised the new engineer. "But it will be hard to synchronize it with the others. Those units are matched when they are made. When one is off balance, it makes the whole system mortal hard to tune. But I'll do my blessed best."

"And, Hal," went on Jay Kalam, "you've been a proton gunner. You can handle the big proton blast needle, if the Legion stumbles on us—though we can't afford a fight, with just four men on a crippled ship."

"Yes, I can do that," gigantic Hal Samdu nodded slowly, his red face very grave. "That's simple. I can do it."

"That leaves you, Jay," spoke up John Star. "We need you to do just what you're doing now. To plan, organize. You will be our commander."

"No——" He started a modest objection, but Hal Samdu and Giles Habibula added their voices; and Jay Kalam became captain of the *Purple Dream*.

The new officer gave his first orders immediately, with the same gravely quiet manner he always had.

"Then, Giles, please get the geodynes into operation as soon as you can—our only chance is to get away before one of these ships catches us in a search beam, and calls the rest of the fleet to wipe us out."

"Very good, sir."

Giles Habibula threw back his head, held up the flagon

until the last drop had trickled from it, saluted too elaborately, and rolled out of the bridge-room.

"John, you may be plotting our course. First we must outrun these ships around us. We'll keep above the asteroid belt, and well away from Jupiter and Saturn and Uranus, with their Legion bases—we can't risk running into another fleet. As soon as we get beyond the danger of their search-beams, we'll head on out toward Pluto."

"Very good."

"Hal, if you please, check the big proton gun. We must have it ready—though we can't risk a fight."

"Yes, Jay."

"And I shall keep watch."

"How many, now?" asked Jay Kalam, hours later. They were still drifting helpless in the void. Watching the betraying red sparks on the telltale screen, John Star answered slowly:

"Seven. And I believe—I'm afraid, Jay, they've found us!"

"They have?"

Intently he studied the instruments, and he agreed at last, his voice edged with apprehension:

"Yes. They've found us. They're moving in, all seven."

Jay Kalam spoke into his telephone:

"Hal, stand by for action. . . . Yes, seven Legion cruisers, all converging on us." He gave positions.

"Giles, the geodynes? . . . Not ready, yet? . . . And you can't depend on the re-wound unit? . . . They've seen us. We must move soon, or never."

A few minutes, and the nearest cruiser came into range, or almost into range, of the proton blast. Jay Kalam spoke into the telephone, and a tongue of blinding violet darted at the cruiser from the great needle in its turret above.

"It's drawing back," whispered John Star, his eye fastened to a tele-periscope. "To wait for the others. But they'll all soon be close enough to fight."

"Ah, Jay, we can try them," whistled Giles Habibula's voice from the receiver, thin and shrill. "Though this crippled unit is still a poor, uncertain crutch!"

Jay Kalam nodded, sharply, and John Star turned to the dials and keys. The musical humming of the geodynes rose, filling the ship with a song of power. Swiftly he advanced them to their utmost output; their sound became higher, keener, until it was a vibrant whining which quivered through every member of the ship.

"Away!" he cried exultantly.

His eyes on the dials, on the red flecks glowing on the telltale screen, he saw that the *Purple Dream* was moving, ever faster, away from the center of that hostile crimson swarm. His own heart responded to the keening whine of the generators; he could almost feel the terrific thrust of the geodynes.

"We're gone!" he cried again. "Off for the Runaway Star! Away to——"

His voice fell. Another note had broken the keen musical whine of the generators—a coarse, nerve-jarring vibration.

Giles Habibula's voice came from the receiver, tiny and metallic and afraid:

"Ah, these wicked generators. I re-wound the unit. But they're off-balance. They won't stay synchronized. That evil oscillation will creep back. It bleeds away the power —and it may shake the mortal ship to fragments!"

"We've lost speed," John Star reported apprehensively from the instruments. "The Legion ships are gaining."

"Adjust them, please, Giles," Jay Kalam pleaded into the telephone. "Everything depends on you."

Giles Habibula toiled. The pure power-song came back, and broke again. The *Purple Dream* flashed on, gaining upon the seven pursuing ships when the geodynes hummed clear and keen, but always losing, falling sluggishly back, when the harsh, disturbing vibration returned.

John Star studied his instruments long and anxiously.

"We're holding them just about even," he decided at last. "We can keep ahead so long as the generators do no worse—though we can't escape them altogether. Anyhow, we can say farewell to the Sun and the System. Even if they follow us out . . ."

"No," Jay Kalam objected quietly, "we aren't ready yet to leave."

"What's the matter?"

"We must have more fuel for the trip out to Barnard's Star—six light years and back. We must have every foot of space on board packed with extra cathode plates for the geodyne generators. And, of course, we must check the supplies for ourselves—food, and oxygen."

John Star nodded slowly.

"I knew we needed a captain. Where——"

"We must land at some Legion base, and get what we need."

"At a Legion base? With all the Legion fleets hunting us for pirates? The alarm will be spread to the limits of the System!"

"We'll land," Jay Kalam said, with his usual quiet gravity, "at the base on Pluto's moon. This is the farthest on our way, and the most isolated Legion station in the System."

"But even it will be warned and armed."

"No doubt. But we must have supplies. We're pirates now. We shall take what we need."

11

The Trap on Pluto's Moon

It was five days' flight to Pluto, most distant outpost of the System; so far that even its sun was but a bright star, its daylight eternal twilight.

Five days—with the full power of the geodynes, whose fields of force reacted against the curvature of space itself, warped it, so that they drove the ship not *through* space, to put it very crudely, but *around* it, and so made possible terrific accelerations without any discomfort to passengers, and speeds far beyond even the speed of winged light. Apparent speeds, a mathematician would hasten to add, as measured in the ordinary space that the vessel went *around;* for both acceleration and velocity were quite moderate in the hyperspace it really went *through.*

Giles Habibula nursed the hard-driven generators with amazing care and energy—his thick hands proved to have an astounding sureness and delicacy and skill; and he had an enormous respect for the ever-increasing swarm of Legion cruisers racing astern, with their threat of successfully prosecuted charges of piracy, if not immediate destruction of the *Purple Dream* and all on board in the consuming flame of their proton blasts.

He adjusted the injured unit until it was all but perfect. For an hour at a time, perhaps, the song of the generators would be clear and keen—but always the harsh discord of the destructive vibration returned.

One by one, the far-flying patrol cruisers of the Legion had joined the pursuing fleet, until sixteen ships were chasing the *Purple Dream*. But, little by little, they were left behind, until, near Pluto, John Star estimated them to be nearly five hours astern.

Five hours, that meant, in which to land at the hostile base, overcome its crew, force them to bring aboard some twenty tons of supplies, and get safely away into space again.

In those days of the flight, John Star found himself thinking often of Aladoree Anthar—and his thoughts were soft music and sheer agony. Though he had known her but a day, memory of her brought a glow of joy to him, and a bitter throb of pain at thought of the human traitors and the monstrous half-known things that held her captive.

The *Purple Dream* hurtled down on Pluto's moon.

Pluto itself, the Black Planet, was naked rock and ancient ice, killing cold and solitude. Its only people were a few hardy miners, mostly descendants of the political prisoners shipped there under the Empire, lonely exiles of eternal night.

Cerberus, moon of Pluto, was a tiny, cragged rock, more desolate and cruel to man than even its dark planet. A dead satellite, it had never lived. Save for the crew of the lonely Legion station, it had no inhabitants.

John Star had more than half expected that the Pluto Squadron of the Legion fleet would be warned and waiting for them, but he field seemed deserted as they came down. He began to hope that the evil web of Adam Ulnar's treason had not been spun so far.

Cerberus Station was a square field, leveled, between ragged black pinnacles. Red-glowing reflectors, spaced along the perimeter, radiated heat enough to keep the air itself from freezing into snow. A long, low building of insulating blocks armored with white metal housed barracks and storerooms. The power plant, which gave energy to fight the enemy cold, must be somewhere underground. The spidery tower of the ultra-wave radio station rose from a black peak beyond the building. Farther, there was only frowning desolation: broken, ugly teeth of mountains, yawning crater-maws, cracked and riven and blasted rock, and strata of ice as old as the stone, all forever dead.

In a uniform which had belonged to Captain Madlok, John Star stepped out into the thin and bitter air, upon the little deck formed by the lowered outer valve. Assuming a confidence which he hardly felt, he waited while two men approached, with a manner of apprehensive hesitation, from the low white building.

"Cerberus Station, ahoy!" he hailed them, his manner as sternly official as possible.

"*Purple Dream,* ahoy," one of them responded, doubtfully—a very short man, very bald, very stout, very red of face, his appearance showing the careless neglect that sometimes comes of long isolation. There was, John Star thought, the equivalent of an entire meal accumulated on the front of his tunic. He wore the tarnished insignia of a Legion lieutenant.

"I am Captain John Ulnar," John Star said briskly. "The *Purple Dream* requires supplies. Captain Kalam is making out the requisitions. They must be aboard without delay."

The short man scowled suspiciously, pig-eyes narrowed.

"John Ulnar?" His voice was a nasal snarl. "And Captain Kalam, eh? In command of the *Purple Dream,* eh?"

His dirty, yellow-stubbled face held a smirk of sullen cunning. John Star watched his shifty-eyed hostility, and suddenly knew that he must be one of Adam Ulnar's men —knew that the web of unguessed treason in the Legion had reached out even to this cold forgotten rock.

"We are." Boldness was the only way. "We're on a top emergency mission, and we must have these supplies at once."

"I'm Lieutenant Nana, commandant of the station." The sullen voice was devoid of military courtesy. With a knowing leer, Nana added cunningly: "The special orders in my file show the *Purple Dream* under Captain Madlok and Commander Adam Ulnar. She's listed as the Commander's flagship."

John Star didn't pause to wonder what his game could be. If he had been warned against them, it seemed strange that he had stayed to meet them peaceably—an unfortified supply base, Cerberus Station showed no evidence of any weapons heavy enough to challenge the *Purple Dream.* If he had received no warning—but there was no time for puzzles.

"There has been a change of command," John Star informed him curtly. "Now here is Captain Kalam."

Jay Kalam appeared beside him, in another borrowed uniform. They swung down the accommodation ladder

72

from the tiny deck, and Jay Kalam offered a document, rapping sharply:

"Our requisition, Lieutenant!"

Glancing up at the ship's low turret, John Star made a quick motion with his hand. The ship's long proton gun lifted instantly out of its housing, and swung out above their heads to cover the long white building. Hal Samdu was at his post.

Nana looked up at the needle with small, blood-shot eyes. His unwashed face showed neither surprise nor any great alarm. He gave John Star a narrow-eyed glare of sullen hostility, and then reluctantly took the requisition.

"Sixteen tons of cathode plates!" His astonishment sounded unconvincing. "Not for one ship!"

"Sixteen tons!" John Star rapped. "Immediately!"

"Impossible!" Nana scowled again at the menacing gun, and muttered evasively: "I can't let you have them without first reporting to Legion Headquarters, for confirmation of your orders."

"We've no time for that. Our mission is top emergency——"

Nana lifted his untidy shoulders, in defiance.

"I'm the commandant of Cerberus Station," he snarled. "I'm not accustomed to accepting orders from——" He paused, and his red eyes narrowed. "——from pirates!"

"In this case, however," Jay Kalam said softly, "I should advise you to do so."

Nana shook his fist, in a rage that looked like bad acting, and Jay Kalam waved a signal to Hal Samdu. The great needle above their heads lifted toward the radio tower on the peak, and blinding incandescence jetted out. The tower crumpled instantly, into hot ruin.

And Nana was suddenly trembling, his unshaven face white and twitching with a fear that looked more genuine than his wrath had been.

"Very well," he whispered hoarsely. "I'll accept your requisition."

"Go with him, Captain Ulnar," said Jay Kalam. "See that there is no mistake or delay."

Nana complained that he did not have all the supplies required. Most of his men were too ill to help with the loading. The cranes and conveyors were out of order. He was doing his utmost, John Star recognized, to delay them until the sixteen pursuing Legion cruisers should have time to arrive.

73

Yet, four hours later, under John Star's stern supervision and the menace of the great proton gun, all the cathode plates were aboard. The cylinders of oxygen were safely loaded, and the supplies of food and wine that Giles Habibula had added to the requisitions. Only the black drums of rocket fuel remained piled beneath the air-lock, and it was still an hour before the pursuing ships should reach them. Yet John Star had caught a gleam of sullen satisfaction in Nana's red pig-eyes that sharpened his uneasiness.

Then Jay leaped from the valve, and came running across the field.

"Time to go, John!" His voice was low, urgent.

"Why? We ought to have an hour——"

Jay Kalam glanced at the curious, staring men gathering to load the rocket fuel, and dropped his voice. "The 'scopes show another ship, John. Nearer. Headed here from Pluto."

"So that was Nana's game!" John Star nodded in bleak understanding. "A nice little surprise for us. Anyhow, we've got to have the fuel. We'll have to take a chance on outrunning Nana's friends."

Jay Kalam's lean dark face was taut with a rare concern.

"This isn't a Legion cruiser, John—it's moving a good deal too fast." Beneath his calm, John Star could sense his deep alarm. "I never saw the like. A black spider of a ship, with things jutting out of a round belly of a hull."

John Star staggered back from the cold apprehension that hit him in the pit of his stomach.

"The Medusæ!" he gasped. "That's the sort of ship that took Aladoree. Nana must have sent for them, to ambush us here. I don't know what sort of weapons they would have——"

"We'll have to go," Jay Kalam cut in. "We can't risk fighting."

"The rocket-fuel?"

"Leave it. Come aboard."

They ran up the accommodation ladder.

Lieutenant Nana stared after them with narrowed red eyes, and muttered something to his men about the drums. They all retreated toward the long metal building—with a haste that was ominous.

The air-lock was sealed. Levers flicked down under John Star's fingers. Blue flame should have screamed from the

74

rockets to send them plunging spaceward—but the *Purple Dream* lay dead!

Puzzled and dismayed, he tried the firing keys again—and nothing happened.

"We're somehow—stuck!" Incredulous, he scanned the dials. "Magnetism!" he exclaimed. "Look at the indicators! A terrific field. But how——? The ship is non-magnetic. I don't see——"

"A magnetic trap," said Jay Kalam. "Our friend Nana has somehow got magnets rigged, somewhere close to the ship. Our hull is non-magnetic; but still the field holds the rocket-firing mechanism and the geodynes out of control. He's trying to hold us, until the ships get here, and——"

"Then," broke in John Star, "we must stop their dynamos."

"Hal," Jay Kalam spoke into his telephone, "destroy the building."

The tongue of roaring violet flame reached again from the shining needle. It swept the long, low metal building from end to end, and left it a flattened tangle of smoking metal and broken brick, flung off its foundations by the sheer thrust of the blast.

"Now!"

Again John Star tried the rockets; again only silence answered.

"The magnets still hold us. The dynamos must be underground, where our blast didn't reach them."

"I can, then!" cried John Star. "Open the lock."

He snatched two hand proton guns, besides the two in his belt already, and darted out of the bridge-room.

"Wait!" called Jay Kalam. "What——?"

But he was already gone; Jay Kalam touched the controls to open the valve for him.

He dropped to the field, ran across to the smoking wreck of the long building, and searched the bare foundations until he found the stair, a shaft hewn through dark rock and strata of old ice. Down the steps he plunged, proton guns in his hands, leaping stray fragments of still-glowing metal.

A hundred feet below, in the cold crust of Cerberus, a heavy metal door loomed in front of him. He turned a proton-blast on it, at full force. It flashed incandescent, sagged, caved in. He leaped over it, into a long, dim-lit hall. He heard the drum of machinery ahead, the hum of dynamos; but another door stopped him. He tried the gun and it was dead—exhausted by that first full blast. Before he could level another, a violet lance stabbed at him from a tiny wicket.

Alert, he flung his body under that blade of killing fire, flat on his stomach. Even though he escaped the searing ray, the conducted shock of it numbed him. But his own blast answered at the same instant, and the glowing wreck of the door was flung back upon the man behind it.

On his feet at once, though his shoulder was blistered and throbbing, he sprang for the door, tossing away his discharged gun and snatching the two from his belt.

A square room was before him, rock-hewn, great dynamos humming in the center of it. Five men stood about it in attitudes of petrified dismay, only Lieutenant Nana's hand groping mechanically for his weapon.

But John Star's guns flamed—at the generators.

Unarmed now, but sure the dynamos were wrecked, he flung his discharged guns in Nana's sullen, blinking, yellow-stubbled face, and ran back down the hall and up the stair, hoping surprise would give him time to get back aboard.

It did. The air-lock clanged again. The rockets washed black pinnacles with roaring blue flame, and the *Purple Dream* flashed upward from Pluto's cragged moon—off at last, John Star exulted savagely, off at last for far-off Barnard's Star, to the aid of Aladoree!

"The delay——" whispered Jay Kalam. "Too long, I'm afraid. That black spider-ship has got too close—we can hardly escape it, now!"

12

Storm in Space

Cerberus, Moon of Pluto, fell behind, a cold gray speck, and vanished.

The Black Planet itself was swallowed in the infinite black abyss, and the splendid star that was the sun began to fade and dwindle in Orion.

They passed the speed of light. The Sun and the stars

behind were visible now only with rays they had overtaken; picked up and refracted in the lenses and prisms of the tele-periscopes to correct the distortion of speed.

Giles Habibula lived, now, in the generator room. Under the care of his fat and oddly steady hands, the geodynes ran almost perfectly. That ominous snarl of destructive vibration went unheard for hours at a time.

And the *Purple Dream* drove on. The tiny worlds of men were lost behind. Ahead, the stars of Ophiuchus slowly spread, but still not even the highest powers of the tele-periscopes could show the faint point of Barnard's Star—so dim in stellar death that it was only the tenth magnitude, as seen from Earth. And only their haunted minds could picture its lone evil world, where Aladoree had been taken.

They drove on, day after day, at the utmost speed of straining generators—and the black flier followed. Light from it would never overtake them, now. The tele-periscopes failed to show its monstrous spider-shape. Only the geodesic telltale screen betrayed it—for the telltale mechanism registered geodesic over-drive fields, instantaneously.

John Star begged Giles Habibula to nurse more thrust from the over-loaded geodynes, and he watched the faint red fleck on the screen. It seemed to stand motionless, now. Whether the generators ran well or ill, its distance never changed.

"They're playing with us," he muttered once, uneasily. "No matter how fast we go, we never gain an inch."

"Just following." Gnawing worry was apparent, even in Jay Kalam's calm. "They can catch us when they like. Or maybe—if their communications equipment is up to it—they'll just signal their friends at home to have our welcome ready."

"I wonder why they don't attack us, now?"

"Waiting to see our plans, I suppose. Or, more likely, they're still hoping for a chance to get the Commander back, alive."

For Adam Ulnar was still locked in the brig, a cheerful and philosophic prisoner with no apparent remorse for his treason; he had asked for paper and was busy writing the memoirs of his long career, for the proud archives of the Purple Hall.

Hopefully now, John Star whispered, "if they won't attack, perhaps we can give them the slip."

Jay Kalam shook his dark head, slowly. "I can see no way."

On they drove, into the star-glittering crystal black of interstellar space. All four of them grew haggard, from want of sleep, from the tension of effort and dread. Only Jay Kalam appeared almost unchanged, always deliberate and cool, always gravely pleasant. John Star's face was white, his eyes burning with anxiety. Hal Samdu, grown nervous and irritable, muttered to himself; he knotted his huge and useless fists, and sometimes glared at imaginary enemies. Even Giles Habibula, incredibly, lost weight until the skin hung in pouches under his hollowed, leaden eyes.

Day by day the Sun grew smaller, until it was dwarfed by Betelgeuse and Rigel, until it was a faint white star, lost amid the receding splendors of Orion.

In the tele-periscopes, Barnard's Star appeared and grew.

Runaway sun! Red, feeble, dying dwarf. Racing northward out of the constellation Ophiuchus, in mad flight from the Serpent and the Scorpion. Long ago christened "Barnard's Runaway Star," from its discoverer and its remarkable proper motion, it was the nearest star of the northern sky and the nearest found to have a habitable planet.

Habitable—so the censored and fragmentary reports of Eric Ulnar's expedition had described it. But the mad survivors of the expedition, rotting away in guarded hospital wards of maladies that the Legion specialists in planetary medicine could neither understand nor cure, had shrieked and whispered of a weird domain of half-known horror. The rulers of that planet were the monstrous Medusæ, and it was scarcely habitable for men.

John Star was watching that ancient, expiring sun one day, an eye of dull red evil in the tele-periscope. Its hypnotic glare brought him foreboding thoughts of Aladoree, imprisoned on its terror-haunted planet. He seemed to see her clear, honest gray eyes, horror-distended, and filmed with soul-searing fear. A cold and helpless wrath accumulated in him.

He started when Jay Kalam spoke:

"Look! Ahead of us—a green shadow!"

Even then his low, restrained voice was tense with dread of the cosmic unknown.

Ahead of them, the tele-periscopes showed that ominous

and eerie shadow, swiftly growing. It shone with the strange dim green of ionized nebular gases, and the dark spreading wings of it blotted out the stars of Ophiuchus, and slowly grew to hide the Serpent and even the Scorpion.

John Star stepped up the magnification of the 'scopes, until he could see the ugly, crawling motion of its vast writhing streams, and the angry currents of strange matter and stranger energies boiling within it.

"An unchartered nebula," he whispered at last. "We had better turn away."

Star-gazing nomads of the Earth, from the beginning, had wondered at those dark clouds against the firmament. Star-roving nomads of space, more recently, had sometimes perished in them. Even yet, however, they were little-known, and all prudent spacemen kept well away from their vast maelstroms of fire and cosmic fury.

Back at the Legion Academy, John Star had listened to a renowned astrophysicist lecturing learnedly on "Intranebular Dynamics." He knew the fine-spun theories of counter-space, of inverse curvature, of pseudo-gravitation and negative entropy. The nebulæ, according to the theories, were the wombs of planets and suns and even of future galaxies; the second law of thermodynamics was somehow circumvented in their anomalous counter-spaces, and radiation trapped in their mysterious depths somehow re-integrated into matter; their final awesome destiny was to re-wind the run-down universe itself. So that famous astrophysicist believed—but he had never ventured near the dark, supernal fury of such a storm in space.

John Star gulped, and his voice came faint with awe. "We're running too near—I'll change our course."

"No," Jay Kalam protested quietly. "Drive on toward it."

"Yes?" Wondering, taut with mounting dread, he obeyed.

The mass ahead tripped the gravity detectors. They had to drop below the speed of light, so that their search beams could guard them from collision. And that strange cloud grew.

Utterly insignificant it may have been, in the scale of cosmic space, so tiny that the System's astronomers had never discovered or charted it. The vast and little-known forces of it could make no threat to the System itself, for the inverse inflection of the counter-spaces was held to cause repulsion from the gravity-fields of suns. On the galactic scale, it was the merest fleck of curious dust.

On the human scale, however, it was big enough—and deadly.

Enormously, its dark and dimly shining arms twisted out across the stars ahead. The 'scopes began to show the terrible detail of it: black dust-clouds, hurtling streams of jagged meteoric fragments, dark banners of thin gases, all whipped with the raging winds of half-guessed cosmic forces, angrily aglow with the eerie green of ionization.

John Star stood rigid with dread, and he felt a chill of icy sweat. But he kept their course on toward it, until they were flashing along no more than a thousand miles from the side of a darkly burning greenish streamer, which seemed to reach out for them like a kind of monstrous pseudopod.

"If it caught us——" His dry throat stuck, and he had to swallow. "Those meteor-streams—hurtling boulders! Those whirlpools of shining gas! The forces inside it—unknown!" He wiped sweat off his set, white face. "I don't think we'd last five seconds."

But Jay Kalam told him, gently:

"Steer a little closer."

"Eh?" John Star muttered, hoarsely. "Why?"

Silently, Jay Kalam pointed at the forgotten red spark on the tell-tale screen, which marked the position of the black ship behind them. It was visibly creeping up, to close the distance which had been fixed so long.

John Star caught his breath. "So they're trying to overtake us, now?"

"More than trying," Jay Kalam reminded him softly. "I suppose they're afraid we'll try to shake them off, in the edges of the nebula. Steer a little closer."

He touched the controls again, with stiff and icy fingers. The racing ship veered slightly, toward that appalling cloud of dim green fire and darkness. A cosmic storm, in very truth—for mad winds of unseen force ripped and twisted black dust and glowing gas into shredded streamers and wild vortices and sprawling tentacles that seemed to writhe and whip in elemental fury.

"Steer a little closer," urged Jay Kalam gently. "And we'll soon find out how much they value Commander Ulnar's life."

John Star moved the controls again, with numb, unwilling fingers, and then turned a tele-periscope on the black ship behind—for even laggard light from it could overtake them, now that they had slowed. A colossal thing, strange as the green and wetly heaving monsters that made its crew. With black rods and vanes and levers jutting in baffling array from the round black hull, it looked like a black spider flying. The main wings had been somehow retracted, but certain smaller vanes moved slightly, now and again, as it came, as if reacting against some unseen medium to control its flight. Perhaps, he guessed, it made use of radiation-pressures.

It grew large in the lenses—dark and strange as the spatial storm ahead.

"They can't attack!" John Star gulped to moisten his throat. "Not if they want to save Commander Ulnar's life."

And Jay Kalam murmured softly: "Try it just a little closer, now."

John Star touched the helm again—and his heart grew sick.

The bright clean song of the geodynes had been ringing like a peal of living power through the ship; he had almost felt the thrust that sent them ahead. But that song changed. Suddenly, now, the snarling vibration of unmatched units came back. Their speed fell off again—and the red spark in the telltale screen came up almost to touch them.

Tense and desperate, John Star guided the sick vessel closer to that stormy wall of dust and green fire and grinding stone, and Jay Kalam watched astern. He said suddenly:

"I'm afraid the Commander won't save us, after all. They're firing—something!"

Out of the belly of that black spider-ship came a little ball of misty white. It followed them, more swiftly than the crippled geodynes could take them, and grew as it came. They watched it in the lenses, frozen with a new wonder and a breathless terror, for it was utterly inexplicable.

A ball of opalescence. It wasn't matter, John Star knew —for no material projectile could have overtaken them so swiftly, even crippled and lagging as they were. It was a swirling globe of milky flame, splendid with rainbow sheens. It swelled behind them. It hid the spider-ship. It covered the belt of bright Orion. It filled the void behind them like a new star born.

A glowing sun—flung after them!

That was quite fantastic, John Star knew. But it grew vast in space, and the hot image of it in the lenses hurt his eyes. And still it swelled, ever more terribly bright.

And it *drew* them!

The *Purple Dream* lurched, rolled toward it.

A sudden dizzy nausea, an intolerable vertigo, overwhelmed John Star. He staggered, stumbled back from the controls, and clutched a handrail. He clung to it, sick and trembling, while the ship spun helpless in the grasp of that pursuing sun.

They fell toward that blinding opalescence. Grimly, his jaw set against the nausea, John Star fought the spin of the stricken ship, battled his lurching way back to the controls—and found the geodynes utterly dead.

The ship dropped, unchecked.

Tossing seas of white opalescence spread out to drown them, vast as the surface of a very sun. Angry, flaming prominences reached out to snare them—and then the thing was gone.

White exploding fire half-blinded them—and it had vanished like a punctured bubble. John Star's baffling sickness ended. Space was black once more behind them, and soon his dazzled eyes could see the belted splendor of Orion. The song of the geodynes came back, and the ship answered her controls.

John Star mopped weakly at his face.

"Never felt—such a thing!" he whispered. "Space itself —dropped from beneath us!"

"A sort of vortex of disintegration, I imagine," Jay Kalam commented softly. "Some such thing was mentioned in the secret reports of the Ulnar Expedition that were sent out to Aladoree at the fort on Mars. Only a hint— they were careful not to tell her much. But there was some reference to an energy vortex weapon—a frightful thing that warped the space-coordinates, making all matter unstable, growing from the energy of the atoms it annihilated, and creating an attraction to draw more matter in. A kind of pseudo-sun!"

John Star nodded, shaken.

"That must be it," he agreed. "The distortion of space must have made the geodynes go dead." He caught a long, uneasy breath. "We can't fight them with the proton gun —not when they start throwing suns!"

"No," Jay Kalam said quietly. "I see only one thing to do—drive straight into the nebula."

"Into that storm!" John Star blinked. "The ship couldn't live a minute, there."

"A minute is a long time, John," Jay Kalam told him gently. "They've fired another shot."

"Another——"

His dry throat seized his voice.

"Turn straight in," Jay Kalam said. "I don't think they'll follow."

For a moment his mind rebelled. He stood frozen at the controls, staring at the angry banners of the nebular storm. One sick instant—and then he had mastered himself. He accepted the danger, and turned the *Purple Dream* into that appalling cloud of dim green fire and darkness.

Death grew behind them. Again a milky ball came from the belly of the black spider-ship, and swelled into a pseudo-sun of devouring atomic flame. Again the cruiser pitched and spun, with geodynes dead, helpless in that greedy grasp. Again John Star was ill.

But the abrupt turn had saved them. That hurtling globe of expanding opalescence missed them, too narrowly, and exploded far beyond them. The released geodynes pealed out again, and the ship sprang ahead—into the nearest angry arm of the nebula.

Into fury and enigma.

John Star had listened to the theories. All positive-entropy processes should be suspended or reversed, the theorists said, in the inverse-inflexure of the nebular counter-spaces. That meant that power-tubes could yield no power, and geodynes could give no thrust. It meant that rockets couldn't fire. It meant that clocks and chronometers would run backwards—and that human machines, very likely, would stop altogether.

That was what the theoretical astrophysicists said—but none of them had ever been inside a nebula, to observe the birth of matter. Only two or three daring spacemen had ever ventured on nebular explorations, into a smaller counter-space lying on the route to Proxima, and they had never emerged.

John Star caught his breath again and tried to nerve himself to meet emergency. The repulsion fields of the meteor deflector would serve to protect the hull from the nebular drift—if the masses were not too large, too numerous, or coming too fast. For the rest, the life of the ship depended on his skill.

The *Purple Dream*, with his quick fingers on the keys, sought a path through the spinning fringe of spiral arms. Whether the theorists were right or wrong, he knew the ship couldn't survive in the nebula's heart. Nothing stronger than grinding boulders would be needed to destroy them. Mysterious womb of worlds, or merely a pinch of common cosmic dust, it could also be their grave.

His flying fingers touched the keys, and the cruiser spun and darted through a dance with black and shining death. It found rifts in the curtains of dust. It recoiled from green, grasping arms. It swam through rivers of hurtling stones. It defied the grasp of the nebula, and fought like a thing alive for life.

From some remote distance, John Star heard Jay Kalam's gentle voice:

"Good work, John! I don't think they'll follow."

And the *Purple Dream* threaded onward through the mazes of the nebula. Walls of green flame were suddenly ahead; the drift lurked in the black dust-clouds, and leaped out with naked fangs of tearing stone. Hurricane-like, the half-known forces of the cosmic storm battered and tore at the ship—forces akin to the dread vortices of sunspots, John Star suspected, and even the deadly drag of the Medusæ's pseudo-suns.

Right or left, up or down, he drove the ship with sure fingers. The radar and the thermal detectors made a continual, useless clamor, until he shut them off. Only human skill and quickness could serve them now.

For a moment he thought they were free. The black ahead was deadly dust no longer, but the frosty dark of open space. Through that glow of eerie green, he saw the beacon of red Antares—and then the geodynes failed again.

The bright keening of the generators was broken suddenly, with that old, heart-breaking vibration. The precious thrust was lost. A black and jagged mass of rock—a nascent world, perhaps—came at them suddenly. John Star's fingers dropped on the keys, but the sick ship failed to answer.

That black-fanged rock came on through the screens. It struck the hull with a clang that reverberated like the very knell of doom. Then there was a silence. John Star listened. He couldn't hear the geodynes—but there was no hiss and roar of air escaping. He knew the staunch hull had held.

Then the ship began to spin. The bright beacon of Antares was suddenly gone, and the rift in the nebula closed. The same wind of force that had hurled the boulder had caught them now. It dragged them back, toward the mysterious heart of the nebula.

John Star tried the dead controls again, and stared fearfully at the chronometer—though he knew that his human mechanism would surely be stopped, quite permanently, before the anomalous forces of the counter-space set time to running backward.

"Giles!" It was Jay Kalam, queerly calm, speaking into the ship's telephone. "We must have power, Giles!"

And Giles Habibula's voice came back from the speaker on the bulkhead, plaintive and abstracted:

"For sweet life's sake, don't bother me now. For poor old Giles is ill, Jay. His head can't stand this wicked spinning—and his precious geodynes never acted so before! Let him die in peace, Jay."

That mad wind of energy swept them on. John Star frantically studied his dials and gauges, and failed to analyze it. Neither magnetic nor gravitic, it must be something of the nebula's own. Here at the unknown borderland of space and counter-space, he thought, even such familiar terms as magnetism and gravitation could have no certain meaning. He watched the chronometer again, waiting fearfully for it to turn backward and knowing he would be dead before that could happen. There was nothing else to do.

"Ah, my poor old head," came the faint and weary plaint of Giles Habibula. "Deadly ill, and spinning like a silly top. Ah, poor old Giles is sick, sick, sick——"

But the sound of the geodynes came back, at first a harrowing growl.

"Sick, sick, sick!" sobbed Giles Habibula. "Ah, a poor old soldier of the Legion, hunted out of the precious System on a lying charge of wicked treason, and dying like a dog in a mortal storm in space. Sick and—ah, *there!*"

The geodynes, abruptly, were humming clear and sweet.

The *Purple Dream* was alive again. John Star turned her out of that savage, sucking current. She nosed through a river of hurtling stones, and drove through a cloud of greenish gas; and ahead was the rift again. The black of space, and bright Antares.

They came out of the last thin streamer of the storm, into the clear dark of space. Ahead were the cold diamond stars; and the greenish shadow of the nebula swiftly dwindled behind—in the vaster cosmic scale, it was just a speck of curious dust.

"Safe!" John Star exulted.

"Safe!" Jay Kalam repeated the word, and smiled a slow, ironic smile. "And there ahead is Barnard's Star."

In the field of the tele-periscope, John Star found the Runaway Sun. It was a red and solitary eye, watching their approach with a cold, steady stare of unblinking menace.

"Yes, we're safe enough, for now," Jay Kalam smiled, a dark taut smile. "I think we're rid of that spider-ship. I think we can reach the planet, now—if we can pass the barrier the Medusæ have set up to defend it."

John Star merely looked at him, with a weary, dim dismay.

"There was something about that barrier belt in the secret reports that came to Aladoree on Mars," Jay Kalam explained. "Not much—Commander Ulnar let her know just enough so she wouldn't suspect his plot. Perhaps he could tell us something more. But I believe the Medusæ have their planet very effectively defended."

He smiled again, gravely.

"Anyhow, John, we're safe enough for now."

13

The Belt of Peril

They went to the cruiser's brig.

"Welcome, John." Adam Ulnar called that cheerful greeting to them, through the bars of the tiny cell. Elder statesman of the Purple Hall, Commander of the Legion, and traitor against mankind, he sat on the edge of the narrow bunk, busy with his memoirs.

"Just a moment, John." Deliberately he finished the sentence he was writing, laid his pen and manuscript aside on the neatly folded blanket, and stood up to meet them. A tall, distinguished statesman. His wide shoulders were proudly erect; his fine head, with the long white hair well-combed and flowing, was bowed to no visible burden of guilt.

"A pleasure, gentlemen." He smiled, and his fine blue eyes held a spark of ironic amusement. "I've too few guests. Come on in. Rough weather we've been meeting, by the feel of the ship."

"But we'll find rougher weather ahead," John Star told him. "Or so I imagine—from all I hear of the Belt of Peril."

That phrase had rather a remarkable effect on Adam Ulnar. His face lost its smile of wary mockery, and froze to a rigid mask. Behind the mask, John Star sensed something like consternation. His hands clenched white on the bars of the cell. He stared from one to the other of them; and seconds had passed before he could speak.

"The Belt——" he swallowed. "You mean we're bound for Barnard's Star?"

"We're going after Aladoree," John Star said crisply. "I understand that Eric's expedition reported some kind of defensive barrier zone around the Medusæ's planet. We want to know what it is—and how to get through it alive."

The fine wrinkles bit deeper into Adam Ulnar's face, and all the cheerful color had ebbed from it. The pupils of his blue eyes were black and big with a sick dismay.

"I don't know what it is." His voice was slow and dull with fear. "I don't know."

"You must!" John Star's voice was a brittle challenge. "You had the full reports, uncensored. Eric must have told you all about it. Let's have it!"

Heavily, the Commander shook his head.

"Eric didn't know," he said. "Even after the Medusæ had made their agreement to help us, in return for a cargo of iron, they wouldn't tell him anything about it. All I know is what it did to the ships of his expedition when they first tried to land."

"And what was that?"

"Enough," Adam Ulnar said. "His fleet approached the barrier zone without any warning of danger, you see— fortunately Eric had been smart enough to bring his flagship to the rear. Only the two lead vessels got into the zone. They never came out.

"What the barrier force is, his engineer couldn't discover. They believed that it is radiant energy—if so, however, it is something different in effect from any gamma or cosmic radiation known to us. The crews of those two unfortunate ships had no time to signal any reports. The ships fell, out of control. Observers on the other vessels reported that they seemed to be disintegrating—falling apart. Later, a few meteor-like streaks were observed in the planet's upper atmosphere. And that was all.

"Eric kept the rest of his fleet outside the barrier until he had established radio and television communication with the Medusæ—which took a considerable time. Afterward, they allowed several of his ships to visit the planet and leave it again—apparently they can open the barrier at will."

John Star eyed him sharply.

"What else do you know?" he demanded. "The men who landed must have learned something about it."

The old man clinging to the bars forced a sick, yellow smile.

"The most of them could never tell what they learned." His dull voice held an echo of dread. "They're the ones who came back to die in the mental wards—if they came back at all. You see, there's something in the planet's atmosphere that isn't good for the flesh or the minds of men. A virus, a secondary radiation excited by the barrier rays, or perhaps a toxic emanation from the bodies of the Medusæ themselves—those stricken scientists could never agree on what it was. But they did prove that men can't go there and live. The effects are extremely variable, and sometimes long delayed. But the onset, when it comes, is sudden and terrible."

"Thank you, Commander," Jay Kalam said, and they turned away.

"Wait!" The shaken voice called after them. "You aren't going on—not into the Belt?"

"We're running through it," John Star assured him.

"We shall try," added Jay Kalam, "to get through it at a very high speed. By surprise. Before those radiations —if that is what they are—have time to take effect."

Holding himself upright, with his white and trembling hands on the bars, old Adam Ulnar looked at both their faces. His pale lips twitched. Bowed, now, his shoulders made a weary little shrug, and he finally spoke.

"I can see there's no dissuading you, John. You're the Ulnar breed, and you won't yield to danger. I believe you're really going to try to run the Belt. I really believe you're ready to land on that monstrous planet, a thing that even Eric wouldn't do."

"I am," John Star said.

"I believe you really are." That white, distinguished head nodded slowly, and a feeble spark of pride came back to the stricken eyes. "I admire your resolution, John. At least you'll die an Ulnar's death.

"Now, if you please, John, I've one last request."

"What is that, Commander?" John Star heard a sudden respect in his own voice, and something close to warmth.

"In my desk, in my stateroom, there's a secret drawer," the bleak-faced old man said huskily. "I'll tell you how to find it. It contains a little vial of poison——"

John Star shook his head. "We can't do that."

"We're kinsmen, John." Adam Ulnar's voice held a broken, pleading quaver. "In spite of our present political quarrel, you must remember that once I did a favor for you. I paid for your education, remember, and put you in the Legion. Am I asking too much in return—a few drops of euthanasia?"

"I'm afraid you are," John Star told him. "Because I think we'll need information from you again, when we come to deal with the Medusæ."

"No, John!" the old man sobbed, wild-eyed and frantic now. "Please, John! You can't deny me death——"

"We ought to bring you the bottle, Commander." Jay Kalam gave him a lean, dark smile. "Just to see what you'd do. Because you've over-played your role."

Adam Ulnar returned that sober smile. His clutching hands released the bars, and his bent shoulders straightened.

"I was trying to turn you back," he confessed. "I've no need of poison, if you do go on—I believe that death in the Belt is as quick as a man could wish." His voice still was taut and urgent. "But every word I've told you is the truth. You'll never land alive—or, if you do, you'll presently be needing that little bottle yourselves, to escape your madness and your pain.

"Bad luck, gentlemen!"

He dismissed them with a casual wave of his hand, and went back to the papers on his narrow bunk.

The *Purple Dream* drove on.

Barnard's Star burned on their right. A swelling, perfect sphere, sharp-edged against the ebon void. A type-M dwarf, old beyond imagination, so far gone in stellar death that their eyes could safely look upon it, with no filters behind the lenses. But its blood-red rays smote to their very brains, with a stark impact of fateful menace.

Straight ahead was its solitary planet, a dim and fearful crescent, washed with that ominous scarlet. World of the monstrous Medusæ, of that black spider-ship, of the waiting Belt of Peril.

The ship drove on, geodynes singing keen and clear. John Star and Jay Kalam stood before the tele-periscopes, watching for the first sign of danger. The red and cloudy planet swelled ahead.

The night-side of it was utterly black, a round blot on the stars. The day-side was a curved and ugly crimson blade, stained with evil blood, clotted with dark rust. Its orbit lay close to the dying dwarf. And it was gigantic, John Star realized; many times the bulk of Earth.

Jay Kalam drew a long, awed breath.

"The forts!" he whispered. "The stations that make the barrier—that's what they must be. A belt of moons!"

John Star found them. Dim and tiny crescents, red as the monstrous planet. He found three, following in the same orbit high above the murky atmosphere of the mighty world ahead; there must be six in all, he guessed, spaced sixty degrees apart.

A ring of fortress moons! The barrier itself must be invisible radiation, but the perfect spacing of those trailing satellites was proof enough of the Medusæ's hostile and scientific craft. John Star's brooding gaze went back to the larger murky crescent.

"Aladoree—there!" His low-breathed words were choked with a sense of incredulous horror. "Beyond those moons! Hidden and guarded, somewhere on that planet. And tortured, I suppose, for the secret of AKKA. We must get through, Jay."

"We must."

And Jay Kalam spoke quiet orders into his telephone.

"Mortal me!" a thin voice came plaintively back from the bulkhead speaker. "For the sake of precious life, Jay, can't we have a single breath of time? Must we go driving like a pack of reckless fools into new and wicked dangers, with never a blessed pause? Can't you give us a moment, Jay—just one single precious moment—to snatch a bite to eat?"

"Give us all the power you can, Giles," Jay Kalam broke in gently. "Because, right now, we're diving toward the barrier zone, depending on surprise and speed."

"Dear life—not now!" gasped Giles Habibula. "Not into that wicked thing they call the Belt of Peril!"

"We are, Giles," Jay Kalam said. "We're going to try it midway between two of their forts, hoping their rays will interfere."

"Sweet life—not yet!" sobbed Giles Habibula. "Give us time, Jay, for a single sip of wine! You couldn't be so heartless, Jay—not to a poor old soldier of the Legion. Not to a miserable, tottering human skeleton, Jay, dead on his feet from toiling day and night to keep his precious geodynes going, and gone to skin and bones for want of time to eat.

"Not that, Jay! Not to poor old——"

But John Star was listening no longer.

Tense at the controls, scarcely breathing, he was driving the *Purple Dream* down toward that vast and evil-seeming crescent of crimson murk, aiming straight between two of those black and tiny moons. And now he saw a fearful thing. Still no visible projectile or ray had come from the fortress satellites, but he saw something happening to the ship—and to him!

The metal bulkheads, and the faces of all the instruments before him, were suddenly luminous. His own skin was shining. Bright atoms were dancing away into the air, swirling motes of many colors. The very metal of the ship, it seemed, was evaporating into iridescent mist. His own body was!

Then he felt it—a sheet of blinding pain.

For a moment he gave way to agony, sick and reeling, eyes closed. He fought grimly to control himself, and lurched unsteadily toward Jay Kalam—who was a shimmering spectre now, clad in a splendid mist of dissolving rainbows.

"What——" His gasping voice came faint and strange, and agony clenched his teeth upon it. "What's this?"

"Radiation——" The bright spectre's voice was thin with pain. "Must dissolve the molecular bonds! . . . Ionized atoms dancing away! . . . Everything melting into atomic mist! . . . Molecular dissolution! . . . Our very nerves —destroyed!"

"How long can——?"

His voice went out. Red agony surged against his brain. Every limb and every tissue shrieked. Even the cells of his brain itself, he felt, screamed protest at this consuming radiation. Every second he thought he had felt the ultimate agony, and every second the agony increased.

He was blind with pain. Pain roared in his ears. Red-hot needles of pain probed every fiber of his body. But still he fought to keep the mastery of himself. He stood rigid over the controls and drove the cruiser down.

Above the agony thundering in his ears, he heard the whine of the hard-pressed geodynes change again to harsh vibration. That ugly snarl increased, until the whole ship shuddered to it. It became terrific. He thought it would break the very hull.

But the vibration ended suddenly. The ship was deathly still. The geodynes had failed completely. Only momentum was left, to carry them on through the radiation-wall.

In the new silence he heard Adam Ulnar screaming in the brig.

"Disintegration . . ." came the faint, hoarse rasp from Jay Kalam. "We're going—invisible!"

He saw, then, that the solid metal of the mechanisms about him was becoming weirdly and incredibly semi-transparent, as if about to dissolve completely in the glittering mist that swirled away from them, ever denser.

He looked at Jay Kalam, through the haze of shattered jewels, and saw a ghastly thing.

That shining spectre-shape was semi-transparent now, bones visible like shadows within misty outlines of flesh. Fiery smoke swirling away from it. It looked no longer human; it was grisly death, melting into nothingness.

Yet it still had consciousness, reason, will.

A sound whispered from it, dry and faint:

"Rockets!"

John Star knew that he was another dissolving ghost. Every atom of his body flamed with unendurable pain. Red agony blinded him, shrieked in his ears, froze his body in a final rigor. Yet he moved, before it overcame him utterly.

He reached the rocket firing keys.

He was sprawled over the control board, the next he knew, weak and trembling. His sick body was limp, dripping with sweat. He dragged himself up, aware that his fearful, agonizing transparency was gone. He saw Jay Kalam, faint and white; saw beyond him a few glistening diamond particles still floating in the air.

"The rockets," breathed Jay Kalam, his voice weak,

uncertain, yet gravely deliberate as ever. "The rockets brought us through."

"Through!" It was a dry, hoarse croak. "Inside the Belt?"

"Inside—and plunging toward the surface."

He fought to recover a grip on himself.

"Then we must brake our velocity, before we smash!"

"Giles!" Jay Kalam called into the telephone. "The geodynes——"

"Don't bother me now!" wheezed the faint and plaintive protest. "For poor old Giles is dying, dying! Ah, the wicked agony of it! And the generators are wrecked, burned up! Destroyed by that fearful vibration! They can never be repaired—not even by the rare and perfect skill of Giles Habibula. Ah, poor old Giles—not all his wits and his rare and precious genius can serve him now. Doomed and dying, far from home——"

"You don't mean it, Giles!" John Star broke in. "You can fix them!"

"No, John, the things are finished, I tell you. Burned up and done!"

"That's true," Jay Kalam said. "I checked them. The geodynes are gone. We've only the rockets to keep us from smashing to smoke."

John Star dragged himself grimly to the firing keys, muttering:

"Now is when we need the fuel we left on Pluto's moon!"

14

Corsair Sun

Down upon the huge, expanding, yellow-red planet the *Purple Dream* was hurtling, rocket blasts thundering forward at full power to check her flight—if it could be checked short of catastrophe.

Jay Kalam watched, gravely anxious, as John Star swiftly took the readings from a score of instruments, set them up on the calculators, and snapped down another key.

"What do you find?"

"A close thing," John Star said slowly, at last. "Much too close. At very nearly the same time, three things will happen. Our velocity will be braked, we'll approach the planet, and the rockets will run out of fuel.

"But that dense red atmosphere hides the surface—I can't tell just how far down it is. If it's too near, we smash before our momentum is checked. If it's too far, we'll be falling again—with all the fuel gone. It has to be just right—or else!"

"Then," Jay Kalam calmly observed, "we await the event. How long?"

"Two hours at full power will empty the tanks."

Jay Kalam nodded his lean, grave head, and turned silently back to his tele-periscope. After a moment he tensed suddenly, and turned to point out a new red spark that had crept unseen into the telltale screen.

"Another black flier," he announced. "Out to see the fireworks when we hit, I imagine—they must have spotted us running past their satellite-forts."

John Star picked it up in his own instrument—a monstrous shape of gleaming black metal; wide vanes moving, strange and slow, about the huge black belly of its hull. Not far above them, it was merely keeping pace with their fall, making no hostile move.

"Waiting to see us smash!" he muttered. "Or to pick us off if we don't!"

"I'm going to get Commander Ulnar," Jay Kalam said abruptly. "I'm going to let him hail them. We've very little left to lose, and everything to gain. Perhaps we can ransom Aladoree. Whatever the Ulnars have offered, the System can afford to raise it—to save her and AKKA."

John Star nodded—perhaps there was a chance. Jay Kalam brought Adam Ulnar to the bridge. The tall Commander was still white and shaken from their passage through the radiation-barrier, but his haggard face smiled faintly.

"Congratulations, John! I never thought you'd get us through."

Jay Kalam told him in a hard, tight voice:

"I'm going to let you talk, Commander. I'll give you a chance to save your life—and to save Aladoree Anthar and her secret for the Green Hall. I'll leave the details to you. But I'm sure the Green Hall would approve any necessary ransom. And I promise you—if you can help us get Aladoree safely back to the System—I promise that you'll go free."

"Thank you, Kalam." The white, distinguished head made him a slight and half-ironic bow. "Thank you for the very touching measure of your trust in me. But it's true that I don't want to die, and true that Eric has blundered very foolishly in his management of the enterprise I planned—for the girl should never have been brought here at all.

"So I'll do what I can."

Sharply, John Star studied that proud face, etched with years but handsome still. For all his hatred of what his kinsman had done, he could see sincerity there, and honor, and reassuring strength.

"Very well," Jay Kalam said. "You can hail them from on board?"

"With the ultra-wave transmitter." The Commander nodded. "The Medusæ, you see, are not sensitive to sound —though Eric's men named them for some terrestrial jellyfish, they're really like nothing in the System. They communicate with short radio waves, directly. I know the code of signals that Eric's men worked out—I used to talk, from the Purple Hall, with the agents they sent to the System."

"Go ahead," Jay Kalam told him. "Get that ship to give us a line, before we crash. Get them to bring Aladoree Anthar safe on board, and to give us what we need to repair the geodynes. And make them open the barrier so we can get away—I don't think we'd survive another passage through it. Promise what you like—but you had better be convincing."

"I'll do what I can."

And Adam Ulnar sat down at the compact panel of the ship's transmitter, his hollowed face visibly strained and eager. He quickly tuned the frequency he wanted, and then began making sounds into the microphone— sounds instead of words, awkward grunts and clicks and whistles.

The reply which came presently from the receiver was stranger still. The voices of the Medusæ were shrill whisperings, dry and eerie, so utterly unearthly that John Star, listening, shuddered to a chill of undiluted horror.

Adam Ulnar, too, seemed to find amazed horror in

95

what he heard. His lean jaw slackened with surprise. He was suddenly trembling, his lax face very white and abruptly pearled with sweat. His staring eyes were black, glazed.

Again he made queer little sounds into the transmitter, his voice so dry that he could scarcely form them. Dry rustlings came back from the receiver. He listened a long time, staring at nothing. At last the alien chirping ceased. Mechanically he reached a white and shaking hand to snap off the transmitter, and he came woodenly to his feet.

"What was it?" breathed John Star. "What did they say?"

"Nothing good," Adam Ulnar muttered blankly. Shakenly he clutched at a handrail to steady himself. "The worst that could have happened. Yet it's something I've dreaded—ever since I heard of Eric's foolish alliance."

His sick eyes gazed at the bulkhead, seeing nothing.

"What has happened?" John Star demanded.

Adam Ulnar rubbed a trembling hand across his sweat-beaded forehead.

"I scarcely dare to tell you, John. Because you'll blame me for it. And I suppose I am to blame—it was I who sent Eric out here with the expedition, so he'd have a chance to make himself a hero. Eric the Second!" He chuckled, without mirth. "Yes, I'm to blame."

"But what have they done?"

His glazed eyes came to John's face in mute appeal.

"Please don't think I planned it, John! But the Medusæ have tricked Eric—and the rest of us, it seems. They bargained to help us restore the Empire, in return for a shipload of iron. Now it seems they intend taking a good deal more."

His gaunt frame shuddered.

"They told me more of their history, just now, than Eric ever learned—and it's quite a history. They're old, John. Their sun is old. Their race was old, on that ghastly planet, before our Earth was ever born. They're too old, John—but they don't intend to die.

"The remarkable motion of Barnard's Star, they tell me now, is a thing of their own accomplishment. Because the mineral resources of their own planet were used up long ago, they've arranged to visit others. In their career across the Galaxy, they live by looting the worlds they pass, and sometimes plant a colony—that's to be the fate of Earth, they tell me."

He shook his white head with a sick, slow motion.

"Please, John," he whispered, "don't think I ever intended that!"

John Star and Jay Kalam stood voiceless with shock. The thing was unthinkable, but John Star knew it must be true. Reason insisted that the Medusæ would scarcely join an interstellar war for a single cargo of iron. And Adam Ulnar's horrified remorse appeared sincere enough.

Dazed, John Star pictured the doom of humanity. The System couldn't fight a science that built these black spider-ships of space and armed them with atomic suns for weapons; a science that fortified a planet with a belt of artificial satellites, and guided a star itself like a red corsair across the Galaxy.

No, the System didn't have a chance—not with the Legion of Space already betrayed by its own Commander's treason, and AKKA already in the hands of the monstrous enemy.

"Please, John!" Adam Ulnar's broken voice was thin with a sick appeal. "Please don't think I intended this. And now, if you please—I really want that little vial in my desk."

Harshly, John Star rasped: "You don't deserve to die!"

"No, Commander," Jay Kalam told him gravely. "You must live—at least a little longer. If we survive the landing, you may yet have a chance to help undo your treason."

He led the stumbling prisoner back to his cell.

Rockets still roaring, the *Purple Dream* fell. Intended only for the delicate maneuvering of takeoffs and landings, the rocket motors were never designed for such a task as this. Braking the terrific velocity which had brought them safely through the radiation barrier was a job for the geodynes—but the geodynes were gone. John Star stood rigid by the controls, fighting for the last ounce of power from the last drop of fuel; fighting to stop the cruiser in time.

The black spider-ship dropped after them. The efficient Medusæ watched—curious, no doubt, to observe the effects of their barrier rays on the wreckage of the ship. And ready, certainly, with some new weapon, if these rash invaders did survive the landing.

Thick red mist came up about the *Purple Dream*.

The black flier following became a dim, vast shadow in

the murk. All else was lost. And still the cruiser fell, toward the unseen world beneath the red-lit clouds. The rockets paused in their even thunder, came back, barked in a loud back-fire—and stopped.

"The fuel is out," John Star whispered. "Still falling —and nothing we can do!"

Hands knotted with an agony of powerless inaction, he peered into the thick, red-lit mist ahead. His straining eyes made out a surface—something smooth and glistening. It flashed up to meet them.

"A sea!" he breathed. "Going down—"

Panic choked him, but he heard Jay Kalam's voice, soft and calm even in the last moment of their plunging fall:

"Anyhow, John, we've got to the planet where Aladoree is."

15

Under the Unknown Sea

"So we're stuck on the bottom of a mortal sea?" observed Giles Habibula.

His mood was not rejoicing. He had the voice of a well-grown and lusty tomcat protesting a weighty tread on its tail.

John Star nodded soberly, and he continued bitterly: "Twenty long, loyal years I've truly served the Legion, since that evil day on Venus, when——"

He checked himself, with a roll of his fishy eye, and John Star prompted:

"How was it you came to join?"

"Twenty years, lad, old Giles has served in the Legion, as stout and true a blessed man, and—ah, yes, in good life's name!—as brave a soldier as ever was!"

"Yes, I know. But——"

"Old Giles has put his past behind him, lad." His voice turned reproachfully plaintive. "He has redeemed himself, if ever a daring hero did. And look at him now, bless his precious bones!

"Accused for a wicked pirate, when for twenty long years he's never done more than—when for twenty eternal years he's been a noble warrior in the Legion. Ah, yes, lad, look at old Giles Habibula. Look at him before you now!"

His voice broke; a great tear trembled in the corner of his fishy eye, as if terrified by the purple magnitude of the nose below, hesitated and dared and splashed down unheeded.

"Look at poor old Giles! Hunted like a dog out of his own native System. Driven like a rabbit into interstellar space. Hurled headlong into this planet of ghastly danger and crawling horrors. Stuck to spend the rest of his cheerless days of suffering in a wreck on the bottom of an evil sea!

"Pitiful old Giles Habibula! For years he's been feeble, tottering, with gray hairs crowning his mortal head. He's been ill and lame. He's been forgotten, stuck away at a lonely, desolate little outpost on Mars.

"Now he's trapped to starve and die in a wreck on the bottom of a fearful yellow sea! Where's the precious justice of that, lad?"

He buried his great face in his hands, and trembled to sobs somewhat resembling the death-struggles of a harpooned whale. But it was not long before he straightened, and wiped his fishy eyes with the back of his fat hand.

"Anyhow, lad," he wheezed wearily, "let's have a drop of wine to help forget the frightful miseries that are piled upon us. And a taste of cold ham and biscuit. And there's a case of canned cheese I found in the stores the other day.

"And I'll tell you about that time on Venus, lad. It was a brave adventure—if I hadn't stumbled over a wicked reading lamp in the dark! For poor old Giles Habibula was clever, then, and nimble as you are, lad."

"No, we've no way to move the ship," John Star repeated, standing on the bridge with Jay Kalam a little later. "She lies in shallow water, though—according to the pressure-gauges, she's less than a hundred feet down."

"But we can't get her to the surface?"

"No. The geodynes are dead, and the rocket-fuel gone —if we had those drums we left on Pluto's moon! And the hull is too heavy to float. Wasn't designed for water navigation."

"Still," objected Jay Kalam, thoughtfully grave, yet

with a calm determination that meant more than another's utmost vehemence. "Still, we can't give up. Not so long as we're alive and on the same planet with Aladoree."

"No," agreed John Star, quietly decisive. "If we could release her, just long enough to find materials and set up AKKA, we'd have the Medusæ at our mercy."

"That is what we must do—what we shall do.

"And now," he added, "let's talk to Adam Ulnar."

They found the man sitting wan and dejected on his cot in the brig, still dazed from the shock of the Medusæ's revelation. The regal pride of the Purple Hall had left him. He was staring blankly at the wall, dry lips moving. At first he was not aware of them; John Star heard the whispered words:

"Traitor! Betrayer of mankind."

"Adam Ulnar," called John Star, torn between pity and scorn for the shaken creature who stared up at them with a kind of listless fear. "Are you willing to help undo your crime?"

A little flicker of interest, of hope, came into the dull, tortured eyes. But the Commander of the Legion shook his head.

"I would help," his voice was dully droning, lifeless, "I'd do anything. But it's too late. Too late, now."

"No, man!" shouted John Star. "It isn't too late. Wake up!"

Adam Ulnar got uncertainly to his feet, his haggard face anxious.

"I'll help. But what can be done?"

"We're going to find Aladoree, and set her free. Then she can wipe out the Medusæ with the power of AKKA."

He sank back, and his voice was wearily bitter:

"You are fools. You are lying in a wrecked ship on the bottom of an ocean. Aladoree is guarded in a fortress that would be impregnable to all the fleets of the Legion—if the Medusæ haven't already tortured the secret from her and done away with her! You are idle fools—though not such fools as I was——"

"Tell us what you know about the planet," rapped Jay Kalam. "The geography of its continents. And about the Medusæ. Their weapons, their civilization, where they would be likely to imprison Aladoree."

Adam Ulnar looked at them dully, out of his apathy of despair.

"I'll tell you the little I know—though it will do no

100

good. I was never here, myself, you know. I had only the reports that Eric's expedition brought back.

"This planet is much larger than Earth. About three times the diameter. Its rotation is very slow, its day about fifteen of Earth's. The nights are fearful. A week long, and bitterly cold—a type-M dwarf hasn't much heat left you know."

His stare was drifting blankly past them; John Star urged him sharply:

"The continents?"

"There is just one large continent—about equal in area to all Earth. There's a strip of strange jungle along the shore, savage and deadly. It grows, Eric said, with amazing rapidity in the long day, and it swarms with fierce, unearthly life.

"Along the east coast, beyond the jungle, is a towering mountain range, more rugged, Eric said, than any in the System. West of the mountains is a vast, high plateau, lifeless, cut up by wild canyons. Beyond is the valley of an immense river that drains almost the whole continent.

"The Medusæ have only a single city left—life is hard on this dying planet, and the most of them have migrated to the other worlds they've conquered—as they mean to conquer ours. That city is located somewhere near the river's mouth—that's as near as I can place it."

"Aladoree?" prompted John Star anxiously.

"She would be in the city, no doubt. A quite amazing place, Eric said, huge by human standards. All built of black metal. Surrounded with walls a full mile high, to keep back the dreadful jungle. There's a colossal fortress in the center, a gigantic tower of black metal. They'd be likely, I imagine, to keep her there—guarded by weapons that could annihilate all the fleets of the System in an instant."

"Anything else you know?" urged Jay Kalam, as the hunted eyes fled back into vacancy.

"No. Nothing else."

"Wake up! Think! The System is at stake!"

He started.

"No—yes, there's one thing I remember, though it won't do you any good to warn you. The atmosphere!"

"What about the atmosphere?"

"You saw that it's reddish?"

"Yes. What—isn't it breathable?"

"It contains oxygen. You can breathe it. But it's filled

101

with the red gas. It does the Medusæ no harm—but it isn't good for men. Its an artificial organic gas, they told me when we talked. They generated it to control the climate—to cut heat radiation at night. They mean to fill the air of Earth with it, no doubt. But it isn't good for men. . . ."

He collected himself with a visible effort.

"You remember that wound on your shoulder, John? That was caused by the same red gas. Squirted on you in liquid form. The Medusæ have learned what it does to human beings. The men of Eric's expedition . . ."

The gaunt man shuddered. "Their trouble came from just breathing this atmosphere. It didn't bother them at once, except for a slight discomfort. But later there was a mental derangement. Their flesh began to rot. And there was a good deal of pain. And then . . ."

"Your doctors treated me, after I was burned on Mars," John Star broke in suddenly. "What was that they used?"

"We had worked out a neutralizing formula. But we haven't the ingredients on board."

"We can live, though, for a time, in spite of it?"

"For a time," he echoed dully. "Individual reactions varied, but usually the worst complications were delayed for several months."

"Then it doesn't greatly matter."

"No," Adam Ulnar spoke with a dull and bitter emphasis. "No, you'll find death, if you manage to leave the ship, in a million quicker forms. Life on this planet is very old, you know. The struggle for survival has been severe. The result is a fauna—and a flora—fit to live with the Medusæ. You'll never survive, outside the ship."

"But we're going to try," Jay Kalam informed him.

"The *Purple Dream*," John Star announced a little later when they were all five gathered on the narrow deck just within the air-lock, "is lying on the bottom of a shallow sea. The water is only about eighty feet deep. We can't move the vessel, but we can get out——"

"Get out!" echoed gigantic Hal Samdu. "How?"

"Through the air-lock. We'll have to swim to the surface, and try for the shore—with the water only eighty feet, it's likely enough that we're just off some coast. We'll have to strip for it. And we won't be able to burden ourselves with weapons or supplies.

"We could exist indefinitely here on board. Plenty of

air and supplies. Perhaps we can survive only a few minutes outside. We may not even reach the surface. If we do, it will be only to meet the dangers of a world where even the air is slow poison."

"My precious eye!" broke in Giles Habibula. "Here we're all stuck to die of slow starvation at the bottom of a fearful sea of evil. And that isn't enough! You want us to swim out like mortal fishes at the bottom of this wicked yellow ocean?"

"Precisely," agreed John Star.

"You want poor old Giles to drown himself like a brainless rat, when he's still got plenty of victuals and wine? Poor old Giles Habibula——"

"You're a fool, John," said Adam Ulnar, with dull and savage emphasis. "You'll never get ashore. You never heard the tales that Eric's men brought back. You don't know the sort of life—plant as well as animal—that fights for survival in the long, red days. How can you live through the nights? You were born on a kind world, John. You weren't evolved to survive on this one."

"Any of you who wish may stay on board," Jay Kalam interrupted quietly. "John is going. And I am. Hal?"

"Of course I'll go!" rumbled the giant, reddening with a slow anger. "Did you think, with Aladoree at the mercy of those monsters, that I'd stay behind?"

"Of course not, Hal. And you, Giles?"

The fishy eyes of Giles Habibula rolled anxiously; he trembled spasmodically; sweat came out on his face; in a dry voice he spoke, with a sudden effort: "Mortal me! Do you want to go away and leave poor wretched old Giles Habibula here to starve and rot on the bottom of this wicked ocean? Life's precious sake!" he rasped convulsively. "I'll go! But first old Giles must have a taste of food to put strength in his feeble old body, and a nip of wine to steady his torn and tortured nerves."

He rolled unsteadily away toward the galley.

"And you, Commander?" demanded Jay Kalam. "Are you going?"

"No." Adam Ulnar shook his head. "It's no use. Competition has bred some very successful life forms in the seas here, I believe, as well as on the land."

The four entered the air-lock, stripped to the skin, carrying their clothing, proton guns, a few pounds of concentrated food, and—on Giles Habibula's insistence—a bottle of wine; all wrapped in a big water-tight bundle.

They sealed the heavy inner valve and John Star opened the equalization tube through the outer; a thick stream of water roared into the little chamber, flooding it, rising ice-cold about their bodies, compressing the air above them. Merciless pressure squeezed them.

The inrush stopped, with water about their shoulders. John Star spun the control-wheel of the outer valve, but the armored door stuck fast.

"Jammed!" he gasped. "We must try it by hand."

"Let me!" cried Hal Samdu, surging forward through the chill water, his voice oddly shrill in the dense air. He set his great back against the metal valve, braced himself, strained. His muscles snapped. Agony of effort twisted his face into a strange mask. His swift breath was harsh and gasping.

John Star and Jay Kalam added their strength, all of them struggling in cold water that came to their chins, fighting for breath in the hot, stale air.

The valve gave abruptly. A rush of water swept them back. Air gurgled out. They filled their lungs out of the trapped air-pocket, dragged themselves out through the opening, and swam desperately for the surface.

Dark water, numbingly cold, weighed on them crushingly.

John Star fought the relentless, overwhelming pressure of it; he fought a savage urge to empty his tortured lungs and breathe. He struggled upward through grim infinities of time. Then suddenly, surprisingly, he was upon the surface of the yellow sea, sobbing for his breath.

Flat and glistening, an oily yellow-red under the cold red sky, the unknown sea stretched away into murky crimson distance. It lifted and fell in long, slow swells.

At first he was alone. Jay Kalam's head burst up beside him, dripping, panting. Then Hal Samdu's red hair. They waited a long time, and at last Giles Habibula's bald dome came up, fringed with thin white hair.

They swam on the yellow sea, and breathed deeply, gratefully—forgetful that every breath was slow poison.

The blank surface lay away from them, a waste of silent desolation. The sky was a cold, lowering dome of sullen crimson; the sun burned low in it, an incredibly huge disk of deeper, sinister scarlet. A dying dwarf, old when the Sun of Earth was born, it seemed too cold to warm them.

"Our next problem!" panted John Star. "The shore!"

"The bundle," muttered Hal Samdu. "With the guns. Didn't float!" Indeed, it had not appeared.

"My blessed bottle of wine!" wept Giles Habibula.

Then they were all silent. Some large, unseen body had plunged above the yellow surface near them; had fallen back with a noisy splash.

16

Black Continent to Cross

They waited, treading water, getting back their breath, while they watched for the precious package which held their clothing and weapons and food, and Giles Habibula's bottle of wine.

"It isn't coming up," John Star despaired at last. "We must strike out for the shore without it."

"It leaked, I suppose," said Jay Kalam. "Or hung in the valve."

"Or it may have been swallowed," wheezed Giles Habibula, "by the monster that made that fearful splash. Ah, my precious wine——"

"Which way is the shore?" demanded Hal Samdu.

Away from their bobbing heads reached the oily, heaving yellow sea, unbroken by any landmark. Oppressively low overhead hung the gloomy sky, thick with the murk of that red poison gas. Far across the sea burned the vast, sullen sun, a blood-red ball. A light breeze touched their faces, so faint it hardly scarred the yellow surface.

"We've two possible guides," observed Jay Kalam, keeping afloat with a calm, unhurried efficiency of motion. "The sun and the wind."

"How——?"

"The sun is low but rising. It must, then, be in the east. That tells us direction.

"As for the wind, there would surely be a sea-breeze on the coast of a continent so large as Adam Ulnar described. At this time in the morning the wind should just be rising from the sea, as the air over the land-mass begins to warm and ascend."

"So we swim with the wind? Toward the west?"

"Our best chance, I think, though the reasoning is based on a very incomplete astronomical and geographical knowledge of the planet. Too bad we couldn't have got a glimpse of the continent, through this murk, as we fell. For it could easily be that we aren't near the coast at all, but simply over some shoal. But I think our best chance is to swim with the wind."

They struck out away from the red sun. John Star with a steady, effortless crawl. Hal Samdu breaking the water with slow, powerful strokes. Jay Kalam swimming with a deliberate, noiseless efficiency. Giles Habibula puffing, splashing, falling a little behind. For a time that seemed hours, they swam, until he gasped:

"For sweet life's sake! Let's rest a bit! What's the mortal hurry?"

"We may as well," agreed Jay Kalam. "The shore may be within two miles. Or it may be two hundred, or two thousand."

They treaded water for a time, and then swam on again with slow, weary determination.

At first they had noticed nothing unusual in the air. But John Star presently became aware of an irritation of his eyes and nostrils, an oppression in his laboring lungs. He found himself coughing a little; presently he heard the others coughing. The unpleasant fate of those survivors of Eric Ulnar's expedition came to his mind, but he kept his silence.

It was Giles Habibula who spoke:

"This red and fearful air! Already it's choking me to death! Poor old Giles! Ah, it's not enough that he should be flung into the unknown ocean of an alien, monstrous planet, to die swimming like a luckless rat in a tub of buttermilk.

"Ah, mortal me! That's not enough! He must be poisoned with this wicked red gas, that will make a raving mortal maniac out of him, and eat the very flesh off his poor old bones with an evil green leprosy! Poor old soldier——"

A tremendous splash cut short his melancholy wheezing; a huge, tapering body, black and glistening, had plunged above the yellow surface behind him, and dived cleanly back.

"My blessed bones!" he gasped. "Some fearful whale, come to swallow all of us!"

Unpleasantly aware that they were drawing the attention of the unknown denizens of the yellow sea, they all swam harder—until the creature leaped again, in front of them.

"Don't exhaust yourselves," Jay Kalam's calm voice came above their frantic splashing. "We can't distance it. But perhaps it won't attack."

Then Giles Habibula sobbed abruptly: "Another monstrous horror!"

They saw a curving, saw-toothed black fin, cutting the oily yellow surface not far away. It swept toward them, cleaved a complete circle about them, and vanished for a time, only to appear again and cut another circle.

"They're making us a precious circus," wheezed Giles Habibula. "And then, no doubt, a wicked feast!"

"Look, there ahead!" boomed keen-eyed Hal Samdu, abruptly. "Something black, floating."

John Star soon made it out, a long black object, low in the water, still veiled in the sullen, red-yellow murk.

"Can't tell what it is. Might be a log. Or something swimming."

"My mortal eye!" shrieked Giles Habibula suddenly; and he fell to furious splashing, purple-faced, desperately groaning for breath.

"What's the matter, Giles?"

"Some—frightful monster—nibbling away—at my blessed toes!"

They swam doggedly on, toward that black and distant object.

John Star felt a harsh, stinging rasp against his thigh; he saw his own blood staining the yellow water at his side. "Something just took off a sample bit of me!"

"They must be just investigating us," said Jay Kalam. "When they find we don't fight back——"

"That *is* a log, ahead!" shouted Hal Samdu.

"Then we must reach it, climb on it——"

"—before these wicked creatures eat us up alive!" finished Giles Habibula.

Driving leaden-weary muscles to the utmost, they struggled on. John Star was toiling for air, every breath a stabbing pain, every slow stroke a supreme act of will. The others, he knew, were as near exhaustion; Hal Samdu's red ugly face was savage with effort; Jay Kalam's white and wet; Giles Habibula, panting, splashing desperately, was purple-faced.

The yellow surface for a time was clear. Then the black, saw-toothed fin came back; it cut the water in a deliberate curve, and came slicing directly at John Star.

He waited until it was near; then he splashed suddenly, shouted, kicked out at it. His bare feet came laceratingly against sharp scales. The fin turned, vanished. For a while the surface was again unbroken.

On they swam, every breath a torturing flame, every stroke an agony. The black log came near, a huge, rough cylinder, a hundred feet long, covered with coarse, scaly bark. On its upper side, at one end, they could see a curious greenish excrescence.

Ahead of them, something splashed again. The curved black fin looped its silent way between them and the log.

They swam on, drawing the energy for every stroke from sheer desperation. The curving rough surface was above them. John Star was all but grasping for it when he felt sharp jaws close on his ankle. A savage tug dragged him strangling under the surface.

He bent himself double, hands jabbing at a hard, sharp-scaled body, free foot kicking. His hands found something soft that felt like an eye. His fingers gouged into it; jabbed, hooked and tore.

The thing writhed under him, rolling and twisting furiously. He jabbed again, kicked desperately. His ankle came free; he struggled for the surface, strangling. His head burst above the yellow water, and he cleared his eyes to see the curved black fin cutting straight at him.

Then Hal Samdu's giant hand clutched his arm from behind, hauled him up; he found himself seated with the others on the great black cylinder of the log.

"My mortal eye!" wheezed Giles Habibula. "That was a wicked narrow——"

He stopped with a gasp, his fishy eyes bulging; Jay Kalam observed quietly:

"We've a companion on board."

John Star saw the thing he had already observed as a greenish excrescence on the other end of the log. A huge mass of muddily translucent, jelly-like matter that must have weighed several tons, in color a dull, slimy green, it clung to the black bark with a score of shapeless pseudo-pods.

Slowly, with baleful, unknown senses, it became aware

of them. Semiliquid streams began to flow within its form-less bulk, as they watched in puzzled horror; it thrust out extensions, flowed into them, and so began an appalling march down the log, toward them.

"What is the fearful thing?"

"A gigantic amœba, apparently," said Jay Kalam. "Look-ing for dinner."

"And he'll find it," estimated John Star, "at his present rate of motion, in about half an hour."

The four men, naked, exhausted and defenseless, sat on their own end of the log, watching thin green arms thrust-ing out, and slow streams of semifluid jelly flowing to swell them. The whole hideous bulk never seemed to move, yet was ever nearer.

How would it feel to be engulfed in it? To be seized by the shapeless, creeping arms, drawn into the avid, bone-less mass, inch by inch, smothered and consumed. John Star caught his breath, and tried to shake off that hypnosis of slow horror, and peered around him desperately.

Sullenly red was the sky above. An angry, brighter red, the enormous, sinister disk of the sun burned low in the east. The wind, freshening out of it, ruffled the surface of the yellow sea. Yellow horizons melted into reddish haze. Around and around the log, in endless circles, sliced a curved, saw-toothed fin.

The colossal amœba reached the middle of the log.

"When it gets here," suggested John Star doubtfully, "we might dive off and try for the other end again."

"And be swallowed alive in the mortal water!" predicted Giles Habibula dolefully. "Old Giles is going to stay where he can see what eats him."

"The wind," said Jay Kalam, "is drifting us toward the shore—I hope. And it should be near, or there wouldn't be driftwood."

The creeping horror was three-fourths of the way down the log when sharp-eyed Hal Samdu shouted:

"The shore! I see land!"

Far off, under the smoky red horizon at the rim of the yellow sea, was a low dark line.

"But it's miles," said John Star. "We must get past this monster, somehow——"

"We can rock the log," suggested Jay Kalam. "Turn it. And run past while our fellow-passenger is underneath."

"And likely spill ourselves off to feed the wicked things in the water when it turns over!"

But they stood up, perilously, on the rough bark, and stepped in unison, at Jay Kalam's word, from side to side. At first their huge craft showed no visible motion; the great amœba continued its unhurried flowing.

Gradually, however, under their combined weight, the log began to spin lazily back and forth, each time a little farther. The wet bark was slippery; Giles Habibula sprawled, once, and gasped in terror as John Star dragged him back:

"Bless my bones! Poor old Giles is no nimble monkey, lad——"

The black fin cut close beneath; his fishy eyes rolled after it.

The nearest reaching arm of formless, avidly flowing green jelly was not five feet away when the log passed the point of equilibrium; it turned suddenly, and set them scrambling desperately on hands and knees to keep on top.

"Now!" breathed Jay Kalam.

Clinging to one another, they scrambled unsteadily along the wet surface, toward the other end, safe again for a time. But the great mass of hungry protoplasm appeared again above the log, green and dripping. Its senses somehow found them. It flowed again.

Twice they repeated that awkward maneuver before the log touched bottom.

A black world lay ahead, ominous and dreadful.

The yellow shallows lapped on a beach of bare black sand. Beyond the beach rose an amazing jungle—a dark wall of thorns. Straight, dead-black spines, flaming with innumerable huge violet blooms, bristling with thousands of barbed and savage points. An impenetrable barrier of woven swords, easily a hundred feet high.

Above the gloomy jungle of thorns rose the mountain ranges; immense peaks towered up, rampart behind gigantic rampart, a rugged, precipitous, sky-looming wilderness of crags, bare, grimly and lifelessly black. The last somber wall drew its ragged edge across the crimson, sullen sky midway to the zenith.

Black sand, black jungle of thorns, black barrier of nightmare ranges, under a scarlet sky; the world ahead was shadowed by a spirit of hostile malevolence; it slowed the heart with nameless dread.

"Ashore!" exulted John Star, as they splashed through the shallows, waving a mocking farewell to the amœba on the log.

"Yes, we're ashore," agreed Jay Kalam. "But, you observe, on an eastern coast. The city of the Medusæ is somewhere on the west coast, the Commander said. That means we have this jungle to cross, and those mountains, and all the continent beyond."

"Ah, yes, a black continent ahead, full of mortal horrors," wept Giles Habibula. "Ah, me, and we've no weapons, we're naked as blessed babes. Not even a bite to eat! Poor old Giles, destined to starve on the alien shores of evil——"

<h1 style="text-align:center">17</h1>

The Rope in the Jungle

"Weapons," began Jay Kalam, "are what we must first——"

John Star caught his breath with pain as something jabbed into his bare foot, and broke in with a wry smile:

"Here's one to begin with. Edge like a razor—warranted!"

He picked up the thing he had stepped on, a wide black shell, with a curving edge. Jay Kalam examined it seriously.

"Good enough," he said. "A useful blade."

He looked for others as they walked up the beach, and found one for each of his companions. Giles Habibula accepted his disdainfully:

"Ah, for life's sake, Jay! Do you expect me, with this feeble thing, to cut a way through those frightful daggers and bayonets waiting for us ahead—waiting to slice us into bleeding ribbons?"

He pointed at the black thorn-jungle.

"And so we're armed," Jay Kalam told him. "As soon as we can cut a spear apiece."

They approached the black, violet-flowering barrier of thorns and spines and hooked spikes. Many of the blades were ten feet long; the close-grained wood seemed hard and sharp as steel. Naked and sensitive as their bodies were, it was not easy for the four to get near the blades they had selected; it proved less easy to cut and shape the iron-hard wood with shells.

Weary hours had passed before each of them was equipped with a ten-foot spear, and a shorter, triangular, saw-toothed dagger. Hal Samdu also shaped himself a great club from a piece of driftwood.

"Ah, so now we set out to cross a whole fearful continent on our bare, blessed feet——" Giles Habibula had begun, with a last regretful look back toward the yellow sea, when his fishy eyes spied something. He ran heavily back toward the beach.

It was their bundle he found, drifted ashore while they worked.

"Our clothes, again!" exulted John Star. "And real guns!"

"And my blessed bottle of wine!" wheezed Giles Habibula, laboring to open the bundle on the sand.

Their hopes for weapons were dashed. The package had leaked; their clothing was sodden, most of the food ruined, the delicate mechanism of the proton guns quite useless from contact with the corrosive yellow water.

Only the bottle of wine was completely undamaged. Giles Habibula held it up toward the red sun, regarding it with a fond fishy eye.

"Open it," suggested Hal Samdu. "We need something——"

Giles Habibula swallowed regretfully, and slowly shook his head.

"Ah, no, Hal," he said sadly. "When it's gone there'll be no more. Not a precious drop of wine on the whole evil continent. Ah, no, it must be preserved for an hour of greater need."

He set it down firmly but carefully on the black sand.

Discarding the useless proton guns, they finished as much of the food as remained edible, and gratefully donned their half-dry clothing—even under the continual radiation of the near sun and the blanket of heat-absorbing red gas, the atmosphere was far from tropical. John Star rudely bandaged the lacerations on thigh and ankle that he had sustained on the way ashore. Giles Habibula stowed the bottle of wine in one of his ample pockets, carefully wrapping it against breakage. And they plunged into the jungle.

Thick, fleshy black stems rose close about them, twisted together overhead in an unbroken tangle, bristling with knife-sharp, sawtoothed blades. The dense roof of thorns hid the crimson sky completely; merely a ghastly blood-hued twilight filtered to the jungle floor.

With infinite caution they picked a way under the tangle of blades, and even caution did not save them. Clothing suffered; each of them was soon bleeding from a dozen minor cuts that throbbed painfully from the poison of the blades. And soon they met a danger more appalling.

"One advantage," Jay Kalam was observing, "is that if the thorns hinder us, they also hinder any enemies that— ugh!"

A little choking cry cut off his grave voice. John Star turned to see him carried off the ground by a long purple rope. Hanging from the crimson gloom above, it had wrapped itself twice about his body, and clapped a flat, terminal sucking-disk to his throat. Struggling savagely, he was helpless in the contracting, inch-thick tentacle. Swiftly, it drew him up into the tangle of black thorns.

John Star leaped after him, dagger lifted, but already Jay Kalam had been carried out of reach.

"Throw me, Hal!" he gasped.

The giant seized him by knee and thigh, flung him mightily upward toward the red-lit roof of thorns. With one grasping hand he seized a coil of the tough purple cable. Immediately it shortened, drawing him higher, forming another loop to throw about his body.

Hanging on with one hand, he sawed at it with his dagger in the other, above Jay Kalam's shoulder. Tough purple skin cut through; a thin, violet-colored fluid streamed out and down his arm—sap or blood, he did not know. Hard fibers, inside, formed a core that did not cut so easily.

A coil slipped about his shoulders, constricted savagely.

"Thank you, John," Jay Kalam whispered faintly, voiceless, but without panic. "But turn loose, while you can."

He sawed and hacked away, silently.

Suddenly there was red in the streaming fluid—it was, he knew, Jay Kalam's blood.

The purple cable contracted spasmodically, with agonizing, bone-cracking force.

"Too—too late! Sorry—John!"

Jay Kalam's white face went limp.

He made a last, fierce effort, as unendurable pressure forced the breath from his lungs in a long gasp of agony. The live cable parted, they fell.

They were, the next John Star knew, outside the jungle.

He was lying on his back in a little glade covered with some soft, fine-bladed plant of a brilliant and metallic blue. Below, over the top of the black thorn-jungle, he could see the oily yellow ocean, a glistening golden desert under the low and sullen sun.

Above towered black mountain ranges. Vast sloping fields strewn with titanic ebon boulders. Bare, rugged, jet-black precipices. Barrier of peaks beyond barrier of somber, Cyclopean peaks, until the jagged dark line of them scarred the red and murky sky.

Jay Kalam lay beside him on the blue grassy stuff, still unconscious. Hal Samdu and Giles Habibula were busy over a little fire by the edge of a tiny, flashing stream that crossed the glade. Incredulous, he caught the scent of meat cooking.

"What happened?" he called, and sat up painfully, his body aching from the inflamed wounds of the jungle thorns.

"Ah, so you're awake at last, lad?" Giles Habibula wheezed cheerfully.

"Well, lad, Hal and poor old Giles got the two of you out of the mortal jungle, after you fell back wrapped in the end of that evil tentacle. It wasn't so far. Here in the valley, Hal threw his spear at a little creature grazing on the blue grass, and I struck sparks with stones to make a fire.

"That's the story, lad. We're through the jungle. But we've got these mortal mountains to climb, when you and Jay are able, and good life knows what dreadful terrors are lying in wait beyond. Ah, if that wicked purple rope is a fair sample——

"Mortal me, lad! This life's too strenuous for such a precious feeble old man as Giles Habibula, that deserves to be sitting somewhere in a blessed easy chair, with a sip of wine to lift his dear old heart from the woe that weighs it down."

He cast a fishy eye at the bulge in his pocket.

"Ah, yes, I've one mortal bottle. But that must wait for the hour of greater need—it will come, soon enough, life knows, with a continent of wicked, crawling horror just ahead!"

Up the mountain barrier they clambered, when Jay Kalam and John Star were able. Over tumbled heaps of colossal black boulders. Up sheer, rugged slopes. Mountain range after wild range they mounted, always to find a wilder, more rugged range beyond.

Slowly the enormous, scarlet sun, which was their compass, wheeled across the gloomy crimson sky, through the long week of its progress. Often they were hungry, and often thirsty, and always deadly tired. The air grew thin and colder as they climbed, until they were never warm, until the least exertion meant exhaustion.

Sometimes they killed the little animals that grazed the blue grass, cooked and ate them while they rested. They drank from icy mountain torrents. They slept a little, shivering in the sunshine, one of them always on guard.

"We must go on," Jay Kalam urged forever. "The night must not catch us here. It will be a week of darkness and frightful cold. We couldn't live through it here."

But it was already sunset when they mounted the last divide. They looked across a vast plateau, lifeless so far as they could see, black and grimly desolate. It was piled with masses of dark rock, riven and scarred from old volcanic cataclysm. A wild waste of utter black. In the darkling sky hung the dying sun, its sinister disk already bitten with fangs of ebon stone.

"We would die here, surely," said Jay Kalam. "We must go on."

And they went on, breathless in the thin, bitter air, as the sun's red disk was slowly gnawed away by the western horizon, and a chill wind rose about them.

18

Night and the City of Doom

For hours they hastened on, across that high black plateau, the bitter promise of approaching night increasing in the air. The huge dome of the sun went down before them. It was gone. In the lurid crimson twilight they came to the chasm's rim.

Sheer walls dropped a full thousand feet. A mighty

gorge crossed the plateau, a huge, cliff-walled trench filled with red, murky dusk.

"A river," Jay Kalam pointed out, "with forest along it. That means firewood and the chance of food. We might find a cave in the cliffs. We must climb down."

"Climb down!" snorted Giles Habibula. "Like a lot of human flies!"

But they found a slope that looked less menacing. John Star led the descent, clambering down over heaps of fallen, colossal black rocks, sliding down banks of talus, scrambling and dropping down sheer precipices. All of them were bruised and lacerated by the jagged rock; all of them took reckless chances, for the dread night came swiftly.

Only the faintest crimson glow marked the slash of sky between the canyon walls when at last they stumbled into the strip of strange black forest at the bottom. They were trembling with cold, violent as had been their exertions; ice-crystals already fringed the river.

Giles Habibula started a blaze, while the others gathered dead wood among the cruel-bladed trees.

"We must find shelter," said Jay Kalam. "We can't live outside."

With torches they explored the frowning canyon wall. John Star came upon a round, eight-foot tunnel. He shouted for the others, and entered, flaring torch in one hand and spear in the other. The air had an acrid fetor and he found great strange tracks on the sandy floor.

The cavern proved vacant. At the rear was a twenty-foot hollow.

"Made to our order," he cried, meeting the others in the entrance. "Some creature has lately used it, but it's gone. We can carry in firewood, and wall up the entrance——"

"Mortal me!" shrieked Giles Habibula, who had been cautiously in the rear. "We're trespassing, and here comes the frightful owner!"

They heard a crashing in the fringe of dark trees, as the thing came up from the river. Then torch-light gleamed yellow and green on a crown of seven enormous eyes, glistened red on close-scaled armor, glinted black on terrible fangs.

It met them at the tunnel-mouth; they had no time to choose to fight or not. John Star and Jay Kalam and Hal Samdu braced their long black spears against the floor to face its charge. Giles Habibula shouted, scrambling back behind them and holding up his torch:

"I'll give you light!"

A river-creature, it must have been, by day, wont to hibernate through the dreadful night. It was serpent-like, thick as an elephant, covered with hard red armor; it had innumerable limbs, the foremost armed with savage talons.

John Star's spear, set against the floor, was driven by the force of its charge into the side of its armored snout.

With a screaming, evil-odored blast of air and sound, the creature tossed up its head, splintering the shaft against the roof. A black tongue, hooked with cruel spines, darted at him. He ducked too late. It impaled his shoulder through garments and flesh, yanked him spinning toward black-toothed, yawning jaws.

He struck with his torch the seven great eyes set in a crown of armor, and thrust it ahead of him into that hot, reeking maw.

The monster screamed again. The tongue lashed, flailing him from side to side of the passage; it drew him back, numb, bleeding, half-conscious, into that black, fetid throat.

Hal Samdu's spear came past him, sank deep in the roof of the yawning mouth. He was vaguely aware of the gigantic club, raining pile-driver blows on the crown of eyes and the armored skull. Then he saw the black fangs, closing down.

His shoulder was bound, when he came to; he was lying by a fire in the cave. The others were busy, carrying in firewood, and great pieces of meat from the huge carcass at the entrance.

" 'Tis fearful cold outside, lad!" Giles Habibula informed him through chattering teeth. "Snowing, with a wicked blizzard roaring down the canyon. The river's already ice. Poor old Giles is too feeble for such a life as this, bless his dear old bones! Killing dragon-monsters in the wilderness of a world where men never ought to be!"

Even by the fire in the cave, the long night reached them with cruel fingers. When they at last emerged again, after the long, grim battle with merciless cold, they found the river a racing torrent. Fed by melting snows, it rose almost to the cave-mouth.

"We shall build a raft," decided Jay Kalam. "And follow the rivers across the continent to the Medusæ's city."

With improvised tools of stone, they laboriously fastened fallen logs together. The slow sun had already reached the zenith when they poled the clumsy vessel out into the rushing stream, to begin the voyage to the black and unknown city by the western sea.

Four painfully built rafts they lost. Two broke up on the rocks, leaving them to struggle ashore as best they might, through angry, icy rapids. One was wrecked by a green, lizard-like water animal. One they abandoned—at the last instant—before it went over a mighty fall.

The onslaught of the red gas in the air was less sudden and severe than John Star had feared. They all developed persistent coughs, but nothing more alarming. He came to suspect that Adam Ulnar had exaggerated the danger.

Week-long days came and departed, and eternal nights of savage cold, when they fastened the raft and came ashore to fight for food and warmth.

Below the thundering fall the canyon was a Cyclopean gorge; the river ran between black and topless walls in perpetual red twilight. Then they came out upon a larger stream that carried them away from the mountains and out across an interminable plain. For endless days they floated between low fringes of black vegetation—plants that died in the bitter nights, and grew amazingly again by day.

The river grew wider, deeper, its yellow torrent swifter. The somber, menacing jungles along its banks mounted ever higher, the animal life in water and jungle and air grew larger and more ferocious. With spear and dagger and club, with fire and bow and fist, they fought many times for possession of the raft.

They had become four lean, haggard men—even Giles Habibula was skin and bone and plaintive protest—black from exposure, ragged, unkempt, shaggy, scarred from many wounds. But they had gained an iron endurance, a new courage, an absolute confidence in one another.

Through all of it, Giles Habibula carried his bottle of wine. He defended it when the camp was attacked by a great flying thing, with splendid wings like sheets of sapphire; a thing that sought their bodies with a deadly, wipping sting. He dived for it when the green river-creature destroyed the raft. Many times he held it up to the red heavens, gazing at it with bitter longing in his fishy eyes.

"Ah, dear life, but a sip of it would be precious now," his plaintive voice would wheeze. "But when it's gone there'll be none—not a blessed drop of wine on the whole evil continent. Ah, I must save it for a greater need."

They were drifting one day near the middle of the river, vast now, a deep, mighty yellow flood, ten miles wide. Awesome walls of black jungle towered along its banks; barriers of violet-flowering thorns, interwoven with deadly purple vines; brakes of towering canes that whipped out at anything moving like living swords; gigantic trees laden with black moss that was blood-sucking death. Above the jungle hung the low, smoky sky, the red sun huge and sullen in the west.

Hal Samdu, at the steering-sweep, roared suddenly:

"The city! There it is!"

Like another black mountain it rose, dim in the red murk, colossal beyond belief. Above the jungle, its smooth walls leaped up, infinitely, incredibly up, to strange ebon towers and huge fantastic mechanisms. A black metropolis, designed by madmen and built by giants.

Breathless wonder and awed unease overcame the four ragged men on the raft, gazing at the city they had crossed the abysm of space and a savage continent to reach. They stood with heads back, gaping mutely at the unguessable, titanic mechanisms that topped the summits of its walls.

"Aladoree!" muttered Hal Samdu, at last. "There!"

"So Adam Ulnar thought," said Jay Kalam. "In that higher central tower—can you see it, dim in the red, above the rest?"

"Yes, I see it. But how can we get there? What good is my club—against those machines on the walls! We are no more than ants!"

"Ah, that's the word, Hal!" said Giles Habibula. "Ants! We're nothing but miserable creeping ants! Ah, me, those wicked walls look a mile high, indeed! And the evil towers and those fearful machines half a mile more on top of them! Nothing but silly little ants! Except—a precious ant could climb the walls!"

The others kept silent. They stared over the river's yellow, raging floor, over the dark jungle barrier, at the black, unbelievable mass of the city against the sky. Jay Kalam stood grave with thought. John Star pictured the girl Aladoree as he last had seen her, gray eyes demurely cool, hair a sunlit glory of brown and red and gold. Could her quiet, fresh beauty really be still living, he wondered, shut up in the mass of somber metal ahead?

The mighty current carried them on. Beyond a bend

they saw the base of the black walls rising sheer from the yellow river; plunging up a full mile, a vertical, unbroken barrier of dead-black metal.

Hours went by, and the yellow tide bore them on.

The city marched up out of the crimson haze, ever more awful, the bulk of it swelling to blot out half the red sky with gleaming black metal, the titanic machines that crowned it frowning down with the threat of unknown death. A palpable atmosphere of dread and horror hung over that unearthly metropolis, a sense of evil power and hostile strength, of ancient wisdom and monstrous science, for it had endured since the Earth was new.

The four ragged creatures on the raft gazed on those marching walls with a hopeless horror. Their minds sank prostrate with realization that unless their puny efforts could free the girl imprisoned there, the makers of this pile of black metal had also shaped the doom of mankind.

The city seemed dead at first, a somber necropolis, too old for any life. But presently they saw movement along the walls. A black spider-ship spread titanic vanes, and rose silently from a high platform to vanish in the red sky eastward.

"We must cover ourselves," said Jay Kalam. "They might be watching."

He had them screen the raft with broken branches, to look like driftwood. And the river carried them on toward the mighty wall. They were gazing upward in awe-struck silence when Hal Samdu cried:

"See them moving! Above the wall!"

And the others could presently distinguish the creatures that moved, still tiny with many miles of distance—the ancient masters of this aged planet!

John Star had glimpsed one of the Medusæ on Mars, that thing in the gondola swung from the black flier, whose weapon had struck him down. A swollen, greenish surface, wetly heaving; a huge, ovoid eye, luminous and purple. But these were the first he had fully seen.

They drifted above the wall like little green balloons. Their eyes were tiny dark points in their bulging sides— each had four eyes, spaced at equal distances about its circumference. From the lower, circular edge, like the ropes that would have suspended the car of a balloon, hung a fringe of black and whiplike tentacles.

John Star could see the superficial likeness, the dome

120

shape, the fringing tentacles, that had earned them the name Medusæ.

In the distance they did not look impressive. There was about them a certain grotesqueness, a slow awkwardness. They didn't look intelligent. Yet in the way they moved, floating apparently at will above the black wall, was a power and mystery that made for respect. And in the knowledge that they were the builders of this black metropolis was room for awe and terror.

The raft drifted on until the black wall shadowed them. Smooth metal towered sheer to the zenith, hiding the machines and the drifting Medusæ. The raft scraped hard metal where it rose from the water; then the boiling yellow current tossed them back again.

"We'll land," said Jay Kalam, "in the edge of the jungle below the wall."

They threw aside the screening branches, and seized long sweeps; they fought for the shore, where the river drew away from that metal precipice.

19

Giles Habibula and Black Disaster

They abandoned the raft when it touched bottom, taking only their crude weapons, and Giles Habibula, his priceless bottle of wine. Hal Samdu stood in the shallows, a giant hand knotted about his club, staring at the dark barrier shadowing the black jungle ahead—staring, helplessly shaking his head.

"How——?"

"There'll be a way," promised Jay Kalam, though even his confidence seemed a little strained. "First, let's get through the jungle."

They attacked the living wall, dared the death that lurked within. Spear-sharp, poisoned spines. Bloodsucking moss. Coiling tentacles of purple vines. Blooms of fatal perfume. Animal death that crawled and leaped and flew.

But the four had learned in a savage school to meet that jungle on even terms. A dozen hours of swimming and floundering through sucking mud, of hacking deadly vines and creeping through *chevaux-de-frise* of venomous thorns, of meeting with level spear or lifted dagger the hungry things that charged from the undergrowth or rose from the mud or dropped from above, and they emerged from the riverbed upon the higher plain—Giles Habibula still with his bottle of wine.

Close on the right hand rose the wall, sheer and black, a mighty, overwhelming mile of it. The plain reached off to the left, covered luxuriantly with fine-leafed grass, a bright metallic blue. It sloped up in the murky distance to blue hills. From blue hills to black city ran the aqueduct.

Jay Kalam's thoughtful eyes surveyed it, a straight channel of dull black metal, miles long, which was carried from hills to ebon city on ancient, soaring arches.

"One chance," he said gravely. "We shall try."

They skirted the jungle to keep out of sight, marched twenty miles, and climbed into the blue hills. They had eaten, slept for a time, but it was still many hours till sunset when they came under the immense dam of black metal below the reservoir.

No guard was visible, but they crept up very cautiously beneath the dam. They climbed slippery, wet walls and flanges of black metal until they came to the lip of the uncovered channel. Below roared the cold clear torrent from the floodgate, three hundred feet wide, dark and deep.

"The water," Jay Kalam observed laconically, "gets into the city."

He dived. The others followed, leaving all but their thorn-daggers. The clear icy torrent rushed them along the black channel; the mighty dam drew back; the city's ramparts marched to meet them. They kept afloat as the yellow river had taught them, and tried to save their strength.

Ahead, in the black wall, appeared a tiny arch. It grew larger, and abruptly swallowed them up. They were in roaring darkness; the arch framed a bit of crimson sky, swiftly dwindling. The steady current plunged on into utter darkness.

Thunder drummed against their ears, increasing, deafening.

"A fall!" warned Jay Kalam.

His shout was swept away. They shot into a battle of

mad waters. Plunging torrents battered them. Merciless currents sucked them down. Savage whirlpools spun them under smothering foam. All in roaring blackness.

John Star gasped for breath, strangled in the foam. He fought the current that carried him down. Down and down! Resistless pressure crushed his body. He endured the agony of suffocation. Desperately he tried to swim, and wild water mocked him. It carried him up—and down again.

When he came up a second time, he contrived to stay afloat; he swam away from the chaos of the fall. They had poured into a vast, cavernous reservoir, completely dark. Its vast extent he could guess only by the rolling thunder of reverberation from its roof.

He shouted as he swam, and heard with keenest joy Giles Habibula's plaintive wheeze:

"Ah, lad, you lived through it! It was an awful time, lad. A fearful thing, lad, to be diving over mortal waterfalls, in this wicked dark.

"But I've still my precious bottle of wine."

Hal Samdu hailed them, then. A little later they came upon Jay Kalam. They all swam away from the thunder, and came at last to the side of the tank which was slick, unclimbable metal.

"Ah, so we must drown, like so many kittens in a blessed bucket!" wailed Giles Habibula. "After all the dreadful perils we've been through. Ah, mortal me!"

They swam along the slimy wall, until they came blindly to a great metal float with a taut chain above it—it must be, Jay Kalam said, the mechanism that measured the level of the water. They climbed the chain.

It brought them up at last, with weary limbs and blistered hands, to the vast drum upon which it was wound. There they saw a feeble gleam of red, and they crept toward it along the great axle-shaft of the drum, wet and slippery with condensation.

Scrambling over the immense bearing of the shaft, they found a little circular hole in the roof of the tank—it must have been left for attention to the bearings. They climbed through it, Giles Habibula sticking until the others pulled him out, and so at last, on top of the reservoir, they were fairly within the city.

They stood on the lower edge of a conical black metal roof, a dizzy drop of two thousand feet below them, and the slope too steep for comfort.

Standing there on that perilous brink, John Star felt a staggering impact of nightmare strangeness and bewildering confusion. Buildings, towers, stacks, tanks, machines, all loomed up about him, a black fantastic forest against the lurid sky, appallingly colossal. The tallest structures reached, he soberly estimated, two miles high.

If this black metropolis of the monstrous Medusæ had order or plan, he did not grasp it. The black wall had seemed to enclose a regular polygon. But within all was strange, astounding, incomprehensible, to the point of stunning dismay.

There were no streets, but merely yawning cavernous abysms between mountainous black structures. The Medusæ had no need of streets. They didn't walk, they floated! Doors opened upon sheer space, at any level from the surface to ten thousand feet.

The stupendous ebon buildings had no regular height or plan, some were square, some cylindrical or domed, some terraced, some—like the reservoir upon which they stood—sheerly vertical. All among them were bewildering machines of unguessable function—save that a few were apparently aerial or interstellar fliers, moored on landing stages—but all black, ugly, colossal; dread instrumentalities of a science older than the life of Earth.

The four stood there for a little time in a shaken bewilderment, caution forgotten.

"Bless my precious eyes!" moaned Giles Habibula. "No streets. No ground. No level space. All a tangle of wicked black metal. We'll get nowhere unless we sprout some blessed wings!"

"That must be the central tower," observed Jay Kalam, "the black fort Commander Ulnar spoke of. Still miles away."

He pointed to a square, forbidding, tremendous pile, towering up amazingly in the red and murky distance, a very mountain of black and alien metal, landing stages which carried colossal spider-ships and large machines of unguessable use, projecting from its frowning walls.

Weary, hopeless, he shook his head.

"We must get back," he whispered, "and hide till dusk."

"Or the monstrous things," apprehensively promised Giles Habibula, "will see——"

"One, I think," broke in John Star, "already has!"

Hundreds, perhaps, of the city's masters had been in view from the moment they came on the roof, greenish hemispherical domes drifting above the confusion of black metal, dark tentacles dangling. All had been far away, insignificant by comparison with their works. But now one had lifted abruptly over the point of the conical roof.

Giles Habibula dived for the hole through which they had emerged. He stuck; before the others could help him the Medusa was overhead.

The sheer size of it was shocking. Those in the distance had been tiny by comparison only. Its green dome, wet and slowly palpitating, was twenty feet through, the hanging, ophidian tentacles twice that in length.

It was infinitely horrible. Vast, bulging mass, gelatinous and slimy, translucently green. Scores of hanging tentacles, slowly writhing—efficient and quite beautiful, no doubt, in the eyes of their owner.

Gorgon's eyes!

Long, ovoid wells of purple flame. All pupil, rimmed with tattered black membrane. Mirrors of a cold and ruthless wisdom, old when the very Earth was new. John Star was not in fact turned to stone. Yet the sheer, elemental horror of that purple stare set off some primeval fear-response. It paralyzed his limbs with tingling cold, slowed his heart, stopped his breath, drenched him with sweat of terror.

Fear-numbed, they stood motionless, until the tentacles had whipped about them, snatched thorn-daggers from their nerveless hands, and pulled Giles Habibula like a cork from the hole. They were lifted, vainly fighting the hard, thin tentacles.

"My mortal wine——" panted Giles Habibula.

It dropped from his pocket. Like a plummet it fell into the chasm below; it fell two thousand feet.

"My blessed bottle of wine!" And he sobbed in the coiling ropes.

Moving by what force they did not know, by what amazing conquest of gravitation, the creature swept aloft with them, above the titanic black disorder of the city, toward—John Star noted it with a certain grim satisfaction—toward the central citadel.

They fought the fear that numbed them.

"Something about that brain," gasped Jay Kalam, even as they were borne away. "Powers that we can't guess. Makes you feel pretty futile."

It carried them into the stupendous building, through a door opening on sheer space, five thousand feet up.

125

Through a colossal green-lit hall. It stuffed them through a rectangular opening in the floor, dropped them without ceremony.

Sprawling in a black-walled room, twenty feet square, they found beside them a man—or what had been a man.

Emaciated, ragged, it was sleeping on its face, breathing with long, rasping snores. John Star shook it, after the Medusa had vanished from above the locked grating overhead, woke it. Stark, feverish terror stared from red eyes in a pallid, haggard face.

It uttered a shrill, hoarse scream of agonized terror; clawed in wild, blind insanity of fear at John Star's hand.

And John Star himself cried out, for the thing was Eric Ulnar.

The handsome, insolent officer who would have been Emperor of the System, become this twisted and pitiful wreck!

"Leave me be! Leave me be!" The voice was thinner and wilder than anything human. "I'll do what you want! I'll do anything! I'll make her tell the secret! I'll kill her if you want! But I can't stand any more! Leave me be!"

"We won't hurt you!" John Star tried to soothe the quivering thing, shocked as he was by the import of its cries. "We're men. We won't harm you. I'm John Ulnar. You know me. We won't hurt you."

"John Ulnar?" Red, fevered eyes stared, wild with a sudden, frantic hope. "Why yes, you're John."

The trembling thing, abruptly sob-shaken, clung to his shoulder.

"The Medusæ!" That wail held more than human woe. "They tricked us! They're murdering mankind! They're bombing the System with red gas, to eat men's bodies away, and make them insane. They're murdering mankind!"

"Aladoree?" demanded John Star. "Where's she?"

"They made me torture her!" sobbed the weak, wild voice. "They want her secret. Want AKKA! But she won't tell. And they won't let me die till she tells. They won't let me die!" it shrilled. "They won't let me die!

"But when she tells, they'll kill us all!"

"A Certain Slight Dexterity"

"My blessed bottle of wine!" sobbed Giles Habibula, plaintively. "I carried it out of the sunken cruiser. I carried it through the jungle of thorns, I carried it up the black and evil mountains. For precious months I carried it on the raft. I risked my mortal life to save it, fighting a wicked flying monster. I dived for it into the horrors of the yellow river. I was near drowning with it in the fall beneath that aqueduct!

"The only bottle of wine on the whole black and monstrous continent!"

His fishy eyes clouded, and the clouds gave forth a rain of tears. He sank down on the bare metal floor of the cell in a stricken heap.

"Poor old Giles Habibula, lonely, desolate, forlorn old soldier of the Legion. Accused for a pirate, hunted like a rat out of his own native System, caught like a mortal rat in a wicked trap to be tortured and murdered by the monsters of an alien star!

"And, ah me! even that is not enough! I'd carried that bottle through a mortal lot of hardship and peril. I'd held it up to the light, many a time, sweet life knows, my old mouth watering. Always I'd save it for the hour of greater need. Ah, yes, for such a time of mortal bleak necessity as faces us now!

"And it must fall! Fall two thousand fearful feet. Every precious drop of it. Gone! Ah, Giles Habibula——"

His voice was overcome by cataclysmic grief, earthquakes of sighs and storms of tears.

John Star questioned Eric Ulnar again. He had slept, that shattered human wreck, his haggard, emaciated body exhausted by the outburst of hysteria. He was calm when he woke, sunk in a sort of apathy, speaking in a dull, weary tone.

"The Medusæ are planning to desert this planet," he said. "They have fought for long ages to keep this mother-city alive. And they've done wonders—making this red gas to keep the atmosphere from freezing, and robbing other worlds to replace their exhausted resources. But now they're coming to final defeat—because the dying planet is spiraling back into the dying star. Even they can't stop that. They have to go."

"They already have an outpost in the System, you say?"

"Yes," continued the lifeless monotone. "They've already conquered the Moon of Earth. They're generating a new atmosphere for it, filled with this red poison gas. And they're building a fortress there, out of this black alloy they used in place of iron, for their base against the Earth."

"But the Legion! Surely——"

"The Legion of Space is destroyed. The last, disorganized remnant of it was annihilated in a vain attack on the Moon. The Green Hall, too, is gone. The System has no organization left. No defense.

"And the Medusæ, from the fort on the Moon, are proceeding with the destruction of the human race. They're firing great shells, filled with the red gas, at Earth and all the other human planets. Slowly, in every atmosphere, the concentration of the gas is increasing. Soon men everywhere will be insane and rotting.

"Only a few of the Medusæ, I believe, have already gone to the System. But their great fleet is now being organized and equipped, to carry the migrating hordes to occupy our conquered planets."

There had been a change in Eric Ulnar's manner. On that first occasion, his voice had been a thin, hysterical scream. Now his dull tones were hardly audible. His face —it still had a sort of pallid beauty from his long yellow hair, worn and haggard and pain-drawn as it was—his face was vacantly calm. He spoke of the plans of the Medusæ with an unconcern that was almost mechanical, as if the fate of the System no longer mattered to him.

"And Aladoree?" John Star demanded. "Where is she?"

"She is locked in the next cell, beside us."

"She is!" gasped Hal Samdu, hoarse with gladness. "So near?"

"But you say she's been——" John Star could not keep a little sob of pain and anger from his voice, "been tortured?"

"The Medusæ want to know her secret," came the lifeless, expressionless reply. "They want the plans for AKKA.

Since they can't communicate with her themselves—she doesn't know the code—they made me try to get the secret for them. But she won't tell.

"We've used different means," his dull drone went on. "Fatigue, hypnotism, pain. But she won't tell."

"You——" choked Hal Samdu. "You—beast—coward——"

He charged across the cell, great hands clenching savagely. Eric Ulnar shrank from him, shuddering, cried out:

"Don't! Don't let him touch me! I'm not to blame! They tortured me! I couldn't stand it! They tortured me. And they wouldn't let me die!"

"Hal!" protested Jay Kalam, gravely. "That won't help things a bit. We need to know what he can tell us."

"But he——" gasped the giant, "he—tortured Aladoree!"

"I know, Hal," soothed John Star, holding his arm, though he shared the savage impulse to destroy this no-longer-human creature. "What he tells us will help to rescue her."

He turned back to Eric Ulnar.

"In the next cell, you say. Is there a guard?"

"Don't let him touch me," came the abject, lifeless whine. "Yes, one of the Medusæ always watches in the great hall above."

"If we could get past the guard, is there any way out?"

"Out of the city, you mean?"

"Yes," Jay Kalam spoke up and his quiet voice held a calm, surprising confidence. "We're going to rescue Aladoree. We're going to take her outside the city, and let her set up her weapon. Then the Medusæ will come to us for orders—unless we decide to destroy the whole city out of hand."

"No, you could never get out of the city," returned the dull voice of that beaten thing. "You can't even leave the hall. It opens over a pit a mile deep. Just a sheer, blank wall below the door. Even if you got down, you'd have no way to cross the city. The Medusæ have no streets; they fly.

"But there's no use even to talk of that. You can't even get out of this cell, or get Aladoree out of hers. The sliding doors are locked. You are unarmed prisoners. Talking of stealing something the Medusæ are guarding in their securest fortress!"

His voice died in dull contempt.

129

With the impatience of a trapped animal, John Star gazed about the cell. A bare metal chamber, square, twenty feet wide. Ten feet overhead was the rectangular opening through which they had been dropped, closed now with a sliding grille of square metal bars. Green light filtered through the bars from the dim, lofty hall above. His eyes, searching for any weapon or device to aid their escape, found no movable thing in the cell. It was simply a square box of that eternal black alloy.

Hal Samdu was pacing back and forth on the hard bare floor, his eyes roving like those of a caged beast, sometimes casting a glance of savage rage at Eric Ulnar.

"You can't get out of this cell, even," insisted that flat, no-longer-human voice. "For they will kill you soon. They will be coming back to make me try again to get the plans from Aladoree. She will tell, this time. They are preparing a ray that burns with all the pain of fire, and yet will not kill her too quickly. But they will let us all die as soon as she tells. They've promised to let me die, when she tells."

"Then," John Star muttered fiercely, "we *must* get out!"

Hal Samdu beat with his fists on the hard black walls. They gave out a dull, heavy reverberation, a melancholy roll of doom; he left blood from his knuckles.

"You can't get out," droned Eric. "The lock——"

"One of us has a certain dexterity," said Jay Kalam. "Giles, you must open the door."

Giles Habibula got to his feet in the corner of the cell, wiping tears from his fishy eyes.

"Ah, yes," he wheezed, in a brighter tone. "One of us has a certain slight dexterity. It came of the accident that his father was an inventor of locks. Even so, it cost him weary years of toil, to develop an aptitude into a skill.

"A blessed dexterity! Ah, as dear life knows, it has never been given the credit it has earned. Ah, me! Lesser men have won riches and honor and fame, with half the genius and a tenth the toil. And to old Giles Habibula his talent and his unremitting effort have brought only poverty and obscurity and disgrace!

"Mortal me! But for that dexterity, I should never have been here, rotting in the hands of a lot of fearful monsters, waiting for torture and death! Ah, no! But for that affair on Venus, twenty years ago, I should never have been in the Legion. And 'twas that dexterity that tempted me then —that, and the fame of a certain cellar of wine!

"Poor old Giles, brought by his own genius to ruin and starvation and death——"

"But now's the chance to make your skill undo all that," urged John Star. "Can you open the lock?"

"Ah, me, lad! The penalty of unjust obscurity! If I had been a painter, a poet, a blessed musician, you would never dare cast doubt upon the power of my art. With my genius, it would be known from end to end of the System. Ah, lad, it was an ill tide of destiny into which I was cast!

"That even you, lad, should doubt my genius!"

Great tears trickled down his nose.

"Come, Giles!" cried Jay Kalam. "Show him."

The three of them lifted Giles Habibula—now an easier task than it would once have been—so that he could reach the barred grating, ten feet above the floor.

He looked at the black case of the lock, fingered it with his oddly sure, oddly delicate hands. He set his ear against the case, tapped it with the fingers, reached up through the bars and moved something, listening.

"My mortal eyes," he at last sighed plaintively. "I never saw such a clever lock as this. Combination. The case is precious tight. No place to insert an instrument and feel it out. And the wicked thing has levers instead of cylinders. Never was a lock like this in the System."

Again he listened intently to tiny clickings from the lock, resting the tips of sensitive fingers against the case, now here, now there, as if vibration revealed the inner mechanism.

"Bless my poor old bones!" he muttered once. "A clever new idea! If we were back in the System, the patents on it would earn me all the fame and wealth that I've been cheated of. A lock that challenges even the genius of Giles Habibula!"

Abruptly he gasped, stooping.

"Let me down! A fearful monster coming!"

They lowered him to the floor. Above, a huge greenish hemisphere floated over the grating. A gross mass of glistening, slimy, translucent flesh, palpitating with strange, slow life. An immense, ovoid eye stared at them with such a dread intensity that John Star felt it must be reading their very minds.

A dark tentacle dropped four small brown bricks through the grating. Eric Ulnar, breaking from his apathy, snatched one of them and gnawed it eagerly.

"Food," he whimpered. "This is all they give us."

A cube of dark, moist jelly, John Star found one of them to be; it had an odd, unpleasant odor, an insipid lack of flavor.

"Food!" wept Giles Habibula, biting into another. "Ah, good life's sake, if they call this food, I'll eat my blessed boots first, as I did in the prison on Mars!"

"But we must eat it," said Jay Kalam. "Even if it isn't palatable. We'll need strength."

The greenish, quivering vastness of their jailor presently floated away from above the grating; they lifted Giles Habibula to resume his battle with the lock.

He muttered in exasperation from time to time; his breath, in the absorption of his effort, became a slow sighing. Sweat stood out on his face, glistening in the dim green light that shone through the bars.

There was, at last, a louder click. He sighed again and raised his face against the bars. Then he shook his head and whispered hastily:

"Life's sake—let me down!"

"You can't open it?" asked John Star, anxiously.

"Ah, lad, so still you doubt?" he breathed, sadly. "The price a man must pay for a precious spark of genius! There was never a lock designed that Giles Habibula couldn't open. Though many an ambitious locksmith has tried, life knows!"

"Then it *is* open?"

"Ah, yes. The bolts just went back. The grate is unlocked. But I didn't open it."

"Why——"

"Because that fearful flying monster is waiting up there in the hall. Hanging still over a mortal queer contraption on a tripod of black metal. Its evil purple eyes would see any move we make."

"Tripod?" shrilled Eric Ulnar, voice edged with a new panic of hysteria. "Tripod? That's the machine they use for communication. They've brought it again, to make me get the secret from Aladoree. They'll kill us all when she tells!"

21

The Horror in the Hall

"Lift me," said John Star, and Hal Samdu's great hands swung him up.

Through the square metal bars of the grating, he could see the walls and ceiling of the vast hall, too wide and too high for the scale of human needs. Made all of the dead-black alloy, it was illuminated by little green, shining spheres strung along the middle of the ceiling.

The Medusa was in view, hanging over the cell and a little to one side. A bulging, enormous hemisphere of greenish flesh, slimy, half transparent, slowly throbbing. Ovoid, foot-long purple eyes, protruding a little—hypnotic and evil. Black tentacles dangling, like the Gorgon's serpent-locks.

Beside it was the tripod mechanism. Three heavy, spike-pointed legs, supporting a small cabinet, from which hung cables fastened to little objects that must have been electrodes and microphone, for picking up Eric's voice and the telepathic vibrations of the Medusæ.

At a sign, the giant lowered him.

"There's a chance," he whispered. "If there are no others in sight—and if we're quick enough."

He told what he had seen, outlined his plan. Jay Kalam nodded grave approval. In quick, breathless whispers, they discussed the details, down to the smallest movement.

Then Jay Kalam gave the word, and Hal Samdu swung John Star up again. This time he seized the grating, slid it swiftly and noiselessly back, in a moment was on his feet in the hall above. Without the loss of an instant he leaped toward the tripod.

Jay Kalam meanwhile came through the opening after him, catapulted by the arms of the giant, and helped Hal Samdu to follow.

An instant after the grating opened, the three stood beside it, working with savage haste to dismember the tripod. Even so, the guarding Medusa had already moved. The green dome of it swept swiftly toward them, thin black appendages whipping out like angry snakes.

Hal Samdu wrenched apart the communicator. One heavy, sharp-pointed leg he thrust to John Star, another to Jay Kalam. The third, with the heavy black case still fastened to it, he brandished like a great metal mace.

Holding the pointed leg like a pike, John Star lunged at a purple eye.

Instinctive terror smote him, the same numbing fear that had struck him twice before from the luminous Gorgon's eyes, the touching off of an age-old response to elemental horror. He felt tingling chills where hair sought to rise, the ice of sudden sweat. Something checked his heart and breath; something froze his muscles.

Immobility of instinctive terror—old inheritance from some primeval progenitor, which had found safety in keeping quiet. Useful, perhaps, to a creature too small to do battle and too slow to run away. But now—deadly!

He had known it was coming. He had braced himself to meet it. He would be ruled by his brain, not by age-old instinct-patterns!

A moment it checked him—just a moment. Then his numbed body responded to desperately urging nerves. He went on, metal point swinging up before him.

The Medusa had taken full advantage of that small delay. The black whip of a tentacle, small as his finger, but cruelly hard, pitilessly strong, snapped around his neck; it constricted with merciless, suffocating force.

In spite of it, he carried out the lunge. Fighting down the blinding agony from his throat, he completed, with every atom of weight and strength behind it, the forward rush, the upward swing.

The point reached the eye, ripped through its transparent outer coat, plunged deep into the sinister purple well of it, between the fringes of black membrane. A pendulous blob of clear jelly burst out, a quick rush of purple-black blood; and the great socket was sunken, sightless, more than ever hideous.

Abruptly increasing its fearful pressure on his larynx, the choking tentacle hurled him forward with a violence that almost snapped his vertebrae, flung him dazed and blind against the metal floor.

With a dogged will that ignored danger and physical pain, he clung to consciousness; he clung to his weapon. Even before he could see he was scrambling back to his feet, dimly aware of the blows of Hal Samdu's club—great soft thuds against boneless, palpitating flesh.

His sight came back. He saw the giant, head and shoulders towering from a very mass of black and angry serpents, shining bronze with sweat of agony and effort, muscles knotting as he swung the metal mace.

He saw Jay Kalam lunge, as he had lunged, to drive his point deep into a purple eye. Saw him instantly wrapped in ferocious black whips that squeezed his body and twisted it and flung it savagely against the floor.

Then he staggered forward again. Black ropes caught his knees before he came within thrusting distance, tripped him. They snatched him aloft with resistless strength, whirled him up to dash him down again.

A huge, malevolent purple eye came before him, as he was flung up—one of the two that remained to the creature. It was too far to reach with a lunge. But he threw his weapon, hurled it deep into the shining target with a twisting swing of his whole body, a long sweep of his free arm.

The serpent dropped him to tug at the spear.

On hands and knees he sprawled beside Jay Kalam, who was still motionless, groaning, weapon at his side. John Star snatched it as he got to his feet, straightening fairly underneath the creature, surrounded by agonized appendages.

On the under surface of the hemisphere, a circle of green quivering flesh, he saw a curious organ. A circular area three feet wide, slightly bulging, that glowed with soft golden iridescence. The light wavered, pulsed rhythmically, with the regular palpitations of the slimy flesh.

With the quick intuition that it must be vital, he thrust at it.

Sensing his attack, the creature fought to avoid it. Hal Samdu, dazed, was flung down at his feet. Black serpents struck. A rope whipped about his waist, tightened fiercely. The same weapon that he had flung into the great eye was now grasped in thin coils; it flailed at him, struck his head with a blinding agony.

He drove on; his point pierced the golden, shimmering circle.

The yellow light went out of it at once. And the Medusa fell, a soft mountain of quaking flesh. Only by a desperate, sidewise fling did he get his body from beneath it in time; even so it caught his legs.

The glowing organ, he was later sure, must have been

the agency of its remarkable locomotion, perhaps emitting some radiant force that lifted and propelled it; perhaps giving it a grasp, in some manner yet inexplicable, upon the curvature of space itself.

Half under it he lay for a while, unable to extricate himself. Still the creature was not completely dead; the dying serpents writhed about him in aimless agony.

It was Hal Samdu who reeled back to his feet to end the battle with a few mighty blows of his club, and then dragged John Star from beneath.

A moment they stood gazing at that quivering mound of slimy greenish protoplasm, tall as Hal Samdu's head, the yet-twitching tentacles sprawling away from the edge of it, three sightless eyes staring horribly.

Utterly hideous as it was, both of them were moved by a contrary impulse of pity for its manifest agony. For its kind had endured in the face of all adversity, perhaps since the planets of the Sun were born. The death of it was somehow dreadful.

"It had tortured *her!*" gasped Hal Samdu. "It deserved to die!"

They turned from it then, to lift Jay Kalam, who was already returning to consciousness, struggling to sit up.

"Only stunned!" he muttered. "So it's finished? Good. We must get on to Aladoree. Before others come. If it called for aid—Hal, please help Giles and Ulnar out of the cell. Must—work—fast!"

He dropped back again. He had, John Star saw, been cruelly hurt when the tentacles flung him down. His fine face was thin and drawn with pain, his grave eyes closed. Gasping, he lay there a moment, then whispered:

"John? Find her. I'll be all right. We must be quick!"

John Star left him then. He ran around that mountain of slow green death, and found another grating in the floor. He dropped to his knees, peering into darkness but faintly relieved by the green rays that streamed through the bars from the hall. At last he made out a slight form, lying on the bare floor, sleeping.

"Aladoree!" he called. "Aladoree Anthar!"

The slender dim shape of her did not stir; he heard her quiet breathing—it seemed strange to him that she should be sleeping so peacefully, so like a child, when the fate of the System depended on a thing she knew.

"Aladoree!" He spoke louder. "Wake up."

She rose, then, quickly. Her quiet voice showed complete possession of her faculties, though it was dull with a heavy weight of apathy.

"Yes. Who are you, here?"

"John Ulnar, and your——"

"John Ulnar!" Her low, tired voice cut him off, cold with scorn. "You've come, I suppose, to help your cowardly kinsman make me betray the specifications for AKKA? I'll warn you now that you're going to be disappointed. The human race is not all your own cowardly breed. Do what you like, I can keep the secret till I die—and that, I think, won't be very long!"

"No, Aladoree!" he appealed, shocked and hurt by her bitter scorn. "No, Aladoree, you mustn't think that. We've come——"

"John Ulnar——" her voice cut him, hard with contempt.

Then Giles Habibula and Hal Samdu dropped by the grating.

"Bless my eyes, lass! It's a fearful time since old Giles has heard your voice. A mortal time! How are you, lass?"

"Giles! Giles Habibula?"

In the voiceless cry that came up from darkness through the bars was incredulous relief, ineffable joy that brought a quick, throbbing ache to John Star's heart. All the contemptuous scorn was gone; only pure delight was left, tremulous, complete.

"Ah, yes, lass, it's Giles. Old Giles Habibula, come on a wicked and perilous journey to set you free, lass. Just wait a few blessed moments, while he works another precious lock."

Already he was on his knees by the sliding grille, his thick fingers curiously deft and steady, moving over the little strange levers that projected from the case of the mechanism.

"Aladoree!" cried Hal Samdu, an odd, yearning eagerness in his rusty voice. "Aladoree—have they—hurt you?"

"Hal!" came her glad, trembling cry. "Hal, too?"

"Of course. You think I wouldn't come?"

"Hal!" she sobbed again, joyously. "And where's Jay?"

"He's——" began John Star, when Jay Kalam's grave tones, weak and uneven, came beside him:

"Here, Aladoree—at your command."

He reeled to the edge of the grating, sank beside it, still weak and white with pain, though smiling.

"I'm so—glad!" her voice came from darkness, broken with sobs of pure joy. "I knew—you'd try. But it was—so far! And the plot—so clever—so diabolical——"

"Ah, lass, don't weep so!" urged Giles Habibula. "Every precious thing is all right, now. Old Giles will have this door open in a moment, and you out in the precious light of day again, lass!"

John Star abruptly sensed something amiss. Quickly he looked up and down the long, high-walled black hall. The vast bulk of the dead Medusa lay motionless, serpent-locks sprawling and still. The floor of dull green light revealed nothing moving, no enemy. Yet something was wrong.

Suddenly it struck him.

"Eric Ulnar!" he gasped. "Did you help him out of the cell?"

"Ah, yes, lad," wheezed Giles Habibula. "We couldn't leave even him for the wicked things to torture."

"Of course," rumbled Hal Samdu. "Where is——"

"He's gone!" whispered John Star. "Gone! Still a coward and a traitor. He's gone to give the alarm!"

22

——Red Storm at Dusk

"Ah, now!" wheezed Giles Habibula. "Ready, lass, to come?"

The lock had snapped; he slid back the barred door.

"Please go down, John," said Jay Kalam. "Help her."

John Star swung through the opening, hung by his arms, dropped lightly on the floor of the cell, beside Aladoree. Her gray eyes watched him doubtfully, greenish in the gloom.

"John Ulnar," she asked, her scornful dislike less open, yet still cutting him deep, "you came with them?"

"Aladoree!" he pleaded. "You must trust me!"

"I told you once," she said coldly, "that I could never trust a man named Ulnar. That very day you locked up my loyal men, betrayed me to your traitorous kinsman!"

138

"I know!" he whispered, bitterly. "I was a dupe, a fool! But come! I'll lift you."

"I was the fool—to trust an Ulnar!"

"Come! We've no time."

"You must be more clever than Eric, if you have the confidence of my loyal men. You Purples! Are you trying, John Ulnar, to get the better of them and the Medusæ too?"

"Don't——" It was a pained cry.

"Please be quick!" urged Jay Kalam from above.

She came to him, then, still doubtful. John Star slipped an arm about her slight body, lifted her foot, and swung her upward into Hal Samdu's reaching arms; then leaped, himself, to catch them.

They stood in the cavernous hall, tiny in its gloomy silent vastness.

Aladoree was thin, John Star saw, and pale, her white face drawn with anxiety and suffering; her gray eyes were burning with a fire too bright, and ringed with blue shadows. Her startled outcry at sight of the hideous mountain of the dead Medusa showed nerves strained to the point of breakdown; yet her erect bearing revealed courage, decision, proud determination.

Torture had not conquered her.

"We're here, Aladoree," said Jay Kalam. "But we've no ship to leave in. No means, even, to get out of the city. And no proper weapons. We're depending on you. On AKKA."

Disappointment shadowed her worn face.

"I'm afraid, then," she said, "that you have sacrificed your lives in vain."

"Why?" Jay Kalam asked apprehensively. "Can't you build the weapon?"

Wearily, she shook her head.

"Not in time, I think. Simple as it is, I must have certain materials. And a little time to set it up and adjust it."

"We've the thing they used for communication with Eric Ulnar." He pointed to Hal Samdu's mace. "Rather battered now. It was electrical. A sort of radio, I think. It would have wires, insulation, maybe a battery."

Again she shook her head.

"It might do," she admitted. "But I'm afraid it would take too long to straighten and arrange the parts. These creatures will soon find us."

"We must take it along," said Jay Kalam.

Hal Samdu unfastened the device from the head of the tripod, slung it to his body by the connecting wires.

"We must do—something!" cried John Star. "Right away. Eric must have gone to give the alarm."

"We must somehow get outside the city," agreed Jay Kalam. "Aladoree, do you know any way——?"

"No. That way," she pointed, "the hall leads into a great shop, a laboratory, I think. Many of them are always there, working. Eric went that way, I suppose, to tell them. The other end is outside. A mile high! There's no way to get down, without wings."

"There might be," mused Jay Kalam. "I remember—a drain, it looked to be. We must see——"

They ran three hundred feet to a great door at the end of the hall, an immense, sliding grate of heavy black bars, crossed, close-set, fastened with a massive lock. Through the bars they saw the black metropolis again—a storm raging over it.

Looming mountains of ebon metal, fantastic, colossal machines of unguessable function, all piled in titanic confusion, with no order visible to the human eye, no regularity of shape or size or position. No streets; chasms merely, doors opening in breathtaking space.

Now the city was lashed with wild violence. The four had weathered other storms on their trek across the black continent, always toward the end of the week-long day, when swiftly chilling air caused sudden precipitation. But this was a wilder fury.

It was almost dark. A lurid pall of scarlet gloom shrouded the city's nightmare masses. Wind shrieked. Yellow rain fell in sluicing sheets; it drenched them, stung them with its icy whip, even in the shelter of the bars. Blinding lightning flamed continually overhead, stabbed red swords down incessantly at black buildings that loomed like tortured giants.

Below the door was a mile-deep chasm, walled in completely by black, irregular buildings. John Star could see no way visible to leave its misty, flood-drenched floor.

Aladoree shrank back instinctively from the chill rain that lashed through the bars, from the ominous glow of the sky and the fearful bellow of the wind and thunder. Giles Habibula hastily retreated, muttering:

"Mortal me! I never saw such——"

"The lock, Giles!" Jay Kalam requested urgently.

"Bless my bones, Jay!" he howled above the roaring

elements. "We can't go out into that! Into that wicked storm, and a fearful pit a mile deep!"

"Please!"

"Ah, if you will, Jay. 'Tis easier, now."

His deft, steady fingers manipulated the levers of the lock, more surely this time, more confidently. Almost at once it clicked; the four men set their shoulders to the bars, and slid the huge grille aside.

Staggering against wind and rain that now drove in with multiplied force, they peered over the square metal ledge. The smooth black wall dropped sheer, under them, for a long mile, sluiced with rain. Jay Kalam braced himself against the howling gusts; he pointed, shouted into the roar of thunder:

"The drain!"

They saw it, besides them, ten feet away. A huge, square tube, supported at close intervals by a metal flange that secured it to the wall. Straight into the pit it fell, dwindling to a thin black line, lost at last in the redly flickering murk below.

"The flanges!" Rather by watching his lips than by sound they caught the words. "A ladder. Too far apart. Inconvenient shape. But we can climb them. Down."

"Bless my bones!" howled Giles Habibula, into the tempest. "We can't do that, Jay. Not in this frightful storm. We can't even reach the mortal flanges! Poor old Giles——"

"John——" Jay Kalam's lips moved, his face a question.

"I'll try!" he screamed.

He was the lightest, the quickest, of the four; he could do the thing if any of them could. He nodded to Hal Samdu, smiling grimly. The giant's hands took him up, hurled him out over the chasm, out into wild rain and bellowing wind.

His arms stretched out, his fingers caught the edge of a metal flange. But the hurricane had his body; it flung him out, over the abysm. Fingers strained. Shoulders throbbed. Muscles cracked. But he hung on.

The merciless gust released him, left him clinging to the flange, drenched and strangled in roaring rain. He tried the flanges, found that they would serve, however awkwardly, as a ladder; he nodded at the others.

He braced himself, then, standing on one leg, the other knee hooked over the flange above, waited, arms free. Jay Kalam was flung out, and he caught him, helped him to a higher position. Then Giles Habibula, green-faced, gasping.

And Aladoree, who said in a queer, muffled tone, "Thank you, John Ulnar," when he caught her in his arms.

Hal Samdu then passed out the gory legs of the tripod, which they slung to their belts. Standing on the narrow ledge, he closed the sliding grate, so that the lock snapped, in hope of confusing pursuit. Then he leaped, through blinding sheets of rain, and John Star leaned out to catch him.

His great weight made an intolerable burden for John Star in his cramped and insecure position. A furious downward gust increased it. John Star felt, as he clung to the giant's wet hand, that his body must be torn in two. But he kept his hold. Hal Samdu caught a flange with his free hand, was safe. And they started down the drain.

The bracing flanges were uncomfortably spaced; it would have been no slight feat to climb down a mile of them under the most favorable circumstances. Now rain fell in blinding, suffocating sheets from the roaring sky; the pitiless wind tore at them. All of them were already half exhausted. But apprehension of inevitable pursuit drove them to reckless haste.

In only one way was the storm an advantage, John Star thought; it had driven the Medusæ to shelter from above their buildings and machines; there seemed no danger of accidental discovery before pursuit started from above. But that advantage they paid for very dearly in the battle with wind and rain.

They were halfway down, perhaps, when Aladoree fainted from sheer exhaustion.

John Star, just below her, had been watching her, afraid that she would slip from the wet flanges. He caught her; he held her until she revived and protested stubbornly that she was able to climb again. Then Hal Samdu lifted her to his shoulders, made her cling to him pickaback, and they climbed on down.

The great chasm's floor, as they descended, became more distinctly visible through the mist of falling water. A vast square pit, a full thousand feet across. Black, blank sides of huge buildings walled it, without a break. The floor was flooded with yellow water from the rain. All the water on the planet appeared yellow in volume, carrying in solution the red organic gas.

Anxiously scanning the flooded floor, John Star could see no possible avenue of escape from it—unless they should climb another of the drains that was discharging its flood into the pit. And they were all too near exhaustion, he knew, to make such a climb, even if that could promise safety.

The torrential rain slackened suddenly, when they were near the bottom. The rumble of thunder diminished; the lurid red sky lifted slightly; the cold wind beat at them with decreasing violence.

John Star's feet had just touched the cold standing water on the floor, when Giles Habibula gasped the warning:

"My mortal eye! The evil Medusæ, coming down to take us back!"

Looking upward, he saw the greenish, black-fringed flying domes, drifting one by one from the hall they had left, floating down swiftly.

23

Yellow Maw of Terror

Standing in ankle-deep water, as the others were finishing the descent behind him, John Star looked desperately about for some possible way of escape from the pit.

Before him lay the sheet of yellow flood water, a thousand feet square. Above it, on every side, stood glistening black walls of tremendous buildings, the very lowest taller than the proud Purple Hall. Here and there the high doors broke them, but none that he saw could be reached by any but a flying creature.

Against the little red rectangle of sky above the chasm, the pursuing Medusæ were drifting down, small, darkly greenish disks against the scarlet.

"There's no way!" he muttered to Jay Kalam, splashing down beside him. "For once—none! I suppose they'll kill us, now."

"But there is one way," said Jay Kalam, voice swift and strained. "If we've time to reach it. Not safe. Not pleasant.

A grim and desperate chance. But better than waiting for them to slaughter us.

"Come!" he called, as Giles Habibula, the last, clambered, groaning and shivering, down into chill water. "No time to waste!"

"Where?" demanded Hal Samdu, splashing after him through the yellow flood, Aladoree still clinging wearily to his back. "There's no way."

"The flood-water," Jay Kalam observed succinctly, "manages to find an exit."

At a splashing run, he led the way to an intake of the flood-drains. A yellow whirlpool, ten feet across, roaring down through a heavy metal grating.

"My bloody, mortal eye!" wheezed Giles Habibula. "Must we dive into the blessed sewers?"

"We must," Jay Kalam assured him. "Or wait for the Medusæ to kill us."

"Bless my dear old bones!" he wailed. "To be sucked down and drowned like a miserable rat! And then vomited out, sweet life knows, to be torn and swallowed by the wicked things in the yellow river. Ah, Giles, it was a mortal evil day——"

"We must lift the lid," urged Jay Kalam, "if we can!"

Hal Samdu had set down Aladoree, who stood shivering and weary, uncertain. Almost swept off their feet by the swirling yellow water, the four gathered along one side of the circular black grating, grasped it, strained their muscles. It did not move.

"A mortal hasp!" cried Giles Habibula, feeling along the edge.

Staggering in the mad current that buffeted his feet, Hal Samdu hammered and levered at the fastening with one of the tripod legs. John Star, glancing up at the square of crimson sky, saw the dark circles of the Medusæ, larger now, midway down.

The giant still beat and pried at the hasp, in vain. John Star tried futilely to help him, and Jay Kalam. The furious swirl of yellow water rushed over it, hindering their efforts, making it almost impossible even to stand.

"It was Eric Ulnar who warned them," said Aladoree, her voice icy with a bitter scorn. "One of them is carrying him. I see him pointing at us."

They renewed their efforts to break the hasp with clumsy tools, panting, too busy to look up even at death descending. At last the twisted metal broke.

144

"Now!" muttered Hal Samdu.

They gripped the bars again, lifted. The grate stirred a little, to their united strength, settled back under the pressure of the roaring torrent.

They tried again, Giles Habibula panting, purple-faced, Hal Samdu's great muscles bulging, quivering with strain. Even Aladoree added her efforts. Still it did not rise.

The Medusæ were fast drifting down upon them. Stealing an apprehensive glance, John Star saw a full score of them, some carrying black implements that must have been weapons, one bearing Eric Ulnar, gesticulating, seated in a swing of woven serpents.

"We *must* lift it!"

They tried again, in new positions, straining fiercely. The grating came up suddenly, relatively light when above the grasp of mad water. They flung it back.

The open pit yawned before them, eight feet across. Angry, swirling water leaped into it in an unbroken sheet, from every side; it was a yellow funnel, foam-lined. Ominous, furious, deafening, the yell of wild waters came up out of it.

Joan Star paused, staring into its savage yellow maw with a sickening wave of horror. It seemed very suicide to dive into that bellowing vortex, suicide in a singularly fearful guise. To be sucked down that tawny, foaming throat, whirled helpless through the sewers below, battered against the walls, finally belched into the horrors of the great river!

And Aladoree! It was impossible.

"We can't!" he shouted to Jay Kalam, above the snarling roar of it. "We can't drag her into *that!*"

"Mortal me!" hoarsely breathed Giles Habibula, the color of his face fading to a pallid, unhealthy green. "It's death! Wicked, howling death, and fearful suffocation."

He reeled back, staggering in the water that tore at his feet.

Jay Kalam glanced at the Medusæ drifting down, very close, now, with their black weapons and Eric Ulnar clinging to his cradle of snakes. He looked gravely at Aladoree, a silent question on his face.

She glanced up at them, her pale face momentarily hardening with scorn. Her gray eyes, still cool and steady, though too bright and dark-rimmed with weariness, looked deliberately from one to another of the four, and then down into the thundering whirlpool.

A long moment she hesitated. She smiled then, oddly; she made a little fleeting gesture of farewell. And she dived into that yellow, bellowing funnel.

John Star was dazed by the suddenness of her action, by the cold, reckless courage of it. It was a moment before he could recover his faculties, put down his own horror of that avid, howling maw. He tossed aside his improvised weapon, then; he gasped a last full breath of air, and followed.

Twenty feet down, he fell with the yellow foaming vortex into a plunging river.

The murky red gloom was extinct in an instant. In complete darkness he was whirled along, beneath the black city. After a little time his struggles brought him to the surface. The drain was racing almost full. His fending arm was bruised against the top of the tube. But he was able to inhale a gasp of foul, reeking air.

He caught breath, again, to shout Aladoree's name, then realized the utter futility of that. Whirling ahead of him in the roaring torrent, she could never hear. Nor would it serve any good if she did.

The passage turned presently; he was strangled in the smother of foam below the angle.

Again, after an indefinite time of waiting, fighting to keep afloat, breathing when he could, he was flung into a deeper, swifter current. Here the drain was all but full. The wild water washed and splashed and foamed against the roof of it; it was seldom he could find an open space from which to fill his lungs.

On and on he was rushed, until he felt that he had fought that savage torrent forever; until his bruised, weary body screamed for rest; until his lungs shrieked for pure air again, and not the foul, foam-filled pockets above the thundering tide.

He could not last another moment, he was thinking, when he plunged into a new, wider channel. The current sucked him under. For seeming hours, deadly, lung-tortured, he fought for the surface; and he came up under racing metal, no air beneath it.

Somehow, he kept the water from his aching lungs. He let the mad current whirl him on. Could Aladoree, he wondered, have endured all this? And the three behind him, if they had dived before the Medusæ came, could they be still alive?

Abruptly he was in a wild fury of roaring foam. He was

drawn down again until a cruel weight of water crushed his chest. Fighting a weary way upward, too nearly life-less to feel any glow of triumph, he saw light in the water.

Up he broke through yellow foam, gratefully sucked in the clear reviving air of the open—quite oblivious of the red and slowly deadly gas that tainted it.

Above, on the one side, was the sullen sky, washed to its full and sinister brilliance by the storm. On the other was the mile-high metal wall of the black metropolis. He had been discharged into the surging flood of the yellow river.

Boiling, scarred with lighter lines of foam, pitted with vortices of angry whirlpools, its turbid tide reached away from him, ten miles wide, so wide that the low, dark line of jungle on the farther bank was all but lost in thick red murk.

For miles below him, it rushed along the base of the mighty wall, until it reached the not less forbidding barrier of the black thorn-jungle.

For months he had voyaged that yellow tide; he had learned to face its thousand perils. But the others had been with him then; they had been on board the raft; they had been armed against the ferocious life of river and air and jungle.

Anxiously, he looked about him for Aladoree—in vain.

When he had breath, he shouted her name. His voice was a thin, useless sound, weak and hoarse, drowned in the roar from the chaos behind him where the flood from the drains met the river's mighty tide.

But he saw her, presently, a hundred yards below him. Her head a tiny thing, bobbing upon the boiling yellow surface. Her body too small, he realized, too frail, too weary, to struggle long against the savage river.

He swam toward her heavily, his limbs all but dead.

The turbid current moved her toward him; it carried her farther again, faster than he could swim; wild water taunted him until, in the near-delirium of exhaustion, he gasped curses at it as if it had been sentiently malicious.

She saw him; she struggled feebly toward him, through rough yellow foam, as they raced along in the shadow of the walls. He glanced back, sometimes, hoping that one of the other three might have come through alive, and saw none of them.

Aladoree vanished before his eyes, when he was not a

dozen feet from her, sucked down by a pitiless current; she appeared again as he was about to dive hopelessly for her, flung up helpless in the freakish water.

He caught her arm, dragged it across his shoulder.

"Hang on," he gasped. And he added with a last grim spark of spirit:

"If you can trust an Ulnar."

With the brief, wan ghost of a smile, she clung to him.

The yellow, swirling foam bore them on, under the mighty, marching walls, toward the river-bend below. There the thorn-jungle waited.

24

"For Want of a Nail"

John Star had never any clear recollection of that time in the river. In the ultimate stages of exhaustion, driven far beyond the normal limits of endurance, he was more machine than man. Somehow he kept himself afloat, and Aladoree. But that was all he knew.

The feel of gravel beneath his feet brought purpose briefly back. He waded and crawled up out of the yellow water, on the edge of a wide, smooth bar of black sand, carrying the limp girl.

Three hundred yards across the dark bare sand rose the jungle. A barrier of black and interwoven swords, it towered forbidding against the crimson sky. It was splashed with huge, vivid blooms of flaming violet that gave it a certain terrible beauty; and it hid death in many guises.

The open sand, John Star knew, was a no-man's-land, menaced from the river and the jungle and the air. But he had scant heed left for danger. Pulling the exhausted girl safely out of the yellow shallows, into the dubious shelter of a mass of driftwood lodged against a sand-buried snag, he fell beside her on the sand. Fatigue overcame him there.

He knew, when he woke, that precious hours were lost. The huge disk of the red sun was already cut in half by the edge of the jungle; the air already chill with a deadly hint of coming night.

Aladoree lay beside him on the black sand, sleeping. Looking at her slight, defenseless form, breathing so slowly and so quietly, he felt an aching throb in his chest. How many times, he wondered, as they lay there, had death passed by on the yellow river, or stared from the wall of thorns—and spared their lives, and AKKA, and humanity's hope?

He tried to sit up, sank back with a gasp of pain. Every individual muscle in his body was stiffly rebellious. Yet he forced himself up, rubbed his painful limbs until some flexibility returned to them, and got unsteadily to his feet.

First he picked Aladoree up in his arms, still sleeping, and carried her higher on the bar, beyond the unseen peril that might strike from the shallows. He made a flimsy little screen of driftwood, to hide them, and found a heavy club; he waited by her, to watch until she woke.

With wary glance he scanned the tawny river, flowing away until the farther dark jungle wall was dim in red haze. He searched the bare waste of somber sand, the black thorn-barrier behind it; the ramparts of the black metropolis, miles up-river, just visible above the jungle. But it was out of the murky sky that danger came, gliding down on silent wings.

The creature was low when he saw it, diving at the sleeping girl behind her little screen of branches. Somewhat it resembled a dragon-fly grown to monstrous size. It had four thin wings, spreading thirty feet. It was, he saw, like the creature that Giles Habibula had once battled for his bottle of wine.

He caught his breath, startled by its strange and wicked beauty. The frail wings were blue and translucent; they glittered like thin sheets of dark sapphire. Ribs of scarlet veined them. The slim, tapered body was black, oddly and strikingly patched with bright yellow. The one enormous eye was like a jewel of polished jet.

A single pair of limbs stiffened under it; cruel yellow talons spread to clutch the girl's body. And its tail, a thin yellow whip, scorpion-like, armed with a terrible black barb, arched down to sting.

John Star leaped straight in the path of it, swung his club for the jet-black eye. But the brilliant wings tilted a little, the creature swerved up; it struck at him instead of the girl. His blow missed the solitary eye; the thin, pitiless lance of its sting came straight at him.

He flung his body down, twisting his blow to fend away the stabbing barb. He felt the impact as his club struck the whipping tail; the venomed point was driven a little aside, yet it grazed his shoulder with a flash of pain.

Scrambling instantly back to his feet, nearly blind with searing pain, he dimly saw the creature rise and turn and glide back again, on translucent blue-and-scarlet wings. Again, it dived, talons set. This time, he saw, the barbed tail was hanging; his club had broken it.

Staggering with agony, he aimed his blow again at the bright jet disk of the eye. And this time the creature did not swerve. It plunged straight at him, yellow talons grasping. In the last instant, dizzy with pain from its venom, he realized that the talons would strike him.

Fiercely, he sought to steady his reeling world; he put every ounce of his strength behind the heavy piece of driftwood, felt it crush solidly home against the huge, black, glittering disk. Then his senses dissolved in the acid of pain.

Vaguely, he knew that it was not flying with him. Dimly, he knew that it was floundering on the sand, dragging his body still locked in its talons. His last blow had been fatal.

Presently the death-struggles ceased; the furry body collapsed upon him. The yellow talons, even in death, were set deep in his arm and shoulder. One by one, when the blinding pain began to ebb a little, he strained his fingers to open them, and he came at last to his feet, faint and ill and bleeding.

Even dead, the thing was beautiful. The narrow wings, spread unbroken on the black sand, were luminous sheets of ruby-veined sapphire. Only the reddened talons and the broken sting were hideous—and the head of it, pulped under his last blow.

Weakly, he reeled away from it, too faint even to pick up his club. He sank down beside Aladoree, still quietly breathing in the dead sleep of exhaustion, peacefully unaware of the death that had been so near.

Sunk in a hopeless apathy of new fatigue and pain, at first he did not even move when he saw three tiny figures toiling along the flat black sand. They must be Jay Kalam and Hal Samdu and Giles Habibula; he knew they must have come alive, by some miracle of courage and

150

endurance, through the drains and out of the yellow river. But he was too deep in exhaustion to feel any hope or interest.

He sat there, by the sleeping girl and the brilliant dead thing, aimlessly watching them come wearily over the black bar, out of hazy red distance.

Three strange, haggard men, each of them with a few tattered bits of cloth still clinging to a worn, exposure-browned body. Bearded men, long-haired, shaggily unkempt. They walked close together. Each of them carried a club or a thorn spear. Their sunken, gleaming eyes peered about with a fierce alert suspicion. They were like three dawn-men, hunting in the shadow of some early jungle; three elemental beasts, cautious and dangerous.

It was strange to think of them as survivors of the crushed and betrayed Legion of Space, the last fighting men of the once-proud System, left alone to defend it from the science of an alien star. Could these shaggy animals decide an interstellar war?

John Star at last found spirit to stand, to shout and wave. They saw him, hurried to him over the bar.

Hal Samdu still carried the black mechanism from the tripod, slung about his great shoulders by its connecting wires. He had dived with it into the drains; burdened with it, he had fought the yellow river.

"Aladoree?" he rasped, hoarse, weary, anxious, stalking up ahead of the others.

"Asleep." John Star found energy for the one word, the gesture.

The giant dropped beside her, eagerly solicitous, a smile of relief on his haggard, red-bearded face.

"You carried her out?" he rasped. "And killed—*that?*"

John Star could only nod. His eyes had closed, but he knew that Jay Kalam and Giles Habibula were coming up. He heard the latter wheezing weakly:

"Ah, precious life! It's been an evil time, a fearful time! Washed through the stinking sewers like garbage, and flung to die amid the wicked horrors of the fearful yellow river. Ah, poor old Giles Habibula! It was a mortal evil day——"

His voice changed.

"Ah, the lass! The lass has not been harmed. And this wicked glittering monster! John must have killed it. . . . Ah, old Giles knows how you feel, lad! A mortal bitter time, we've all been through!"

151

His voice brightened again.

"This dead creature—the flesh of it is good to eat. 'Tis like the one I fought so mortal hard for my bottle of wine —that precious wine I never got to taste! We must have a fire. I'm fearful weak from hunger. Ah, poor old Giles, dying of hunger——"

John Star drifted away, then, a second time, into blissful sleep.

It was colder, when he woke. His body was numb and stiff, though a sheltered fire of driftwood blazed beside him. Dread night was coming apace; the sun's angry disk now completely gone, the sky a low dome of baleful murky twilight. Bitter wind blew across the river, toward the jungle.

Giles Habibula was by the fire, grilling meat he had cut from the dead flying thing. John Star felt gnawing hunger; it must have been the fragrance of the roast that awoke him. But he did not eat at once.

Jay Kalam and Hal Samdu were beside Aladoree, beyond the fire. The little machine that the giant had brought so far, they had taken apart. The pieces of it were spread out before them, on a flat slab of driftwood. Coils of wire and odds and ends of metal and black plastic.

He stood up, hastily, despite the stiffness of his body, and hurried to them. In their absorption, they did not look up. Before Aladoree was an odd little device, assembled from the black metal parts, from rudely carved fragments of wood. She was fingering the remaining bits of metal, anxiously, one by one, rejecting each with a little hopeless shake of her head.

"You're setting it up?" John Star whispered eagerly. "AKKA?"

"She's trying!" breathed Jay Kalam abstractedly.

John Star glanced across the black jungle-top, toward the towers and machines of the black metropolis, remote in the red twilight. It was sheer impossibility, he felt, that the crude little device on the sand should ever do injury to those colossal walls.

"I must have iron," said Aladoree. "A tiny bit of iron, the size of a nail, would do. But I must have it for the magnetic element. Except for that, there's everything I need. But there's no iron here."

She laid down the tiny device, hopelessly.

"We must fine ore, then," said John Star. "Build a furnace, smelt it."

Jay Kalam shook his head gravely, wearily.

"We can't do that. No iron on the planet. The Medusæ, you know, first promised to conquer our System for the Purples, just for a shipload of iron. In all our wandering, I saw no trace of iron deposits."

"We can't build the weapon, then," Aladoree said slowly. "Not here. If we could only get back to the System."

"The ship is lying wrecked, somewhere on the bottom of the ocean."

Numbed with bleak despair they stood there, shivering in the chill wind that came up across the river. Over the dark thorn-jungle they stared, at the walls and towers and unguessable mechanisms of the dark metropolis. Old before the dawn of man, it would stand invincible when the last man was gone.

From those far walls and towers, abruptly, green flame burned. They saw titanic forms rising, the black spider-shapes of the Medusæ's interstellar fliers. A monstrous swarm rose up as the far thunder of green-flaring rockets rolled over the jungle and the river, and vanished at last in the blood-red sky.

"Their fleet!" whispered Aladoree. "Flying away to the System, with all their hordes, to occupy our planets. Their fleet, already gone! If we had found a bit of iron—— But it's too late. We've already failed."

25

Wings Above the Walls

"All for the want of a mortal nail!" commented Giles Habibula, in a voice that might have softened the heart of a statue of iron.

"Ah, me! That the lack of a blessed nail could mean so much!"

He was huddled on the black sand, a heap of dejection, carelessly holding a smoking piece of meat on a stick, above the sheltered driftwood fire.

"Poor old Giles Habibula! Ah, that he should live to

see such a fearful day! Better—ah, sweet life knows, far better—that he should have died as a blessed babe! Better that the law should have taken its cruel, pitiless course, that time on Venus!

"A fearful reward it is, in dear life's name, mortal fearful, for twenty years of loyal service in the Legion. Accused for a precious pirate. Imprisoned and starved and tortured! Ah, yes, driven out of his own native System, to this hideous world of frightful horror!

"Poisoned by the very mortal air, doomed to howling insanity and death by slow, green rot. Hunted by a million mortal monsters. Forced to scuttle like a rat through the wicked black city. Driven like a miserable rat to drown in the stinking sewers. Now face to face with a fearful death, in the cold of the dreadful night. And the one bottle of wine on the whole black continent smashed before he'd had a taste of it!

"Mortal me! It's more than a man can endure. Too mortal much, in life's dear name, for a poor old soldier of the Legion, sick and lame and feeble, with his wine spilled under his very eyes!

"And now, for the want of a nail, the whole human System is lost! Ah, me, for the lack of one precious bit of iron, all humanity doomed to die before the invasion of the monstrous Medusæ! Ah, good life knows, it's a mortal evil time! A mortal bitter time! Poor old Giles Habibula——"

There was a crackling sound from the driftwood fire, a whiff of bitter smoke. He stirred himself abruptly, rose with a final doleful wail:

"Ah, me! Misfortunes never come alone. Now the mortal meat is burned!"

And he went back to the bright-winged thing that John Star had killed, to cut another steak from its furry body.

By the glittering, sapphire-and-ruby wings that lay forlorn on the black sand, the others were standing in a dispirited little group, shivering in the increasing cold wind that blew out of the deepening red twilight.

From the river bar they were staring, beaten and beyond hope, at the walls and towers and machines of the black metropolis, looming weird against the darkling scarlet sky, above the dark thorn-jungle.

An overwhelming sense of failure, of the inevitable doom overtaking them and all humanity, rested oppressively upon them; despair held them in dead silence.

The keen blue eyes that peered above Hal Samdu's red beard caught a black space flier—a colossal spider-ship of the Medusæ, riding eerie green jets—moving toward the somber walls above the yellow river. He pointed, silently followed it.

"Is that——?" John Star cried, with a sudden painful leap of his heart. "Beneath it—could it be——?"

"It is," Jay Kalam said gravely, "the *Purple Dream!*"

"Your ship?" cried Aladoree.

"Our ship. We left it wrecked, under the yellow sea, with Adam Ulnar on board."

"Adam Ulnar!" Her voice was edged with scorn. "Then he has gone back to his allies."

She looked at John Star oddly.

"It looks," he admitted, "as if he had. He could communicate with the Medusæ by radio. He must have called them, got them to raise the ship and help repair it."

They watched the *Purple Dream,* flying under the vast black vanes of the Medusæ's flier, its tiny torpedo shape no more than a silver mote. Blue flame burst from its rockets as it approached the black city, and it slanted down athwart the red sky, the other huge machine hanging near above it, on green wings of distant thunder. It slowed; it came at last to rest on a tower of the black wall, in full, maddening view of them. The black ship landed close beside it.

For a few minutes they all stared at it, silent with the intensity of their desires.

"We must get that ship!" Jay Kalam whispered, at last.

"It would take us to the System," breathed Aladoree, voiceless. "We could find iron. We could set up AKKA. We could save at least a remnant of humanity."

"We could try," agreed Jay Kalam. "They would follow us from here, of course. With those weapons that throw flaming suns. The Belt of Peril is still above us; we'd have to get through that again. All their invasion fleet will be guarding our System, now. And the hordes of them, in that new fortress on the Moon . . . But," he whispered, "we could try."

"But how?" rasped Hal Samdu hoarsely.

"That's the first question. It's miles to where the ship is, across the jungle. On top of that smooth wall, a mile high. Nothing could reach it but a flying thing. And that black flier is beside it, apparently to guard it. How?"

His eyes fell, then, on John Star, who was staring fixedly

155

at the wings of the creature he had killed, glittering beside them on the black sand.

"What is it, John?" he demanded, his low voice strangely tense. "You look——"

"Nothing could reach it except a flying thing?" John Star said slowly, absently. "But I think—I think I see a way."

"You mean—to fly?"

Jay Kalam searched his intent, haggard face; puzzled, he glanced at the long, splendid wings at which John Star was staring, sheets of sapphire, veined with red.

"Yes. I used to fly," said John Star. "At the Legion Academy. Gliding. One year I was gliding champion of the Academy."

"Build a glider, you mean?"

"It could be done—I believe it could. Those wings are long enough. Strong. The thing's body was larger than mine. And the wind is blowing across the river, toward the jungle and the walls. There would be rising currents."

"Here are the wings. But the rest——?"

"Not much would be needed. The wings are already ribbed. We need posts to brace them together, but we could cut canes in the jungle. And twist fiber cords to lash them together."

"There isn't much time."

"No. It will soon be too cold to work. Just a few hours. But we've no shelter, no weapons. We'd never live through the night. No, Jay, it seems the only thing."

"Yes!" Jay Kalam spoke suddenly, accepting the idea. "Yes, we shall try. But it's a desperate undertaking, John. You realize that. An uncertain craft—if we can build one that will fly at all. The danger you will be discovered. The difficulty of getting on board; and then getting the better of Adam Ulnar, with only a thorn dagger. Even if you get to the controls, there's that spider-ship on guard."

"I know," John Star said soberly. "But it seems the only thing."

So they set out, in the face of every conceivable obstacle and danger, to do the impossible, first searching for tools, for sharp-edged shells, for rocks that would serve as knives and hammers, for the iron-hard jungle thorns.

Measuring the bright wings, John Star drew on all his old knowledge for a design into which they would fit, sketched it with charcoal on a slab of bark.

Then, in increasing cold and darkness, with the glistening wings, with struts and braces shaped from jungle cane, with twisted fiber cables and members shaped from the tough thorn wood, he labored hour after hour to construct the glider, while the four others roved the beach and the jungle fringe for materials.

They did not rest until it was finished, a simple thing, frail and slight. Merely the four bright wings, braced together, with fiber thongs to fasten them to John Star's body. They bound it on him, and he ran with it a few times down the sand bar, into the bitter wind, the others hauling him with a rope of twisted bark, to try its balance.

He thrust two thorn-daggers into his belt, then, and fastened a long black spear to the frame beside him. He ran down the sand, the others tugging on the rope. He rose, cast it off.

His strange craft came up unsteadily, swerved and dived toward the sand. He righted it with a desperate twist of his body—he could control it only by shifting his weight. And he soared up in the strong current that rose over the jungle.

He looked down, once, at the tiny group on the bar of black sand—three ragged men and a weary girl whose hopes had sent him up. Four tiny figures, alone in the red dusk. He waved a hand; they waved back.

Heart aching queerly, he soared on. He could not fail them, for they would surely die unless he took the ship. Jay and Hal and Giles—and Aladoree! He could not let them die, even if their safety had not meant the survival of humanity. Over the black thorns, now. Sheer disaster if he fell here. When he found time to look again, the four were lost in the shadow of the jungle-edges.

His old skill came back swiftly. He found his old elation again in the sweeping, soaring flight; there was a lifting joy even in the difficulty of managing his tricky craft, even in defying the black thorn-jungle.

Keeping within the rising currents above the jungle's edge, he worked steadily up-river, toward black and mighty walls—grown vague, now, in the thickening red gloom, the *Purple Dream* no longer visible. At first he had been doubtful of the frail machine, but he soared with increasing confidence, presently fearing only that the wind should change, or the Medusæ discover him. Then unexpected danger came.

Up from the black forest came gliding another creature, like the one which had supplied his wings. It circled him;

it climbed above him; it dived at him again and again, sting and talons ready, until he knew that it meant to attack.

He shouted at it and vainly waved his arms. At first it seemed alarmed, but then it dived again, nearer than before.

He unbound the black spear with cold-stiffened fingers, and set it before him. The thing dived a last time, slender sting curved, yellow talons set. It came straight at him. He met it squarely, spear aimed at its single black eye.

The point went home. But the rushing body struck his fragile craft with a force that made its flimsy structure creak. Flung off balance, John Star slipped toward the jungle, after the body of his attacker.

Equilibrium recovered, just clear of the thorns, he rose again. But the fiber-bound frame had been weakened and warped by the impact. It snapped and groaned alarmingly as he soared, its flight more startling and unstable than ever.

But at last he reached the stronger, gusty current that rose against the walls of the black city. Up he was carried, up, fearful that each moment would see his bright wings folding, his body spinning back to the yellow river.

So at last he came level with the tower. He made out the *Purple Dream*, a tiny spindle of silver, lying on the huge black platform in the vast shadow of the spider-ship that guarded her. The nightmare city stretched away beyond; the machines on the high platforms were an army of black giants, crouching in the red twilight.

Over the landing stage he swept, and down.

The gust carried him too fast, he was almost swept over the wall and into the city; the glider cracked and fluttered. His body was slowed and shuddering with the probing cold, numb and unresponsive.

But his feet touched black metal in the shadow of the *Purple Dream*. He slipped free of the binding thongs, and discarded the bright wings. He ran silently toward the air-lock, thorn dagger in hand, alert for the unknown obstacles ahead.

26

Traitor's Turn

The air-lock, to his relief, was open, the accommodation ladder down to the metal platform. He was up the steps in an instant, across the lowered valve, and upon the long, narrow deck inside, beneath the curve of the hull, where he came face to face with Adam Ulnar.

At their parting, months before, on the bottom of the yellow sea, Adam Ulnar had seemed a beaten man, shattered, crushed with the discovery that he and his cause had been betrayed by the Medusæ, broken with the knowledge that he had unwittingly betrayed mankind.

He was different now.

Always tall, impressive of figure, he was once more erect, confident, coolly resolute. Freshly shaven, long white hair combed and shining, neatly groomed in Legion uniform, he met John Star with a hearty smile of surprised welcome on his handsome face.

"Why—why, John! You surprised me. Though I had hoped——"

He started forward, extending a well-kept hand in greeting. And John Star leaped to meet him, menacing his throat with drawn thorn dagger.

"Keep still!" he whispered harshly. "Not a sound!"

He felt the contrast between them. A strange figure he presented, he knew; grimy, exposure-blackened, haggard from fatigue, half naked. With shaggy head and many months' growth of beard he must look more beast than man. An uncouth animal, facing a polished, confident, powerful man.

"Adam Ulnar," he breathed again, fiercely, "I'm going to kill you. I think you well deserve to die. Have you anything to say?"

He waited, shuddering and stiff with cold. Suddenly he was afraid that he could not strike this serene, smiling man, whose personality roused instinctive admiration and quick pride in their kinship—for all his black treason.

"John!" protested the other, his voice urgently persuasive. "You misunderstand. I'm really delighted that you came. My unfortunate nephew told me, a little while ago, that you had been here, and had drowned in the sewers. Knowing you and your companions, I could scarcely believe that all of you had perished. I was still hoping to be of some assistance to you."

"Assistance!" echoed John Star harshly, still threatening his throat with the dagger. "Assistance! When you are responsible for everything that's wrong!"

"I want all the more, my boy, to help you, because I realize my own responsibility. It's true that you and I have different political views. But I never had any desire to help the Medusæ to colonize our planets. I have no other purpose, now, than to undo what I've done."

"How's that?" demanded John Star, with a sick fear that this smooth, compelling voice might win his confidence, and betray it again.

Adam Ulnar made a gesture to include the ship about them.

"I've already done something. You must admit that. I've had the cruiser raised and repaired, in the hope that it might carry AKKA back to the System in time to avert total disaster."

"But the Medusæ raised it."

"Of course. They tricked me; it was my turn—if I could do it. I got back in communication with them, and asked to join them. I agreed to aid them with my military skill, in the conquest of the System. And I asked them to raise the *Purple Dream,* fit it up for my maintenance.

"They raised the cruiser, and repaired her, well enough, but I'm afraid they haven't a very high opinion of humanity. They don't seem to trust me as far as we Purples trusted them. The black flier outside has been standing guard over me, day and night. You know the sort of armament it has—those guns that fire atomic vortices."

"You've seen Eric?" demanded John Star suspiciously. "He's with you?"

"No, John. He isn't with me now. He told me how the Medusæ had made him try to force the girl to reveal her secret. He told me all about your arrival and escape. And he told me how he went back to warn the Medusæ—he didn't think you had a chance to get away, and he hoped to earn their favors."

"The cowardly beast!" muttered John Star. "Where is he?"

Adam Ulnar nodded, a shadow of pain on his handsome face.

"That's what he was, John. A coward. Even though his name was Ulnar. A pitiful coward. He made the first, foolish alliance with the Medusæ, because he was a coward, because he was afraid to trust my own plans for the revolution.

"I knew, then, John, that I'd made a mistake. I knew it was you who should have been Emperor, not Eric. Even then, it might not have been too late—if you had been willing to take the job."

"But I wasn't."

"No, you weren't. And perhaps you were right, John. I'm losing my faith in aristocracy. Our family is old, John; our blood is the best in the System. Yet Eric was a craven fool. And the three men with you—common soldiers of the Legion—have shown fine metal.

"It hasn't been easy for me to change, John. But I had time to think, under that yellow sea. And I have changed. From now on, I shall support the Green Hall."

"Yes?" John Star's voice was hard with skepticism. "But answer my question. Where is Eric? Both of you——"

"Eric will never betray mankind again, John." The voice was edged with pain. "When I found how he had sent the Medusæ after you, when you were escaping—I killed him." He winced. "My own blood as he was—I killed him. I broke his neck with my own hands."

"You—killed . . . Eric?"

John Star whispered the words very slowly, his haggard eyes anxiously scanning Adam Ulnar's face, now stern with its pain.

"Yes, John. And killed part of myself with him, for I loved him. Loved him! You're the heir, now, to the Purple Hall, John."

"Wait!" snapped John Star, savagely, pressing the dagger closer, while he searched the gauntly handsome, pain-shadowed face.

"Very well, John."

With a curious little smile, Adam Ulnar folded his arms, backed to the wall, stood watching him.

"You don't trust me, John. You couldn't, after all that has happened. Go ahead, then; drive your weapon home, if you feel that you must. I shan't defend myself. And as I die I shall be proud that your name is Ulnar."

John Star came toward him, crude weapon lifted. He gazed into the fine, clear eyes. They did not waver. They seemed sincere. He could not kill this man! Though doubt still lurked in his heart, he lowered the black thorn-blade.

"I'm glad you didn't strike, John," Adam Ulnar, said, smiling again. "Because I think you will need me. Even though we have the cruiser repaired, there are obstacles ahead of us, yet.

"The black flier, here, is on guard. If we get away from that, they can send a whole fleet after us. The Belt of Peril is still above—it is weaker, I've recently learned, above the poles of the planet, but even there it's a very effective barrier.

"Even if some succession of miracles lets us get to the System, humanity is already crushed, disorganized. We would receive no aid; we could be attacked, even, by miserable human wretches already insane from the red gas.

"We'd have to deal with their fleet, and the black fort on the Moon, from which they are shelling all the System with that red gas. Eric says they dismantled all their gas plants here, months ago, and moved them to the Moon —that must be why the concentration of the gas is getting so weak in the air here.

"Already, John, we may be too late. We may be the sole survivors, with no chance of surviving very long ourselves. If we're going to try at all, we've very little time."

"I'll trust you, Adam," said John Star, striving to put down a lingering doubt. He added swiftly: "We must pick up Aladoree and the others. They're down by the river, without shelter from the cold, or any real weapons. They'd soon die in this night!"

"To move now with that black flier on guard," protested Adam Ulnar, "would be suicide. We must wait some opportunity——"

"We can't wait!" He was harsh with desperation. "We've the proton gun. If we took them by surprise——"

Adam Ulnar shook his head.

"They dismantled the needle, John. Removed it. The cruiser is unarmed. They took even the racks of hand weapons. Your thorn is the only weapon we have—against those suns they throw!"

John Star set his jaw.

"There's one way!" he muttered grimly. "A way to move so fast they'd have very little time to strike."

"How's that?"

"We can take off with the geodynes."

"The geodynes!" It was a startled cry. "They can't be used for a takeoff, John. You know that. They can't be used safely in any atmosphere. We'd fuse the hull with friction-heat! Or crash into the ground like a meteor!"

"We'll use the geodynes," said John Star, harshly. "I'm a pilot. Can you run the generators?"

Adam Ulnar looked at him for a moment, strangely; then he smiled, took John Star's hand, and squeezed it with a quick, strong pressure.

"Very good, John. I can operate the generators. We shall take off with the geodynes. . . . I wish you had been my nephew."

John Star felt a responding emotion, checked by that little doubt which refused to die. So many had trusted this tall, commanding man; his treason had been so appalling!

They parted. In the little bridge-room, John Star inspected the array of familiar instruments; he tested them swiftly, one by one. All the iron, he saw, had been replaced by other metals. But everything seemed to function as it should. He peered through a tele-periscope.

The Medusæ's guarding flier lay beside them, one vast strange vane extending overhead. Against the dim red glow lingering in the murky west, it loomed evil and gigantic; it looked more than ever like some hybrid spider-thing, swollen to Cyclopean dimensions.

The low, clear music of the geodyne generators became audible, and rose to a keening whine. Adam Ulnar's voice came crisp from the bulkhead speaker:

"Generators ready, sir, at full power."

John Star's brief, grim smile at the "sir" was checked again, by sharp mistrust. Swiftly he estimated the position of the bar on the river, planning the thing he meant to do. For the slightest error, he realized, meant instant annihilation.

Fingers on the keys, he peered back into the tele-periscope.

He remembered the air-lock, then, and touched the button that closed it. That act, he knew, might betray them. But if he had left it open, mere air-resistance would have torn it away.

Tensely he waited, one second, two, and three, for the

motors to work. A long, slender black cone projected abruptly from the huge black sphere of the flier's belly. It swung toward them. A weapon!

Four! Five! He heard the clang of the closing valve and touched a key.

The tower platform and the black flier vanished instantaneously. Yet, since that unimaginable force was applied equally to the entire ship, there had been no perceptible shock; the geodynes had flung them away with a rapidity incalculable—and perilous!

Dim crimson gloom spun about them. A black shadow met them.

Driven with lightning speed to meet this desperate emergency, John Star's fingers leaped across the keys. Years of training now found their test. He had often imagined, in the days at the Academy, that such a thing might be done, half longing for the chance to try it, yet half fearful that the chance might come.

After the merest instant of acceleration, he reversed the geodynes for another split second, to check an inconceivable velocity.

And the *Purple Dream*, a moment before upon the black wall, was plunging down toward the flat yellow river, still at a frightful speed, her hull incandescent from friction with the air. Desperately, he flung down the rocket firing keys, to check the remaining momentum before they struck.

A desperate game, this playing with the curvature of space itself, in the very atmosphere of a planet. Human daring and human skill, pitted against titanic forces. Savage elation filled him. He was winning—if the rockets stopped them in time!

Down on a dark sand bar hurtled the incandescent ship. Down to the bank of a freezing river. Rockets thundering at full power to the last moment, she struck the sand heavily; she plowed into it, steam mantling her red-hot hull.

By the narrowest margin—safe!

Safe, at any rate, until the Medusæ had time to strike.

Hot valves flung open. Four passengers came aboard. Half-naked, haggard passengers, dead-weary, stiff with cold. The air-lock clanged behind them; the *Purple Dream* thundered away again, blue blasts licking black sand.

Geodynes cut in at once, she plowed with an utterly reckless velocity upward through the dim red afterglow.

John Star felt a moment of wild triumph, before he recalled the belt of fortress satellites ahead; recalled the six light years of interstellar space beyond; remembered the fleets of the Medusæ, guarding the System, and the occupation force waiting in their new black citadel on the Moon.

Behind, he saw huge machines stirring along the walls and towers of that nightmare metropolis. A full score of the spider-ships lifted on jets of green fire, to pursue. More than a match for the *Purple Dream* in speed, armed with those weapons that fired suns of annihilating atomic flame!

27

The Joke on Man

The red murk above grew thin. The *Purple Dream* burst upward into the freedom of space, where her incandescent hull could cool. The planet drew away beneath them, a huge and featureless half-moon of dull and baleful orange-red.

Up from it followed the swarm of spider-ships. The recklessly sudden start of the cruiser had left them too far behind to use their fearful weapons at once. But swiftly they closed the gap.

Ahead was the Belt of Peril.

Sinister web of unseen rays spread from the six trailing forts in space. Mighty secret of an elder science. Dread zone of unknown radiation that melted molecular bonds, to let stout metal and tortured human flesh dissolve away into a mist of free atoms.

Remembering Adam Ulnar's new information that it was weaker over the poles, John Star set his course northward. He drove the cruiser at the utmost power of the geodynes, sick already with his dread of the barrier, sick at thought of what Aladoree must suffer within it. But there was no choice.

The *Purple Dream* plunged into the wall of unseen radiation, John Star alone on the bridge.

Fiery mist swirled suddenly away from his body, from bulkheads and instruments. Mist of excited or ionized atoms, dancing points of rainbow light. White, searing pain probed his body, screamed in his ears, flamed before his eyes. Atom by atom, the ship and his body were dissolving away. Limp with suffering, he fought to keep awareness, to keep the hurtling cruiser within the narrow passage of partial wave-interference above the pole.

His body, grown luminous and half-transparent, was immersed in shining agony. He could scarcely move the keys. Red flame burned away his very brain.

Part of him was startled, inexpressibly, by a sudden laugh, strange and harsh and wild. A mad laugh. Lunatic! It shook him with a sickness of new horror, for he knew that the one who had laughed was himself.

He had just thought of a terrific joke!

Like those survivors of the first expedition, the same part of him knew, he was going mad! Long exposure to the red climate-control gas had overtaken him at last. Gone mad! And doomed to die of slow green decay!

He was laughing. Laughing at a monstrous joke. The joke was the death of the System, by madness and green leprosy. And its point, the death of those who tried to save mankind, by the same slow decay. A fearful joke! So terribly funny!

Millions, all the human billions, laughing foolishly, inately, as their flesh turned to foul green rot and fell away. And those who had thought to save them—the very first to die. What a cosmic joke! Men laughing at the face of red pain. Men and women laughing while their flesh turned green! Laughing, until their bodies fell apart, and they laughed at death!

What a universal joke!

His hands slipped away from the keys; he was doubled up with laughter.

Would the Medusæ see the point, as they rained the bombs of red gas on the planets? Or was their monstrous race too old for laughter? Had they forgotten how to laugh, before the Earth was born? Or had those green and palpitating bodies the power of laughter, ever?

He must ask Adam Ulnar. He could communicate with the Medusæ. He could find out. He could tell them the joke—the cosmic joke, a whole race laughing as it died.

He tried to stand up, but laughter wouldn't let him rise. He rubbed his hands together. They felt dry, papery. Already the scales were forming on his skin. His flesh would flake away until his bones were bare. He was a joke, himself! What a joke!

He lay on the floor and laughed.

Dimly, then, he became aware of something he must do. Red flame lapped at his brain; he was sick with suffering. And there were others. Others? Yes, Jay and Hal and Giles. And Aladoree! He could not fail them! But what was the thing he must do?

It was to drive the cruiser on, he remembered vaguely, through the Belt of Peril. Then this intolerable pain would cease. It would leave the others. Aladoree! So beautiful, so weary. He must not let her suffer this!

He fought the laughter. He tried to forget the joke. He battled the agony that consumed his nerves. Doggedly, he dragged his limp body back to the controls.

On through the radiation barrier he drove the *Purple Dream*. He watched the semi-transparent instruments through a haze of colored light. He moved the keys with shining hands. He was shaken again and again with laughter.

He knew, finally, that they were beyond the barrier. The red pain faded; the unearthly luminescence departed from the instruments; the dancing rainbow glitter slowly dissipated from the air. But still he sobbed with laughter.

Jay Kalam came finally into the bridge, haggard and pain-drawn, but calmly efficient. Already, since they had passed the barrier, he had shaved and found a new uniform. He was neat again, lean and brown, gravely handsome.

"Well done, John," he said quietly. "I'll take the bridge a while. I've just been talking with the Commander about our chances of outrunning the fleet behind us. He says——"

John Star had struggled desperately to listen, to keep silent and understand what Jay Kalam said. But the joke —it was so terribly funny. He burst into mad laughter again, a wild tempest of laughter that sprawled him on the floor.

He must try to tell Jay Kalam about the joke. Jay Kalam could appreciate it. Because, very soon, he would be laughing too, as his own body turned to green decay. But, for the racking laughter, he could not speak at all.

"John!" he heard Jay Kalam cry, aghast. "What's the matter? Are you—hurt?"

Jay Kalam helped him to his feet; held him until he could stop laughing and shake the tears out of his eyes.

"A joke!" he gasped. "An immense joke! Men laughing as they die!"

"John! John!" The grave voice was faint with inexpressible horror, "John, what is it?"

He struggled to forget the joke. There was something else he had to tell Jay, something else not quite so funny. He checked another fit of sobbing laughter.

"Jay," he whispered, "I'm going mad. I can feel it on my skin, and I can't stop laughing—though I guess it isn't really funny. You must take the controls. And have Hal lock me in the brig——"

"Why, John!"

"Please lock me up. I might—I might even harm Aladoree. . . . And go on to save the System."

The laughter came back; he clung to Jay Kalam, sobbing out: "Wait a little, Jay. Let me tell you the joke. So very, very funny. Millions of men laughing—while they die. Little children, even, laughing while their flesh decays. It's the biggest joke of all, Jay. A cosmic joke on the whole human race."

Laughter overcame him. He fell shaking to the floor.

The next he knew, beyond laughter and delirium, he was strapped to a berth in a cabin, and Giles Habibula was bathing his body with a pale, luminously blue solution, evidently the same which Adam Ulnar's close-mouthed physician had used on the wound where the liquid gas had burned him, long ago in the Purple Hall.

"Giles," he whispered, and his voice came hoarse and weak.

"Ah, lad!" wheezed Giles Habibula, smiling. "You know me, lad, at last! It's mortal time you did. You'll laugh no more—promise old Giles?"

"Laugh. What have I to laugh at?" Vaguely he remembered some great joke, but what it was, he could not say.

"Nothing, lad!" gasped Giles, relieved. "Not a precious thing. And you'll be on your blessed feet again, lad, by the time we reach the System."

"The System? . . . Oh, I remember. Does Jay think we can escape the black fleet?"

"Ah, lad, we left them long ago. We flew close to the red dwarf star. They would not follow—its gravitational field stopped their propelling mechanisms. Some of them fell in it. So did we—mortal near! Ah, a wicked fight we had to drive clear of it, lad." ·

"So I was laughing? . . . I almost remember. I thought that red gas had got me. But that doesn't seem so funny. Am I sane again, Giles?"

"Ah, yes, you seem to be, lad. Just now. Adam Ulnar had this solution. The things made it up, to a prescription he had, while they were repairing the ship. It neutralizes the gas—if one has not been exposed too mortal long. The fearful green scales went from your skin days ago. But we were afraid——"

"Did any of the others——"

The wheezing voice fell. "Yes, lad. The precious lass——"

"Aladoree?" Pain throbbed in John Star's hoarse cry.

"Ah, yes. All the rest of us escaped; we all used this solution. But the dear lass caught it when you did, lad, in that fearful Belt of Peril—the shock of that radiation seemed to bring it on."

"How is she, Giles?"

"I don't know, lad." He shook his head. "The evil green is all cleared from her precious skin. But still she is not herself. She lies, as you lay, in a dead trance we can't wake her from. She was mortal weak and weary, you know, lad, when it took her.

"Ah, lad, it's bad. Mortal bad. If she doesn't wake she cannot build the blessed weapon. And all our trouble has been in vain. Ah, it's a wicked time! I like the lass, lad. Dear life knows I'd hate to see her die!"

"I—I—" whispered John Star, through his agony of apprehension and despair. "I—love her, too, Giles."

And he sobbed.

John Star was able to return to the bridge by the time they entered the outskirts of the System, passing Pluto and Neptune. All the familiar planets, they saw in the teleperiscope, had turned a dreadful red. Even Earth was a dull spark of sinister crimson.

"Red," breathed Jay Kalam, his lifeless tone edged with horror. "The air of every planet is full of the red gas. I'm afraid we're too late, John."

"Even if we aren't," John Star whispered bitterly, "Aladoree is still no better."

"We'll land on Earth, anyhow. Find a piece of iron. And wait. Perhaps she'll wake—before the last man is dead."

169

"Perhaps. Though her pulse, Giles says——" He broke off, and muttered fiercely: "But she can't die, Jay! She can't!"

They were slipping past the Moon, five days later, toward Earth. Aladoree still lay unconscious, her strong heart and her breath grown desperately slow. Her frail body, weakened by exhaustion, by captivity and torture, by months of exposure to the red gas, was fighting desperately for life itself. The others watched her, kept her warm. They bathed her lax body in the neutralizing solution, helped her swallow a little broth or water when she could. They could do no more.

The Moon was a red world of menace. John Star scanned it through a tele-periscope. Naked since before the birth of Man, its rugged mountains were shrouded now in deadly crimson gas; the new human cities were mounds of lifeless ruin. On a bare plateau of lava, he saw the Medusæ's fortress!

Unearthly citadel! A replica of the black metropolis on their own doomed planet. Tremendous walls and towers of that black, enduring alloy, bristling with fantastic black machines—the instruments of a science that had survived through uncounted ages, had conquered many worlds.

"The hordes of them are waiting there," said Jay Kalam somberly. "Manufacturing the red gas. Bombarding the planets with shells of it. And their invasion fleet is stationed there. If they discover us——"

His voice fell. He had seen the same thing that shocked John Star with horror. A flaring burst of cold green flame above a black landing stage. A black flier rising, following them toward Earth!

"Perhaps they have already. But we may have time to land ahead of them, and look for a piece of iron."

"But Aladoree is still in that dreadful trance," John Star muttered. "Unless she wakes, to build AKKA, we have no weapon."

On they plunged, toward the red murky Earth, fearfully watching the black spider-ship crossing after them from the newly crimson Moon.

28

The Green Beast

Into the atmosphere of Earth, red-hazed with poison now, the *Purple Dream* dropped, over western North America, to land at last by the Green Hall, on the brown mesa beneath the mile-high, rugged Sandias.

John Star volunteered to leave the cruiser, to look for iron. There had been none aboard when the ship came back into their possession. Space-craft are non-magnetic, since magnetic fields interfere with the operation of the geodyne; and the Medusae, refitting the vessel, had removed the few bits of precious iron and steel from the instruments.

"Carry this," Jay Kalam told him, and gave him his old thorn-dagger. "And be cautious if you meet men. They may be mad, dangerous. . . . And hurry. We must get iron, and slip away, somewhere, before the black ship comes. We must hide, and wait for Aladoree to wake."

Dropping outside the air-lock, John Star paused to stare in horror at what remained of the System's proud and splendid capitol.

The sky was clouded with a scarlet murk, through which the mid-afternoon sun burned with a blood-red, evil light. Bare mesas and cragged mountains were turned strange and grim and incredibly desolate under the dreadful illumination.

The Green Hall had been destroyed by a great shell from the Moon.

On the edge of the grounds, where once had been wide, inviting lawns, a ragged crater yawned, rimmed with torn, raw rock. Beyond the pit the building lay in colossal ruin, a mountain of shattered emerald glass, from which protruded skeletal arms of twisted, rusting steel.

A moment he waited, horror-struck. Then, remembering the urgent need of haste, he plunged forward through a rank growth of weeds, through the bare skeletons of trees that the liquid gas must have killed, across dead lawns piled with rocks flung from the crater and shattered fragments of green glass.

Curious, he soon had cause to reflect, how hard it is to find even a nail when it must be had. He found assorted metal objects: a bronze lamp-stand, a little figurine of cast lead, the charred, twisted aluminum frame of a wrecked air-sled. Even a great steal girder flung from the building, many times too heavy to carry.

He hurried on, desperately searching the devastated grounds for any fragment of iron small enough to move, with an occasional anxious glance at the lurid sky. If the Medusæ *had* seen them, if the black ship was coming to attack them——

He stumbled around a great heap of broken green glass, and came face to face with green horror.

It had been a man. A gigantic man. It must have survived through the days of terror by sheer brute strength. Nearly seven feet tall, its body half naked, half clad in the ragged, filthy fragments of a Legion uniform—the uniform of the Green Hall Guards. Its skin was a mass of bleeding sores, scabbed and crusted horribly with hard green flakes. Red-rimmed eyes, green-clouded, hideous, stared from the horror of its face, half sightless. Its lips were gone. With naked fangs it was gnawing avidly at a fresh red bone that John Star knew, shudderingly, from its shape, to be a human humerus.

Sight of this man-beast, crouching, gnawing, snarling, sickened him with pitying horror. For it meant far more than one man's fate. It epitomized the doom of all humanity, under invasion by an older and more able race—a wise, efficient race, now proved by the crucial test better fitted to survive.

Involuntarily he had cried out at sight of that green, doomed beast. Then, realizing the danger, he tried to slip away. But it had already become aware of him. It made a curious, half-vocal, questioning sound—hoarse and flat and queer, for its vocal cords were evidently too far decayed for articulation. The red-rimmed, clouded eyes peered hideously, and found him. It came toward him, lumbering, shambling, bestial.

"Stand back!" he shouted sternly, tension of panic in his voice.

The effect of his sharp command was curious. For that shambling thing straightened suddenly to military erectness. It came to attention. Stiffly it raised an unspeakable, green-crusted paw in salute. But that was no more than a mechanical reaction left over from its forgotten humanity. It slumped back into the same stooping posture; it lumbered on toward him.

"Attention!" he shouted again. "Halt!"

A moment it paused, and then came on faster. Formless, protesting sounds spewed from its lipless mouth. And John Star stood, faint with horror, trying to understand its cries, until it uttered an abrupt, eager, animal squeal, and broke into a crouched and stumbling run.

He knew, then, that it was stalking him for food.

Swiftly he looked behind him for a path of escape; he realized with a wave of sick apprehension that it had trapped him. Its animal cunning was not yet gone. Mountains of broken green glass hemmed him in. He must face it.

True, he had the black thorn. But he was not so strong, he knew, as he had been before his own long sickness. And this avid, mewing animal was well over twice his weight. The green decay, apparently, had not yet greatly wasted away its strength.

He hoped, as they came to grips, that the tricks of combat he had learned in the Legion Academy would make up his disadvantages. But as one horny, green-scaled paw seized his dagger wrist in a clever, cruel hold, he knew that it had once been another Legionnaire. Its crazed brain had not forgotten how to fight.

The dagger dropped from his paralyzed grasp. Foul green arms locked him in a crushing embrace. Then it tried an old trick of his own. A knee in his back, the other locked over his thighs; his shoulders twisted, twisted, until his back would break.

He struggled vainly in the merciless hold, blind with pain and panic. The hard green scales were harsh against his body; fetor of decomposition sickened him. His efforts failed, and he felt a giddy sickness.

Naked fangs slashed at his shoulder; the thing made an eager whine. It was hungry.

Sheer desperation brought his old cool composure back, then. Through the mist of agony he imagined himself back at the Academy. He smelled the reek of leather and rubbing alcohol and stale sweat. He heard an instructor's bored, nasal monotone: "Twist your body, *so;* drive your elbow into the plexus, *so;* slip your arm here, *so;* then lock your leg and turn."

He did it, as the dry old voice whispered in his memory, hardly aware where he was, knowing only that the torturing pain would cease when he had done it, and he would be free to search for a nail.

Snap!

He rose slowly, beside that quivering mass of greenish decay. He staggered on again among the shattered Green Hall's ruins, scanning the battered earth. He must hurry! If the black flier came . . . It was a child's toy that caught his eye. A rusty, broken little engine that could no longer move its tiny burden—but might yet save the System.

He tore the shaft out of it, assured himself that it was good gray iron, and hastened back toward the cruiser.

Clambering over a heap of broken green glass, he looked up, and saw the black spider-ship. It was slanting down, across the red and murky sky, already very near.

At a dogged, weary run, he staggered back into view of the *Purple Dream*. Tiny torpedo shape of silver, a pygmy in the shadow of the huge, black-vaned machine plunging down on hot green jets above the dark Sandias. It was still beyond the yawning crater, a quarter mile away.

Hopelessly, a needle-pain of exhaustion stabbing at his heart, he stumbled on. The cruiser was unarmed; the weapons on the black flier could annihilate it in an instant.

Wondering dimly, as he ran, he saw a little group appear on the lowered valve of the air-lock, and hurry down the accommodation ladder. Jay Kalam and Hal Samdu and Giles Habibula, he recognized them, carrying the inert figure of Aladoree.

The valve closed above them; and Adam Ulnar had not appeared.

They ran away from the cruiser; evidently it was about to take off with Adam Ulnar at the controls. But why? Still running grimly on, John Star remembered his old doubt. Had his famous kinsman turned again? Had he put the others off to go back to the Medusæ? John Star could scarcely believe that. Adam Ulnar had seemed sincere. But——

Then the *Purple Dream* moved.

It plunged forward in the fastest take-off he had ever witnessed. It leaped away so swiftly that his eyes lost it. They caught it again, flashing toward the spider-fiier, its hull already incandescent.

Even as he realized that it was driven, not by the comparatively feeble rockets, but by the terrific power of the

174

geodynes, it struck the round black belly of the enemy craft with a burst of blinding light.

Flaming, the black invader fell with a curious deliberation out of the red sky. It struck the barren slopes of the Sandias, rolled down them, still looking queerly like a black and monstrous spider in the slow agony of death.

John Star's old, haunting doubt was gone.

"You are the last Ulnar," Jay Kalam greeted him with a solemn new respect, when he came up to the lonely little group on the edge of the mesa. "Adam Ulnar said he was trying to pay a debt. And he told me to tell you, John, that he hoped you would be happy in the Purple Hall."

John Star dropped on his knees by the limp, white-faced girl on the ground, whispered anxiously:

"Aladoree! How is she?"

"Ah, me, lad," dolefully wheezed Giles Habilula, fixing a pillow under her head, "she seems no better. No better! It's the same evil trance she's been in for mortal weeks. She may never wake. Ah, the poor lass——"

He flung a tear out of his fishy eye.

They tried to make her comfortable, under a little shelter made from the branches of a shattered tree. They found rude clubs to defend her if the green beasts should find them. Hal Samdu and Giles Habibula went to search for food and water; they returned in the dim and lurid sunset, empty-handed.

"Mortal me!" wailed Giles Habibula. "Here we are lost in a fearful desert, all death and dead ruin, without food or drink for ourselves or the lass! Ah, me! And frightful, mewing creatures are roving all about us, hunting for mortal human food. Ah, it's a wicked time!"

The Moon came up in the scarlet dusk, a huge and blood-red globe, above the rugged ramparts of the dark Sandias. And they saw, against its pocked and sinister face, a little cluster of tiny black specks, creeping about, growing, expanding. A little swarm of black insects that became steadily and ominously larger.

"A fleet coming down from the Moon," whispered Jay Kalam. "Since that one ship did not return . . . A whole fleet of their spider-ships, coming to make sure we are destroyed. They'll be here in an hour."

29

AKKA—and After

"She must wake," whispered John Star. "Or she never will!"

"I'm afraid so," agreed Jay Kalam. "I imagine they'll destroy the very mesa, with those atomic suns. To be sure we trouble them no more . . . But there's no way—"

"She must wake!" John Star muttered again.

With a sort of fierce tenderness, he lifted Aladoree from where she lay. Her body was limp, relaxed. Her eyes were closed, her pale, full lips parted a little, her fine skin very white. He could scarcely feel her pulse; her breath was very slow. Deep, deep, she was sunk in the coma in which she had lain so long.

So lovely and so still! He held her fiercely in his arms, staring up in mute, savage defiance at the red and black pocked Moon. She must not die! She was his! Forever— his! So warm, so dear! He would not let her die.

No! No, she must wake, and use her knowledge to build the weapon and destroy the menace of that red Moon. He must wake her, so she could be his forever!

Unconsciously, he had been whispering it to her. And he spoke louder now, in a desperate appeal. He called to her, trying without actual hope to shout through her coma, to make her realize the desperate need that she should wake.

"Aladoree! Aladoree! You must wake up. You must. You *must!* The Medusæ are coming, Aladoree, to kill us with the opal suns! You must wake up, Aladoree, and build your weapon. You must wake up, Aladoree, to save what's left of the System! You mustn't die, Aladoree! You mustn't! Because I love you!"

He always believed that his appeal reached through to her sleeping mind. Perhaps it did. Or perhaps, as a medical scientist has suggested, it was the irritating stimulation of the red gas itself that roused her, outside the *Purple Dream.* That does not greatly matter.

She sneezed a little, and whispered sleepily:

"Yes, John, I love you."

He almost dropped her, in his eager start at her response, and she came wide awake, staring about in amazed alarm at her strange surroundings.

"Where are we, John?" she gasped. "Not—not back on that planet——"

She was gazing in horror at the red Moon in the red-bathed sky.

"No, we're on the Earth. Can you finish the weapon, quickly, before the Medusæ come? We brought the parts you made by the river."

She stood up, looking dazedly around her, clinging uncertainly to John Star's arm.

"Can this be Earth, John, under this terrible sky? And that the Moon?"

"It is. And those black specks are the spider-ships of the Medusæ, coming down to kill us."

"Ah, the lass is awake!" wheezed Giles Habibula, joyfully.

And Jay Kalam hurried forward with the small, unfinished device that Aladoree had built back on the other planet, useless for want of a little iron.

"Can you finish it?" he asked, still calmly grave. "Quickly? Before they come?"

"Yes, Jay," she said, equally calm, seeming to recover from her first bewilderment. "If we can find a bit of iron——"

John Star produced the broken shaft of the toy engine. She took it in eager fingers, examined it swiftly.

"Yes, John. This will do."

Dusk was red in the west. Ghastly night came down. Under the red, rising Moon the four stood silent about Aladoree and her weapon, tense with hope and dread. They were alone on the mesa, cold in that dreadful light. Behind them was the murdered Green Hall, a stark skeleton of dead human hopes, terrible and quiet against the murky afterglow. Before them the mesa sloped up to the rugged Sandias, beneath the baleful Moon.

Silence hung over them—the awful silence of a world betrayed and slain. Only once was it broken—by a fearful, hideously half-vocal howl of agony and terror from the ruin.

"What was that?" the girl whispered, shuddering.

It was something no longer human, stalked by another hungry beast, John Star knew. But he said nothing.

Aladoree was busy with the weapon. A tiny thing. It looked very simple, very crude, utterly useless. The parts of it were fastened to a narrow piece of wood, which was mounted on a rough tripod, so that it could be turned, aimed.

John Star examined it—and failed entirely to see the secret of it. He was amazed again at its simplicity, incredulous that such a thing could ever vanquish the terrible, ancient science of the Medusæ.

Two little metal plates, perforated, so that one could sight through their centers. A wire helix between them, connecting them. And a little cylinder of iron. One of the plates and the little iron rod were set to slide in grooves, so that they could be adjusted with small screws. A rough key—perhaps to close a circuit through the rear plate, though there was no apparent source of current.

That was all.

Aladoree made some adjustment to the screws. Then she bent over, sighting through the tiny holes in the plates, toward the red Moon, with the black specks of the enemy fliers against it. She touched the key and straightened to watch, with a curious, lofty serenity on her quiet, pale face.

John Star had vaguely expected some spectacular display about the machine, perhaps some dazzling ray. But there was nothing. Not even a spark when the key was closed. So far as he had seen, nothing had happened at all.

For a strange moment he fancied he must still be insane. It was sheer impossibility that this odd little mechanism—a thing so small and so simple that a child might have made it—could defeat the Medusæ. Efficient victors over unknown planets and unknown ages, what had they to fear?

"Won't it——?" he whispered, anxiously.

"Wait," said Aladoree.

Her voice was perfectly calm, now without any trace of weakness or weariness. Like her face, it carried something strange to him. A new serenity. A disinterested, passionless authority. It was absolutely confident. Without fear, without hate, without elation. It was like—like the voice of a goddess!

Involuntarily, he drew back a step, in awe.

They waited, watching the little black flecks swarming

and growing on the face of the sullen Moon. Five seconds, perhaps, they waited.

And the black fleet vanished.

There was no explosion, neither flame nor smoke, no visible wreckage. The fleet simply vanished. They all stirred a little, drew breaths of awed relief. Aladoree moved to touch the screws again, the key.

"Wait," she said once more, her voice still terribly —divinely—serene. "In twenty seconds . . . the Moon . . ."

They gazed on that red and baleful globe. Earth's attendant for eons, though young, perhaps, in the long time-scale of the Medusæ. Now the base of their occupation forces, waiting for the conquest of the planets. Half consciously, under his breath, John Star counted the seconds, watching the red face of doom—not man's now, but their own.

". . . eighteen . . . nineteen . . . twenty——"

Nothing had happened. A breathless, heartbreaking instant of doubt. Then the red-lit sky went black.

The Moon was gone.

"The Medusæ," Jay Kalam whispered, as if to assure himself of the unbelievable, "the Medusæ are gone." A long moment of silence, and he whispered once more: "Gone! They will never dare—again!"

"I saw—nothing!" cried John Star, breathlessly. "How——?"

"They were annihilated," said Aladoree, strangely serene. "Even the matter that composed them no longer exists in our universe. They were flung out of all we know as space and time."

"But how——?"

"That is my secret. I can never tell—save to the chosen person who is to keep it after me."

"Mortal me!" wheezed Giles Habibula. "Ah, the blessed System is safe at last. Ah, dear life, but a mortal desperate undertaking it's been to save it. You must be precious careful not to fall into hostile hands again, lass. Old Giles will never be able to go through all this again, sweet life knows!

"Ah, me! And here we're left in the middle of the desert, in the wicked dark—and the Moon will never rise again!"

His voice had snapped the tension that held them.

"John——" breathed Aladoree.

No longer was it the voice of a goddess. Its awful

179

serenity was gone. It was all human, now, weak and shaken, appealing. John Star found her in the darkness. He made her sit down, and she sobbed against his shoulder with happy relief.

"Ah, lass," groaned Giles Habibula, "good cause you have to weep. We all may perish yet, for want of a mortal bite of food!"

The *Green Defender*, newest cruiser of the Legion of Space, flashed down to the Purple Hall, on Phobos, nearly a year later. Though one red gas shell had fallen on that tiny moon of Mars, during the Medusæ's bombardment, the great building had not been injured. The neutralizing solution had cured those affected by it; it had dissipated, combined into harmless salts, until the dark sky of the little world was free from any stain of red.

The cruiser dropped on the landing stage that crowned the central purple tower. The new Commander of the Legion came gravely down the accommodation ladder, and John Star came eagerly to meet him. Greetings over, they paused, looking down at the luxuriantly green convexity of the little planet, with grim memories of the last time they had been together here, when they took the *Purple Dream*.

"Not much trace left of the invasion," remarked Jay Kalam.

"No, Commander," replied John Star, with a little smile at the title. "Not one case of the madness left uncured, in all the System, I understand. And the red gone from the skies. It's already history."

"A splendid estate, John." With admiration, Jay Kalam's glance roved the richly green, curving landscape. "The finest, I think, in the System."

John Star's face clouded.

"A responsibility I had to assume." His voice was almost bitter. "But I wish I were back in the Legion, Jay. With Hal and Giles. I wish I were back in the guard of Aladoree."

Jay Kalam smiled. "You're—fond of her, John?"

He nodded, simply. "I was—am. I hoped—until that night, when she used AKKA. I realized then what a fool I was. She's a goddess, Jay. With the secret she has a power —a responsibility. I saw that night that she had no time for—for love."

Jay Kalam was still gravely smiling.

"Did it ever occur to you, John, that she's just a girl? Even though it may be interesting to destroy a planet, she can't be doing it all the time. She's apt to get lonesome."

"Of course," John Star admitted wearily, "she must have other interests. But she was—simply a goddess! I couldn't ask her. Anyhow, it could never be me!"

"Why do you think that, John?"

"For one thing, my name. Ulnar. I couldn't ask her to forgive that."

"But the name needn't worry you, John. The Green Hall, recognizing your distinguished service, has officially changed your name to John Star. That's one thing we came to tell you."

"Eh?" he gasped.

Then Aladoree came through the air-lock, Hal Samdu and Giles Habibula behind her. Her face sedate, gray eyes cool and grave, the clear sunlight working miracles of red and brown and gold in her hair, she looked at John Star in demure inquiry.

"Since the Purple Hall is now the strongest fortress in the System," Jay Kalam explained hastily, "the Green Hall requests you to assume the responsibility of guarding Aladoree Anthar."

"If you are willing, John Ulnar," added the girl, eyes twinkling.

His throat was dry. He searched in a golden mist for words, uttered them with an effort.

"I'm willing. But my name, it seems, is John Star."

Still grave, but for her eyes, she said: "I shall call you John Ulnar."

"But you said——"

"I've changed my mind. I trust one Ulnar. More than that, I——"

She was suddenly too busy to finish the sentence.

"Ah, me!" observed Giles Habibula, approvingly watching the two.

" 'Tis evident we're welcome, with the lass. Mortal evident! Especially the lass! Ah, and it looks like a good enough place for a poor old soldier of the Legion to pass his remaining years in peace. If kitchen and cellar bear proper proportion to the rest of the building.

"Ah, Hal, if you can forget your precious pride in all those medals and decorations that Jay has showered on you since the Green Hall made him Commander of the Legion, let's look about for a mortal bite to eat."

THE COMETEERS

1

The Prisoner of Phobos

Phobos spun on the time of Earth—for the ancient conquerors of that moonlet of Mars had adjusted its rotation to suit their imperial convenience. They had clad its dead stone with living green, and wrapped it in artificial air, and ruled the planets like captive islands from its palaces.

But their proud space navies had been beaten and forgotten long before these middle years of the thirtieth century. All the human islands around the sun were free again, and the youngest heir to the tarnished memories of that lost empire was a restless prisoner in the humbled Purple Hall.

Night was fading now into an ominous dawn, as the long crescent of Mars came up like a blood-rusted scimitar before the sun. Beneath its reddish light, a glass door slid open and he came out of the towering central pylon into the wide roof-garden on the western wing.

A slight young man, he wore the green of the Legion of Space, without any mark of rank or service decoration. With a frown of trouble on his boyish face, he paused to search the dark sky westward. Another man in green burst out of the door behind him.

"Bob Star! Where—ah, lad, there you are!" The older soldier of space was short and bald and fat, his tunic patched with the emblems of a long career but now unbuttoned in his haste. "Can't you wait a moment for poor old Giles Habibula?"

"Sorry, Giles." Bob Star turned quickly back, his thin, sunburned face warmed with a smile of amused affection for his panting bodyguard. "I tried to slip away, but only for a glance at the sky. Must you follow every step I take?"

"You know I must," the fat man puffed. "Hal and I have your father's orders, to guard your life every instant with our own. And the great John Star is an officer who expects obedience."

"The great John Star!" A momentary bitterness edged the young man's voice, before he saw the other's outraged loyalty. "I suppose my father's really great." He nodded soberly. "I know he's the hero of a terrible war and the owner of Phobos and my mother's husband.

"But why must he have me guarded like a criminal?"

"Please, lad!" Giles Habibula came waddling anxiously to his side, through the transplanted shrubbery that made the garden a fragrant bit of the far-off Earth. "Perhaps your father's sterner than old Giles would be, but he's only trying to make a soldier of you. And you know why you must be guarded."

"For my own safety." His trim shoulder lifted impatiently. "So my father says. But I'm a graduate of the Legion Academy, with honors enough. I've been taught how to fight. Why can't he trust me to defend my own life, like everybody else?"

"But the stake is more than your life, lad." Giles Habibula looked quickly about the empty walks, and drew him cautiously farther from the door. "And your danger more than John Star's doing. It's no secret to Hal and me that you have been named by the Council to receive your mother's trust."

Apprehension thinned Bob Star's brown face.

"You mean—AKKA?" His voice dropped with a wondering awe when he spoke of the mighty secret known by that brief symbol. The most precious possession of the united human planets, it was a weapon of most desperate resort, a power so awesome that each legal keeper of it was sworn to reveal it only to the next.

"That's your appointed duty, lad," the old man was breathing solemnly. "The noblest destiny a man can dream of—to be sole custodian of that great weapon, as your precious mother is. It was the order of the Council that you be guarded, from the day you were chosen. Hal and I are proud to serve you. Why fret about it?"

"But I'm not keeping any secret now," he protested restlessly. "None except the fact that my mother is to give me AKKA when her doctors say it's no longer safe with her—a day that I hope won't come for another twenty years and more. Must I stay a prisoner all the time I wait?"

"Perhaps the orders seem a trifle strict." The old man's bald head bobbed sympathetically. "But why fume about it? If we're confined to Phobos, it's still a precious scrap of paradise. We've all the comforts of the greatest palace in the System. To say nothing of the privilege of a noble cellar filled with famous vintages. Tell me, what's so mortal bad about it?"

"Nothing, really." Bob Star's fingers lifted nervously to touch a scar on his forehead, a pale triangular ridge that didn't tan. "I know it's a tremendous honor to be chosen keeper of AKKA, even though I didn't want it. But I couldn't sleep last night, and I suppose I got to brooding."

"Your head?" Giles Habibula had seen his fingers on the scar. "Is that the trouble, lad? Is that old concussion causing pain again?"

He dropped his hand self-consciously, his face drawn stern against the old man's sympathy. That throbbing pain had not come back—but only because it had never really ceased. The nature and the consequences of that old injury were secrets of his own, however, guarded as stubbornly as he meant to guard the weapon called AKKA. His lips tightened silently.

"If it's just a mood, I know the cure for that!" Giles Habibula beamed at him hopefully. "A platter of ham and steak and eggs, with hot brown bread, and a pot of coffee to wash them down. And then perhaps an apple pie. You got up too mortal early, dragging a poor old soldier out of his bed without a blessed bite to eat. Let's go back to breakfast!"

"Later, Giles." Bob Star spoke absently, peered at the dark sky again. "But first I want to look for something."

"Whatever it is, we'll never find it on an empty belly." The old man was peering with a sudden dismay at the grim lines of strain, which made that searching face seem for a moment prematurely old. "But what's the matter, lad? You're too young to look so grave."

"I couldn't sleep," Bob Star kept looking at the sky. "I don't quite know why. But my windows were open, and while I was lying there I happened to see something among the stars."

"Yes, lad?" The wheezy voice of Giles Habibula seemed curiously apprehensive. "And what was that?"

"Just a little greenish fleck," Bob Star said slowly. "In Virgo, near Vindemiatrix. I don't quite know why, but it got on my nerves. It went out of sight, when Mars began to rise. I don't know what it was, but I'm going to have a look at it, with the telescope yonder."

He started on toward the shining dome of the small ob-

187

servatory he had set up at the end of the garden—so that he could rove the stars with its electronic screens and his own restless mind, in spite of his imprisonment.

"Wait, lad!" The fat man's voice was sharper. "You wouldn't drag a poor old soldier of the Legion out of his blessed sleep in the middle of the night, just to look at a star?"

"But it isn't any ordinary star." He swung back to Giles Habibula, with a frown of disturbed perplexity. "Because I know it wasn't there a few nights ago—I happened to be searching that same sector of the sky for an asteroid that seems to have strayed off the charts. It couldn't be a nova—not with that strange, pale green color!"

"Forget it, lad," the old Legionnaire whined persuasively. "Any star can have a wicked look, to a man without his breakfast."

"I don't know what to think." He shook his head uneasily. "The object got to haunting me, while I lay there watching it. It got to seeming like an eye, staring back. It made me—afraid." He shivered, in the thin wind across the roof. "I don't know why, but I am really afraid."

"Afraid?" Giles Habibula gave the brightening sky a hurried, fishy glance. "I don't see anything to fear. And we're no cowards, lad. Neither you nor I. Not with the proper victuals in us—"

"Perhaps it's a comet." Still frowning, Bob Star swung back toward the observatory. "It looked like one—it was a short streak of that queer, misty green, instead of the point a star would show."

He shrugged uncomfortably.

"But then any comet should have been detected and reported long ago, by the big observatories. It hasn't been —I've been reading all the astrophysical reports, with nothing else to do! I can't imagine what it is, but I'm going to have a look."

"Don't, lad!" The wheezy voice sharpened, with a puzzling urgency. "Let's not meddle with fate."

"How's that?" He peered sharply at the old man's seamed, bland face. "What's wrong with you?"

"I've seen trouble—and I don't like it." Giles Habibula nodded unhappily. "I know we've had a peaceful time this last year, since Hal and I came back with you from Earth. Ah, a happy time, with little to do but fill our guts and sleep. But I've lived through things to chill your blood."

Bob Star backed away, watching him anxiously.

"I've known the mortal times some men call adventure," he went on dolefully. "I was with your father, along with Commander Kalam and Hal Samdu, twenty years and more ago, when we went out to the Runaway Star, to fight the wicked Medusæ for your dear mother's life and her precious secret."

"I know," Bob Star nodded. "The four of you were the heroes who rescued my mother's weapon and saved the human planets. But what has that to do with this fleck of green mist in the sky?"

"Only that I've had enough," the old man said. "Listen, lad, to a word of kind advice. Heroism is damned uncomfortable. Let's forget this monstrous comet. It might have waited until my poor old bones were laid to rest—instead of coming to upset my last days with such frightful talk."

He shook his head forebodingly.

"Poor old Giles! He had only sat down, with a bottle of wine in his trembling fingers, ready to stretch his legs before the fire and doze away into the last blessed sleep, when this fearful comet came, to start him awake with the threat of another stellar war. Ah, in dear life's name—"

"Stellar war!" Bob Star seized the old man's pudgy arm. "Then the danger isn't just imagination?" His hard fingers tightened. "And you knew about that green comet —how long ago?"

The old man squirmed and shook his head.

"No, no, lad!" he muttered hastily. "There's nothing at all to worry about, not here on Phobos. You just dragged me out of sleep too mortal sudden. My poor old wits are still fogged and groggy. You must pay no heed, lad, to the babblings of a battle-shaken veteran of the Legion."

"What about the comet?"

"Please, lad! I know nothing. In life's name—"

"It's too late, Giles." His fingers sank deeper. "You've already talked too much. If you don't want to tell me what this is all about—and why it's being kept from me—I can ask some awkward questions."

"Then stop it, lad!" the old man moaned. "You needn't shake me like a dying rat."

Waiting breathlessly, Bob Star released his arm.

"A whisper in the Legion. I've no secrets of the Council, lad. And it was your own father who ordered us to keep it from you. You won't let on that Giles breathed a word about it?"

"My own father!" Bitterness heightened Bob Star's anxiety. "He thinks I'm a weakling and a coward."

"Not so, lad," muttered Giles Habibula. "He was just afraid the worry of it, and the mortal shock, might be too much for you."

"He doesn't trust me," Bob Star whispered. "But tell me about this comet—if that's what it is."

"I've your promise, lad, not to tell him?"

"I promise," Bob Star said. "Go on."

Cautiously, the old soldier drew him across the grass, into the shelter of a clump of white-flowering frangipani. He glanced uneasily about the great roof, and up at the mighty central tower of the Purple Hall, which was already ablaze in the sunlight above them.

"The fearful thing was first seen ten weeks ago." His nasal voice sank to a hissing whisper. "Picked up by the great free-space observatory at Contra-Saturn Station. It was plunging toward the Solar System, with a velocity that threw the astronomers into fits."

He caught apprehensively at Bob Star's arm.

"But you'll remember, lad? You'll not give poor old Giles away, for the stupid blunder of his tongue? Your father's a stern man. Even though he and I are comrades of that great voyage to the Runaway Star. You'll remember?"

"I keep my word," Bob Star said. "But what's so alarming about this comet?"

"It's like no other," the old man wheezed. "It's no frail thing of pebbles and ionized gas, and it's larger than any other comet ever was. The astronomers don't know what it is. But it's twelve million miles long, lad—imagine that! And it has a thousand times the mass of Earth. It can't be any member of the System, they say. A strange body, driving out of the black gulf of space amid the stars."

Bob Star had drawn back dazedly.

"I see," he whispered huskily. "And what else about it?"

"The astronomers are tearing out their hair, lad. So your father told us. Because the thing has upset all their calculations. Its motion is all wrong. When the pull of the sun should have begun to increase its speed—it stopped!"

The old man's shifty,-red-rimmed eyes looked quickly out across the garden, and up at the dark sky, and hastily back at Bob Star again. It shook him to see that Giles Habibula was frightened.

"What stopped it?"

"Nobody in the System knows." The rusty voice dropped lower. "Now it's just hanging there. Five billion miles out —far beyond Pluto! That's isn't the motion of any kind of comet, Bob. A space ship might stop that way—if you can imagine a space ship twelve million miles long!"

"What else?" Bob Star stood taut with a mixture of dread and excitement. "What's happened since?"

"That's all I know—except that the Council is alarmed. You can't blame 'em! That's why your father was called to Earth, to meet with them at the Green Hall. They've ordered a censorship on any news about the comet—as if the people can't be hurt by a military secret!"

"I wonder what they're planning?"

"That's top secret, but I know the talk of the Legion." The old man turned to glance furtively behind him again. "I suppose you've heard of the *Invincible?*"

"The new battleship?"

"The greatest ship the System ever built." Giles Habibula beamed with a momentary pride. "A thousand feet long, and armed with a vortex gun—the great new weapon that won our war with Stephen Orco. A thing almost as dreadful as your mother's secret device."

"I know," Bob Star whispered impatiently. "But what about it?"

"I've no high secrets, lad," the old voice rasped. "All I know is the talk of the Legion. But I hear the *Invincible* is to carry some sort of expedition out to discover what's inside that green cloud—to operate the comet like a ship!"

Fat fingers tugged again at Bob Star's sleeve.

"You'll remember, lad?" Giles Habibula begged. "You won't tell your father?"

Bob Star stood very straight in that undecorated uniform, his dark head uncovered to the cold and distant sun rising now beneath the fading scimitar of Mars. The fingers of his right hand were tracing, as they often did, the triangular scar on his forehead. His tanned face was bleakly set.

"Don't worry, Giles," he said quietly. "I won't tell."

Abruptly, then, he exploded: "So my father told you to keep it from me? He's afraid I couldn't stand the shock! Why doesn't he order you to rock me to sleep in your lap?"

2

The Keeper of the Peace

Bob Star hurried on again toward the observatory dome. Giles Habibula limped hastily after him, peering at the dark sky and starting at every rustle of the wind in the shrubbery, as if his fishy eyes had already seen some unpleasant visitant descending from the comet to the roof.

Outside the little dome, Bob Star paused. He stood at the end of the roof, beside a low parapet of purple glass. Far beneath lay Phobos—a moonlet so tiny and so rugged that it seemed like a solitary mountain peak beneath the palace, floating alone in space, detached from any world at all. Yet it was green with transplanted forests, and spangled with artificial lakes.

He could remember when it had been large enough, and lovely to him, a dazzling triumph of the planetary engineers, its narrow valleys filled with all the adventure he could seek. But that was in his boyhood, before he went away to the Legion Academy. It was just a prison to him now.

Giles Habibula sat down on a bench in the sun. He fumbled in the pockets of his unbuttoned uniform and found a little empty flask, with a graduated scale along the side. He held it up to the sunlight, and his eyes dwelt gloomily upon a single lonely drop of the wine he loved.

"Go on, lad," he whispered sadly. "If you must look into the ghastly face of death! Poor old Giles will wait here for you. He's good for nothing now, but to roast his aching bones in the sun."

Inside the chilly gloom of the observatory, Bob Star sat down at the telescope. Its mechanisms whirred softly, in swift response to his touch. The great barrel swung to search space with its photoelectric eyes, and the pale beam of the projector flashed across to the concave screen.

Bob Star leaned to watch the screen. It was a well of darkness. White points danced in it. The brightest, he knew, was the third-magnitude star Vindemiatrix. Near it he found a patch of pallid green, oddly blurred.

He stepped up the electronic magnification. Vindemiatrix and the fainter stars slipped out of the field. The comet hung alone, and swiftly grew. Its shape was puzzling—a strangely perfect ellipsoid. A greenish football, he thought, kicked at the System out of the night of space—by what?

"Twelve million miles long!" he muttered huskily. "Which means it can't be any sort of solid matter. With that low density, it has to be hollow. But what's inside?"

Using ray filters and spectroscope, with the full power of the circuits, he strove to pierce that dull green veil, and failed. He sprang to his feet and stopped the instrument, impatiently snapping his fingers. Outside, he walked heavily to where Giles Habibula sat.

"It's no use," he muttered. "I found the cloud around it, but I failed to see inside. Nothing gets through—not a ray!"

He shivered again. For he had never seen anything so bafflingly weird, so strangely terrible. The comet was dreadful with the forbidden mystery of the dark interstellar wastes from which it had come, and its very vastness overwhelmed his mind. It was something beyond the range and scale of men, as men are beyond the microscopic infusorians swarming in a water-drop.

"Well, lad, you've seen it." Giles Habibula was rolling cheerfully to his feet. "The best astronomers in the System have done no more. Let's eat, before we perish."

Bob Star nodded silently, his mind still numb with consternation. They were halfway back across the roof, when the old soldier paused, pointing westward as abruptly as if he had seen the comet.

Turning, Bob Star saw a white arrow with a head of pale blue flame. It wheeled above the rusty crescent of Mars, and grew in the sky. A rustling whisper came into the air. The shubbery shook to a roaring gale of sound. A silver spindle flashed overhead, so near that he could see the black dots of observation ports, and recognize the *Phantom Star.*

"My father!" He felt the roof quiver faintly, as the landing ship came down on the great stage that topped the central tower. "He'll know all about the comet, and what the Green Hall has done."

"Your mother is waiting in the Jade Room," a guard

in the corridor told Bob Star. "There was an ultrawave message from John Star. He's coming to meet her there."

The Jade Room was enormous, its high walls paneled with jade-green glass and polished silver. On two sides, vast windows overlooked the darker green and brighter silver of the landscaped moonlet. The floor and the massive furnishings were of Venusian hardwoods, shining ruby-red.

His mother, she who had been Aladoree Anthar, sat quietly in a great chair that made her seem almost tiny. She looked up as he came in, and a quick smile brushed the pale trouble from her face. He could guess how grave her thoughts had been, but she said only:

"You're up early, son."

He paused inside the door, feeling painfully awkward. She was very lovely and he knew she intended to be kind. Yet, when anything reminded him of her great trust, she became a personage, too aloof and great to be his mother. He asked nervously:

"Father's coming here?"

"He just landed." Her breathless gladness made her seem human again. It made him want to run to her and put his arms around her. Somehow it filled his eyes with tears. He had started impulsively toward her, when he heard what she was saying:

"Your father sent a message ahead to ask me to wait for him here, alone. Perhaps you had better go outside, Bob, for just a few minutes."

That stopped him. He stood looking at her. His fingers were twisting savagely at a button on the front of his tunic. It came off in his hand, and he glanced down at it blankly.

"Why, Bob!" His mother came quickly toward him from her throne-like chair. "Is something wrong? What makes you look so strange?" She caught his arm gently. "You're shaking. Are you ill?"

He shook his head, blinking angrily at his tears.

"I'm all right," he muttered huskily. "If you didn't treat me this way!"

"Bob!" Her face looked hurt. "I didn't mean to seem unkind—"

"You're too kind!" he broke in harshly. "But I want to be trusted. I want a chance to live—even if it means a chance of getting killed. I can't stand to be shut up here, when things are happening." He caught a sobbing breath.

194

"If you want to be really kind, send me out to explore the comet on the *Invincible*."

She stepped back quickly, her face suddenly pale.

"I didn't know you knew," she whispered. For a moment she was silent, and then she shook her head regretfully. "I'm sorry, Bob," she said. "I had no idea you felt this way. John and I are very proud that you were chosen to be the next keeper of the peace." She looked at him anxiously. "Doesn't that promise you danger enough?"

"But how can I ever learn to face danger?" he demanded bleakly. "If you and father keep on treating me like a child. Guarding me like a prisoner!"

"I hope we haven't sheltered you too much." Moving closer to him, she seemed to hesitate. "There—there's something I'd better tell you, Bob."

He stiffened, at the sudden gravity of her voice.

"You know you made a very brilliant record at the academy, Bob—your father and I are very proud of that. Only one student ever finished with a higher average. He was Stephen Orco."

He winced from that name, his fingers drifting instinctively toward the scar on his forehead.

"When you graduated, Bob, the commanding officer told us he was worried about you. He thought you had driven yourself too hard, trying to beat Orco's marks. He showed us a report from the staff doctors. They agreed that you were near a nervous breakdown, and they advised a year of complete rest for you before you were given any duty. He warned us not to tell you about the report until you were better."

She smiled at him hopefully.

"I'm sure you're all right now," she said. "But that's why you've been here."

Bob Star was staring past her, at the windows and the ragged near horizon.

"It wasn't overwork that hurt me," he whispered faintly. "It was Stephen Orco—"

But his mother wasn't listening. He turned, and saw that his father had entered the room. John Star came striding across the wide red floor, trim and straight as always in the green of the Legion. Hard and slender, he looked little older than his son. He came straight to Aladoree, and administered a brief, soldierly kiss, and handed her a heavy, sealed envelope.

"Darling," he said, "this is an order from the Green

Hall Council." Gravely preoccupied, he turned to his son. "Robert," he said, "I wish to see your mother alone."

Bob Star stood speechless. The jade-green walls were cold as ice. The red floor was a terrible emptiness. His knees were going to buckle, and he had nothing to hold to.

"Please, sir—" His dry throat stuck.

"Let him stay, John," his mother said quickly.

"If it's about the comet," he muttered hoarsely, "I've already seen it."

"It is," John Star looked at Aladoree, and nodded abruptly. "You may sit down, Robert."

He collapsed gratefully into a great chair and clung to the cold red hardwood, trying to stop the trembling of his hands. He saw his mother's wide gray eyes lift slowly toward John Star, from the document she had taken from the envelope. Her face was white with an incredulous dismay.

"John." Her voice was very quiet. "This is an order for me to destroy the object in Virgo, at once, with AKKA."

John Star's nod had a military severity.

"The resolution to destroy the cometary object was approved by the Council eight hours ago," he said briskly. "I brought the order to you at the full speed of the *Phantom Star*—a record crossing."

The big gray eyes rested for a time on John Star's face.

"John," his mother asked very softly, "do you know what you are asking me to do?"

"Certainly." John Star looked at her with an annoyed impatience. "I spoke before the Council, in favor of the motion. The vote was very close. There were sentimental objections."

"Perhaps I'm sentimental," she answered quickly. "But I don't want to destroy that object—not unless we must. Because it's something very wonderful—so wonderful that none of our scientists will undertake to say what it is."

She stepped quickly toward him.

"Can we just erase it from existence, without ever knowing?"

"We can—we must!" Still standing, John Star had drawn his lean body very straight. "Consider the arguments for the destruction of that unknown object and the beings who appear to operate it like a ship—the news reporters had coined a word for them, before we set up the censorship. The Cometeers!

"Their science must be immensely ahead of our own

—except that they probably don't possess your weapon. And their hostility is as certain as their power!"

An oratorical ring had come into John Star's voice, as if he were quoting phrases from his talk before the Council.

"On Earth, everywhere in the System, the law of survival has set even the most closely kindred forms of life to killing one another. The Cometeers can't be our kinsmen, in any degree—they may be something we couldn't recognize as life at all.

"Logically, they must be our enemies.

"The peculiar motion of the cometary object is itself sufficient evidence of some purpose in relation to our planets. That purpose is necessarily for the benefit of the Cometeers, because they are obviously a successful and hence a selfish type of life—however they may look!"

Aladoree was shaking her head.

"I'm not so sure of your logic."

"The sentimentalists in the Council tried to question it," John Star answered. "Fortunately, the Cometeers have already given us more convincing evidence of their hostile intentions."

He paused dramatically, and Aladoree asked softly:

"How is that, John?"

"They have already visited most of our planets."

"People," Bob Star broke in, "have actually *seen* them?"

"Not exactly." John Star didn't look away from his wife. "The creatures of the comet are—or made themselves for the occasion of their visits—invisible. But they've left signs enough."

Aladoree asked quickly, "What have they done?"

"They came in some massive machine, whose drive-fields were powerful enough to disturb our ultrawave communications. Evidently their first object was to investigate our defenses—the invisible ship always landed near some Legion stronghold. On Earth, twenty-four hours ago, the raiders killed four guards—with a frightful weapon. They entered a locked vault, which we had thought impregnable. They escaped with a precious military secret."

John Star stepped quickly toward his wife. Suddenly he was no longer the soldier and orator, but only a man, anxiously begging.

"Please, darling!" he whispered. "I know you have the right to veto the first order. And I know what a terrible

197

responsibility you carry. I think I understand your feelings. But this danger's too great and near to be denied. For all we know, one of the invisible Cometeers may be with us now, in this very room!"

He glanced quickly about that jade-and-silver chamber. Agony whitened his lean face, and tears shone in his eyes. Impulsively, he swept Aladoree into his arms. Bob Star stepped quickly back, astonished; he had almost forgotten that his father was a human being, as well as a soldier.

"Won't you do it, darling?" he was pleading. "For your sake—and for mine!"

Gravely, Aladoree pushed his arms away.

"What was the secret," she asked, "that the Cometeers got?"

John Star turned to look at his son. His lips drew tight. He nodded slowly, as if in reluctant admission of Bob's right to be here.

"They learned," he said, "that the man known as Merrin is still alive."

Bob Star watched the new dismay that swept the color from his mother's face. He saw the slight, shocked movement of her head. Her voice, when at last she spoke, seemed oddly quiet.

"It makes all the difference, if they know about—about Merrin. It leaves us no choice." She nodded unwillingly. "If they've found out—that, then they must be destroyed."

3

The Fulcrum and the Force

Bob Star stood watching his mother, frowning with a puzzled anxiety. With the stern regret with which she had made that terrible decision still lingering on her face, she had turned quickly away from him and his father. She was bent now over a small table of polished Venusian scarletwood, busy with a few little objects she had gathered from about her person: her watch, a pen and a mechanical pencil, a metal ornament from her dress, an iron key.

"Must I go?" he whispered.

She looked up at him, with a grave little smile.

"You may stay," she said. "Since one day you are to become the keeper of the peace. Though there's very little to see." She glanced at the harmless-seeming objects on the little table. "You could watch a thousand times without learning the secret," she added, "because the control of AKKA is more than half mental."

She was busy again. With a deft skill that seemed to show long practice, she unscrewed the barrel from the pen and removed two tiny perforated disks from the back of the watch. Upon the mechanical pencil, whose working parts provided a fine adjustment, she began assembling a tiny, odd-looking contrivance. The platinum chain of the ornament seemed to form an electrical connection, and the clip from the pen would function as a key.

Bob Star peered at it, and whispered unbelievingly.

"Is that little gadget—all there is?"

"It's all there is to see." Her fine eyes came back to him for an instant, frowning with the gravity of her task. "This little device is merely the lever," she said. "The force that moves it is mental. The fulcrum on which it works—" Her pale lips drew stern. "The fulcrum is the secret."

Bob Star shook his head, staring at that tiny instrument.

"You mean that you destroyed the Moon, when those other invaders from the Runaway Star had made their fortress there—with only that for a weapon?"

"With the same sort of lever." She glanced at John Star, and he gave her an awed little smile, as if they both were living again through that dreadful instant. "I made that one from bits of wreckage from the bombed Green Hall, and parts of a broken toy."

Bob Star leaned closer, dazedly.

"It seems impossible that you could destroy anything so vast as the comet—with only that!"

"Size doesn't matter," she said quietly. "Neither does distance. This little device you see is only the lever, remember, through which that force can be applied to any object in the universe." She glanced up again, still frowning with her preoccupation. "The effect is a fundamental, absolute change in the warp of space, which reduces matter and energy alike to impossible absurdities."

Bob Star was silent for a moment, breathless. He shrank back a little, shaken with a startled dread, from this gravely smiling woman. She was his mother no longer, but something as strange and terrible as the Cometeers must be. Shining on her face was a calm, passionless serenity.

"Mother—mother," he whispered huskily. "You're like —like a goddess!"

It seemed strange that she should hear him, in her remote detachment. But she turned to him soberly, and said: "It's lonely, Bob—being a goddess."

Her eyes left him. For a few moments she worked in silence, assembling the device. But presently she paused again, to look up at him.

"Bob, there's one thing you ought to know now, since you've been chosen to be the next keeper. That's the reason there must be only one keeper—the reason you must wait for the secret, until the doctors find that it is no longer safe with me."

He stood listening, cold with a troubled expectation.

"There is one limitation to the use of AKKA." She hesitated, frowning at him soberly. "Even the existence of that limitation is a high secret, which you must not repeat."

He nodded, waiting breathlessly.

"To use the same figure of speech," she said quietly, "there is only one fulcrum."

"Huh?" His breath caught. "I don't understand."

"There's just one fulcrum," she repeated quietly. "That is not a literal statement, but it's all I can say before you are to be entrusted with the secret. What you must understand is simply this: If two people know the secret, and try to use their levers at the same time, neither can succeed. It would be entirely useless to the two of us, if we tried to use it independently."

"I see." He stepped toward her quickly, moved by a sudden dread. "What happens to you?" he whispered sharply. "After you have told me?"

"Nothing painful." Her gray eyes looked up again, shining with a serenity that he couldn't understand. "You can see that the knowledge must not be left where it might be unsafe."

"You mean—" He knew what she meant, but suddenly he couldn't say the words. "Aren't you afraid?"

She shook her head. To his amazement, she was smiling.

"I don't mind," she whispered softly. "You won't, after you have been the keeper of the peace as long as I have. I suppose that last duty of the keeper must seem a terrible penalty, to you today. But there comes a time when you see that it is the final, most fitting and most precious reward for our special service."

"I—I can't see that." That waiting duty became suddenly vast and dreadful in his mind, and he felt small with a new humility. "But I'm sorry—mother." He reached out to touch her arm with a diffident caress. "I'm sorry I've been fretting so—about waiting here with nothing much to do."

She reached to catch his hand and squeeze it sympathetically, and then stopped quickly again over the queerly toy-like device on the little table, which was a lever to thrust whole planets into annihilation. When he saw the look on her face—the calm authority that was almost divine and the willing acceptance of ultimate death as its price—his own restless impatience began to seem petty childishness. She finished some final adjustment, and straightened to face John Star.

"It's ready," she said.

"Then use it."

She picked up the tiny device, and carried it to the vast west windows. Following, Bob Star was shaken with a puzzled dread. He wet his lips, and whispered hoarsely:

"Can you use it safely, here inside the building? And find the comet, without a telescope?"

"I can." She glanced back gravely. "It's mental force that moves the lever. There's no danger to anything except the object at which it is directed. And a telescope would be only in the way, because light's too slow to show the target where it is. What I've called the fulcrum, remember, is something outside space and time."

She had turned to lift the small device, her slender hands white with her tension but yet oddly steady. She seemed to be sighting through the peepholes in the two tiny metal disks—though the comet, now by day, was invisible to Bob Star's eyes. Her finger was moving to touch the key when John Star sprang to catch her arm.

"Wait!" he gasped.

Beyond them, Bob Star saw a pale blur of blue flame in the sky. He heard the whisper and the rushing and the thunderous roar of rockets. The air was alive with quivering sound, and he glimpsed a mountain of white metal, flashing above the window. Then the red floor trembled, and the rockets were suddenly still.

"It's the *Invincible!*" In that abrupt silence, John Star's taut voice seemed oddly small and far away. "Commander

Kalam must have followed me—I can't quite imagine why!" He turned slowly from the window, to Aladoree. "I think you should wait, until we know."

Bob Star had run to join them at the window. A thousand feet below and a mile away, he saw the enormous ship —far too large for the stage on the tower, it had come down in the forest. The trees beyond it were uprooted and blazing from the rocket blast.

Even from its height, it looked literally invincible, and the shining might of it gave him a momentary sense of pride in the Legion and mankind. It was the most magnificent machine that men had ever made. The geodyne drive put the stars within its reach. New refractory alloys made its bright hull invulnerable. Its great weapon, the atomic vortex gun, could desolate planets.

A rocket plane lifted from the hull, as he watched, and climbed swiftly toward the stage above the tower. His mother's eyes followed it, bright with hope.

"That must be Jay," she whispered. "We must wait."

She lowered the device she had been aiming toward the comet, and Bob Star turned from the mighty miracle of the *Invincible* to peer at it once more.

"It's so small!" he protested breathlessly. "Made of such common things! It looks so insignificant—beside the *Invincible*. As if it couldn't really destroy—anything!"

"This is only the lever." She lifted it on her small palm, almost casually. She must have seen the awed wonder in his eyes, for she added quietly: "I carry it taken apart and the parts disguised, as another measure of security. Yet, even if the assembled instrument fell into hostile hands, there would be no danger. No manipulation of the instrument itself can have any effect, unless you know the fulcrum and the force."

Bob Star came to attention, with a quick salute, when Jay Kalam entered the room. Oddly, although he had been commander of the Legion for nearly twenty years, he looked far less soldierly than John Star. He was slender and dark and tall, with no trace of military stiffness in his bearing. His green-and-gold uniform was worn with a confident assurance, but it failed to disguise the grave reserve of the scholarly gentleman.

"John!" He spoke from the doorway, his voice quick with urgency. "Aladoree! Have you destroyed the object in Virgo?"

She moved toward him anxiously.

"Not yet," she whispered. "In another second—but we saw your rockets—"

"Then don't!" His thin face relaxed, and the breath sighed out of him. He came on into the room, smiling slightly now. "I was afraid I had got here too late," he said huskily. "The Council has rescinded its order—"

"What's that?" John Star's voice was brittle as the snap of breaking glass. "Why?"

Deliberately, the tall man drew another heavy envelope from an inside pocket of his tunic, and handed it gravely to Aladoree. She opened it hastily, and her gray eyes smiled again as she read the document.

"I'm glad you got here, Jay," she whispered softly. "You have saved me from murdering—something that must be very wonderful!"

"Why is this?" John Star's lips were tight, his narrow face pale and stern. "Why was the order rescinded?"

The grave commander of the Legion swung quietly toward him.

"John," he said soberly, "you know the Council was divided on ordering the destruction of the cometary object. I myself oppose it—as the murder of something greater than a planet. After you departed, I got permission to speak before the Council, in favor of a more moderate policy."

"But—Jay!" John Star's voice was sharp with his apprehensive urgency. "We know already that the Cometeers are hostile. We know they've found out about Merrin. Every moment the comet exists increases our danger. It must be destroyed!"

The tall commander shook his head.

"I know your arguments, John," he said slowly. "And we all admit that the situation is extremely grave. We must take stern measures to assure the safety of the System. But we aren't justified yet in annihilating the object —without even finding out what it really is. While it's true that the Cometeers have been scouting our military establishments, it's quite possible that they are only trying to protect themselves from the hasty use of some such weapon as Aladoree's. For all we know, their purpose in approaching the System may be entirely peaceful."

"Jay, you're a pacifist at heart." Restrained anger cracked in John Star's voice. "You've no business in the Legion!"

"I'll not be guilty of the murder of an unknown world,"

Jay Kalam answered softly. "Not just out of panic. My business in the Legion is the protection of civilization—and what does that mean, without justice or mercy? If we attempt the needless destruction of the comet, I feel that we're asking for the same sort of fate.

"Anyhow, John, I was able to convince several members of the Council that they had been unduly swayed by your war talk. The first motion was to send an ultrawave message to call you back, but I pointed out the probability that the Cometeers might intercept and decode the order. I could see an actual danger there—because I can feel the weight of your arguments, John, even though I favor moderation. You had been gone only two hours, and I thought we could overtake you with the *Invincible*. It seems we were nearly too late."

"You'll wish you had been too late." John Star's face looked pale and rigid, and his voice sounded hoarse and stern and terrible. "And the System will!" He nodded bleakly at the document Jay Kalam had brought. "That paper is the death-warrant for mankind."

An ominous quiet hung in the Jade Room. Silently, at last, Aladoree walked back to the scarletwood table and stooped to take apart her harmless-seeming weapon.

"I hope you're wrong, John," Jay Kalam said.

"But I'm not," John Star answered flatly. "I've no desire to be needlessly ruthless. But my duty is to guard the keeper of the peace, and I can't afford to let mistaken emotions stand in the way. I know this, Jay: by saving the comet you are murdering the System."

4

The Man Called Merrin

A terrible, taut stillness reigned for a little while in the Jade Room. John Star stood motionless and alone on the vast red floor, his pale face set like a mask of death. Something made the others shrink back from him.

Bob Star heard the sudden catch in his father's breath, and saw the wet glitter in his eyes. The guardian of the keeper was suddenly also a man defending his wife. He strode to Aladoree and turned, with his arm around her waist, to look almost defiantly at the commander of the Legion.

"Well, Jay?" His voice was flat and hard and dry. "If we can't destroy the comet, what are we going to do?"

"The Green Hall voted to leave that in my hands," Jay Kalam said. "I considered the situation carefully, while we came out from Earth. I've worked out a plan that I think is safe."

"Yes?" John Star waited, grimly intent.

"There are three things we must do," the lean commander said deliberately. "We must protect the keeper. We must guard the prisoner known as Merrin. We must find out as soon as possible whether the existence of the comet is any actual danger to the System.

"The first task is your duty, John."

John Star nodded silently, his arm drawing tighter around Aladoree.

"But I doubt that she's safe any longer, here in the Purple Hall," Jay Kalam added. "Phobos is well defended —but so was that vault in the Green Hall, which the Cometeers raided. With their invisibility, they would probably be able to land and enter the building undetected. What was left of the men guarding that vault shows that they have strange and terrible weapons."

"I'm quite aware of that!"

"Then I suggest that you take Aladoree away from here, on the *Phantom Star*, at once. I don't want to know where. You may select your own destination. Keep it secret. You can send some members of the Council the necessary information about how to communicate with you, if it does become necessary to use AKKA—a simple set of code signals, for ultrawave broadcast, ought to be sufficient."

"Yes, sir." John Star gave him a brisk salute.

"The defenses of the man called Merrin," he continued deliberately, "are already as good as the Legion can make them—except in one particular. I'm going to call upon your son, to make them complete."

He turned to Bob Star, his dark eyes searchingly intent.

"Are you ready, Bob, to undertake a very important and very dangerous duty, for the Legion and the System?"

"Yes—yes, sir!" Bob Star's voice tried to stick, but he was trembling with an incredulous joy. Dismay shook him, when he heard his father's quick protest.

"Robert isn't ready for duty," John Star said. "I was planning to take him with us, when we leave on the *Phantom Star*."

"No!" Bob Star gasped. "Please—I want something to do."

John Star merely shrugged at that, but Aladoree caught his arm.

"Bob and I have been talking, John," she said quickly. "He feels that we have been shielding him too much, and I believe he's right. I think he really needs a chance to prove himself."

"Thank you, mother!" Bob Star whispered, and he turned eagerly to the grave commander. "Please—I want to try—whatever I can do. I want to try—and I'll do my best!"

"This will need your best." And Jay Kalam turned to John Star. "John," he said quietly, "for this service I must call upon your son. No other man will do. You recall the adjustment of the Jovian Revolt. There's the matter of a promise given—and I intend to respect the honor of the Legion, even in such times as these."

John Star turned slowly back to his son. Watching him uneasily, Bob could see the stern reflection of some searching question on his face, but at last he nodded, without ever asking it. He swung abruptly back to Jay Kalam.

"Yes, I suppose we must go on keeping our word." His voice seemed cold and harsh. "You may give Robert the necessary orders."

Bob Star felt an ache in his throat. He wanted to thank his father, but the bleak set of John Star's face checked the words. He lifted his arm in an impulsive salute, and John Star returned it stiffly.

"For the third matter," Jay Kalam said again, "I am going out to the object in Virgo, on the *Invincible*. We shall keep in contact with the Green Hall, so long as possible, with tight-beam ultrawave. I intend to discover the true nature of the object and the purpose of its enigmatic motion. I hope to find that it isn't quite so dangerous as you think."

John Star stepped forward quickly, and shook the commander's hand. He seemed to swallow, and then said huskily, "Jay!"

"I fully expect to be seeing you again, John," Jay Kalam said evenly. "If we don't return, however, I suppose it will be advisable to destroy the object. It will take us about five days to reach it and five to return. Give us two more. If we haven't come back in twelve days, John, you may consider us lost—and forget my protests against destroying the object."

He paused, turning to Bob Star.

"Bob, you will come with us on the *Invincible* to the prison of the man known as Merrin. We'll have time on the crossing for me to explain the details and the great importance of your duty. You may make your farewells. We are leaving at once."

Bob Star turned breathlessly toward his mother.

His father was beckoning the commander aside. "Jay, I've decided where to look for our new sanctuary. We'll be leaving Phobos within two hours. As for communication—"

Cautiously, John Star lowered his voice.

The woman who was also the keeper of the peace moved quickly to meet her son. Her tall loveliness caught his heart with a sharp pang of yearning affection, and the tender softness of her voice, when she spoke, brought back to him all the bittersweet of childhood. She took both his hands in hers, and drew him to her with a quivering urgency. Her eyes swept fondly up and down him, and he saw her swelling tears.

"Bob," she breathed, "kiss your mother! You haven't kissed me, Bob, since the day you went away to the academy—nine years ago. And I think—" Her clear voice shuddered. "I'm afraid, Bob, that we shall never be together again!"

He kissed her. A sudden cruel tension had closed on his chest. Her troubled loveliness swam in his tears.

"My beautiful, beautiful mother!" he whispered. He drew back to look at her, with a puzzled unease. "But you didn't want to destroy the comet," he said quickly. "I thought you weren't afraid, even—to die."

"That?" She shrugged away the penalty of her secret. "But I wish—I almost wish that Commander Kalam had landed half a minute later. Because I'm still afraid your father is right."

"Why?"

She stood silent for a moment, fear cold on her face.

"Jay will tell you about the man we call Merrin," she said huskily. "I saw him only once. That was after he became the prisoner of the Legion. He was shackled and well guarded. Yet, somehow, he was terrible."

She stood staring toward the jade-and-silver wall, her eyes fixed and somber as if her mind were seeing something more disturbing.

"He was a giant, Bob." Dread still trembled in her voice. "There was a kind of splendor in him, and a terrible strength. He was a helpless captive, yet his face was shining with an unconquered power. He seemed like—well, something more than just a human being."

She caught Bob's arms, her strong hand quivering.

"He seemed superhuman—immortal and almost invincible and entirely contemptuous of mankind. His mind must be as powerful as his magnificent body—but his emotions can't be quite human. You have to admire him. But you must fear him, too. I don't quite know why, because there certainly isn't much harm left that he can do.

"He didn't speak to me, Bob. He simply turned for an instant to look at me, as they were leading him across to his cell—taking mincing little steps, because of the leg irons. His blue eyes were burning—and they were cold as ice. They were undefeated, carelessly unafraid.

"He laughed at me, as he went on, from a distance I could never reach across. Something in him hadn't been beaten—and never will be! You must guard him well, Bob. For in him you are guarding the lives and the happiness of all your honest fellow men!"

Astonished and puzzled, he whispered, "I will."

"Come, Bob," Jay Kalam was saying. "It's time to go."

He embraced his mother.

"I love you, Bob," she was breathing. "And I'm—oh! so afraid!" Her slight, straight body was trembling against him. "Be careful, son. Don't let the man called Merrin get away!"

"Good-bye, Robert." His father shook his hand, speaking with an unaccustomed tremor of emotion in his voice. "Whatever happens, don't ever forget that you are now an officer on duty with the Legion of Space."

"Yes, sir." Bob Star wondered about that unspoken question he had seen in his father's troubled eyes, and he tried hard to answer it. "I won't forget!"

He went out of the Jade Room with Commander Kalam, and paused abruptly when he saw Giles Habibula, sitting half-asleep on a seat in the wide corridor outside.

"My bodyguards?" he asked quickly. "Are they coming?"

The commander's dark face warmed, as if to the glow of old memories.

"Giles and Hal?" He nodded quickly. "They're good men—we served together, you know, long ago. Bring them on board."

A concealed door behind the chart room of the *Invincible* opened into a long chamber that Bob Star was surprised to find in a warship of space. Golden light from hidden sources fell upon the rich sheen of heavy rugs. The pale ivory walls were hung with exquisite Titanian tapestries. The massive furnishings, in silver and black, were luxuriously simple. The long bookshelves and the optiphone, with its tall cabinets of the recorded music and drama of several planets, revealed the scholarly aesthete in the master of the room.

The *Invincible* was now driving outward from the sun, away from yellow-red Mars and the greenish fleck of Phobos. Her humming geodynes—electromagnetic geodesic deflectors, in the language of the engineers—acted to deflect every atom of ship, load, and crew very slightly from the coordinates of the familiar continuum of the four dimensions, so that the vessel was driven around space-time, rather than through it, by a direct reaction against the warp of space itself.

In that hidden room, however, even the vibrant droning of the geodynes was shut away, as if they ran in another space. Nothing gave the faintest sense of the ship's tremendous acceleration and velocity. The crispness of the cooled artificial air suggested springtime in the woods of far-off Earth.

"Sit down, Bob." Jay Kalam nodded at a great chair, but Bob Star felt too tense and breathless to sit. "I'm going to tell you about the prisoner we call Merrin, and the unfortunate circumstances that place this grave duty upon you."

"This man—" Bob Star was trying to seem calm, but his dry voice trembled and sank. "This man you call Merrin—is he—is he Stephen Orco?"

A shadow of troubled amazement crossed the commander's lean face.

"That is a high secret of the Legion." His low voice was taut and his dark eyes searching. "A secret you had no right to know, before today. How did you find out?"

"My mother described the prisoner, back there in the Jade Room," Bob Star said. "I knew Stephen Orco, and he knew there couldn't be another like him. But I thought—" His voice caught, and his troubled fingers came absently up to that pale, triangular scar on his forehead. "I thought he was dead."

"I'm glad that's how you knew." The commander seemed to relax. "Because Stephen Orco is dead—and buried—to all except a trusted few." His face turned grave again. "When did you know him?"

"Nine years ago." Bob Star's voice was hoarse with emotion. "On Earth, at the academy. He was in the graduating section, during my first term. He was handsome, brilliant. At first I was attracted to him. But then—"

He broke off abruptly, his face pale and hard.

"What happened, Bob?" Jay Kalam's tone was warm with a puzzled sympathy. "Did you quarrel?"

"It was our affair." Bob Star nodded bleakly. "For years I meant to find him, as soon as I graduated, and—settle it. But then he showed the Legion what sort he is, with the Jovian Revolt. And I thought he got death for his treason." He peered at the tall commander. "Wasn't that the sentence?"

"It's what the public records show," the commander said quietly. "But you must tell me about you and Stephen Orco."

"I can't!" A sort of panic shook Bob Star. "I haven't told anyone—not even my own parents."

"I need to know," Jay Kalam insisted softly. "Because your singular duty now must be a consequence of that incident—whatever it was."

Bob Star stood looking for a moment at Jay Kalam, his face hard with a long-remembered bitterness. He nodded soberly.

"You know the tradition of hazing at the academy?"

"The officers have always tolerated it," Jay Kalam said. "It is believed to be good for discipline."

"Maybe it is—usually." Bob Star shrugged impatiently, as if to shake off the burden of that old bitterness. "Anyhow, you know the rule that each new cadet must accept and obey one command from each man in the graduating section?"

The commander nodded quietly.

"I suppose it isn't bad, usually," Bob Star went on. "The graduates are learning to be officers, and the new boys learning discipline. The commands are commonly harmless,

210

and I suppose the custom usually makes for comradeship as well as discipline."

A cruel emotion quivered in his voice.

"But Stephen Orco was no usual student. A giant of a man. He was remarkably good-looking, and a great athlete. His hair was red as flame. His eyes were peculiar —a bright, cold blue, and always shining with a clever malice. The instructors used to say he was the most brilliant cadet ever at the academy."

Bob Star's narrowed eyes were staring past Jay Kalam at the dark-hued patterns of a priceless Titanian hanging. In the pain of that old injury, he had forgotten his first awe of the tall commander. His words fell swiftly, hard as slivers of ice.

"Stephen Orco had no real friends, I think. All the boys must have been secretly afraid of him. Yet he did have a kind of popularity. His remarkable strength and his malicious wit made it uncomfortable to be his enemy. More than that, he had a kind of evil fascination.

"He was a born leader. His reckless audacity matched his uncommon abilities. He could dare anything. And he had a pride to match his capacities. It made him try to excel in everything—usually with success. It seemed to me that he had a jealous enmity toward every possible rival. He loved no one. He was completely selfish in every friendship.

"From the first day, he hated me."

The commander looked faintly startled, beneath his grave reserve.

"Do you know why?"

"Jealousy, I suppose," Bob Star said. "He knew I was John Star's heir. He assumed that I would be chosen to take my mother's place as keeper of the peace." He shook his head. "There couldn't have been any other reason."

"Did he mistreat you?"

"From the first day." Bob Star's nervous fingers traced that scar again. "He injured me in every way he could. He tried to keep me from winning any honors—perhaps he wanted to keep me from qualifying to be keeper. He did his best to turn all the instructors and the other students against me. He used me for the butt of his cruel practical jokes. He made things pretty rough for me, until he graduated."

He paused unhappily, biting his quivering lip.

211

"I've tried to forget what he did to me," he whispered. "But there was one thing—"

"Yes?" the commander urged him. "What was that?"

"It was one night, just before the end of the term," he went on abruptly, his low voice quick and breathless. "I was walking alone on the campus—I was worn out from my first examination in geodesic navigation, and upset because somebody had poured ink over all my notes and a finished term paper in my desk—I suppose Stephen Orco was responsible for that, too, though I never really knew.

"Anyhow I met him in the dark, with three of his friends. Or perhaps I shouldn't call them friends—it was fear that held them around him, not affection. They stopped me. Stephen Orco asked me if I had obeyed that customary command from him. I said I hadn't. He turned to the others. They whispered. I heard the others snicker. Then he came back to me, and gave me his command."

Bob Star paused, white-faced.

"What was that command?"

"He ordered me to repeat a statement after him. An ugly thing. He wanted me to say that I wasn't John Star's son. He wanted me to say that my father's infamous cousin, Eric the Pretender, had been my mother's lover, and that I was that traitor's son. He wanted me to say that I was a coward and a weakling, unfit to be the keeper. He wanted me to swear, on my honor as a future officer of the Legion, that his monstrous lie was true.

"Of course I wouldn't." Bob Star's low voice was hoarse again with that remembered pain. "One of his friends objected that the hazing tradition gave him no right to go so far, but one glance from Orco was enough to shut him up.

"We were near the academy museum. It was closed and dark, but one of the men had been doing research on the old weapons displayed there, and he had a key. Orco made him open the back door, and they dragged me into the building.

"They took me down into a little basement room, where they wouldn't be interrupted—for I had made friends of my own, in spite of Orco. They did various things to me, but I didn't speak. Stephen Orco's terrible pride was burning cold in his eyes. I think my stubbornness made him angry—if you can imagine that.

"He exhausted the customary penalties, and thought of new ones. He was clever, and he had a taste for such work.

Even after his three companions got frightened, he wouldn't agree to let me go.

"Finally, he sent one of the others up to break open a display case and bring him down a rusty torture implement that dated from the last corrupt reigns of the Empire, when the democratic Greens were about to overthrow the power-rotted Purples. A device invented to break political prisoners. It was called the Iron Confessor."

"Huh?" The commander peered suddenly at that pale scar, with dark, startled eyes. "I think I remember seeing that display. Isn't the thing a sort of helmet?"

"There's a wide iron ring that goes around the head," Bob Star said huskily. "And a sort of three-edged blade that can be forced through a hole in it, as the screws are tightened, into the scalp and the skull of the victim.

"I think Stephen Orco was showing his jealousy, then. He couldn't forget that I came from the old imperial family. If he had been John Star's son—or the Pretender's either—I think he would have been plotting to restore the Empire. Anyhow, he called that torture device the Purple crown, and I could see the savage envy in the way he made me wear it."

Jay Kalam stood staring at the scar. "He didn't do—that!"

"He made his men hold me," Bob Star said. "He put that ring on my head, and tightened the screws until I felt the blood running down my face. He kept commanding me to repeat the wicked lie. Still I wouldn't do it, and my silence seemed to goad him.

"The Iron Confessor was more than the ring and the blade. There was another part, that had been smashed before it was put in the museum. Orco repaired that, while his men held me there with that blade in my skull. I don't know exactly what it was, or how it worked—I didn't have much attention left, just then, for mechanical details. But Orco said it used supersonic vibration, tuned to stimulate the pain centers of the brain. It looked like a radio amplifier. A cable ran from it to that three-edged blade. What it did was to transform a voice into sensations of intolerable pain.

"Stephen Orco stood in front of me, when he got it hooked up. The room was dark, but I could see his face in the glow from the tubes of that device. The hair red like flame. The blue eyes triumphant and mocking and

213

terrible. He began talking into a little microphone, and that thing turned his voice into great waves of red agony beating at my mind.

"It felt unendurable. But I was already exhausted from trying to get away. The others were all grown men, and trained athletes. I was twelve years old, growing weak from loss of blood, and already half-unconscious with pain. There was nothing I could do.

"Orco kept on talking, gradually twisting the dials of that fiendish device to step up the intensity of agony. The Iron Confessor had been invented by my own family, he said, to extract confessions from enemies. It was guaranteed, he said, to make anybody confess anything.

"He said it was based on the secret principles of political conversion first discovered by a party called the Reds, a thousand years ago. The tuned ultrasonic vibrations from that blade could destroy the synaptic patterns of my brain, he said—to break my will and make the truth of everything he told me.

"And I was terribly afraid for a while—afraid of yielding to him. But suddenly, even with that knife in my skull and his voice burning like a flame into my brain, I felt that I was strong enough. I felt that nothing he could do would beat me. I looked up at him, and told him to do his worst, and promised to kill him whenever I got the chance.

"That seemed to heighten his anger. He stepped up the pain of that vibration again, and he said he was going to fix me so that I'd be afraid to kill anybody. Then he repeated that wicked lie, and kept commanding me to swear that it was true.

" 'Say it, pup!' he would shout at me, his voice trembling with his own fury and transformed to pure agony flaming out from that blade in my skull. Then he would turn up the amplifier. And then he would shout again, 'Say it, pup!'

"I didn't say it—not at least so long as I was conscious. But I'm not sure what really happened, toward the end. It was a kind of nightmare. That dark room, and his face proud and angry and dreadful in that faint glow of light, and his voice hammering at my mind with red agony.

" 'Say it, pup!'

"I knew at the end that my will was weaker than that machine. And I must have finally given in—I'm afraid I did." Bob Star stood shuddering for a moment, his thin hands clenched. "I don't know what happened," he repeated huskily. "But it's hard to imagine that Stephen Orco gave up before I spoke."

"The next thing I really knew, I was in bed in the infirmary, with my head bandaged and a nurse giving me a shot of something to quiet my nerves. She told me that Stephen Orco and his friends had brought me there about dawn. Their story was that they had found me wandering on the beach, under the cliffs, with my head slashed open.

"I told everybody that I had fallen in the dark, and hurt myself accidentally."

"Why did you do that?" Jay Kalam shook his head, in puzzled reproof. "Why didn't you report the truth? Stephen Orco would have been punished and discharged from the Legion—he would never have had the opportunity to lead the Jovian Revolt."

"It was our quarrel," Bob Star whispered hoarsely. "Ever since those vibrations of pain were burning into my brain, I've meant to kill him, if I could." He shook his head and muttered again, uncertainly, "—if I could."

"How's that?" The commander gave him a long, troubled look. "Assuming that it became your duty to kill Stephen Orco, and that you had the means at hand, couldn't you do it?"

"I don't quite know." Bob Star shivered again. "I can't remember what happened at last, or whether I really gave up. He kept promising to break me, so that I could never kill anybody. I'm afraid—afraid he did. Because I think my brain was damaged by the ultrasonic vibration—if that was what it was. There's still a pain throbbing in my head. A little hammer of red agony, pounding day and night. In nine years, it hasn't stopped."

Bob Star's face was white, and sweat had broken out on his forehead.

"I wasn't a coward—before that night," he whispered hoarsely. "I wasn't the weakling he wanted to make me." He sank abruptly into the big chair, looking miserably up at Jay Kalam. "But now, commander—I don't know."

5

The Honor of the Legion

The tall commander of the Legion stood for a time scraping thoughtfully with one lean finger at the lean angle of his jaw, studying Bob Star.

"I'm glad you've told me this," he said at last, his voice quiet and very grave. "I understand the way you feel, because once I thought it would be impossible for me to kill a man." His dark eyes closed for a moment, and his face drew stern as if with some memory of pain. "But sometimes it must be done. I learned that long ago, and found that I could do it."

He stepped forward abruptly.

"And so must you, Bob. You can—and must! As things stand now, it is very likely to become your duty to take the life of Stephen Orco."

Those softly spoken words brought Bob Star out of his chair.

"How is that, commander?" He was trembling, and he had to gasp for his breath. "I'd give anything for the chance!" Something checked his eager voice, and something made him bite his lip. "But I'm afraid—afraid I couldn't do it."

Chimes rang softly, then. A massive door swung open, to admit once more the deep-toned, vibrant song of the geodynes that drove the battleship. A steward came in, pushing a little wheeled table. He saluted.

"Breakfast, commander," he announced. "For two."

Jay Kalam motioned silently for him to go. The heavy door closed behind him, and once more it seemed that the long, ivory-walled room was somewhere far from the racing ship.

"Why might it be my special duty to kill Stephen Orco?" Bob Star was whispering. "And how does it happen that he's still alive, now so long after his execution was announced?"

"A strange affair." Jay Kalam stood frowning gravely,

ignoring the covered table the steward had left. "An unfortunate aftermath of the Jovian Revolt. The full history of that rebellion has never been made public, but I must outline it to you now—so that you will understand the peculiar status of Stephen Orco, and the supreme importance of your present duty."

Bob Star nodded, listening breathlessly.

"Orco himself is a sinister riddle, from the very beginning," the commander went on gravely. "Many people besides yourself have found him queerly inhuman. Perhaps he is. Our investigators have been at work ever since he turned traitor, and still they have discovered nothing whatever about his origin."

"But I remember his parents," Bob Star broke in. "They visited the academy, not long before—that night." He found his fingers on that scar again, and dropped them self-consciously. "He gave a party for them. He made a point of inviting all my friends, and leaving me out."

"They were only foster parents," Jay Kalam said. "His adoptive father, Edward Orco, seems to have found him, when he was just an infant, under peculiar circumstances. Orco was a wealthy planter. He had extensive holdings through the asteroids. His home was on Pallas. Our investigators learned what we know about the finding of Stephen Orco from his old servants.

"It happened nearly thirty years ago. Orco was cruising in toward Mars in his space yacht. He and his wife had been visiting some of their properties scattered through the smaller asteroids, and they were coming to Mars for the social season. Their route had taken them far off the usual space lanes.

"Some forty million miles off Mars, their navigator discovered an unusual object, adrift in space. It had tripped the meteor-detectors, but it was obviously no common meteorite. The navigator's report aroused Orco's curiosity enough so that he turned back to examine the object.

"It proved to be a cylinder of magnelithium alloy, eight feet long. It had a carefully machined screw cap, which was sealed at several points with masses of black wax. Impressed upon each seal, in scarlet, was a curious symbol: the looped cross—the *crux ansata,* which is an ancient symbol of life—above crossed bones.

"Orco had gone out in a space suit to examine the object. He decided to bring it aboard, through the airlocks, and open it. His wife objected. The crossed bones, she insisted, meant danger. The shape and dimensions of the object rather suggested a coffin, and she thought that it might contain a corpse, dead of some dreadful contagion.

"But Edwin Orco was a hardy man. It was not timidity that had won his fortune, out on that high frontier. And his curiosity must have been burning. In the end, he had the cylinder dragged into the air-lock. Then, when no member of his crew proved willing to touch it, he shut himself into the chamber with it. He broke the seals, and unscrewed the cap.

"The walls of the cylinder were heavy, and carefully insulated. Inside, it was fitted with tanks of oxygen, water, and liquid food. There were heaters and thermostats and condensers to dry the air. In brief, except for lack of power, the thing was a miniature space ship.

"In the midst of the apparatus, in a kind of cradle, lay Stephen Orco. A red-haired tot, not a year old. He was naked, and there was nothing to identify him. Apparently he was never able to tell anything of his past history. Edwin Orco advertised discreetly for information, offering large rewards, but nothing was ever forthcoming.

"Stephen Orco must have had, as you say, some unusual fascination. One glimpse of the child's wide blue eyes won Edwin Orco's childless wife. The couple adopted the infant. They gave it every advantage their wealth could buy, even to securing the appointment to the academy."

"His own brilliance would have been enough to win him that," Bob Star put in. "He could have had any scholarship he wanted."

"Anyhow," Jay Kalam went on, "he graduated with top honors. He went into service, and got the rapid promotions that his abilities seemed to earn. Within four years, he had his own ship. Not two years later he was placed in command of the Jupiter Patrol.

"The Jovian satellites, I suppose you know, were settled largely by exiled Purples—enemies of the democratic Green Hall. They were moved there when the Empire was overthrown, two centuries ago."

"I know," Bob Star agreed. "My own grandfather was born on Callisto."

"Within a year after he assumed command of the Jupiter Patrol," the commander continued, "we began to receive ultrawave dispatches from Stephen Orco, reporting an unexpected uprising of the Purples. He stated that he had the situation well in hand, however, and asked for no reinforcements.

"For several weeks we did nothing—until a band of fugitives reached Ceres in a space yacht, with the information that Stephen Orco was himself the guiding spirit of the revolt, and that the fighting had begun when his conspirators attacked men in the Patrol. Civilian friends of the Green Hall were being systematically murdered.

"I recalled every possible Legion ship to the Martian yards, from as far away as Mercury and Contra-Saturn—"

"I remember when we heard about it, in the classroom at the academy," Bob Star put in. "I hadn't seen Stephen Orco since the time they tortured me. I tried to get into the fleet, to even that old score, but my request for duty was never approved."

"Your father asked me to ignore it," Jay Kalam said. "I didn't know what you have just told me—or you might have had a chance to get your man. Because that was the most serious crisis the Legion has faced since Eric the Pretender brought those monstrous invaders back from the Runaway Star to help him restore the Empire.

"As soon as the fleet was gathered in the Martian yards, I took your mother aboard the flagship. From the reports coming back from Jupiter, I was already sure we were going to need her weapon.

"Our outward flight was not opposed. We approached Callisto without meeting any hostile action, and I dispatched an ultrawave message, calling on the mutineers to surrender. The answer was something like a sun, fired at us from the fortress above the city of Lel."

"The sun-gun?" Bob Star whispered. "I heard rumors, you know, in spite of the censorship and the way my father tried to shield me."

"The correspondents named it that," Jay Kalam nodded. "The weapon was an improvement over something the monsters of the Runaway Star had used against us twenty years before. An energy vortex, which wraps the coordinates of time and space to make all the heavy elements as unstable as plutonium—and creates a resistless attraction to draw more matter into its terrible whirlpool of atomic annihilation."

His dark face had stiffened.

"Stephen Orco must be as brilliant as you say. He had designed that dreadful thing from scraps of information the exiles of Callisto had got from the creatures of the

Runaway Star while the Purples under Eric were in alliance with them. But somehow he had multiplied the range and power of it. That first shot destroyed two of our finest ships. I saw at once that Orco's weapon could reach every planet in the System, with those atomic shots.

"Your mother had already assembled her own secret weapon. As much as I dislike wholesale destruction, I asked her to wipe out the city of Lel with all its surrounding fortifications.

"You saw the instrument of the peace, Bob, back there in the Jade Room. Your mother must have told you that the working of it is not spectacular. I was not surprised that nothing seemed to happen when she tried to operate it. But I could see her expression of puzzled fear when he turned to me, a moment afterward.

" 'It doesn't work,' she whispered.

"One glance at the screen of a tele-periscope was enough to show that the fortifications of Lel were still unchanged. I was able to step up the magnification enough to see the atomic gun itself—a colossal skeleton tube of metal girders, set up on a mountaintop beside the city.

"While I was looking, another vortex came spinning toward us. A sort of spiral nebula in miniature, in which meteors and ships exploded as furiously as if they had suddenly turned to pure plutonium. That second shot caught three more cruisers, and your mother saw at once that we had been defeated.

"Someone else, she told me, had come upon the principle of AKKA. She tried to explain, without compromising her secret, that the weapon utilizes a singular instability of the universe which is such that any master of the device can prevent its use by any other."

Bob Star was nodding.

"She spoke to me about what she called a fulcrum," he said. "The device she puts together is a lever, and the mind supplies the force, but there is only one fulcrum." His breath caught sharply. "Had Stephen Orco discovered —that?"

The commander nodded bleakly.

"Your mother's failure was sufficient evidence, she said, that another master of AKKA was fighting us. Her weapon wouldn't work again, she told me, until that other person was dead—or at least until his instrument had been taken from him.

"Of course your mother was able to keep Orco from

220

using the secret against us, but his atomic gun itself was enough to beat our fleet. We lost six more vessels as we fled. A triumphant ultrawave message from Orco followed us.

"His message was insolently phrased. It confirmed your mother's belief that he was the new master of AKKA. It demanded that the Green Hall recognize him as the supreme ruler of an independent Jovian Empire.

"But even that wasn't enough to satisfy Orco's imperial ambitions. He demanded trading rights and other concessions on every planet, and humiliating limitations upon the strength and movements of the Legion. It was clear that he planned to dominate the whole System."

Jay Kalam stood rigidly straight amid the rich simplicity of that great, soundless room, in the racing battleship. His lean face was grimly set. His dark eyes were narrowed sternly. The vibrant ring of his low voice seemed to Bob Star like an undying echo of mighty deeds.

"We were defeated," he said softly. "But not vanquished. The Legion has never been vanquished, Bob. You must remember that."

"Yes, sir." Instinctively, Bob Star stood straighter.

"While the politicians on the Council stalled for time and debated how to answer Orco's ultimatum, we set out to build our own atomic gun. We had our spectrographic observations of those hurled suns, and a few hints your father found in the Pretender's private papers, in the library of the Purple Hall.

"That information was incomplete and some of it inaccurate. But your father made a brilliant guess about how the deformation of space-time increases nuclear stability. I did what I was able. It was your mother—aided, perhaps, by her own secret science—who showed us how to control the movement and growth of the field of instability.

"We built, and set up on Ceres, an atomic gun fully equal to the one on Callisto. Stephen Orco had been organizing his new empire and dispatching his ultimatums without much haste, because he thought we were completely at his mercy. The successful erection of our atomic gun on Ceres was a surprise that defeated him.

"Neither weapon could destroy the other, for the control fields of each could deflect approaching shots. Stephen Orco's weapon was powerful enough, given time, to desolate every planet in the entire System—one shot from

Callisto reduced ten thousand square miles of Mercury to smoking, radioactive lava.

"But our weapon was equally effective. It was a simpler task to blot life from the moons of Jupiter than from the rest of the System. We should have finished first. And Stephen Orco, as you say, is a remarkably brilliant man. He saw at once that he was defeated. He was too intelligent to carry on a clearly hopeless battle. He immediately offered to surrender, when our first vortex struck Callisto.

"He demanded, however, that we guarantee his life. He required the personal word of every member of the Green Hall, and of myself, for the Legion, that we would protect his life at every cost. He made an odd exception, however, with regard to you, Bob—until today, I didn't understand why."

Bob Star leaned forward, to ask hoarsely, "What was that?"

"I think I recall his words," said Jay Kalam. "Here's what he said:

"'Leave out Robert Star. He and I already have an engagement regarding my life. If that young pup has the guts to kill me, let him do it.'"

That challenge jerked Bob Star forward. He was trembling. His thin face tightened, and his nails dug into his palms. The triangular scar on his forehead turned white.

"He needs killing," he whispered harshly. "But I'm afraid—afraid I couldn't do it." His mouth had fallen a little open, and he stood mopping at the sweat on his pale face. "I can't remember all that happened, but I know the Iron Confessor did something to my brain. Orco said he was going to break me. And I'm afraid—afraid—"

"So am I." The commander smiled bleakly. "But we are soldiers of the Legion." For a moment he was silent, his dark face stern and grave. "The word of an officer of the Legion has seldom been broken, except by a few such men as the Pretender and Orco himself. Mine will not be broken. I am not going to kill Stephen Orco."

His somber eyes dwelt upon Bob Star.

"But since he made that mocking exception in your case, Bob, it may become necessary for us to take advantage of it. Understand, I'm not commanding you to kill him. What I'm going to do is to leave you at his prison, with an independent authority to take whatever action you see fit. Your orders will be simply not to let Stephen Orco escape."

"Yes, commander." Bob Star wet his lips. "I—I understand."

"It's unfortunate that we had to spare the traitor's life." Jay Kalam frowned regretfully. "Your father was opposed to that concession. I urged the Council to agree to it, however, because it might have cost billions of lives to carry on the war long enough to kill him.

"Perhaps it seems surprising that Orco was willing to trust the Legion, but he evidently knows our standards of honor—even though he chose to disregard them, in his own career. The terms were settled, anyhow, but he became our prisoner—no doubt the most dangerous man that locks ever held."

"He must be." Bob Star stepped quickly backward. "If he knows my mother's secret!"

"He has been well guarded," Jay Kalam continued. "We announced that he had been condemned and executed—to discourage the efforts of possible rescuers. In a secret place, we built the strongest fortress that our engineers could devise. He is held there, under the name of Merrin, dead to the world outside.

"But not," the commander added quietly, "to the Cometeers."

"Eh?" Bob Star felt stiff with dismay. "How's that?"

"The creatures of the cometary object have discovered that Stephen Orco is alive," Jay Kalam said soberly. "That's the reason your father was so set upon the immediate destruction of the comet."

"How—" Bob Star gulped to find his voice. "How did they find out?"

"Certain information about Stephen Orco, including the location of his prison, was kept in a vault in the Green Hall. The vault was believed to be impregnable, and it was always guarded by trusted men.

"But the invisible beings from the comet slipped into the building. They killed four guards—with some unknown agency. They picked locks that Giles Habibula himself had tested and failed to open. They carried off the documents relating to Stephen Orco."

"If they should set him free—" Bob Star shook his head, apprehension gray on his face. "I don't like to think of that. Stephen Orco has no loyalty to mankind. If the

223

Cometeers are going to be our enemies, he would gladly join them."

"It's hard to believe that, of any human being." The commander lifted his head, smiling gravely. "Anyhow, I still hope to find that the Cometeers intend to be our friends. If they fail to reciprocate our gesture of friendship, remember your duty." His voice rang hard. "Don't let Orco escape!"

Bob Star sank back into the big chair, shuddering. His thin face was a mask of agony, and the scar of the Iron Confessor was lividly white. His tortured eyes stared up at Jay Kalam, mutely pleading.

"I'll try," he whispered miserably. "But I'm—afraid!"

6

The Girl in the Wall

The *Invincible* drove down toward the south pole of Neptune. The eighth planet was a vast and inhospitable world of pale twilight and bitter night. The enormous installations of the planetary engineers, running through long centuries, had finally cleared the poisonous methane and ammonia from the air, generated enough free oxygen to support human life, and raised the surface temperature many degrees. There were cities over the rich mines in the equatorial regions, but the immense polar continent was not yet ready for colonization. A frozen wilderness larger than all Earth, blanketed with freezing, everlasting fogs, it was marked on the interplanetary charts:

Uninhabited and dangerous; shipping keep clear.

In disregard of that warning, the *Invincible* landed three degrees from the pole. Bob Star and his two bodyguards came down a ramp, to a dark frozen plain. Already shivering, they ran away from the ship. Rockets thundered behind them. They dropped flat to escape the sudden hot hurricane of the jets. The ship lifted and vanished in the cloudy, greenish twilight, carrying Jay Kalam forward on his mission to test the good will of the Cometeers.

A squad of Legionnaires came out of the foggy dark.

They challenged the three, examined their credentials, and guided them to a fortress standing on a low and barren hill. They were almost upon it before Bob Star could see anything. Abruptly, then, a vast and massive wall loomed out of the greenish gloom.

"The wall is ring-shaped, sir," the guard officer informed him, with an awed respect for Jay Kalam's signature upon his papers. "There's a circular field inside, where our four cruisers are lying now. But you don't see the real prison at all. It's a buried cylinder of perdurite. Merrin's cell is a thousand feet below the field."

A ponderous, armored door admitted them to the hundred-foot thickness of the wall. Bob Star asked immediately to see the prisoner. And at last, beyond confusing, narrow passages walled with gray perdurite, behind huge cylindrical doors that were elaborately locked, beyond hidden elevators and grimly alert guards in turrets of vitrilith, he looked upon the man he must kill.

A huge door let him into a small square room, where two sentries watched. Its farther wall was a thick, shining sheet of vitrilith. Beyond that impregnable transparency was Stephen Orco's cell.

The prisoner sat in a big chair, reading. He held a glass of some red drink in one great hand, and his splendid body looked relaxed in a green dressing gown. Bob Star could see the angle of his handsome face, and the light smile clinging to his wide, womanish mouth.

"This is Merrin, sir," the officer said. "He was sealed beyond that vitrilith wall when the prison was completed, two years ago. No one has talked to him since. The cell is soundproof, and the guards are ordered to ignore any sort of signal he may attempt. All metal objects are kept from him. Air, water, and liquid foods are pumped to him through screened tubes from another room accessible only to the commanding officer—"

He broke off to indicate a small red button on the gray wall beside him.

"I must warn you, sir. Don't touch that button. It is connected to a valve that would fill the cell with lethal gas. Our orders, however, are to preserve the prisoner's life as a trust of the Legion."

Bob Star scarcely heard the man's last words above the sudden ringing in his ears. Abrupt sweat chilled him. He swayed with a sick faintness. The little red disk stared at him, like a sinister eye.

225

He had to touch it—that was all.

And the score of nine years would be settled. An intolerable burden would be lifted from him. Even the old pain, he felt, would go, and the System would be safe from the malign genius of Stephen Orco—

He was aware, then, that the prisoner had seen him. The blue eyes, cold and burning with a reckless defiance, had lifted from the book. The handsome face smiled mockingly. Stephen Orco got lazily to his feet and came strolling to that transparent, unbreakable wall. He pointed at the red button, and slapped his leg with silent merriment. His full lips formed a derisive, soundless greeting.

Bob Star felt a sudden desire to speak to him. This was their first meeting since that night of torture. He tried to hope that his haunting fear would somehow vanish, an illusion born of pain, when he met Stephen Orco under these new circumstances.

Yes, the officer said, there was a telephone, but its use was forbidden.

"You saw my orders," Bob Star insisted. "It's necessary for me to speak with Merrin."

After a conference with the commandant, it was arranged. Bob Star was left alone in the square, gray room outside the crystal wall. A magnetic speaker thumped, and then he heard the clear, rich baritone of Stephen Orco:

"Greetings, Bob! I'm amused at your efforts to touch that red button."

Bob Star felt his face stiffen.

"Laugh if you like," he muttered harshly. "But I can do it—if I must."

"Try again, if you like." Orco's taunting laughter rang loud from the speaker. "No, you'll never do it, Bob. Not since that night with the Iron Confessor—I've seen too many times what that ultrasonic pulse does to brain tissue and the thing called courage. I've never been afraid that you would kill me. And I'm certain no other will—because of a foolish code the Legion has."

Shuddering with a sick humiliation, Bob Star swung desperately toward that red button. He reached for it grimly—but his old fear yelled, *you can't!* A numbing chill struck down his hand. He staggered back, his shoulders sagging with defeat. Tears blurred his eyes. His hands knotted impotently.

"I'm really glad to see you," Stephen Orco's voice was booming. "Because you must have been sent here upon the foolish hope that you could destroy me. That means that my already rather fantastic defenses are considered inadequate. I conclude therefore that I have powerful allies outside, and that I may hope shortly to be set free."

"Not if I can prevent it!"

"But you can't, Bob. I've beaten you." Bob Star was astonished and disturbed to see the black enormity of hate that peered suddenly through that mocking levity. "I've broken you, forever."

Orco's voice was suddenly lower, a breathless, thickened rasping, monstrous and clotted with his hate.

"When I first learned of your existence, while I was only a child, it filled me with fury to think that an utterly incompetent weakling, through no effort or merit of his own, should one day become the most powerful of men —while I had nothing. I resolved then, before I had ever seen the gilded boy of the Purple Hall, to crush you and take all your heritages for myself."

Stephen Orco paused. His wide mouth broke into a sudden, brilliant smile of satisfaction, and his tone was light again when he resumed: "You weren't hard to break, Bob. The Iron Confessor killed all the danger in you, that first night. Afterwards, I admit, ethical questions disturbed me, but time soon answered them. Consider it this way: One of us has AKKA given to him; the other must discover it by his own efforts. Which better deserves it?"

"The keeping of AKKA isn't any sort of selfish advantage," Bob Star answered huskily. "It is a tremendous task that fills the life and finally demands the death of the keeper." He caught his breath. "But how—how did you discover it?"

The prisoner smiled patronizingly.

"I'm going to tell you, Bob," he said blandly. "If only to establish my superior rights to the secret and the perfect justice of my actions. I might remark, by the way, that I don't intend to let the care of the secret become any sort of distressing mortal burden to me. The trouble with you, Bob, is just that you weren't big enough for the job."

He shook his head mockingly, at Bob Star's trembling impotence.

"Anyhow," he continued easily, "I simply followed the methods of investigation that should have suggested themselves to any person of intelligence. I collected the data available, formulated hypotheses to explain them, tested

227

the hypotheses by experiment, and so finally arrived at a satisfactory conclusion.

"While I was still at the academy, I obtained secret access to a secret library, and studied there all the existing accounts of the use of AKKA since the time of its discovery by your mother's great ancestor, Charles Anthar —while he himself was a prisoner, guarded almost as carefully as I am.

"The last recorded use of the weapon had been to destroy Earth's old satellite—after it had been seized and fortified by the Pretender's unsuspecting allies. With my foster father's space yacht, I searched the orbit the satellite had followed. I finally found three small metallic buttons.

"No larger than the end of my thumb, they were all that remained of the Moon. I have since come to realize how very fortunate I was to find a single atom. It was only because your mother was working hastily, with a crudely improvised instrument, that the annihilation of the heavy elements was not quite complete.

"Some months of careful work, in a laboratory financed by my foster father's funds, revealed the nature of the partial effect of AKKA upon those metallic specimens. From effect to cause was a matter of mathematical reasoning. It remained but to test alternative hypotheses, and elaborate the surviving construction—and the secret was mine."

The prisoner paused, smiling again.

"Don't you agree with me, Bob, that such abilities merit reward? I am certainly the most gifted of men; reason assures me that I am therefore their rightful ruler. And I should have been that already, Bob—but for one blunder."

Hoarsely, Bob Star whispered, "What was that?"

"I failed to kill your mother." Stephen Orco shrugged carelessly. "The trouble was that I didn't see, until too late, the singular limitation of the weapon. I didn't try to use it until she was also trying. It failed for both of us, and that blunder put me here. But it's one I shan't repeat, when I find another chance."

He chuckled maliciously.

"I'm not afraid to tell you that," he added cheerfully. "Because I know you can't touch that red button—not even to save your mother's life."

Bob Star knew then what he must do, but still he couldn't do it—at any rate, not yet. Wearily, he signaled for the guards and had the telephone disconnected. With the prisoner sealed again in that tomb of silence, he waited alone in the little outer room, bleakly resolved to stay there until he could press that button—or until the need was gone.

Stephen Orco had calmly returned to his chair and his book. He relaxed in the green robe, sipping at his drink, apparently oblivious of any danger to his life. Twice again Bob Star left the hard bench where he waited, trying to touch that button.

The simple act was utterly impossible. The effort did nothing but accelerate that unceasing throb of pain inside his head and turn him faint with illness. He gave up for the time, desperately hopeful that the stimulus of emergency would nerve him for the deed, if any crisis came.

Hopelessly, he stumbled back to the bench.

His eyes, as he sat there, widened abruptly. His breath sucked in, and his lean hands clenched. He leaned forward, staring at the hard gray wall. For he thought that its surface had begun to shimmer with vague, moving shadows.

The massive door was still locked behind him. The alarm gongs were silent. The sheet of vitrilith was still intact, and the lounging giant beyond it still ignored him. There was no hint of another presence with him—none save the creeping shadows on the wall. He watched them, breathtaken.

A misty blue circle flickered against the gray. Ghostly shadow shapes darted through it. Abruptly then, as if some tri-dimensional projector had come suddenly into focus, the hard armor of the wall melted into an amazing scene.

He looked into a curious chamber, sunk now like a deep niche into the cell wall. Its surface followed tapering spiral curves, and the color of it was an absolute black, spangled with small crystals of brilliant blue that were various as snowflakes.

The girl stood inside the sudden hollow in the wall, upon a many-angled pedestal of blue transparency. An unsteady flame burned deep within that great sapphire block, and its fitful light danced against the tiny flakes of blue.

Vividly real against that spiral shell of darkness and blue fire, the girl stood watching him. Her expression had a desperate, almost agonized intentness. One slim white arm was thrust out and upward, in what seemed a gesture of warning. The pale oval of her face was grave with the expectation of danger, and her bright lips parted, as he watched, as if she had spoken some warning word.

No sound reached him, however, and the silence brought him a sudden doubt of what he saw. With a bewildered shrug, he got up from the bench and started uncertainly toward the wall. Her solemn brown eyes followed his movement in a way that made him sure that she was really watching, and she stopped him with an imperative gesture.

She turned, then, to point through the transparent slab at Stephen Orco, who now seemed absorbed in his book and drink. Keeping her distressed golden eyes on Bob Star, she gestured urgently toward the red button that he had failed to touch.

He started toward it again, and again all the agony of the Iron Confessor rose up out of the past to stop him. He turned helplessly back toward the girl, with a sick misery in his eyes. She plainly wanted him to kill Stephen Orco—and he wondered suddenly if her panic-stricken loveliness could be nothing more than hallucination, the vivid symbol of his own impotent desire.

She saw him turn, and a tragic sadness shadowed her face. The light died in her golden eyes. White knuckles lifted to her mouth, in a gesture of bleak frustration. Suddenly then, she started as if she had heard some silent voice. She shuddered, beckoning him toward the red button again, desperately and hopelessly.

Then, as the urgent pleading of her face changed to sad compassion, a bomb of cold flame exploded in the blue pedestal. Sapphire sparks danced across the crystal rime upon the spiral walls. Blue radiance filled the niche, and slowly died. Dark shadows thickened, and silently dissolved.

The gray wall was whole again.

And Bob Star was once more alone. He swayed, trembling. Tears of defeat and despair burned his eyes. He flung his head and looked sharply at Stephen Orco, who was just setting down his empty glass, his attention still lost in the book.

Confusion roared in Bob Star's mind. Had she been real? All his doubts had been suspended, in that last moment of his useless effort and her sad departure, but now the question hammered at him. A living person

—where? Or only a tormented projection of his own unendurable predicament.

He jumped when the gong shattered the silence in the room. Harshly, from a speaker beside it, rasped a hoarse command: "Emergency stations! Secure all doors! Stand—" The voice choked strangely. "Quick!" It was a ragged whisper now. "Invisible things—I can't see—"

Now! Bob Star's breath gasped out. He must act now, or betray the Legion. Fighting a numbing inertia, he swung toward the gray wall. The push button winked at him, a red, malicious eye. He was aware that Stephen Orco had laid aside the book, to watch him with a careless amusement.

He contrived to take another halting step. Abrupt sweat chilled him. His ears were roaring again. For the effort had plunged him back into the grasp of the Iron Confessor. Once more he felt the pressure of that cold steel band around his head, and the cruel thrust of that three-edged blade, and the burning agony of the unendurable vibration. He could see Stephen Orco's furious face against the darkness of that room, and hear his savage voice, amplified and changed to unbearable pain:

"So you don't like it, pup? Then you had better change your mind. Because you'll never be able to do anything about it. I'm fixing you now so you can't kill anybody. This machine is stronger than anybody's will. When it gets through breaking you, you'll stay broken. Even if you weren't a sniveling coward before, you'll be one now.

"You can't kill me. You can't kill—"

Those taunting words echoed again in his mind, with the imperative effect of a post-hypnotic suggestion. He couldn't kill—but he must! The image of that frightened girl in the wall came back to spur him on, and he took another dragging step toward that push button.

But still he couldn't kill—

Something was wrong with the lights in the room. They were turning green. Or was there a green light shining through the massive door behind him. The crisis was here. Now he had to act, and there were only two more steps—

A greenish mist had flooded the room, rising swiftly against the transparent barrier that separated him from Stephen Orco—or was it only in his eyes? The gray walls swam, until he thought they were going to dissolve into another inexplicable vista.

231

His skin began to prickle strangely. Something numbed all his sensations. Stiffness seized his limbs. He thrust his arm out frantically toward that red push button—or tried to. But he no longer had an arm. Darkness annihilated everything. He didn't know when he hit the floor.

7

The Beast of the Mists

The muttered thunder of descending rockets awoke Bob Star. Bitter cold had stiffened his cramped limbs, and his eyes opened upon oppressive green twilight. He found himself sprawled upon frozen ground, still numb with that tingling paralysis which had robbed him of consciousness.

Groping desperately for recollection, he found a disturbing conviction that the gap in his consciousness had contained something unthinkably hideous—something that his mind had sealed away, to preserve its sanity.

After a moment, however, the sickening fact of his own failure came back. Despair swept away that other disquieting half-memory, and he sank back for a time in a crushed and hopeless apathy, until the increasing sound of the rockets became too loud to be ignored. Gasping in a great breath of that icy air, he sat up stiffly.

He was bewildered to find himself at the very brink of an appalling chasm. The flat and barren face of Neptune broke, not a dozen feet from where he had lain, into a dreadful pit of greenish darkness. He stood up to look into it, and found only misty emptiness. It seemed to have no farther walls, nor floor. He swayed back from it, giddily.

The scrape of a foot jarred his nerves. He spun apprehensively, and then grinned with a shaken relief when he found his two bodyguards behind him, safely back from the rim of the inexplicable pit, staring up at a vague blue flickering in the cloudy dark above.

"Aye!" boomed Hal Samdu. "It's a ship."

"And time we were rescued!" gasped Giles Habibula. "Dear life knows we've been waiting long enough, dying in this wicked cold."

"Giles!" Bob Star called anxiously. "How did we get here? And what's this pit?"

"Ah, lad!" The fat man came waddling toward him, flinching visibly from the nearness of that dreadful precipice, yet beaming with a surprised relief. "Wē thought you'd never wake, before you died of cold."

The gigantic strength of Hal Samdu swept him to his feet. Clinging weakly to the two men, he felt Giles Habibula's sob of gladness.

"A long time we waited, lad. Mortal long—"

"The pit?" He peered at it blankly, as Giles Habibula dragged him apprehensively back from the brink. "Where are we?"

"That's where the prison was." The old soldier's voice was a thin rasp of dread. "After the raiders had taken the prisoner away, a red light shone down from the sky, where their invisible craft must have been. Beneath it, the walls crumbled into nothing. The very ground turned into red fire, and sank away. Ah, lad, that fearful pit is all that's left of the prison and the garrison and the Legion cruisers that were lying inside the wall. I don't understand—"

"So he got away?"

Bob Star turned heavily back toward that strange chasm, feeling sick enough to throw himself into it. He had failed the Legion, and the consequences numbed his mind. Nothing mattered now. Dull, incurious, his eyes lifted to that fitful, shifting glare of rocket jets burning through the clouds.

"It's landing near!" Giles Habibula was wheezing gratefully. "The Cometeers escaped with the prisoner, and all the rest are dead, but we at least are saved."

"Tell me," Bob Star whispered urgently. "How did we get away?"

"We didn't, lad," Giles Habibula answered. "The prisoner spared our lives—I don't quite know why. He told us he was really the great rebel, Orco—but I suppose you knew that."

"I did," Bob Star nodded bleakly. "My duty here was to kill him, if there was danger of his escape." In spite of himself, he sobbed. "But I—I couldn't do it."

"Hal and I were waiting for you in the corridor outside." Generously, the old man seemed not to see his bitter tears. "Of a sudden, my poor old nerves were shocked by a frightful alarm. Gongs were ringing, and men running half-naked to their stations.

233

"Most of them never got there. They fell, lad, struck down by things they never saw. And a greenish mist dimmed my own old eyes. My ailing body failed me. I went down helpless with the rest—perhaps a bit before the rest, for safety's precious sake.

"Yet for a time I clung to my dim old wits, when Hal and all the rest seemed to know nothing. I heard the clatter of locks, and saw those great doors turning. Then I could hear some sort of fearsome creatures passing through—things I couldn't see.

"Presently the prisoner Orco came walking out of his cell, speaking and making gestures to what seemed to be just empty air. He was answered by uncanny hoots and booms of sound, fit to freeze your blood. And your own body came after him, lad, floating—carried by something I felt grateful not to see.

"The prisoner pointed out Hal and me, and something came to lift us—what it was, I don't know. But we were carried from the prison and dumped here on this frosty ground—without a blanket or an extra jacket or even a blessed bite to eat.

"Near us was some great ship—there was nothing I could see, but I heard machinery running, and the clang of the air-locks opening. My poor old heart came near stopping when the prisoner spoke to me. His voice was right before me, but you couldn't see him anywhere.

"'You are Giles Habibula, the pick-lock?' he greeted me. 'I bow to the fame of your accomplishments.' He laughed a little, but in a way I didn't like. 'I think we are brothers.'

"Then his voice went black with hate. 'I believe that you two are the insufficient bodyguards of the cringing fool who calls himself Bob Star,' he said. 'I understand that he will be conscious again. Tell him that I have spared his life once more—to repay him for sparing mine!'

"He laughed, as if that were some sort of ugly joke. 'Tell him you three are the only men alive on this continent,' he went on. 'Tell him it's five thousand miles to the sea, and nine thousand more across the ice packs to the Isle of Shylar. I'm afraid he won't live to reach it—but he'll live to wish he had touched the button.'

"He didn't say what button, lad. But he laughed again —it was a fearful thing, that thick laughter from the empty air. And then he said, 'Tell Bob Star I'm going now to repair a blunder I made—a blunder in the disposition of his mother.'

"A valve clanged then. Something hooted and boomed —perhaps his new friends were calling him. The air-locks rang shut, and the green fog swirled, and the ship you couldn't see was gone—with not a jet to push it.

"For a few minutes there was silence. When I dared to lift my feeble head, I could see the marks the landing skids of that great ship had cut into the frozen ground. I had almost found the courage to get up and go back to the fort to look for help—it's a good thing I didn't!"

The old soldier shuddered.

"Because a beam of pale red light came down from the sky—I suppose from that ship. It cut through the clouds, and shone down upon the fort. A fearful thing to see! The walls dissolved into mist and sparks and fiery dust, and the very ground sank away, until the fearful pit you see was cut into the planet."

Giles Habibula shivered.

"Ah, me, lad! The Cometeers are fearful enemies. I almost wish that rocket hadn't come back to save us. If we live to leave Neptune, it will only be to watch mankind destroyed by weapons we don't know and enemies we'll never even see."

"Don't say it, Giles!" Hal Samdu's gigantic fists were knotted stubbornly. "If we live, it will be to fight for the System and the keeper of the peace. Come!" He turned impatiently. "We must look for the Legion craft, before it goes away and leaves us."

That unsteady glare of rocket jets had vanished in the clouds but Bob Star had felt a faint shock when the ship struck the frozen plain.

"It came down too hard," he whispered anxiously. "I think the rockets were misfiring, from the way the jets flickered. I'm afraid it crashed."

They stumbled through the bitter darkness along the lip of that chasm, toward where the jets had vanished. What they found at last was no bright Legion cruiser, but only a pile of twisted wreckage.

"Dear life!" gasped Giles Habibula. "This is no more than the nose of some unfortunate vessel. It will never serve to carry anybody out of this fearful land. We're still to freeze and die here, as Orco and his strange friends planned—"

Bob Star was peering dully upward at the wreck. Great

plates of armor were twisted and blackened, and massive beams projected through the torn flesh of the ship like broken bones. Ports were shattered, like eyes blinded. Rocket tubes were crushed, and a colossal proton gun had been hurled from its turret. This murdered craft must have been a Legion battleship—

His heart came up in his throat. He staggered back from the wreckage, and shook his head blankly. He saw Giles Habibula and Hal Samdu staring at him.

"The *Invincible*—"

Numbing despair had paralyzed his voice, but he needed to say no more. The mighty *Invincible* had been reduced to this battered fragment. That meant that Jay Kalam's gesture of friendship had failed. It meant that the Cometeers had no friendly purpose—and now, since they had liberated Stephen Orco, that arch-traitor could defend them against AKKA.

"Ah, so!" Giles Habibula moaned bitterly. "It's only a miserable bit of the great *Invincible*. And the coffin, no doubt, of poor Jay—"

"Perhaps he's still alive." Bob Star clutched eagerly at that faint hope. "His quarters were forward, in this section. And somebody must have been alive, to fire those rockets—"

"Before the crash," the old man muttered. "But now I see no sign of life."

Yet it was he who spoke, after Bob Star and Hal Samdu had failed to get inside this fragment of the craft.

"Lad," he asked, "you say the forward valve is clear?"

"It is," Bob Star said. "But locked."

"Then help me reach it."

They lifted him into the wreckage, to the mechanism of a great entrance valve. He clung to a twisted beam before it, peering in the darkness at the lock.

"Ah, me!" he whispered sadly. "Why must a fighting ship be secured like a precious safe? Have they no trust in the men of the Legion?"

Bob Star, watching, marveled at the quick, deft certainty of the old man's pudgy fingers. He was hardly surprised when something clicked beyond the blackened armor plate, and whirring motors began opening the outer valve.

"Do you know, lad," Giles Habibula wheezed triumphantly, "there's not another man in all the System who could pick such a lock? The fact is that it might have

236

troubled me—if Jay hadn't called on me to help his experts design it! But let's look for him."

The bridge was dark and empty. They paused to read the last neatly written entry in the log:

> Wreck falling toward south pole of Neptune. Geodynes gone and rockets crippled. Will attempt to land at prison base. General order: The Cometeers are our enemies, and the Legion will fight to the end.
>
> Kalam

"Jay!" Hal Samdu's great voice was booming apprehensively. "Where are you, Jay?"

"In his den, of course!" Bob Star whispered suddenly. "It's soundproof."

He ran back through the chart room to the hidden door, rang, and waited. The little door opened. Golden light spilled out, and then he saw the tall commander of the Legion.

"I thought I was alone—" Jay Kalam's low voice rang with a sudden joy. "Bob! Hal—and Giles! I had given you up."

He brought them into the luxurious simplicity of that long, hidden room, and closed the door. Hal Samdu's gigantic frame relaxed to the warmth of it, and Giles Habibula hurried back to the galley to bring hot food, but Bob Star could find neither comfort nor appetite.

"I tried—" he burst out suddenly. "I really tried, commander!" He set down a cup of steaming soup, unable to swallow. "But I—couldn't." His thin face was twisted with a savage self-reproach. "I'm just the coward Orco said—"

"Don't say that." Jay Kalam shook his head. "I'm too familiar with the effects of such devices as the Iron Confessor to blame you at all. But I wanted to give you a chance to test yourself—partly for your own sake."

"Thank you, commander," Bob Star whispered bitterly. "But I failed! I let Stephen Orco get away, to plot the murder of my mother and lead the Cometeers against the System—"

"No." Jay Kalam's voice was gravely decisive. "If there is any fault, it is my own, for holding a standard of honor too high. Perhaps I should have ordered Orco killed. I know I should have let your mother destroy the cometary object."

"Are you sure?"

The commander nodded grimly.

"The way the Cometeers received our attempted gesture of friendship proves that they are absolutely devoid of the high qualities I had hoped to find. But let me tell you!

"Not three hours after we had left Neptune, the telltale screens began to flash. There was nothing we could see with the tele-periscopes, but the gravity detectors betrayed an invisible object of fifty thousand tons, approaching behind us—as if it had followed us from Neptune.

"In hope of establishing peaceable communication, I ordered the heligraph room to flash a signal: *We are friends*. I am certain, from all the recent reports of invisible raiders, that the Cometeers know us well enough so they can read such messages.

"They are no longer our friends, however. Before we had time to repeat the signal, the *Invincible* was caught by some tremendous unseen force. The geodynes were helpless against it. Like a pebble on a string, we were drawn toward that hostile craft.

"Can you conceive an invisible beam of energy, Bob —a tubular field of force, a mathematician might call it— strong enough to drag the *Invincible* against her fighting geodynes, five thousand miles in five minutes? That's what happened.

"Then a red light burned for a moment among the stars—in the direction of that invisible ship. And the *Invincible* was destroyed. All the afterpart of the ship was somehow—annihilated!"

"Aye!" Giles Habibula put down his spoon long enough to shudder. "I've seen that fearful light. I watched it melt the prison away, and leave that dreadful pit."

"I wonder what it could be." The commander rubbed his lean jaw thoughtfully. "Matter can't be destroyed—even your mother's weapon, Bob, must act in some way to keep the universe in balance, even while it seems to cancel planets out. I've been wondering what happened to the ship and the prison. I believe I know."

He nodded soberly, while the other bent nearer.

"Matter can't be destroyed," he repeated softly. "But it can be transformed. I believe that red light was the visible effect of something that dissolves atoms into neutrinos—those tiniest particles of mass, that can pass through any sort of matter undetected."

"That must be the answer," Bob Star agreed, a little

238

relieved to find any sort of explanation for that giddy pit, yet chilled with colder awe of the unknown powers of the Cometeers.

"Anyhow," Jay Kalam resumed abruptly, "some forty men were left alive with me. I made no effort to stop their rush to the life rockets. The vortex gun was wrecked; we couldn't fight. I remained aboard alone.

"The six little rockets drove back toward the fort here —a tiny swarm of blue stars, dwindling swiftly in the dark of space." His dark eyes closed for a moment, as if with pain. "They had gone only a little way," he said huskily, "when that red light burned again. The little blue stars reddened and went out."

Hal Samdu's big, gaunt face flamed with anger.

"So they murdered the survivors?" he muttered.

Jay Kalam nodded grimly.

"That is our measure of the Cometeers—and of Stephen Orco! For it seems from what you say that he is now their ally."

Bob Star stood peering at him dazedly.

"Which way did they go, commander?"

"As far as I could follow them with the detector, Bob, they were returning toward the comet."

"We must follow," Bob Star whispered. "Stephen Orco must be destroyed."

"He must." Jay Kalam grinned without mirth. "He has certainly forfeited his immunity." He shrugged wearily. "I was hoping to get help at the fort—"

"But now there's no help for us," Bob Star muttered bitterly. "The only men on the whole frozen continent, without a ship—"

Hal Samdu broke in, "Bob, we aren't the only men."

"What!"

"Ah, so, there are others—enemies!" wheezed Giles Habibula. "In this monstrous confusion of disasters we've had no time to tell you, lad. But some stranger came up to us through the fog, while you lay unconscious there by the pit."

"Why do you call him an enemy?"

"He's no friend of mine!" The old soldier shivered. "At first I thought him a chance survivor of the garrison, and I called out to him. The answer was a shot from a proton gun. The flash went wide, thanks be to the fog. Then Hal flung a rock, and the stranger fled, snarling and whimpering like a hurt beast."

"Eh?" Jay Kalam seemed to catch his breath. "You're sure this fellow didn't come from the fort?"

"Sure as death, Jay. I saw him in the flash of his gun, and I know it's many months since he was washed and shaved to pass inspection. A bearded, hairy, shaggy brute, clad in faded rags."

"Strange." The commander whistled softly. "I wonder—"

8

Death on Neptune

Bob Star asked, while they were still within the ivory-walled luxury of Jay Kalam's quarters on the wrecked *Invincible,* "Can't we signal for help?"

The commander shook his head. "The signal house was destroyed, with all the spare equipment in the stores."

"But we can't just do nothing," Bob Star whispered. "If I had another chance—" He sank into bitter silence for a time, until a flicker of hope aroused him. "Couldn't we build something that would fly, out of the wreckage?"

"I was satisfied to land it as safely as I did," Jay Kalam said quietly. "The best yards the Legion has could never put this mountain of broken metal back in space again."

"Isn't there anything—" Bob Star had to bite his lip, to stop a sob of frustration.

"We must search, I think, for that stranger in the fog," the commander said quietly. "If he wasn't a member of the garrison, it seems likely enough that he might have some means of communication with the outside. Not a very hopeful plan, but I see none more promising."

They had searched three days for that shaggy stranger, but it was something else that Bob Star found. He paused in the foggy night. The light tube wavered in his hand, as if the thin beam fled from what it had discovered. Giles Habibula crouched close to him, whispering apprehensively:

"In life's name, what is this?"

Jay Kalam and Hal Samdu came up through the freezing dark, and they all bent to peer at what Bob Star had found: bits of torn and bloodstained cloth, a little pile of frozen viscera, a few gnawed bones, a hollowed skull still covered with scalp and yellow hair.

"This green cloth—" Bob Star picked up a torn sleeve. "It came from a Legion uniform."

"Ah, so!" Giles Habibula's voice was a thin moan of terror. "Some poor soldier of the Legion was eaten here by the fearful monsters of the dark, as we may be—"

"He must have strayed from the garrison—but I wonder what ate him." Bob Star paused to peer around them in the greenish gloom, and he couldn't keep from shivering. "I thought there was no wild life on this continent."

Jay Kalam bent suddenly to pick up a bright, blood-splashed object. He turned it beneath the light. It was an enameled lapel pin of white metal—the figure of a bird, grasping a tiny scroll. The commander leaned to study it, and his breath came out between pursed lips.

"No," he said softly, "this man didn't come from the garrison here. I used to know him." He paused and straightened, gazing soberly out into the foggy dark. "He had pale, timid blue eyes under that yellow hair, and his voice was soft as a woman's. He used to paint pictures— dainty little landscapes. He wrote what he thought was poetry, and read it aloud to his friends. It seems queer that such a man should die this way—"

"Who was he?" Bob Star whispered.

"Justin Malkar was his name—his men used to call him Miss Malkar. But only behind his back, because he was really a competent officer. His crew admired him enough to give him this pin, the last time his ship came back to Earth. A well selected gift. He was weak as a woman for such gaudy trinkets."

The commander bent gravely to lay the pin back on a rock beside the scattered bones, and Bob Star said:

"I wonder what brought him here."

"His weakness, I suppose," Jay Kalam said. "And Stephen Orco's power. He must have been several years older than Orco, but they held the same rank when they were ordered to join the Jupiter Patrol. Orco soon dominated him. His ship was one of the first that went over to the mutineers. Yet he wasn't a bad man; Orco simply understood and used his peculiar weaknesses.

"When the mutineers surrendered, Malkar's ship was

missing. It was the *Halcyon Bird*, a powerful new cruiser. Orco told us that it had been destroyed by our atomic shot. We soon discovered, however, that Mark Lardo had fled upon it—Lardo was a wealthy Callistonian planter who had been Orco's chief lieutenant.

"We suspected that their plan was for Lardo to come back on the cruiser and set Orco free. For the last two years, the Legion has been scouring space for the missing ship, but this is the first trace—"

He looked down again, at the glint of that bright pin on the rock.

"But what could have attacked him?"

"I think we'll know the answer," Jay Kalam said softly, "when we find the bearded stranger who shot at Giles and Hal."

He reached to unsnap the cartograph from his belt. He had brought that tiny instrument to map their movements. He opened the cover and peered at the record strip.

"We're nearly seven miles from where the prison used to be," he said thoughtfully. "Until we have more information, we must assume that Justin Malkar died somewhere near his ship. Our logical next step is to explore this vicinity, following a widening spiral—"

"Ah, so!" Giles Habibula nodded apprehensively. "Let's get away from these bones, before that monster comes back to pick them!"

They tramped on again, shivering in the fog. Bob Star led the way around crumbling boulders, up frozen slopes, across shallow valleys of eternal night. Jay Kalam watched the glowing instrument, and softly called directions.

They had found no other clue, and they had swung back toward the shelter of the wreck, when Bob Star turned aside toward something looming in the darkness like another boulder. A vague shadow, it took on reality as he stumbled wearily toward it.

The gleam of metal checked him. He made out the black ovals of observation ports, and the bulge of a gun turret. A trembling hope took his breath. He heard Jay Kalam calling him, and ran back silently.

"Quiet!" he whispered. "That's a ship—"

His words were cut off by a beam of blinding light that struck the frosty ground beside them.

"They heard us!" he gasped. "Get down—"

They dropped flat, scrambled for cover behind a rock.

A sudden sword of violent flame stabbed the rock, spattering incandescent fragments.

"Bob?" whispered Jay Kalam. "Giles? Hal? All safe?"

"Aye, Jay," rumbled Hal Samdu. "But where are the others?"

"Bob?" the commander called again. "Giles?"

But the frozen dark made no reply.

Bob Star, standing nearest the ship, barely escaped the flaming beam from the great proton gun. He felt the shock of it as he dropped, and saw the slender needle swinging after him, still faintly glowing from that first discharge, a pointing finger of death.

He scrambled desperately away from it, toward the ship itself. The needle reached the bottom of its travel, and flamed again. Frozen rocks exploded behind him, but the shock reached him only faintly. Safe beneath the reach of the needle, he ran back to the main entrance valve. An instant's inspection told him it was locked.

"Lad! Where are you, lad?" The frightened voice of Giles Habibula startled him. "Ah, the wicked things that can happen to a poor old soldier of the Legion!"

Bob Star saw him scuttling toward the hull with a surprising agility, to escape the reach of that glowing gun.

"The first flash blinded me," he whispered bitterly. "I ran in the wrong direction, and now we're trapped against the ship. If we try to get away, they can cut us down."

"Here, Giles!" Hope touched Bob Star again. "Can you open this lock?"

"Perhaps—if you'll just be patient." Giles Habibula fumbled in his pockets. "Ah, here it is—the same bit of wire that let us into the *Invincible*." He started toward the valve, and shrank back abruptly. "But why, lad? Myself, I'm content enough to have it safely locked—and no fighting men rushing out to kill us."

"Open it," Bob Star said. "If you can—"

"I can—if I must." He was already busy with his scrap of thin wire. "Strange are the wheels of genius!" he wheezed sadly. "Never could I use my great gift in peace and comfort—when anybody sends for me to test a lock, within the safety of the law, it's apt to seem impregnable. My ability seems to sleep until the screen of danger rouses it. It is ever sluggard, without the tonics of haste and danger—"

Motors began to hum, lowering the outer valve.

"Well!" He retreated hastily. "It's your own folly, lad!"

Bob Star sprang into the open chamber of the air-lock. Listening, he heard quick, cautious footsteps approaching along the deck inside. He flattened himself back against the curved metal wall, next to the inside valve, and waited breathlessly. The blunt nose of a proton pistol came into view.

Few such situations had been neglected in his very thorough course at the Legion Academy. And he was master of all he had studied—until the situation where he must kill flung him back into the grasp of the Iron Confessor.

He caught that weapon and the hand that held it. His quick tug tumbled a thickset, bearded man out through the inner valve, into the narrow lock chamber. The stranger was twice his weight, but his long training told. His quick thrust found a vital nerve, and he tossed his bearded attacker out of the lock.

"Giles," he called softly. "A prisoner for you."

Silence met him on the cluttered deck. He found the bridge deserted, the chart room vacant. He climbed warily into the darkness beneath the blazing searchlight, but the gun turret was also empty. The bearded man had been alone. He went back to the valves and shouted into the bitter night:

"Commander, the *Halcyon Bird* is ours!"

The prisoner was recovering consciousness in the icy cell, with Giles Habibula sitting on his head. "I am the Viceroy of Callisto," he was snarling thickly. "I am Mark Lardo, friend of the great Orco. If it's food you want, I'll show you how to find it."

Bob Star and Jay Kalam were in the bridge room, twelve hours later. Disorder and filth had vanished. The torn charts were patched and back in their racks. Bob Star was cleaning and inspecting the navigation instruments, while the commander frowned over the cruiser's tattered log. Hal Samdu, who had been clearing rubbish from decks and living quarters, entered to report: "Jay, the prisoner in the brig is howling like a wolf."

"I suppose he's insane," Jay Kalam said. "That wouldn't be surprising. Anyhow, we can't do much for him. Have you finished?"

"Aye, Jay, she begins to look like a proper Legion ship. Have you learned yet how she came to lie here?"

"Here's part of it." The commander nodded at the soiled

and crumpled pages of the log. "It seems from these entries that Justin Malkar wanted to surrender, along with Stephen Orco. He expected no special immunity, but his conscience had overtaken him. He was ready to pay for his treason.

"He wasn't allowed to surrender. Mark Lardo, who had been Stephen Orco's court favorite, came aboard with a dozen of his armed henchmen. From that point, the entries are somewhat obscure. From the facts we know, however, it seems clear enough that Lardo was really planning to rescue Stephen Orco."

He frowned again at the torn and bloodstained pages.

"The puzzling thing to me is how he knew the location of the prison. It would appear from these dated entries that he knew it before the prison was built—as if Stephen Orco had been clever enough to guess where we would locate it!"

"Even that might be possible." Bob Star couldn't help shivering. "He always seemed inhumanly intelligent."

"Anyhow," Jay Kalam continued, "it seems clear enough that Justin Malkar deliberately sabotaged the rescue attempt, perhaps to atone for his own crimes. The plan, apparently, was to land on Triton, which is almost uninhabited, and wait there until the chance came to rescue Orco—when he was moved into the new prison.

"That Malkar wrecked the plan seems clear enough, when you read between the lines. Though he was a competent officer, he managed to wander far off his course on the voyage out to Triton—deliberately wasting fuel.

"Until the end, he let the plotters believe that he was with them. He contrived to use up the last scrap of cathode plate and the last drop of rocket fuel, in landing here. Although the fort wasn't a dozen miles away, the estimated position of the disabled ship that he entered in the log is a thousand miles from here."

His eyes lifted from the last mutilated page.

"The rest we must read from other clues. It seems likely that Malkar hoped to reach the fort and arrange for the capture of his companions. He failed—perhaps his sabotage was discovered. Anyhow, the vessel lay here without fuel and with very little food aboard—most of the supplies had been consumed during the wait on Triton.

"And Mark Lardo is now the sole survivor."

"The remains we found—" Horror took Bob Star's voice.

"That carnivorous beast was Mark Lardo." The commander nodded, his lips drawn thin. "It would appear that he contrived to lock his companions outside, where the cold would kill and preserve them. His ruse must have been some story of a rescue vessel landing, but apparently he had no idea, until the Cometeers attacked the fort, that it stood almost beside him in this fog."

"Ah, the cannibal!" Giles Habibula came shuffling feebly in, his face greenish. "The galley's filled with human bones!"

Jay Kalam sat smiling sternly.

"The artist in the queer soul of Justin Malkar ought to be pleased," he murmured, "with the retribution he arranged for Mark Lardo. Listen to him!"

Faintly, from the distant brig, they could hear the ceaseless hoarse screaming of the madman. "Don't turn me out! They are getting hungry—Malkar and the others. Don't turn me out."

Shuddering, Giles Habibula closed the door.

"Ah, Jay, it was a heavy task you set me," he muttered. "But I've cleared up the power rooms, as you wanted, and inspected all the rockets and geodynes."

All three swung toward him anxiously, as Jay Kalam asked, "Are they in working order?"

"So far as I can see." The old soldier nodded. "But the cathode plates for the generators are all gone, to the last ounce. And the rocket fuel left in the tanks wouldn't move the ship a precious inch!"

9

The Field of the Comet

Giles Habibula remained on guard while the others tramped the frozen miles to the wrecked *Invincible*, and came back toiling to pull a makeshift sledge loaded with heavy drums of rocket fuel. Then the old man primed the injectors, and Bob Star, navigator, took his stand on the bridge. With jets roaring blue, the *Halcyon Bird* broke free of the frost and soared through green dusk to the wreck.

For many hours, then, they labored to carry cathode plates and more drums of fuel from the intact stores beneath the chart house of the dead *Invincible*. Giles Habibula scoured the galley and stocked it again, and before they were ready for flight he had a hot meal waiting.

"So now we're off for the Green Hall?" he wheezed gratefully, as they ate. "To gather all the fleets of the Legion against this traitor and his monstrous friends—" He peered at the commander, and started apprehensively. "We are bound for the precious Earth, or at least the Legion yards on Mars—aren't we, Jay?"

Sternly grave, Jay Kalam shook his head.

"I'd be afraid to try to go back," he answered softly. "In fact, I'm almost afraid to try to call any Legion installation. Because I'm afraid we *are* the Legion."

"We—" Giles Habibula gasped. "In life's sweet name what do you mean?"

"The Cometeers have destroyed the *Invincible* and liberated Stephen Orco," Jay Kalam said. "That means war to the hilt. They've nothing to gain by any more delay, and every reason for moving at once, with adequate forces, to wipe out the Legion and kill the keeper of the peace—"

"My mother—" Bob Star bit his trembling lip. "What can we do?"

"I have been considering our action, and I have reached a decision." The tall commander straightened, rubbing thoughtfully at his unshaven chin. "We're going to take off at once, in the direction of the comet—"

"Please, Jay!" sobbed Giles Habibula. "Don't make such ghastly jokes!"

"I think we're safer for the time being on a course toward the comet than we would be on Earth." Jay Kalam sat looking at him sadly. "With the keeper of the peace stalemated, our forces had nothing left to match whatever weapon it was that crumbled the fortress here into that pit."

"Ah, don't say such things!" Giles Habibula squirmed and blinked at him. "Can't we even ask for help?"

"Not without a grave risk that the enemy will intercept our messages—and answer them with that annihilating beam," Jay Kalam said. "It might be wiser not to attempt any signal at all, but I have decided that we must chance a call to the Legion relay station at the atmospheric engineering plants here on Neptune, as we take off."

"And if—" Bob Star tried to swallow the croak in his throat. "If they don't answer?"

"Then we must take the further risk of sending a message to the Green Hall," the commander said. "I think the safest channel for that would be tight-beam ultrawave, through the Contra-Saturn relay station."

"But the answer will take many hours—" Bob Star protested.

"No matter who answers—the Legion or the Cometeers—we won't be waiting," Jay Kalam told him softly. "If it does turn out that we are the only effective force the Legion has left, I want to keep in action. If we could only kill or recapture Orco, remember, that would still reverse the whole situation."

Jay Kalam rose from the table, adding quietly, "Please plot a course for the comet, at full power. Don't worry about hoarding any fuel for return."

"But you tried it once!" Giles Habibula started to rise and sank back weakly, his pale eyes rolling. "You had a ship with a thousand times our fighting power." He shuddered apprehensively. "Out there is the mortal wreckage of it."

But elation was surging up in Bob Star. In spite of all the commander's forebodings, the means to escape bleak Neptune had lifted his spirits. He wanted the clean freedom of high space and the blood-hastening song of speeding geodynes—and one more chance.

"Shame, Giles!" Hal Samdu was rumbling. "If we've any chance to destroy that human beast before he can harm Aladoree—let's be off!"

His angry glance fell dully to his fork, and Bob Star saw that his great fingers had absently crumbled the metal.

The commander sent him to the gun turret, Giles Habibula to the power room, and Bob Star back to the bridge. And they burst at last from freezing clouds into the clear immensity of open space. The power tubes were burning, and life came back to the cruiser's dead transmitter.

Using a narrow beam and limited power, with all the equipment carefully shielded, Bob Star called the relay station at the atmospheric plants. There was no answer. He increased the power and tried again, but all he heard was the dry hiss of static.

"That's enough." Jay Kalam stopped him. "We can't

risk using more power, or wasting more time." He gave Bob Star a brief message in code. "This is my general order, reporting the destruction of the *Invincible* and the liberation of Orco, and commanding the Legion to fight to the last—if there is any Legion left to obey. Get it off to Contra-Saturn, and head for the comet at full acceleration."

A dimly green, flattened ball, Neptune was falling away into a blackness pierced with stars and webbed with pale nebulae. Bob Star shut off the rockets, after that last message was sent, and cut in the geodynes. The sense of motion ceased, under that different sort of thrust, but the greenish planet dropped away with a magical swiftness, drawing toward the smaller ball of Triton.

Behind them, the far-off sun flamed bright but tiny in the frosty dark, shrunk to a splendid star. Great Jupiter and tawny Saturn were faint flecks beside it on the screens of the tele-periscopes. The smaller Earth could not be seen.

Bob Star was not looking back, however; his eyes were on the comet ahead. He was alone on the bridge. The only sound besides his breathing was the high-pitched humming of the hard-driven generators. The pale green oval blot of the comet absorbed his uneasy thoughts. What, really, was it?

What were the Cometeers?

Obviously, they were intelligent. Superintelligent. They were invisible, or could make themselves so. The armament of their unseen scouting vessel had destroyed the System's greatest fighting ship, and dissolved that prison-fortress on Neptune into nothingness.

Men knew no more of the Cometeers, but Bob Star tried apprehensively, now, to picture them. Could they be human? He wanted to believe they were, for their humanity meant to him the reality of the girl—or the vision—he had seen within the prison wall.

"Lad, lad!" old Giles Habibula had chided him. "You're dreaming. I think your father kept you shut up in the Purple Hall too long, when you should have been out looking for such a girl to call your own. But you mustn't mistake your lovesick dreams for the truth."

"Dreams?" he protested quickly. "The girl I saw is as real as you are, Giles! And in terrible trouble—because, somehow, of Stephen Orco and the Cometeers. I still believe we'll find her, if we ever reach the comet."

Jay Kalam, however, had been equally skeptical.

"If the girl you think you saw was real, Bob, she couldn't very well be a native of any planet in the System. We have no inkling of any scientific principle that would enable the projecting of such an image as you describe, without terminal equipment. You want to believe that she's an inhabitant of the comet—perhaps a member of some friendly faction there. But the odds against that are billions to nothing."

Bob Star whispered, "Why?"

"The forms possible to life are so infinitely various," the commander answered deliberately, "the structural adaptations of protoplasm to environmental influences are so amazingly complex, that on all the planets of all the suns of all the universe, there probably never was and never will be another race precisely like our own."

Jay Kalam smiled at him, with a grave kindness.

"I'm afraid Giles is right, Bob. I think you should regard that incident as purely subjective—a product of your own unconscious fears and wishes, reacting to the stimulus of the agency that made you unconscious. Rather than human beings, the Cometeers are more likely something you wouldn't recognize as life at all."

Bob Star stood watching the greenish blot of the comet in the tele-periscope, until the ship and the world ceased to exist. He and that great green eye were alone in space. And the eye was drawing him onward, into its own unknown chasm.

If the Cometeers weren't human, what were they? Tentacled monsters? Animate vegetables? Crystal life, prism-shaped? Or could the entire comet, he wondered, be a single sentient entity? Might its intelligence exist not in discrete individuals but somehow as an attribute of the whole?

Horror took root in his mind, feeding upon his own fantastic speculations. Trying to find escape from those terrors of his own imagination, he went back to the astronomical task he had begun at the Purple Hall: looking for that remote asteroid which had wandered from where it should have been. He failed to find it anywhere, but he discovered something else.

"Something's wrong with Pluto," he told Jay Kalam, when the commander came to relieve him. A harsh rasp of wondering dread edged his weary voice. "I've rechecked my observations a dozen times, and the answer is always the same. It is drifting out of its orbit—toward the comet! I know that sounds insane, and I hardly expect you to believe—"

"But I do." The commander's dark face showed no skepticism, but only consternation. "It fits in with the secret reports we have been receiving from the Contra-Saturn observatory. A number of small asteroids have been drawn from their orbits into the comet—perhaps by the same sort of force that grasped the *Invincible*. Now it seems they're taking planets."

"If they can do that—" Bob Star stood voiceless, trembling with his fearful expectations.

The tall commander shrugged, with a grave acceptance of whatever might come.

"You're tired, Bob," he said. "Go back to your quarters and get some sleep."

Bob Star reeled away like a run-down robot. He dropped, fully dressed, upon his berth. But sleep evaded him—because the green eye of the comet still watched him. It had followed him into his cabin, and it searched his very mind.

The thin whine of the generators was an eerie, hypnotic melody. His numbed brain broke it into weird minor bars. When it carried him at last into an uneasy half-sleep, fear went with him. Nightmares came, in which the Cometeers pursued him, shapeless and unseen.

He woke again, with the distant screams of Mark Lardo in his ears, and stood his watch, and tried once more to sleep. For four such haunted days, the ship drove on toward the comet. At last, with a bleak satisfaction in his voice, he could report to Jay Kalam:

"In five hours, at our present rate of deceleration, we ought to reach the surface of the object."

"If the Cometeers let us!"

Bob Star left the bridge. Too restless to sleep, he made a tour of the cruiser. In the power room, he found Giles Habibula sitting on the floor beside the geodynes, fat legs spread wide. Empty bottles lay scattered around him, and he was very drunk. At sight of Bob Star, he started apprehensively.

"Mortal me!" he gasped. "You gave me a fearful fright, lad. My first fancy was to see some monstrous thing creeping in to destroy me. Ah, it's a fearful voyage!"

He fumbled among the bottles, and found one not quite empty.

"Sit down, lad, and share a drop of wine. The precious warmth of it will thaw a little of the cold terror from your heart. Ah, poor old Giles would have made a sorry soldier, Bob, but for the red courage that comes foaming from the bottle!

"It's a sad thing, lad, but the age of man has ended. Those monsters are to rule the System now. Perhaps we're lucky to be among the first to meet the Cometeers—to die before we know what they really are. But I want to meet them drunk." He tipped up the bottle again.

Bob Star went back to the tele-periscopes, and watched the comet grow. The sharp-edged, greenish oval of it looked the size of an egg, and the size of a man's head. It spread across the black of space. It swallowed the stars; became a sea of green, overflowing all the heavens.

He and Jay Kalam examined it with every instrument the ship possessed.

"I can't make anything out of it." The commander shook his head, baffled and visibly afraid. "That green surface is a perfect geometric ellipsoid. It is absolutely featureless. At this distance, we ought to be able to see anything as small as a house or a ship or a tree. But there's nothing at all."

"The raiders were invisible," Bob Star remarked.

"And it may be that they live on the surface we see." Jay Kalam rubbed thoughtfully at the dark angle of his jaw. "But I don't think so. More likely, I think, that green surface will turn out to be a kind of armor—though of no material we know. The hull, let us say, of an enormous ship. It does move like a ship. Our next problem may be to get inside."

And still the object spread. It had covered half the stars, when the alarm gongs rang. Apprehensively, Bob Star sprang to the instruments. He took swift readings from the glowing dials, and integrated the results upon a calculator.

"We've met a powerful repulsive field," he told Jay Kalam. "It's already absorbing more of our momentum than the geodynes are."

He called the power room, to order the braking of the generators stopped, but still that repulsion mounted. He called Giles Habibula again, to meet it with the thrust of the geodynes. At quarter speed—At half—At full thrust—

He turned at last to the commander, shaking his head in bewildered defeat. "All our forward speed is gone," he whispered hoarsely. "We're drifting back from the comet now—against the full power of the geodynes."

"That seems to show that the green surface is really a kind of armor," Jay Kalam said slowly. "A barrier of the same kind of energy, perhaps, that is drawing Pluto toward the comet."

"Anyhow, we can't get through." Bob Star straightened, trying not to show his sick despair. "From the readings I got, that repulsion must increase to infinity at the green surface. Nothing could break through—" A shrill scream of terror cut off his voice.

"It's the madman," he whispered hoarsely, "Mark Lardo."

The bubbling shriek came again: "They're here! And they're hungry! Don't—don't let them eat!"

Bob Star turned back to his instruments, to read the intensity of that repulsion again. The prisoner had been screaming at intervals ever since his capture—though never with such an ungoverned abandon as this. He started, when he felt Jay Kalam's hand on his arm.

"Bob." The commander's low voice was dry with dismay. "I think there is—something—with us, aboard."

He wanted to deny that, because it was too monstrous to be true. He had heard nothing, certainly. His eyes had seen nothing. Yet, somehow, even before Jay Kalam touched his arm, his mind had been shrinking away from some fearful, unseen presence.

"Look!" The cry burst harshly from his lips. "The green—"

A greenish mist was obscuring the instruments before his eyes. His body tingled to a sudden, stiffening chill. All his sensations were somehow blanketed. Very faintly, he heard Jay Kalam whisper: "Is this what happened at Orco's prison?"

He couldn't answer. His body had become a clumsy, unresponding machine. He realized that he was falling. Dully, from a vast distance, he heard the thin, mad screams of Mark Lardo:

"Don't let it eat—"

10

The Cometeer

Bob Star picked himself up painfully from the deck of the narrow bridge. His limbs were numbed and tingling uncomfortably. A dull, persistent ringing faded slowly from his ears and left a dreadful silence in the ship. The screams of Mark Lardo had ceased. He realized abruptly, with a sense of sick defeat, that he couldn't hear the geodynes.

Jay Kalam was moaning, where he had fallen, and Bob Star bent to examine him. His body was queerly lax. The skin was flushed, and cold with sweat. Heart and breath were irregular and slow.

Bob Star turned back to the instruments. The geodesic indicators showed axial deflection zero, field potential zero. The ship was being flung away from the comet, helpless now in that field of repulsion.

"Our visitor?" Jay Kalam spoke faintly, from where he lay. "Gone?"

"I think so." Bob Star went stiffly to help him get up.

"What was it?"

"I don't know." Bob Star tried to swallow the dry fear in his throat. "I didn't see anything except that green haze—"

"I wonder if it really was a haze?" Jay Kalam was still swaying giddily, but a grave alertness had come back to his thin face. "Or was it perhaps the effect of a radiation which short-circuits nerve fibers. Legion engineers have experimented with radiation that seems to do that." He glanced at a chronometer. "How long were we unconscious?"

"Perhaps ten minutes," Bob Star said.

Jay Kalam sent him to see what had happened to the others. A stifled groan led him to the gun turret. Hal Samdu was just dragging himself up behind the great proton needle, stiffly flexing his mighty arms.

"Aye, Bob," he rumbled. "What came upon us?"

"I don't know yet. Tell me, Hal, what did you see—or feel?"

Hal Samdu shook his head.

"I saw nothing. A monstrous shadow crept into the ship. Then the green mist was in my eyes, and I couldn't see anything. This stiffness seized my body, and I couldn't move. That's all I know."

Bob Star was descending toward the power room, when a strangled whimpering led him back to the brig. He looked through the bars, at Mark Lardo. Shocked horror spilled out his strength.

Gasping, trembling, he clung weakly to the bars, staring at the thing in the cell. Mark Lardo had been big—a shaggy, powerful human brute. But this shrunken creature looked hardly larger than a child. Its skin was uncannily white and hideously shriveled. It lay inert on the deck, mewing feebly.

"Lardo." Bob Star's voice was thick with his horror. "Mark Lardo—can you hear me?"

The thing moved a little. The shrunken head rolled back, and Bob Star staggered away from the bars. He had seen its eyes. They were sunk deep into that tiny skull, and queerly glazed. He thought they must be blind. Smoky, yellow shadows swirled through them. They were the eyes of nothing human.

Sick to the very heart, Bob Star stumbled away.

Even though insane, the Mark Lardo of an hour ago had been a man, massive and powerful, his great, wild voice ringing through the ship. This wasted horror was no longer human. It had less than half the bulk of Mark Lardo, and little indeed of the savage, animal life.

Bob Star stumbled down the steps into the power room, and stood swaying at the bottom. "Giles," he called hoarsely, "have you any wine?"

Giles Habibula was leaning disconsolately against one of the geodyne generators. His fat arms were flung across it in a sort of sick caress. He was sobbing, and he didn't seem to hear.

"Giles," Bob Star called again, "I want a drink."

He heard, then, and came slowly across the room.

"Ah, lad!" He was drunk no longer, but weeping bitterly. "You find me at an evil hour, lad. My poor geodynes —like a dear friend murdered! I think we both need a drink."

He found a full bottle, in a box that should have held

255

tools. Bob Star gulped down half of it. Giles Habibula finished what was left, and wiped a forlorn yellow face with the back of his hand.

"I'm an old generator man," he muttered huskily. "But never did I run a set of geodynes so powerful as these were, or so sweetly tuned. They always answered my touch as if they were alive, lad. They sang me a song. They loved me, lad—more than any woman ever did.

"But now they're dead, lad—dead. Killed and mutilated. Every coil has been cut into a thousand useless bits of wire. Every grid and filament has been twisted out of shape. The very cathode plates are warped, so that they can never be tuned again."

"They look all right," Bob Star protested.

"Ah, so," the old man wheezed sadly. "Their shining beauty is left. But the precious life is gone. I sat here, too full of wine—wine and caution—to stop the thing that killed them." He turned to fumble for another bottle. "But let's drink again, and speak no more of the fearful thing I saw."

"You saw it?" Bob Star took the bottle, and pulled him toward a bench. "Sit down, Giles, and tell me what you saw."

"Let me drink, lad," he begged hoarsely. "Let me drown that monstrous recollection, for dear life's sake, while I'm still sane!"

Bob Star held the bottle from him.

"Ah, well, I'll tell you what I saw," he muttered at last. "If you think it may help us guard your precious mother. But it wasn't what I saw that froze my poor old bones. It was what I felt—the cold, foul breath of mortal evil."

"Just what did you see?"

"The ache of coming harm has been gnawing at me ever since we left Neptune," Giles Habibula wheezed. "Even wine couldn't kill it, altogether. Suddenly, a little while ago, I knew that some fearful thing had crept into the ship. I heard Mark Lardo howling louder.

"I should have fled from it, but there was nowhere to go. And soon I couldn't move, for that green mist came and chilled my poor old body. I couldn't move a finger, not even to lift a precious drop of wine. Ah, so, lad! I was sitting here on the deck, with the bottle between my knees. I never needed a drink so much, in forty years of soldiering, but I couldn't get the blessed bottle to my lips.

"Then the thing came down into the power room. I

could hardly turn my dim old eyes to see it, for that paralysis. It came partly down the companionway and partly through the bulkheads. Even the metal shells of the geodynes were no barrier to it. It walked across toward them—"

"What was it like?" Bob Star broke in huskily. "A man?"

"Don't ask how it looked!" the old man begged. "Let's drink—and forget the wicked wonder of it."

"Please!" Bob Star urged. "For my mother's sake."

"Ah, if we must." His fear-glazed eyes rolled upward. "Ten feet tall it stood. A thing of moving fire! The head of it was violet, bright and tiny as a star, and cold as ice, wrapped in a little cloud of purple mist.

"The foot of it was another star, hot and red, in the middle of a little moon of reddish mist. Between the violet star and the red one was a pillar of greenish light. Spindle-shaped. It kept whirling; it was never still.

"Around the thicker middle of the spindle was a broad green ring. Some crystal, maybe. It seemed solid—but still it wasn't too solid to pass through the bulkheads. That's the way it looked, as near as I can tell you. But the horror of it was the way it made you feel."

"So that was how it looked?" Bob Star nodded bleakly. "Now, tell me what it did."

"It did enough to my precious geodynes, life knows," the old soldier moaned. "It was alive, lad. It was never still. The pillar of mist kept spinning. The two stars beat like hearts of light, in the little moons of colored mist around them. Only the green ring shone with a steady glow.

"It came across the floor, lad, to my precious generators. The mist swirled out—an arm of it reaching through the solid metal of their cases. And the song of them changed to a fearful, hurt sound. It was their cry of death.

"The thing left them in a moment and came toward me." His fat bulk shook. "I thought I was gone, lad. The creature was hungry—with a foul and noisome greed. It yearned for the life of me, lad. And it reached out with that green fire to kill me, the way it killed the geodynes.

"But then Mark Lardo screamed again." Giles Habibula sighed. "That's all that saved me, lad. The evil creature saw me to be an old man, weak with many infirmities, and my flesh poisoned with the wine. It heard the madman scream—I saw it stop and listen. And it left me, for the sweeter meat of a strong young man.

"It floated away through the metal of the ship, not bothering about the door. And I sat listening to that screaming. It changed, lad. The last scream was something to turn the blood to ice in your very heart, lad. And that was all I heard."

Bob Star stood speechless, thinking of the whimpering, shriveled thing it had left in Mark Lardo's cell. Giles Habibula took the bottle from his hand and turned it up. His yellow throat pulsed convulsively until the last drop was gone.

The creature in the cell was not yet dead when Bob Star forced himself shakily back. It was no longer able to move itself, however, because a dreadful disintegration had already set in. Seeing that it would not long possess any kind of life at all, Bob Star called Jay Kalam. They went voicelessly into the cell to gather it up, and nerved themselves to strip it of Mark Lardo's garments, which now were far too large.

By the time they had laid it on the bunk in the cell, the shrunken fingers and toes were beginning to come away. No attempt at medical aid was possible, yet the last sickening indications of life lasted for more than an hour. There was no sign of intelligence, but the expression of that doll-sized head and the whimpering sounds it uttered made Bob Star believe the thing was still aware of agony.

At last the smoky yellow went out of the eyes. They were left terribly white, obviously blind, and shimmering with the same iridescence that now covered the rest of the body. The thing moved no more. The glowing remains continued to crumble, until Bob Star and Jay Kalam rolled what was left into a blanket, and flung it out of the ship into space.

Jay Kalam spent two hours, afterwards, with a small specimen he had kept for analysis. He came back from his tests with an expression of baffled unease.

"That wasn't human flesh," he told Bob Star. "Several of the elements found in the body were entirely lacking; others were present, but in the wrong proportions. The chemical structure of the protoplasm had been queerly changed.

"Something fed upon Mark Lardo," he concluded huskily. "It consumed some ninety pounds of his weight. The thing it left in the cell was neither human nor really alive."

"Commander," Bob Star whispered, "what—what do you think it was?"

Jay Kalam frowned thoughtfully.

"We expected to find no familiar sort of life on that object. But I believe the thing Giles saw was, in its own way, alive. It showed intelligence and purpose. It moved. It—fed."

His voice had caught, and his pale face stiffened, but he went on in a moment, almost calmly:

"It must have been, in a sense, material—it consumed ninety pounds of matter from the body of Mark Lardo. Yet it was sufficiently free of the ordinary limitations of matter to travel through solid metal."

He shrugged uncomfortably.

"Perhaps we should have expected something of the sort," he added. "Because the Cometeers have obviously advanced far above us, scientifically—whatever their moral lag. They must be able to manipulate matter and energy, perhaps even space and time, in ways still beyond us."

Bob Star stood silent for a time, clinging grimly to his old belief in the humanity of the people of the comet—for that meant, to him, the reality of the girl he had seemed to see in the wall of Stephen Orco's prison. But his faith in her existence died, before the silent horror that still stalked the ship.

"I've read an old legend," he whispered suddenly, "of creatures that were believed to suck the blood of the living—"

"The vampire." Jay Kalam's dark head shook, as if with a helpless protest against what they had seen. "A feeble and inoffensive myth beside the Cometeers."

He paused to draw a long, rasping breath.

"We had wondered what they want," he muttered huskily. "Now I think we know. I think they have come to the System for—food."

A harsh, inarticulate rumbling came from Hal Samdu. "Fight!" he sobbed. "We must fight. Giles, you must fix the generators."

Tears shone in the old man's eyes.

"It can't be done," he gasped. "My proud beauties—they were murdered by the Cometeers!"

Bob Star returned with Jay Kalam to the bridge. "We are now beyond the field of repulsion," he reported, when he had taken observations. "But we're still flying away from the comet at a high velocity, and helpless to do anything about it." He laughed bitterly. "With only the rockets—"

At that moment the telltales flamed red. The alarm gongs clanged. He spun to scan the screen of the bow tele-periscope, and gasped breathlessly, "Asteroid ahead!"

11

Murdered Asteroid

Bob Star's fingers swept to the rocket firing keys. The *Halcyon Bird* trembled to thundering exhausts. Blue torrents of flame flared into the dark void ahead, lighting the screens of the tele-periscope.

"An asteroid?" Jay Kalam whispered. "You're certain?"

"I am," Bob Star said, too busy to turn. "The gravity detector shows a mass dead ahead. Millions of tons. The deflector fields wouldn't swing it an inch. But I've changed our course with the rockets—I think enough—"

"An asteroid—" Jay Kalam paused thoughtfully. "The condensation theories of cosmogony have indicated the existence of such tiny bodies at the fringes of the system. But I don't believe one has ever been discovered so far from the sun. We're a billion miles outside of Pluto's orbit—"

At the tele-periscope, Bob Star had sharply caught his breath.

"I see it," he cried. "It's still far-off, and safely to the left—"

His breath caught again, and he bent closer to the screen.

"What is it?" Jay Kalam whispered.

"The thing is only a tiny, irregular rock," Bob Star answered uncertainly. "Probably no more than half a mile in diameter. But I believe—" suppressed excitement crept into his voice—"I believe it's inhabited!"

"Bob!" protested the commander. "That's impossible, almost. When it's so remote—uncharted—"

"The light-diffusion," Bob Star insisted, still watching

the screens, "indicates an atmosphere. And so small a body couldn't hold an atmosphere without an artificial gravity-field. I'm sure—"

"Planetary engineering is expensive, Bob," Jay Kalam reminded him. "Especially when the equipment would have to be brought so far. It would have been nearly impossible for anyone to develop such a remote asteroid secretly—"

"There!" Bob Star whispered. "I have it again, with a higher power."

He looked around suddenly, his lean face shining with wonder.

"It is! It is inhabited, commander! I see vegetation—it has been landscaped! And there's a building—a long white building! A ship lying beside it—a small geodesic cruiser. And an ultrawave tower on the little hill behind it!"

Jay Kalam's hand closed hard on his shoulder. "Can you land there, Bob?"

"Land?" Bob Star turned from the screen to read the other instruments. "I don't know," he said slowly. "Our relative velocity is very high. It would take a lot of rocket fuel to stop without the geodynes."

"We must—if we can," Jay Kalam urged him. "For we're helpless, on this wreck. If we can land, we should be able to secure the use of the ship you saw. Or at least to signal some Legion base for aid."

Intent over his instruments, Bob Star had hardly seemed to hear. At last he read the final integration from the calculator, and turned swiftly to the rocket fuel gauges.

Anxious, Jay Kalam asked: "What do you find?"

"I think we can do it," Bob Star said. "With just about enough fuel left to fry an egg. We won't be able to leave the asteroid again—unless we get the other ship, or at least a new supply of rocket fuel."

"Try it," Jay Kalam said.

Again the rockets thundered response to the firing keys.

"I'll find Hal Samdu," the commander said, "and send him back into the proton gun turret. And you keep alert, Bob. Because I think we aren't very likely to meet a friendly reception. Honest folk are not apt to frequent a secret refuge a billion miles outside the System. Frankly, the asteroid puzzles me.

"The obvious guess is that it's a criminal hide-out. But it's pretty remote from any possible scene of operations.

Pirates could hardly find it a convenient rendezvous. There wouldn't be much profit in running synthetic drugs so far. I don't know what to expect—except hostility."

And even in that the commander was disappointed. Bob Star scanned that tiny world alertly, as the *Halcyon Bird* dropped upon it with rockets flaming blue; and Hal Samdu waited at his great proton needle. But no challenge came from the ultrawave tower. No hidden proton guns stabbed out. No stir of motion greeted the descending stranger. The tiny white spindle of the geodesic cruiser lay motionless upon the rocket field, beside the enigmatic quiet of the long white building.

The *Halcyon Bird* came at last to rest upon the level gravel of the little field, beside that other ship.

"Well!" Bob Star laughed uneasily, pointing at a fuel gauge that read *Empty*.

Jay Kalam was peering through the observation ports, with wonder on his face.

"Queer," he whispered, "that our arrival doesn't create some commotion. Strange ships don't land here every day."

Bob Star looked out. Beyond the slim, bright hull of the motionless ship, he could see the white walls and pillars of the building. It was a vast, rambling structure, and every gleaming surface reflected expensive artistic simplicity. A tiny artificial lake burned like a flake of pale silver, beyond it, under the purple darkness of the star-pierced sky. And all about it slumbered the silent, exotic beauty of the landscaped grounds.

Such small planetoids are never round. The surface of this one was a maze of pinnacles and cliffs, ravines and chasms. Pale grass and rank, livid woodland covered the more level slopes. Many-hued lichens splashed the projecting rocks with green, scarlet and gold.

A slow smile of bemused admiration was creeping over Jay Kalam's thin face.

"Why, it's a fairyland," he whispered softly. "A dream!"

His shining eyes moved from one strange vista to another, drinking in the peaceful, haunting beauty of lichen-painted rock masses, the gay laughter of shimmering gardens, the cool smile of the silvery lake, and the simple welcome of the long white house.

Beside him, Bob Star felt a strange, painful joy stealing into his heart. Every shrub and tree called to him with a limpid voice of enchantment. The whole tiny planet reached out to him alluring, soothing arms of magic. They rocked his spirit in a cradle of peace. The rest of the System seemed abruptly very remote, the disasters of mankind queerly unreal. And he knew that it would be very hard to go away.

"Can't you feel it, Bob?" Jay Kalam was whispering again. "Can't you feel the hand of a genius, in the balance and the rhythm and the pattern of every rock and plant and patch of grass? Can't you hear an artist singing, in the line and mass and color of it?"

Bob Star nodded silently.

"This world is haunted, Bob, if anything ever was." He went on softly, "Haunted by the spirit of the man who made it. It calls to you from every vista—with joy or peace or laughter or pain. Or sometimes with terror, where the rocks are wild and dark, and those pale, livid trees are twisted like monstrous dwarfs."

Something made him shiver.

"But it's dead. Its maker is dead." His low voice carried a strange, half-absent conviction. "He's dead, and his spirit is trying to call to us, from the beauty he created."

Abruptly he shook his head.

"I somehow got that feeling," he said briskly. "But we've no time to be talking nonsense, Bob. We must be finding out what's wrong here—why everything is so still. And seeing if we can get that ship."

They left Hal Samdu watching in the gun turret. Cautiously alert, gripping proton pistols, the three others descended from the air-lock of the *Halcyon Bird*. The synthetic atmosphere of the tiny world was fresh and cold, sparkling with the fragrance of the gardens. An uncanny silence haunted it.

Quickly, they crossed the bare gravel of the rocket field, toward the other ship. No name was painted on its tapering silver sides. It was small, but new in design, modern and swift, patterned after the latest geodesic cruisers of the Legion.

"A good ship," Jay Kalam said. "And her valves sealed, her ports closed, as if she were ready for flight."

"Ah, so," muttered Giles Habibula, in a feeble, apprehensive tone. His eyes were darting this way and that, with a furtive, nervous quickness. His seamed yellow face was pale, his fat limbs trembling. He contrived to walk so that he was between Bob Star and the commander.

"Ah, so." he repeated. "But it isn't." He was pointing at a dark, oily patch upon the gravel beside the ship. "The

263

drain valves to her fuel tanks have been opened," he said. "Her precious fuel has all run out to waste upon the gravel."

"That's so," said Jay Kalam, under his breath.

Giles Habibula shivered. "I don't like this stillness, Jay. The place is too fearful silent. Ah, some dreadful hand has touched this little world, Jay. It's dead, Jay. Dead! And no longer any fit dwelling for the living!"

They had come to the sealed entrance valve.

"It's locked, Giles," Jay Kalam said. "Will you open it?"

"If you wish." The old man nodded reluctantly. "But it's nothing good we'll find within. The ache in my poor old bones tells me so. We'll find nothing but the ghastly tracks of horror."

He fumbled in his big pockets for a scrap of wire, and waddled heavily to the lock.

Bob Star looked anxiously around him. Silence was sawing at his nerves. The long white house behind them was largely built, he saw, of native stone. But its white, inviting luxury had been expensively finished with metal, glass, and tropical woods imported from the distant System—its materials represented the peril and the enormous cost of many a voyage of billions of miles. Its dark windows stared at him vacantly. A depressing spirit of empty desolation came out of it, and touched his soul with a cold chill of dread.

"While we wait, Bob," Jay Kalam said, "will you take a look at the ultrawave station? See if the transmitter is in working order. And if the automatic printers have been taking down any newscasts. It would take days to get an answer to any message, at this distance. But perhaps we can learn how the System has been faring."

He hastened away across the tiny field, and up the cragged height where the spidery tower stood. Eerie stillness dogged him. It was hard to keep from looking behind him.

He pushed open a swinging door, and entered the tiny rock-walled room beneath the tower. Horror thrust him back. Every piece of equipment in the room was useless. The receivers were dead. The printers were silent. The transmitter had been wrecked, as cleverly and completely as the geodynes of the *Halcyon Bird*. Every wire had been cut into many pieces. Every tube had been destroyed. The plates of every condenser were twisted, strangely corroded.

264

But the silent horror was shrieking at him from what lay on the floor. It had been a man. There were scattered garments. A little pile of gray, ash-like dust shimmered with pale, unpleasant colors. He saw dark stains, where some liquid had run. The Cometeers had been here before him.

He shut the door upon the thing within the room, and went shakily back down to the rocket field. Jay Kalam and Giles Habibula were still standing beneath the sealed entrance valve; he told the commander in a hushed voice what he had found, and asked Giles Habibula:

"You can't open it?"

"Ah, lad!" Sadly, the old man shook his head. "Have you no faith in my precious genius? I could have opened it in a moment, lad—but I waited for you to come back. Old Giles is too old and feeble, lad, to be recklessly loosing upon himself such frightful evil as is locked within the ship—"

He touched the lock again, and humming motors lowered the valve. Side by side, Bob Star and Jay Kalam mounted it. On the deck within they found crumpled garments, piled with iridescent ash, and darkly stained where some strange fluid had run. Jay Kalam shrank back, shivering.

"Giles," he whispered hoarsely, "see if the geodynes are ruined."

"But come with me," the old man begged. "Old Giles is no mortal fool, to go blundering off alone—"

Another heap of weirdly shining ash stopped them at the door of the power room. Giles Habibula peered with apprehensive eyes at the gleaming generators, and sorrowfully shook his head.

"Murdered!" he wheezed. "Destroyed, like our own. This ship is as useless as the *Halcyon Bird!*"

"The ship must have been about to depart, when it happened," Jay Kalam murmured thoughtfully. "The valves were closed, the crew at their places. I suppose the owners of the place were trying to escape. But they must have left clues for us—"

His slender hands had clenched, as if with sudden agony. A dark pain tightened his face.

"That's all that's left for us to do," he added bitterly. "To play detective! For we're marooned here, without any way to depart or to call for aid. There's nothing else we can do—"

12

Out of the Wall

For a time they stood in silence, upon the silent deck of the dead ship. Beside them lay the gray, glowing heap of something that once had been a man. A black despair had chained them to it, until Jay Kalam abruptly lifted his shoulders.

"The only thing I see," he said, "is to explore the asteroid, and learn as much as we can about the men who lived here. Perhaps we can uncover some resource. Perhaps there's a reserve of rocket fuel, or even a new set of geodynes. We can begin with a search of this ship. There may be documents—"

They found eleven more piles of glowing dust, where men had died. Two were on the small bridge. Bob Star left them, to examine the log. The positions entered in it told that the ship had made many voyages to Pluto, the equatorial colonies of Neptune, and certain of the smaller asteroids. But it contained no hint of the business or identity of her owners. Jay Kalam made a more perplexing discovery. He came from one of the cabins, carrying a ring and a little black book.

"I found these," he said, "in the dust where a man died. He may have been the owner of the ship; his suite was the choice one, and very elaborately furnished. I don't know what to make of it."

He showed Bob Star what he found. The ring was plain gold. It had a broad black set, deeply inscribed, in scarlet, with the outlines of crossed bones, and a looped tau cross. That same symbol was stamped in red upon the black cover of the book. Its thin pages, Bob Star saw, were filled with penned hieroglyphs, meaningless to him.

"It's a diary, I imagine," Jay Kalam answered Bob Star's inquiring frown. "The difference in the color of the ink seems to show many brief entries, made at different times. It ought to be interesting, but it looks like some sort of shorthand, probably in cipher. I'll see what I can do with it."

"Perhaps we'll find more papers in the mansion," Bob Star suggested hopefully.

"I doubt it. The business of these people seems to have made them very cautious." He was studying the ring again, and the red emblem on the book, with a worried frown. "This symbol is what puzzles me."

Bob Star bent to peer at that curious design of looped cross and crossed bones.

"Was that the sign—" His voice caught, and he began to tremble.

"That was it." The commander nodded soberly. "The symbol on that sealed magnelithium cylinder in which Edwin Orco found the strange infant he named Stephen." His pale lips drew stern. "I think the secret of this asteroid will be useful to us—if we can only find it."

They went on to the great, rambling white-walled house, and climbed to the broad verandah. Bob Star stepped shakily over the sinister glow of a pile of grayish ash, beside a wide dark stain and a discharged proton pistol. He hammered on a great door of wrought silver, which bore, in red enamel, the crossed bones of death and the looped cross of life.

Silence let them in, to meet the austere welcome of brooding death. Exploring the lofty, dimly lit halls, and the vast magnificence of deserted rooms, they were astounded again and again at the evidence of lavish luxury. One glimpse into the immense kitchen almost banished the apprehension of Giles Habibula.

"Ah, lad!" His seamed face was shining. "Here's abundance! Whoever he may have been, the master of this place knew the secret of life. No finer victuals and wines could be gathered from all the System!"

He gasped for breath, licking his fat blue lips.

"We need live no longer in that mortal coffin of a wreck, Jay—save the one of us on guard. Life knows how long we may be marooned upon this gloomy rock. Forever, it seems likely. We may as well dine and drink—"

His voice died abruptly when they came again upon the shining ash of another man.

In one vast, long, dim room, they found a great library of magnificently printed volumes. The lofty walls were hung with the work of famous painters. Niches were set with fine sculpture. An alcove held a fine optiphone and

267

many thousands of records, which set Jay Kalam's dark eyes to glowing.

"This was a secret kingdom," he said softly. "It was a great mind's dream of paradise, transmuted into reality by some extraordinary power of accomplishment. A shining light of genius is reflected everywhere: in the beauty that sings from the gardens, in the architecture of this building, in this wonderful room—"

"Ah, so, Jay," put in Giles Habibula. "And don't forget the kitchen and the precious cellar."

"A true artist," the commander went on, gently. "A supreme creator—his mark is everywhere." He was staring around with a baffled frown. "And his capacities included a genius for anonymity: we haven't found a letter, a photograph, a memorandum—not even a monogram, except the one on the ring and the book."

Jay Kalam had returned to the *Halcyon Bird,* to attempt to wrest the secret from the shorthand diary, when Giles Habibula made another discovery. Bob Star and Giles Habibula were crossing the library, when the old man abruptly halted.

"Lad," he said, his voice thin and hollow in the vastness of the room, "there's a hidden passage in the wall of the alcove yonder."

With a skeptical interest, Bob Star inquired: "How do you know?"

"How do you know, lad, which way is up and which way is down?" He sighed heavily. "It's a feeling, lad, a blessed instinct. A matter of subconscious observation. A precious aptitude, refined by long training. Old Giles Habibula was not always in the Legion, lad. Before that night when a woman let him down, he was a free agent, living by his genius.

"Men can't hide their treasures from Giles Habibula, lad. For their minds work alike, as their locks do." His thin voice sank confidentially. "When you wish to find something a man has hidden, lad, merely consider the kind of man he is, the circumstances he was in, and you'll go straight to the hiding place."

"Do you really think," Bob Star inquired doubtfully, "that there's a secret passage here?"

"Think?" echoed the old man, scornfully. "I know it." He pointed. "That wall, you see, is thick enough to conceal a narrow passage."

"But I don't!" Bob Star protested. "It looks thin enough—"

"That's because the pillars and hangings are cunningly designed to hide the thickness of it—a clever optical illusion." He was waddling toward the alcove. "The entrance should be in that odd corner. It's well concealed from the rest of the room, and convenient to the steps within."

His thick, deft, oddly sensitive fingers were rubbing and tapping at the richly polished panels of red Venusian hardwood.

"Ah, so," he breathed. "Here's the door. The dust, you observe, is broken in the crack."

"I don't observe," Bob Star said. "But if you think it really is a door, I'll break it down."

"Wait, lad!" Giles Habibula protested indignantly. "It might be broken down. But there's no aesthetic satisfaction in the breaking down of doors. That's a crude admission that craftsmanship has failed. The very thought is a twisted blade in the heart of genius, lad.

"The means of opening the door are at hand, and we have but to lay our fingers on them. A switch, no doubt, for the mechanism is doubtless electrical. The master of this house," he said slowly, "was elaborately methodical, and himself a great genius." Heavy lids drooped briefly over his fishy eyes. "Ah, so!" he wheezed. "The optiphone, of course! Some trick with the dials—"

His thick fingers touched the knobs. Silently, the scarlet panel swung inward, and white lights flashed on beyond.

"Walk ahead, lad," he asked. "And keep your weapons handy. It's possible that someone is yet alive in the hidden space below. And life's too precious to be wasted, in any desperate encounter with proton pistols—"

Bob Star walked eagerly ahead, down a long, narrow flight of winding, rock-hewn stairs. He found no living thing below, however. What he did find merely increased the haunting enigma of the asteroid. At the foot of the stair, cut into the very heart of the tiny world, was an enormous chamber. It contained an elaborate biological research laboratory. There were powerful microscopes, radiological and chemical apparatus, ovens, incubators and vats of ghastly specimens—most of them human. The Cometeers, apparently, had found the place as readily as had Giles Habibula. The dust of seven human beings lay shimmering on the floor.

Back aboard the *Halcyon Bird,* Jay Kalam listened to Bob Star's account of the find, with thin lips compressed. He didn't speak, and Bob Star asked: "Have you deciphered the diary?"

"No," the commander shook his head. "It's more difficult than I had expected."

Time went by upon the planetoid, each hour a new drop of bitterness in the cup of the four Legionnaires. One hope faded, and another. They found no signal apparatus, no spare geodynes, not even an extra drum of rocket fuel. The mystery of the lonely rock still evaded them. Jay Kalam reported no progress with his efforts to read the secret diary.

At last, from the bridge of the helpless *Halcyon Bird,* Bob Star watched Pluto approach the pallid ellipse of the cometary object. For many days it had been plunging outward from its former orbit. He waited with a troubled wonder to see it checked by that field of repulsion, but nothing stopped it. It struck that sea of shining green, and vanished.

He turned the tele-periscope back to Neptune. It reassured him for a moment to find that next planet in its place, but then he saw the gap between Neptune and Triton looked too wide. The satellite was already on its way.

"Triton!" he muttered huskily. "Then Neptune—and finally the Earth." His lean hands clenched helplessly. "But there's nothing we can do—"

That same night, he was striding restlessly, alone, through the silent gloom of a great hall in the white mansion. Pale lights burned cold on high walls paneled with black and scarlet. The white floor was hard white metal. He paused upon it suddenly, staring unbelievingly at a panel in the wall.

He had seen a moving shadow there. It brought back a shadow and vision that had come to him in the fort at Neptune, and a face that had not yet faded from his uneasy dreams. Trembling with eagerness, he stepped quickly toward the shadow. In spite of himself, he was whispering:

"Come back to me! Please come back—"

The shadows darkened and began to glow, somehow sinking back beyond the surface of the black-and-scarlet wall. A pure blue light was born among them, brighter than their flaming edges. His heart paused when they rushed together, and became a perfect, luminous reality.

It seemed to him as if a deep niche had suddenly been cut in the wall. Its shape was a tapered spiral. It was black. It flamed with innumerable lights, from scattered crystal flakes of blue. A many-angled pedestal of purest sapphire burned within it.

Upon the pedestal, as before, stood the girl.

Her beauty brought an ache to his throat. Her sweet body glowed white against the darkness and the sapphire flame of the spiral chamber. His first glimpse brought a confused and yet indelible impression of her straight, slim perfection, of the massed midnight of her red-glinting hair, of the pale, tragic oval of her face, and the wide, sad eyes of golden-flecked brown.

In a moment he saw that she was hurt. Her white robe was torn and stained with red. She swayed upon the vast sapphire. The pallor of pain was on her face, and her eyes were deep and dark with agony. He could see that she was fighting desperately against weakness and pain—and against something else. Bob Star sensed a terrific, invisible conflict, in which her mind was making some supreme exertion—

He started toward her, impulsively driven to her aid.

Two yards from the wall, he checked himself. She wasn't here. She was simply a shadow in the wall. She was no more here than she had been in the prison on Neptune, two billion miles away. Just a shadow—

Or not even that. Perhaps she was mere hallucination, the daughter of a brain that Stephen Orco had cracked with the Iron Confessor. The red hammer of pain, not still for nine years, beat behind that scar—and it seemed to him now that the blue fire in the crystals behind the girl danced in time to its beat.

He realized abruptly that she hadn't motioned him to keep away, as she had done before. Her tragic eyes were fixed on his face, anxious, pleading—and dilated with desperate effort. Reeling on the great sapphire, she held out her arms toward him. And her image flickered, oddly. It was just, he thought afterwards, as if he had been seeing her through a great sheet of some perfectly transparent crystal, and this barrier had been withdrawn.

He was startled, then, to hear her voice. It was a low, breathless cry—but somehow relieved and glad. Some strange joy washed the pallor and the agony of effort from her face. Her slim body relaxed, and she fell toward him.

A shadow, falling? Fighting the numbness of incredulity, Bob Star sprang forward. He swayed with an utterly astonished delight when her warm, real weight came into his arms. For a moment she seemed lifeless. Then brief animation stirred her. She looked back toward the empty chamber, where sapphire flame still shimmered upward from the vacant pedestal. A curious call, a single liquid, bell-clear note, broke from her lips.

Immediately the sapphire exploded like a great bomb of light. Blue flame filled the niche. It faded to a swirling confusion of shadow. And the shadow died upon the black and scarlet wall. As if exhausted, the girl went limp in his arms again. He stood for a moment holding her, staring at the polished blankness of the wall.

"A shadow?" he whispered, and turned with her. He carried her back through the dim length of that great hall, and across the wide, columned gallery, and out upon the gravel of the rocket field, to the *Halcyon Bird*.

Giles Habibula met him below the air-lock.

"Well?" he challenged the old man. "Don't you think she's real?"

"Real enough." The fishy eyes warmed with approval. "And I'm glad to see you forgetting your sickly dreams. A good thing for you. Ah, and she's a lovely lass. Tell me, lad, isn't she fairer than your vision?"

"No." Bob Star laughed. "Because she is the vision."

Staring, Giles Habibula gasped, "Where did she come from, lad?"

"Out of the wall," Bob Star told him, and laughed again at his baffled doubt.

"Don't make fun of poor old Giles." He straightened. "Jay wants you," he announced. "On the bridge, right away."

"Why?"

"I don't know, lad—but I can see that he's disturbed."

"I'll come," he said. "But first I must find a place for her."

There were vacant cabins aboard the *Halcyon Bird* and Giles Habibula waddled ahead to open a door and turn down the covers on a berth.

"What ails the precious lass?" he wheezed.

The girl had seemed unconscious. But the golden eyes fluttered open as Bob Star's arms drew away from her.

Her oval face was strained again, anxious. She struggled to sit up, clutching urgently at his arm. He tried to make her lie back.

"Don't worry," he told her, smiling. "Just take it easy. Everything will be all right—"

Her voice interrupted him. It was low and husky with effort.

Bob Star shook his head. He could sense the liquid beauty of her language, but it was completely strange to him. He caught not one familiar word—nor had he expected to. Yet she turned to Giles Habibula, as if puzzled, disconcerted, by his lack of comprehension.

The old man cocked his yellow head to listen.

"Ah, lass," he muttered, "your voice is precious sweet. And it's evident you have something to say you think important. But your tongue is one old Giles never heard before."

Still fighting a deadly weariness, the girl turned back to Bob Star. Her weary voice ran on, raggedly. Her white face was a mute appeal.

"I'm sorry." He shook his head. "But we can't understand. When you're rested, we'll find some way—"

Her fingers closed on his arm, with a convulsive, frantic strength. Her voice went louder, higher, and sobs were breaking in it. Tears of baffled frustration glittered in her golden eyes.

"What could she be trying to say?" Bob Star peered helplessly at Giles Habibula. "When she came before, it was to warn me about the Cometeers—"

Her fingers relaxed from his arm. She slipped back to the berth again, unconscious.

"This cut on her shoulder?" Bob Star bent over her apprehensively. "It can't be serious?"

"Ah, no, lad. Just a scratch. Rest and sleep will soon repair her strength. Old Giles will dress her little wound, lad. His old hands have yet a certain skill. Don't forget Jay wants you on the bridge."

"Bob," the tall commander greeted him, in a low voice which yet betrayed a suppressed anxiety, "will you please check the orbital motion of this asteroid, and our motion with respect to the cometary object."

Jay Kalam stood watching while Bob Star read the positions of the sun and Jupiter and Sirius on the calibrated screens on the tele-periscope, and bent to tap out his quick calculations.

273

"I see the answer on your face." The commander nodded at his expression of startled apprehension. "It checks with my own. The asteroid has been caught in another tubular field of force. Apparently we are to be drawn out into the comet, along with the larger planets."

13

Fuel for the Comet

The cometary object hung close ahead.

To watch the last sunset, Kay Nymidee had scrambled with Bob Star's aid to the top of a high, bare pinnacle, beyond the rocket field. They were sitting, side by side, on a cushion of scarlet moss. Their feet dangled over a precipice.

Beneath lay the irregular convexity of the tiny world, molded by the dead genius of its unknown master into vistas of fantastic, haunting beauty. Grassy slopes smiled with peace, and bright masses of flowering woodland laughed joyously. But above them, everywhere, rugged peaks and ridges stood solemnly and gorgeously strange in lichen-coats of green and gold and scarlet.

And the purple blackness of the sky was a vault of never-fathomed mystery. Day might illuminate the face of the asteroid, but never its sky. Now the sun was setting, behind Bob Star and the girl, a point of blue-white splendor, attended by the tiny flecks of Jupiter and Saturn. It cast black, knife-sharp shadows of the two upon the cragged opposite wall of the gorge.

Before them, above black shadows and flaming lichens, the comet was rising—for the last time. The ellipse of it came up like a featureless mask of hideous green, peering malevolently over the edge of the tiny world. Its leering face was near, now, and huge.

Bob Star caught the girl's hand; Kay Nymidee clung to him with an apprehensive grasp.

"*Temyo ist nokee,*" she murmured, in her own strange tongue. Her voice was deep and husky with dread.

"Yes," he whispered, "I suppose we'll soon be inside the comet. But there's nothing we can do—" He checked himself, and forced a smile. "But don't you worry, darling—"

Nearly a week had passed since her inexplicable arrival on the asteroid; and now she seemed almost recovered from whatever ordeal she had undergone. The scratch on her shoulder was healed, her fair skin glowing again with health.

Through their efforts at communication, Bob Star had learned her name—Kay Nymidee. He had learned that her home had been indeed in the comet. He had found that she hated and feared the Cometeers—whom she called *aythrin*.

But that was all.

She had appeared disappointed and bewildered by the failure of the Legionnaires to understand her language. She had tried, desperately, to learn their own, making Bob Star point out objects, to teach her nouns, and act out the meaning of simple verbs. A brilliant and eager student, she could already make a good many simple, concrete statements. But anything more abstract than the greenness of grass or the sweetness of wine was still beyond her reach.

Bob Star glanced at her, and again her breathtaking beauty held his eyes. The sinking, distant sun, catching her head from behind, filled the mass of her dark hair with living gleams of red. Her face was a wide oval of white beauty, though now the green rays of the comet had overcast it with a look of strange foreboding.

Wide, golden, her eyes were on his face. In the failing light, the pupils were great pools of tragic darkness. They were haunted with consuming sorrow, with a sick despair that he yearned to brush away. But they lit, when he looked into them, with a wistful golden light. A tender smile glowed for a moment on her face.

Bob Star caught her against him, impulsively.

"Kay—" he whispered. "Darling—"

For a moment she relaxed against him, but then dread stiffened her. Her haunted eyes went back to the comet, and her face in its green light was once more stark and strange.

"*Mahnyanah*—" came her fear-roughened whisper. "*Mahnyanah*—"

275

Bob Star released her.

"That's right," he whispered bitterly. "We can't relax for an instant, so long as Stephen Orco is alive—"

"Staven Or-rco!"

She seemed to clutch at the name, with a puzzling desperation. Her urgent voice repeated it, with that odd accent. Her slim arm swept out toward the fearful, rising face of the comet. And then she was talking furiously at Bob Star, once more, in her liquidly beautiful, incomprehensible tongue.

He shook his head, helplessly.

"Staven Or-rco!" He caught the name again, but that was all he understood. Her voice rose higher. Tears began to glitter in her eyes. She caught his shoulders, as if to shake him into understanding. But she gave up at last, sobbing in his arms.

The blue point of the sun had set, and the comet reigned. Its greenish, awful face spanned the dark sky from horizon to zenith. Visibly, terribly, it grew. Beneath its unearthly light, the great building was warped into an unreal palace of nightmare. Trees sprawled under it in black masses, like dark monsters crouching. The higher, barren rocks glittered beneath it like fantastic spires of ice.

The *Halcyon Bird* had become a green ghost ship, when Bob Star and the girl came stumbling back to it. The others were waiting outside the air-lock, staring at the fearful sky. They looked ghastly; the strange radiance had turned their flesh lividly pale; their faces seemed like masks of horror.

There was to Bob Star something grotesquely incongruous in the scholarly calm of Jay Kalam's voice, speaking quietly to Giles Habibula.

"Obviously," he was saying, "the Cometeers are able to generate and control some force analogous to gravitation. We have an inkling of the possibilities, from the geodyne and our own gravity cells, but their tubular fields of that unknown force have infinitely more range and power."

Giles Habibula was nodding automatically, his face lifted toward the onrushing comet and ghastly in its dreadful light.

"They must have an engineering science a million years ahead of ours," Jay Kalam's even voice went on. "When you think of the tremendous power required to pluck a planet out of its orbit, or to drive the comet itself like a ship—"

His voice fell away into a chasm of breathless silence.

With appalling speed, now, the green edges of the comet were rushing outward. They were like green curtains dropping toward every horizon. Bob Star had to swallow, to find his voice. It sounded harsh and rasping in the dreadful silence. He asked Jay Kalam:

"Shall we go aboard?"

"If you wish," the commander answered quietly. "The ship is helpless; I don't know that it offers any sort of safety. I don't know what the danger is. You may do what you wish. For myself I'm going to stay out here on the field, so that I can watch until—whatever happens."

Bob Star caught Kay Nymidee's arm, and drew her a little toward the air-lock. But she shook her head, and looked up again at the expanding sea of the comet. Waiting beside her Bob Star had a sudden unpleasant sensation that the asteroid was falling, with their bodies beneath— falling into a tremendous green abyss. The pale, sharp edges of it rushed down to the horizon, and the whole sky was a dome of flaming green.

He heard Jay Kalam whisper: "We're about to strike that green barrier."

A thin wail quavered from the lips of Giles Habibula.

"A frightful time!" he sobbed. "What use is genius now?"

Bob Star put his arms around Kay Nymidee, and moved her a little into the shelter of the shining ship. What would happen when they struck? Woud they ever know?

He waited, breathless. He could feel the quick beat of the girl's heart against his side. There was an odd little flicker in the green vault of the sky. But nothing happened. Waiting became unendurable. Shakily, he whispered:

"When, Jay? When—"

He heard Jay Kalam draw a deep, even breath.

"We've passed the green barrier," the commander said. "We're already inside the comet. Just look at the sky!"

Bob Star walked unsteadily beside Kay Nymidee, away from the hull of the *Halcyon Bird*. His bewildered eyes swept the sky. It still was green, an inverted bowl of pale, weird-hued flame. But it was swarming, now, with strange heavenly bodies.

His startled glance swept them. They were mottled disks like dark moons, strung across the green. They were of many sizes, colored with a thousand merging shades of red, orange, yellow, and brown, all splashed with an eerie green. They were clustered planets, crowding the green sky. The patches were continental outlines. The vast areas of green, he thought, must be seas, reflecting the sky.

"A sun!" Jay Kalam was gasping. "A captive sun!"

And following his gravely pointing arm, Bob Star saw a great ball of purple flame. Its hot color was fantastically strange against the green. It was huge—it looked three times the size of the System's sun, as seen from his home on Phobos.

Kay Nymidee had stepped quickly a little away from him. Her slender white arm, trembling, was pointing at one of the swarming dark planets, which was not mottled like the rest, but a smooth disk of indigo. Between that planet and the captive sun, Bob Star saw three glowing purple lines.

"Bob, Jay! Hal, Giles!" The girl was calling them all by their names, softly accented. And still she was pointing at the featureless disk of violet-blue. "*Aythrin!*" she cried urgently. "Staven Or-rco!"

She ran to touch the green-glinting hull of the *Halcyon Bird,* and then gestured as if it had risen toward the indigo world.

"Staven Or-rco!" she repeated, and ground her small hands together, as if obliterating something.

"See!" Bob Star whispered. "She wants us to go to that blue planet. Stephen Orco is there, with the Cometeers —she calls them *aythrin.* She wants us to go there, and kill him."

The girl had watched him as he spoke, brown eyes shining. Now she seized his arm, speaking at him furiously in her own language. She nodded, shook her head, shrugged, made faces, gesticulated. Bob Star put his hands on her shoulders, to try to calm her.

"It's no use," he told her. "We can't understand. And we can't fly the *Halcyon Bird,* if that's what you want—"

"She has something more to tell us," said the commander. "I wonder if she couldn't draw it?"

He found writing materials in his pockets, and thrust them into her hands. Eagerly, she drew a circle, and pointed at the great indigo disk. Then she made some marking within the circle, and held out the paper, talking rapidly again.

"The circle means the planet," Bob Star said. "But the marking inside—"

He had to shake his head, as the other did. And tears of frustration came suddenly into her eyes. She flung the paper down, with an angry, bewildered gesture, and burst into stormy tears.

"It's too bad." Jay Kalam shook his dark head regretfully. "I'm willing to grant, now, Bob, that she's a native of the comet—although her humanity seems contrary to orthodox science. It's likely enough that she came to bring us information of some sort about the Cometeers and Stephen Orco.

"But nothing she knows is going to help us. Without any common background of languages or culture, or even of thought-forms, it would take her months or years, brilliant as she evidently is, to learn enough English to convey any complex or abstract ideas."

He turned abruptly, and squinted at the purple sun.

"We must go aboard, Bob," he said, "and take what observations we can. We must discover as much as we can about the comet—and what is happening to us." Something mushed his voice. "I think," he added, "that we won't have much time for observations."

"Why?"

"I believe the asteroid is falling into that captive sun."

For a time, on the bridge, they worked silently. Bob Star was speechless with the ever-renewed impact of the comet's wonder. It was Jay Kalam, still gravely collected, who began to put their discoveries into words.

"This object we've called a comet," he began quietly, "is a swarm of planets. We've counted one hundred and forty-three. Since we entered on the forward side of the asteroid, we must have seen nearly all of them. We knew already, from its gravitational effect on the System, that the comet's mass is nearly a thousand times that of Earth. The captive sun accounts for rather less than half of it. The average mass of the planets, then, must be over three times that of Earth. They've been built into a ship. The green barrier is the hull—an armor of repulsive force. The planets are arranged inside of it, spaced about a great ellipsoid—"

"What I don't see is how such a system could be stable." Bob Star looked up uncomfortably. "Such great masses, so closely crowded—what keeps them from collision?"

"They must be held in place with those same tubular fields—beams of force, set to balance gravity. The frame, so to speak, of the ship." The commander spoke deliberately, half-absently, as if to set his own ideas in order. "The captive sun is at one focus of the ellipsoid. The planet which disturbs Kay so much is at the other—"

"And look at it!" Bob Star was peering at the screen of a tele-periscope. "The surface of it seems absolutely smooth, but look at those machines! A little bit like our proton needles—but they must be enormous, to be visible at this distance! One of them stands under each one of those three purple beams, between the planet and the captive sun—"

"I believe I get it!" Jay Kalam's low voice quivered with restrained excitement. "The captive sun can't be any ordinary star—not with that purple color. I believe it's artificial—an atomic power plant.

"That triple beam is probably the transmission system that taps its power. And, if that's true, the blue planet must be the control room of the ship. Those smaller machines around the three large ones probably distribute the energy to operate it.

"It must take enormous power to hold and propel all these planets and protect them with that barrier of repulsion. Atomic fission wouldn't be enough. That plant must annihilate matter—"

His breath caught, and his lean face tightened.

"I couldn't find Pluto among all those planets," he whispered hoarsely. "I think that's the reason why."

Bob Star peered at him blankly.

"I think the Cometeers wanted it for fuel," he said. "I think they have already stripped it of whatever they wanted to preserve, and flung what was left into that atomic furnace."

He was silent for a little time. His face looked haggard and rigid as a mask of death.

"That seems to complete our picture of the Cometeers." His voice remained oddly calm. "They are universal marauders. They rove space from sun to sun. They pillage planets, and feed upon the life they find. They seize the planets themselves, to build into the swarm, or to burn for fuel—"

"And that's what they want with this asteroid?" Bob Star shivered.

"I think so." Jay Kalam nodded, curiously quiet. "The Cometeers have already once raided the asteroid. Probably they have no further interest in it, except as a speck of fuel." Absently, he was stroking his lean jaw. He asked presently, very softly, "How long have we, Bob?"

Bob Star remained standing for a moment in a dark reverie; he started nervously, and turned to busy himself hastily with tele-periscope, calculator, and chronometer. He straightened at last, and wiped cold sweat from his forehead.

"Three hours—" he whispered, huskily. "Just three hours—"

14

Orco's Voice

Jay Kalam closed the door of the bridge room with a weary finality. For a moment he leaned heavily against it. Then, with dragging feet, he followed Bob Star across the deck, and out through the open air-lock.

Kay Nymidee and Hal Samdu and Giles Habibula were still outside, on the gravel of the rocket field, beside that deserted mansion. They looked ghost-like in the pale green radiance that shone from all the sky.

Hal Samdu stood bolt upright. His great, gnarled hands were clenching and opening again, convulsively. His shaggy head was flung back, and his blue eyes were fixed upon the indigo disk of the master planet. His rugged face was grimly savage.

"If Stephen Orco is there," he was rumbling, harshly, "we must go after him—and kill him. For Aladoree—"

Giles Habibula and Kay Nymidee sat side by side on the gravel. The girl was marking little diagrams with her finger, on the ground, and talking urgently at the old man. He was patiently listening, wearily shaking his head.

"Old Giles is sorry, lass," he said gently. "But it's no use—"

They all looked up when Jay Kalam and Bob Star came down from the valve.

"Well, Jay?" boomed Hal Samdu. "Now we are within

281

the comet, with Stephen Orco. How shall we move to kill him?"

Jay Kalam stepped back a little, wearily, to lean against the green-washed hull of the *Halcyon Bird*. His dark eyes closed for a moment, and his long face, in that unearthly light, became a stiff mask of pain.

"Still, Hal," he said slowly, "there's nothing we can do."

He looked at Giles Habibula and the girl, with weary pity.

"In three hours," he said, "the asteroid will fall into that atomic furnace. We still have no means to leave it."

Hal Samdu's massive face twitched to a spasm of pain. Brokenly, he gasped, "Aladoree—"

Giles Habibula surged apprehensively to his feet. His bald head rolled back, his small eyes peering fearfully at that growing ball of purple fire.

"Just three hours?" he gasped convulsively. "For life's sake, Jay, can't you give us more than that?" His eyes rested for a moment on the commander's stiff face, and he shook his head. "Poor old Giles!" he sobbed. "What a reward for all his genius, and his life of faithful service to the Legion and the System—to be burned for fuel, within the bowels of a monstrous comet!"

He blinked his eyes and blew his nose.   •

"Wine," he whispered. "There's wine in the house. Precious, potent, ancient wine—chosen and aged by that other genius who used to own this rock. Fine old wine, too rare to burn for fuel—"

A vague smile smoothed the apprehension from his face, and he lumbered heavily away toward the great white mansion. Listening, Bob Star caught the faintly whistled notes of a sad but lively ballad of the Legion, *The Sparrow of the Moon*.

Hal Samdu was still standing rigid, watching the indigo planet. The muscles of his angular, weather-beaten face were working; he was muttering inaudibly. The commander's tall body sagged against the hull of the *Halcyon Bird,* as if the life had gone out of it. Bob Star swung to Kay Nymidee, who was looking from him to the purple sun, with apprehensive bewilderment.

"Come on, Kay," he said huskily. "Let's walk."

She smiled. *"Se,"* she said softly. *"Ahndah."*

They crossed the level of the rocket field, and climbed up into a welter of rocks beyond. The incrusting lichens had changed color strangely under that green sky, so that the wild peaks were fantastic as the spires of a fairy city.

Bob Star made her sit beside him on a mossy ledge. His arms closed around her. He could feel her trembling. Staring away into the green sky, her eyes great pools of somber dread. They were lost, bewildered, helplessly riding a dead world to doom. Yet he drew her close to him, and tried to think only of her white beauty—

Giles Habibula was beneath them among the rocks, panting with excitement.

"Come, lad!" he puffed. "The dalliance of love is the food and drink of youth, I know. But it must await a time less torn with mortal urgency. Come!"

"What's wrong now?" Bob Star made no move to rise, for nothing mattered, now.

"Jay bids you come and aid us to load the *Halcyon Bird* with rocket fuel."

"Rocket fuel!" exclaimed Bob Star, dazedly. "There's none."

"But there is!"

Bob Star helped the girl down from the ledge, and they followed Giles Habibula.

"Where—" he whispered breathlessly. "Where did Jay find rocket fuel?"

"Ah, lad!" The old man shook the bald dome of his head, which shone greenish in the light of the comet. "Ever the same is the fate of genius: it stumbles unknown into an unmarked grave. It wasn't Jay that found the precious fuel. It was poor old Giles Habibula."

"How did you find it?"

"Poor old Giles had started to seek wine with which to pull the fearful fangs of death. But, beneath this mortal green sky, his aged spirit, weak and feeble as it is, rebelled against extinction. Ah, so! His precious genius awoke to the shocking touch of peril, and refused to be destroyed. It recalled Jay's theory that the owners of the asteroid must have hidden their fuel away against space pirates. It recalled the nature of that other genius who built this place.

"Ah, and it set his old finger on the hidden fuel!"

They were crossing the rocket field. The old man's fat arm pointed toward the switch-box, built in the wall of the white house, which controlled the flood-lights.

"I simply walked to that box, lad, and opened it. There is a deftness that lingers in my old hands, lad. I found the secret of the box, that would have evaded any other. And there's the fuel!"

They came around the green-bathed hull of the *Halcyon Bird*. Beyond, not a dozen yards from her air-lock, a little cylindrical metal house had risen through the gravel. Hal Samdu was rolling black drums of rocket fuel from the door of it.

Bob Star ran to aid him. No more than two hours later, Bob Star, with the commander and Kay Nymidee, climbed to the bridge of the *Halcyon Bird*. Urgently, the girl pointed through an observation port at the indigo disk of the master planet.

"*Aythrin!*" her soft voice cried eagerly. "Staven Or-rco! We go?"

The commander turned to Bob Star. "Can we make it?"

"We can try."

His fingers touched the firing keys. Blue jets washed the gravel field, and roared against the white columns of the deserted mansion. The *Halcyon Bird* was alive again, and away into the green chasm of the comet. The asteroid fell behind them, to dwindle and vanish against the ominous face of the purple sun.

Bob Star felt a pang of regret at its destruction. For it was in the cradle of its haunting, exotic beauty that he had come to know Kay Nymidee. His love for her had spread, somehow, to its laughing groves and the wild splendor of its lichen-painted rocks and the peace of the long white house above the smiling lake.

He thought unhappily that now its mystery could never be solved. After days of effort, Jay Kalam had confessed that he had failed to decipher the book that seemed to be a diary. The anonymity of its writer was now forever secure. The purpose of that hidden laboratory, the meaning of the looped cross of life above the crossed bones of death, the possible connection between the asteroid and Stephen Orco—those riddles were beyond answer now.

"Have we fuel enough," the commander was asking, "to reach the master planet?"

"The tanks aren't half full, but we had time to load no more." Bob Star was silent for a time, frowning as he read the calibrated screens and tapped out his calculations. "I believe we can do it—"

His voice caught as the telltales flashed and the gongs began to ring. Startled, he swung back to the instruments.

"The power beam—if that's what it is," he whispered huskily. "Between the planet and that atomic engine. It has caught us, with its own field of force. A danger I hadn't expected."

He paused to read the screens again, and swiftly calculated a new course for the ship.

"I think we can keep free, but this costs fuel." Checking his figures again, he shook his head and bit his lip. "I'm afraid we'll land a little too hard for comfort."

Stern-faced, abstracted, he turned again to screens and calculator, fighting a silent battle to conserve every precious drop of fuel.

In hours, perhaps the flight was long. But always it seemed to Bob Star that they had hardly left the asteroid before the *Halcyon Bird* was slanting down out of a pallidly green sky that swarmed with many-colored worlds, toward the dark, strangely level surface of the master planet.

That great world seemed a perfect sphere of indigo, unbroken by mountain or sea. It appeared absolutely featureless, save for the overwhelmingly colossal machines, red and mysterious beneath their pale domes of greenish radiance, that were scattered about it at distances of hundreds or thousands of miles.

As that dark, strangely forbidding surface expanded before them, Kay Nymidee pointed through an observation port at the looming bulk of one of those machines.

"Go—" she said eagerly, and groped for a word, "there!"

Bob Star nodded, and set the nose of the *Halcyon Bird* toward it. Then he looked doubtfully at a fuel gauge.

"I'll try," he whispered.

But the needles crept inexorably toward zero. The even drumming of the rockets was interrupted by a warning cough. He shook his head, and brought the *Halcyon Bird* to a jarring landing upon the strange flatness of the indigo world, with rockets dead before the ship was still.

"The tanks are empty," he muttered blankly. "The ship won't move again."

Kay Nymidee seized his shoulder, and pointed imploringly at the crimson cyclopean mass of the machine ahead, a bewildering and fantastic enigma of red metal, within its transparent shell of shimmering green.

"Sorry, Kay." He shook his head again. "We just couldn't make it."

The mute reproach in her brown eyes changed slowly to frightened dismay.

"Perhaps we can walk, if we aren't discovered," Jay Kalam suggested hopefully. "Kay seems determined to take us to the machine. And it doesn't look so far—"

"The distance is deceptive," Bob Star told him, "because of the vast size of the planet, and the remarkable clearness of the atmosphere, and the lack of any other object for comparison."

"How far is it?"

Bob Star looked at his instruments.

"According to my last observation," he said, at last, "that machine is about a hundred and twenty miles from us."

The hostile impact of an alien world struck the five with shocking violence when they left the air-lock of the useless *Halcyon Bird*. It was five hours later. They had spent the time in preparing to undertake a desperate march of more than a hundred miles. Bob Star and Hal Samdu were dragging two sledges improvised from metal doors torn from within the ship, packed with food, water, and weapons.

The runners sang musically across the flat infinity of the planet's surface. The puzzling substance of it was absolutely smooth, hard and slippery underfoot. Nowhere, so far as they could see, was it broken by any irregularity. At first they found walking difficult; Giles Habibula fell sprawling twice. As a compensatory advantage, however, the sledges, once started, glided along with little effort.

"A whole world, armored?" marveled Bob Star. "Is it metal?"

"It isn't metal." Jay Kalam shook his head. "I took time to examine it, after I finished those atmospheric tests—though I still don't know what it is." He shrugged uneasily. "Something harder than diamond and tougher than steel. Acids don't affect it. It neither absorbs nor radiates heat. Perhaps it isn't actually matter at all, but another stable energy-field, more or less like that green barrier."

Surprisingly, his tests had found a breatheable atmosphere. A rich oxygen content made up for the low barometric pressure. The surface gravitation, Bob Star had reported, was slightly less than Earth-standard. Since the planet had four times the diameter of Earth, that meant that its relative density must be extremely low.

At a little distance from the *Halcyon Bird*, Jay Kalam paused, and they all looked back. The silvery cruiser lay small and lonely upon that blue, jewel-smooth plain. It was the only object upon the infinite world behind, a solitary gleam under the pale green sky.

Blue flame, as they looked, gushed suddenly from the gun turret. The bright hull glowed swiftly red, and flames exploded from the ports. The five went on, regretful, for it had been a faithful ship.

"They'll surely find the wreck," Jay Kalam said. "But I hope they'll think we died in it."

They plodded on, wearily dragging the sledges, toward the red riddle of that enormous machine, a hundred miles away. Bob Star's eyes rested on it, with an apathetic fascination. It stood on a square platform, which might be, he estimated, two miles high and ten in length. The machine towered above it, so immense that he dared not attempt to guess its height.

The blood-red stuff of it shone like metal. There was a lofty frame of colossal beams and girders. There were moving parts, so intricate, so strange, that he could readily find no name or explanation for them. In particular, his eye was caught by a vast, shimmering white object, shaped like a flattened orange, that moved irregularly up and down between two colossal plates of crimson. The whole was enclosed in a transparent greenish dome that seemed somehow akin to the sky.

Despair took hold of him.

"Against the scale of that machine," he muttered, "we're no more than five flies."

They plodded on. In the pellucid atmosphere, the machine always looked almost near enough to touch. And always it retreated mockingly at their weary efforts. At last, at the plaintive insistence of Giles Habibula, they halted. The *Halcyon Bird* was lost to view. They huddled in a lonely little circle by the sledges, on that shimmering vastness. They drank, ate sparingly, and tried to rest.

There was no wind. The cool air was oppressively still. The green sky did not change. There were no clouds.

"The planet doesn't rotate," Jay Kalam commented. "There is no weather, nor even any time. It is a world without change."

A terrible silence overhung them. Nothing lived or moved or gave voice upon all the empty plain. The green sky was equally devoid of life or motion. The cold disk of the purple sun hung steady, high above the straight horizon. They could see the glowing lines of the triple beam converging toward it. The multitudinous planets of the swarm stood motionless in the pale green void. They neither rotated nor changed position.

Giles Habibula wiped sweat from his yellow brow with the back of his hand.

"Ah, me!" he moaned. "A fearful world to die in! Upon one journey of forlorn hope, old Giles carried a bottle of wine through the mortal hardship of a continent larger than the precious Earth. But then he fought enemies he could understand. He never felt such need of the bright strength of wine." He fumbled in the packs on the sledges, and found a bottle of some rare vintage from the asteroid. Watching with a jealous eye, he offered it to each of the others in turn, and at last drained it gratefully.

Even Jay Kalam was worn to confessing despondency.

"It's true," he agreed bleakly, "that things were never quite so bad for us, not even on the Runaway Star. Though the things we fought then were able scientists and terrible foes, they were still defeated refugees from their own environment.

"But the Cometeers have conquered theirs. The creatures of the Runaway Star were things that we could sometimes kill, but the Cometeers aren't flesh." His thin lips set. "I doubt very much that any weapon men ever made could destroy one of them."

Startled, Hal Samdu peered at him. "Not even Aladoree's?"

He shook his head. "AKKA will destroy anything material—but I'm not certain that the Cometeers are material at all."

"Ah, so, Jay," croaked Giles Habibula. "Our plight is desperate. In seeking to balk the Cometeers and destroy Stephen Orco, we are no more than five ants making war on all the System—"

His voice wheezed into silence. His dull eyes, staring into the green sky, seemed to film. The breath went out of him.

"A good thing!" he gasped. "A good thing we drank the wine."

Bob Star saw a distant object, skimming swiftly toward them through the green. It came from the direction of the *Halcyon Bird*. Jay Kalam caught at Giles Habibula's arm as he started away.

"Don't run," he said. "There's nowhere to go. If we crouch down, perhaps they won't see us."

Bob Star was huddled beside Kay Nymidee. He caught her hand, and it closed upon his with a desperate pressure. Her face was drawn, white with strain. Her pale lips quivered. Overwhelming terror shuddered in her eyes. Pity for her stabbed him like a blade.

A nerve-severing sound tore him away from the girl. He jumped, startled, terrified. For a moment he could not identify the sound. Then he knew that it had been Giles Habibula's scream. Now the old man was trembling, sinking slowly backward upon his knees. His moon face was yellow-gray, contorted with dread. His small round eyes were fixed, glazed, bulging.

"What is it, Giles?"

"Mortal me!" the old man sobbed. "It's the fearful thing—or another like it—that ate Mark Lardo!"

Bob Star looked up then, and found the object he had glimpsed a moment ago in the far distance now already upon them. For the first time, his horror-filmed eyes rested upon one of the Cometeers.

It was hanging in the air, close beside them.

Floating low was a tiny star of red, veiled in a misty crimson moon. Ten feet above it hung a violet star, wrapped in a violet fog. The red seemed hot as the core of a sun, and the violet as cold as outermost space.

A mist swirled between the moons. There was life in its motion; it was like a throbbing artery of light. Red star and violet star beat like hearts of fire. Girdling the misty pillar was a wide green ring. It was the only part of the creature that looked at all substantial—and even it, Bob Star knew, could pass through the hard alloys of a space cruiser's hull.

His dazed mind first received the thing with startled incredulity. He blinked, and looked down at the dark plain, and rubbed his eyes. But the thing had not gone when he looked again. And its hideous reality ate into his mind, like a corrosive poison. He fought the queer, numbing horror that came flooding from it.

"Just colored lights," he muttered. "Moving mist. Shouldn't be afraid—"

But mind-killing dread swept into him. His numbed senses perceived a terrible entity within, beyond, those colored lights; an alien mind supernally powerful and completely evil. Every atom of his body reacted to it with automatic, shocked revulsion.

And the incessant beat of that old, strange pain, behind the triangular scar of the Iron Confessor, was suddenly redoubled. Every throb of it became a sickening, staggering blow against the naked tissues of his brain.

He braced himself against fear and pain. Swiftly, half-unconsciously, his fingers had been slipping fresh cells into his two proton pistols. The two weapons came up, now, together.

The emerald ring looked to be the most material part of the being. He pointed the guns at that, and pulled the firing levers all the way, to exhaust the cells in one single blast. Those two blinding swords of violet ruin would have cut through a solid foot of tempered steel. They would have electrocuted any living being—as the System knew life—at the distance of a mile.

But, like phantom swords, they flashed through the green ring, harmless.

Quivering to the shock of icy dismay, Bob Star recalled Jay Kalam's opinion that no human weapon could injure the Cometeers.

"Kay—" despair rasped from his leathery throat, "Kay—"

His voice stopped, as if to the touch of death. For out of the pillar of swirling light another voice had spoken, whose careless, mocking levity was the most appalling thing Bob Star had ever heard.

"That's rather useless, Bob." It was the voice of Stephen Orco.

Bob Star staggered backward. That light, ringing voice was more terrible than all the shining horror in the air.

"You had your chance, Bob," said the voice. "When I was in prison on Neptune, you had only to touch a little red button. But you failed. I'm afraid you'll never succeed. For now, Bob, I've a body that cannot be destroyed."

"You—" dread drew his tone to a quivering edge. "You're—*that?*"

"I am what you see, Bob. One of the drivers of the comet."

A low, mocking chuckle rang inside the shining being. There was a little silence, and then the clear voice spoke again:

"Perhaps, Bob," it suggested lightly, "you would be glad

to hear of your mother? It must be some time since you left her."

Bob Star leaned forward, sick and trembling. A gloating satisfaction in that careless voice cleft his spine like a cold axe. Hoarsely, through stiff, unwilling lips, he forced the whisper: "What about her?"

"I was alarmed for your mother, Bob," the liquid mockery of Stephen Orco's voice flowed on. "For she has been lost. My new associates searched the System for her, in vain. I was somewhat worried, for her life is the only barrier before me, now.

"But her capture has just been reported to me. It appears that your father, on his *Phantom Star,* was taking her away from the System, toward the star 61 Cygni. My associates have overtaken them. And I hope soon, Bob, to meet your mother, here within the comet."

15

The Cattle and the Herdsmen

Bob Star woke from a singular dream.

In the dream he had thought that his body had been exchanged for the shining form of one of the Cometeers. And this bodiless entity, himself, was flying through the green vacancy of the comet's interior. Ahead of him, fleeing in a similar shining guise, was Stephen Orco.

This Stephen Orco, of the dream, was carrying away a woman. He was going to consume her, in some dreadful way. Only a shrunken husk would be left, bleached, wrinkled, hideous. And even the whimpering husk would die, and crumble to iridescent ash and fluid. Sometimes the woman was his mother, and sometimes she was golden-eyed Kay Nymidee.

Somehow, even in his bodiless form, Bob Star carried a weapon. He had no picture of its shape, but it was something that could destroy Stephen Orco, and save the changing woman. But a terrible fear was beating him down, out of the green abysm. His shining shape was reeling under the incessant blows of a great red hammer of pain. Stephen Orco's voice was shouting furiously at him, turned to agony by the cruel mechanism of the Iron Confessor:

"You can't! You can't kill anybody!"

He woke, and knew that it was the low, anxious voice of Kay Nymidee that had roused him.

"Sa daspete!" she was urging. "Sa daspete!"

He was lying down, with his head on her knees. Her hands were cool on his forehead, and they seemed to soothe the old pain behind the scar. He looked up to find her anxious face oddly blurred and strange beneath pale green light. He tried to rise, and discovered the numbness of his body. Hideous as his dream had been, recollection came back. Ringing in his brain, he heard again the lightly mocking voice of Stephen Orco:

"I'm not going to hasten your destruction, Bob. A ship has been ordered here, to pick up you and your companions. You will be taken, along with a load of the prisoners from Pluto, down into this fortress of my new companions. And ultimately—"

A chuckle had come from that shining thing.

"Have you ever seen the way we feed, Bob?" that bright voice murmured. "Well, you're going to. But while you're waiting for that, there's something else I want you to think about.

"I can't be killed.

"You've already proved that, with your own guns. And it's no use clenching your fists and shaking your head —your face confesses your reluctant admiration of my new physical equipment. Certainly, it's admirable enough. Space is no barrier to me now, neither is any material wall. But its best feature is immortality.

"My new body is truly eternal, Bob. It has mass and potential energy. But its mass is in no form you know as matter, Bob, and its energy is beyond the comprehension of your physics. Not even your mother's weapon could destroy it.

"These deathless dwellings for intelligence are the supreme achievements of my new associates, Bob. You had not guessed that they were artificial? But the drivers of the comet once were beings of flesh. Not far different, perhaps, from mankind. But they became impatient with frailty, incapacity, death. They called upon their high science for a means of transferring their minds to eternal constructs of specialized energy.

"The Cometeers agreed to make me one of their number, to secure themselves from your mother's weapon—AKKA could destroy all their somewhat elaborate equipment and possessions of course, even though it could not directly annihilate their bodies.

"And now, Bob," the gay voice mocked him, "I shall be forced to leave you. Your parents, as I told you, are being brought into the comet. I must go to welcome your mother."

Stephen Orco chuckled at the mute agony twisting Bob Star's face.

"I wish to discuss with her the principle of AKKA. There are points not clear from my own research. And when our discussions are ended, Bob—

"If you wonder why we must feed the way we do—it's because even these indestructible devices of life are incomplete. They were designed to be eternal vehicles for intelligence, and they can preserve our minds forever, against all possible assaults. Yet their very perfection becomes almost a flaw.

"Because they aren't the bodies we used to own. Their senses are superior, but not the same. The mechanisms of emotion were largely omitted from their design, as useless heritages of the flesh. The consequent penalty we must pay for our undying perfection is a periodic hunger for the emotions and sensations we have lost.

"With their usual ingenuity, however, my new friends have found a way to satisfy that hunger. The vital energy of our immortal mechanisms requires occasional renewal, from the transmutation of ordinary matter. By taking that matter from bodies like those we used to own, in a way that stimulates the most intense emotion and sensation, we are able to satisfy both those recurrent appetites—the physical and the spiritual, so to speak—at the same time.

"Since our minds came from a number of vastly different races, we must each keep our own herds of the proper creatures. I am arranging to maintain a human colony, Bob—you and your companions will presently see the arrangements.

"I'm planning, however, to make my first meal upon your mother. I understand from my new friends that the close rapport of mind and emotion set up during the feeding process will enable me to pick her thoughts of all I want to know. And then——"

The shining thing chuckled softly.

"Have you seen what is left, after one of us has eaten, Bob? Can you see your mother, so? Small as a child, shriveled and colorless, whimpering for death? When you do see that, Bob, I've a question for you. I'm going to ask you if the nameless castaway of space hasn't matched the pampered darling of the Purple Hall."

The sardonic voice had faded then, as green mists thickened to veil the Cometeer. . . .

Bob Star moved uncertainly again, fighting the lingering stiffness of that paralysis, and Kay Nymidee helped him to sit up. Blinking to clear his eyes, he saw that heatless purple sun in the green sky again, and the slick blue flatness of the master planet. The two improvised sledges lay close beside him. Jay Kalam and Hal Samdu and Giles Habibula were unpacking them hastily, flinging aside the spare proton guns and extra cells they had carried.

"Ah, so," he heard Giles Habibula wheeze mournfully. "The monster ruined them, every one, the way that other did my precious geodynes aboard the *Halcyon Bird*." He saw Bob Star, and brightened. "Ah, lad, old Giles is glad to see you up again. We thought you would never wake——"

"There!" Hal Samdu was rumbling. "It must be the ship he said was coming for us."

Lurching stiffly to his feet, Bob Star peered into the green sky.

He saw a flying thing, slanting down toward them. It was a thick, horizontal saucer shape, red as that colossal machine standing above the blue horizon. Its upper face formed a deck, which ringed a low red dome. It came with no roar of rockets, nor any visible means of propulsion.

Bob Star caught apprehensively at Jay Kalam's arm.

"What——" he whispered hoarsely, "what can we do?"

"Nothing, but try to preserve our lives," said the weary-voiced commander. "And watch for some chance—some miracle of fate—for so long as we live——"

The red disk came down gently, at some little distance. The deceptive conditions made distance and size difficult to estimate, but it suddenly looked much larger than Bob Star had first supposed it.

The clang of some metal thing—perhaps the cover of a hatch—jarred Bob Star, even in his hopeless apathy. He heard raucous hoots, and answering reverberations that were like the booming of great drums. These were the same uncanny sounds, he realized, that he had heard from the invisible ship which carried Stephen Orco away from Neptune. A great, square opening gaped suddenly back in the crimson side of the disk. A square door had fallen outward, to form an inclined gangway. Marching down that incline came monstrous things.

No longer—despite the unsolved enigma of Kay Nymidee's humanity—did Bob Star expect to find beings like men within the comet. Yet he was not prepared for the mind-shaking impact of the things that came down the gangway.

There were eight, of three different sorts.

The foremost was a ten-foot sphere of some silvery metal, surrounded with a dark equatorial band. At first Bob Star thought that it was rolling; then he saw that only the band turned, sliding about the globe. Each pole was a dark, glittering bulge that looked like a faceted eye. About each bulge were spaced three long, gleaming metallic tentacles, now coiled close to the hemispheres.

The two creatures behind were slender cones in shape, nearly twenty feet tall. They were bright green; their skins had an oily luster. Their bases, apparently, were elastic, inflated membranes, expanded to hemispheres, upon which they bounded forward with a curious, astounding agility. The slender upper parts of the cones were flexible necks. The dark, pointed organs that tipped them turned this way and that, like singular heads. Green cones bouncing upon pneumatic cushions—they looked like grotesque nursery toys, but there was nothing toy-like about their air of deadly purpose.

The remaining five were slender tripedal giants. Their lean bodies, vaguely suggestive of the human, stood perhaps fifteen feet tall. They were covered with a dully glistening, dark-red armor, like the chitin of gigantic insects. Each had six slender upper limbs, forming a kind of fringe about a cluster of stalked organs, where the head should have been. They carried a kind of harness slung with a variety of curious implements or weapons.

"Mortal me!" gasped Giles Habibula. "Are these fearful things the lords of the comet? And not the shining monsters?"

"I don't think so." The commander stood gravely watching their approach. "I imagine these are the slaves of the

Cometeers. Herdsmen, perhaps, of the things they breed for food—"

He fell abruptly silent.

The white sphere turned a little aside, a few yards away. It halted, resting on the dark belt. Hoarse, raucous hoots came from it—like commands. The green cones answered, with dull booming reverberations that seemed to come from their inflated pedal membranes. The scarlet, three-legged creatures made no sound. But they came on with the cones, spreading out as if to encircle the five by the sledges. Bob Star broke at last out of his trance of horror, reaching automatically for his proton guns.

"Wait, Bob," Jay Kalam muttered wearily. "Our weapons have all been ruined. We can't resist—"

"But, Jay—" protested Hal Samdu, "we can't give up—without a fight!"

"We must," Jay Kalam insisted quietly. "We must preserve our lives, and hope for some opportunity—"

The giant made a mute, hurt sound.

"Surrender?" he rumbled incredulously. "Legionnaires don't surrender!" Catching up a dead proton pistol, like a club, he strode out to meet the nearest bounding green cone. "We can't give up," his voice came back. "Not with Aladoree still in danger—"

Kay Nymidee ran after him, as if to catch his arm, calling urgently.

"Pahratee!"

She was too late. The thin, flexible upright tip of the green cone whipped over toward him. From the dark, tapered organ at the tip of it, which was like a pointed head, there flashed a thin and blinding ray of orange light.

Hal Samdu crumpled down, groaning with helpless agony.

"We can't resist," Jay Kalam repeated hopelessly. "Help me carry him, Bob. We'll go aboard—if that's what they want. There's nothing—"

His quiet voice broke off, with a breathless exclamation. And Bob Star was amazed when he turned and spoke to Kay Nymidee, with strange words as soft and liquid-toned as her own.

The prison-hold filled nearly all the lowest level of the disk-ship. The vast circle of it, some five hundred feet across, was broken only by a doorless wall, perhaps enclosing the engine rooms, which shut off a part of the center. There were no ports, and the only light was a dim red glare reflected from the high metal ceiling. The ventilation was bad, sanitary conveniences were few, and the hold reeked with the odors of its occupants.

The entrance was a massive grille of red metal bars, at the top of a long ramp. One of the white spheres remained on guard beyond the grille, but none of the cometary beings came into the hold.

The five new prisoners were pushed through the door, and left upon the ramp. Examining Hal Samdu, who was still unable to speak or to sit up, Bob Star and Giles Habibula found a small, circular inflamed patch on his temple.

Bob Star and Jay Kalam had attempted to carry him as they came aboard, but one of the thin red giants had taken the limp body from them, in its fringe of clustered arms. And they had meekly followed.

The miserable thousands imprisoned in the hold were mostly sitting or lying on the bare metal floor. They were clad in haphazard fragments of clothing; only a few had odd little bundles of their possessions. Their unwashed faces were haggard with fatigue and despair, and the sound that rose up from all of them was a weary murmur of hopeless apathy, without any light or laughter.

On the ramp, Bob Star was accosted by a gaunt, gray-faced man who had been stalking like a tired specter, across the great floor, stepping over recumbent bodies to look at the face of every slumbering or weeping child.

"Have you seen my son?" the weary stranger rasped. "A blue-eyed lad, with curly yellow hair. His name is John—after the great John Star. Have you seen him?"

Bob Star shook his head, and saw hope extinguished by despair.

"Where do you come from?" he asked.

"From Pluto." The blood-shot eyes looked at him with a dull curiosity. "My name is Hector Valdin. I was a worker in the platinum mines of Votanga." His gnarled hands made a heavy gesture. "These people—they were my friends and neighbors there. But now—"

"What brought you here?"

"Don't you know?" The gaunt man peered at him. "Well, they say something happened to all the Legion bases. I met a man who saw the end of Fort Votanga. The batteries began to fire—and stopped. A red light shone down on the walls—and they crumbled away. There was only a great pit left."

The weary man shrugged vaguely.

"I don't know what that was. But a green thing began growing in the sky. It was a comet, men said. And Pluto was being dragged inside it, somehow. I don't know—"

His teeth ground together in sudden, savage pain.

"But then these monsters came. They burned our houses, to drive out our women and children, so that they could catch them. They're taking us somewhere. I don't know where. But my son John is lost." The red eyes came pleadingly back to Bob Star's face. "You haven't seen a little blue-eyed lad—"

So this, Bob Star thought bitterly, was to be the fate of all humanity.

"Do the creatures ever come in here?" His question came of some vague and hopeless impulse toward escape. "Do they ever open that door?"

"They never come among us." Hector Valdin shook his head. "The door hasn't been opened since we were herded into the vessel—save to admit you."

"How do they clean the floor and feed the prisoners?"

"They don't clean the floor," Hector Valdin said. "And the only food they give us is a sour slop that runs into troughs by the wall."

The hopeless eyes searched Bob Star again with a weary wonderment.

"Where was your home?" he asked. "I think I never saw you in Votanga."

Bob Star had looked away from him, across the hopeless murmuring misery of the thousands sitting and lying on the floor, and then back at the massive locked grating at the top of the ramp.

"It doesn't matter, if you don't feel like talking." Hector Valdin shrugged. "Most of us are still too dazed to know just what happened." He straightened wearily. "Anyhow, friend, I must go on now, to look for my son John—"

A sudden blue light had come into Bob Star's eyes. And a smile had come over his thin face, a hard and dangerous smile.

"Wait, Hector Valdin!" His voice had a bright and eager ring. "I'll tell you who we are, and how we came to be here."

"Never mind," the gaunt man muttered. "It doesn't really matter. I must find John—"

"Wait!" Bob Star called urgently. "If you honor the name of John Star—"

And Hector Valdin came back, with a little of the leaden

apathy already lifted from his face. And others, near at hand, gathered around them to listen. For Bob Star's voice rang strong with an urgent, compelling eagerness. And he spoke magic names, from the glorious history of man.

". . . Jay Kalam, who is commander of the Legion . . . The big man, just sitting up, is Hal Samdu, who went with my father and the others out to the Runaway Star. . . . Giles Habibula—he can open the door, to let us out into the ship! . . . My mother, the keeper of the peace. She is a prisoner, now, about to be murdered. . . ."

Bob Star talked on. He groped for stirring words. He was a little surprised at the confidence, the ringing strength, in his voice. For in his heart he knew there was no hope. He knew they were all cattle for the Cometeers.

He knew that Stephen Orco could not be killed.

Yet soon many men were listening to him. A quick interest was penetrating the leaden despair upon their weary faces. And the bright finger of hope transfigured now one and now another—

16

John Star's Son

The first conversation of Jay Kalam and Kay Nymidee was curiously hard to interrupt. It had begun, out upon the jewel-smooth armor of the planet, when the girl called out for Hal Samdu to stop, and the surprised commander addressed her in her own language.

Even in the presence of their captors, her face shone with sudden delight. She ran joyously to the commander, and threw her slim arms about him. She lifted on tiptoe to kiss both his lean cheeks. Then, almost ignoring the creatures herding them into the ship, she was talking at him furiously. And Jay Kalam replied, awkwardly, haltingly, but as if he understood.

They scarcely paused when their captors pushed them down into the prison-hold, and locked the massive grate behind them. On the ramp inside, they kept on talking. Kay Nymidee spoke very fast. Her white face showed a great play of expression, smiling with joy, frowning with the effort of making her meaning clear; it was bright with hope, shadowed again with apprehension.

Jay Kalam's dark face, in contrast, was intently fixed. For the most part he merely listened, his dark brow furrowed with the effort of comprehension. But frequently he broke in, to beg the girl to repeat, or to ask some halting question.

Bob Star came to them more than once, and went away again when they gave him no attention. Men were following him, now, led by words like golden banners blowing. That still amazed him, for he was only a boy, afraid, half-disabled from a strange and ancient injury. But they did, and he went on, rejoicing in the magic of those words.

Kay Nymidee came running to him at last. She called something and seemed hurt again because he didn't understand.

"She's asking," Jay Kalam said, "if you know Spanish."

"Spanish?"

"Yes. That's her language."

"Spanish? How does she know Spanish?" He was bewildered. "Isn't she a native of the comet?"

"Kay is," the commander said. "But her race isn't. I told you how improbable—"

"How does that happen? How did her people get into the comet?"

"An odd story." Jay Kalam stroked at the dark angle of his jaw. "But credible enough, with what we know of the Cometeers. The bare facts are all she has been able to tell me. Kay's Spanish, you see, and mine are almost two different languages. Mine is due to an interest in the plays of Lope de Vega, who wrote fourteen hundred years ago. Hers is the Spanish of a thousand years later, still further changed by four hundred years of adaptation to an alien environment. Her accent is so unfamiliar that it is the merest accident that I recognized her tongue at all —when she told Hal Samdu to stop. And her scientific words, of course, are nearly all totally unfamiliar. That makes her message peculiarly difficult to understand."

"Four hundred years?" Bob Star gaped at him. "Have the Cometeers been here before?"

Jay Kalam shook his head, explaining:

"You may recall, Bob, from your history books, that during the latter part of the twenty-sixth century the Andean Republic passed through a brief golden age. For a few years, in science and nearly all the arts, as well as in wealth and military power, it was the leading nation of Earth.

"The climax of that splendid era was the *Conquistador* expedition. In the greatest geodesic cruiser that had ever been built, a hundred men and women left Santiago upon what was planned to be the System's greatest voyage of science and exploration.

"The *Conquistador* never returned.

"The hundred had been the intellectual flower of the republic. Their loss may have been the blow that broke the golden age, because the northern lands soon resumed their supremacy, and Spanish is now almost a dead language."

"The *Conquistador*—?"

"It was captured by the Cometeers," Jay Kalam said. "Apparently their ships were continually sent ahead, at velocities far beyond the speed of light, on scouting expeditions—I suppose in search of planetary systems worth raiding.

"Such an invisible scout met the *Conquistador*, somewhere beyond Pluto. Her entire crew was carried back to the comet, which was then some hundreds of light-years away.

"Many of the prisoners were kept alive, and eventually a few of them escaped. Aided by other enslaved beings, they got away from the master planet, in a captured ship, and reached one of the outlying planets of the cluster.

"For two generations they existed as miserable fugitives, until the survivors found their way into a great cavern, where they weren't immediately discovered. They had learned the plans of the Cometeers and they determined to warn and aid the System. Kay Nymidee is their daughter —after four hundred years.

"They made scientific progress. The projector that brought Kay to the asteroid is their most brilliant achievement. I don't entirely understand her explanation, but apparently it operates by warping space-time to bring two remote points so close together that light—or even, finally, a material body—can cross the gap.

"The machine, anyhow, was developed by Kay's father. And he had been using it to send Kay into the secret places of the Cometeers, after their secrets. They detected it when she was trying to warn you, on Neptune. They

301

raided the cavern. Kay is the only one who escaped. At the last moment, her father used the machine to send her to you, upon the asteroid."

Bob Star caught eagerly at his arm.

"What has she been trying to tell us?" he gasped abruptly. "About Stephen Orco and the Cometeers?"

"The Cometeers can be destroyed," Jay Kalam said. "But Kay doesn't know how. She knows only that the means exist. She says the Cometeers are ordinarily immortal. But their rulers possess some secret agency that can destroy them—something invented by the ancient designers of their artificial bodies. She has no idea what it is, but she does know where the secret is kept."

"Where?"

"In a fortress deep inside this planet—you remember Kay's drawing?"

Breathless and trembling, Bob Star nodded.

"Well, this planet is a world truly dead—cold to the center. It is honeycombed with cavernous hollows, as we might have suspected from its low mean density. The chief stronghold of the Cometeers, where they guard that secret, is down somewhere near the center of the planet. Kay has been trying to guide us to it."

Bob Star stood frowning at the grave commander, his brief hope already crumbling.

"The information is very useful now!" he muttered bitterly. "When we are prisoners, unarmed and condemned! When the weapon that can kill Stephen Orco is hidden in the middle of an armored planet, fifteen thousand miles beneath us, and guarded with all the science of the Cometeers!"

Bob Star was never satisfied with his part in the rebellion of the prisoners. True, the plan of action—if anything so vague, so wild, so desperately hopeless could be called a plan—was his. And it was he, at last, who led the rush from the hold.

But those five mad seconds never contented him.

Hector Valdin had gone with him through the weary apathy of the prison-hold. He had introduced Bob Star to his fellow miners, his old neighbors, simply as John Star's son. And Bob Star had touched them with the greatness of the System, the old glory of mankind. He stirred them with the great names of John Star and Commander Kalam; of Hal Samdu and Giles Habibula; of Aladoree, the beloved keeper of the peace. They rose to follow the bugle of those names.

And Bob Star had come at last to Giles Habibula, demanding: "Giles, can you open the door?"

"Why, lad?" The old man started. The yellow moon of his face went ashen. "In the precious name of life, why should I open the door?"

"Can you?" Bob insisted.

"That monstrous globe is watching," whispered the old man. "And there are fearful hordes above—"

"But you can?"

"Ah, the sad fate of genius!" He shook his head, dolefully. "Yes, lad, I can open the door. I watched the working of the lock as they let us in, and I've been looking at the thing for hours since, until I can see every part within the case. It's a combination affair, with disks and tumblers, worked by sliding rods. The design is good—though not good enough to baffle poor old Giles Habibula. But why—?"

Jay Kalam, with whom Bob Star had discussed the piece of reckless audacity he called a plan, said soberly: "Do it, Giles."

"Not yet!" The old man shuddered. "Not beneath the eye of that fearful globe—"

"We'll try to distract it," Bob Star promised.

He made a sign to the gaunt, gray-faced miner. Hector Valdin lunged toward Kay Nymidee, grasping for her, as they had planned. She screamed, stumbling toward Bob Star. Bob Star swung at his haggard ally. Others rushed to circle them. A noisy riot swept up and down the ramp.

Meanwhile, Giles Habibula crept trembling to the massive lock at the top of the ramp. Shouting, Jay Kalam was pushing his way toward the center of the milling throng. And gigantic Hal Samdu was fighting now, with a grim and silent earnestness, as if he forgot it was make-believe. And Giles Habibula came lumbering at last down the ramp, gasping for Bob Star. His face was yellow-green, glistening with sweat.

"Lad!" he wheezed. "Lad, the door is unlocked. You may go through, if you are such a fool—"

Bob Star led the cheering mob up the ramp. He reached the massive red grating, and his clear voice called a ringing command. Magically, then, the mob became a terrible and desperate army. Hal Samdu and Hector Valdin helped him fling aside the unlocked grating. And he led the rush

303

upon the white sphere beyond, to pit bare human flesh against its metal might.

It was a mad thing; Jay Kalam had made him see that. These thousands behind him were weaponless, already once beaten. Even if they took the ship, they were far indeed from the well-guarded secret that could kill Stephen Orco.

But Bob Star led his crush of silent, empty-handed men against the metal sphere. They lifted it, and surged with it toward the red wall of the corridor. It was hooting a raucous alarm; and the white tentacles seized the bodies of men, to beat men down with living flails.

Others took the places of the fallen. Bob Star had made death itself a victory to the men behind him. And a supernal thing strode among the prisoners as they marched from the hold, something greater than any man. It was that intangible, ineffable power that touched a few beasts in the wilderness of early Earth, and created the unity that is mankind and the glory of the far-flung System.

It was that something, transfiguring human flesh, that smashed the hooting sphere against the red metal wall, again and again, until the faceted eyes were shattered, and its surface was crushed in, until the deadly tentacles were still and the hooting ceased—and then tore it into fragments, to make weapons.

That same power led the ragged horde down the corridor, to meet the guard: Another argent sphere, hooting hoarse commands. Three of the tall green cones, bouncing upon distended bases, booming their threats, flashing orange-red rays from their narrow, pointed heads. A full score of the red-armored, three-legged giants, with strange colors flashing from the stalked organs where their heads should have been, their tentacular limbs clutching golden weapons.

It was hopeless, as Jay Kalam had warned. It was useless, utter folly. . . .

But that supernal power would not be stopped. Bob Star led the way to meet that alien band, shouting, flourishing one of the tentacles of the dismembered globe, which had stiffened now into a silver spear. A great eager voice rolled up behind him.

That, for Bob Star, was the end of the battle.

He had flung his argent spear at one of the green, bounding cones. He saw it strike the oily, glistening skin, and sink deep. He plunged forward, to grasp it and strike again. But he saw the green neck flex, so the narrow head pointed at him; he saw the beginning of an orange flash.

Then a red and merciless spear of pain drove through the pale old scar on his forehead, and thrust deep into his brain. Red agony exploded through his skull, and faded slowly into darkness. Faintly, as his sick consciousness went out like a dying flame, he heard the thundering, triumphant shout:

"Take the ship!"

17

The Human Rocket

Bob Star woke once more from the same strange dream.

Again his body had been the shining, weightless body of one of the Cometeers. And again he was pursuing the eternal, supernal form of Stephen Orco, who fled with a woman—his mother, sometimes, and sometimes Kay Nymidee. Once more he had been crushed down by a great hammer of red pain, and overwhelmed by the old fear that yelled:

"You can't—You can't kill—"

His trembling hand was pressed against his forehead when he woke. There, above that old scar, the skin felt swollen and painful to his fingers—where that organic ray had struck him. The old agony still throbbed beneath it, as if the three-edged blade of the Iron Confessor still stabbed intermittently into his brain.

Awake, he still felt as strangely weightless as he had been in that dream. He found that he was floating in the air, and the lack of gravitation made him giddily uncomfortable. He had to swallow a sudden sense of panic, when he found no support beneath him. Groping desperately for something substantial, he looked around him blankly.

Around him were the hard blue walls of a shaft or pit, perhaps fifty feet square and a hundred deep—too large a chamber, he decided, to be part of the prison-ship. After a moment of twisting and peering, he discovered his old companions.

Giles Habibula was clinging to what seemed the bottom of the pit, where a circle of slender rods of red metal projected from the polished wall. His deft, sensitive fingers were sliding the rods in and out, twisting them; the yellow globe of his head was cocked as if to listen.

Jay Kalam and Kay Nymidee were near him, equally weightless, busy with some unfamiliar instrument. From a rectangular case of red metal they were taking wires and coils and odd-looking parts of scarlet metal, and little round black cells.

It took him a moment longer to locate Hal Samdu. Bruised somewhat, covered with bloodstained bandages, the giant was clinging to the edge of the pit, peering out as if on guard. One great hand clutched a long rod of yellow metal—a weapon, Bob Star knew, that must have been taken from one of the lean, red-armored beings.

Beyond him, beyond the square mouth of the pit, yawned a dark, cavernous abysm. Far distant in it he could glimpse rugged walls of dark rock, and part of a machine that must have been fantastically huge, faintly illuminated with a ghastly crimson light.

A curious sickness came upon Bob Star as he tried to move, as if every tissue of his body clamored for the certainty and the orientation of weight. Yearning for something to cling to, he floundered about in the air until his foot kicked the wall.

The action had surprising results. It sent him hurtling, head foremost, across the fifty feet to the opposite wall. Dismayed, he flung out his arms to fend for his head. The undue force of the gesture sent him spinning back across the pit. Giles Habibula reached away from the circle of rods to catch his ankle.

"Better cling to this bit of rail, lad," he advised absently. "Or you'll be smashing out your wits before you ever get them back. For we're almost at the center of this fearful planet, and nearly free of gravity. One step could carry you a mile—"

"At the center of the planet?" He shook himself dazedly. "Tell me, Giles—"

The old man had returned to his business of twisting and sliding the scarlet rods.

"Ah, lad," he wheezed, abstractedly, "you've been out for a mortal long time—the ray from that creature struck your old wound; I think it almost killed you."

306

"The ship?" Bob Star asked eagerly. "Did we take the ship?"

"Ah, so, we took the ship." He slid the rods in and out, listening with his ear against the case. "Thanks to the mad courage you had put into the prisoners, lad—they overwhelmed our guards like a wild sea. Aided, too, by the unrewarded genius of a poor old soldier in the Legion. And by the miner, Hector Valdin; he led them on—until he died."

The absent voice had faded, and Bob Star asked:

"If we're at the center of the planet, how did we get here?"

"We were already in the cavernous space outside when we took the ship," said Giles Habibula. "The core of the planet is a hive of the Cometeers and their cattle."

He shuddered, but oddly his thick fingers didn't seem to pause or tremble.

"When the ship was ours," he went on, "Jay and the lass took command. They had us disembark here, an hour ago. Our comrades went on with the ship, to seek some refuge in the caverns. Ever since, I've been toiling with this lock.

"It's nothing simple! The number of possible combinations would make your head spin, lad. To open it by trial and error would take from now until the sun grows cold. Ah, me! the Cometeers are clever—

"But the lass bade me open it, lad. She says their inner stronghold is somewhere beyond, where they guard the weapon that we must take."

Bob Star nodded—and bit his lip. "I'm sorry, if my talk has bothered you—"

"Not so, lad," protested the old man. "Talk but oils the working of my precious genius. But this lock is a fearful test for it. Never was such a riddle built into cold metal, lad. And never was old Giles so unfit to draw out the answer. For he's ill, lad. The stark hand of death is close upon him."

But his fingers didn't cease their labor. Bob Star glanced at Jay Kalam and Kay Nymidee, who still were busy over the intricate thing in the red metal case.

"What's that?"

"Some blessed contraption Jay tore out of the control room of the ship before we came off. From the wonderment on his face, I doubt that he knows himself what it is."

Bob Star was about to let go the rail he held, to try to reach them, when a sudden, unendurable sickness seized him. Here, near the planet's heart, he had no weight. Directions had no meaning. His surroundings had begun to spin, dizzily. At one moment, the blue shaft was horizontal. The next, it was an inverted pit, and he was clinging precariously to the roof of a vertiginous abyss.

Giles Habibula, beside him, was doubled up again, his moon face greenish, sweat-beaded.

"Jay!" he gasped hoarsely. "I'm sick—deathly ill! The wine we found on that asteroid—I think it was poisoned! I'm dying, Jay. Dying—"

"Not yet, Giles," Jay Kalam called. "We all feel upset, from being without weight. It is the same as the space-sickness they used to have on the old rocket fliers, before the invention of the gravity cell. Some people are almost immune, as I am. Others never become adjusted to it.

"Anyhow, Giles, you must open the lock. All we have done is useless, unless we get through this door."

"I can't do it, Jay!" The old man was swearing and panting. "I'm too mortal ill. The torture of a dying body destroys my concentration. For life's sake, Jay—"

"You must, Giles. For the keeper of the peace!"

Giles Habibula sighed, and bent again to his task.

"Ah," he sobbed, "genius draws a bitter lot—"

Kay Nymidee was still busy over the red metal case. Now Bob Star heard her utter a little cry of satisfaction. She held up a dark, opalescent prism, and swiftly explained something to Jay Kalam. He nodded gravely, and rapidly they began to reassemble the mysterious device.

A dull, coughing explosion drew Bob Star's eyes to the square mouth of the pit. Pale smoke had puffed from Hal Samdu's captured weapon. Beyond, he saw a white globe approaching. It came sailing through the air, black belt spinning, crystal eyes glittering, white tentacles sprawling. In the midst of his consternation, Bob Star found time to wonder briefly if it were all machine, or if it contained a living brain.

He heard its abrupt, hoarse hoot of alarm, close on the explosion. Hal Samdu fumbled a moment with the golden weapon. Then he hurled it spinning toward the silver globe, and came plunging down the shaft, to sprawl against the bottom of it.

"Aye, Jay!" he rumbled apprehensively. "We are discovered. A horde of the monsters coming. I destroyed one —but the golden gun would not work again—"

His voice stilled to a terrific vibration that thundered down the shaft. It was the clang of a huge gong, deep as the note of a hammered planet. And suddenly, beyond the silver sphere, an alien horde was following into the pit: huge green cones, and red, grotesque giants in golden harness. Another globe brought up the rear.

They were swimming through the air.

Bob Star shivered to the uproar: the raucous howling of the spheres, the deep, incessant drumming of the cones. And, above all, the thunder of the gong, like the sobbing in unison of all the bells ever cast, a soul-chilling throb of alarm.

"Hasten, Giles," urged Jay Kalam.

"Ah, Jay!" begged the old man, frantically. "Have mercy!"

"You must," the commander told him soberly. "Or we shall die."

And, as calmly as if he could not hear that hideous onslaught, Jay Kalam was still busy with the enigmatic mechanism in the long red case. Now he was fastening five wires to a binding post. Kay Nymidee, eagerly aiding him, twisted one of the wires around Giles Habibula's fat arm. She made each of the others hold the end of a wire.

The gong still thundered its warning. Bob Star watched the monstrous throng come down, until he could see the pattern of the tread on the black belts of the spheres, see the multiple heads of the silent giants.

"I had hoped," he heard Jay Kalam's calm voice, gravely regretful, "that they would follow the ship, and give us time—"

Hal Samdu rumbled imploringly: "Hurry, Giles!"

"In life's name," gasped Giles Habibula. "When I'm already dying—"

The foremost silver sphere was now close upon them. Its white tentacles whipped out toward Kay Nymidee. Bob Star set himself to leap at it in futile, bare-handed desperation.

"Wait!" breathed Jay Kalam.

He made some quick, final adjustment within the rectangular red case. A faint, momentary humming came from it, low at first, running up the scale of sound until it became ear-piercingly shrill, then inaudible. And it seemed to Bob Star that the light abruptly changed, as if a shadow had flickered across them. The nightmare throng was indefinably distorted; it appeared somehow withdrawn, as if seen through an inexplicable veil.

Besides that, he sensed nothing. But the white sphere jerked back its grasping tentacles. The alien horde was abruptly silent, as if with consternation. Monstrous things rebounded from the walls, retreating.

Beside him, Giles Habibula sighed deeply.

"Ah, me," he gasped, with a vast relief. "It's done!"

Wearily, he wiped his pale yellow face with the back of his hand. And Bob Star perceived that the entire bottom of the shaft had begun slipping away, like an enormously massive sliding door. A dark slit appeared at one side of the shaft, and widened. And presently they were looking down a great, square well, walled with jewel-smooth indigo, into another world, where a small green sun was shining, cold and dim.

Jay Kalam was the first to speak, his voice faint with awe.

"So this," he said, "is the hidden fortress of the Cometeers."

Bob Star was amazed at the extent of the space beyond that mighty door. When they had pushed themselves through the shaft, and Giles Habibula had touched something that closed the vast barrier behind them, they all paused in a shuddering astonishment.

Bob Star's sense of directions had changed again, and it now seemed that this vast, dimly lit void was above them. It must have been fifty miles in diameter, he thought —perhaps five hundred. It was roughly spherical. The walls of it were partly wild cliffs of natural rock. And partly they were tremendous flat surfaces of that hard blue armor.

Machines loomed far away, in that twilit vastness, larger than any he had seen on the surface of the planet. They must be the engines, he thought, that ran upon the power of that captive sun to drive the clustered worlds of the comet like a ship. He felt that he could almost sense that flow of illimitable energy, and it gave him a sense of crushed futility.

It made him ill again. Suddenly he was clinging like a fly to the roof of this hollow world, and sick with the invincible fear that he was falling into the cold green sun at the center of it. Then the green globe and the dim,

310

cyclopean machines began to spin over and under him, over and under, until he shut his eyes, retching.

Faintly, he heard Kay Nymidee speaking, with awe and terror in her nervous voice, and the elation of a desperate daring.

"Kay says the weapon we seek is locked in the green sphere," Jay Kalam interpreted. "Two of the Cometeers, she says, are always stationed outside of it, on watch. Even those guards can't enter the sphere itself, for the metal of it is impregnated with forces that form a barrier to the energy-fields of their bodies. Only a few of the rulers of the comet are able to pass that barrier.

"Kay and her father studied it with their projector, she says. But they were never able to penetrate the barrier. Kay doesn't know how to enter, or what may be within."

Nauseated, trembling, Bob Star forced his eyes open. He peered uneasily at Kay Nymidee and the others—he dared not look again into that giddy void. Jay Kalam was gravely alert. Hal Samdu seemed grimly belligerent, but Giles Habibula was still greenishly ill.

"We must lose no time," Jay Kalam went on decisively. "The slaves are bewildered for the moment. But they saw the door open, and they'll report what happened. The Cometeers themselves won't be so easy to confuse. Somehow, we must reach the green globe."

Bob Star stole an apprehensive glance at it—a small, dim green sun, far out in that sickening chasm of spinning emptiness.

"How can we get there?" he whispered. "It's miles and miles away—and floating free—"

"Not floating," Jay Kalam said. "It must be suspended by those tubular fields. But still," he admitted, "there's nothing we can climb."

"Then," Bob Star whispered hopelessly, "how—?"

The commander said quietly, "We can jump."

Bob Star gaped. "Jump?"

"Certainly. There's no gravitation here to stop us. If we don't miss the globe, and go sailing on beyond—"

Instinctively, Bob Star's hands clutched at the railing beside the great door. Even the idea of a plunging fall through that directionless pit made him sick again. But Jay Kalam made them all crouch in a little circle upon the jewel-hard surface of the mighty door, holding hands. He had fastened the red, rectangular metal case to his belt; they all clung to the wires that ran from it.

"When I give the word," he said, "we all jump toward the green sphere."

To Bob Star, it began to spin again, over and under him. It took all his will to keep his eyes upon it. Dimly, he heard the commander counting. He heard the quiet, "Now!" He leapt, with all his strength, into that dizzy gulf.

For a moment he was too ill to be aware of anything. Then he knew that they were all clinging together, a helpless little huddle of flying figures, drifting through the confused vastness of a hollow world. The green sphere seemed a very tiny and distant goal. And they were quite helpless now to stop or turn.

"I'm afraid," said Jay Kalam, "that we're going to one side."

It was very strange, to Bob Star, to hear that voice, as always cool and grave and perfectly modulated. A frightened whisper, a choking gasp, a scream, would have been in better keeping with the nightmarish horror of that flight. For the small green sun was whirling over and under them again. All meaning and direction had vanished from the vastness of that dim cavern. His sickness came back, made intolerable by the lack of anything substantial to cling to. He compressed his lips in silent agony.

"The damned Cometeers—these on guard?" he heard Hal Samdu's booming question. "Won't they see us?"

"Not so long as we hold these wires," Jay Kalam answered. "Though, of course, it's possible they may detect us with other senses than sight."

Fighting his sickness, Bob Star looked along the glistening red wire that he grasped, to the instrument at Jay Kalam's belt.

"We aren't—?" he gasped. "We aren't—invisible?"

Sitting in empty space as calmly as if he rested in a chair, the commander nodded soberly.

"Kay and I took the invisibility mechanism out of the captured ship," he said. "In my haste to remove it, I got it out of adjustment. We had some difficulty in discovering the principle of it, so that we could repair it—our success is due to Kay.

"It seems to create a special sort of energy-field around objects electrically connected with it," he explained. "Light rays striking on side of the field are absorbed, and instantly reradiated from the other—as if they had gone straight through."

"Then how can we see?" Bob Star asked. "If there's no light inside?"

"That field, Kay says, has another effect. It absorbs other vibrations—apparently from the infrared end of the spectrum—and reradiates them as visible light, here inside the field, for the convenience of the user."

"That's one danger," the commander added softly. "Though those slaves couldn't see us, Kay believes that the Cometeers themselves are sensitive to the infrared. If so, they will be able to see a shadow where we are—"

Another wave of illness swept away Bob Star's attention. During that fall—for to him it was a fall, through the giddy pit of some strange hell—time lost its meaning. He settled into a passive, agonized endurance. By turns, he opened and closed his eyes. He watched the dizzy spinning of that remote green sun, amid the monstrous mechanisms that drove the comet. He closed his eyes, and hung bathed in the silent eternal thunder of their power. And his illness did not cease.

With one hand he clung to Giles Habibula, who was still sick, green-faced and groaning. And he gripped the hand of Kay Nymidee. She was silent and pale, but sometimes, when he could see her face, she smiled a little. Time had seemed suspended. But at last Bob Star realized that the cold green ball was drawing near, but somewhat to one side. Jay Kalam was saying:

"Yes, we're about to miss it."

"Ah, so," sighed Giles Habibula. "And it's my fault, Jay. I was too slow, when we jumped. Too weak with this mortal illness. I dragged you all aside—"

Bob Star shut his eyes, sick with defeat.

"Flying on by," he muttered hopelessly. "With no way to turn."

He was amazed to hear Jay Kalam saying, "But there is a way—at the cost of one of us."

He whispered, "How?"

"One of us," the commander answered, "must turn loose and kick away, so that the reaction will push us toward the globe. We are flying like a ship in space—and one of us must be the rocket."

"That would work!" Bob Star exclaimed eagerly. Then dismay choked his voice to a whisper. "But he would have to let go the wire, and leave the field. He would be visible again. And the Cometeers—"

"Aye, Jay," Hal Samdu was rumbling, "just tell me what to do."

"No," Bob Star protested quickly. "I'll be the one—"

"Bob," said the commander, quickly, "you must stay with us."

He gave Hal Samdu brief directions. And the giant crouched against the huddle of their drifting bodies, and then kicked powerfully away. His sprawling body spun away through dim emptiness. It seemed to flicker, oddly, as it passed the veil of invisibility. It grew small, hurtling away into the greenish twilight.

Giles Habibula was abruptly sobbing, noisily. For a moment Bob Star felt the salt sting of tears in his own eyes, and an ache in his throat. But then he saw the pale, green ball again, almost upon them. And he gasped hoarsely:

"Look—there!"

For he had seen one of the shining guardians of the globe. A magnet of living light, with the red star and the violet for poles and the misty spindle between them like the field of a magnet turned to animate flame. It was more than alive. It was wondrous and beautiful and infinitely dreadful.

They drifted close to it—and it paused abruptly in its slow flight about the sphere. Bob Star's breath stopped. His skin felt cold with a sudden sweat, and his body tensed uselessly. He hung helpless in the air; there was nothing he could reach and nothing he could do.

For an instant the creature stood still. The pulsation of the bright stars ceased. And the misty spindle seemed frozen into a pillar of greenish ice. Then burning life returned. The Cometeer darted away, in the direction Hal Samdu had gone.

"It was Hal that it saw," Jay Kalam whispered. "But it will soon be looking for us."

A moment later, they thudded against the cold, hard metal of the faintly glowing sphere. They crouched upon it, held by a slight attraction. More like an asteroid than the green sun it had first appeared to be, it was, Bob Star thought, perhaps half a mile in diameter.

Kay Nymidee was whispering swiftly to Jay Kalam.

"She says the weapon is inside," he interpreted quietly. "This ball is a kind of safe."

"Ah, so!" gasped Giles Habibula. "And what a safe!"

314

18

At the Empty Box

Every safe, Jay Kalam reasoned, must have a door. They searched, shuffling very carefully across the coldly glowing metal, walking by the aid of its slight gravitation. At last they came to a square, twenty-foot depression, surrounded by a low metal flange.

Giles Habibula scrambled down into the pit, and examined a triple circle of projecting metal rods.

"Ah, me!" he moaned with dismay. "If that last lock was difficult, this one is impossible. The masters of the comet couldn't open it themselves, with all their precious science, if ever they lost the combination. What a lock! You could try possible combinations at random till the universe runs down, and the odds are a million to one the door would still be closed."

His thick fingers, so uncannily sensitive, so amazingly deft, were already swiftly busy, sliding the rods in and out, twirling them. Intently he was listening, although Bob Star could hear not the faintest sound.

The others clung to the flange above him. Bob Star, at intervals, was still acutely ill. And momentarily he expected to see the dread, shining pillar of one of the Cometeers materialize beside him, perhaps to speak with the triumphant voice of Stephen Orco.

Urgently, Jay Kalam inquired at last, "Can't you do it, Giles!"

The old man looked up to wipe sweat from his sick yellow face with the back of his hand. He shook his head. "It's a fearful test of my genius, Jay. Never was such a lock built in the System. The emperors of the comet must not trust their own guards."

Wearily, he bent again.

"Opening locks," he muttered absently, "is largely a matter of point of view. To any of you, a lock is something to prevent the opening of a door—and it does prevent it. But old Giles sees a lock as a means of opening the door—and it is."

He groaned, and spat.

"Or at least," he amended, "it should be. But old Giles never met such a lock as this."

Kay Nymidee had seized Jay Kalam's arm, to whisper frantically.

"Hasten, Giles," he pleaded. "Kay says they'll surely find us soon. Our invisibility, remember, is a trick of their own. It can't baffle them long."

The old man looked up again, his small red eyes round with unexpected anger.

"For life's sake," he burst out, "have you no patience?

"Here is Giles Habibula, a feeble old soldier, faint and retching in his last illness, dying far from home. Ah, so, a dying man, taxing his genius to the last precious ounce, to solve a riddle that would baffle all the scientists and mathematicians and doddering philosophers in the System for the next thousand years!

"In the name of precious life, can't you let him work in peace, without screaming in his ear—"

"Forgive me, Giles," the commander begged hastily. "I'm sorry. Go on."

The old man shook his head, muttering, and bent again to the triple circle of projecting rods. His deft hands paused at last, and a faint vibration whispered through the faintly glowing metal. The floor of the pit began to slip aside, and Giles Habibula scrambled hastily for the flange at the edge.

"A desperate trial!" he gasped. "But the door is open—"

Bob Star crept forward to watch the widening slit, which revealed a deep, square well, walled with coldly shining metal. The way was open, to the weapon that could kill Stephen Orco! That triumphant thought swept him forward eagerly—and then halted him, with smashing agony.

For he couldn't kill Stephen Orco. He couldn't kill anybody. He had been trying to think that he was slowly conquering that crippling obsession—until the battle to take the prison-ship, when the organic ray from that cone-shaped creature stabbed into his head. But its merciless thrust had brought back all the torture of the Iron Confessor—he wondered dully now if that orange-colored ray had carried an ultrasonic component that acted on the same pain centers of the brain. Whatever the effect, it had speeded

316

the merciless beat of that old pain, and reinforced that imperative injunction.

He couldn't kill—

"Come on," Jay Kalam was urging. "We've no time to spare."

They pushed themselves into the square pit. Hundreds of feet they dropped, aided now by the feeble gravitation of the metal sphere, and struck another door, studded with three more circles of projecting rods.

"Another lock," muttered Giles Habibula. "But now I know the principle."

He touched something, and the first door closed ponderously behind them. He bent to the second lock.

"Never," he wheezed abstractedly, "was my genius so fearfully tried. And never fired by such dire emergency! Ah, me! this day will mark the death of Giles Habibula! This monstrous safe may well become his tomb."

The shining metal murmured again, and the enormous mass of the inner door slipped aside. They followed the square passage on beyond, into a small, square room which must have been near the center of the sphere. It was flooded with the greenish radiation of the walls, and the passage behind them was the only entrance.

The little chamber was empty, save for a massive, rectangular box of the scarlet metal, three feet long, fixed to the inner wall. Its sides were covered with intricate hieroglyphic designs in silver and black. Upon the top of it was another triple circle of projecting rods.

Moaning under his breath, Giles Habibula applied himself.

As the inner door, also, closed behind them, Bob Star clung to the glowing wall, regarding the box with a certain incredulous awe. Already he was a little disappointed. His vague expectations had included something more impressive than this red chest, so small that one man might almost have carried it.

"It's no use," he whispered. "No use!"

For what manner of weapon, hidden in so small a space, could defeat the tremendous science whose awe-compelling evidence had surrounded them so long?

He went cold and rigid with alarm when another vibration whispered through the palely shining metal. Kay Nymidee began to tremble. From her white, drawn lips came a strained, unconscious little cry.

317

"The outer door," Jay Kalam whispered. "They are coming."

"Ah!" gasped Giles Habibula. "Here! It's open!"

Bob Star sprang apprehensively to his side, to help throw back the lid of the scarlet box. He hardly knew what he had expected to find. He couldn't imagine what might destroy that shining thing which now held the mind of Stephen Orco. He peered anxiously into the box, and his jaw fell slack open upon a voiceless cry of dismay.

For it was empty.

For a moment he felt numb and faint with consternation. Intolerable vertigo came back. He was shaken with painful, futile retchings. The green walls of the small, square room spun about him. Quivering cold with sweat, he clung to the edge of the empty box.

"Jay, it's all in vain," he heard Giles Habibula's weary murmur. "There's nothing—" The old man's breath went out, with a hopeless sigh. "Ah, me!" he wheezed. "Never did fate perpetrate such a fearful jest!

"Never did men ever struggle so, for no reward at all." His bald head shook sadly. "We roved the frozen night of Neptune's polar desert to find a ship, and fought a mad cannibal for it. We voyaged the perilous wastes of space, until the shining monster met us. We dwelt amid the haunting horror of the asteroid, and entered the terror of the comet upon it. We plunged close to death in that atomic furnace. We took that ship when they tried to make cattle of us, and came fifteen thousand miles upon it, into the core of an armored planet. We worked locks that were fearful difficult, and made our bodies into a living ship of space—ah, poor Hal, who perished for us! Now old Giles Habibula has exhausted his precious well of genius, to break into the strongest safe in all the universe.

"But all in vain. The thing is empty—"

Sobs choked his voice.

Moved by a thought that the weapon might be really in the box, perhaps concealed by another invisibility-device, Bob Star groped for it hopefully. His searching fingers found only hard, bare metal. With a helpless shrug, he looked up at Jay Kalam and Kay Nymidee.

Ghostly white, the girl was staring down into the empty box. Her bloodless face had gone flaccid with despair. Her eyes were wide, dull with the death of hope. Her body looked limp, nerveless—he thought she would have fallen, had there been gravitation to make anything fall.

Jay Kalam was rigid and silent, ashen-faced. Though he somehow had kept his expression of grave composure, it had no meaning. His eyes were blank windows into vacant space, with no light in them. His lean, slender fingers were twisted together, with a mute agony.

The girl's dull eyes crossed Bob Star's, without warmth or recognition. She began talking as if to herself, in a dead, husky whisper. Jay Kalam interpreted her words, but it seemed to Bob Star that he did so like an automatic machine, without himself comprehending anything.

"I am the last of my people. For twelve generations we have dwelt inside the comet. We have survived through times when death would have been welcome, for one thing —to destroy the Cometeers before they could destroy mankind. My father lived and died for that, and all my people did. Now at last I thought we had a chance. But we have lost—"

His voice grew slow, and faded away, as if he had been a machine running down. Giles Habibula was still slumped over the empty box. He was weeping noisily, blowing his nose. His fat fingers were restlessly exploring the smooth red metal, in aimless search.

Straightening convulsively, Bob Sar whispered, "Can't we do—anything?"

Jay Kalam shook his head. His teeth had cut his lip, and his lean chin was bright with blood. The grave restraint of his face made a strange contrast with that scarlet stain. He shook his head and licked his lip, and seemed dully surprised at the taste of blood.

"We can only wait, now—for them—"

Dazed, hopeless, Bob Star stared vacantly into the empty box. They had failed, and they were doomed. The old pain beat stronger and faster against his brain. The ancient fear seized him; it would never die.

Sickness came back. He crumpled down beside moaning Giles Habibula, in trembling, agonized despair. He scarcely heard the remote whisper of the inner door, opening, but the dry and voiceless gasp of Kay Nymidee drew up his eyes.

He saw the Cometeers.

Two of them, dropping into that small green room. Out of the nearer pillar of bright mist came a low chuckle of careless triumph. It was the reckless laugh of a mocking

319

god. Listening dully in his apathy, Bob Star heard the familiar, ringing baritone of Stephen Orco:

"Greetings, Bob. Allow me to present my colleague, who is the nominal ruler of the comet."

The violet star dipped slightly, as if it had made a mocking bow.

With a certain dim, lethargic interest, Bob Star stared at the shining lord of the comet. It, he supposed, was responsible for the monstrous joke of the empty box. Were the Cometeers, he wondered, indeed completely invulnerable? Had this tremendous, guarded vault been but a fantastic hoax, designed to support the authority of this shining emperor?

"Your remarkable enterprise," the easy voice of Stephen Orco continued, "has alarmed my colleague, who is going to take steps for its immediate termination. I regret your untimely passing, Bob, but your outrageous indiscretions have made it impracticable for me to preserve your life any longer."

If the voice had gibbered or whispered or shrieked, Bob Star thought, the horror of it would have been easier to bear. For there was a dreadful discrepancy between the terrible burning wonder that spun before his eyes and that careless tone of laughing levity.

"Before you die, Bob, wouldn't you like to hear of your parents? They are quite near, you know—so near that your unfortunate companion, Hal Samdu, was brought upon his capture to their prison-ship. That is how I came to be aware of your extraordinary activities.

"Your mother, you will doubtless be relieved to know, is yet uninjured. But she has been displaying a foolish and useless reluctance to enter any discussion with me of the principles of AKKA—a reluctance which is soon to have a festive end. I had planned for you and your companions to be present at the banquet. But the impatience of my imperial colleague puts that out of the question."

There was a little pause, and Bob Star observed an anxious, restless movement of the misty pillar spinning within the thing that was master of the comet.

"It is a pleasure," resumed the brightly sardonic voice of Stephen Orco, "to be present at a crisis in universal history. And, as I interpret the somewhat apprehensive behavior of my colleague, as we entered, this is indeed a crisis. I believe that your audacious indiscretion in forcing your way into the chamber of generation is going to result

320

in an order for the immediate total extermination of mankind. A somewhat solemn occasion, don't you agree?"

An untroubled chuckle rang from that column of living light.

"Not that I'm going to feel any compunction about assisting with the execution—"

The bright shape of the ruler of the Cometeers had moved again, as if impatiently. A shadowy arm of that bright haze reached out—and Bob Star felt a tingling of his skin. A greenish mist began to blur his vision. This, he thought, was the ultimate moment.

"Wait, Orco!"

Dimly, through the sudden rushing in his deafened ears, Bob Star heard Jay Kalam's strained and husky voice.

"Wait—if you want to know how you can assist so calmly with the extermination of mankind. Because I can tell you why, Stephen Orco. I know who—what—you really are."

Bob Star was aware of reprieve. The tingling numbness receded from his limbs. He could see again, and the roaring faded from his ears. He heard the mocking challenge of Stephen Orco's voice:

"Well, Commander Kalam?"

Jay Kalam paused as if to choose his words, and spoke at last with a strangely cool deliberation.

"Stephen Orco," he said, "we first tried to enter the comet upon a small geodesic cruiser. A shining monster came aboard; it wrecked our generators and killed an old associate of yours, one Mark Lardo."

"I am aware of the incident—none better," Orco's voice cut in impatiently.

Listening, Bob Star wondered vaguely at the commander's purpose. He was fighting for time, obviously. Yet what, in this ultimate extremity of defeat, was the value of time? In a moment, however, his wonder was lost, in his consuming interest in Jay Kalam's revelation.

"We landed the wreck upon an uncharted transplutonian asteroid. It had been inhabited. Its people had been destroyed by the Cometeers. They left us a fascinating mystery. A thousand things told us that the owner of the asteroid had been an able scientist and a gifted artist. Everything on that tiny world proclaimed his genius—and his amazing wealth. It was hard for us to imagine why such a man should have hidden himself on that lonely rock, outside the System."

321

"But why is your problem of any interest to me?" inquired the voice from that shining thing.

"Because it explains your difference from other men," Jay Kalam said. "Your unusual gifts, your desire for superiority, your hostility to mankind."

"Go on," said Orco's voice. "But be quick."

And it seemed to Bob Star that the nearer shining thing made a restraining gesture, to halt some act of the ruler of the comet.

"One remarkable feature of the riddle," the commander continued, "was a very complete biological laboratory, cleverly hidden beneath the dwelling. Another was the emblem that strange exile had chosen to mark his belongings—the *crux ansata* and crossed bones, in red, on a black background. You may recall that the same emblem—the symbol of life above the symbol of death—is associated with the puzzle of your own origin?"

The shining being came a little nearer; the restless whirling of its green-and-argent pillar seemed to pause; Bob Star sensed its compelling interest.

"When the asteroid was dragged into the comet—"

"Thank you." The bright being chuckled. "Your penetration of the outer barrier had perplexed my new associates. But go on."

"The asteroid was flung into that power plant," Jay Kalam continued. "But not before I had solved its riddle. The exile," he explained, "kept a diary in a secret shorthand, which I was able to read." He paused to shake his head, at Bob Star's stifled gasp of unbelief. "What I read," he went on soberly, "I have kept to myself until now—because of its unpleasant aspects."

"Let's have it," rapped the voice from the pillar of light. "My colleague will not submit to restraint much longer."

"That fantastic exile," the commander went on, still deliberately grave—"was a man named Eldo Arrynu. A native of Earth, he was educated there and on Mars in biological science. Eldo Arrynu was peculiarly brilliant, in artistic as well as scientific directions. His early career was distinguished, until he was sentenced in disgrace to a Martian prison for conducting illegal biological experiments."

Jay Kalam paused to get his breath—still fighting, Bob Star realized, for time.

"With a year after his imprisonment, he was pardoned, in reward for a brilliant emergency operation that saved the warden's life. He vanished. And the Legion was never able to find him again—although we had evidence enough of his diabolical activities.

"What he did, of course, was to take refuge upon this uncharted asteroid. In prison, apparently, he had formed connections with a powerful ring of space pirates and interplanetary smugglers, who had used it as a base. He soon became the leader of the ring, evidently, and turned its criminal activities in a new and terrible direction.

"On that asteroid, he became the source of the most insidious traffic that has ever disgraced the System, one the Legion has fought in vain to suppress. It's the profits of that monstrous traffic that transformed a barren rock into a hidden paradise—"

"Be brief," warned the voice of Stephen Orco. "Or die."

"The illegal experiments of Eldo Arrynu," Jay Kalam continued, still gravely unhurried, "had been in the synthesis of life—the grisly consequences of such efforts long ago forced the council to outlaw them. Working on that asteroid, Arrynu carried his forbidden work to a triumphant completion. The business that brought him such enormous wealth was the manufacture and sale of androids."

For a moment the nearer shining thing seemed frozen. Red star and violet star ceased their regular beat. And the misty spindle between them was congealed into a pillar of green-white crystal. Then it broke into quivering motion, and one startled word came out of it:

"Androids!"

"Eldo Arrynu," amplified Jay Kalam, "had come upon the secret of synthetic life. He generated artificial cells, and propagated them in nutrient media, and learned how to control their development by radiological and biochemical means.

"He was an artist, as well as a scientist. The genius of creation must have possessed him. The medium of his great art was living, synthetic flesh. He achieved miracles—diabolical miracles—"

The commander's lean face had grown dark and hard, as if with the pain of festering memory.

"It is a sorry commentary upon human civilization," he said grimly, "that a wealthy man should give half his fortune for a hundred pounds of synthetic protoplasm. But many did—enough to give Eldo Arrynu the wealth he desired."

His hard jaws clenched suddenly, until they went pale.

323

"Nor can I blame them altogether," he whispered. His dark eyes seemed to stare into a terrible window of the past. "For there was one, arrested by the Legion for her owner's murder. She was the spirit of beauty, made real; she was a true artist's dream of grace. To look at, she was the very soul of womanly innocence. To listen to, her golden voice—"

His lean throat worked to a convulsive swallow.

"It became my duty to destroy her. But—almost—" His dark eyes looked suddenly, gratefully, at Bob Star. "But for the memory of your mother, Bob, I might have brought disgrace upon the Legion—"

He collected himself, and his eyes swept back to the restless shining forms.

"The criminal activities of the ring did not stop with the mere sale of the androids," he said. "Because the flawless, enthralling perfection of their bodies frequently concealed the most unspeakable evil. The luckless purchaser of their matchless loveliness often found that the price included the remainder of his fortune, even if not his life.

"Eldo Arrynu wrote black pages into the records of the Legion—

"But," the commander went on, "if he failed to provide his creations with any moral restraints, Eldo Arrynu seems to have had no difficulty in endowing them with extraordinary cunning—or even, sometimes, with an exceptional intelligence."

Jay Kalam paused momentarily, and continued almost casually:

"You must already have guessed what I'm about to tell you, Stephen Orco. You aren't a man. You are a synthetic monster from the laboratory of Eldo Arrynu."

The frozen violet star dipped as if it had bowed. The sardonic voice of Stephen Orco spoke out of the misty pillar, ringing as if with a careless amusement:

"Thank you, Commander."

"Your case," Jay Kalam went on, "is fully discussed in the diary. Eldo Arrynu took exceptional pains with your creation. His sublime artistic genius must have got the better, temporarily, of his practical business instincts. He designed you to be a perfect being, a true superman.

"Soon, however, after you emerged from his vats and incubators, he perceived the fatal flaw in you—the cold fiend, sleeping. He saw that his supreme effort had fallen far short of humanity, in the most vital direction possible.

"The diary records a curious struggle. One entry praises your physical perfection and your remarkable intelligence; it glows with his love for you—for he did love you, with the absorption of an artist in his masterpiece, and the devotion of a man for his son.

"The next entry, however, is a gloomy record of doubts and misgivings, filled with evidences of the fiendish coldness that all Arrynu's arts could never eradicate from you. It ends with the determination to destroy you.

"Unfortunately, however, that strange exile could never quite bring himself to the task. His love and his well-founded fear drove him at last into a regrettable compromise. He sealed you into a magnelithium cylinder, with everything necessary to preserve your life, and cast you adrift in space, far from the asteroid.

"By concealing his identity from you," said the commander solemnly, "he hoped to escape the consequences of his folly. But even so, you destroyed your own maker, Stephen Orco, when you loosed the Cometeers upon the System.

"It's possible that your long, helpless confinement in the cylinder had some further adverse influence in the formation of a character that was never good. Some part of your insatiable appetite for power and superiority must be by way of compensation for that imprisonment.

"But you were never human—"

"I'm grateful, Commander," Stephen Orco's voice broke in, carelessly mocking as ever. "But I fail to perceive any advantage to you in revealing my origins. Certainly, it isn't going to make me any more generous to the human cattle on which I feed to know that I was never one of them."

The bright mist chuckled.

"If you expected gratitude—"

The voice paused abruptly, as the shining ruler of the Cometeers made an imperative forward motion, and then it added quickly:

"Now you may prepare to die."

19

The Man Who Broke

Listening to the commander's quietly spoken narrative, staring at the luminous and beautiful thing that was now Stephen Orco, Bob Star had been shaken with a savage conflict of strange emotions.

For his great enemy had never been anything more human than this thing of frozen fire! That fact explained part of the fear and hatred that had twisted and smothered him ever since that dreadful night at the academy. It was no man that had driven the dull blade of the Iron Confessor into his skull, but a thing already inhuman.

With that knowledge, the pulse of pain behind that old scar seemed to weaken and waver in its beat for the first time in nine years. He dared again to feel that he might somehow find strength to defy the crippling command that Orco's transformed voice had burned into his brain. His empty hands tightened, hungry for a weapon.

He was crouching beside the empty box. Old Giles Habibula was still bent over it, clinging to the sides of it when the waves of retching shook him, still sobbing noisily and frequently blowing his nose.

"Now you may prepare to die." The hurried final words of Stephen Orco seemed to echo in his mind. "Because my imperial colleague seems peculiarly apprehensive about your presence in the chamber of generation—"

Bob Star felt the slight, unobtrusive pressure of the old man's trembling arm against his side, and then the cold weight of the small object Giles Habibula pressed into his hand. A light of understanding burst over him; he knew why the commander had wanted time.

Turning to shield the object with his body, he stole a quick glance at it. A puzzling weapon—if it were a weapon. A polished cube of some hard black stuff, not quite two inches on an edge. Its surface had the cold, soapy slickness of a polished gem. It felt oddly heavy—though it was weightless now, he could feel the inertia of its mass. Projecting from one face was a red, knurled knob.

Clutching it, Bob Star tried not to show his abrupt, breathless tension. It must be the weapon—and he knew that he himself must use it, instantly. The attention of Stephen Orco and the ruler of the Cometeers was probably still on the commander. That might give him time to strike.

But he couldn't kill—

Or—could he? For one frozen moment, as his quivering fingers closed on that harmless-looking instrument, it seemed to him that he was back in that dark basement room at the academy museum, nine years ago. The rusty metal band of the Iron Confessor was around his head again, and that three-edged blade driven once more into his skull, with Stephen Orco's taunting voice vibrating from it in waves of ultimate agony.

"So you don't like it, pup? This rusty crown of your proud forefathers! But no matter how little you like it, you'll never do anything about it. Because this ingenious little device was made to break men. You may be able to defy your conscience and the law, or even to forget your honor as an officer of the Legion, but you'll never disobey the Iron Confessor.

"And you can't kill me, Bob. You can't kill—"

His trembling fingers had relaxed to drop the black cube, because he couldn't use it. But then Kay Nymidee must have glimpsed it, for he heard her catch her breath. The bright image of her flashed into his mind, and his surge of tortured emotion swept him back again to that dark room.

He could feel the sticky pull of his own seeping blood drying on his face, and taste its salt sweetness on his lips. Once more he saw the wild rage on Orco's handsome face, dim in the glow from the tubes of the Iron Confessor. He heard the tramp of the night watchman's feet in the corridor above, and then the whispered voices of Orco's friends.

Those things had been forgotten, buried beneath his fear and pain. The footsteps and those protesting voices—frightened and defiant, when he heard them now. Hazing was in the academy tradition, but this thing had gone too far. If Bob Star died, the truth would certainly come out. Murder. All Stephen Orco's cleverness wouldn't be enough to save them from court-martial.

But Orco had grown too angry to listen to them.

"Say it, pup!" That dreadful voice came flooding through

327

Bob Star's brain again, transformed to red agony by the vibration of that three-edged blade. Once more it repeated all the unspeakable lies that Orco wanted him to swear. And again it insisted, mercilessly, "Say it, pup."

But he had never said it.

"He has got you beaten, Orco." Now he heard those other voices, sharpened with increasing fear as the watchman's steady footfalls paused in the corridor. "You can't break him—not even with the Iron Confessor. Don't you know he's John Star's son?"

The buried truth came rushing back.

"I give up!" Those long-forgotten words were Stephen Orco's—and the hush of fear had swept the rasping anger from his voice. "He's tougher than I expected. Let's get him out of here—and fix up a story for him. He's John Star's son, remember. Too proud to go telling tales."

"Aren't you, pup?" Stephen Orco had turned to speak into that cruel device again, before they removed it. "You'll forget it, won't you, pup?"

For nine years, he had forgotten.

All that came flashing through his mind while he clutched that cold black cube. He was John Star's son— and Stephen Orco had been the one who broke. Somehow, his fingers were suddenly steady. He lifted the cube, twisting at that tiny scarlet knob.

A pale beam of silver light shone from the opposite face of the cube. He twisted the little instrument, to sweep that beam toward the shining things.

"Bob! You can't—"

But he could. That startled, apprehensive outcry became a harsh scream. It faded into a bubbling note of ultimate agony—which might have come from a dying victim of the Iron Confessor.

His glance had followed that beam of silver light. Even before it struck those two shining beings, they seemed to freeze. For an instant they hung motionless. Their radiance died. They became two ghostly wisps of pale gray dust. The dust swirled, and then there was nothing.

Stephen Orco and the emperor were dead.

The green walls rushed away from Bob Star, and time seemed to pause. For an instant his very victory was somehow appalling, because it had shattered the whole orientation of his life. But then he knew that the old throb of pain had died behind that scar—perhaps, Jay Kalam later sug-

328

gested, the painful thrust of that organic ray had somehow helped erase the marks of the Iron Confessor.

The cold walls came back, and he heard the glad little sob of Kay Nymidee. An eager smile had swept the shadows of ominous foreboding from her face, for the first time since he had known her. She was suddenly in his arms, almost hysterical at first, and then happily relaxed.

Wonderingly, Jay Kalam picked up the black cube, which Bob Star had dropped back into the empty box. It had become covered with feathery crystals of frost. He brushed them away, and tried the red knob again. Nothing happened.

"It seems to be dead," he said. "Exhausted."

"Perhaps I turned the knob too far," Bob Star said. "The thing seemed to kick back in my hands. I think the mass of it decreased. It was growing very cold before I dropped it."

The commander nodded, watching the white frost come back.

"I suspect," he said thoughtfully, "that you released a great deal of energy, of some sort that we can't perceive—" He caught his breath. "Did you notice?" His low voice had quickened, with more emotion than he often showed. "Both those creatures were stricken—or seemed to be—before the white ray touched them!"

"Huh?" Bob Star peered at the mass of glittering frost, and back at the commander's grave face. "Do you think—"

"A very little of that energy was enough to kill these two." Jay Kalam's lean finger scraped at the dark stubble on his bloodstained chin. "We don't know how. But Orco told us the Cometeers were stable fields of energy. Perhaps this instrument generated some key vibration, adjusted to destroy that stability. If that is so—and if the range of this weapon is as great as it should have been to enforce the authority of that shining emperor—then I imagine that we have won a very decisive victory."

Deftly juggling the frosty cube, he replaced it in the box.

"Where did you get it?" he asked Giles Habibula. "We thought the box was empty."

"Ah, so it was." The old soldier blew his nose again. His fat hands still clung to the box, his pudgy fingers caressing the oddly intricate designs on its sides. His illness had vanished.

"Then," Bob Star whispered, "how—?"

"This pattern was the key," wheezed Giles Habibula. "It

329

made me wonder from the beginning, for the makers of this safe had wasted none of their cunning on useless ornament anywhere else. The figures of it led my fingers to a hidden rock. The combination rods are set level with the surface—to make the black circles in the design. I had just found it, when those fearful creatures came upon us. I gave Jay a signal to distract them, while I set out to open it.

"Mortal me!" He shuddered. "The precious genius of Giles Habibula could never endure another such trial. His poor old heart would stop. As it was, death was breathing on him when he found the combination—and saw that queer device lying where there had been nothing!"

"Where had it been?" Bob Star asked. "Under a false bottom, do you think?"

"Nothing so simple!" Giles Habibula shook his head. "I can see through false bottoms, blindfolded. Life knows where it was!" He peered at the commander. "What do you think, Jay?"

Reflectively, Jay Kalam rubbed his chin.

"The Cometeers knew more of space and time than we do," he said slowly. "Their tubular force-fields are evidence of that—as their own bodies were. That weapon may have been hidden somewhere across our universe, linked to a field that would draw it back when the lock was worked. Or it may have been outside our frame of space and time altogether—such a thing would not have been impossible for them."

"It's lucky you had read that diary." Bob Star looked up at him, frowning. "But still I wonder why they let you delay them so long. When the ruler of the Cometeers found use here so near his secret, I wonder why he didn't kill us instantly."

"I was wondering while I was talking to Orco." The commander nodded gravely. "And I've a guess to offer. I don't think the shining emperor had been quite frank with his new ally. Orco seems to have been allowed to believe that his wonderful new body was entirely invulnerable. And you recall that he referred to this place as the chamber of generation—he had probably been deceived about the nature of the secret guarded here. I suspect that the ruler of the Cometeers kept quiet about the weapon, holding it in reserve to counter Orco's knowledge of AKKA.

"If that's the way it was, Orco must have been quite confident of his new-found immortality, and free of any alarm, until the end. His imperial companion was obviously apprehensive, and impatient to be done with us. But, in such circumstances, he would have been unable to take any very precipitate action without the danger that Orco would find out the truth—and the Cometeers have a new emperor—"

Jay Kalam was interrupted by a bulky missile that came plunging down the square well of the entrance, and thudded heavily against the coldly glowing metal. It gasped for breath, and straightened, and became the body of Hal Samdu. It still bore the marks of battle, but joyous blue eyes were shining through the reddened bandages.

"Aye, Bob," the giant rumbled. "I told your mother you would be here."

"My mother?" Bob Star whispered. "Is she—safe?"

"Aye," said Hal Samdu. "She's waiting on that saucership, outside. And your father, too. The strange slaves of the Cometeers are all around them, but you needn't mind them now. They're our friends, now that we have killed their shining masters—"

"The Cometeers?" Jay Kalam broke in. "How many did we kill?"

"Every one," boomed the bandaged man. "So John Star has learned from the slaves. I don't know what you did, but the slaves are rejoicing because the monsters are all destroyed, out to the limits of the comet."

"I had begun to hope so." Jay Kalam's dark eyes fell to the small black cube, which looked more than ever harmless now, with the film of frost thawing from it. "Yet I scarcely dared—"

Hal Samdu's great hand caught Bob Star's arm.

"Come, Bob," he said, "to your mother."

John Star was waiting at the entrance valve, to welcome them to the ship. His hard body looked trim and soldierly as ever in the green of the Legion. Bob Star was secretly amazed when his father kissed him. And a lump came up in his own throat when John Star called him, for the first time in many years, not Robert, but Bob.

They entered the ship, and climbed to the upper deck. Far back, beyond the central dome, were ranked a score of the strange slaves of the Cometeers: silvery globes, slim, green, cone-shaped things, lank, many-limbed red giants. The creatures stood motionless and silent, and Bob Star could sense their awe of these insignificant bipeds, who had wiped out their shining masters—an awe that had good cause, now that Stephen Orco was dead, and Aladoree's weapon effective once more.

She came to meet them, walking with the light, quick grace he remembered. Even in the gloom of this hollow world, her brown hair shone with reddish glints and her cool gray eyes were luminous with joy. Rejoicing to the comfortable pull of the ship's gravity cells, which swept away his lingering vertigo, Bob Star ran to take her in his arms.

"My son!" She kissed him, laughing. "You've grown a frightful beard!"

She embraced Jay Kalam and Giles Habibula, who long ago had been her bodyguards. And then Bob Star presented Kay Nymidee, with his arm around her waist.

"Mother, here's a stranger. She's alone. All her people were murdered by the Cometeers. She doesn't speak much English—but she will, soon. I want you to make her welcome. For it was she who showed us where to find the weapon that killed the Cometeers. And because—because I love her."

Kay whispered something, softly, smiling at his mother. His mother took his hand, and hers, and put them together. Kay laughed a little, her fingers squeezing his, and suddenly he was longing to be with her in the peaceful beauty of the gardens of Phobos, which would no longer be a prison to him now.

"I'm glad, Bob," his mother was whispering. "Glad—" She paused, and they listened to his father's crisp voice:

"—then, Jay, what can we do with the comet?"

"There are, I believe, three possible alternatives," the commander answered thoughtfully. "The keeper of the peace may be requested to destroy the entire comet—an irrational action, which I still oppose. Or it may be kept and governed as a permanent part of the System. Or the liberated slaves, if they are capable of operating it, may be allowed to depart with it. I should prefer the third choice, but of course the final decision is a matter for the Council.

"In any case, the comet offers us a magnificent accession of knowledge." His grave eyes shone with a quick enthusiasm. "I'm already planning to return immediately, as soon as we have safely returned the keeper of the peace to the Purple Hall. I want to bring teams of experts in every branch of learning—"

Bob Star felt very tired, and the commander's ringing voice began to matter less than the warmth of Kay's arm against him. Faintly, as if from some vast distance, he heard the plaintive whine of Giles Habibula:

"Come along, Hal, and let's see if we can't find some proper human food and drink—"

ONE AGAINST
THE LEGION

ONE AGAINST THE LEGION

1

The Deadly Invention

"Unusual. Important. Indubitably dangerous." The low, grave voice of Commander Kalam, without losing its deliberate calm, had emphasized each word. "You have been selected for this duty, Captain Derron, because the Legion feels that you have earned implicit trust."

After four grim years, that scene was still as vivid in the mind of Chan Derron, as if a red-hot die had stamped it there. For that strange assignment had turned all his life, out of beckoning promise, into the dark incredible web of mystery and terror and despair.

"Yes, sir."

Chan Derron saluted briskly. He stood eagerly at attention, waiting in that huge, simply furnished chamber in the Green Hall that was the office of the Commander of the Legion of Space.

A big man, lean and trim and straight in the green of the Legion, he looked steadfast as a statue of bronze. His hair, rebellious against the comb, was like red-bronze wire. His skin was deeply bronzed with space-burn. Even his eyes held glints of unchanging bronze. His whole bearing held a promise of uncrushable strength that it warmed the Commander's heart to see.

Beneath his military readiness, however, Chan Derron's heart was thumping. He was proud of the uniform that had been his for less than a year; fiercely proud of the decorations he had already won in the war with the Cometeers. And he was desperately eager to know what was coming next. His breath caught, and he watched the lean, dark face of Jay Kalam.

"I have ordered all of Admiral-General Samdu's fleet to assist with this assignment—it is important enough to justify that," the Commander was saying. "But the crucial duty is such that one ship—and one man, Captain Derron —must be trusted to carry it out."

Chan Derron tried to swallow the little lump of eagerness in his throat. A duly commissioned captain—he mustn't tremble like a wide-eyed cadet. After all, he was twenty-two. But the low-voiced question startled him:

"You know of Dr. Max Eleroid?"

"Of—of course," he stammered. "If you mean the geodesic engineer? The man who redesigned the geodyne, and invented the geopeller? At the academy we studied his text on geodesy."

"So you were an engineer?" The Commander faintly smiled. "Dr. Eleroid," he said, "is probably the greatest physical scientist living—although his dread of publicity has kept him from becoming widely known. And he has just done something new."

Chan Derron waited, wondering.

"This morning," Jay Kalam said, "Eleroid came into this office, with an assistant behind him staggering under a box of equipment. He was frightened. He begged me to take him and his invention under the protection of the Legion.

"The invention is his most important, he said, and his most dangerous. He had decided not to work it out at all, he told me—until the System was placed in danger by the coming of the Cometeers.

"He set out to complete it, then, as a weapon. It is a little too late for the war. But he intends to entrust it to the Legion as an adjunct to AKKA in the defense of mankind.

"Yesterday, anyhow, he found evidence that an intruder had been in his laboratory—that's somewhere west, in the Painted Desert. This unknown spy has him baffled and very thoroughly scared. Only two people had been trusted with any details of his work, he said—his daughter, and this assistant, Jonas Thwayne. He has no clue to the spy's identity; but he gives him credit for being a remarkably clever man."

The Commander straightened sternly.

"That's the background of the matter, Captain Derron. And here are your orders."

"Yes, sir."

"We are going to aid Dr. Eleroid with a field test of this invention—it has never been tested, he says, except on the minutest scale—and then, if the test is successful, he will leave it in your hands.

"You will go back aboard your cruiser and proceed at once to Rocky Mountain Base. There you will find awaiting you twenty workmen, with atomotored excavating equipment, explosives, and building materials. You will take them aboard, and then rise without delay on a course for the New Moon. You follow me, Captain?"

"I do, sir."

"When you have reached an altitude of two thousand miles," Jay Kalam continued, "you will open this envelope and proceed to the spot designated inside."

Chan Derron accepted a small green envelope, sealed with the wings of the Legion in dark green wax, and put it in an inside pocket of his tunic.

"You will land at the designated spot, and disembark the workmen and equipment. At a point you will select, they are to dig an excavation twenty feet square and twenty deep. In that, working under your orders, they are to build a room armored with two feet of perdurite, provided with a stair and a concealed door with a special lock —you will be given the specifications.

"This task must be completed by twelve noon, tomorrow, Legion time. You will put the men and equipment back aboard the *Corsair*. The cruiser will return at once, under your first officer, to Rocky Mountain Base. And you, Captain Derron—"

Chan Derron caught his breath, as the Commander suddenly rose.

"You will remain on guard, near the hidden door. You will keep your ultrawave communicator, emergency rations, and your proton needle and bayonet. You will stand guard while Dr. Eleroid and his assistant land, enter the hidden chamber, and test the invention.

"Finally, if the experiment is successful, Dr. Eleroid will deliver his apparatus and notes into your care, for the Legion. You will call your cruiser to return, go aboard with Eleroid, the assistant, and the machine, and come

339

back at once to Rocky Mountain Base. Is that all clear, Captain Derron?"

"Clear enough, sir," said Chan Derron. "If you feel that one man is enough—"

"Samdu's fleet will be on duty to see that there is no outside interference," the grave Commander assured him. "For the rest, we must rely upon secrecy, precision of action, and division of knowledge. Upon you, Captain Derron, rests the final responsibility." His dark eyes stabbed into Chan's. "This is as great a trust as the Legion has ever given any man, but I believe you are equal to it."

Chan gulped. "I'll do my best, sir."

"The Legion can ask no more."

The matter already appeared grave enough, perhaps, but Chan Derron was not used to being depressed by the details of his duty. The mystery surrounding this affair he found pleasantly exciting, and the faint hint of danger was like a tonic to him.

On his way back to the *Corsair*—the trim little geodesic cruiser that was his proud first command—he was humming a song. He had never been to the New Moon, then. But he had often seen the artificial satellite, careening backward across the sky of Earth. And soon, no doubt, with Commander Kalam trusting him with such important assignments as this, he should have a furlough earned— his heart leapt at the promise—on the gay New Moon.

Striding toward the vast space-port that sprawled brown across the desert mesa beside the Green Hall's slender spire, he kept time to the popular tune, whose age-hallowed sentiments ran:

> *Where first we danced,*
> *On the bright New Moon,*
> *Where we romanced,*
> *On the far New Moon,*
> *I lost a million dollars—*
> *But I found you, dear!*

He strode aboard the slim silver *Corsair*. In his bright expectations, this strange duty had already taken him to some far planet. When he came to open the sealed envelope, however, his ship two thousand miles out toward the New Moon, the destination he read was back on Earth —a barren islet in the bleak Antarctic Ocean.

The *Corsair* dropped among screaming birds. Chan selected a level spot on the highest granite ledge, a hundred feet above the gray unresting sea. The twenty workmen fell to. Humming atomic drills sliced into the living rock. A web of structural metal was flung across the pit. Rock debris was fused into massive walls and roof of adamantine perdurite.

Next day the cruiser departed on the very stroke of noon. Left alone among the settling birds, that soon covered even the hidden door, Chan Derron shuddered to something colder than the bitter south wind.

Beyond this black pinnacle, and the green-white chaos that forever roared about its foot, the polar sea ran empty and illimitable. Low and yellowed in the gray northward sky, the sun glinted on the summits of a few icebergs. So far as he could tell, he might have been the only man upon the planet. And a sudden bleak fear rose in him, that all Commander Kalam's elaborate precautions against the unknown spy had not been enough.

Once more, anxiously, he inspected his proton blaster. Perfected since the cometary war to replace the lighter proton pistols that had served so long, it projected an intense jet of nucleonic bullets far swifter and more deadly than any solid projectile. The holster became a stock, for accurate long range work. A folding bayonet snapped out for use at close quarters.

Chan tried to find comfort in the fine, silent mechanism, in its chromium trimness and its balanced weight. But the lonely wail of the bitter wind, the empty hostility of the cold sky and the ice-studded sea, awoke in his heart a brooding apprehension.

He shouted with relief when the *Bellatrix*—the long bright flagship of Admiral-General Hal Samdu—plunged down through a cloud of shrieking birds. Two men were put off, and a heavy wooden box. The *Bellatrix* roared back spaceward. In seconds, it had vanished.

Chan Derron had never seen Dr. Eleroid, but he knew the scientist now from his portrait in the geodesic text. Eleroid was a big, slightly awkward, slow-moving man, with a red, rugged, genial face. But for his eyes, he might have been taken for a butcher or a bartender. His eyes, however, wide-set and seen through heavy lenses, possessed the magnetic power of genius.

Eleroid was still afraid. That was obvious from his anxious peering about the islet, from a sudden start when

341

the white-cloaked assistant touched him, from the relief on his broad face when Chan strode to meet him.

"Glad to thee you, Captain." His deep soft voice had an occasional lisp. "Where ith the vault. We must hathen!"

Chan indicated the door, disguised with a slab of natural rock, and returned to help the small, perspiring assistant with the box. Dr. Eleroid watched it very anxiously, and lent his own strength to help them down the narrow stair.

They set the box down in the middle of the bare, square, gray-armored room. The assistant was rubbing at red weals on his thin hands. Suddenly he began to sneeze, and covered his face with his handkerchief. Max Eleroid gestured imperatively toward the stair.

"You are to stand guard, Captain." His voice was hoarse with tension. "We'll lock the room. I'll call you, by ultra-wave, when we are done." His trembling hand touched Chan Derron's arm. "Keep a vigilant watch, Captain," he begged. "For the thafety of the System may be at stake."

The massive door thudded shut. Chan moved a little away, and the birds settled over it again. Rock and sky and sea were empty as before. The south wind was more biting, the northward sun feebler. Pacing back and forth, he shuddered again.

His apprehension, he was trying to tell himself, was silly—when something touched him. At first he thought that only a bird had brushed him. Then he felt the fatal lightness of his belt and his hand flashed with well-trained swiftness for his blaster. He found that it was gone!

He stared around him, bewildered. Rock and sky and sea were ominously vacant as ever. What could have happened to the weapon? He could see no possible answer. The screaming birds mocked his sanity. This clearly meant danger—the operation of some unknown and hostile agency. But how was he to meet it? Samdu's guarding fleet must be somewhere not far beyond that bleak gray sky. He would call the Admiral—

But his own signal was already humming from the little black disk of the ultrawave communicator, that hung by its cord from his neck. He touched the receiver key and slapped the instrument to his ear.

"*Help!*" It was Max Eleroid. "Thith man—" The lisping voice was queerly muffled, choked. "*Thith man—he ith not—*"

An odd purring hum came out of the communicator, and then it was silent.

2

Adequate Evidence

The same disturbing message had been picked up by the fleet. When the *Bellatrix* landed, not an hour afterward, Chan Derron was found staggering aimlessly about the rock.

"My blaster's gone!" he gasped to the Admiral-General. "If it hadn't been taken, I might have been able to cut a way in, in time to help."

"Where is your vault?" demanded the rugged old spaceman. His huge ugly face was ashen gray, and the anxious gestures of his great scarred hands had already set all the stiff white mass of his hair on end. "We'll have a look."

Chan pointed out the scarcely visible seam.

"It's locked." His voice trembled with the dread of the hour that he had waited. "Eleroid locked it, on the inside. I tried it, after he called. You'll have to cut through the perdurite."

"If we can—" Hal Samdu's battered hands clutched, in tortured indecision. "If only old Giles Habibula were here! He has a gift for locks—but he's off on Phobos, beyond the sun from us now, eating and drinking himself to death at John Star's table." He shook his head. "I don't know quite what to do—"

"We can't wait, sir," Chan Derron urged him. "I'm afraid to think what must have happened in that room. Haven't you equipment, on the battleship, that can cut through that door—"

His voice dropped into a chasm of incredulity.

For the huge Legionnaire had bent and seized the projecting knob of rock that formed a disguised handle for the massive slab of armor, balanced on its pivots in the doorway, as if he would break the lock with his own unaided muscles. And the door swung smoothly open.

Hal Samdu straightened to stare grimly at Chan. "Locked, eh?"

343

Chan Derron stepped dazedly back, and a black wind of terror blew cold about his heart.

"It was locked!" he gasped. "I tried it!"

But a cold deadliness of doubt glittered abruptly in the blue eyes of the Admiral-General. His big hand deliberately hauled out his own proton needle and he covered the weaponless Chan.

"Hold him, men," he commanded. "I'm going to look inside." Hal Samdu and his officers went down into the small square chamber. In the garish light of the tube still burning against the ceiling, they found Dr. Max Eleroid and the man in white. They were both sprawled still, and the slighter body of the assistant was already stiffening into the rigor of death.

Rivulets and pools of darkening blood stained the new gray perdurite. Both men had been stabbed. And the weapon still protruding from the back of Dr. Max Eleroid was a service blaster, of the new Legion type, holster-stock and bayonet locked in place. There was nothing else left in the bare, bright-lit room. The long wooden box, with its contents, was gone.

Staggering and gasping for breath, as if he too had been stricken, Hal Samdu came back up the stair, carrying in his great quivering hand the blaster with a thin red drop trembling on the point of the fixed bayonet. He thrust it into Chan's bewildered face.

"Captain, do you know this weapon?"

Chan examined it.

"I do," he gulped hoarsely. "I know it by the serial number, and by the initials etched into the butt. It is mine."

Hal Samdu made a choking, furious sound.

"Then, Derron," he gasped, when he could speak, "you are under arrest. You are charged with insubordination, gross neglect of duty, treason against the Green Hall, and the murder of Dr. Max Eleroid and his assistant, Jonas Thwayne. You will be held in irons, without bail, for trial by court-martial before your superior officers in the Legion. And God help you, Derron!"

Chan was swaying, paralyzed. A great far wind roared in his ears. The black rock and the shining battleship and the threatening men in green around him, all dimmed and wavered. He swayed, fighting for awareness.

"But I didn't do it," he gasped. "I tell you, sir, this can't be—"

But icy jaws of metal had already caught his wrist, and the great ruthless voice of Hal Samdu was roaring at him:

"Now, Derron, what did you do with Eleroid's invention?"

What did you do with Eleroid's invention? . . . *What did you do with Eleroid's invention?* . . . WHAT DID YOU DO WITH ELEROID'S INVENTION? . . . *WHAT DID YOU DO . . .*

Chan Derron heard that question a million times. It was shouted at him, whispered at him, shrieked at him. He ate it with prison food, and breathed it with dank prison air. It was beaten into him with men's hard fists, and burned into his brain with the blaze of cruel atomic lights.

He was commanded to answer it, threatened, begged, tricked, drugged, flung into solitary, starved, promised freedom and riches, picked to mental shreds by the psychologists and psychiatrists, offered fabulous bribes—and threatened again.

Of course he couldn't answer it.

Because of that fact alone he was kept alive, even after he hungered for the quiet freedom of death.

The court-martial had indeed, when at last the torture of the trial had ended, returned a triple sentence of death, on two counts of murder, and one of treason. But that had been commuted by Commander Kalam, the day he embarked on the great research expedition to the green comet, to life imprisonment at hard labor in the Legion prison on Ebron.

Chan heard that news in his cell with a sense of sick frustration. He knew that now he would not be allowed to die, any more than he was let live, until that unanswerable question was answered. And the great grim prison on the asteroid, as he had foreknown, brought him no escape from those angrily and incredulously demanding voices.

The person, even the person of a convicted criminal, was legally safeguarded by the Green Hall. And the tradition of the Legion was against cruel and unusual methods. The safety of mankind was a greater end, however, than the letter of the law, and the Legion existed to guard that safety.

The court-martial had found adequate circumstantial evidence that Chan Derron had killed Max Eleroid and his assistant, and then, failing to escape with the unknown new device, had somehow disposed of it. The case was absurdly simple. There was only that one question. The entire organization of the Legion moved as ruthlessly to extract the answer from Chan as rollers pressing the juice from a grape. Therein the Legion failed—but only because the answer was not in him.

Chan lived two years in the prison on Ebron.

Then he escaped.

For two years more the Legion hunted him.

3

The Sign of the Basilisk

"No." Jay Kalam lifted weary eyes from the documents stacked before him, on his long desk in the tower of the Green Hall. "Tell Gaspar Hannas I can't talk to him." His voice was dull with fatigue. "Not tonight."

For he was deadly tired. In command of the great research expedition to study the sciences and the arts of the half-conquered comet, he had spent three strange, exhausting years among those scores of amazing worlds beyond the barrier of green.

For months more, at the permanent depot of the expedition at Contra-Saturn Station, he had toiled to direct the first preliminary analysis and classification of the results of the expedition—recording the hundreds of tremendous discoveries gleaned from those ancient captive worlds.

Then another, more urgent duty had called him back to Earth. A few apprehensive statesmen in the Green Hall were gaining support for a movement to order the destruction of the departing comet with AKKA. The Commander, in return for the free cooperation of the liberated peoples of the comet, had promised to let them go in peace. Leaving young Robert Star in command of the half-secret, heavily fortified depot, he came back to fight before the Green Hall for the life of the comet.

Now at last the victory was won. The new Cometeers were gone beyond the range of the greatest telescope, pledged never to return. And Jay Kalam felt slow and heavy now with his long fatigue. A few more reports to complete—secret documents dealing with the dreadful matter-annihilating weapon of the Cometeers—and then he was going to John Star's estate on Phobos, to rest.

"But Commander—" The distressed, insistent voice of the orderly hummed through the communicator. "Gaspar Hannas is owner of the New Moon. And he says this is urgent—"

The Commander's lean face grew stern.

"I'll talk to him when I get back from the Purple Hall," he said. "We've already sent Admiral-General Samdu, with his ten cruisers, to help Hannas catch his thief."

"But they've failed, sir," protested the orderly. "An urgent message from Admiral-General Samdu reports—"

"Samdu's in command." Jay Kalam's voice was brittle with fatigue. "He doesn't have to report." He sighed, and pushed thin fingers through the forelock of white that he had brought back from the comet. "If the thief is really Chan Derron," he muttered, "they may fail again!"

Settling limply back in the chair behind his crowded desk, he let his tired eyes look out of the great west window. It was dark. Beyond the five low points of the dead volcanoes on the black horizon, against the fading greenish afterglow, the New Moon was rising.

Not the ancient satellite whose cragged face had looked down upon the Earth since life was born—that had been obliterated a quarter-century ago, by the keeper of the peace when Aladoree Anthar turned her secret ancestral weapon upon the outpost that the invading Medusae had established there.

The New Moon was really new—a glittering creation of modern science and high finance, the proudest triumph of thirtieth century engineering. The heart of it was a vast hexagonal structure of welded metal, ten miles across, that held eighty cubic miles of expensive, air-conditioned space.

Far nearer Earth than the old Moon, the new satellite had a period of only six hours. From the Earth, its motion appeared faster and more spectacular because of its retrograde direction. It rose in the west, fled across the sky against the tide of the stars and plunged down where the old Moon had risen.

The New Moon was designed to be spectacular. A spinning web of steel wires, held rigid by centrifugal force, spread from it across a thousand miles of space. They supported an intricate system of pivoted mirrors of sodium foil and sliding color filters of cellulite. Reflected sunlight was utilized to illuminate the greatest advertising sign ever conceived.

The thin hand of the Commander had reached wearily for the thick sheaf of green-tinted pages headed: REPORTS OF THE COMETARY RESEARCH EXPEDITION, J. KALAM, DIRECTOR. REPORT CXLVIII: PRELIMINARY ACCOUNT OF METHODS AND EQUIPMENT FOR THE IRREVERSIBLE REDUCTION OF MATTER TO RADIANT NEUTRINOS.

But the rising sign, as it had been designed to do, held his eyes. A vast circle of scarlet stars came up to the greenish desert dusk. They spun giddily, came and went, changed suddenly to a lurid yellow. Then garish blue-and-orange letters flashed a legend:

Tired, Mister? Bored, Sister? Then come with me—The disk became a red-framed animated picture of a slender girl in white, tripping up the gangway of a New Moon liner. She turned, and the gay invitation of her smile changed into burning words: *Out in the New Moon, just ask for what you want. Gaspar Hannas has it for you.*

"Anything." Jay Kalam smiled grimly. "Even the System's foremost criminals."

Find health at our sanatoria! flamed the writing in the sky. *Sport in our gravity-free games! Recreation in our clubs and theatres! Knowledge in our museums and observatories. Thrills, and beauty—everywhere! Fortune, if you're lucky, in our gaming salons! Even oblivion if you desire it, at our Clinic of Euthanasia!*

"But all the same," Jay Kalam whispered to the sign, "I think I'll still take the quiet peace of John Star's home on Phobos—"

The Commander stiffened, behind his desk.

For the great sign, where a green flaming hand had begun to write some new invitation, suddenly flickered. It went out. For an instant it was dark. Then red, ragged, monstrous letters spelled, startlingly his own name!

"KALAM!" Darkness again. Then the fiery scarlet symbols: *"G-39!"*

An explosion of red-and-white pyrotechnics wiped that out. One blue spark grew into an immense blue star. The star framed the Moon Girl again. She laughed, and a white arm beckoned.

But Jay Kalam was no longer watching the sign. For G-39 was his call in the secret emergency intelligence code to be used only in cases of grave necessity. A little chill

348

of cold forewarning shook his hand, as he touched the communicator dial.

"All right, Lundo," he hold the orderly. "Get me Gaspar Hannas on the visiwave!"

Builder and master of this gaudiest and most glittering of all resorts, Gaspar Hannas was a man who had come up out of a dubious obscurity. The rumors of his past —that he had been a space-pirate, drug runner, android-agent, crooked gambler, gang-boss, and racketeer-in-general—were many and somewhat contradictory.

The first New Moon had been the battered hulk of an obsolescent space liner, towed into an orbit about the Earth twenty years ago. The charter somehow issued to the New Moon Syndicate in the interplanetary confusion following the First Interstellar War had given that gambling ship the status of a semi-independent planet, which made it a convenient refuge from the more stringent laws of Earth and the rest of the System. Gaspar Hannas, the head of the syndicate, had defied outraged reformers—and prospered exceedingly.

The wondrous artificial satellite, first opened to the public a decade ago, had replaced a whole fleet of luxury liners that once had circled just outside the laws of Earth. The financial rating of the syndicate was still somewhat uncertain—Hannas had been called, among many other things, a conscienceless commercial octopus; but the new resort was obviously a profitable business enterprise, efficiently administered by Hannas and his special police.

His enemies—and there was no lack of them—liked to call the man a spider. True enough, his sign in the sky was like a gaudy web. True, millions swarmed to it, to leave their wealth—or even, if they accepted the dead-black chip that the croupiers would give any player for the asking, their lives.

The man himself must now have been somewhat beyond sixty. But as he sat, gigantic and impassive, at the odd round desk in his office, watching the flowing tape that recorded the winnings in all the halls, sipping the dark Martian beer that never intoxicated him, no onlooker could have guessed his age within a score of years —or guessed anything at all that moved behind his face.

For the face of Gaspar Hannas, men said, had changed with his fortunes. His old face, they said, had reflected his real nature too well. It had showed the scars of too many battles. And it was printed, they whispered, on too many notices of reward.

The face of Gaspar Hannas, now, like the flesh of his great idle hands, was very white—but whiter still, if one looked closely at its vast smooth expanse, were the tiny scars the surgeons had left. It was oddly blank. The only expression that ever moved it was a slow and meaningless smile—a smile that made its white smoothness like the face of a monstrously overgrown idiot child's.

The eyes of the man, set far apart and deep in that white bald head, were sharp and midnight black. Beyond that idiotic smile, they had a contradictory keenness. But their dark piercing fixity never revealed what was passing in the mind of Gaspar Hannas.

Such a face, men agreed, was singularly useful to a man in his trade. It was what Jay Kalam waited to see upon the shining oval plate of the visiwave cabinet. (One of the System's first useful developments from the conquered science of the comet, this instrument utilized the instantaneous achronic force-fields that the lovely fugitive, Kay Nymidee, had used to escape from the comet.)

The plate flickered, and Jay Kalam saw the vast smooth features of the New Moon's master. And now not even that senseless smile could hide the apprehension devouring the vitals of Gaspar Hannas. For his whiteness had become a ghastly pallor. He was breathless, and his whole gross body trembled.

"Commander—Commander!" His great voice was dry and ragged-edged with fear. "You've got to help me!"

"What do you want, Hannas?" Jay Kalam asked flatly. "And why was it necessary to use my emergency call—when you already have a Legion fleet detailed to guard your establishment?"

Still Gaspar Hannas smiled that silly baby-smile, but his blank forehead was beaded with fine drops of sweat.

"Admiral-General Samdu gave the authority," he gasped. "He agrees that the situation is urgent. He's here with me now, Commander."

"And what's the trouble?"

"It's this man—this monster—who calls himself the Basilisk!" The huge voice was hoarse and wild. "He's ruining me, Commander. Ruining the New Moon! Time knows where he will stop!"

"What has he done?"

"Last night he took another patron. The high winner

at baccaret—Clovis Field—a planter from the asteroids. My police escorted him, with his winnings, to his yacht. They got him there, safe. But he was taken out of the sealed air-lock, Commander—with all his winnings!"

Jay Kalam brushed the white forelock back into his dark hair, impatiently.

"One more gambler robbed?" His tired eyes narrowed. "That has happened many a time on the New Moon, Hannas—when you didn't think it necessary to call the Legion."

A queer tensity stiffened that white, foolish smile.

"Robbed—but that isn't all, Commander. Clovis Field is dead. His body has just been found in the pre-crematory vault at the Euthanasia Clinic. And his right hand is closed on one of those little black clay snakes that this Basilisk uses to sign his crimes!"

"What killed him?"

"Strangled!" boomed Gaspar Hannas. "With a green silk scarf." In his deep black eyes, behind that mindless mask, Jay Kalam saw the glitter of a terrible light. Accusing or triumphant—he didn't know which. "It is embroidered in gold, Commander," said the great voice of Hannas, "with the wings of the Legion of space!"

Jay Kalam's lean face tensed.

"If any Legion man was guilty of this crime, he will be punished," he said. "But I see no need to call on me so soon. What's the matter with your own police? You have ten thousand of the toughest men in the System. Put them on the trail."

The black eyes had a glazed expression.

"Commander, you don't understand. It—it's uncanny! The air lock on the yacht was sealed—and stayed sealed. The vault was locked—and not unlocked. Nobody could have done the things. *Nobody*—"

"I advise," said Jay Kalam, "that you examine some of your own employees. You say that Admiral-General Samdu is with you? Please put him on."

The smooth white face was replaced by a cragged ugly red one, equally gigantic. Beneath his snow-white hair, the features of Hal Samdu were still with an awed bewilderment.

The Commander smiled a greeting.

"Wel, Hal, what is your emergency?"

The battered red face twisted, and the blue eyes of Hal Samdu grew dark as if with pain.

351

"I don't just know, Jay." His deep voice was worried. "There's not much you can put a finger on." His own big fingers were clenched into baffled fists. "But it *is* an emergency, Jay! I know it. I can feel it. The beginning of something—dreadful! It may turn out to be as bad as the Cometeers!"

Jay Kalam shook his tired dark head.

"I don't see anything that grave—"

Hal Samdu leaned forward and his great battered impotent fist came up to the screen.

"Well, Jay," he rumbled, "maybe you'll listen to this!" His voice sank, with an unconscious caution. "I've been on the Derron case you know, ever since we got back from the comet. Well, I haven't caught him—there was never such a man! But I've got clues. And, well—"

His tone dropped lower still.

"Commander, I've got evidence enough that this Basilisk is Chan Derron!"

"Quite possible." Jay Kalam nodded.

"There was no Basilisk until after Derron got out of prison," argued Hal Samdu. "Soon after, there was. He began with small things. Experiments. He's trying out his power—the weapon he murdered Max Eleroid to get! Time knows how he hid the thing on that rock, when we combed every square inch—unless he could have used a geopeller. But he has it—some frightful unknown thing!"

The great hands twisted together, in a baffled agony.

"And he's getting more confident with it. Bolder! Every job he tries is more daring. And time knows where he will stop!" The great rugged knob of his Adam's apple jerked. "I tell you, Jay, the man who robbed and murdered Clovis Field can do anything—*anything!*"

Hal Samdu's voice dropped again. It was cracked and shaken with alarm.

"I don't like to speak of this, Jay, on the wave. But if this Basilisk—if Derron—can do what he did tonight, then *she* isn't safe! Or—*it!*"

Jay Kalam stiffened. He could not fail to know what Hal Samdu meant by *she* and *it*. He and the giant, with old Giles Habibula, had been too long the guards of Aladoree Anthar and the priceless secret that she guarded; the mysterious weapon, designed by the symbol AKKA, whose very existence was the shield of mankind.

If the keeper of the peace was—

352

"All right, Hal," he said. "I'll come out to the New Moon—"

"And one thing more, Jay—" The rugged face remained stiffly anxious. "Bring Giles Habibula!"

"But he's on Phobos," protested the Commander, "and Mars is a hundred degrees past opposition. It would take half a day to get him. And I don't see—"

"Call John Star," begged the big Legionnaire, "and have him bring Giles to meet you. Drunk or sober! For we'll need Giles, Jay, before this thing is done. He's getting old and fat, I know. But he has a gift—a talent that we'll need."

"All right, Hal," Jay Kalam nodded. "I'll bring Giles Habibula."

"Thank you, Commander!" It was the great hoarse voice of Gaspar Hannas. Into the visiwave plate, beside Hal Samdu's unkempt head, the smooth white face of Hannas crowded, smiling idiotically. "And—for Earth's sake—hurry!"

Jay Kalam put through his call to Phobos by ultrawave—the faster visiwave equipment, still experimental, had not yet been installed there. He ordered the *Inflexible*—powerful sister ship of the murdered *Invincible*—made ready to take off. He was on his feet, to leave the office, when he saw the little clay serpent.

It lay on the thick green sheaf of the report that he had been working over a few minutes before. And, beneath it, was a folded square of heavy, bright-red paper.

"Huh!" His breath caught sharply. Now how did *that* come here?

He looked quickly around the room. The heavy door was still closed, the orderly sitting watchful and undisturbed beyond its vitrilith panel. The windows were still secure, the grates over the air ducts intact.

"It *couldn't*—"

Certainly he had seen no movement, heard no footsteps. The Cometeers had known invisibility, but even an invisible man must have opened a door or a window. Baffled, aware of a cold prickling touch of dread, he shook his head and picked up the serpent.

That was crude enough. A roughly molded little figurine, burned black. It lay in a double coil, head across the tail, so that it formed the letter *B*.

Where *had* it come from?

Then delicate hands trembling a little, he unfolded the

heavy red sheet. The impression of a black serpent, at the top of it, formed another *B*. Beneath it, in a black script precise as engraving—the ink still damp enough to blot his fingers—was written:

My Dear Kalam:
  Since you are going out to the New Moon, will you kindly take Gaspar Hannas a message from me? Will you tell him that nothing—not even the protection of the Legion of Space—will protect his most fortunate patron, every day, from the fate of Clovis Field?

  The Basilisk

4

The Pawn of Malice

The Solar System is curiously flat. The two dimensions of the ecliptic plane are relatively crowded with worlds and their satellites, and the cosmic debris of meteors, asteroids, and comets. But the third is empty.

Outbound interplanetary traffic, by an ancient rule of the spaceways, arches a little to northward of the ecliptic plane, inbound, a little to the southward, to avoid both the debris of the system and danger of head-on collisions. Beyond these charted lanes, there is nothing.

A tiny ship, however, was now driving outward from the sun, parallel to the ecliptic plane and two hundred million miles beyond the limits of the space-lanes. Its hull was covered with thin photoelectronic cells capable of being adjusted to absorb any desired fraction of the incident radiation—making the vessel, when they were in operation, virtually invisible in space.

Not thirty feet long, and weighing too few tons to have perceptible effect on the mass-detectors of a Legion cruiser beyond ten million miles, the ship had power to race the fleetest of them.

Her geodynes were of the new type designed by Max Eleroid. Far more powerful than the old, they were yet so delicately matched and balanced that the ship could be landed on a planet, or even worked into a berth, without the use of auxiliary rockets.

The *Phantom Atom* had compact accommodations for a crew of four. But only one man was aboard—now staring grimly at his own picture, fastened beside another on the metal bulkhead behind the tiny, vitrilith-windowed pilot bay.

ONE HUNDRED THOUSAND DOLLARS REWARD!

That was the heading, in bold crimson letters, above the full color picture. Beneath it was a block of smaller black type:

This sum will be paid by the Legion of Space, for aid and information leading to the capture or the death of Chan Derron, escaped convict, believed to be known also as the "Basilisk."

Description: Stands six feet three. Earth-weight, two hundred ten. Hair, bronze. Complexion, deeply space-tanned. Eyes, gray. Slight scars on face, neck, and back, such as due to extreme interrogation.

This man is physically powerful, intelligent, and desperate. A former captain in the Legion, he was convicted of murder and treason. Two years ago he escaped from the Legion prison on Ebron. Clues of him have been found on several planets.

Officers of all planets are warned that Derron is a dangerous man. He was trained in the Legion academy. He is believed to be armed with a mysterious and deadly instrumentality. It is advised that he be disabled before he is accosted.

Jay Kalam
Commander of the Legion of Space

Four years had made a difference between the picture and the man. The picture, taken after his arrest, looked bleak and grim enough. But Chan Derron, in those four bitter years, had grown harder and leaner and stronger. Some frank boyish simplicity was gone from his dark-tanned face, and in its place was something—savage.

He turned from the picture to another posted beside his

own. His great brown hand saluted it, and a brief, sardonic grin crossed his square-jawed face.

"Comrades, eh, Luroa?" he muttered. "Together against the Legion!"

He had taken the other notice from the same Legion bulletin board, in old mud-walled Ekarhenium, on Mars, where he had found his own. The two notices were displayed side by side, at the top of the board—offering the two biggest rewards. And he had been dazzled by the sheer, startling beauty of the other face.

A woman's face, wondrous with something beyond perfection. Beneath the dark, red-gleaming hair, her features were regular and white—and something shone from them. Her eyes were a clear green, wide apart, with the slightest hint of a slant. Full-lipped and red, her long mouth smiled with a hidden mockery.

A woman's face—but she was no woman.

For the text beneath her picture ran:

Rewards totalling two hundred and fifty thousand dollars will be paid by the Legion of Space, the Green Hall Council, and various planetary governments, for the being named Luroa, pictured above, living or dead.

She is not a human being, but a female android.

The history of the android traffic is perhaps not generally known. But for many years, at his laboratory hidden on a remote planetoid, a gifted criminal biologist, Eldo Arrynu, engaged in the manufacture of these illegal synthetic beings. He headed a ring of criminals that made a vast income through smuggling these dangerous creatures to wealthy purchasers throughout the system.

Stephen Orco, the male android whose unprincipled cunning came near destroying the system during the war with the Cometeers, is typical of these illicit creations: perfect of body, brilliant of brain, but morally monstrous.

The entity Luroa was the last creation of Eldo Arrynu, and she is believed to be the last android in existence. The scientist refused to sell her. He kept her with him, until the attack of the Cometeers. She escaped, however, when all others on the planetoid were killed. Since, she has been the gifted and ruth-

356

less leader of the remnants of this interplanetary gang.

Beyond the single picture above, discovered in the records on the planetoid, no description of the android Luroa is available. Nothing is known of her surviving associates.

Officers are warned that this sinister being possesses a mind of phenomenal keenness, that she is pitilessly free of all human scruples, and that her alluring beauty is her most deadly weapon. She is fully trained in many lines of science, physically more powerful, and far quicker than most men, and skilled in the use of all weapons.

Officers are advised to destroy this being upon identification.

> Jay Kalem
> Commander of the Legion of Space

"A quarter of a million, darling!" Chan Derron whispered. "And I think you're worth it—on looks alone!" The hard grin seamed his dark face again. "For your own sake, I hope they haven't got you overestimated as much as they have me."

He blew the smiling picture an ironic kiss, from his big brown hand, and then bent again to the hooded view-plate of the chart cabinet. Miles of microfilm, within the instrument, intricate reels and cams and gears, ingenious prisms and lenses, could give a true stereoscopic picture of the System, as it would appear from any point in its stellar vicinity, at any desired telescopic power, at any time within a thousand years. The integrators could quickly calculate the speediest, safest, or most economical route from any one point to any other.

The big man found the light fleck that was Oberon, outermost satellite of cloudy-green Uranus. His great hands deftly moved the dials, to bring it into coincidence with the tri-crossed hairs in the view-plate. He read the destination from the indicators and set it up on the keys. And then, while the humming mechanism was analyzing and re-integrating the many harmonic factors involved in moving the *Phantom Atom* across a billion miles of space, to a safe landing on that cold and lonely moon, his bronze-glinting eyes went back to the smiling picture on the bulkhead.

"Well, Luroa," he said slowly, "I guess it's going to be

good-bye." He waved a grave farewell, to her white and mocking loveliness. "You know, we could have made quite a couple, you and I—if I had just been what the Legion takes me for!"

His bronze head shook, his brown face wistful.

"But my lady, I'm not. I'm no reckless pirate of the spaceways—unless by dire necessity. I'm just a plain soldier of the Legion, in incredibly and peculiarly bad luck. I haven't got any 'mysterious and deadly instrumentality.' "

His head lifted a little. His eyes lighted. His voice softened, confidentially.

"But I've one secret, Luroa!"

Smiling again, he pointed at a series of figures on the log-tape beside the hooded glass.

"No secret weapon," he whispered. "And nothing like the secret of your life, Luroa. But it's enough to mean new hope to me." His great head lifted, with a fierce little gesture of pride. "It means one more chance."

A moment he looked silently at the smiling picture and the green-eyed loveliness of Luroa looked back, he thought, almost with a mocking comprehension.

"It was like this, my dear," he said. "The last time Hal Samdu chased me, I got a hundred million miles ahead of his fleet, running out north. I got far beyond visual range. Or beyond the normal range of the mass-detectors. I was rigging up a new hook-up, trying to find if old Hal was still on the trail, when I found—something else."

He shook his finger at her.

"Don't ask me what it is, Luroa. It's too far off, with whatever albedo it has, to show even a point in the system's best telescope. But the mass is of the order of ten million tons, and the distance approximately ten billion miles, estimated by triangulation.

"Doesn't matter, what it is. A chunk of rock, or a projectile from Andromeda. I'm going out there. Just one more landing first, at some out-station, to get food and cathode plates. And then I'm off. I'll find out what it is. And do a bit of research I have in mind. And—well, wait."

Chan Derron's air of lightness was growing very thin. A hoarse little break came in his voice.

"Wait," he whispered slowly. "With all the equipment on the little *Phantom Atom* to manufacture food and air and water with atomic power, I can last a lifetime—if I must. I can wait and listen. Even at that distance, I ought to pick up something with the visiwave—enough to know if Chan Derron can ever come back."

He tried to grin, again, and waved his hand at the picture of Luroa.

"Till then, my darling," his voice came huskily, "I guess it's good-bye. To you and the Legion and the System. To every man and woman I ever knew. To every street I ever walked. To every bird and every tree. To every living being I ever saw.

"Good-bye—"

Chan Derron gulped suddenly. He turned quickly away from the two pictures on the bulkhead, and looked out into the depthless dark of space. His eyes blinked, once or twice. And his great tanned hands stiffened like iron on the vernier-wheel of the *Phantom Atom*.

The geodynes made a soft musical humming. There was a slow muffled clicking from the automatic pilot. Chan Derron stared northward, into the star-shot dark. There— somewhere in Draco—lay that unknown object, the only possible haven left.

It would be like this, always, he thought. Silence and darkness. He would hear the murmur of his machines, and his own rusty voice, and nothing else. He would talk too much to himself. He would look across the cold dark at the bright points of other worlds. And wonder—

Tchlink!

It was a soft little sound. But Chan Derron stiffened as if it had been the crash of a meteor's impact. He spun, and his hand flashed for the blaster hanging in its holster on the bulkhead. Then he saw the thing that had made the sound, lying on the view-plate of the star-chart cabinet.

The breath went out of him. His hand dropped from the weapon, helplessly. His great shoulders sagged a little. For a long time he stood staring at it, with all the strength and hope running out of him like blood from a wound.

"Even here!" His bronze head shook, wearily. "Even out here."

Slowly, at last, he picked up the sheet of heavy red paper, that had been pinned beneath the crude little serpent of black-burned clay. He read the neat black script:

My Dear Captain Derron:
Congratulations on the brilliance and the daring of your last escape. Samdu has long since turned back,

to try to guard the New Moon—from me! For the moment, you are safe. But I must give you two points of warning.

You will find alarm and danger waiting for you on the moons of Uranus. For the Legion base there has been tipped off that you are on your way.

And you will be held responsible, Captain, I fear, for the things that are going to happen on the New Moon at every midnight—whether you are there or a billion miles away.

Your faithful shadow,
The Basilisk

Stark dread had driven its stunning needle into Chan Derron's spine. He stood dazed, motionless. The mockery of that message swam and blurred upon the red page. And a slow, deadly cold crept into his paralyzed body.

It was more than frightening to know that his every act was followed by a sinister and inescapable power. Frightful to know that the incredible arm of the Basilisk could reach him, even here. Omniscience! Omnipotence! The powers, almost of a god, in the hands of—what?

Almost he could feel that fearful presence with him. He peered about the tiny pilot bay. It was dimly lit with the shaded instrument lights and the faint starlight that struck through the ports. He snapped on a brighter light. He wanted to search the ship. But of course that was no use. There couldn't be anybody here. The mass-detectors with his new hook-up would have given automatic warning of the approach of the mass of a man's body, within a million miles of the ship.

He caught his breath, trying to shake off that shuddery chill, and in spite of himself he began to talk.

"Why keep after me?" he begged the empty air. "I suppose you picked me to take the blame at first, just because I happened to be there outside when you murdered Dr. Eleroid. But haven't I suffered enough—for nothing at all?"

His great clenched fists came up against his breast. He choked back the words—trying doggedly to keep loneliness and strain from cracking his mind. But he couldn't stop the stream of bitter recollection. Ever since his escape in the light cruiser he had since rebuilt into the *Phantom Atom,* he had been in flight from that merciless and omnipotent tormentor. All he wanted was a chance—half a chance—to find a new identity and begin a new life—anywhere!

But that man—if it was a man—who hid behind the name of a fabulous dragon and confused his other victims with a trail of clues pointing always at Chan himself—the Basilisk wouldn't let him get away.

There was the time he landed at a lonely plantation on Ceres, hoping to buy supplies with a few pounds of platinum he had mined from a chance strike in the meteor drift. He found the planter and his wife murdered, their mansion plundered, and a Legion cruiser approaching. He barely got away—to find the loot in his own cabin aboard the *Phantom Atom*.

His bronze-gray eyes began to blink when he thought of the time in old Ekarhenium, when he had left the little ship hidden in the desert and found an honest laboratory job. The first day he worked, his new employer's office safe was robbed—and the plunder found in Chan's own desk.

"And that's not half!" In spite of him, his savage emotion burst into speech again. "There was the time I left the *Phantom Atom* on an eccentric orbit around Venus, and dropped down the shadow cone with a geopeller. Buried my space suit in the jungle and slipped into New Chicago. That time you let me think I had got away—"

He tried to laugh, and caught a sobbing gasp of breath.

"Until I began seeing my face on all the telescreens! Wanted for another killing—" He shrugged heavily. "That murdered guard at the Terrestrial Bank, with my face on the film of his gun-camera—I don't know how you did it.

"But isn't all that enough?"

Choking back the useless words, he stared around the pilot bay again. He was alone. There was only the automatic pilot, clucking softly now and then as it set the cruiser back on course, and the silent serpent of black clay lying on that thick red sheet, and the cold feel of mocking eyes upon him.

"All right, Mr. Basilisk!"

He snatched the serpent, suddenly, and hurled it to shatter into black fragments on the deck. A savage anger took his breath and shook his limbs and roared in his ears.

"Look out!" He gasped harshly. "Because I'm through running away. I don't quite know what I can do—or how —against you and all the Legion. But—look out!"

He stopped the geodynes, and swung grimly to the chart cabinet. The view-plate showed him the greenish point of Earth, and presently the silver atom of the New Moon beside it. He read its position on the calibrated screen, and turned to the calculator to set up his first hopeless move against his unknown tormentor.

5

"At the Blue Unicorn—"

The mighty *Inflexible* slipped gently into a berth against one of the six vast tubular arms of the New Moon's structure. Massive keys locked her trim hundred thousand tons of fighting strength into position. Her valves opened, to communicate with the artificial satellite.

Thre men in plain clothes were sitting at a table in a long, richly simple chamber hidden aft the chart-room of the flagship. The slender man had chosen conservatively dark, exquisitely tailored civilian garb. The white-haired, rugged faced giant had attired himself in lustrous silks that reflected every bright hue of the New Moon's mirrors; he had left behind his tinkling sheaf of medals with a visible reluctance. The careless gray cloak of the third fell loose on his short but massive figure; a heavy cane was gripped in his pudgy yellow hand.

"For life's sake, Jay, what's the mortal haste?" The round, blue-nosed face of Giles Habibula looked imploringly at the tall Commander. "Here we've just sat down to get our precious breath, after that frightful dash across the void of space. We've had but a whiff of dinner, Jay. And now you say that we must go!"

Great Hal Samdu looked at him grimly.

"The dashing could have harmed you little, Giles," he rumbled, "when you were fast in a drunken sleep. And if you've had but a whiff of Jay's good food—then a whole taste would founder a Venusian *gorox!*"

Jay Kalam nodded gravely.

"We're at the New Moon, Giles. Gaspar Hannas is waiting for us, at the valve. And we've a job to do."

Giles Habibula shook the wrinkled yellow sphere of his head, and turned fishy pleading eyes to the Commander.

"I can't stand it, Jay," he whimpered. "It's a turn I can't endure." He pointed a trembling yellow thumb at his protruding middle. "Look at Giles Habibula. He's an old, old man, Giles is. He must ration his precious wine. He must have a cane to aid his limping step. He'll be dead soon, Giles will."

The pale eyes blinked.

"Ah, so, dead—unless the scientists come at the secret of rejuvenation. And precious soon! There's a specialist, Jay, on this very New Moon, whose advertising promised that—but John Star wouldn't let me come!"

He sighed, sadly.

"Aye, the whole world plots for the death of poor old Giles. Look at him, Jay. He was drinking up his last miserable drop of happiness at the Purple Hall. For Phobos is a pleasant world, Jay. The sun in its gardens is kind to the aches in an old man's bones. John Star is a generous host—not always rushing famished guests away from his table, Jay!

"Ah, and it's a comfort to see Aladoree every day—to see her so happy with John Star, Jay, after all the fearful dangers they've come through. A comfort to be near, to guard her, if trouble comes again."

His seamed face smiled a little.

"It gives a lonely, friendless old soldier a tiny mite of happiness, Jay, to dandle Bob Star's daughter on his knee. And to see Kay herself still so lovely, after all the horror of the comet, and so eager for Bob's visits home. The next one, the doctors say, is sure to be a son—but that's a secret, Jay!"

Leaning heavily back in his chair, the old man sighed again.

"Old Giles was happy on Phobos, Jay—happy as the shattered wreck of a dying Legionnaire can be. He had his bit of supper, amid the dear familiar faces. He sipped his precious drop of wine. He dozed quietly away—ah, so, and it might have been into a poor old soldier's well earned last repose! But—no!"

His pale eyes stared accusingly.

"He wakes up in a strange cramped bunk. And he finds he is upon a cruiser of the Legion, shrieking through the frigid gulf of space. Ah, Jay, and his dimming old senses feel the shadow of a frightful danger, rushing down upon him! That's an evil way to serve a defenseless old man, Jay, in his miserable sleep. The shock might stop his heart!"

His fat hands clutched the edges of the table.

" 'Tis a fearful thing, Jay, to alarm folks so! Ah, it made me think of the Medusae. And that evil man-thing Orco, and the fearful Cometeers." He leaned forward, earnestly. "Tell old Giles there's no alarm, Jay! Tell him it's only a monstrous joke."

His small eyes looked anxiously back and forth, between the grave face of Jay Kalam, and the grimly rugged one of Hal Samdu. His wrinkled face faded slowly, to paler, sickly yellow.

"Life's name!" he gasped. "Can the thing be so mortal serious? Speak, Jay! Tell old Giles the truth, before his poor brain cracks."

Rising beside the table, Jay Kalam shook his head.

"There's little enough to tell, Giles," he said. "We have to deal with a criminal, who calls himself the Basilisk. He has got some uncanny mastery of space, so that distance and material barriers apparently mean nothing to him.

"He began in a small way, nearly two years ago. Taking things from secure places. Putting notes and his little clay snakes in impossible places—I recently received one in my office in the Green Hall.

"He keeps attempting something bigger. There have been murders. Now he has served notice that he is going to rob and murder one of the New Moon's patrons, every day. If he goes on—well, Hal is afraid—"

"Afraid?"

Hal Samdu crushed a great fist into the palm of his hand, and towered to his feet.

"Afraid," he rumbled. "Aye, Giles, I'm sick and cold with fear. For if this goes on, the Basilisk can take the keeper of the peace as easily as any luckless gambler—"

"The keeper?" In his own turn, lifting himself with the table and his cane, Giles Habibula heaved anxiously to his feet. His pale eyes blinked at Jay Kalam. "Then why can't she use—AKKA?" His voice had dropped, almost reverently, as he spoke those symbolic letters. "And so end the danger?"

The Commander's dark head shook regretfully.

"Because we don't know who the Basilisk is, Giles," he said. "Or where. Aladoree can't use her weapon, without a target to train it on. If we can ever discover the precise

364

location of the Basilisk in space—before he takes her—that is all we need to know."

"Aye, Giles," Hal Samdu rumbled urgently. "And that is why we sent for you. For you have a gift for opening locks, and discovering hidden things."

Giles Habibula inflated himself.

"Ah, so, Hal," he wheezed. "Old Giles had a spark of genius once—a precious glow of talent that has twice saved the System. And little thanks he got for the saving of it. Ah, once—but it's rusted now. It is dying. Ah, Jay, you might better have left old Giles to his peaceful sleep on Phobos."

His small eyes were blinking at them, swiftly.

"But we must seek the identity of this master of crime. Have you no clue, Jay? No precious clue at all?"

"Aye, Giles," broke in Hal Samdu again. "We've clues enough. Or too many. And they all tell the same story. The Basilisk is the convict, Derron."

"Derron?" wheezed Giles Habibula. "I've heard the name."

"A captain in the Legion," Jay Kalam told him, "Chan Derron was convicted of the murder of Dr. Max Eleroid and suspected of the theft of a mysterious device invented as a weapon for use against the Cometeers. The model was never recovered. Derron escaped from the prison on Ebron, two years ago. The activities of the Basilisk began soon after."

A green light blinked above the door.

"The orderly," Jay Kalam said. "We must go. Gaspar Hannas is expecting us, and we've only two hours."

"Two hours!" gasped Giles Habibula. "Jay, you speak as if we were condemned and waiting to die."

"It's two hours until midnight, New Moon time," Jay Kalam explained. "That is when this criminal has promised to appear—and we may have a chance to trap him."

Giles Habibula squirmed uneasily. "How do you hope to do that?"

"We are taking steps," Jay Kalam answered. "First, the ten cruisers of Hal's fleet are on guard against the approach of any strange ship. Second, within the New Moon, Gaspar Hannas has promised the full cooperation of his special police—they'll be on duty everywhere. Third, we will be waiting within the New Moon ourselves, with a score of Legion men in plain clothes."

365

"It is this man Derron, that we must take," grimly added Hal Samdu. "There's evidence enough that he's the one we want. Gaspar Hannas has raised the reward for him to a quarter of a million. We've papered all the New Moon with his likeness. The guards, and the players, too, will be alert. If he comes here tonight, we'll get him!"

"Ah, so, Hal!" wheezed Giles Habibula. "But if all you've told me is true—if distance and walls mean nothing to this strange power with which the Basilisk is armed—then perhaps he can strike down the poor gambler without coming here himself."

"Anyhow—" and Jay Kalam beckoned toward the door where the green light was blinking still—"we must go. If he comes, we may take him. If he doesn't, we may still discover some clue. Anything—"

His lean jaw set.

"Anything to tell us where he is, so that he can be destroyed."

Gigantic Hal Samdu stalking ahead, Giles Habibula waddling and puffing and laboring with his cane behind, they went out of the Commander's apartment, out through the chart room and the great armored valves of the *Inflexible,* into the New Moon.

Gaspar Hannas met them. Huge as Hal Samdu, he was dressed in loose flowing black. The black emphasized the whiteness of his monstrous soft-fleshed hands and his vast smooth face. His black, deepset eyes were distended and darting with fear. Sweat shone on his forehead and his white bald head. But his blank face greeted them with its slow and idiotic grin.

"Gentlemen!" he gasped hoarsely. "Commander! We must hasten. Time draws short. The guards are posted, and I've been waiting—"

His voice choked off, abruptly, and he started back from Giles Habibula. Leaning heavily on his cane, the old man was peering at him. The old soldier's yellow face broke into a wondering grin.

"In life's name!" he wheezed. "It's Pedro the Shar—"

The mindless smile congealed on the white lax face of Gaspar Hannas, and his huge hands made a frightened gesture for silence. His eyes swept the fat man swaying on the cane, and he whispered hoarsely:

"Habibula. It's been fifty years. But I know you. You're Giles the Gh—"

"Stop!" gasped Giles Habibula. "For I know you—

366

Gaspar Hannas—in spite of your artificial face. And I've more on you than you do on me. So you had better hold your mortal tongue!"

He steadied himself, with both hands on the cane, and his pale eyes blinked at the giant in black.

"Gaspar Hannas!" he wheezed. "The great Gaspar Hannas, the New Moon's master! Well, you've come a long way, since the time of the Blue Unicorn. You must have eluded the posse in the jungle—"

The big man lifted his hand again, fearfully.

"Wait, Habibula!" he gasped. "And forget—"

"Ah, so, old Giles can forget—for a price." The old man sighed. "Life has served us mortals different. Here you have made a mighty fortune. Men say the New Moon has made you the System's richest man. Your poor old comrade is but a penniless veteran of the Legion, starved and friendless and ill." He quivered to a sob. "Pity old Giles Habibula—"

"In fifty years, you have not changed!" Admiration rang in the husky voice of Hannas. "What do you want?"

The yellow face was suddenly beaming.

"Ah, Mr. Hannas, you can trust the discretion of Giles Habibula! The luxury of your accommodations here is famous, Mr. Hannas. The excellence of your food. The vintages of your wines."

Gaspar Hannas smiled his senseless smile.

"You are the guests of the New Moon," he said. "You and your comrades of the Legion. You shall have the best."

The fishy eyes of Giles Habibula blinked triumphantly at his companions.

"Ah, thank you, Mr. Hannas!" he wheezed. "And I believe that duty is now carrying us into your salons of chance. It's many a long year, Mr. Hannas, since old Giles risked a dollar for more than fun. But this meeting has brought the old days back, when the wheels of chance were meat and drink—aye, and life's precious blood—"

Gaspar Hannas nodded, and his smile seemed to stiffen again.

"I remember, Giles," he said. "Too well. But come. We've no time to waste on games." He looked at the old soldier again, and added reluctantly, "But if you really wish to play, the head croupier in the no-limit hall will give you a hundred blue chips."

"I, too, remember," sighed Giles Habibula. "At the Blue Unicorn—"

"Five hundred!" cried Gaspar Hannas, hastily. "And let us go."

Jay Kalam nodded, and Hal Samdu stalked impatiently ahead.

"Ah, so," gasped Giles Habibula. "Post your guards. And set your traps. And let's go on to the tables. Let your bright wheels turn, your precious blood race fast as the numbers fall. Let brain meet brain in the battle where wits are the victor. Ah, the breath of the old days is in my lungs again!" He waddled ponderously forward.

"There'll be no danger from this Chan Derron," he wheezed hopefully. "There's no human being—aye, none but old Giles Habibula himself—could pass Hal's fleet and the New Moon's walls and all these guards, to come here tonight.

"And as for your precious Basilisk—I trust he'll prove to be no more than some hoax—*In life's name, what was that?*"

Some little dark object had fallen out of the air before him. It had struck the floor and shattered. From the fragments of it, however, he could see that it had been the small figurine of a serpent, crudely formed of black-burned clay.

6

"You're Chan Derron!"

The old Moon has been eclipsed two or three times a year, whenever the month-long circuit of its orbit carried it through the diminishing tip of Earth's shadow cone. The New Moon, nearer the planet, plunged through a brief eclipse every six hours. Upon that fact, Chan Derron made his plan.

During his strenuous years at the Legion academy, Chan had somehow found time for amateur theatricals. Often enough, in these last two fugitive years, his actor's skill had served him well. And now he called upon it for a new identity.

He became Dr. Charles Derrel, marine biologist, just returned from a benthosphere exploration of the polar seas of Venus, now in search of recreation on the New Moon. His bronze hair was dyed black, his bronze-gray eyes darkened with a chemical stain, his tanned skin bleached to a Venusian pallor. A blue scar twisted his face, where the fangs of a sea-monster had torn it. He limped on the foot that a closing valve had crushed. His brown eyes squinted, against unfamiliar sun.

"That will do." He nodded at the stranger in the mirror. "If you ever get past the fleet and the guards."

Another bit of preparation, he took the geopeller unit out of a spare space suit and strapped it to his shoulders under his clothing. (The geopeller, invented by Max Eleroid, was a delicate miniature geodesic deflector, with its own atomic power pack. Little larger than a man's hand, controlled from a spindle-shaped knob on a short cable, it converted an ordinary space suit into a complete geodesic ship. A tiny thing, yet already it had brought many a spacewrecked flier across a hundred million miles or more to safety.)

The *Phantom Atom* drifted into the Earth's shadow cone, beyond the old Moon's orbit. It dropped inertly Earthward. Hal Samdu's patrolling cruisers set red points to blazing on the detector screens, but they would not discover Chan so easily, for the few tons of his ship were as nothing, against their many thousands. And the powerful, ever-shifting gravitational, magnetic, and electrostatic fields of the Earth far reduced the sensitivity of any detector in the planet's close vicinity.

The Earth grew beneath him. A great disk of denser darkness, it was ringed with supernal fire, where the atmosphere refracted the hidden sun's rays into a wondrous circle that blazed with the red essence of all sunsets. The silvery web of the spinning sign slid into that ring and vanished in the dark.

With a careful hand on the vernier-wheel, straining his eyes in the faint red dusk, Chan Derron found it again. He piloted the *Phantom Atom* to the motor-house that controlled a great flimsy mirror of sodium foil out at the rim of that vast wheel, and locked the ship against it with a magnetic anchor.

Slipping into white, trim-fitting metal, Chan snapped

369

his blaster to its belt, and went out through the valve. One bolt from his blaster severed the power leads. And he waited, at the mirror's edge, until the sun came back. The great sheet burned with white fire, and the little ship behind it lay hidden in total darkness. But if the mirror turned—

At last the technician arrived, sliding up a pilot wire from the metal star of the New Moon's heart, carrying a kit of tools to repair the disabled unit. Gripping the control-spindle of the geopeller, Chan flung himself to meet him.

They sprawled together in space. The technician, after his first surprise, displayed a wiry strength. He groped for his atomic torch, that would have cut Chan's armor like paper.

"I've got a blaster." Vibration of metal in furious contact carried Chan's words. "But I don't want your life—only your number and your keys."

"Derron!" The man's face went white within his helmet. "The convict—we were warned." Chan grabbed for the torch. But the fight had gone out of the other. Limp with terror, he was gasping: "For God's sake, Derron, don't kill me. I'll do anything you want!"

His name, it seemed to Chan, had grown stronger than his body! And more dangerous than any enemy. Swiftly, he took the prisoner's tools, his work-sheet, his keys, and the number-plate—a black-stenciled yellow crescent—from his helmet. With the man's own torch, he welded the shoulder-piece of his armor to the motor-house.

"In three hours," Chan promised, "I'll be back, and let you go."

He grasped a sliding ring on the pilot wire, and the geopeller sent him plunging down five hundred miles to the New Moon's heart. The wire brought him to a great platform, on one of the vast tubular arms of the central star. He dropped amid half a score of other men, all with kits of tools, and hastened with them into a great air-valve.

His own face looked at him, from the wall of the valve. *$250,000 REWARD!* shrieked crimson letters. *LOOK!* This man may be beside you—*NOW!*

At a wicket, as he filed with the others out of the valve, he turned in his captured work-sheet. "Inspect and repair Mirror 17-B-285" was the order at its head. He scrawled at the bottom of it, *Defective switch located and repaired.*

How long would he have, he wondered, before some

other repairman, sent out to do a better job, would find the first welded to the motor-house beside the *Phantom Atom?* But if he had won just three hours—

In the locker rooms, where the men were squirming out of their metal, hastening under the showers, gratefully donning their clothing, he saw that ominous poster again. And all the talk he heard was of Chan Derron and the Basilisk, and whether the two could be the same, and whether the promised robbery and murder would be carried out at midnight.

Chan Derron found the locker to which his borrowed number corresponded. He hung up his suit, hastily donned the somewhat-too-small lounging pajamas and loose cloak that he discovered there, and thrust himself into a group of tired men bound for home and supper.

"Keep yer optics hot," advised a little mechanic beside him. "Any big man you see tonight might be good for that quarter million. You don't know who—"

"You don't know who," Chan agreed.

He left the workmen, and a little door let him out upon the vast, noisy open space beneath the docks, thronged with incoming passengers from the space liners above. He closed the door, and sighed with relief. For he had passed the fleet, and the New Moon's walls, and the alert inspectors scrutinizing every man that came down the gangplanks above. He was safe—

"Your reservation check, sir?"

It was an attentive, dark-skinned Martian porter. The grimy paper sticking from the pocket of his yellow uniform, Chan saw, was another copy of that notice of reward. With a worried frown, Chan patted his borrowed pockets.

"Oh, I remember!" He squinted and blinked. "Left it in my baggage. Can you get me a duplicate?"

Were the dark eyes studying his scar? He eased the crippled foot.

"Yes, sir. A temporary check. Your name, sir?"

"Dr. Charles Derrel. Marine biologist. From Venus, en route to Earth. Two days here." He squinted again. "Can you get me some dark glasses? Not used to the light. The clouds on Venus, you know—"

The check, evidently a necessary passport to the New Moon's wonders, was presently procured. Chan dispatched the porter to look for non-existent baggage, and hurried on alone. The transit bands—a series of gliding belts whose moving coffee-tables and bars were crowded with bright-clad vacationists—carried him through endless enormous halls, past glittering shops and the tall black portals of the Hall of Euthanasia. But Chan had eyes for nothing until he saw the Casino—for it was there that he might hope to meet the Basilisk at midnight.

Transparent and illuminated from within, the pillars at the entrance looked like columns hewn from living gems. Ruby and emerald, they were covered with a delicate rime of gold. Tiny beneath their unbelievable glitter, a woman stood waiting.

He swung off the belt.

The girl was tall, with a proud grace of poise that he had rarely seen. The wealth of her hair was platinum white; her fine skin was white; she wore a fortune in white Callistonian furs. And her eyes, he saw, were a rare true violet.

He hurried on, to pass her.

She was utterly beautiful. Her loveliness set a painful throb to going in his throat. He could not help a twinge of bitterness at thought of the double barrier between them—her obvious wealth and reserve, and his own more than desperate situation. If he had been some idle billionaire, he was thinking bleakly, perhaps returning from his colonial mines and plantations, she might have been waiting for him—

His heart came up in his mouth.

For the girl was coming swiftly toward him, across the vast gold-veined emerald that floored the entrance. The white perfection of her face lit with a welcoming smile. Her eyes were warm with recognition. In a joyous voice —but one too low for any other to hear—she greeted him by name:

"Why, Chan! You're Chan Derron!"

Rooted with wonder, Chan shuddered to those syllables that made his body worth a quarter of a million dollars, living or dead. The smile of admiration congealed on his face. Moving with the weightless life of a flame, the girl came up to him, and eagerly seized his nerveless hand in hers.

7

The Luck of Giles Habibula

The salons of chance occupied a series of six immense halls radiating from the private office of Gaspar Hannas, which was situated at the very hub of the New Moon's wheel. The walls of the office were transparent from within, and Hannas, from the huge swivel chair within his ring-shaped desk, could look at will down any one of the halls.

They were huge and costly rooms. The walls bore expensive statues, expensive murals, golden statues set in niches. And their polished floors were covered with thousands of tables of chance.

Beneath each hall ran an armored tunnel, unsuspected by most of the players above, where their losses were swiftly examined for counterfeit, counted, tabulated, and dispatched to the impregnably armored treasure vault beneath the office of Gaspar Hannas. A continuous tape, fed through a slot in the circular desk, revealed minute by minute the New Moon's gains and losses. The losses all appeared in red but that color was rarely seen.

"The laws of probability," Gaspar Hannas always insisted, smiling his fixed and mindless smile, "are all I need. Every game is fair."

And cynics, it had been suspected, were apt to find their doubts very unexpectedly terminated in the Hall of Euthanasia.

The six halls, tonight, were more than commonly crowded. For the whisper of the Basilisk had run over all the New Moon, and a great many thrill-seekers in their gayest silks and jewels had turned out to see what would happen at midnight. The play, however, as recorded on the endless tape, was somewhat slow—too many had heard that the highest winner was unlikely to keep his winnings.

Gaspar Hannas, for once, was not watching the tape.

He was walking with the three Legionnaires through the Diamond Room, where no limit was placed upon the stakes. Hal Samdu, in his great gnarled hand, carried a tattered notice of reward.

"This convict, Derron," he insisted. "He's your Basilisk."

And he refreshed his memory, from time to time, with another look at the bronze-haired, space-tanned likeness of Chan Derron.

"Yonder!" Jay Kalam paused abruptly. "Derron was a big man. There's one as big."

They followed his grave dark eyes.

"Ah, so!" Giles Habibula was puffing mightily, from keeping pace with Hal Samdu's impatient stride. "A majestic figure of manhood. And a lovely lass at his side!"

The man stood like a tower above all the restless, bright-clad players. His hair was dark, dark glasses shaded his eyes, and his skin had a singular pallor. A long scar marred his face.

The blond girl beside him was equally striking. With a queen's proud grace, she wore a lustrous cloak of priceless white Callistonian fur. A queer white star-shaped jewel—it looked, Jay Kalam thought, like a hugely magnified snow-crystal—hung at her throat.

"Six-feet-three!" Hal Samdu caught a gasping breath, and the poster trembled in his mighty hand. "He can't hide that—and the paleness and the dark hair and the glasses could be disguise!" He beckoned to one of the soldiers in plain clothes, trailing unobtrusively behind. "We'll arrest him, and soon find out."

Jay Kalam's head shook sharply.

"Shadow him," he whispered. "But if he is Derron— and the Basilisk—we must see more of his methods. Meantime—"

He breathed something to Giles Habibula.

"In life's name, Jay!" The small fishy eyes of the old man rolled at him, startled. "Don't ask me that! Don't command a poor old soldier to throw away his life!"

"Remember, Giles." Hal Samdu caught his shoulder. "It's for the keeper of the peace."

Giles Habibula winced, and heaved himself away.

"Don't mangle me, Hal!" he gasped. "For life's blessed sake! Of course I'll do what Jay desires. Aye, for the keeper—" He turned ponderously to the white giant in black. "Ah, Mr. Hannas," he wheezed, "now I must have your order for a thousand blue chips."

"A thousand! A million dollars worth?" The idiot's smile stiffened upon the face of Gaspar Hannas, and he looked protestingly at Jay Kalam. "Commander, this is blackmail!"

"No blacker," whispered Giles Habibula, "than the bloody career of Pedro the Shark!"

"I'll give it to you!"

Clutching the order, Giles Habibula waddled toward the table. A smart jab with his cane, in the ribs of a purple-clad woman as corpulent as himself, made him a place beside the green-cloaked giant and the girl in white. He presented the order to the startled croupier.

"A thousand blue chips, mister—or make it a hundred of your mortal diamond ones."

He turned to the pale tall stranger.

"Begging your pardon, sir," he wheezed. "But my poor old hands scatter the chips, they tremble so. And your lucky touch, I see, has won a fortune for the lovely lass beside you. Would you kindly place my bets, sir?"

"If you like." The big man relaxed. "How much are you playing?"

Giles Habibula gestured at the stacks of his chips.

"The million," he said. "On thirty-nine."

Even here in the Diamond Room, such a play made a stir. Spectators crowded up to watch the wheel. With his small eyes half closed, Giles Habibula watched the croupier flick the ball into its polished track, and then lift his hand dramatically over the wheel.

"Eh!" he muttered. "Not when old Giles plays!"

He turned to the man and the girl.

"Thank you, sir!" he puffed. "And now we await the turn of luck—or skill!" His leaden eyes lit with a sudden admiration of the girl's proud grace. "A lovely thing!" he wheezed. "As lovely as you are, my dear—that blue tapestry from Titan!"

His cane pointed suddenly across the table, held with an odd sure steadiness in his pudgy yellow hands, so that its polished green head was precisely opposite the still up-lifted hand of the croupier, across the wheel.

The croupier gulped and whitened. His hand dropped, dramatically, as he followed the racing ball.

"Ah, and that golden nymph!" The cane fell, precisely as the hand, pointing to a statue in its niche. And the quick eyes of Giles Habibula came back to the girl in white. "Dancing as you might dance, my dear!"

The croupier stood trembling. His pale face ran sudden little rivulets of sweat. And the clicking ball fell at last into the slot. Blank, distended, stricken, the eyes of the croupier came up to the seamed yellow face of Giles Habibula.

"You are the winner, sir," he croaked. "At forty to one!"

"Precisely," agreed Giles Habibula. "And none of your chips or scrip—give me forty millions in good new Green Hall certificates."

The quivering fingers of the croupier tapped the keys before him, and presently a thick packet of currency popped up out of the magnetic tube. While hushed spectators stared, he counted out forty crisp million-dollar bills.

Tembling suddenly as violently as the other man, Giles Habibula snatched up the forty stiff new certificates. He swung hastily, and his fat arm struck the pale man in green, scattering the bills out of his hand.

"My life!" he sobbed. "My forty millions! For Earth's sweet sake, help a poor old man to save his miserable mite!"

After the first awed moment, there was an excited scramble after the bills. Giles Habibula, stooping and snatching, fell against the tall man. The stranger caught him and helped him back to his feet.

"Ah, thank you, sir!" Small eyes glittering, he was avidly seizing and counting the returned money. "Thank you. Thank you generously, madam!" He heaved a vast sigh of relief. "Ah, it's all here! Thank you!"

He waddled triumphantly back to where his three companions were ostensibly watching another table. Ignoring the peculiarly pale and sick-looking smile on the face of Gaspar Hannas, he dropped something into Jay Kalam's palm.

"Ah, Jay," he panted, "it cost me mortal peril—aye, and the last desperate exertion of my failing genius—but here are your suspect's keys, and his reservation check."

"Mortal peril?" echoed Gaspar Hannas, faintly. "It cost me forty million dollars!"

The Commander studied the oblong yellow card.

"Charles Derrel," he muttered. "Marine biologist, from Venus." His dark eyes narrowed. "It's just a temporary check—'original mislaid.' And the initials—Charles Derrel and Chan Derron!"

Hal Samdu's great fists clenched.

"Aye, Jay!" he whispered. "Shall we arrest him now?"

"Not yet," said the Commander. "Wait for me here."

He walked quickly to the table, and touched the tall man's arm. The stranger turned very quickly to meet him. And the quickly checked movement of his arm told the Commander that some weapon hung ready beneath the green cloak.

"These were dropped when the money was being picked up, just now." Jay Kalam allowed a glimpse of the keys and the yellow card. "If you can identify the check—"

The stranger stared through his dark glasses, speechless. But the girl stepped forward. Her gracious white arm slipped through the stranger's and she gave Jay Kalam a smile that took his breath.

"Of course he can." Rich as a singer's, her voice was quick and positive. "Or I can identify him. Sir, this is Dr. Charles Derrel. Recently from Venus. My fiance."

"Thank you." With a sudden intense effort of memory, Jay Kalam studied the girl. "Who, may I ask, are you?"

The proud, impersonal violet eyes met his.

"Vanya Eloyan." She spoke as if she were saying *I am a princess*. "From Thule."

The Commander bowed, and dropped the card and the ring of keys into the stranger's powerful hand. The girl smiled dazzling thanks, and then took her companion's arm and turned him back to the table.

Rubbing thoughtfully at his lean, dark chin, Jay Kalam found his own companions at another table, where the wheel paid one hundred to one. Giles Habibula, his moon-face intent, was pointing with his cane, across the spinning wheel, toward the stupendous magnificence of a mural depicting the old Moon's end.

The croupier behind the table, with a desperate illness in his eyes, was staring slack-jawed at Gaspar Hannas. His hand moved, in a convulsive gesture, to mop his brow. And the old man's cane moved swiftly also, pointing.

"And there," he wheezed, "stands the lovely likeness of Aladoree!"

"Restrain yourself, Habibula," rasped Gaspar Hannas. "Or you'll destroy the New Moon as surely as she did the old! For honor's sake—"

The number fell. The croupier's mouth opened in a

strangled moan. He gulped, and made a helpless little shrug at Gaspar Hannas.

"You are the winner, sir," at last his voice came squeakily. "Twenty million played, at one hundred to one. You have won two billion dollars." He tapped uncertainly at his keys. "We'll have it for you in a moment, from the vaults."

The great white hand of Gaspar Hannas caught the old man's cloak.

"Habibula," he croaked huskily, "have you no mercy? In honor's name—"

The fishy eyes of Giles Habibula blinked reprovingly.

"Ah, me! But that's a strange word to hear from you, Gaspar Hannas! Precious little honor has been found in anything your foul hands have touched, in the forty years that I have known you." He turned back to the table. "I want my two billion."

In hundred-million-dollar Green Hall certificates, the first his blinking eyes had ever seen, his winnings were pushed toward him. With that amazing quick dexterity that his fat hands sometimes displayed, he shuffled through them to check the count.

"Pedro," he wheezed sadly, "you shouldn't begrudge me this—not when all your New Moon's splendor is built upon the cornerstone of my poor old brain. For I find you still using the same simple devices I invented for the tables of the Blue Unicorn!"

He patted his crackling pocket, contentedly.

"It would serve you right, Hannas, if I played all the night. Ah, so! Even if I broke your New Moon, and made you beg for the black chip of admission to your own Euthanasia Clinic!

"But I won't do that, Hannas." He swung heavily on his cane. "Because I'm more honest than you ever were, Pedro—aye, there's a limit to my stealing. Ah, so, one more play is all I want. Just one billion dollars, Hannas, at a hundred to one."

Gaspar Hannas staggered, and his white jaw slackened.

"Habibula!" he husked. "In the name of Ethyra Coran—"

"Don't utter her name!" gasped Giles Habibula. "To show you why not, I'll just play two billion!"

"You can't do that!" Hannas choked. "I—I think that table's out of order. We're closing it—"

"Then I'll find another," wheezed Giles Habibula.

But Jay Kalam touched his arm.

"Better keep close beside us, Giles," the Commander whispered. "Move slowly, so that the plain-clothes men can gather in around you. And you had better keep your own eyes on Dr. Derrel, for you've got just twenty minutes now."

"I?" Giles Habibula blinked at him. "You make me feel like a convict on Devil's Rock waiting for the ray." He touched his pocket again, with a sidewise look at Gaspar Hannas. "I know he'd slit my poor old throat in an instant, Jay. But surely, with so many of you here, he wouldn't dare. For Pedro was ever a white-livered coward at the core."

"I was speaking, Giles," Jay Kalam told him gravely, "of your danger at midnight, when the Basilisk has threatened to strike."

"The B-B-B-Basilisk?" Giles Habibula stuttered through ashen, quivering lips. "Aye, the mortal Basilisk! You told me he had threatened to abduct and murder some luckless p-p-p-player. But why should he pick on m-m-m-m-me?"

Gaspar Hannas caught his breath, and his white baby-grin seemed for an instant genuinely mirthful.

"Didn't we tell you, Giles?" asked Jay Kalam's grave, astonished voice. "Didn't we tell you that the Basilisk has promised to come at midnight—in eighteen minutes now, to rob and murder the highest winner?"

"And your two billions, Habibula, are the richest winnings in the New Moon's history." The great voice of Gaspar Hannas had a ring of savage glee. "But I'll cash them, if you like—for one black chip!"

8

The Man Who Flickered

Giles Habibula began to tremble. His bulging middle quivered. Drops of sweat stood out on his furrowed yellow face. His small eyes seemed to glaze. His teeth chattered violently, and then, false to him, fell out on the floor.

"Ahuh!" he gasped. *"Yuh—whuh—!"*

He began tearing furiously to get his winnings out of his pocket. Jay Kalam recovered and returned the teeth. He took them clattering into the cavern of his mouth, and cried piteously:

"Jay! Ah, Jay, why didn't you tell me? A poor blind old man, tottering on the very brink of life, a creeping famished toothless wretch. Jay, would you let old Giles thrust his neck into the very noose of death?"

"You've Hal's fleet to guard you," the Commander sought to reassure him, "and ten thousand of the New Moon's police. We'll protect you, Giles."

"Aye!" An eager fighting glint lit the blue eyes of Hal Samdu. "We've set a trap for this Basilisk—and now you've baited it well, Giles, with your two billion dollars!"

"Ah, no!" sobbed Giles Habibula. "Old Giles will bait no traps—not with his poor old flesh!" He was staggering back to the table he had just left so triumphantly. "How long did you say, Jay?" he gasped. "Eighteen minutes—to lose more than two billion dollars?"

The croupier went white again, to see him returning.

"Hasten, man!" The old soldier gasped. "Call for the bets, and spin your ball! In life's mortal name, is this place a hall of chance—or the black Euthanasia Clinic?"

The croupier gulped and whispered hoarsely:

"Place your bets, gentlemen! Bets on the table!"

The leaden eyes of Giles Habibula were peering along the row of players.

"Some mortal fool has got to win," he croaked. His glance fell upon a little gray man, opposite: a dried-up wisp of humanity, whose pale anxious eyes, through heavy-lensed glasses, were peering at endless rows of notations in a small black book. His thin nervous fingers were tapping at the keys of a compact, noiseless computing machine. Only three blue chips remained before him on the board. Giles Habibula called to him, "Brother, do you want to win?"

The little stranger blinked up at him, in near-sighted bewilderment.

"Sir," came a shrill piping voice, "I do. More than anything else in the world. I have been laboring many years —I have made twenty million calculations—endeavoring to perfect my system of play. I have three chips left."

"Forget your mortal system," wheezed Giles Habibula. "And play your three chips on one hundred and one."

The little man scratched his gray head uncertainly, peering vaguely back at his book and his calculating machine.

"But my system, sir, based on the permutations of numbers and the gravitational influence of the planets—my system—"

"Fool!" hissed a mousetrap-faced female beside him. "Play! Old blubber-guts has got something! He just cleaned up a couple of billions!"

She set a stack of her own chips on one-hundred-one.

Giles blinked, and the croupier spun his ball.

The little gray man looked at his machine, and put one chip on forty-nine. The fat yellow hands of Giles Habibula, handling the green certificates as if they had been incandescent metal, laid the stack of his winnings on the double-zero.

"Two billions and a few odd millions," he told the chalk-faced croupier. And his voice dropped to a rasp of deadly menace. "And don't you move until that ball stops. Don't take a mortal breath! I'll handle the relays."

He looked back at the little gray man.

"On second thought, brother," he wheezed, "your forty-nine will win. Due to gravitational influences!" He thrust the green handle of his cane abruptly into the croupier's pasty face. "You stand still!"

The cane lifted, with a slow, deliberate sweep, and the ball clicked into the slot.

"Forty-nine is the winner!" Sobbing with pale faced relief, the croupier snatched up the sheaf of bills from zero-zero. With a trembling wand, he raked in the other bets. He pushed a stack of a hundred chips to the small gray man.

The bleak faced woman made some sound, very much under her breath, and abruptly departed.

"My system!" piped the frail little man, excitedly. "At last—it wins!"

His thin fingers recorded the play in his little black book. They tapped the silent keys of his machine. He peered at the dial, and then pushed the stack of his chips back upon the number forty-nine.

The colorless eyes of Giles Habibula glittered at the croupier.

"Forty-nine," he predicted, "will win again."

The croupier licked his dry lips. His glazing eyes shot a despairing glance at Gaspar Hannas. He hoarsely called for bets, and spun the ball, and watched its clicking circle with a kind of white horror on his face.

And forty-nine won!

"My system!" The gray man clutched with shaking hands at chips pushed toward him. "For twenty years," he whispered, "Dr. Abel Davian has been thought a visionary fool. But now—" His heavy lenses stared about the hushed, wondering table. "Now, sirs, he must be acknowledged a mathematical genius!"

"He's still a fool." Gaspar Hannas spoke to Jay Kalam, not troubling to lower his contemptuous voice. "A pathological gambler. I've seen thousands like him—egotistical enough to think they can invent some lunatic system to cheat the mathematics of probability. They never know when they've had enough, until they finally come begging for a free black chip. Davian probably will tomorrow, when he has lost what he wins tonight."

The commander nodded with a glance of pity at the trembling man, whose frantic fingers were stabbing now at the keyboard of the calculator. He turned slowly back to the master of the New Moon, his dark face drawn firm as if to veil some unspoken accusation.

"An old client, eh?"

"He has been fighting for twenty years to break me." Blinking implacably, Hannas stood watching Davian enter the results of his play in the little black book. "I've got to know him well, from all the times he has come whining for me to cash his worthless I O U's. I even met his wife, on their first trip out to my old ship—a charming girl, who tried for years to save him, after he had thrown away everything they had, before she finally realized that euthanasia is the only cure for his kind. He used to have a responsible position in the statistical department of some research firm. Look at him now—a ragged nobody."

Hannas chuckled, with a mirthless scorn.

"They're all alike," he said. "They lose everything, and the syndicate pays their way home. But they aren't content. They never learn. They've got to get even. They sell their homes. They break their relatives. They borrow from their friends, until they have no friends. They live in squalor, and scrape and beg and steal—and keep coming back out here to try again to break the bank."

"An unfortunate case." Jay Kalam turned thoughtfully from the white-faced gambler, to study the idiot smile of Hannas. "Don't you ever feel responsible?"

"I didn't invent human nature." Hannas shrugged disdainfully. "But the syndicate doesn't encourage such patrons. The personal disasters they bring upon themselves tend to reflect on our establishment, and too many of them finally become bitter and desperate enough to create unpleasant public scenes by killing themselves at the tables, or even sometimes attacking our own people, instead of decently requesting that free black chip."

He sniffed derisively.

"They're all alike," he repeated. "This Davian is only a little more persistent than the rest—"

Jay Kalam glanced at his chronometer and touched the big man's arm.

"Twelve minutes to midnight," he said softly. "I think we had better be moving along. But signal your men to keep their eyes on this Dr. Derrel."

They went on across the vast floor, Hal Samdu stalking impatiently ahead. Laboring and puffing, Giles Habibula fell behind. Sweat broke out on his yellow face.

"In life's name!" he sobbed. "Jay, Hal, can't you wait for poor old Giles? Would you leave him alone with the fearful Basilisk at his heels? Can't you feel the tensity of doom in the very air, aye, and see the stark print of fear on every mortal face?"

Jay Kalam had paused, and the old man snatched at his arm.

"Come, Jay!" he gasped. "For life's sake, let's make ready for the moment. Let's stand against the wall, Jay, and gather all our men about us, with blasters ready—"

"Shut up, Giles!" rapped Hal Samdu. "There's no danger, but to the winner. None, I think, if we surround this Dr. Derrel—"

"My mortal life!"

It was an apprehensive croak from Giles Habibula. Trembling, his arm was pointing at a table where the play had stopped. A tall man dressed in white was setting upon it some bulky object wrapped in brown canvas.

Giles Habibula stared anxiously, as he uncovered it. A square black box was revealed, with polished brass rods projecting from the sides and the top. A little instrument-board was wired to the box, and a set of phones that the man slipped off his head.

"Who is he?" Giles Habibula had caught the arm of Hannas. "In life's precious name, what is that machine?" His thin voice quavered. "I don't like the look of such strange machines—not when we're dealing with such an unknown monster as the Basilisk!"

"That's only John Comaine," said the rusty voice of Gaspar Hannas. "We'll speak to him."

He lead them to the man whose brain had conceived the New Moon. Comaine, in his white laboratory jacket, looked robust and athletic. His stiff blond hair stood on end. He had a square stern mask of a face, with slightly protruding, emotionless blue eyes. He nodded to Gaspar Hannas, in stiff and uncordial greeting.

"Comaine," said Hannas, "this is Commander Kalam and his aides; they have come to hunt the Basilisk."

The glassy, bulging eyes looked at them briefly, coldly.

"Gentlemen." His voice was dry, metallic, inflectionless. "I am attacking the problem in my own way. I built the New Moon. I am going to defend it."

Giles Habibula was gaping at the black box.

"Ah, so, Dr. Comaine. And what is that?"

"The operations of the Basilisk," Comaine said briefly, "display the use of an unfamiliar scientific instrumentality. The first step, obviously, is to detect and analyze the forces used."

And he turned abruptly back to his instrument panel.

"Ah, so," wheezed Giles Habibula. "You are right. And that is that!"

And they went on among the tables, watchfully scanning the thousands of players. An increasing tension charged the air. Play had almost stopped. A nervous hush was spreading, broken now and then by a voice too loud, by a laugh that jangled with unadmitted fear. Many who had come to watch the work of the Basilisk seemed to regret their early courage, and there was an increasing trickle of silent men and women toward the doors.

Abruptly Giles Habibula stopped again.

"I know that man!" He pointed furtively ahead. "Aye, forty years ago, at the Blue Unicorn! He is Amo Brelekko!"

"Naturally you know him," rasped the great voice of Gaspar Hannas. "For you and he and I were three of a kind, in those old days."

"Ah, what's that?" Giles Habibula inflated himself, indignantly. "In life's name, Hannas, I'll not have you say three of a kind!" His fat lips made a sharp, startling sound, as if he had spat. "Neither you nor the Eel ever did a mortal thing, but Giles could do it quicker and smoother and more silently, with precious less danger from the law!"

His leaden eyes went back to the tall man strolling toward them. Amo Brelekko was gaunt to the point of emaciation. His huge head was completely bald. A long hatchet nose accented the knife-like sharpness of his face. He now wore brilliant purple lounging pajamas, and a flaming yellow robe. A great diamond pinned his tunic, and the lean yellow claws of his fingers were glittering with rings.

"Amo the Eel!" whispered Giles Habibula. "You wouldn't know that forty mortal years had gone. He looks just the same. He had the swiftest hands I ever knew—aye, beside my precious own!"

His pale eyes blinked shrewdly at the New Moon's master.

"What is he doing here, Hannas? You couldn't let him play. He knows your tricks as well as I do."

The white giant smiled his silly smile.

"Brelekko has been here since the New Moon was built," said Gaspar Hannas. "I offered him ten thousand dollars a day to play for the house. He refused. He said that he would prefer to take his money from the other side of the table.

"And he does. But he is more moderate than you were, Habibula. He limits his winnings scrupulously to ten thousand dollars a day. I don't regret his presence. His spectacular methods of play make him a valuable advertisement."

"Aye, he'd be good." Giles Habibula nodded. "Though he was only a youth when I knew him, he already showed a precious promise, in the quickness of his hands."

"Brelekko is a gifted man," agreed Gaspar Hannas. "He's a skilled amateur magician—sometimes he gives a special performance for our guests. His brain is as clever as his hands. He invented the game of hyper-chess, and none can beat him at it."

"I never tried," muttered Giles Habibula.

"His suite is equipped as an astrophysical laboratory," Hannas went on, "with an observatory dome outside, on the New Moon's hull. By avocation he is a brilliant scientist, by vocation the greatest gambler in the System—"

The leaden eye of Giles Habibula had begun to glitter.

"Except," Gaspar Hannas added very hastily, "of course, yourself."

His great white hand beckoned, and Amo Brelekko came to meet them. When his dark eyes found the waddling old man in gray, however, he stopped abruptly. Gems glittered in a sudden arc, as his lean hand flashed toward his armpit.

But the thick cane of Giles Habibula was first. It snapped up level with the gaunt body of Amo Brelekko, and his yellow hand tensed on the head.

"Still, Brelekko!" His thin voice rang cold with menace. "Or I'll burn you in two." As the jeweled hand dropped, his voice softened. "Ah, me, Brelekko," he wheezed, "after forty years, can't we forget?"

"I'll never forget, Habibula." The speech of Brelekko was a voiceless rasping. "Not in forty centuries!"

"Then you had best restrain yourself, Amo," advised Giles Habibula, grimly. "At least until midnight has passed."

The fleshless, cadaverous face of the gambler made an unpleasant grimace.

"So you are here to hunt the Basilisk, Habibula?" his rasping whisper asked. "There's an ancient Terrestrial proverb, 'Set a thief to catch a thief.'" His laugh was queerly muted like his voice, a kind of chuckling hiss. "But I think even that will fail. For the Basilisk is a better thief than you ever were, Habibula."

Giles Habibula caught a choking breath, and the cane lifted swiftly. But Amo Brelekko, with a mocking little gesture of his thin jeweled hand, had turned toward a distant table, where there was a little stir of sudden excitement.

"We'll soon know," he whispered. "For yonder is the winner, I believe—the man in danger. And midnight is almost at hand."

Like a yellow skeleton stalking, he hurried toward the table. The three Legionnaires and Gaspar Hannas hastened after him. The most of the players, when they came to the table, had drawn a few paces back—out of apprehensive respect, it seemed, for the ominous promise of the Basilisk—so that only a few were left about the table, at the center of a hushed, whispering ring of spectators.

Most of those few yet at the table were the plainclothes men of the Legion. But the big pale man who gave the name of Charles Derrel had pushed through to join them, with the tall blond beauty at his side. Brelekko turned to stand beside the croupier, peering through a monocle at the wheel. The engineer in white, John Comaine, had moved his mysterious equipment to the end of the table; the phones were on his head, and he was fussing with the instrument panel.

The only actual player left at the table—and, obviously, the focus of all the expectant strain that filled that hushed, watching circle—was the little ragged man, Abel Davian.

His stacks of chips were taller now, and he was trembling with elation. His heavy spectacles were awry, and his withered skin, beneath the garish atomic lights, was filmed with bright sweat. His threadbare tunic was torn open at the throat. With a feverish wildness, he set down the last play and tapped the calculator and pushed out another bet.

Giles Habibula had stopped, panting apprehensively, in the circle of tense onlookers. But his three companions pushed forward to the table, and the little gambler peered up at them. His near-sighted eyes blinked in recognition.

"Thank you, Mr. Hannas," his thin voice piped. "My system has won me twenty million dollars—a fair return, I think, for all my bitter years of washing dishes and living on nothing and saving pennies for your tables. And now I'm going to surprise you."

With a nervous, greedy, haste, he raked in his winnings.

"You used to laugh at me, Mr. Hannas, when I came to ask some small favor." Resentment flashed in his hollowed eyes. "You used to say that I was habitual, and you said habituals couldn't quit. But I'm going to take my money home." His shrill voice quivered, in pathetic defiance. "Good-bye, Mr. Hannas!"

He asked the croupier for an empty money-bag. His hurried hands began stuffing it with his winnings. Blue chips, and the glittering disks of synthetic diamond worth ten times as much. The gold-colored New Moon scrip. Crisp Green Hall certificates.

Jay Kalam snatched a glance at his chronometer, and made an imperative gesture to the alert Legionnaires about him.

"Five seconds!" he whispered. "Guard this man."

Little Abel Davian picked up the bag of his winnings and his calculator and his little black book, and shuffled wearily away from the table. He paused to make a jerky, nervous little gesture of farewell.

"No, Mr. Hannas," he muttered. "I'm not coming back—"

Jay Kalam stiffened where he stood, and caught his breath.

His ears heard a most peculiar noise: a deep vibrant hum. It was like the purr of a monstrous jungle cat in its suggestion of ominous and ruthless power, yet mechanical in its even rhythm. And it had an uncanny penetration—it throbbed through all his body; it made his bones ache and his head throb and his teeth chatter.

Abel Davian—flickered! Exactly, the Commander thought, as if some perfectly transparent curtain had dropped between them. And his thin, stooped little body seemed for an instant queerly frozen, like a motion picture when the projector stops.

Then Abel Davian was gone.

Even in that stunned and breathless instant, Jay Kalam was aware of the crackle of discharged electricity, of the tingling of his skin. He knew that a sudden force pushed him violently toward the spot where Abel Davian had been, instantly tugged him as violently back.

And then, still swaying and sick to his heart with a cold nausea of fear, Jay Kalam ran his hand before staring, utterly unbelieving eyes. For there beside the table, in the exact spot from which the little man had been so strangely snatched away, was something else! Something—monstrous!

9

The Thing from Nowhere

Chan Derron, when the blond girl greeted him by name at the Casino's resplendent entrance, stood for an instant shocked and cold. Then, looking into her shining violet eyes, he let himself respond a little to her smile, and returned the warm pressure of her hand.

"Can we talk for a moment?" he asked, and nodded aside from the busy portal.

"But come with me, inside." Her voice was a golden song that rang in his heart. "I've a table reserved for us in the grille beside the Diamond Room. We can talk as we dine. And then—"

The music of her voice missed a note, and through the violet depths of her eyes flashed something black and cold as transgalactic space.

"Then," she said softly, and once more the radiance of her smile set a pain to throbbing in his heart, "we shall play."

"Wait, please!" Chan Derron caught his breath, and tried to quiet the wild pulse hammering in his ears. He made his eyes look for a moment away from the girl's disturbing beauty, while he mastered his face and his voice. He turned back to her.

"I'm sorry," he said. "Very sorry—because you are the most beautiful woman I've ever seen. But I think you have mistaken my identity. I am Dr. Charles Derrel. Here from Venus, en route back to Earth. I'm sorry, but we've never met before. And I don't know this—did you say— Chan Derron?"

Her fine, proud head shook slightly, and her lustrous platinum hair shimmered in the changing light from the immense, jewel-like columns of the Casino. There was something subtly mocking in her violet eyes, and Chan noticed for the first time that they were very slightly tilted.

"I could not mistake your identity," she said softly. "And if you don't know Chan Derron, I'll refresh your memory."

Her slim quick hands opened a white bag, and allowed him a brief but sufficient glimpse of his own features, beneath the screaming type that offered a quarter of a million dollars in reward. The bag snapped shut, and her white smile dazzled him.

"Now, Charles," she asked, "shall we dine?"

Something in the way she spoke, something far beyond the light, inviting music of her voice, was hard as the great white jewel at her throat, cold as a planet whose sun is dead. Chan Derron tried to conceal the tiny shudder that ran through his big body.

"Whatever you say, my dear," he told her.

Inside the massive, gold-rimmed portal, they had to show their reservation checks. Chan glimpsed the girl's. The name on it was Vanya Eloyan. Residence, Juno. But it was a yellow temporary check, like his own.

In the dining room, which occupied a triangular space between two of the radiating halls, Chan seated the girl

389

at a secluded, fern-hidden table. She declined champagne, and so, cautiously, did he.

"Vanya Eloyan," he said softly, relishing the name. "Of Juno." He looked up at her white, dynamic loveliness. "But I think you are a girl of Earth, Vanya. I've never met a colonial with quite your manner, though your accent does suggest that you were educated at the Martian universities. In science, I should say. And music. Am I right?"

The white perfection of her face was fixed, suddenly, with a solemnity of purpose almost tragic, though still the sheer beauty of it kept an ache in Chan's throat.

"I prefer not to speak of myself." Her voice, for all its music, was cold as the sun of Neptune. "I came to meet you here, Chan Derron, to ask you a question." She leaned a little forward, her splendid figure tense; her violet eyes lit with a fire bright and terrible. *What did you do with Dr. Eleroid's invention?*"

All the blood ran out of Chan Derron's face, leaving it the ghastly gray-white of the pigment he had used. A cold blade cleft his heart. Icy, strangling hands stopped his breath. The strength ebbed out of him. His big body sagged toward the table.

In the prison on Ebron he had heard that question ten thousand times, until the very syllables brought back those years of torture. He had been fighting for two years to escape it. It was a little time before the dryness of his throat would let him speak, and then he said:

"I didn't kill Dr. Eleroid. I didn't take his invention. My conviction was unjust. I've been the victim of something—monstrous! Believe me, Vanya—"

Her eyes glinted with the chill of a polar dusk.

"I don't believe you, Chan Derron." Her low voice rang with a deadly resolution. "And you won't escape until I know what you have done—what you are doing—with Dr. Eleroid's secret."

The desperate, ruthless intensity of her ready poise and her searching face made her seem to Chan the most terrible but yet the most beautiful thing he had ever seen. And suddenly he was startled by some mocking familiarity.

"Remember, Chan Derron," her cold voice warned him, "with two words I can end your life tonight—and the amazing career of the Basilisk!"

Chan Derron drew a long uneven breath, and settled slowly back in his chair. He was staring at the figure of white loveliness across the table. He stared while a silent waiter brought their food, and silently departed. And the thing he saw was more alarming than her icy threat.

For the make-up on her perfect face had dissolved and shifted. Her violet eyes in his mind, had turned a clear ice-green. The platinum splendor of her hair had become a glory of red-lit mahogany. Yes, indeed, he knew her face!

He had studied every feature of it, for lonely hours, on the picture posted beside his own on the bulkhead of the *Phantom Atom*. This splendid and deadly being was no woman! She was Luroa, the last survivor of Eldo Arrynu's synthetic android monsters. The price on her life matched that on his own.

Chan Derron smiled gently, and eased the dark glasses on his face.

"You know two words," he whispered softly. "But I know one—Luroa."

There was a flicker of white tension on her face, he thought. The flash of something dark and deadly in the deep pools of her eyes. But in another instant she was smiling at him radiantly.

"The food, Dr. Charles," she said, "is too good to be neglected—and we must be in the Diamond Room before midnight."

When they were in the gaming room, the girl bought a stack of chips—displaying a sheaf of green certificates that seemed to speak of the sinister skills of Luroa. They played, he placing the chips at her direction. And they won. Perhaps, Chan thought—he had few illusions about the role of chance at the New Moon's tables—because the magnet of her beauty always crowded the table where she played.

Her violet eyes were watching him very closely, he could tell, and seeing all that happened about them, and measuring the minutes that fled. She was waiting, he realized, for midnight—and for him to betray himself as the Basilisk.

"Vanya," he whispered once, when they had a moment alone, "I only came here to hunt this criminal. If you'll let me—"

"Wait," she returned inexorably, "until midnight."

When the three Legionnaires came upon them, Chan Derron recognized the Commander and Hal Samdu at once. Even in plain clothes, they were unmistakable to any veteran of the Legion. For a little time he put hope

391

in his disguise—fervidly regretting that he had not been six inches shorter.

The return of his check and keys, however, by Jay Kalam, convinced him that he had been identified—and that the short fat man's spectacular maneuvers had been no more than an elaborate accompaniment to the picking of his pocket.

It surprised him that the girl spoke so promptly in his defense. His sense of her surpassing beauty kept rising above his fear of her—even above his cold instinctive horror of the android. When the Commander had gone, he turned to her with a little smile of relief, and gratitude.

"Thank you, Vanya."

Her smile of response was breath-taking—but all intended, he swiftly realized, for the spectators. For her golden voice dropped softer than a whisper; pitilessly cold, it rang ominously in his ear:

"No thanks are due me, Chan Derron. Kalam and Samdu and old Habibula know you as well as I do—and my identification meant nothing to them. They are just waiting—as I am—for midnight."

And midnight came.

The girl, as the moment stalked upon them, had gripped Chan's arm. Her small fingers sank desperately into his flesh—as strong, he thought, as an android's must be. And her keen violet eyes were watching every move he made, he knew, as sharply as he watched the promised victim of the Basilisk—gray, tattered, trembling little Abel Davian.

Her other hand, he noticed, and wondered at it, was toying constantly with the great white jewel at her throat. What manner of jewel, he was asking himself in that final moment, was this huge gem that had the prismatic sheen and the intricate hexagonal perfection of a great snowflake?

Chan Derron heard that hideous, feral purring. He saw little Davian flicker, grow queerly rigid—and saw that he was gone. He felt a breath of dank and ice-cold air. He was flung toward the spot where Davian had been, and dragged instantly back.

Then—hardly aware that he was strangling to a whiff of some choking, acrid gas—he was staring with bewildered and incredulous eyes at the monstrous thing that had appeared in Davian's place. It was like nothing men had found in all the System.

Standing on three thin, swaying, rubbery-looking legs, it reared twelve feet high. Queerly teardrop-shaped, its body was covered with close-set, green-black scales. Three huge eyes, of a dull and lurid crimson, glared from its armored head. Its enormous, jet-black beak yawned open to reveal multiple rows of saber-like teeth. An unpleasant fringe of long green serpentine tentacles hung beneath the beak.

A greenish slime was dripping from the fearful body to the polished floor, exactly, Chan thought, as if the creature had just that instant been snatched out of the muck of some primordial jungle. Beneath the slime, its dark scales had an old, metallic glint. And there was that strangling, pungent reek, which Chan slowly recognized as the odor of chlorine.

For a little time it stood almost motionless, twisting that frightful, long-beaked head, so that those three enormous red eyes, which looked in three separate directions, could survey all the circle of puny humans about it.

A queer strained hush had fallen on the Diamond Room. For a moment there was not even a scream. Then those nearer, choked and blinded with the breath of chlorine that had come with the creature, began to stumble uncertainly back. The first sound was a hysterical laugh, that became a thin sobbing scream. And then the hush became an insane stampede.

But already the thing had moved. Three wings were abruptly extended from its armored back. Queerly, they *unrolled*. They were translucently green, and delicately ribbed with darker emerald. One on each side and the third, tail-like, behind, they raised and fell, one by one, experimentally, and then became a blur of motion.

Out of that fearful beak came an appalling bellow. Reverberating against the lofty vault of the Diamond Room, a wild echo out of unknown jungles, it hastened the fugitive thousands. And the creature itself, with an ungainly but amazing swiftness, ran forward on the three swaying limbs. Its wings made a mounting thunder of sound, and the wind rushing from them was choking with chlorine.

"Back, Vanya!" gasped Chan.

Chan sprang after her. But the great wing struck his head and crushed him down. Falling, he glimpsed the girl standing in the monster's path. Both her hands, he saw, were lifted to her strange white pendant.

Then the green tentacles, squirming snake-like beneath that beak, snatched her up. The thing lifted with her above the expanding ring of panic-stricken fugitives, and flew with her swiftly down the hall.

"Get him!" It was the great voice of Hal Samdu, roaring vainly against the shrieking tumult. "Get Chan Derron!"

Blind and coughing from the chlorine, the giant was staggering about, blinking his eyes, waving a long, bright blaster. Jay Kalam, beside him, strangled and voiceless, was trying to call to the plainclothes men.

"Aye, get him!" wheezed Giles Habibula from beneath a table. "And get the mortal monster!"

"Half a million!" Gaspar Hannas bellowed. "To the man who gets Chan Derron!"

Stunned dismay and poison gas, Chan realized, had given him a few free seconds. And, strapped to his body beneath the green cloak, he had the compact geopellor unit from his spare space suit. The control cable ran down his sleeve, and his fingers gripped the handle. A swift pressure on it—and he rose silently from the midst of his enemies. Flying high beneath the vault of the Diamond Room, he soared after the monster and the girl.

White, silent proton bolts stabbed after him. Plaster exploded from the painted vault, raining down into the panic on the floor. He breathed the sharpness of ozone, and felt one faint shock.

But the geopellor, for all its compactness, was swift. Chan pursued a darting zigzag. Seconds, only, had gone, when he came to the end of the long Diamond Room. But the monster, with the girl, had already vanished.

The trail they had left was plain. The alien creature must have overlooked the wide doorway, for a ragged opening yawned in the top of the vault. Chan twisted the spindle in his hand. The geopellor flung him up through it.

And his brain, refreshed by the rushing wind of his flight, reached a swift decision. This moment—when he was free and in the air, while the monster was creating a diversion—this was obviously his chance to escape. And dread impelled him to flight, for the girl's accusation and the encounter with Jay Kalam had brought back all the horror of the Devil's Rock.

But he hadn't come to escape. He was hunting the Basilisk, and the monster was the one visible clue to the identity and the methods of that criminal. A shudder tensed his straight-extended flying body. But he knew that he must follow the monster.

The girl herself, he tried to tell himself, didn't matter.

The pitiless synthetic brain of Luroa was a greater danger to him than all the Legion. It would be better if the monster destroyed her. Yet, in spite of himself, the thought of Vanya Eloyan spurred his frantic haste.

Beyond the hole in the massive wall—which could only have been torn, he thought, by some sort of explosion, and which therefore meant the monster was armed with something far more formidable than tentacles and fangs —beyond, he plunged into the corridors of the New Moon's museum.

The monster and the girl were gone from sight. Far down one hall a little cluster of people were running frantically. Beside a glass case stood one of the attendants, with a yellow crescent on his uniform. Chan dropped out of the air beside him.

"Which way?" he demanded.

The man stood wooden, glassy-eyed. His arms made a sudden defensive gesture, against Chan—although the geopellor had been used occasionally in sport, it was still new enough so that a flying, wingless man must have seemed almost as startling as the monster.

Chan shook the attendant. "Which way did it take her?"

"It couldn't be!" the man sobbed. "There isn't such a thing!" His eyes came into focus again, and he stared at Chan's face as if doubting its humanity. "A thing carrying a woman?" he whispered. "It went on up, into the unfinished spaces. That way!"

He pointed—and then bent suddenly, very sick.

Twisting and squeezing the spindle, Chan darted upward again. Wind shrieked in his ears, and tore at his cloak. He found another shattered hole in the ceiling, and plunged through into an incompleted part of the New Moon.

Above bare floors, naked beams and girders and cables soared upward into gulfs of darkness. Unshaded atomic lights burned here and there, like stars in a metal universe. They cast blue, fantastic shadows. It was thousands of feet through that network to the black curving metal of the New Moon's hull.

Chan Derron peered, bewildered for a moment, into that blue mysterious chasm of sinister shadows and spidery metal. His right hand dragged the blaster from beneath his cloak. Then he heard the monster.

The awesome bellow reverberated weirdly through the maze of empty steel, rolling thunderously back from the metal hull, but it gave some clue to direction. The geopellor flung Chan upward again. And at last, on a high platform that the builders had used, he came upon the creature and the girl.

A far blue light cast a grotesque web of black shadows across the scene. The girl lay motionless. Green-black nightmare crouched over her, that hideous beak yawning wide. The serpentine tentacles were writhing about her throat.

The geopellor hurled Chan forward. The blaster flashed in his extended right hand. The first white bolt struck the dark-scaled body with a flare of green incandescence. Without harm, it seemed. And the green tentacles flung up a weapon.

Another service blaster of the newest Legion design, identical with his own!

The merest fraction of its energy would have meant slow death, from radiation sickness. A little more would have killed him instantly, by ionizing his brain tissue. But his second bolt into the monster's central crimson eye, took instant effect. The blaster fell. Queerly stiffened, the creature toppled toward the girl.

Ignoring a voice of fearful protest in his heart, Chan sent himself forward. The same arm that held the blaster slipped under the girl. The geopellor lifted them both. The monster came crashing down behind them. The diaphanous green wings, when it struck, abruptly unrolled. They remained rigidly extended, and the thing did not move again. Chan dropped beside it, and set the girl upon her feet.

Her lithe body had moved again in his arms, and now she gasped for breath, smiling at him shakenly. Her synthetic loveliness made him glad, for a moment, that he had saved her life.

"Thank you," she whispered, "Chan!"

Her voice was velvet magic. Her violet eyes slowly closed toward his. And then, with an unexpected pantherine quickness, she was gone from his arms. A sudden, numbing blow from her elbow had struck some nerve center in his neck. A clever, savage strength had wrested the blaster out of his hand.

He swayed dazedly. Here, far from the gravity plates in the "bottom" of the New Moon's hull, their attraction was somewhat decreased, and it required a little time for muscles to adjust themselves to lessened strains. When he recovered his balance, the girl was already backing alertly away from him, covering him with his own weapon.

"Well, Mr. Basilisk!" her soft voice mocked him. "Let's see you get away this time!"

Chan caught his breath. The blue darkness and the shadowy strands of steel spun about him. He had foreseen this danger from the girl—and yet the very peril of her beauty made it all incredible. His hands tightened on the spindle of the geopellor. He had small chance of distancing the bolt of protons, but the power of the little unit could hurl his body against her—

"Still, Chan Derron!" her voice rang sharply. "Open your hand." The blaster gestured alertly.

His fingers relaxed. He tried, hopelessly, to protest.

"Vanya, you *can't* believe that I'm the Basilisk. For, all the time, you were there at my side—"

"Silence!" The bright weapon lifted, imperatively. "I was there—close enough to feel the mechanism strapped to your body, Derron. And the wires in your sleeve."

Narrowed, her violet eyes had a deadly glint.

"I had you then, Derron—until you sent your little pet to carry me away. Now I've got you again—and this time you won't escape." He wondered again at the fingers of her left hand, lifted to that strange white jewel at her throat. "But still I'm going to give you one more chance."

He saw the tension in her hand, and the ruthless purpose behind the white perfect mask of her face. Cold as sleet, her voice whipped at him:

"What did you do with Dr. Eleroid's invention?"

Sick, helpless, he shook his head.

"Where is the machine you control with the instruments on your body—"

He knew she was going to fire, when he didn't answer. He could hurl himself at her with the geopellor. Two deaths, instead of one. But her pitiless beauty—

That monstrous purr came suddenly. The girl and everything beyond her flickered abruptly, as if a wall of vitrilith had dropped between. He saw her hand stiffen on the blaster, saw the white bolt's flash.

The last thing he saw was her strained face, with its grim suspicion changed to amazed and bitter certainty. Her image dissolved in a chasm of star-glinting darkness. And Chan Derron was hurled into black and airless cold.

10

The Clue on Contra-Saturn

"You say it's dead?" quavered Giles Habibula. "Jay, you're sure the fearful thing is dead?"

High in the shadowy web of blue-lit metal beneath the New Moon's shell, the grotesque monstrosity sprawled stiffly on the bare platform. Jay Kalam and Hal Samdu and Gaspar Hannas stood peering down at it, but Giles Habibula hung apprehensively back near the elevator that had brought them up.

"Quite dead," Jay Kalam assured him. "Chan Derron evidently beat us to it—who would have guessed he was wearing a geopellor under his cloak? And then got away—with the girl!"

"Got away!" It was a pained moan, from the gigantic, black-clad master of the New Moon. "And all our guests know he did. There's a panic at the docks. Every vessel going out is already booked to capacity. In twenty-four hours there won't be a visitor in the New Moon—and not many of our own employees—unless the Basilisk is caught."

The great white hands of Hannas clenched, impotently.

"The Basilisk has ruined me, Commander!" he rasped. "Or Chan Derron has. Already."

"Keep your men after him." Jay Kalam's gesture swept the dusky labyrinth of shadow-clotted steel. "He could be here—anywhere. With that woman—" His dark brow furrowed. "There was something about that woman—you observed her, Hal?"

"Aye, Jay," rumbled Hal Samdu. "She was beautiful— far too beautiful for any good. She had the same evil beauty that belonged to those androids of Eldo Arrynu."

"Android!" Jay Kalam started at the word. "She could be! She could be Luroa—Stephen Orco's list sinister sister!" He set his lean fingers deliberately tip to tip. "The New

398

Moon would be the natural hunting ground of such a creature, and Chan Derron the sort of confederate she would seek. But she didn't look like—"

"Ah, Jay, but she did!" protested Giles Habibula, plaintively. "That was mortal evident! The hair and the eyes were changed, and make-up cunningly used to alter the shape of her face—ah, it was a lovely one! But still it was that she-monster's."

Jay Kalam spun on him.

"Why didn't you speak?"

Lifting his cane defensively, Giles Habibula stumbled apprehensively back.

"Jay, Jay," he whined plaintively, "don't be too severe on a poor old soldier." He sighed heavily, and one fat yellow hand clutched at his heart. "Giles is an old, old man. His eyes are blurred and dim. But still he can relish the sight of beauty, Jay. And that girl was too beautiful to be stood before your blaster squad. Ah, she was a dream!"

"If you were any other man, Giles, you'd stand before a blaster squad yourself."

The Commander turned decisively back to Gaspar Hannas.

"Remind your police," he said, "that this female android is worth two hundred and fifty thousand dollars. That makes three quarters of a million, now, for the two."

"I'll make it an even million, Commander," the white giant gasped. "To save the New Moon—"

He stumbled away toward the elevator.

Jay Kalam was rubbing reflectively at his jaw.

"Perhaps Luroa ought to stand beside Derron on our suspect list," he said slowly. "We know the Basilisk is clever, utterly ruthless, and superbly trained in science— and that description certainly fits the android. She must be either the Basilisk or his confederate—or else she came here to snatch his prize away!"

He turned methodically to the rigid thing Chan Derron had slain. Hal Samdu was already playing his light-tube over it, while Giles Habibula prodded rather fearfully at its armored body with his cane.

"Ah, such a horror!" the old man wheezed. "And it came out of nothing—"

"It came from somewhere," Jay Kalam broke in gravely, "and it brings a new complexity into the situation. It's no native of the System. And like nothing we found in the comet. It means—"

"Jay!" It was an astonished gasp, from Giles Habibula. "Jay, look here!" The prodding cane trembled in his hand. "This mortal thing was never alive!"

"What's that?"

"See!" the old man wheezed. "The scales of it are metal, fastened on with rivets. The wings are neither flesh nor feathers—they're blessed cellulite. It had no muscles to make them beat, bue this rotating shaft. These serpentine tentacles that raped the poor lass away, are all of metal disks and rubber and wire. And the fearsome eyes have lenses of vitrilith.

"Jay, the thing's a mortal robot!"

"So it is, Giles." He bent over it. "Hal, may I have your light?"

He peered into one of the huge, glassy orbs, felt the frail-seeming elastic stuff of the wings, inspected beak and tentacles and limbs, studied the patch of scorched metal scales, and the fused pit where the central eye had been. At last he stood up, decisively, and returned the light-tube.

"Ah, Jay," inquired Giles Habibula, "what do you discover?"

"A good deal," said the Commander. "A number of inferences are immediately obvious. A thorough scientific investigation will doubtless suggest as many others."

He turned to Hal Samdu.

"Hal, you take charge of this—mechanism. Send to Rocky Mountain base at once for a crew of research technicians—get as many men as possible who were with us on the cometary expedition—and have them disassemble it.

"Make a thorough microscopic, chemical, bacteriological, and spectrographic study of surface specimens and the material of every part. Photograph every part, before and after removal, under ultraviolet light. Make—but your crew will know what to do. Tell them to neglect no possible source of information—for this thing is our one tangible clue to the methods and the headquarters of the Basilisk.

"Have your men write up a complete report of what you find, and all possible deductions as to where this machine was built, by whom, for what purpose, and how

it could have come to the New Moon. One word more
—guard the robot and your results with the utmost care!"

"Yes, Commander." Hal Samdu saluted, eagerly, and
a joyous smile lit his big ugly face. "Aye, and it's good
to have something really to do, Jay, at last!"

And he stepped after Hannas into the elevator-beam.

"Now, Giles," the Commander continued, "there are
three men I must learn more about. I know the overwhelming weight of evidence that Chan Derron is our
Basilisk—perhaps with the android's complicity. But, in a
case so grave, we can't afford to overlook any other possibility. Admitting that the Basilisk must have a brilliant,
pitiless, and scientific mind, there were three others present
in the Diamond Room who might possibly be suspect."

"Eh, Jay?" The small fishy eyes of Giles Habibula
blinked. "Who?"

"The engineer," began Jay Kalam, "John Comaine—"

"Ah, so," agreed Giles Habibula. "I didn't like the look
of his mysterious box. And the others?"

"The gambler, Brelekko," said the Commander. "And
Hannas, himself."

"Hannas! And Brelekko?" The old man nodded. "Ah, so,
I guess they all three fit your classification. I know less of
this Comaine. But if two men ever were ravening wolves,
Jay, they were Hannas and Brelekko!"

"You know them, Giles. Were they always friends, as
now?"

"Friends, Jay!" The leaden eyes peered at him. "Ah,
Jay, they were bitter enemies as ever fought—the three
of us, each against the rest. Ah, so! And if any of us had
been less a man than he was, the others would have picked
his precious bones!"

"Tell me about it, Giles."

"It was forty years ago, and more, Jay." Leaning on the
cane, he heaved to a sorrowful sigh. "When Giles was still
a man—aye, a fighting man, not the miserable old soldier
dying before you now. He was back on Venus, on furlough
from the Legion—"

"Furlough, Giles?" inquired the grave Commander. "For
five years?"

Giles Habibula sucked in his breath, indignantly.

"The charges of desertion were never proven, Jay," he
wheezed. "Ah, all that was a wicked plot of my enemies,
to wreck the career of a loyal Legionnaire—"

"Never proven," put in Jay Kalam, solemnly, "because

all the documents in the case mysteriously vanished from the files of the Legion."

"I know nothing of that." The fishy eyes blinked. "Jay, Jay! If you've nothing better to do than turn up all the malicious lies that were invented by human demons like Hannas and Brelekko to ruin the bravest soldier that ever risked his life to save the System—"

His thin voice broke, piteously.

"Forget it, Giles." A faint twinkle lit the dark eyes of Jay Kalam. "Just tell me what happened on Venus."

"Ah, thank you, Jay," wheezed the old man, gratefully. "You were never one to dig up mortal skeletons to haunt a poor old soldier with!"

He balanced himself on the cane.

"I went back to the Blue Unicorn, Jay. It was on a little rocky island off New Chicago. The wildest place—and the richest—in all the System. But it was a woman that brought me there, Jay."

He sighed, and his colorless eyes looked far away into the shadowy cavern of raw metal.

"Ah, Jay, such a woman as you wouldn't find in all the whole System today—not unless you picked out the android Luroa. Ah, no other could be so beautiful or so quick or so brave. Her name was Ethyra Coran."

He gulped, and his thin voice trembled.

"The three of us loved her, Jay. Ah, so, every man on Venus was mad with her beauty—but we three were better men than the rest. We knew the matter lay between us. And, for her precious sake, we had to pretend a sort of friendship.

"Amo Brelekko was just off the Jovian liners. He wasn't using that name, then. Or the name he had used on the liners—for one ruined man had killed himself, and another had been murdered. He was made of money. Young as he was, he already had a skill—none but I could ever win from him at cards. He had a voice, then—and not that ghastly whisper. And the same gaudy dress and glitter of jewels he wears today. He had a gentle, flattering way with women—aye, Jay, many a poor lass had given him her soul, and perished for it.

"Gaspar Hannas had come from none knew where. He was known as Pedro the Shark. There were a thousand whispers about his past, but he wore a different face then —and none who had seen it cared to ask the truth. From wherever he came, he had brought a fortune with him, and he found more at the Blue Unicorn. Money and blood —ah, Jay, I've seen sights I can't forget!

"Gaspar Hannas was a man precious few lasses would have dared to refuse, but Ethyra Coran had a courage to match her beauty and her wit. Ah, so, and precious few men would have cared to be the rival of Pedro the Shark. But that was in the old days, Jay, when old Giles was still a man."

The old man's eyes chanced to fall again upon the monstrous robot on the floor, and he started back apprehensively, as if he had not seen it before.

"Ah, the hideous machine! I could make a long story, Jay. Aye, a story of cunning and passion and death that would freeze your heart. For the Shark and the Eel were ruthless, cunning beasts, and I—you know that Giles was ever honest and straightforward, Jay, and simple as a precious child—I had to grapple for their fearful weapons, to hold my own. To make the story short, Jay—"

He paused, and a happy smile crossed his round yellow face.

"I got the girl—aye, and a mortal lovely prize she was!"

His smile twisted into a triumphant grin.

"As for Hannas and Brelekko, why each of them, Jay —through a neat little device of my own—blamed his defeat upon the other. Ah, and then they became enemies indeed. The quickness and the craft of Brelekko matched the brutish strength and the ruthless courage of Hannas, however, and each failed to destroy the other."

"And you think they are still enemies?" the grave Commander asked.

"Deathly enemies," insisted Giles Habibula. "How could they be friends? When Brelekko must be madly jealous of all the wealth and power Hannas has found in the New Moon. When Hannas—aye, and justly—must hate Brelekko for knowing his past and his tricks, for hanging on him like a leech, and winning at his tables.

"Ah, so, Jay, in either of them you have brains enough —and mortal evil, too—to make your Basilisk."

"Possibly." Jay Kalam frowned doubtfully. "Though there's not a shred of evidence against any man except Chan Derron. We'll see them again, below."

When Hal Samdu had returned, with a guard of Legionnaires, to take charge of the robot for his crew of scientists, they went down again to the luxurious quarters that Gaspar

Hannas had placed at their disposal. The Commander sent for Amo Brelekko.

Yellow and almost skeletal, strutting in his gaudy silks, great jewels glittering, the gambler made a fantastic figure. The insolence of his swagger, Jay Kalam thought, must have been put on to cover a deep unease. His dark eyes shot an insanely malicious look at Giles Habibula.

"Brelekko," asked the grave Commander, "as a clever man, on the spot from the beginning, intimately acquainted with the persons involved—what is your opinion about the Basilisk?"

The hawk-face remained a bleak tense mask.

"Obviously the criminal must be an able scientist," the voiceless gambler replied. "Obviously, he knows the New Moon intimately. Obviously, also, he dislikes Gaspar Hannas. I know one man, Commander, who fits those three conditions."

"So?" wheezed Giles Habibula. "Besides yourself?"

The dark unblinking eyes darted at him, venomously.

"Who is that?" Jay Kalam prompted.

"The man who built the New Moon," rasped Brelekko. "John Comaine."

"But isn't he employed by Hannas?"

"John Comaine is the slave of Gaspar Hannas," Brelekko whispered. "I know the story—I alone, beside the two of them. A young man, a brilliant scientist but mad with the thirst for wealth, Comaine came to the battered hulk of a condemned space ship that was the first New Moon. He lost too much—money that was not his to lose. Hannas let him pay the debt with his science—and then held the new crime over him. Comaine tried at first to escape, but every effort left him deeper in the power of Hannas. Yet I think he still has the pride and the heart of a scientist. I know he first dreamed of the New Moon, Commander, not as a gambling resort, but as a super-observatory and laboratory of all the sciences, to be stationed out in Neptune's orbit. It was the ruthless power of Hannas that turned his dream of Contra-Neptune into this. Would it be very strange, Commander, if a scientist, revolting against half a lifetime of such slavery, should make his science strike back?"

"Perhaps not," Jay nodded slowly. "Thank you, Brelekko."

He detailed two plain-clothes men to shadow the gambler, and sent for John Comaine. When the engineer appeared, stiffly awkward, the square stern mask of his slightly pop-eyed face hiding any emotion, the Commander asked him the same question about the Basilisk.

Comaine shook his big blond head, impassive as a statue.

"The Basilisk is a scientist," said his flat harsh voice. "I know, Commander, because I have been attempting to set my own knowledge against his. And I have failed to match him. I have met only one mind equal in ability to the feats of the Basilisk—the mind of Dr. Max Eleroid."

"But Eleroid is dead!"

"My only suggestion, Commander," the engineer said flatly, "is that the cadaver in question was not accurately identified."

Two more operatives were sent to follow Comaine.

An orderly, in the Legion green, was admitted.

"Commander Kalam." He saluted. "We have reports from the principal stock exchanges on all the planets. As you surmised, sir, the shares and obligations of the New Moon syndicate fell precipitately with the news of what happened here—to about three per cent, in fact, of their former value.

"The financial reports confirm your belief, Commander, that a behind-the-scenes battle has been in progress for control of the syndicate. One group has now capitulated, evidently, so that the other is able to buy at its own price."

Jay Kalam nodded gravely.

"Has the buyer been traced?"

"It has always been very difficult to discover anything about the affairs of the New Moon Syndicate, sir. They are handled by very devious means. The Legion has exerted pressure, however, upon several brokers. The reports indicate, almost surely, that the buyer is Gaspar Hannas!"

"Eh?" Old Giles Habibula started. "But Hannas is the New Moon's master, already."

"He is head of the syndicate," Jay Kalam told him. "Originally he was sole owner of the enterprise. But the cost of constructing the New Moon, while the actual sum has never been revealed, must have been staggering—far beyond the resources of Hannas. He was forced to sell a vast amount of stock, and the syndicate incurred tremendous obligations. Out of that situation comes the chief reason for suspecting that Hannas himself is the Basilisk."

"Eh, Jay?" Giles Habibula turned pale and began to

perspire. "And here we're in the New Moon, in the very clutch of his mortal power! But why Hannas, Jay?"

"Even through the cloud of legal confusion that is always kept around the dealings of the syndicate, it's clear that Gaspar Hannas was about to lose the New Moon. Now the activities of the Basilisk have enabled him to buy back control at his own price. There—in the difference between bankruptcy and the System's greatest fortune—you have motive enough, I think."

"Aye," agreed Giles Habibula. "But you said this Basilisk must be a scientist—and Gaspar Hannas is no scientist."

"But he has a very able one—if Brelekko told the truth—completely under his thumb. John Comaine." Jay Kalam rubbed abstractedly at his jaw, and then his dark eyes went abruptly to Giles Habibula. "However," he said, "all the weight of evidence still rests against Chan Derron.

"For Chan Derron took Dr. Eleroid's invention—which is probably the very scientific agency that makes possible the feats of the Basilisk. He has been connected with every crime. He was here, loaded down with concealed instruments, when little Davian was taken. And once more he has mysteriously escaped.

"I was for a long time reluctant to believe that so fine a Legionnaire as Captain Derron was, could have turned to such a monster as the Basilisk. But the presence of the female android accounts for that. It may be that Luroa was the mysterious spy who first frightened Dr. Eleroid! And then she met Chan Derron."

Somberly, his dark eyes looked far away.

"He would not be the first man degraded and destroyed by the fatal allure of those inhuman things."

"So, Jay," sighed Giles Habibula, "some of them were mortal beautiful!"

Jay Kalam's glance came back to the old man, suddenly intent.

"Giles," he said softly, "I've an idea!"

"Eh, Jay!" The fishy eyes blinked uneasily. "You're getting too many ideas about a poor crippled old hero of the Legion, Jay."

"You are ordered, Giles, to find Chan Derron."

"But we're all looking for Derron."

"So we are." Jay Kalam's lips tightened sternly. "But I'm afraid you haven't been exerting your full capacities." His low voice lifted slightly. "Giles, as Commander of the

406

Legion, I order you to find Derron and the woman with him. By any means you can. You will work alone—but keep in touch with us by ultrawave and call for any aid you need."

"Find the Basilisk?" Giles Habibula paled and squirmed. "How do you think—?"

"Use your own methods," Jay Kalam told him. "But you've been boasting enough of your cloudy past—you might pretend to be another criminal. Whatever you do, learn everything you can. Discover the location of the Basilisk's headquarters—find a target for the keeper of the peace. Trap Derron and the android."

Giles Habibula licked his fat blue lips. He gulped. His seamed face turned greenish-yellow, and glittered with sweat. He gasped for breath, and mopped with a trembling hand at his bald brow.

"Jay!" he wheezed at last. "Are you out of your mind? In all these years, hasn't Giles given enough to the System—aye, given all his precious genius!—without being flung into this web of fearful horror?"

His pudgy fingers quivered on Jay Kalam's arm.

"In life's name, Jay, stay your cruel command! Ah, think, Jay! Poor old Giles might be snatched from beside you at this very moment—to be found perhaps in the black Euthanasia vault, with the blade of the Basilisk in his poor dead back!"

"Remember," Jay Kalam said gravely, "that it's for the keeper."

Giles Habibula caught a sobbing breath.

"For the keeper," he wheezed, sadly. "For her, Jay— I'll go."

Then the Commander of the Legion went suddenly tense, and his lean face went a little white.

Krrr! Krrr! Krrr!

The tiny sound, peculiarly penetrating and insistent, was humming from the communicator hung by its thin chain about his neck. The Commander's lean deliberate hands, drawing the little black disk from under his clothing, trembled slightly.

"It's Legion Intelligence," he told Giles Habibula. "An emergency call."

Giles Habibula watched apprehensively as he touched the dial, whispered a code response, and lifted the little disk to his ear. The straining ears of the old Legionnaire failed to hear anything. And the face of Jay Kalam didn't lose its grave, contained reserve. But his failure to breathe, and his frozen stiffness, betrayed enough.

"You've had bad news, Jay," whispered Giles Habibula, when at last the Commander lowered the disk and broke communication. "Aye, mortal bad!"

Jay Kalam nodded, very slowly. His lean face, beneath that one white lock on his forehead, looked the oldest that Giles Habibula had ever seen it.

"That was one of the subordinate officers calling from the depot of the cometary expedition at Contra-Saturn." His voice was very quiet. "The depot has been robbed, Giles. All our files and specimens rifled."

"Eh, Jay!" Giles Habibula blinked at him. "The secrets of the Cometeers!"

"All our most valuable—or most dangerous—notes were taken, Giles. Weapons and instrumentalities that we had planned to guard for centuries until our civilization might be mature enough to assimilate them safely. All gone!"

"Was it—the Basilisk?"

The stricken head nodded again.

"A little black clay snake was found on Bob Star's desk, inside the vaults—none of the locks on the vaults, by the way, were disturbed. As usual, there was a clue. Dropped on the floor was a yellow reservation check from the New Moon. It was dated yesterday. And the name on it was Dr. Charles Derrel."

"Derrel?" gasped Giles Habibula. "But, Jay, it isn't six hours since I picked that check out of Chan Derron's pocket—and Contra-Saturn, by the swiftest cruiser, is three days away!"

"The best proof yet," Jay Kalam said gravely, "that the Basilisk is Chan Derron." His lean hand gestured sternly. "Get him, Giles."

"But—Bob?" Giles Habibula was wheezing anxiously. "You say a subordinate was speaking? Where was Bob Star?"

The face of Jay Kalam had stiffened bleakly.

"The office said that Captain Robert Star is mysteriously missing from the depot," he said faintly. "Giles, I'm afraid Bob Star is already in the hands of the Basilisk. Alive or not—I'm afraid to guess."

Giles Habibula lifted himself laboriously to his feet with the cane.

"Bob, the poor lad!" he sobbed. "Now my duty's plain enough—but how am I to find the Basilisk?" His head shook hopelessly. "How can one poor old man track down the monster that strikes here at midnight and a billion miles away before the dawn?"

His pale eyes rolled.

"Or—in life's precious name—what if I do find him? And the mortal android? One poor old soldier, to face the System's two most frightful criminals. Aye, to face all the evil power of the Basilisk! And that woman, whose very beauty is a false mirage and a consuming flame and a poisoned blade!"

He blinked, and caught a gasping breath.

"But for all that, I must go. Farewell, Jay. Farewell! And please tell the keeper that poor old Giles Habibula was loyal to the end." He thrust out a trembling hand, and the Commander grasped it. "For it is mortal likely, Jay, that Giles Habibula will never be seen alive again."

And he waddled slowly out into the corridors of the New Moon.

11

The Unearthly Robot

Back in the rich, soft-toned simplicity of his hidden, ray-armored apartments aft the chart rooms of the mighty *Inflexible,* once more in the trim gold-and-green of his uniform, Jay Kalam sat waiting impatiently. The deep muffled song of the geodynes reached him briefly, as a door was opened. And Hal Samdu came stalking in, looking worried.

"Well, Hal?" the Commander's quiet reserve did not conceal his eagerness. "What is your report on the robot?"

The big gnarled hands of the Admiral-General laid a thick green envelope on the desk. They clenched, as he raised them, with a savage force.

"If I could only get my fingers on this Derron—" His great voice was thick with an agony of frustration. "To think, Jay, that all the Legion can give the keeper no promise of safety!"

"I know it's appalling." The Commander nodded, white-lipped. "But your report?"

"In the envelope," said Hal Samdu. "I got together twenty men, half of them veterans of the cometary expedition, all of them specialists in some field of science. They took the robot-thing apart, and studied every piece of it, by every possible means. The lab work was finished, twelve hours ago, at base. Since, they've been discussing and checking the meaning of their discoveries, and writing up the report."

Jay Kalam leaned forward, anxiously.

"What did they find?"

Hal Samdu shook his rugged white head.

"I'm no scientist, Jay. You know that. It's all in the envelope."

"But," the Commander asked, "in brief—"

"As you surmised, Jay, it's an illegal robot. It makes use of biophysical principles forbidden in the same Green Hall statutes that outlawed the androids. The most similar illicit model in the museum was taken shortly after the war with the Medusae. It was built by a young Dr. Enos Clagg, who was run down by the Legion and sentenced to three years on Ebron."

"The details?"

Scowling with a painful effort to be clear, Hal Samdu touched one big knobby finger with another.

"First, Jay," he rumbled, "they concluded that the thing was designed by a human engineer—a man trained on Earth or Mars."

Jay Kalam nodded. "Why?"

"Because so many familiar engineering principles were used in its construction. There were none of those strange freaks of design—strange to us—that we found in the machines of the Cometeers.

"The thing was driven by an atomic power tube. There were pinions, shafts, cams, cables, levers—all used precisely as a supremely good human engineer would use them, if you set him to build a mechanical imitation of —of whatever monster the thing was copied from."

Jay Kalam was rubbing reflectively at his jaw.

"That fits Derron well enough," he said. "He took high honors in the engineering section at the academy. But, for that matter, it also fits the female android, or Hannas, or Brelekko, or Comaine. What else, Hal?"

The gigantic Captain-General bent down another gnarled finger.

"Second," he said, "they agreed that the thing was built outside the System."

Jay Kalam nodded again, without surprise. "Where?"

"On a planet somewhat larger than the Earth, they concluded, comparatively near a dying red sun—a star of the type designated as K9e. The surface gravitation of the planet is about 1.250 g—about one and a quarter times Earth-gravity. The atmosphere is denser than Earth's. It contains sufficient free oxygen to sustain human life—but also enough free chlorine to be very unpleasant."

The Commander was listening intently.

"The basis of those conclusions—"

"The metals of the robot, in the first place. They are mostly aluminum and beryllium bronzes. They are alloyed according to standard metallurgical formulae. But spectrographic analysis proves that they were not smelted from any ores mined in the System. The impurities are small in quantity, yet the metallurgists declare that the evidence is conclusive.

"The deposits of corrosion, in the second place, on the body of the thing. They contained chlorides, due to the action of free chlorine. And you recall the stink of chlorine in the air, when the thing appeared?"

Jay Kalam nodded, frowning intently.

"In the third place, Jay, there is the sort of life they found in the green slime clinging to the thing. Microorganisms of types unknown in the System. I'm no bacteriologist, and you'll find details in the report. But those are queer things. They perish, in the normal conditions of the System, for want of chlorine. And thrive on the chlorine in some of the common bactericides. Some varieties break down chlorides, and liberate free chlorine. If such organisms ever get established in the oceans of Earth—" Hal Samdu's rugged face set grimly. "I hope Derron doesn't think of that!"

The Commander was asking, "What else?"

"They attacked the problem from another angle," Hal Samdu continued. "The robot-thing was obviously a mechanical reproduction of a living original. It has many features, such as the scales, beak, teeth, gill, and nostril-vents, which, being useless to a machine, prove that conclusively. And those things also tell a great deal about the alien environment in which the original lived."

411

Jay Kalam held up a lean hand.

"One question, Hal. Why should the robot have been copied after such an original?"

"The scientists discussed that, Jay. Besides any possible intention to deceive other creatures of that world, or to mislead and terrify the people of this—"

The rugged brow of the Admiral-General furrowed with a frown of concentrated effort.

"Besides that, Jay, there is the general speculation that machines designed to operate efficiently, under any given set of conditions, must frequently follow the same principles that life has found most efficient under those conditions—the very words of the report! Why don't you just read it, Jay?"

But the Commander motioned silently for him to go on.

"From the dimensions of the thing, and the amount of power provided for the functioning of its limbs and wings," Hal Samdu resumed laboriously, "particularly from the size, strength, weight and camber of the wings themselves, in relation to the total weight—from all that, the scientists arrived at fairly precise data on the atmospheric density and surface gravity.

"From a study of the cooling system, insulation, and lubricants used—all checked against the optimum temperature conditions for those chlorine-loving micro-organisms —they closely estimated the temperature of the planet.

"The photo-cells that served as eyes for the thing revealed a good deal. From their sensitivity, the adjustment of their iris diaphragms, and the nature of the color filters used, it was possible to determine very exactly the intensity and the color of light to which they were adapted—the light of a K9e sun, within a certain range of distances.

"One deduction checked against another, to verify and refine the first approximations. I've been able to give you but a clumsy sketch of it, Jay. Aye, the science of the System has become a fine and powerful instrument!"

"Too powerful," Jay Kalam said, "in the hands of the Basilisk! But what else, Hal? Anything on how the robot arrived in the New Moon—and how Davian was taken away?"

Hal Samdu shook his shaggy white head.

"There was no real evidence, Jay, but one of the geodesic physicists has a theory. He thinks the Basilisk must be using some application of the same achronic forces the visiwave does—the same sort of warp in the geodesic lines that brought Kay Nymidee out of the comet. You'll find his whole report in the envelope, but he admits that his idea is too vague to be of any practical use. With our data from the cometary expedition, we might have worked out something—but that's gone."

"Then," Jay Kalam demanded, "have you anything on the location of this star?"

"It's in the envelope, Jay," Hal Samdu continued desperately. "The astrophysicists did another remarkable piece of work. They listed all the K9e stars in telescopic range —they are not very luminous, you know, with a surface temperature just above three thousand, and therefore the number known is relatively small.

"They checked off nearly half which are binaries, and hence could have no planets. Most of the rest were eliminated because spectrographic studies revealed no trace whatever of absorption by free atmospheric chlorine. When they were done, Jay, only one star was left."

The Commander rose abruptly. "What star is that?"

"They showed it to me in the telescope—and showed me the faint dark lines of free chlorine in the spectrograms. It's a faint red star in the constellation Draco, known as Ulnar XIV. Its distance is eighty light-years."

"Eighty light-years!" Jay Kalam's thin lips pursed. "No man has been so far—none except the Basilisk! It would take us two years to reach it, at the full power of the *Inflexible*—and we should arrive without any fuel left for action or return."

His dark head shook slowly. Thin, unconscious fingers combed the one white lock back from his forehead. His dark eyes stared at Hal Samdu, with a fixed intensity.

"Hal—" he whispered suddenly, hoarsely. "Hal—I see but one thing to do. It's a terrible thing—it is terrible for life, the child of a star, to destroy a star. And we've no certainty that even that would end the Basilisk—we may have spun our assumptions out too far."

He caught his breath, as if with an effort.

"However, I'm going to order the destruction of the star Ulnar XIV." His dark eyes closed for a moment, as if against some dreadful sight. "Another time, I waited too long—to urge the keeper to annihilate the green comet. Great as a star may be, the life of the System matters somewhat more to us."

"Aye," Hal Samdu rumbled solemnly. "Strike!"

The Commander of the Legion found the small black

413

disk of his communicator. His thin, trembling fingers turned the tiny dials, and tapped out a code signal. His thin lips whispered into it. Hal Samdu sat watching, his face rigid as a statue's.

At last Jay Kalam lowered the instrument.

"It is unfortunate that no visiwave equipment has yet been installed on Phobos," he said. "I am communicating direct, by ultrawave. But Mars is now more than a hundred million miles away. It will take nine minutes for the message to reach the keeper. In ten, the star Ulnar XIV should have ceased to exist in the material universe—although terrestrial astronomers will naturally not be able to detect its disappearance for another eighty years!"

He paced a nervous turn across the end of the big silent room, beyond the desk.

"Twenty minutes," he muttered. "Before we can get any reply—"

"What was that?"

Hal Samdu was suddenly peering about the empty room, blaster level in his big gnarled hand.

"Didn't you hear it, Jay?" he demanded. "A muffled purr! Or feel a breath of bitter cold?"

"I heard nothing, Hal." Jay Kalam sighed, wearily. "We've been under too much strain. I'll order you something to drink. And look through the report, while we're waiting."

He broke the seal on the big green envelope.

"Eh!" His jaw fell slack. "This is no report."

"But it is, Jay! It hasn't been out of my sight."

Out upon the desk the Commander poured a score of neatly tied packets of little yellow slips.

"These are I O U's!" he gasped. "Payable to the New Moon Syndicate. They must have come from the vaults of Gaspar Hannas! And here—here—"

His trembling fingers had found a familiar sheet of stiff crimson parchment. It bore the serpentine monogram. Upon it, in that precise familiar script, was written:

My dear Commander:
    Admiral-General Samdu's brilliant summary has given you a sufficient idea of the genuinely brilliant work of his investigators, and I believe that circumstances will very shortly prove the document to be no longer of value to you.

The Basilisk

"Derron!" Waving the blaster, Hal Samdu was peering wildly about the great armored room. "We can't escape him—not even here! If Giles doesn't get him—"

Jay Kalam was still staring at the red sheet, with dull lifeless eyes, when:

Krrr! Krrr! Krrr! shrilled the tiny, piercing emergency call from his communicator. With stiff fingers he groped again for the little black disk, set the dial, and held it to his ear.

Hal Samdu, watching, saw his face grow taut and white. The instrument at last dropped out of his fingers, and he swayed over the desk, holding himself up with trembling arms.

"It wasn't the reply," Hal Samdu was rasping hoarsely. "There hasn't been time! What has happened, Jay?"

The lusterless, glazing eyes of Jay Kalam stared at him.

"The worst, Hal," he whispered. "That was a frightened bodyguard calling from Phobos—the call crossed ours. The Basilisk has struck again. This time he has taken them all. John Star. And Bob's wife and her child. And—"

He made a little shrug of hopeless defeat.

"And—the keeper of the peace!"

12

The Plundered Vault

That mighty, feral purr receded. The icy cold was gone. Chan Derron could breathe again. Swaying unsteadily, still on his feet, he tried to see where he was, but a smothering darkness wrapped him. His heart was hammering. His breath was a rapid gasping. Cold goose pimples still roughened his body. He had been snatched from before the menacing weapon of Vanya Eloyan, he knew, by that uncanny agency of the Basilisk—and his very vanishing, the girl would take for absolute proof that he was himself the criminal!

But now—*where was he?*

In some confined black space. His feet scraped on a metal floor, and the swift ring of the sound told him that walls were near. He stumbled forward, and his hands came upon a barrier of cold metal.

Was this the Euthanasia Clinic—and the thought drove a cold blade of panic into him—where another victim of the Basilisk had been found murdered? Was death waiting for him, in this thick darkness, now? What was *that?*

He crouched and spun. Intently he listened, but there was no sound beyond the prompt echo. His eyes strained vainly into the blackness. His hand swept instinctively toward the holster under his cloak. And then he remembered, with a sinking sickness in his heart, that the girl had disarmed him.

Something brushed his shoulder. He put up a defensive arm, and something tapped it again. He tried to quiet a pounding heart, and groped before him. His cold fingers caught a swinging pendant. He pulled at it, and a blue-white glare of atomic light blinded him.

For a moment he had to cover his eyes. And then, staring about, he blinked again in wonder. This was indeed a vault—just before him was the ponderous lock-mechanism of an armored door that must have weighed two hundred tons—but in no crematorium.

For the long shelves that lined the branching narrow corridors were stacked with the heavy bags and rolls and packets that held the symbols of wealth, all neatly sorted into chips and scrip and coin and currency. And every bag and roll and packet bore the yellow crescent that was the New Moon's emblem. This, the dazed realization broke upon Chan, was the New Moon's treasure vault!

Then he noticed a curious thing. The scrip of the New Moon Syndicate, the chips used at play, and the bags of coin were all apparently intact—but upon the shelves labeled to contain Green Hall certificates, there were only stacks of rough clay bricks. The vault had been looted! What remained was almost worthless—all the real money was gone, with only mocking clay left in its place!

And his tall body went suddenly rigid and cold. For the vault would presently be opened—probably it had been locked, for safety, because of the Basilisk's promised raid. When it was opened, the Legion of Space and the New Moon police would find the man they thought they wanted—cornered.

In the silence of the vault, Chan began to wonder if the man who had put him there still watched him. His strained nerves could feel alert and hostile eyes upon him. Imagination pictured the Basilisk laughing at him—a low thick chuckle, he thought of it, cold, diabolical, inhumanly gloating.

"Well, Mr. Basilisk?" He couldn't stop his own wild, ragged voice from talking into the mocking silence. "What am I to do now? Sit down and cry? Tear my nails out scratching at the wall? Hang myself from the shelves? Or just let them find me?"

It was hard to keep from screaming. He paced up and down the metal floor, driven with a savage, futile energy. Apprehension painted a vague sinister presence, leering from beyond the shelves.

"Well, can you hear me?" he choked. "How does it feel to be a god, Basilisk? To watch every man in the System? To follow all who try to escape your power, wherever they go? To take what you want? And slay whom you will?"

He shook his fist against the bare metal wall.

"It may feel pretty great—to your twisted brain—whoever you are. But you won't last forever! For some poor devil will get you—somebody that you've mocked and tortured and battered until all that keeps him alive is a little voice that says *kill him, kill him, kill him!*

"Somebody, Basilisk, like me."

Then it happened that his aimless pacing brought him to the scrap of paper on the floor and it happened that his wildly staring eyes glimpsed the scrawled symbols on it. With a wondering exclamation, he snatched it up, smoothed it with his fingers, studied it anxiously.

A small oblong sheet, torn across one end. Scratched upon it, in hasty pencil marks, were three heliocentric space-time positions, followed by a series of numbers in which Chan could see neither relation nor meaning.

The first position designated was that of the New Moon, he recognized—the position it had occupied at the moment of that midnight on which the Basilisk had taken the little gambler, Davian.

The second position—and the thing that had first caught Chan's eye—was a point located in the constellation Draco, at a distance of some ten billions of miles from the Sun. That was the location of the unknown object Chan had discovered when he fled northward from the Legion fleet, the object to which he had been planning to escape when the pursuit of the Basilisk drove him to turn and fight.

The third position was also in the Dragon—but at a

heliocentric elevation which Chan quickly interpreted into the amazing distance of eighty light-years.

After a few moments of study, Chan Derron slipped the crumpled scrap very hastily into the pocket of his tunic, and fervently hoped that the Basilisk wasn't looking —after all, he told himself, a presumably human brain must be limited in its power of attention.

The millions of tons of that object in space had been an utter mystery. This bit of paper seemed good evidence that it was connected with the operations of the Basilisk. And the discovery opened the faintest possible chance—

His fists were clenched.

"If I can get out," he muttered, "out of here and out of the New Moon and back to the *Phantom Atom*—if she's still safe where I left her—if I can get aboard her, and escape the Legion fleet, and get out to that object—"

His voice fell to a soundless whisper.

"If I can do all that, Mr. Basilisk—look out!"

Great shoulders square again, he strode to the lock. Its bolts and levers were uncovered for him to see—bright metal bars weighing many tons. But they were yet secure. His desperate strength and frantic eyes could discover no way to move them.

"If Giles Habibula were here—" he muttered.

Wistfully he recalled the fabulous exploits of the old Legionnaire in picking the locks of the Medusae and opening the guarded vaults of the Cometeers. Habibula, doubtless, with all this mechanism open before him, could have opened the door at once.

But Chan Derron was completely baffled.

He was standing back, panting, sweat-drenched from useless effort—when something clicked, concealed motors hummed, and the great bolts began to slide slowly back as if of their own accord.

It would be the men of Gaspar Hannas, of course, opening the vault. Chan Derron's hand flashed automatically to his armpit, to find only the empty holster of his blaster and the straps that still held the compact unit of the geopellor to his body.

Weaponless, he could only wait, watching the appallingly deliberate well-oiled movement of the bolts. In the geopellor, ironically, lay power to carry him across a hundred million miles of space, but it was useless now. At last the bolts were withdrawn, and the ponderous disk of the door swung slowly open.

"Hasten, you fools!" a great harsh voice was booming. "I must see if all is safe." That must be Gaspar Hannas himself, driven wild with a well-founded fear for his treasure. "If the Basilisk can do all the things he has done, these locks are worthless."

"And there he is!" It was a triumphant shout, from a half-glimpsed man in the yellow of the New Moon's police. "Trapped!"

The violet, blinding tongue of a proton jet whipped through the widening opening. And the voice of Gaspar Hannas bellowed:

"Forward, men! We've got him! He's worth half a million—remember—dead or alive! And the woman—if she's with him—half a million more!"

Chan Derron had stepped swiftly aside, at the first flash of the ray. He waited, listening. There must be a score of men without, he knew from the little sounds of feet and breath and weapons, and they were alertly advancing. He snatched the swinging cord and snapped off the lights in the vault.

"Come out, Basilisk!" boomed the tremendous voice of Gaspar Hannas. "With empty hands! Or we'll come in and get you!"

Crouching in the darkness, Chan called a desperate last appeal:

"I'm not the Basilisk, Hannas." His voice stuck and quivered. "I'm Chan Derron. More a victim than anyone. If you'll listen to me, Hannas—"

"Forward, men!" thundered Hannas. "He admits he's Derron, and we've caught him in the vault! Burn him up!"

The door was swinging wider. Out of the darkness, Chan watched the men creeping forward. Narrowed eyes fearfully searching, proton guns uneasily ready.

He gulped and tried to still the shuddering dread in him.

"You are afraid of me," he called. "Every one of you. I can see the sweat of fear on all your faces. I can see fear crawling in your eyes. Well, you had better be afraid. But it is the Basilisk you ought to fear, and not the man his monstrous tricks have loaded down with suspicion. I, too, am hunting the Basilisk. And now I have some information. I can help you—"

The great voice of Hannas cut him off:

"You've got too much information, Derron! But it is going to die with you. *Get him, men!*"

And the men in yellow slipped forward again.

Chan Derron caught his breath, and snatched one of the mocking clay bricks off the racks. And his fingers gripped the little black control spindle of the geopellor, at the end of the cable that ran down his sleeve.

"If you can!" he shouted. "But you won't get your treasure, Mr. Hannas! Your vault is stripped clean. Here's what the Basilisk left!"

He flung the little brick, so that it shattered against the face of the door. Fragments pelted the men beyond. Half a dozen blinding jets leapt, as nervous fingers contracted. One man, sobbing an oath of fear, dropped his weapon and ran—until an officer's swift beam cut him down.

"Empty?" came the stricken voice of Hannas. "Empty—"

This was the moment. Chan filled his lungs with breath —for the speed of the geopellor made breathing almost impossible. He squeezed and twisted the control handle. And the compact little unit on his shoulders lifted him. It flung him toward the wall of guns.

Bright proton guns flung up to stop him, but their deadly violet lances stabbed behind him. He was already driving bullet-like down one of the long corridors beneath the gaming halls.

"After him, you cowards—"

The great roaring voice of Gaspar Hannas was whisked away, upon the shrieking wind. But the rays could overtake him. Thin lines of fire cut straight to the armored wall ahead. One hissed very near, and ionized air brought Chan a stunning shock.

Teeth gritted, fighting the darkness in his reeling brain, he twisted the little spindle back and forth. The geopellor flung him from side to side, in a swift zigzag, with a savage straining force.

Greater danger awaited him at the long hall's end. Once he stopped to seek an exit, he would make a fair target for the men behind—and the first bull's-eye worth half a million dollars.

He bent his twisting flight toward the floor, and blinked his streaming, wind-blinded eyes. And he saw a small door swing open ahead. A huge man in white filled it completely, carrying a bag of potatoes.

Chan checked his velocity a little—but perilously little —and aimed his bullet flight for the fat cook's burden. He saw the man's eyes begin to stare and widen, and he set his own body for the impact.

The geodesic field shielded him somewhat, but it was still a dazing blow. The cook was hurled flat in the doorway. And Chan, beyond him, came into a kitchen bigger than he had ever dreamed of. Acres of stoves; endless white conveyor tables loaded with dishes and food. All but deserted, now, for the New Moon was being emptied, by fear of the Basilisk.

Beyond the kitchen, in the narrow quarters of the servants, he realized that he had lost his direction. Behind him was a tumult of fear and menace. Half those who glimpsed his flight screamed and fled or hid. But another half, made daring by the magic promise of that half-million, shouted to the pursuers behind, or snatched at weapons of their own.

But the geopellor was swifter than all the hue and cry. Chan dropped upon his feet, walked breathless around the turn of a corridor, and met a yellow-capped porter hastening with a bag.

"Which way," he gasped, "to the docks?"

"That way, sir." The man pointed. "To your left, beyond the pools. But I'm afraid, sir, you'll find the ships all booked—"

His mouth fell open as Chan lifted into the air and soared over his head.

"The Basilisk!" he began to scream. "This way! To the docks!"

The pursuit followed his voice. But Chan's plunging flight had already carried him into the "hanging pools" that were one of the New Moon's novel attractions—great spheres of water, each held aloft by a gravity-plate core of its own, each illuminated with colored light that turned it to a globe of changing fire.

The swimmers had fled. Chan threaded a swift way among the spheres. He heard an alarm siren moaning behind him. And suddenly the gravity-circuits must have been cut off, for the shimmering spheres of water turned to plunging falls.

Already, however, the geopellor had flung him over the rail of a high balcony. He burst through a door beyond, and came into the vast space at the docks. The immense floor was crowded, now, with gay-clad thousands, swept into panic by fear of the Basilisk, fighting for a place on the out-bound ships.

Leaning for a moment against the balcony door, Chan caught his breath. He must have a space suit. There were space suits in the locker rooms beyond this frightened crowd, beside the great valve where he had entered the New Moon. He could fly across the mob, he thought, in seconds and with little risk. But sight of him flying would surely turn fear to stark panic. Many would doubtless be trampled and maimed.

After a second, he went down the steps on foot, and pressed into the fighting throng. That was the longer way. It meant the danger that the valve-crew would be warned against him. Yet he could not take the other way.

It took him endless minutes to push through fringes of the crowd. He heard the distant sob of sirens, and the thunder of annunciators beating against the voice of the mob. He knew the hunt was spreading, and was uneasily aware of his head towering above all those about him.

But he came at last to the little door marked *Employees Only,* and slipped through it into the locker rooms. Here was less confusion than he found anywhere —the workers in the great sign were used to danger. He hurried to the locker where he had left his armor, stripped off his borrowed clothing, flung himself into the space suit, and strode toward the great air lock.

The inner valve was open. A crew of silver-armored technicians were just marching out. Chan entered, as the last of them came through, and made an urgent gesture to the man at the controls. That man had already stiffened, however, listening.

"Warning!" a magnetic speaker was crackling. "Close all locks—until Derron is caught. This man is now attempting to escape from the New Moon. There is a half million reward for him, dead or alive. Derron is six feet three, believed—"

Chan saw quick suspicion change to deadly certainty in the eyes of the valve-keeper. He heard the beginning of a shout and caught the glint of weapons. But the geopellor was already lifting him toward the lock. His bright-clad fist shattered the glass over the emergency lever—intended to be used only if the great valve was closing on a man's body. He pulled down the lever.

The gate before him flung open, as the one behind automatically clanged shut in the face of pursuit. A blast of air spewed him out. The geopellor stopped his spinning flight, and brought him up to the platform where he had

422

landed. He found the wire marked Sector 17-B, snapped the belt of his suit to it and squeezed the little spindle. The geopellor flung him out along the wire.

Five hundred miles to go. The great sign spread its web about him, silver wires shining bright against the dark of space. Great mirrors flashed against the sun; filters glowed red and blue and green. He glimpsed the gibbous Earth, huge and mistily brilliant, so near that he felt he could almost touch the ragged white patch that was a cyclonic storm over Europe.

Five hundred miles—but he pushed the geopellor to a reckless pace, for a warning must be flashing out, he knew, over the wires about him. In four minutes—no more—he had released himself from the pilot wire, beside the silver ball of the control house.

His searching eyes found the *Phantom Atom*. The tiny ship was safe, still hidden behind the great foil mirror. The geopellor carried him to its valve and he flung himself inside.

The first intimation of disaster came when he saw that the prisoner he had left there, space armor welded to the housing, was gone. His heart stood still. Was this some new trick of the Basilisk? He opened the inner valve, and came face to face with a man waiting for him in the corridor.

A very short fat man, with protruding middle and bald spherical head and wrinkled yellow skin. The same man —no mistaking him!—whom Jay Kalam had sent to pick his pockets in the Diamond Room. The intruder was blinking ominously, with pale small eyes. His fat hands held a thick cane pointing at Chan's body—and a deadly little black orifice was visible in the ferrule that tipped it.

"Come on in, Mr. Basilisk!" he wheezed triumphantly. "And match your mortal wits against Giles Habibula!"

The Hundredth Man

Hope came to the Legion with the first ultrawave message from Giles Habibula. Uncharacteristically laconic, it ran: *Aboard Derron's ship. Bound for mysterious object near Thuban in Draco. For life's sake, follow!*

And the Legion followed. Jay Kalam put the mighty *Inflexible* at the head of Hal Samdu's fleet of ten geodesic cruisers. At full power they reached northward, toward Alpha Draconis—which once had been the pole star of Earth. Toward what destination?

Every officer in the fleet was trying to answer that question. Every electronic telescope and mass detector was driven to the utmost of its power searching for any mysterious object. By the time they were one day out from the New Moon, part of the answer had been discovered.

Jay Kalam, tired and pale from the long strain of the chase, restlessly pacing the deep-piled rugs of his sound-proofed and ray-armored chambers in the heart of the *Inflexible,* paused at the signal from his communicator, and lifted the little black disk to his ear.

"We've found it, Commander!" came an excited voice from the bridge. "Forty-four minutes of arc from Alpha Draconis. It's still invisible—albedo must be very low. But the mass detectors indicate an object of nearly twenty million tons.

"A puzzling thing, Commander. This object, whatever it is, must be a newcomer to the System. We estimate the distance from the sun at a little less than ten billion miles. Any object of that size would surely have been discovered by the Legion's survey expedition, five years ago—if it had been there then!"

Jay Kalam put the communicator to his lips.

"Can you identify the object?"

"Not yet," came the reply. "Until we can pick it up on the screens, we won't know whether it's just a rock—or something else."

"Keep tele-periscopes focused on the spot," Jay Kalam ordered. "And use every instrument to search space ahead of us, until we pick up Derron's ship. Keep communications standing by for another message from Giles Habibula, and the vortex gun ready for action."

Shift and changing shift, the gun crew stood ready about the ponderous weapon. In every observatory on every racing ship, men searched the dark void amid the stars of the Dragon ahead. And the communications men waited for further word from Giles Habibula.

But the weary Commander of the Legion, sleeplessly pacing the silent empty luxury of his apartments upon the flagship, restlessly combing his white forelock back with anxious thin hands, received other messages. They came by visiwave from the System behind—for the hard-driven fleet was already beyond the range of ultrawave communication. Their import was all of alarm.

The first message came from the captain in charge of the plain-clothes men who had been detailed to shadow the three suspects on the New Moon—Amo Brelekko and John Comaine and Gaspar Hannas. All three had vanished.

"John Comaine mysteriously disappeared from his laboratory, with two of our men on duty outside the only door," the report stated. "Gaspar Hannas had locked himself in his empty treasure vault. His scream for aid was heard by communicator. When associates opened the vault, he was gone. Amo Brelekko was removed from the floor of the Diamond Room, as the little gambler Davian had been—and in his place, before the few appalled spectators left on the New Moon to see it, was dropped a decaying human skeleton which has been identified as that of a female android."

That made little sense to Jay Kalam. He pondered the implications of it, and then dispatched a message to the captain, asking for further information. The reply, relayed from Rocky Mountain Base, informed him that this officer had now also vanished.

Krrr! Krrr! Krrr!

The penetrating beat of his emergency signal announced the next message, and he heard the ragged voice of a distraught Legion Intelligence officer reading a note from Lars Eccard, Chairman of the Green Hall Council. All sixty members of the Council had been threatened with abduction, by the Basilisk. No ransom was demanded, and no escape was offered—

425

"Chairman Eccard's dictation was interrupted at that point," the shaken voice continued. "Staff members rushed into his chambers and found him gone. Reliable reports from subordinate officers already confirm rumors that every member of the Council has disappeared."

The whole Green Hall—kidnapped! Staggered by that blow, Jay Kalam slumped heavily behind his desk. Those sixty men and women had formed the supreme government of the System. The chosen representatives of the local planetary governments, of capital and labor, of the various professions and sciences—they had all been snatched away.

"Why?" The tired red eyes of the Commander stared across his great empty desk, at the black bunkhead. "Why take them?"

With an uncanny promptness that startled him, the beat of his emergency signal answered. What he heard, when he put the communicator to his ear, was a rasping whisper, distorted in transmission.

"I'll tell you why, Commander," it mocked him. "I took them because I want the System to know my power. I want every man on every planet to shudder and grow pale when he thinks of the Basilisk. I want men to look on me as they once regarded angry gods.

"For I have suffered injuries that must be avenged.

"To establish my new supremacy, I am taking one hundred men and women from the System. They have been the leaders of the foolish attempt to destroy me, and therefore I can deal with them without compunction. I shall use them without remorse for the text of a lesson to mankind. One, out of the hundred, will be allowed to survive and return, to bring that lesson to the rest of mankind."

An unpleasant chuckle rasped from the instrument.

"One hundred, Commander!" croaked that thin, mad voice. "You already know the most of them. Aladoree, the keeper of the peace. John Star. Bob Star, and his wife and their child. A few more of your most conspicuous Legionnaires. Two dozen private individuals—among them three men from the New Moon, Hannas and Comaine and Brelekko. The sixty members of the Green Hall Council —to let them consider all they have done to the Purples."

The humming whisper gave way again to that sardonic chuckle, Jay Kalam's hand tensed and trembled on the little

426

black disk, and his aching body was cold with sudden sweat.

"The total now is ninety-nine," that husky rasping ran on. "I need one more to complete my hundred. Knowing the other ninety-nine, Commander Kalam, I need not tell you who the other is to be."

With that, the humming whisper ceased. Jay Kalam dropped the Communicator. His swift hand snatched the blaster from his belt; he spun to search the empty room —knowing all the time that such precautions were futile.

Nothing happened, however, in the long moment that he held his breath. He made himself holster the weapon again, and groped for the communicator to call Rocky Mountain Base, now a billion miles behind and more, through the visiwave relay.

"Did you pick up that message?" he asked hoarsely. "Is triangulation possible?"

And back across that void, that light would have taken many hours to bridge, the voice of the operator came instantly, consternation not hidden by its humming distortion.

"We heard it, Commander. But triangulation was impossible—because the message was transmitted from our own station! We haven't yet discovered how our transmitter circuits picked it up. But guard yourself, Commander Kalam. You got the threat against yourself?"

"I did," Jay Kalam said. "If I am kidnapped, Hal Samdu will take my place and the Legion will carry on."

He dialed off, called Hal Samdu on the *Bellatrix,* and told that veteran spaceman of these disastrous new developments.

"Draw up beside the *Inflexible,* Hal," he said, "and come aboard. You will take command if I become the hundredth man."

"Aye, Jay." The rumble of Hal Samdu came thinned and furred through the communicator. "But what of Giles —have you heard anything?"

"Not yet," Jay Kalam told him.

"I'm afraid for Giles, Jay." The deep voice seemed hoarse with alarm. "It's true he's an old man, now, and not so clever as he used to be. This Derron is powerful and desperate—and it's a whole day, now, since we heard anything."

Jay Kalam lowered his communicator, with a helpless shrug—and instantly the throb of the emergency signal bade him take it up again. He touched the dial, and put the little black disk to his ear.

"Jay! Do you hear me, Jay?" It was the long-awaited voice of Giles Habibula, thinned, muffled with the hum of the instrument, and hoarse with some desperate anxiety.

"I do, Giles," he said into the little disk. "What is it?"

"Turn back, Jay," came the faint, wheezing voice. "For life's sake, turn your fleet back to the System. Call off your bloodhounds of space, and leave us be."

"Turn back?" cried Jay Kalam. "Why?"

"Ah, Jay, there's been a monstrous error. This is not the Basilisk I've caught. My companion is but an honest, luck-less man. And your chase is a fearful blunder, Jay. It is drawing you far out into space, and leaving the System defenseless.

"In Earth's name, Jay, I beg you to turn back."

"Giles!" the Commander shouted. "If you're speaking under torture—"

A dead click told him that the other instrument had been dialed off. He was trying to call back when the softer note of the ship's signal rang. He heard the excited voice of the executive officer.

"We've got it, Commander! Derron's ship. Dead ahead, toward that object in Draco. Only forty tons—which is why it took us so long to pick it up. But it has power enough, apparently, to hold its lead. We have the range. What is your order?"

Jay Kalam's hand tightened on the communicator. A cold wind seemed to blow around him, blowing away the ship, and blowing away the years. He saw Giles Habibula, a stout little man, strutting, grinning, as he had been when they were privates together. He knew Habibula was on the ship ahead. But the rushing of that wind became the rusty whisper of the Basilisk, jeering at him. No man, not even a friend, could be weighed against his duty to the Legion.

"Do you hear me, Commander?" the executive officer was insisting. "What is your order?"

Jay Kalam slowly closed his eyes, and opened them again. His lean hand made a slow salute. Low and forced, his voice said:

"Fire at once with the vortex gun. Destroy the vessel ahead."

Samdu's battleship, the long *Bellatrix*, was slipping in beside the mighty flagship when the first vortex was fired.

428

Watching through the ports of an air-lock, the Admiral-General saw the great blinding knot of atomic disruption spinning out ahead, flaming wider as its expanding fields of instability consumed all the matter in its reach.

"Well, Mr. Derron," the gigantic spaceman muttered with a grim satisfaction, "or Mr. Basilisk—now let's see you get away!"

Hard-driven geodynes were pushing the two colossal ships through space—or, more accurately, around it—at effective speeds far beyond the velocity of light. But they came together so gently that their crews could feel no shock. Air valves were joined and sealed. And Hal Samdu stalked impatiently aboard the great flagship.

"Quick!" he boomed to the officers who received him. "Take me to Commander Kalam at once."

But, when swift elevators and moving cat-walks had brought them to the hidden door behind the chartroom, the Commander of the Legion failed to answer their signal.

The alarmed executive officer came to unlock the armored door. Hal Samdu stalked ahead into the soft-lit luxurious apartments of Jay Kalam. Silence met him, and emptiness. The Commander of the Legion was gone.

"Poor old Jay," rumbled Hal Samdu. "The hundredth man!"

He turned abruptly upon the officers about him.

"Derron's ship is still in range? Then fire again with the vortex gun. Keep firing till you get it."

14

Man and Android

Facing Giles Habibula in the narrow space within the valve of the *Phantom Atom*, Chan Derron caught his breath. Still he was weaponless—and the black tiny hole in the tip of the old man's level cane looked at him like a deadly eye.

"Habibula?" his startled voice echoed. "Not the great Giles Habibula?"

Chan was weaponless—but the heavy little pack of the

429

geopellor was still strapped to his shoulders, its control spindle still gripped in his hand. It could make a living projectile of his body. His hand began to close.

"Wait, lad!"

The old man lowered the menacing cane. His fishy eyes rolled fearfully and his wheezing voice was hoarse with a desperate appeal.

"For life's sake, lad, forget your mortal tricks. There's no need for you to crush old Giles Habibula to a bloody pulp with your blessed geopellor. For he's no enemy, lad. Ah, no! He comes to you as a precious friend!"

Chan Derron studied the old man with a grim suspicion. And then he saw, behind Giles Habibula, the money stacked on the deck. Thick packets of new Green Hall certificates, bound into great bales and piled high against the bulkheads. The wrapper on every packet was printed with a yellow crescent. Here was the treasure of Gaspar Hannas, taken from the New Moon's vaults!

His hand jerked tense on the little black spindle.

"You aren't—" he gasped hoarsely. "You aren't the Basilisk?"

Giles Habibula quivered. The seamed moon of his face turned slightly green. He caught a croaking, asthmatic breath.

"No, lad!" he gulped. "In life's name—no! I'm just a poor old soldier. Ah, but a hunted fugitive, lad. A friendless deserter from the Legion."

"Deserter, eh?" The dark-stained eyes of Chan Derron narrowed. "If you really are the famous Giles Habibula, why should you desert? And what are you doing here?"

Giles Habibula blinked his colorless eyes.

"Thank you, lad," his thin voice quavered. "Ah, so, lad, from the bottom of my failing old heart, I thank you for calling me famous. For the Legion has forgotten me, lad."

He wiped his eyes with the back of a fat hand.

"Once old Giles Habibula was the hero of the Legion," he sighed. "Aye, of the whole precious System. For his noble courage, lad, and his blazing genius, have twice saved the very life of mankind—once from the hateful Medusae, and again from the frightful Cometeers. And what reward has he got, lad?"

He choked and sobbed and gasped for breath.

"A beggar's reward, lad. Old Giles is forgotten. His precious medals tarnish in a box. The few miserable dollars they gave him are all drunk up. A lonely, hopeless old

430

soldier, dying on the ungrateful charity of those who had been friends—ah, lad, but life was mortal black—until he heard of your exploits!"

A brighter look came over his yellow face.

"Ah, so, lad!" he cried. "You're the sort that old Giles was, in the days when he was young. A bold man, aye! Reckless and dashing. Not caring whether he drove to sunward of the law, or to spaceward. Taking his wine and his gold and his love wherever he found them! Ah, lad, old Giles has come to you, to beg you to help him find his own lost youth."

The hand of Chan Derron tightened again on the spindle.

"Don't lad!" gasped Giles Habibula. "Don't—for life's sake. It's known to all the Legion that you're the Basilisk. Ah, so, and that's a thing of which you should be precious proud—to stand alone against the law of all the planets, and mock the Legion of Space."

Chan Derron shook his head, protestingly.

"But I'm not the Basilisk," his voice broke hoarsely. "I'm just his victim. He has planted a hundred bits of evidence, to pin suspicion on me. Look at this money taken from the vaults of Hannas."

Giles Habibula nodded, and his yellow face broke into a happy smile.

"Ah, so, lad!" he wheezed. "Look at it—millions and millions of dollars. Enough to keep a man in wine and women and luxury for a whole lifetime. Or two men, when the life of one is already run to the end. Shall we take off with our loot? Ah, it will be like the old days, lad—living in flight from the Legion?"

The eyes of Chan Derron narrowed to an accusing stare.

"You admit you were an outlaw in the old days," he muttered. "You're famous for your way with locks. And you have learned all the scientific tricks of the Medusae and the Cometeers. I believe *you* are the Basilisk, Giles Habibula."

"Life, no, lad!" The old man turned pale. "Don't think that—"

"If you aren't," rapped Chan Derron, "tell me one thing: how did you find the *Phantom Atom*, when all the Legion failed?"

"Easy, lad," wheezed Giles Habibula. "Among the keys I lifted from Dr. Charles Derrel in the Diamond Room, was one stamped: *Controlhouse 17-B-285.* One question told me that the mirror that motor turns was out of order. That's how I knew where to meet you. But surely, lad, you don't think—"

Soberly, Chan Derron shook his head.

"I believe you're hunting the Basilisk," he said. "So am I. And I've a clue—which is more than I believe the Legion has—besides those the Basilisk has planted to pin his crimes on me. You may come with me, if you like."

The small leaden eyes blinked at him, blankly.

"I told you, lad, that I came to seek the Basilisk," Habibula wheezed at last. "If you are not the monster—and if you can take me to him—then I'll go with you."

Chan gestured briefly toward the compact living apartments aft.

"Make yourself at home," he said. "I am going forward. We have got to slip out of the sign, and elude the fleet, and get to an object I have discovered near Thuban, in Draco. We've cathode plates enough to reach it, but not to return. I shall expect you to stand a watch, later."

"Ah, so, lad. You can depend on Giles Habibula."

Chan Derron went up into the pilot bay, and Giles Habibula waddled back to the galley. There, preparing an extravagant meal out of the slender stock of supplies he found, he made an immense deliberate clatter of pots and pans.

Presently his deft pudgy fingers tuned the visiwave relay hidden under his cloak. Keeping up the noise to cover his voice, he put the communicator disk to his lips and dispatched his first brief message to Commander Kalam:

"Aboard Derron's ship. Bound for mysterious object near Thuban in Draco. For life's sake, follow!"

He finished getting the meal, tasting copiously from every dish, and carried a loaded tray forward to the pilot bay. Chan Derron was towering in that tiny space, concentrated on instruments and controls. His great hand motioned Giles Habibula impatiently back.

"What's the trouble, lad?" the old man demanded.

"We've a race on." Chan Derron's intent eyes didn't look away from the controls. "Samdu's fleet picked us up. We'd outrun them if we had enough margin of fuel. As it is—I don't know. But leave me alone."

Giles Habibula shrugged philosophically, and carried the tray back to the galley. Deliberately, he demolished its contents, belched and yawned, and looked hopefully about the shelves.

"A mortal pity," he sighed, "that the Basilisk didn't use his fearful magic to pick us up a few bottles of wine. If he'll let me join him——I know a few good, well-guarded cellars—aye, vintages five centuries old—that his instrument might reach."

He pried himself upright again with the cane, labored aft, and tumbled into one of the tiny staterooms. Soon a series of softer sounds rose against the keen hum of the hard-driven geodynes: whistle and flutter and sob and moan, whistle and flutter and sob and moan—the snore of Giles Habibula.

When the regularity of those new sounds had become well established, another person slipped out of the rearmost of the four tiny cabins. A woman. The quick grace of her tall slim body spoke of unusual strength. Platinum-colored hair framed a face of surpassing loveliness. Alertly watchful, her clear eyes were violet.

Moving with no sound audible above the hastening song of the geodynes and the snoring of Giles Habibula, she went swiftly forward. One slender hand clung near a singular jewel, like a great white snow-crystal, that hung from her throat. And the other, with the practiced and familiar grip, held a proton blaster of the newest Legion design.

She came to the little opening in the bulkhead behind the pilot bay, and stood watching Chan Derron, with the ready weapon leveled at his heart. His broad back was toward her, his whole big body was tense. He seemed absorbed in his task. His great hands moved deftly over the controls as he fought to drag from power cells and geodynes the last possible quantum of energy.

For a long time she watched him.

Once a telltale flashed suddenly. Chan Derron started. His big hands moved convulsively, and the steady musical note of the geodynes rose higher in the scale.

"In tomorrow's name!" she heard him mutter. "For one more ton of cathode plates—"

An unwilling little glisten had come into her eyes. Her blond head flung angrily. She caught her breath, and lifted the blaster. He would never even know.

But the Basilisk ought to know. All his crimes had earned a long, long taste of the bitterness of death. She let the blaster sink again and watched. Telltales and detectors told her that the fleet was in pursuit. Set up on the keyboard of the calculator, she could read the destination of the *Phantom Atom*—a point in Draco, ten billion miles from the sun. And every taut movement of Chan Derron reminded her that this was a desperate race.

What was located at the point? And why the haste to reach it? Her pressure on the blaster's release would destroy all hope of answering those questions. That was the only reason, the girl told herself, that she must wait. But she turned suddenly, and went swiftly and soundlessly back down the corridor, toward the cabin where she had been concealed.

The whistle and flutter and sob and moan of Giles Habibula's snoring had never faltered. But, the instant after the girl had passed his cabin door, it ceased abruptly, and a wheezing voice softly advised:

"Stop, lass, right where you stand."

The girl spun very swiftly, the proton gun leaping up in her hands. She found Giles Habibula standing out in the corridor. His thick cane was leveled at her body, and her own weapon dropped from the look in his slate-colored eyes.

"Ah, thank you, lass," he sighed. "It would be a shameful pity to destroy a thing as lovely as you are. And I beg you not to force my hand. For I know you, lass. Old Giles could never forget the mortal beauty of Luroa."

Something swift and cold and deadly flashed in the violet eyes. The blaster jerked again in the girl's strong hand. But it was met by an instant motion of the cane. Her reply was a smile—so lovely that the old man blinked and gasped.

"And I know you," her smooth voice said. "You are Giles Habibula. I don't think any other man could have caught me as you did."

The yellow face beamed at her.

"Ah, so, I am Giles Habibula. Aye, and forty years ago you would have heard my name—or a dozen of my names—in the underworlds of every planet. For Giles Habibula, in the old days, was as great an operator—as bold and clever and successful— as you have been in yours, Luroa."

The girl still smiled her dazzling and inscrutable smile.

"But now it seems that the two of us," wheezed Giles Habibula, "are after another outlaw as great as we have been—greater, aye, unless we prove otherwise by catching him."

His flat leaden eyes blinked at her.

"Shall we join forces, lass?" he asked. "Until we have destroyed the Basilisk." His round yellow head jerked aft, toward Chan Derron in the pilot bay. "With my own precious genius," he said, "and with the deadly cunning and the fearful strength and the mortal beauty that Eldo Arrynu gave to you—ah, no lass, with all of them we cannot fail."

He peered at her, anxiously.

"If you will join me, lass—man and android, against the Basilisk!"

For an instant the girl's white loveliness had seemed frozen, so that the wonder of her smile seemed a hollow, painted thing. But then her face abruptly softened. She slipped the blaster into a holster that her furs concealed, and held out a strong slender hand to Giles Habibula.

"I'm with you, Giles," she said, "until the Basilisk is dead." And the old Legionnaire wondered at a difference in her voice. Somehow it seemed naive, bewildered, troubled—somehow like a child's. "Come, Giles," she said, and beckoned toward the cabin where she had hidden. "There's something I must tell you."

15

The Dreadful Rock

The rock, black and naked, broke a lonely sea. The sea had a muddy, green-black color, cut with long strips of floating yellow-red weed. Its surface had an oily, glistening smoothness. The sky above it was a smoky, greenish blue. And the luminary that rose very slowly in it, baking the rock under merciless rays, seemed larger than the sun. It presented an enormous crimson disk, pocked with spots of darkness. The infra-red predominated in its radiation, so that its dull light brought a sweltering heat.

Upon the summit of the rock, an uneven granite bench not fifty yards in length, were crowded one hundred men and women. Their bodies were slowly cooking under the unendurable rays of that slowly rising sun. They were parched with thirst, for the ocean about them was an undrinkable brine. And they all were coughing, strangling, weeping, gasping with respiratory distress, for the green in the air was free chlorine.

They were the hundred the Basilisk had taken.

The last arrival, Jay Kalam, remembered hearing a sudden, queerly penetrating purr, as he stood in his chamber aboard the *Inflexible*. A resistless force dragged him into a frightful chasm of airless cold. But even before the breath could go out of him, light came back—the dull sinister radiation of this dying star. The feral purr receded, and he found himself sprawling on this barren rock.

Chlorine burned his lungs. A savage gravitation dragged at his body. Heat struck him with a driving, blistering force. And he was sick with an utter hopelessness of despair.

"Commander Kalam!" choked a voice. "You?"

It was Lars Eccard, the abducted chairman of the Green Hall Council, red-eyed and gasping, who aided him to his feet. He peered with smarting eyes about the bare summit of the rock, and saw many that he knew—even bent as they were with continual coughing and masked inadequately against the toxic gas with scraps of dampened rags tied over their nostrils.

He saw Bob Star and a few other Legionnaires who had been taken, standing guard with their blasters on the highest points of the rock. And beyond them, wheeling and soaring and diving in the poison yellow-green haze that hung upon the poison sea, he glimpsed a dozen living originals of the monstrous robot that had appeared in the Diamond Room of the New Moon.

"They have attacked many times, Commander," rasped Lars Eccard, beside him. "Thus far we have always beaten them off, but all the weapons are nearly dead."

"I have my own blaster."

Jay Kalam touched his weapon, but the lean old statesman shook his head.

"It will help, Commander." He paused to cough and sob for breath. "But not for long. For the tide is rising. Already, since dawn, it has come up a hundred feet. Another hundred will cover the rock. And there are things in the water more deadly than those in the sky."

Jay Kalam climbed a little higher on the rock, with Lars Eccard stumbling behind him. All the haggard, white-masked faces he saw were familiar to him, for these were the hundred foremost citizens of the System.

A woman lay on a little shelf of stone. Improvised bandages covered her arms and shoulders. A small golden-haired girl knelt beside her, sobbing. Her bandaged hand patted the child's head.

"That is Robert Star's wife," said Lars Eccard. "One of the winged monsters snatched her up. She was almost beyond the cliffs, before Bob killed it. It dropped her, and fell into the sea. The things that dragged it under the water were terrible indeed."

A fit of coughing seized Jay Kalam. It left him breathless, trembling, blinded. His lungs were on fire. Lars Eccard tore a scrap off his tunic, and gave it to him.

"Wet this, Commander," he said. "Tie it around your face. Water absorbs chlorine."

On a higher ledge, they came upon a dozen men and women kneeling in a circle. All wore the rude masks, and one or another of them was always coughing. But they seemed to ignore the flesh-corroding death they breathed, and the black-winged death that wheeled and screamed above them, the crimson death of heat that beat down from the immense and lazy sun, and the manifold and hidden death beneath the acid, monster-infested sea that rose inexorably about the rock. Each had before him a little heap of pebbles, and their red half-blinded eyes were upon a pair of dancing dice.

Lars Eccard looked down at them and shrugged.

"If it helps them to forget—"

Gaspar Hannas was the banker at that game. His broad face, beneath its yellow-stained mask, showed a slow and senseless smile. And the same eagerness moved his great white hands to draw in the pebbles he won, as if they had been diamond chips on the tables of his own New Moon.

John Comaine, the big blond engineer, did not play. He squatted across from Hannas. His long square face had a wooden impassive look, and his glassy protruding eyes were fixed upon his old employer with what seemed a well-suppressed hostility. Beside him was the queer, box-like instrument he had set up on the New Moon to detect the mysterious agency of the Basilisk.

Amo Brelekko was rolling the dice. A white handkerchief covered half his face, but otherwise he seemed unchanged since the Diamond Room. His gaudy garments looked immaculate. The rays of the low red sun splintered from his jewels. His thin yellow hands manipulated the cubes with a deft and incredible skill.

For all that old skill, however, he rolled and lost. The winner, whose thin nervous hands snatched eagerly for the pebbles, was a little gray wisp of a man whose stooped and tattered figure seemed vaguely familiar. He set the play down in a little black book, and then tapped swiftly at the keys of a compact, silent little calculating machine. And suddenly Jay Kalam knew him. He was Abel Davian, the little gambler the Basilisk had taken from the New Moon's Diamond Room.

The yellow-stamped money bag, that must still hold the twenty million dollars of his fatal winnings, lay disregarded on the rock beside him. But he pushed out a handful of black pebbles, and took the dice from Brelekko. Perspiration rolled from his shrunken skin, as he shook the cubes, and threw. He lost, and bent again with a worried frown to his calculator.

"Strange animals, men," muttered Lars Eccard.

Beyond in a shallow rocky cup that John Star guarded, they discovered his wife, Aladoree. She was kneeling, her proud slight body shaken ever and again with paroxysms of dreadful coughing. Her quick hands were busy with some odd little instrument on the ledge before her, improvised from stray bits of wood and metal. She looked up, and saw Jay Kalam. A weary little greeting smiled above her mask, but he saw the death of a hope in her eyes.

"We had expected to see you, Jay," came John Star's hoarse voice. "But on the *Inflexible*."

Jay Kalam looked down at the crude simplicity of the half-completed instrument. This harmless-seeming toy, he knew, was the supreme weapon of mankind, capable of sweeping any known target out of existence. He breathed the symbol of its power:

"AKKA?"

The coughing woman who was the keeper of it shook her head.

"The instrument isn't finished," she whispered. "The parts for it that I was wearing, disguised as jewels, have been taken from me. We haven't found materials enough. I need wire for the coil."

Jay Kalam fumbled for the small black disk of his ultrawave communicator. "Perhaps the parts of this will help."

"Perhaps." The haggard woman took it from him. "But even if the instrument is completed, I don't see how it

438

can serve us. For the Basilisk's identity, and the seat of his strange power, are still unknown. We don't even know where we are."

"But we can guess," Jay Kalam told her. "We made a fairly conclusive identification of the star from which the Basilisk's peculiar robot came. From the abundance of free chlorine here, and the appearance of the sun above —it is pretty obviously type K9e—I believe that this is the same star. That means that our own sun ought to be eighty light-years southward. When night comes, so that we can see the constellations and the Milky Way—"

"When night comes," John Star broke in huskily, "we won't be here. The tide floods this rock."

"In that case—"

Jay Kalam choked and coughed. It was a long time before he could catch his strangling breath, and see again. He looked soberly, then, at the tortured man and the wan-faced woman before him. They were waiting, very grave.

"In that case," he whispered again, "I see but one thing that we can do. A very desperate thing. But it offers the only hope there is."

"Jay—" John Star gulped. "You don't mean—"

The grim dark eyes of the Commander met the patient, luminous gray ones of the keeper.

"If you can complete the instrument," he told her quietly, "I think you must use it immediately to destroy this sun, this planet, everything in this stellar system. Even ourselves."

The woman's fine head nodded gravely.

"I'll do that," she said. Her quick hands were turning the little disk of the communicator. "And the parts of this," she told him, "will supply everything I need."

"Wait," croaked John Star. "First—couldn't we use it to report our position and our plight? There's still the Legion—"

The Commander shook his head.

"This is just an ultrawave unit," he said. "With no visi-wave relay, it would take eighty years for our call to reach the System, and eighty years for the answer to come back —and there's no receiver anywhere sensitive enough to pick up the signals. Even the visiwave relay, that filled a whole room on the *Inflexible,* had a maximum theoretical range of less than half a light-year.

"No, John. I think our only hope—"

Krrr! Krrr! Krrr!

439

The tiny, piercing beat of the emergency signal checked him. It came from the instrument he had handed Aladoree. Wonderingly, she gave it back. What he heard, when he put it to his ear, was the muted and distorted whisper of the Basilisk.

"My dear Commander," it said, "I am forced to interfere with your reckless sacrificial scheme. For quick annihilation from the keeper's weapon is not what I had planned for ninety-nine of you. I prefer to let you live long enough to pay for all the insults and injuries that have been heaped upon me. I want to give you time to realize that the person who suffered so long as the smallest and the most scorned of men is now the greatest—the Basilisk. And when you know the truth, when you have made adequate atonement, I want to watch you perish in the manner I shall choose.

"As for the hundredth man," that gloating whisper continued, "his death by AKKA would spoil my victory. For I intend to return him alive to the System, to tell mankind of my sweet revenge. You may assure your companions —if you wish to revive their hopes—that one of them is destined to survive."

The whisper ceased. Jay Kalam dropped the little instrument, and stared about the bare black rock. He saw the little circle of kneeling men and women, still intent upon their game of futile chance. He saw Bob Star's wife, who had been Kay Nymidee, rising weakly to take their sobbing little child into her arms. He saw Bob Star himself, a lean lonely figure at the end of the rock, standing guard against the monstrous winged things that soared and dived upon the wind beyond.

"I wonder—" He choked and coughed and gasped for breath. "I wonder if the Basilisk isn't somewhere near, with his base and whatever equipment he uses. Because we got his voice by ultrawave, without any relay."

The choked little gasp from Aladoree brought his eyes back to her haunted, stricken face. Her slender arm was pointing, trembling. And Jay Kalam saw that the half-completed instrument of AKKA was gone from the bench of rock before her. In its place was a little black serpent, crudely shaped of clay.

16

The Geofractor

"But I am not Luroa."

The violet-eyed girl had closed the door of the tiny cabin upon the racing *Phantom Atom,* and now the keen endless whine of the hard-driven geodynes came but faintly to her and Giles Habibula.

"Eh, lass?" The old man blinked his colorless eyes. "But you are!"

Perched earnestly on the edge of the narrow bunk in front of him, for his mass overran the only chair, the girl flung back the lustrous mass of her platinum hair, and peered gravely back into the old soldier's face.

"I'm no android, Giles Habibula," she insisted. "I'm as human as you are. I'm Stella Eleroid. I'm the daughter of Dr. Max Eleroid—who was murdered by the Basilisk."

A cold light flashed in her violet eyes, and her white face was hardened with a grimness of purpose that seemed to freeze its beauty into marble.

"When I knew the Legion had failed," her cold, low voice ran on, "I set out to track down this killer and to recover the geofractor—that was his last and greatest invention, the thing that Derron killed him for."

"Geofractor?" echoed Giles Habibula. "What in life's name is that?" He lurched ponderously forward, his small eyes squinting into her face. "But you're Luroa, lass," he insisted. "I saw your picture on the posters. There's a difference in your eyes and your hair, and I'll grant you to be a gorgeous actress—but you'll never fool old Giles."

"I can explain."

With an impatient gesture, the girl caught his massive shoulder. The old man looked a long time into the white, taut beauty of her face, and at last all the doubt melted from his eyes as he smiled.

"You see, Giles," she said, "my father and Dr. Arrynu were boyhood friends. They roomed together at Ekarhenium. Each had a vast respect for the abilities of the other.

My father used to say that if Arrynu had chosen to live within the law, he could have been the greatest biologist or the greatest artist in the System. Sometimes, during his long exile, Arrynu paid secret visits to the earth, and my father always entertained him. I think he hoped until the end to persuade Arrynu to give up his illicit researches and turn his gifts to something better."

She paused for an instant, biting her full lip.

"I had admired him, since I was a girl," she continued more slowly. "And on his last clandestine visit, he—well, discovered me. He had always ignored me before, but this time I was older. Seventeen. He began making violent love to me. He was a vigorous and passionate man. The romance of his outlaw life had always intrigued me. He told me about the luxuries and the beauties of the uncharted asteroid where he had his secret stronghold, and begged me to go back with him.

"And I would have gone. I was young enough—insane enough. I thought I loved him." Her gray eyes looked beyond Giles Habibula, and for a moment she was silent. "I've sometimes wished I had gone. In spite of everything he did, Eldo was the greatest man I've known—except, perhaps, my father.

"But I told my father, the day we were to leave. He was terribly upset. He began telling me things I had only guessed before, about the unpleasant side of Arrynu's character—the illegal researches, the manufacture of outlawed drugs, the ring of criminals Arrynu had gathered and dominated.

"In spite of all that, I was still young enough and mad enough to go, until my father went on to tell me about the androids—the synthetic things like Stephen Orco, but most of them female, that Arrynu had made and sold. Lovely but soulless criminal slaves, that usually robbed and murdered their pleasure-seeking purchasers and then returned to Arrynu to be sold to another victim.

"That convinced me. I refused to see Arrynu again. My father talked to him, just once more. I don't know what was said, but that was the end of their odd friendship. Arrynu returned to his hidden planetoid. I know now what he did there."

An old brooding horror darkened the eyes of the girl.

"He made the thing he called Luroa. Her body had the superhuman strength of the androids. Her brain had the same inhuman, pitiless criminal cunning he had given

442

Stephen Orco. But she was modeled after me. From photographs and his own memory, he created a likeness almost exact."

"Ah," breathed Giles Habibula. "Ah, so. But lass, how does it come that you have been playing the role of that mortal android?"

"Arrynu kept Luroa with him," the girl said, "until the Cometeers, guided by that monster he had made himself, fell upon his little secret world. Arrynu was killed. But Luroa escaped. Daring and brilliant and ruthless, she assumed the leadership of her maker's interplanetary gang. Her exploits soon got the Legion on her trail. It was then that she conceived her most diabolical scheme."

The eyes of the girl were almost black, and she paused to shudder. Her hand groped for the great white jewel at her throat, as if it had been a precious talisman.

"Luroa knew she had been made in my likeness. She planned to steal my identity. She was going to abduct me, from the laboratory where I was trying to carry on my father's work. She was going to kill my brain with drugs, and let the members of her gang deliver me to the Legion and collect her own reward. And she would step into my shoes."

"Ah, a fearful plot!" Giles Habibula leaned forward anxiously. "And what happened?"

"My father had warned me of such a possibility," the girl said gravely. "After his death, suspecting that she had been responsible, I made certain preparations. When Luroa came, I was ready. It was not she who won, but I."

Giles Habibula surged to his feet and pulled her unceremoniously to him and set a very enthusiastic kiss upon her lips.

"Good for you, lass!" he cried. "So you beat the android at her own mortal game? But why didn't you report the matter to the Legion? And claim your just reward?"

The girl's face grew very sober again.

"It might have been hard to prove that I was not Luroa. Besides, that same day I learned that my father's murderer had escaped from the Devil's Rock." Her voice was still and cold. "And the theft of a document from the laboratory a few days later proved that he was using my father's geofractor. I knew that the Legion had failed— and must continue to fail, against that terrible invention.

"But Luroa, I thought, might not fail. I became Luroa."

443

"A well-played part," applauded Giles Habibula. "But, lass, tell me about this stolen invention."

The girl sat down again on the edge of the bunk. Her platinum head inclined a moment, listening to the fighting whine of the geodynes. Her slender hand unconsciously touched the ready butt of her proton blaster, and then the great white crystal at her throat.

"Don't worry, lass," Giles Habibula urged her. "I gave our position and course to Commander Kalam and the fleet. Derron will have no time to look for stowaways. But this mortal invention?"

"You know," she told him deliberately, "that my father was a geodesic engineer."

"Ah so, the greatest," wheezed Giles Habibula. "His refinements made the old-type geodynes seem primitive as ox-carts. He invented the geopellor, that Derron is so ready with."

"Derron's good with stolen discoveries." Her white hands clenched, and slowly relaxed again. "But the geofractor," she said, "is based upon a principle totally new —affording a complete, controlled refraction of geodesic lines.

"The instrument utilizes achronic force-fields. My father independently discovered the same new branch of geodesy of which Commander Kalam's expedition got some inkling from the science of the Cometeers."

"Ah, so," Giles Habibula nodded. "Kay Nymidee used something of that sort to escape from the comet."

"But the geofractor, as my father perfected it," the girl said, "had a power and a refinement of control that the Cometeers apparently never approached. Its achronic fields are able to rotate the world lines of any two objects within a range of several hundred light-years."

"Aye, lass." Giles Habibula smiled as if he understood. "But in other words—?"

"The geofractor projects two refractor fields," the girl told him. "Each unit is able to deflect the geodesic lines of any object out of the continuum, and wrap them back again at any point within its range. Which means," she smiled, "that the object, in effect, is snatched out of our four dimensional universe, and instantly set back again at the other point.

"There are two coupled units," she explained, "timed to perfect synchronism, so that each creates a perfect vacuum to receive the object transmitted by the other. That prevents the atomic cataclysms that might result from forcing two objects into the same space at the same time.

"That explains why the Basilisk—" she caught her breath, "why Derron has such a way of putting clay snakes and bricks and robots in the place of the things he takes. It balances the transmitter circuits, and saves power."

Giles Habibula exhaled a long, amazed breath.

"So that's the geofractor!" he wheezed. "Ah, a fearful thing!"

"So Derron has made it," the girl whispered bitterly. "But my father intended it for purposes of peaceful communication. He dreamed of a timeless interplanetary express service. He even hoped to make wide stellar exploration possible, so that human colonists could spread across the galaxy.

"Yet he realized the supreme danger of his discovery. I doubt that he would ever have finished it at all, but for the bitter straits of mankind in the cometary war. He completed it only as a weapon of last resort—and he provided a shield against it."

"Eh?" Giles Habibula stared at her. "A shield?"

The girl touched her white, six-pointed jewel.

"This contains a tiny, atom-powered achronic field-coil," she told him. "It is adjusted to create a spherical barrier zone, that the search and refractor fields of the geofractor cannot penetrate.

"It is all that has defended me, thus far, from Derron's stolen power. And he has tried more than once to take it from me—as when he sent that robot to the New Moon to attack me—though he bungled, that time, by killing his own monster too soon."

Giles Habibula blinked and squinted at her.

"Now, lass," he queried, "now that we know all this —what shall we do about it? Derron is driving out with us toward some unknown object in Draco, and the fleet is pressing mortal close behind us."

"That object," said Stella Eleroid, "must be the geofractor."

"Eh!" Giles Habibula started. "But that was a small thing, Jay Kalam said. He said one man could carry it."

"The model was, that Derron took," the girl agreed. "It would have had power enough to carry one man—and itself—away from the island where my father was testing it—the only wonder is that Derron didn't escape with it

445

then, himself, instead of attempting his stupid pretence of innocence.

"But it had far too little power for these recent feats. A huge new machine must have been constructed—probably it was built on a planet of another star, possibly with the labor of such robots as the one sent to the New Moon. The thief has had four years, remember, and the model itself solved all problems of transportation."

"But, lass—" Giles Habibula shook his head, doubtfully. "If Derron was in the New Moon, and this evil machine ten billions of miles away, then how could he have been the Basilisk?"

"Remote control," said Stella Eleroid. "The device was perfected by my father. Something small enough for a man to carry in one hand, but powerful enough to operate the geofractor from almost any distance, with tubular fields of achronic force. Since those same fields can be adjusted to pick up energy, as easily as to transmit it, they can be used for observation as well as control, with no time-lag, and no pickup equipment required."

She saw Giles Habibula's puzzled scowl.

"That means Derron can operate the geofractor from almost anywhere," she said. "He's loaded now with the remote-control apparatus—I felt the hidden wires in his sleeve." Her white face tightened. "There on the New Moon, he must have felt like a god traveling incognito—able to spy on anybody in the system with no danger of detection, and ready with the geofractor to snatch away everybody who dared oppose his power-madness. Or almost everybody."

Nervously, she touched the white jewel again.

"Then, lass, shall we just wait and keep you hidden?" Giles Habibula urged uneasily. "Until Derron brings us to his fearful machine—"

Crash!

Something splintered the cabin door behind them. Slivers flew around them, and Chan Derron's wide shouldered bulk was framed in the ragged opening. One hand clutched the control spindle of his geopellor, and the other leveled the bright needle of a proton blaster.

The girl's hand darted for her weapon. But Chan's fingers tightened on the spindle, and his big body came toward her with the fleetness of a shadow. The nose of his blaster caught hers, and flung it against the bulkhead.

446

A simultaneous kick sent Giles Habibula's thick cane spinning.

The geopellor lifted Chan back to the shattered doorway.

"Some spare blasters in the chest," he gasped. "And I'm not quite deaf."

His weapon covered them while he caught his breath.

His narrowed eyes swept the white, defiant beauty of the girl, and he smiled grimly.

"Listen," he said softly. "Miss Stella Eleroid—I'm glad you're not Luroa! And Giles Habibula—I thought you had been a loyal Legionnaire too long to desert! Listen—" His weapon gestured emphatically. "I heard all you said. And now we are going to be three together against the Basilisk. For I am going to convince you that I didn't murder Dr. Eleroid."

A little shudder swept the girl's taut body. The savage hate in her eyes drove Chan a step backward.

"Think so?" her voice whipped at him. "I don't!"

"Ah, lass—wait!" The small eyes of Giles Habibula rolled at her apprehensively. "We'll listen."

"What you said about the geofractor," he told the trembling, defiant girl, "explains the circumstances of your father's murder."

"Then tell me how it happened," she challenged him coldly. "You ought to know!"

"I had that armored room ready, when your father and another man landed with the working model they were to test," he said quietly. "They went inside and locked the door. I stood guard outside. Admiral-General Samdu, not an hour later, found the door unlocked—that fact is what convicted me. He found Dr. Eleroid's body, and aonther, but the working model was gone.

"The body of the assistant was already stiff in *rigor mortis*. That was a point they failed to explain, in the case against me. They simply disregarded it." Chan Derron's jaw set grimly. "But *rigor mortis* never begins in less than two or three hours after death. The other body found in that room with Dr. Eleroid had been dead probably ten or twelve hours."

His somber eyes went back to the girl's intent white face.

"You have explained how it must have happened," he told her. "The murderer had already killed your father's assistant. He had hidden the body, and taken the assistant's

447

place. It was the murderer who went down into that room with your father. Don't you think that is possible?"

The platinum head of Stella Eleroid nodded very slowly, as if unwillingly. Her violet eyes, still very dark, remained fixed on Chan Derron's face with an intensity almost hypnotic.

"It is possible," she whispered reluctantly. "Because my father suffered from an extreme myopia—he couldn't recognize anyone ten feet from him. And that day he must have been completely absorbed in his experiment." She nodded again. "But go on."

"The murderer—the real Basilisk—is obviously a very clever man," Chan continued. "We know he had already been spying on your father. He must have planned the thing very carefully. His risk was great—but taken for a tremendous stake.

"Once in that locked room, he watched your father test and demonstrate the invention. And then, when he had learned all he had to know, he killed the inventor. He used the geofractor to bring the stiffened body of the actual assistant from wherever he had hidden it. He used it again to take the blaster out of my belt. He drove the bayonet into your father's body, and unlocked the door, and finally removed himself and the working model—leaving everything arranged to convict me of the crime."

He searched the girl's fixed white face.

"You believe me," he whispered hoarsely. "Don't you, Stella?"

"I—I don't know." She shook her head. "I want to—but who is the Basilisk?"

"Ah, that's the mortal question!" Giles Habibula gasped. "Perhaps you speak the truth, Captain Derron—and if you do, this criminal has done you a fearful wrong indeed. But there's still a monstrous mass of evidence against you."

"Won't you trust me?" Chan begged hopelessly. "Just until we reach the geofractor. I think it will tell us who our enemy really is."

"My orders are to bring you back," the old soldier said bleakly. "And the fleet is already close behind us. But, if you're willing to surrender, I'll take your case to Commander Kalam—"

Chan Derron's face set grimly.

"I'll not surrender," he said. "I know the fleet is close behind. And we haven't cathode plates to keep up full speed—they may soon be in range, with the vortex gun. But I'm going on to the geofractor. If you won't help—"

His weapon gestured ominously. A dull green gleam flashed from a finger of the hand that held it, and Giles Habibula blinked.

"Eh, lad!" he gasped. "Your ring—where'd you get that ring?"

"It was my mother's," Chan Derron said. "She had the stone reset for me."

"Let me see it." The old man held out a trembling hand. "It's Venusian malichite? Carved into a die? The spots all threes and fours?" He scanned Chan's big body with an odd intenseness. "Tell me, lad—who was your mother? Where did you get this stone?"

"The jewel belonged to my grandmother." Chan stared at him blankly. "She was a Venusian singer. Her name was Ethyra Coran!"

"Ethyra Coran!"

The eyes of Giles Habibula were suddenly brimming with tears. His big body heaved out of the chair. He pushed Chan's blaster unceremoniously aside, and flung his arms about him.

"What's this?"

"Don't you see?" wheezed Giles Habibula. "Your mother was my own precious daughter. You're my own blood, Chan Derron. The grandson of Giles Habibula!"

"Then—" Chan freed himself, stared into the beaming yellow face. "Then—will you help me?"

"Ah, so!" the old man cried. "And gladly! For no grandson of Giles Habibula could be the Basilisk.

With a grave and silent question in them, the eyes of Chan Derron looked at the girl. For a long moment, her level violet eyes met his, dark with another question. At last she nodded slowly.

"We'll give you a chance, Chan Derron," she said. "If you can find the Basilisk."

17

The Final Gamble

The pursuing fleet crept up behind, in spite of Giles Habibula's frantic appeals to the Commander. The first shot from the vortex gun came after the *Phantom Atom:* a vast expanding field of atomic instability that burned strange with deadly radiations and sucked at the fugitive ship with a ruthless attraction.

"Let me tune your geodynes!" gasped Giles Habibula, as the tiny vessel fought that consuming maelstrom. "I've been an engine man for fifty precious years, and I can coax the generators to more than they can do."

And, indeed, when his deft hands had returned her geodynes, the tiny vessel began to draw ahead again. The second whirling field of atomic disruption groped after them with weaker fingers; the third flamed and died far behind. And the *Phantom Atom* was many hours ahead of the fleet, when they came to the geofractor.

Chan Derron's brain was staggered by that machine's immensity, and baffled by its strangeness. Against the star-shot dark of space hung two great spheres of blacker blackness. Three colossal rings, set all at right angles, bound each of them; and between them, connecting them, was a smaller cylinder of the same dully gleaming metal.

"It looks a little bit like a twenty-million ton peanut," he muttered. "But I never saw anything so black as those great globes!"

"They are not anything," said Stella Eleroid. "They are simply holes in the continuum of our universe. That blackness is the darkness of a lightless hyperspace.

"It is through those holes that the geodesics are refracted," she said. "They are held open by the achronic field coils in the rings about them. There are four rings about each globe of force—the three that you see, and a fourth that has been rotated into hyperspace.

"Except for size—miles, to feet—this machine is almost identical with my father's model. The controls, no doubt, and the atomic power tubes that activate the field coils, are in the central cylindrical structure."

"Eh?" murmured Giles Habibula. "And we may find the Basilisk there?"

"We may," the girl said. "But I think not. The remote-control system would make it needless for him to remain here. But doubtless the machine is safeguarded. We may meet some of his robots."

"But that mortal power?" The eyes of Giles Habibula rolled fearfully. "The force that snatches men away—"

"It can't reach us." The girl touched her white jewel again. "So long as this device is intact, and we keep close together. But if we separate—or it is lost—"

"Ah, lass, we'll cling to you!" cried Giles Habibula. "And defend it well!"

Circling the dark mass of the geofractor, that hung in space like an elongated planetoid, they found an entrance valve in the wall of the enormous cylinder between the two black spheres. No weapon, nor any sign of alarm, met their approach. Magnetic anchors held the *Phantom Atom* beside the valve, and the three emerged, clinging close together, in white space armor.

A massive and intricate combination lock stopped them at the outer valve.

"Ah, here is a barrier that could stop all the Legion," muttered Giles Habibula. His fingers, in their flexible metal gloves, began spinning the dials. He set his helmet against the heavy door, to listen. "All the Legion!" he wheezed again. "But not the precious dying genius of old Giles Habibula."

The colossal armored door slid deliberately aside, and they came into the great chamber of the valve. Another lock, at the inner gate, yielded as readily, and they emerged into the mysterious interior of the machine.

Chan's first impression was of staggering immensity. A a dull violet light, from endless banks of gigantic power tubes, gleamed dimly upon the square masses of huge transformers, black cables writhing like incredible serpents, and the maze of titanic girders that supported all the mechanism.

His armored hand gripped his blaster, but no movement met them. No living thing was visible. There was no sound save that from the generators and transformers—a humming so mighty and deep that it became a roar.

Already, with a swift certainty of purpose, Stella

Eleroid was leading the way along a narrow cat-walk, out through that web of unknown energies. Giles Habibula opened another locked door, and they entered a long dim-lit chamber that was obviously a control-room. Illuminated dials and gauges shone in endless rows, signal lights flashed, signal bells rang, automatic switches made an endless muffled clicking.

Eerily, this room was also empty. Sweeping it with the muzzle of his blaster, Chan Derron shuddered. This mass of untended mechanism was somehow uncanny, as if it had been itself alive.

"The Basilisk is not here," said Stella Eleroid. "I hardly expected him to be. But I believe I can operate the geofractor—I was my father's assistant, until he decided the job was too dangerous for me. We can disconnect the remote control, and use the search fields to look for him."

"Good," Chan said. "I think I know where to look. Try the vicinity of the red star Ulnar XIV, about eighty light-years north. Here are the heliocentric co-ordinates of the position."

He gave her the scrap of paper he had found in Hannas' vault. She turned to the long maze of untended controls. She held hurried little conferences with Giles Habibula, as the old man went to work beside her, his fat hands as familiarly skillful, Chan thought, as if they had built everything they touched.

Gripping his blaster, peering this way and that, Chan kept an anxious watch. It began to seem to him that the humming emptiness of this space was more terrible than a horde of the Basilisk's robots would have been—until he heard a familiar feral purr, and saw green-winged horror flapping at the farther end of the long room.

This time he knew that the central crimson eye was a vulnerable point. His white ray flashed. The monster fell, sprawling weirdly over a bank of dials, before it could lift the Legion-type blaster in its own green tentacles.

"Don't worry," Chan called to Giles and the girl. "I got it!"

But the violet eyes of Stella Eleroid were startled and grave.

"We had the remote control disconnected half an hour ago," she told him. "The arrival of that monster means that the Basilisk has another geofractor in operation— somewhere!" She paused to shudder. "He may send us something else!"

Chan Derron resumed his apprehensive watch.

"We've found it, Chan!" came the girl's eager voice an hour later. Her eyes were fixed upon a tiny, shielded screen, in a little oblong control-box. "The place where the geofractors must have been built. It's on a great planet that circles the red star. In the middle of a high plateau, there's a clearing in the jungle. Mines. Furnace stacks. Metal roofs of factories. The foundation, miles long, where the geofractors must have been built. A sort of robot-city—I see thousands of the winged robots, wheeling about. Some of them fighting, I think, with their real-life originals at the edge of the jungle. The Basilisk must have begun by building robots, and setting them to build others—"

"But the Basilisk, himself?" broke in the anxious nasal wheeze of Giles Habibula. "Where's the mortal Basilisk?"

Stella Eleroid shook her platinum head—and Chan wondered briefly which was real: the blond curls and violet eyes of Vanya Eloyan, or the red-mahogany hair and grey-green eyes he had learned to know from the posters of the android Luroa?

"There are no human beings in sight," she said. "Only those robots."

"Keep searching, lass!" gasped Giles Habibula. "The criminal must be somewhere. And all those people he took away."

Chan Derron stood his endless watch. The girl moved delicate controls and watched a screen inside that hooded box.

"Here!" she whispered at last. "A spot that must be ten thousand miles from that city of robots, in the middle of a reddish ocean. There was a shadow that the search field could hardly pierce—a barrier field, I suppose, set up by some device like my own."

She touched the white jewel.

"But I've broken through it—the device is not quite so perfect as my father would have made it. I can see a tiny rock, crowded with people fighting—"

Her voice died away. She bent closer, shaking her head as if with pity.

"People?" Chan whispered sharply. "Who?"

"I can't see," she whispered. "All their faces are masked—maybe against some gas, because they're all coughing. A ragged, pitiful lot. The water seems to be rising, and they are most of them fighting for higher places

453

on the rock. Creatures like that robot are flying over them, and great black armored monsters are leaping out of the rising sea."

Giles Habibula was blinking intently over her shoulder.

"Ah, so!" he breathed. "The luckless victims of the Basilisk. There's Kay, the poor lass—all bandaged. Her child—and Bob Star!" His thin voice became a sort of wail. "And there's the keeper—ill. Unconscious, it looks. And John Star lifting her to a higher place. Ah, frightful death is hovering near them all."

He caught a sobbing breath.

"Aye, and now I see those three scoundrels from the New Moon. Hannas and Brelekko and John Comaine. They are playing some dice game—all but Comaine. And the little gambler, Abel Davian, is with them—still with his book and his mortal calculator. Playing their blessed lives away, for pebbles, while wicked death creeps down upon them!"

His quivering fingers caught the girl's arm.

"You must set them back on Earth," he gasped. "And quickly—before they all perish!"

But she shook her head.

"I can't do it," she said helplessly. "That barrier field is almost as good as mine. It takes all the power we have to drive a search field through it. We can't get through with a refractor field—not to pick up even one of them."

Chan Derron was beside her, breathless.

"Then, Stella," he demanded, "can you set me on the rock?"

"No," she told him. "That's as impossible as lifting them away. But why?"

His dark-stained eyes were narrowed and savage.

"I think the Basilisk is there on the rock—hiding inside that barrier field and watching his victims die," he said grimly. "I'm going after him. If you can't set me on the rock, drop me as near it as you can."

"Into that dreadful sea." Her eyes were dark with concern. "Chan, you'll be killed!"

"Thanks, Stella." He grinned at her, very briefly. "But I think the Basilisk is one of those people on the rock —and I have one clue to his identity. I'm going to test it— if there's time enough. Won't you help?"

"I'll help." A brief light shone in her eyes and was extinguished with dread. "Go to the other end of the room.

454

Beyond the range of my barrier field. And—" her voice caught. "Goodbye, Chan!"

He was already striding away.

"Aye, farewell," Giles Habibula called after him. "My grandson!"

At the other end of the long, dusky control room, Chan Derron paused and raised his hand. The girl looked at him for a moment, and then turned very suddenly to the little box beside her.

A savage, penetrating vibration throbbed through all Chan's body. The girl and old Habibula and the strange room were all whipped away. He was flung through frigid blackness, into a world of yellow-green mist.

Green-winged horror flapped and screamed beside him. He fell through the haze, toward the dark flat sea where larger creatures plunged now and again above the oily surface. The geopellor could have checked him, but still he dived, because he thought the Basilisk might be watching from the rock.

A dark armored shape rushed at him, beneath the surface. The bolt from his blaster made a volcano of steam. He drove on through it, and reached the rock, and climbed upon that with greenish slime dripping from his silver armor.

The highest peak of land now stood not five feet above the tide, which still lapped visibly upward. Those left on the rock were fewer than a hundred now; soon there would be none at all.

He knew most of the masked, gasping, heat-parched human things clinging to the rock, but they paid him little heed. Many were too far gone to care, but one wild creature challenged him, with a blaster, unsteadily leveled, as he tugged to open the face plate of his helmet.

"The Basilisk!" A calm restraint still ruled the rasping voice, and he recognized the Commander of the Legion. "He's come to mock us!" Jay Kalam cried. "Kill him."

That feeble cry went unheard, however, and the blaster, exhausted with firing at the winged things above, flickered harmlessly and died.

"The wrong man, Commander," Chan whispered swiftly. "I'm not the Basilisk—but I do have evidence that he's hiding here among you. Will you let me look for him?"

The chlorine-reddened eyes still seemed sane.

"If we've been wrong—" Jay Kalam choked and coughed

and nodded weakly. "Go ahead, Derron. Whatever you find, we've little more to lose."

"Guard the keeper." Chan thrust his own blaster into the Commander's startled hands. "I think the Basilisk is here—but I want to make a test."

Stripping off the metal gloves of his space armor, he flung them down on the rock and gathered up a handful of small black pebbles. He strode on to the level ledge, scarcely a foot above the water now, where Hannas and Brelekko and the little Abel Davian and a few other masked, strangling men and women still knelt about their futile game, while John Comaine looked on with an expression of stolid hostility from beside his mysterious black box.

He paused a moment to peer at that box. The remote-control device that operated the geopellor was surely something no larger. He wished for an instant that he had kept the blaster—but still he had the test to make. He dropped to his knees, beside gaunt Brelekko, and heaped the pebbles before him.

"I've come to join your game," he said.

The yellow, bright-ringed claw of Brelekko shook the dice and rolled them. He said nothing at all. But Gaspar Hannas, smiling behind his bandages that mindless smile that was the only one upon the rock, gasped hoarsely:

"Welcome, stranger. Though our game must soon be over—for all but one of us. That's the real gamble, now. Because the Basilisk has promised, Commander Kalam says, that one of us is to be returned alive to the System."

"One of you." Chan nodded bleakly. "But that's no gamble, because it lacks the element of chance. The man to be saved is the Basilisk himself."

"Huh!" Gaspar Hannas gulped and stared and shook his head. "He couldn't be here—"

"There's evidence that he is," Chan said. "I suppose cowardice has helped to bring him to this least expected hiding place, here among his hopeless victims; and I imagine, too, that he is getting a sadistic satisfaction out of watching them die." He paused to look sharply at the broad face of Hannas, but its white idiocy still was unchanged. "Let's play, he said. "And please ask Dr. Comaine to join us."

Hannas made a gasping grunt at John Comaine. The big engineer nodded sullenly. Stiffly awkward, and moving with a visible reluctance, he left his instrument and came to kneel in the circle.

Chan took the dice from the talons of Brelekko, and rolled a seven. Raking in the pebbles he had won, he brushed the fingers of Hannas and Brelekko. He lost, and put the dice in the hand of tattered little Abel Davian— and watched that lean gray hand with narrowed eyes.

The ragged little gambler was tapping the keys of his silent calculator again, when Chan saw the angry red welts lifting on his fingers. Chan was leaning to peer at the calculator, when muted screams, from throats burned raw with chlorine, drew his eyes upward.

The sullen sun stood now at the zenith, and against its dull-red face he saw the black shape of the geofractor —or the stand-by machine, this must be; the one that had been used to send that attacking robot into the other. The black shadow of it was spreading swiftly across that sinister disk.

It was falling!

Cold with fear, he understood this desperate last gambit of the Basilisk. The criminal had shielded this rock against the refractor fields. The barrier must be maintained— against Stella Eleroid, at the controls of the other geofractor. But, even if the stand-by machine couldn't reach through the barrier, it would still fall through.

Swiftly, it grew in the sky. Watching it, listening to the gasps and sobs of all those who waited hopelessly for its millions of tons of metal to crush them into that acid sea, Chan failed for a moment to hear the deep sudden purring in the air around him.

When he did hear it, and knew that the barrier had been lifted, he moved very quickly. His great hand snatched the little calculating machine out of Abel Davian's swelling fingers. He smashed it against the ledge, seized a rock, and crushed the fragments to scrap and dust.

"Why, sir?" The little gambler blinked bewilderedly at him through thick lenses. "What are you doing?"

"Conducting an allergy test," Chan rapped at him.

"I don't understand you, sir!"

Chan glanced up at the stupendous shape of the falling geofractor and around him at the silent exiles crouching on the rock. They awaited its impact, he thought, almost with gratitude.

"We've probably three minutes." He grinned bleakly at

Abel Davian. "And you ought to be interested in this test —since you are the one who showed a positive reaction."

"I—what do you mean, sir?"

"Four years ago," Chan Derron told him, "when I helped Dr. Eleroid's psuedo-assistant carry his working model of the geofractor down into that armored room where he was killed, the man contrived to keep me from seeing his face—he muffled himself against the cold, and made me walk in front, and kept leaning over the box. However, it happened that my hand touched his. I saw rapid red swellings rising upon his fingers, and I noticed that he sneezed."

Chan's darkened eyes stabbed at the cringing gray man.

"When I learned a little while ago how the crime was carried out, I happened to remember that you began to sneeze as you came toward me in the Diamond Room on the New Moon, just before you vanished—and I had wondered already how it came that you had the audacity to win on that particular night. All that was enough to suggest the possible utility of your portable calculator."

Rigid, pale, Abel Davian stood feebly shaking his head.

"I contrived to touch your hands, just now," Chan's harsh voice raced on. "And I observe again the symptoms of an extreme allergy sensitive to my body. That is a rare but proven phenomenon—the proteids of one human body acting as allergens to another. Its very rarity made the identification quite positive—even before I had confirmed it by proving that your calculating machine was the portable remote-control box through which you operated the geofractors, Mr. Basilisk."

Ashen, palsied, the little man was cowering back from him. His hunted eyes flashed up at the enormous bulk of the falling geofractor, swelling ever more swiftly in the greenish sky. They came back to Chan, magnified by the thick lenses, lurid with a triumphant hatred.

"What if I am the Basilisk?" his shrill voice whined defiantly. "I'm still the winner—because I've had my revenge, and none of you can escape. If we had three minutes—now I think we've less than two."

"Perhaps it doesn't matter." Nodding almost abstractedly, Chan turned from that colossal falling mechanism and the silent people waiting for it. "But still there's something I'd like to know." He scowled at the trembling gambler. "Why should you want revenge—upon so many of us?"

"Because my people were Purples." Savagery twisted

458

Davian's thin gray face. "My mother's family had once been favorites of the emperors. I believe my real father was Eric the Pretender. It was the Green Hall that crushed the empire, and drove us into exile." His narrow shoulders stiffened with a supercilious pride. "But for all of you—the Legion and the Council and the keeper of the peace, I should have been a prince of the Purple Hall."

"I see." Chan Derron glanced sadly at the limp, unconscious form of the keeper of the peace and John Star standing guard beside her—and his breath caught.

"But that isn't all you've done," Davian's bitter voice ran on. "I've been trying all my life to recover something of the wealth and honor that was rightly mine—and all of you have always crushed me back again, into hunger and rags and shame."

"Eh?" Chan looked at him sharply. "How's that?"

"I studied science," rasped the little man. "I took the name of Enos Clagg, because you all had come to hate my father's—"

"Enos Clagg?" Chan nodded in recognition. "And you built illegal robots!"

"Military robots," Davian whispered huskily. "I hoped to restore the empire with them. But we were betrayed to the Green Hall. The Legion tracked me down. I served three years on Ebron—dreaming of ways to settle the score."

Scarcely listening to him, Chan had looked back at that enormous falling machine. Now its black mass filled half the sky. A fantastic greenish twilight was falling fast upon the rock. A chlorine-poisoned wind stirred suddenly.

"After I was pardoned from Ebron," Davian's bitter voice rushed on, "I saw that I must be more subtle. I came to Earth, with a little money my mother had saved, and took the name I wear. I met a girl, and fell in love, and married her. She wanted me to forget my plans, and for a little while I almost did."

His savage eyes flashed at Gaspar Hannas.

"Until we visited his gambling ship," he said. "I had studied the mathematics of probability in my cell on Ebron. I was hoping to win back the lost wealth of the Purples. But Hannas robbed me. Hannas and Brelekko and Comaine!" His cracked voice lifted wildly. "They've robbed me again and again, every time I scraped up money to go back—and laughed at me because they said I was habitual. That's why they're here—to watch me win one game!"

"But you have lost." Chan's voice was lifted, above a sudden deep vibration in the air. "Because the daughter of Dr. Eleroid is at the controls of your other geofractor —and evidently this rock is no longer shielded from it, since I smashed your control box. Just look around you! Already, the keeper and many of the rest have been returned to the System."

All the rock was trembling now to a mighty purring. By twos and threes, by little groups, the haggard victims of the Basilisk were vanishing. Familiar articles of furniture, bits of Terrestrial shrubbery and sod, used to balance the circuits, showed that they had been replaced on some kinder planet. In a few moments Chan was left alone with Abel Davian, beneath the many million tons of the falling geofractor.

"But I don't think you'll escape, Mr. Basilisk." His big hand made a hurried gesture of farewell. "Because Stella Eleroid knows certainly, by now, that you—and not I— killed her father."

Then that deep vibration quivered through Chan's body. Some pellucid screen, it seemed, had fallen between his eyes and the gray stricken face of Abel Davian. The green thickening twilight became a total darkness. And he knew that Stella Eleroid had lifted him from the peril of the rock.

NOWHERE NEAR

1

The Man Who Liked Machines

Nowhere Near was the name of a point in space. Five black light-years from our Legion base at the closest star, sixty more from old Earth, it was marked by the laser beacon and little else. A relief ship came once a year—when it could get through the anomaly.

The last Legion ship had not got through, and half our personnel were overdue for rotation. Odd types, they had volunteered because they had expected to enjoy loneliness and mystery and danger. Most of them had found long ago that they did not.

Our supplies came late, on a private craft chartered for the emergency. A painless but powerful geodesic flyer, the *Erewhon* looked like a scarred veteran of less legal missions. Her captain was a squat, shambling man, hard of eye and close of mouth—the sort of civilian likely to need refuge in the hazardous fringes of Nowhere.

Instead of the men and women we needed to relieve our weary crews, she brought only two passengers—an old soldier and a girl. A queer story and a queerer riddle came with them. The story—all I could learn of it—was told to me by Captain Scabbard when he came aboard the station with a sealed pouch of orders from our sector base.

The old soldier and the girl, as he told the story, had boarded the chartered flyer in some haste, along with their odd cargo, just before it lifted.

Trouble came with them.

His spacemen were not the finest sort, Captain Scabbard admitted. They were not used to discipline, and he suspected that some of them were relieving the hazardous tedium of the long voyage to Nowhere with smuggled drugs. They baited the old soldier and tried to make love to the girl.

They were used to free companions, the captain said, and they couldn't understand such a girl. Her proud aloofness just inflamed them. Even the ship's mate joined the game. On the mate's watch, they got the soldier drunk, locked him in his stateroom and attacked the girl in her room.

Captain Scabbard was still confused about the ending of the story. The girl had disabled two of her attackers, with some unexpected trick or weapon. Angered, the others became uglier than ever. She screamed for the soldier.

Less drunk than he had seemed, the soldier picked the lock and came out to join the fight. Though he had been disarmed, he and the girl fought five able spacemen. Two had finally fled. The other three, Captain Scabbard believed, had been killed.

"But we couldn't find the bodies." His eyes flickered uneasily back toward the lock, where his passengers were waiting to come aboard the station. "I ain't makin' no formal charges. They ain't makin' none. The soldier told me to just forget the incident. But the mate and two more are gone, and we couldn't find the bodies."

He shivered apprehensively.

"Maybe you never stopped to think how hard it is to get rid of a dead body in a stateroom on a sealed space flyer. It ain't just hard—it's impossible! In my time around Nowhere I've seen a lot of funny things, but I ain't never seen nothing to match that soldier and his girl!"

That's part of what made the story queer.

I thanked Captain Scabbard and told him that I would interview his passengers before I let them come aboard the station. He grew angry. He was afraid of them, I soon realized. He wanted to get them off his ship, but I stood firm.

We had troubles enough already. Nowhere Near had an ugly name in the Legion, for good cause. Duty there was both dull and dangerous.

A third of our thirty-man crew was normally rotated each year, but the last relief complement had been aboard that lost ship. An unwise search had cost us twelve more lives. The station commander, cracking under the strain, had committed a strange suicide by steering a rescue rocket into the heart of the space called Nowhere.

His death had left me the acting commander, although my actual promotion had only now arrived in Captain Scabbard's green-sealed pouch. I was still very young, very conscious of my peculiar duty. With only sixteen men and two free companions, I was standing guard against a danger that none of us understood.

Old enough to be cynical, most of the men under me had a bitter feeling that Nowhere Near was a forgotten stepchild of the Legion. They had been cruelly jolted when they learned that the *Erewhon* had brought us no replacements for the missing men or relief for those who had already served long beyond their normal tour of duty. I was prepared for trouble—but not asking for it.

"You are under charter to the Legion," I reminded Captain Scabbard. "That means your port and flying orders come from me. This is no place for tourists, and I don't want the sort of problem you have just reported. Your passengers will have to convince me that they have some legitimate business here."

Grumbling sullenly, he agreed to let me interview them in the station lock. When he sent them to meet me there, the first thing I saw was the old soldier's shocking sloppiness. Out of uniform, he wore a flaming yellow civilian sweater and shapeless old fatigue pants, one leg tucked inside his oversize spaceboots and the other dropping outside. He was short and thick and flabby—scarcely fit for his heroic role in Captain Scabbard's tale. Yet he came waddling through the great steel valves as confidently as if he had come to take command of the station.

The nurse followed him, immaculate in white. A glowing, bronze-eyed, athletic girl, she looked too young and fresh and lovely to be so far from the stars men had mastered. A gasp of admiration came from the lock sergeant behind me. My own pulse was quickening—until I saw her ring.

The ring was a heavy platinum band set with an odd black stone. An unpleasant gem, the dull black stone was carved into a grinning skull with hot ruby eyes that glowed like live coals. That ugly death's-head struck me with a puzzling shock of evil, because it seemed to deny her clean, strong vitality.

"Captain Ulnar?" Neglecting to salute, the old soldier stopped to stare at me with eyes like flat wet pebbles. "Captain Lars Ulnar? You want to talk to us?"

"If you want to come aboard the station."

"Why else do you think we've come forty trillion miles on Scabbard's miserable bucket of rust?" His round face was baby-smooth and baby-soft, and it reddened now like an angry infant's. "We were expecting a warmer welcome. My name's Habibula. Corporal Giles Habibula."

His bald pink head nodded toward the girl.

"Nurse Lilith Adams. We're here as guests of the blessed Legion. You have orders to supply us rations and quarters in the station."

"I've received no such orders."

"Our visit was arranged through Legion channels." His indignant voice was nasal and high, oddly irritating. "Orders to expect us were sent you a year ago."

"The ship last year was lost."

"We're well aware of that." He grimaced pinkly. "We've been sweating for a miserable month at your sector headquarters, waiting for a brass-capped fool to arrange our passage on the *Erewhon*. We were warned that our papers had been on that unlucky ship. We had duplicates sent you more recently, in care of Commander Star."

"Commander Star?"

"Ken Star, commander of the Legion survey ship *Quasar Quest*." Indignation buzzed in his high nasal voice. "He'd taken off before we got to sector base. He must have left our papers here."

"Commander Star has not been here." My first astonishment was changing to irritated disbelief. "Not for years, anyhow. I've seen his name in the station records. He was the first commanding officer, years before I got here. I've never seen him."

"Life's precious sake!" The old man's mud-colored eyes rolled apprehensively toward the silent girl. "I'm afraid poor Ken has blundered into mortal trouble." He lurched forward as if he meant to pass me. "Well, Captain, it looks as if you'll have to take my precious word about those orders."

"Hold it, soldier!"

The riddle was growing queerer. No Legion survey ship had been expected at the station. The old soldier's tale of lost orders was a bit too pat. He looked too clever. Besides, with his improper uniform and his failure to salute and his irritating insolence, he had ruffled my sense of military fitness.

"If you are a soldier!" I stepped in front of him. "Have you ever been taught Legion courtesy and discipline?"

"Mortal well, Captain." He stopped, but did not salute. "For most of a mortal century, I've been offering Legion courtesy to officers who deserved it. I've gladly saluted Commander Kalam and Admiral-General Samdu and the great John Star. But I'm not saluting you."

He blinked shrewdly at me, as if daring me to react.

"Giles!" The girl spoke for the first time. Her low voice was lovely as her face, gentle in cool reproof. "Don't be a fool!"

"I mean no disrespect, sir," the old man wheezed. "If you had read those orders, you would know that I am honorably discharged. We are here as special guests of the Legion—as civilians."

"Nowhere Near has several missions." Now more annoyed than puzzled, I spoke stiffly. "Our first mission is simply to warn shipping away from a dangerous and mysterious anomaly in space. Our second is to observe and report every fact we can discover about the nature and the cause of that anomaly. We have no facilities to entertain civilian guests."

"Captain Ulnar—please!" The girl stepped forward urgently. "I'm sure Commander Star will arrive with our orders soon. At least you must let us wait for him."

I hesitated, because she troubled me. She belonged somewhere else, I thought—perhaps in some fortress like the Purple Hall, along with old masters and old ivory and all the proud creations of man's great past. She looked too thrillingly alive, certainly, for this deadly exile at the brink of Nowhere.

"You'll have to answer some questions," I said. "Captain Scabbard gave me a very brief account of an incident on the *Erewhon*. He says the two of you killed three able spacemen. He couldn't learn how you disposed of the bodies."

Old Habibula's stone-colored eyes squinted blankly out of his pink baby-face. The girl stiffened slightly, lovely and lean and grave, her eyes darkening.

"What happened?" I demanded. "What happened to those three men?"

"Three pirates!" gasped old Habibula. "They got what they mortal well deserved."

"That may be," I agreed. "But I am responsible for the safety of this station. I want to know exactly how they got it. Nurse Adams, what have you to say?"

"A dreadful experience." Her head lifted proudly in her stiff white cap. Her tawny eyes met mine—alert, searching, somehow tragic. "I can't talk about it."

The desperation in her voice touched my heart—but I was young enough to feel that my new duty at Nowhere Near required the same kind of desperation. I looked at old Habibula to recover my severity.

"You'd better talk about it," I said, "if you want to come aboard."

Neither spoke.

"Then I suppose that ends our interview."

I turned to leave them in the lock.

"Wait!" old Habibula whined angrily behind me. "We've got our rights, even as mortal civilians. The Green Hall guarantees our democratic freedoms. You can't make us say anything you might take to be incriminating."

"True enough." I paused at the inner valve. "But I can't afford to let strangers with incriminating secrets inside Nowhere Near."

"Strangers?" His gasp was almost a sob. "Captain, don't you know the history of the precious Legion? Have you never heard of poor old Giles Habibula, who fought in the war against the wicked Medusae, and fought against the invisible Cometeers, and fought against the fearful human monster who called himself the Basilisk?"

"What if I do?" Reviewing dusty memories of history lectures back at the Legion academy on old Earth, I made a rapid calculation. "Don't try to tell me that you are that Giles Habibula. He'd be dead of old age by now."

"I am—almost!" he gasped. "Life knows I'm mortal old—and waging a war to save my precious life!" Sadly, he shook his pink and hairless baby-head. "Perhaps it's true there's an evil stain across my past. I must confess that I once picked locks for a living. But all that has been atoned for—a million times atoned for, to the living glory of the Legion, with my precious sweat and blood and brains."

He stopped to catch a sobbing breath, his dull-colored eyes squinting at me cunningly.

"When Ken Star arrives, he'll tell you who we are," he whined. "Ken Star will vouch that we are not the miserable criminals you seem to take us for."

"Please—C-Captain!"

466

The girl's voice had an anxious little catch. When I looked at her, her young loveliness became an aching throb in my throat and wild magic in my imagination.

"Commander Star's—our friend." She hesitated oddly. "I know he'll soon be here to assure you that we aren't criminals of any sort—that we do have legitimate business here."

Her bronze eyes were wide and warm, bright as if with tears.

"Captain, you can't send us back to Scabbard and his gangster crew." The quiver in her voice dissolved my resolution. "At least you've got to let Giles tell you why we're here. You've just got to, Captain!"

Frowning to conceal unsoldierly feelings, I came slowly back to them. The riddles around them had begun to tease my curiosity. I knew that old Habibula was deliberately baiting me, but I couldn't guess why. I was still convinced I didn't want them on the station, yet the girl had lit a glowing coal of longing in me.

"All right." I swung as coldly as I could to old Habibula. "Why are you here?"

"Because I like machines."

2

North of Nowhere

The old soldier moved toward me across the lock. His rolling, cautious gait, in the low G-force here near the axis of the spinning station, convinced me that he was at least a veteran spaceman. His pale eyes measured the shining steel valves, caressed the red-painted pumps, read the winking lights of the lock monitor.

"What machines!" His nasal voice lifted happily. "What divine machines." He gave the girl a pink baby-grin. "Look at 'em, Lil! Such machines are food and precious drink to me."

I too admired fine machines. I had spent three years polishing and turning and loving the great space machine

467

that was the station. For a moment I wanted to like Giles Habibula.

"Very well." I tried to be gruff. "But this is no mechanical museum. If you have any honest reason for visiting Nowhere Near, what is it?"

"We're conducting an experiment." His flat, shallow eyes flickered evasively from me to the girl. "A mortal important experiment! Though I told you I'm retired, the Legion has asked another desperate service of me. The Legion medics have made me a miserable human guinea pig, for a research that's likely to end in my death."

"Now we're getting somewhere." I thought I saw a glimmer of light. "What is that research?"

"You know I'm old." His baby-head shook sadly. "Dreadful death is crowding close upon me—a poor reward for all the hardship and danger I've endured to help defend the precious human race. But still I've not forgot the spirit of the Legion. I've volunteered to give my few last years to this rare and desperate experiment."

"Yes?"

"Lilith Adams is my very special nurse." He gave her a fond pink smile. "I'm her guinea pig for a new serum the Legion medics have invented. The hazards are unknown, for the serum has never been tested. I fear the research will end in my death."

Hunching his thick shoulders in the flame-yellow sweater, he shivered.

"That's why I've come to Nowhere Near," he wheezed. "To sweat out these fearful final years among the machines I love. Perhaps to perish here—a precious human sacrifice for the glory of the Legion and the welfare of mankind."

"What's the serum for?"

"Age!" he gasped. "It's supposed to immunize me to what the medics call the cumulative biochemicals of senescence. We've come to wait here till we discover whether it works. If it does, the medics promise I'll be immortal. But it's a frightful gamble!"

"So you want to live forever?"

"I'll do my best, sir." He shot a murky glance at me. "I'm a veteran of the Legion, and I've not forgot our magnificent tradition. I've come to devote myself to this desperate experiment, to the brink of death itself—even if it takes a thousand mortal years!"

I stood for a moment just admiring his bluff.

Cool and tall and curiously sure in her clean white garb, Lilith Adams looked gravely at him and seriously back at me. I was almost smiling, but her lean and lovely face showed no hint of amusement.

"I'm afraid you've picked an unfortunate spot for this kind of research," I told them. "No miracle serum is likely to protect either one of you against the hazards of Nowhere. I'll respect your orders, of course—if Commander Star does bring any orders about you before the *Erewhon* leaves. But surely you can see that Nowhere Near is no old folks' home. There's not a man of us here who wouldn't give a month's pay for half an hour of sun and wind and sea and sky, back on Earth. Why can't you test your serum there?"

Stubbornly, the old man shook his pink and hairless head.

"I've seen too much of Earth." His pale eyes fluttered uneasily. "I've seen too many human beings—too mortal much of their yelling and crowding and fretting and scheming and lying and killing and stinking. That's why we've come to Nowhere Near."

"There are new planets enough," I argued patiently, "if you really don't like Earth. Virgin worlds, where you can really get back to nature. Seas that men have never sailed, plains that men never plowed, creatures never hunted, mountains never climbed. When Nowhere gets on my nerves, I like to dream of those new worlds—"

"I've seen new planets." The old man blinked. "I've met raw nature, on the fearful world of the Runaway Star. Monsters in the sea and monsters in the jungle and monsters in the air—dreadful death in every breath we took!"

He gave me a pink, solemn scowl.

"I'm looking for my lost youth. If I do find it here, with Lilith's precious aid, I'll owe all my thanks to the computers that designed her new serum and the automated factories that made it. I'll owe no thanks to nature—natural death would have killed me years ago!"

Shuddering massively, he paused to gasp for air.

"I don't like nature and I don't trust people." His clay-colored eyes shifted belligerently. "Look at the wicked natural mystery you call Nowhere. Look at Captain Scabbard and his brutal crew. Nature and men—fearful nature and monstrous men!

"Give me machines—like your great station here.

"Machines I understand. Take nature. This natural space

469

called Nowhere—so I gather from the miserable men who infest the fringes of it—is a dreadful riddle that the best brains in the Legion have failed to unlock, after endless years of trying. Take men. I've seen how even the precious innocence of Lilith Adams can awaken unsuspected evil in the worst or best of men. You take nature and men. I'll take machines!"

He dropped his smooth baby-hand on the sleek black case of the lock monitor, with an air of familiar affection.

"Machines I know and trust. I can see how they work and fix 'em when they don't. Machines I love, because they exist to work for men. Left to herself, nature always kills us—unless our wicked fellow men are quicker to the death. But I think machines can save my poor old life, with Lil's precious serum."

Staring at the two of them, I had to shake my head. The riddle was growing queerer. Though I had been amused by old Habibula's agile loquacity, I couldn't decide what to believe of his story. The pink glow of his skin and the vigor of his fight on the *Erewhon* seemed to argue for a real rejuvenation.

Yet he seemed too cunning, too bold, too eloquent. I couldn't believe that any normal man would hate his natural world as heartily as he claimed to, or love machines as much. Certainly I couldn't believe that any sane veteran of the Legion would willingly retire to Nowhere Near.

Lilith Adams was even more perplexing.

Though nurses are often beautiful and sometimes virginal, I had never met a nurse—or any girl at all—who looked quite so breathtaking, or seemed so aloofly untouched and untouchable, or who possessed her quiet air of absolute command. I couldn't help thinking that she was far more wonderful than any possible machine. Yet, like Captain Scabbard, I was somehow afraid of her.

I looked at old Habibula.

"If you don't like nature, why've you come here to the edge of Nowhere—which is probably the greatest natural peril in the universe?"

"Because I trust machines," he droned solemnly. "If some mortal peril does come out of Nowhere, nature will be no blessed help to us. Men cannot defend us. Our precious machines will be our only friends. I know no better machine than this whole station is, made to keep

470

us snug and cozy here in space, trillions of miles from mobs and weather and dirt—"

The lock phone purred. The watch officer was calling me. Captain Scabbard had finished his unloading—except for the two passengers and their baggage. Anxious to get away from Nowhere, he wanted his flight orders. One of our free companions and three men I couldn't spare had asked to leave on the *Erewhon*. The magnetometers showed a dangerous new magnetic flux around a rock near the center of Nowhere. A dozen other problems called for my attention, and I had to end the interview.

"Sorry."

When I saw the quiet desperation that tightened the girl's perfect face and darkened her tawny eyes, I felt a stab of genuine regret, but I tried to keep my voice crisply firm.

"My job's to keep the station safe," I said. "You've failed to explain what happened to those spacemen on the *Erewhon*. You've failed to give me any believable reason for being here. You've failed to show me any official permission. I can't allow you aboard."

Old Habibula turned crimson, wheezing and sputtering incoherently. The girl straightened, looking straight at me. Her eyes had a terrible directness.

"Captain Ulnar," she asked abruptly, "why are you here?"

I didn't want to tell her. I knew I didn't have to tell her. Yet somehow her searching eyes required the truth.

"The reason—the reason is my name." Stumbling awkwardly, I confessed that painful fact. "Lars Ulnar is the wrong name for advancement in the Legion. Ulnar was a great name once—made great by many generations of space pioneers—but it has been disgraced by evil men. I volunteered for Nowhere Near because I had to prove that I was better than my name."

Her probing eyes were merciless.

"So you are kin to Commander Ken Star?"

"Distantly." Puzzled, I met her desperate eyes. "He is John Star's younger son. John Star was John Ulnar, before the Green Hall rewarded his heroism with a better name. But I've never met Commander Star—and I've no reason to expect him here."

"For life's precious sake!" bellowed old Habibula. "We just told you he's on his way."

I ignored that insolent outburst.

"My own people come from another branch of the family tree," I told the girl. "We've had our small part in the conquest of space, but we were never great. Never traitors, either. We never shared the glory of the Purple Hall, but we can't escape its shame."

For another cruel moment, her darkened eyes studied me.

"Perhaps you can," she whispered. "I hope you can."

I waited for another moment, hoping she would show me some genuine reason to let them stay. I thought she was going to speak, but she only caught her breath and turned away. I left them in the lock, the old man whimpering like a punished animal.

Captain Scabbard looked ugly when I told him that he had to keep his passengers, but he didn't wait to argue long. Our instruments showed a violent new disturbance raging out in the anomaly. If he feared the old soldier and the girl, he was more afraid of Nowhere.

I had to let the disenchanted free companion go with him. Her enlistment had expired, and I failed to persuade her to stay. A pert brunette named Gay Kawai, she had been the life of the station, but now, since I had seen Lilith Adams, she was suddenly old and fat and commonplace.

With regret, I refused leave to the three men who had asked to go with her. Their Legion enlistments had another year to run, and I had no replacements for them. Along with half a dozen other silent, bitter men, they attended Gay Kawai to the valves. Their morale, I saw, was going to be a problem.

Captain Scabbard took his flight orders, muttering that he hoped never to see me again. The valves *thunked* against their seals. The *Erewhon* was gone, with the soldier and the girl.

At first I was almost grateful for that new activity out in the anomaly, because it gave Gay Kawai's unhappy friends something else to think about. By the end of the next shift, however, we had too much to think about. The magnetometers were running wild. The drift meters showed erratic but intense gravitic fields. The stars beyond Nowhere were visibly reddened and dimmed.

At the first peak of the disturbance, our laser search gear picked up two uncharted objects. One appeared north of Nowhere. At a range of half a million miles, it was jaggedly angular, three miles long. From mass and color and magnetic effects, we identified it as an iron asteroid.

The other object gave us more trouble, because the anomaly was affecting all our instruments. We first detected a jet of ionized gas, then a tiny solid nucleus moving in our general direction. When the gas flared again, turning it directly toward the station, I knew that it had to be some piloted craft.

We tried to signal, with radio and ultrawave and laser phone, but no answer came back through the roaring forces of the anomaly. The station was armed—as we had need to be, against such men as Captain Scabbard. We manned the proton guns and fired a warning bolt.

The reply was a flickering, reddened laser beam.

"Calling Nowhere Near." The words wailed faintly through interference and distortion. "Corporal Habib . . . Nurse Lilith Adams . . . sweet life's sake, don't fire on us! . . . in escape capsule . . . from Scabbard's mortal *Erewhon* . . . Now you'll have to take us in!"

3

On the Brink of Anomaly

We held our fire and signalled the escape capsule to the north docks. When it was sealed station-side, the lock sergeant made it fast, talked through an open hatch, and reported by intercom to me.

"It's the same windy old soldier, sir. With the same lady nurse. Acting queer as ever, sir. They won't come off the capsule. They won't let me inspect it. They won't even talk to me. They ask to speak to you."

Old Habibula gave me an innocent baby-grin when he saw me in the dock chamber. He scrambled out of the capsule, puffing and wheezing even in the low-G field, and came rolling to meet me.

"Impudent puppy!" His hairless head bobbed toward the lock sergeant. "My cargo's my own blessed business. I won't have such insolent meddlers filching it away. I don't trust people!"

"Giles means most people." Lilith Adams spoke quietly from the capsule. "But we've come back to place our faith in you, Captain Ulnar."

"Have you decided to tell me what happened to Captain Scabbard's mate and those two spacemen?"

She looked down through the hatch at me, her bronze eyes as cool and aloof as the luminous Clouds of Magellan. When I turned to old Habibula, his brick-colored eyes blinked evasively. Neither said a word.

"You have no rights here—not even as spacemen in distress." I didn't try to hide my exasperation. "Perhaps I can't leave you out to die in Nowhere, but I'll have to hold you in the station brig." I tried to scowl at the girl. "Unless you care to tell me why you're here."

"For life's sweet sake!" The old man reddened with a hurt surprise. "Lil's too young and proud and fine for any wicked brig, and something in me never loved confinement—that's why I learned my precious art with locks!"

His flint-colored eyes squinted at me shrewdly.

"If you want to be a mortal military bureaucrat, I guess we'll have to tell you why we've come back. I think the blessed truth will make you grant that we do have legitimate business at Nowhere Near."

"I'm listening."

"We left here as unwelcome guests on Scabbard's ugly tub, thanks to your peculiar sense of your duty to the Legion." His nasal whine lifted resentfully. "Scabbard's crew of hairy cavemen were all cursing Nowhere—whatever that is. The geodynes were stalled and half the instruments were dead. We were still on rocket astrogation, eight hours out, when we picked up a laserphone signal."

"You did?" Glancing up at the girl, I found her eyes upon me, darkly intense, yet queerly serene. "Laserphones don't function well in the anomaly."

"A call from Commander Ken Star—we told you he was coming!" His dun-colored eyes rolled triumphantly at me. "When you hear about that call, you'll let us in your precious station. You'll thank us for coming back, and keep us safe while you send help to Ken."

"We'll see," I said. "Let's hear about the call."

"I don't trust people," old Habibula wheezed. "That's why I took a mortal risk to bug Scabbard's cabin and the laser room, so that I could eavesdrop on the ship's phone. That's how I heard the signal."

His slaty eyes rolled at me.

"The call came on the distress channel," he panted. "Faint and fading, but the laserman pieced it together. Commander Star was on the laserphone himself. Said he was headed here on the *Quasar Quest*—just like we told you."

He paused to puff, squinting as if judging my reaction.

"But the survey ship's in trouble," he wheezed again. "Caught in the spreading anomaly. Space-drive out. Rockets dead. Drifting into Nowhere. Commander Star was calling for help, but he got none from Scabbard."

Old Habibula must have seen my unbelief, because his smooth moon face grew pinker.

"We're telling you the blessed truth." His hollow voice lifted belligerently. "Scabbard was scared—maybe he ain't as tough as he looks. He'd been drinking, but he took the laserphone. He replied that we were already too near Nowhere. Our own geodynes were stalled. We had no rocket fuel to spare. He said he'd report the call, if we got back to sector base. But he refused to render aid."

Old Habibula stiffened defiantly.

"That's why we left his stinking ship. I conferred with Lil. We knew you'd want to help Commander Star, and now we've come to bring his distress message to you."

His dust-colored eyes blinked alertly at me.

"Ain't that enough to satisfy you?" he whined impatiently. "Now will you let us inside your precious station?"

"Not yet." I stood frowning doubtfully. "Why did Scabbard let you leave his ship?"

"He didn't." Old Habibula grinned. "He'd got too drunk to care. I told you I've a certain craft with locks, and Lil can be persuasive. We gathered up our cargo, and commandeered the escape capsule, and left Scabbard sleeping." He drew a rasping breath. "Now you've got to let us in —and send help to poor Ken Star!"

"If all this is just a hoax, it's a pretty clumsy one," I exploded. "A liar ought to do better. I don't know what to believe—but in any case we have no ships or men left to waste on rescue attempts."

"Please, Captain Ulnar." The girl spoke from the capsule, her vibrant voice urgent, yet queerly serene. "If you do hope to escape the shame of the Purple Hall, we have brought your chance. You must take us in!"

I stood for a second looking at her. Spotless in white,

bronze eyes intensely dark, she looked aloof and cool and alluring. At any other place, at any other time, she might have stirred me. On Nowhere Near, however, with the anomaly growing around us, I couldn't afford to let her become anything more than another baffling factor in a problem that promised no solution.

"I'll take you in," I told her. "But I'll have to make a search for weapons or any kind of contraband. Get out of the capsule."

"You'll find no weapons," old Habibula huffed. "Nor contraband, neither." His muddy eyes rolled toward the lock sergeant behind me. "Like I told that insolent pup, my cargo is my own blessed business."

"Quiet, Giles!" the girl called softly.

Sullenly quiet, old Habibula held up his hands while I prodded his flaming sweater and his sagging pants. The hard lump in his right pocket turned out to be a leather-padded blackjack. The left pocket gave up a ring of keys, a rusted nail, a twist of steel wire, a worn pair of brass knuckles, but nothing more deadly.

When I looked at the girl, she jumped from the capsule. Flying like a white bird in the low-G field, she alighted on the deck and turned before me, lean arms lifted, waiting to be searched. Light flashed white on her platinum ring, glowed cold on that small black skull.

Somehow I could not touch her, but I saw no unnatural bulge. Leaving the sergeant to guard them, I scrambled into the capsule. Old Habibula's plaintive whine came after me.

"When you reach my precious cargo, remember our desperate experiment. Remember Lilith's precious serum. Remember all the years we'll need, to prove I really am immortal. We have come supplied."

Stooping in the narrow capsule, I inspected his cargo. I had been prepared for the loot of some crime as fantastic as his tale of immortality. I was prepared for smuggled weapons—perhaps for a plot to seize the station for a base of Scabbard's pirates. I was even prepared to find medical equipment and supplies for a legitimate longevity experiment.

What I found was caviar and wine.

"A mortal small reward for all my desperate years of service with the Legion," his plaintive wail followed me. "But don't you doubt it's real! The best black caviar, packed in permachill for interstellar shipment all the way

476

from Earth—every can cost a fearful fortune. Selected wines from old Earth—the choicest vintages of the last hundred years. Don't you damage it, in some fool search for stolen jewels or nuclear devices!"

That odd cargo, more than old Habibula's unlikely tale of that distress message from the *Quasar Quest,* more than the remote and lovely desperation of the girl herself, made up my mind. Though few retired corporals are pensioned off on caviar and wine, those heavy crates fitted no pattern of danger to the station that I could perceive.

"I'm accepting you as guests, not as prisoners," I told them. "But only on a temporary basis. Your status depends on how you behave, and on the truth of what you've told me, and on what else happens out in Nowhere."

"Thank you, Lars Ulnar!" The girl's quiet voice brought a lump to my throat. "You'll be glad you trusted us."

I gave them quarters out in the full-G ring, programmed the station computer to issue their rations and supplies, and asked the lock sergeant to look after their cargo. By that time Ketzler, the watch officer, was buzzing me.

The anomaly was still spreading around us, he reported. The disturbance at its heart had never been more violent. The intense magnetic flux had wrecked our best magnetometer. Reports of increasing gravitic drift were disturbing the men.

Ketzler was beardless and solemn, even younger than I. A loyal junior officer, he had been patiently in training for the time when our rotation plan would let him take my place, but now this crisis began to erode his half-learned authority. Even on the intercom, I could hear the tremor in his voice.

"I'm afraid—afraid of trouble with the men, sir. Especially those old hands whose leave we had to deny. I've heard some ugly talk."

"I know they're bitter," I admitted. "But I'm not afraid of them."

I spent the rest of the watch checking instrument readings and doing what I could to bolster morale. After all, I told Ketzler, there wasn't much the men could gain by mutiny. The *Erewohn* was gone. Our emergency craft, though mutineers might seize them, were none of them fit for the long voyage out to any inhabited planet. Even though the station was drifting toward Nowhere, we were all safer inside than out.

Haunted by old Habibula's tale about that call from

Commander Star, I had the duty crew probe the region north of Nowhere with every available instrument. They picked up nothing, yet I knew the search was inconclusive. The raging interference was violent enough to drown any possible laser or radio signal.

Because I had to present a confident appearance, as much as for any other reason, I called Lilith Adams to ask her and old Habibula to meet me in the mess hall for dinner.

"Delighted!" Her cool voice was oddly calm, yet oddly tense. "Captain, could you show us the station, too? And tell us more about the anomaly and this new disturbance? We've heard some alarming rumors."

The truth would be more alarming than the rumors, but I didn't tell her that. I did agree to take them around the station before dinner—for at least two reasons. I wanted to show the crew an air of duty-as-usual. I wanted more clues to the riddle of our uninvited guests. Perhaps I also wanted to please the girl.

Methodically building an image of steadfast calm, I took time for a shower and a shave before I went to pick up our guests. Brushing the dust off my best uniform, I caught myself whistling with anticipation.

On the way to meet them, I stopped at the control center. The desperate tension there almost cracked my image of sure authority. Ketzler was still on duty with the new watch, though he should have been in bed.

The center was a big, drum-shaped room, buried at the heart of the ice asteroid. It spun slowly on its own axis, so that the rim of the drum was an endless floor. One round end was a projection screen for our electronic telescopes; the other held the electronic chart where the computer integrated all the instrument readings to make a visible map of Nowhere.

I found Ketzler sitting rigid at the computer console, staring up at the shifting glow of the chart. It showed an ugly black-bellied creature, crouching at the center of a great web of shining lines that reached up and down all the way to the curving floor.

The black belly of the creature was the heart of the anomaly, the region where all our instruments failed. Its spreading purple legs were the charted zones of anomalous gravitic force. The bright lines of the web were lines of magnetic force—already spread far beyond the tiny, bright green circle that marked the position of Nowhere Near.

478

Ketzler jumped when I touched his shoulder.

"How's it going?" I ignored his nervous response. "Think it's peaking out?"

"Not yet, sir." His glasses were pushed crooked on his haggard face, and they magnified his bloodshot eyes. "It's the worst it has ever been—and still getting wilder. The gravitic drift has got me worried, sir."

He pushed a button that lit a curving row of bright yellow dots on the chart. The dots were numbered. Each one showed a charted past position of Nowhere Near. They marked the trail the drifting station had followed, always closer to that creature's belly.

"It's sucking us right in." He looked at me cross-eyed through the sweat-smeared glasses. "Even with our position-rockets going full thrust. We can't control the drift, sir."

"We've done all we can," I assured him. "If something does happen, I'll be at dinner—"

Uneasily, he licked his dry lips.

"Before you go, sir, we've a couple of things to report. That new iron asteroid we picked up north of Nowhere—it's gone again!"

He pointed to a red dot on the chart.

"Another thing, sir—before you go to dinner." I heard a dull echo of reproach in his hollow voice. "The laser monitors have just picked up what seems to be a distress signal from that same direction. No intelligible message, but we got what I think is part of the name of a ship. I think it was something *Quest*."

4

The Enemy Machine

In spite of such disquieting developments, I tried to carry an air of hearty confidence. Of course the anomaly was dangerous, I reminded Ketzler. Its dangers were our business at Nowhere Near, and we were attending to them.

However tired or frightened or resentful, the duty crews were still at work. Our undamaged instruments were still

479

following what went on. The computer was still plotting. The position rockets were fighting at full thrust to keep us out of Nowhere.

We could do no more.

Even if Habibula's unlikely tale was true, even if the *Quasar Quest* was fighting for her life against the half-known forces in the anomaly, there was no help we could give. Our lean resources were fully committed. If the cosmic menace of the anomaly had been ignored or underestimated, if our needs had been neglected, the errors had not been ours. We could not correct them now.

Even to myself, I dared not admit that we were near a very desperate extremity. Shrugging off Ketzler's anxious question, I advised him to get some rest and went on to keep my date with Lilith Adams and Giles Habibula.

She had changed her severe white uniform for something blue and sheer, though she still wore that ugly, red-eyed skull. Even at full-G, her motion had the flowing grace of flight. She smiled and took my hand. Her touch lit rockets in me.

"Captain Ulnar, you are very kind."

Her warm voice gave me a giddy feeling that the terrible disturbance of the anomaly had already swallowed me. She was walking at my side, alluring in that translucent blue, yet somehow out of reach. Excitingly near and real, she was yet somehow wrapped in that untouchable aloofness that I could not understand.

"Giles has gone on to the mess hall for a snack before our tour," she said. "Can we pick him up there?"

A pang of jealous speculation stabbed me. If their queer tale was even partly true, if old Habibula was actually recovering his lost youth, it struck me that such a girl as Lilith Adams might be a more important part of the experiment than all his precious wine and caviar.

We found him in the mess hall. Still appallingly unmilitary in the same blazing yellow sweater and the same shapeless fatigue pants, he was sitting at a table with our one remaining free companion, a plump redhead named Gina Lorth. They had split a bottle of his wine. He was acting younger than his age and as free as the companion.

"Ready, Giles?"

Showing no concern about the companion, Lilith had spoken in that cool tone of unconscious but absolute command that told me she was far more than nurse or playmate. Giles Habibula lurched to his feet, almost upsetting the startled redhead. Suddenly he was sober. His awed respect assured me that Lilith's unknown role in this affair was something more than to prove his recovered youth.

"For sweet life's sake!" he wheezed. "Don't shock me so."

"Come along, Giles. Captain Ulnar is going to show us over the station."

With a sad glance at the wine left in the bottle, he gave it to Gina and came puffing after us.

"Lil's precious serum!" His flat, bright, rock-colored eyes squinted at me craftily. "It's giving back my youth, but at a fearful cost. Gnawing hunger and desperate thirst —and a yen I haven't felt for fifty mortal years!"

I showed them Nowhere Near.

The station was a lean doughnut of inflated plastic and steel, just thick enough for rooms on both sides of a two-level corridor. It ringed a thousand-foot hall of interstellar ice—frozen water and methane and ammonia—that would have been a comet if it had ever drifted close enough to a star.

That spinning doughnut made the rim of a half-mile wheel. The spokes were plastic tubes that held power lines and supply ducts and elevator shafts. The hubs were thick cylinders that projected from the poles of the ice asteroid. An inner slice of each cylinder, spinning slower than the spokes, was pierced for the valves that let ships enter the air docks. The outside end of each hub, driven with a counterspin that kept it at null-G, held its telescopes and laser dome motionless with respect to the stars.

Old Habibula appeared to enjoy the tour. His affection for machines seemed genuine. He lingered fondly about the atomic power plant shielded deep in the ice. He wanted to see the biosynthetic batteries that recycled our water and restored our air and produced the most of our food. He admired our intricate research gear. Somewhat to my surprise, he even seemed to understand it.

"One question, Captain," he wheezed at me. "You're showing us a lot of lovely machines, modern as tomorrow. What I can't quite see is the prehistoric design of the station itself. Why this spinning ring with its clumsy imitation of gravity, when you could have used gravitic inductors?"

"Because of the anomaly," I told him. "Space is different here—nobody knows precisely how or why. Gravitic and electric and optical devices don't work well—you know what happened to the space-drive on Scabbard's ship."

His earth-colored eyes blinked apprehensively.

"What is this mortal anomaly?"

"A spot in space where the common laws of nature don't quite fit," I said. "If you want the history of it—"

"Let that wait till dinner, Giles," Lilith put in gently. "I'd like to see the station first."

She still puzzled me. Though she didn't claim to love machines, she seemed at home with them. Her quiet questions showed a keen brain, I thought, and a surprising technological background.

We were just entering the observation dome at the north hub of the station, where the night of space came into the station itself, drowning the faint red glow of the instrument lights in icy midnight.

We were in zero-G there, and I handed old Habibula and the girl little hand-jets. Both knew how to use them. Leaving Habibula admiring the gloomy forest of bulky instruments bolted to the inside wall, Lilith soared easily away toward the vast invisible curve of the transite dome that looked out toward Nowhere.

"Captain Ulnar," she called. "Come with me."

Soft and clear, her voice held that odd tone of sure command. Surprised at myself, I followed her silently. She had paused above the looming instruments, trim and small and perplexing against the vaster riddle of the anomaly.

For a few moments she drifted there, looking out at the dust and mist of stars and the universal dark. Looking past her toward galactic north, I could see where a few stars were slightly blurred and reddened. Even that took a practiced eye. The fearful shape of Nowhere revealed itself only to our special instruments. Yet something gave me a sudden queer feeling that she knew more about it than I did.

"Tell me something, Captain." She turned quickly to me, her face grave and lovely in the cold starlight. "What is the atomic composition of this dome?"

When I told her that it was a transite casting, it turned out she knew not only what transite was made of—she knew that the process of manufacture had been changed three times since that remarkable synthetic was first invented. She began to ask for precise technical specifications: date of manufacture, isotope analysis, index of refraction, density and curvature and thickness.

Though such questions seemed trivial to me, her manner was deadly serious. Young then, I still had an excellent head for numbers. I had prepared myself carefully for the duties of that first command, and I was able to tell her promptly what she wanted to know.

"Thank you, Captain." Her lean, pleased smile set my head to spinning like the station. "Now we'd like to hear all about Nowhere."

As the hand-jets carried us in retreat from Nowhere and the star-frosted spatial night, back to the faint red glow of the instruments and the drifting bulk of old Habibula, I felt more than ever troubled by the riddle of our visitors. Though I was finding new facts, they fitted no pattern that I could understand.

"We've heard rumors about this anomaly," Lilith was saying. "It seems to be a dreadful thing—"

"I ain't afraid of it," old Habibula puffed. "Not since I've seen all these fine machines. You can trust my judgment. I've a sense for danger, that has cost me mortal dear. And I ain't afraid of Nowhere."

We were on our way back to the ring. Leaving the fanjets in the rack, we caught D-grips on a moving cable. It lifted us through a cavernous hollow. It swung us above the dim-lit tanks and tangled pipes of the catalytic plant that converted the frozen gases of the asteroid into fuel for nuclear rockets and drinking water for us. It carried us flying above the massive metal bulge of the control drum, toward the main elevator.

"Far and away, I'm the oldest veteran of the Legion," old Habibula boasted. "In the bad old times, I've seen wicked perils that would blind your blessed eyes. I fought the mortal Medusae and the evil Cometeers and the monstrous Basilisk. But precious peace has come to the human system now. My trusty sense of danger finds no feel of peril here. I'll put my faith in these machines—"

The penetrating whine of my lapel intercom interrupted him.

"Captain Ulnar!" Hoarse excitement rasped in Ketzler's voice. "We've just got another fragmentary call from that ship in distress. The *Quasar Quest.* Commander Ken Star. And listen to this, sir!"

Old Habibula and Lilith were flying ahead of me, clinging to the D-grips. When Ketzler paused, I heard the girl catch her breath, heard the old soldier's wailing exclamation.

"They're under attack, sir!" Raw fear rasped in Ketzler's voice. "Something has followed them out of the anomaly. Some kind of enemy machine. A hundred times as big as the ship. Star says he's disabled. He says the thing is gaining on him.

"The last few words were interrupted, sir. But I interpret them to mean that Star has been forced to abandon ship." Ketzler's voice lifted toward the jagged brink of panic. "I thought you'd want to know at once, sir. What shall we do, sir?

"What shall we do?"

5

The Impossible Rocks

For a moment I was busy with Ketzler. My first impulse was to reprimand him for that indiscreet intercom broadcast, which surely would damage station morale. Considering his extreme agitation, however, I let that wait.

"Perhaps the message is a hoax." I spoke with more conviction than I felt. "In any case, our duty is to carry on. Keep monitoring everything. Keep our guns manned. Keep me informed."

"Yes, sir." His voice sounded very lonely. "We'll carry on, sir."

Lilith Adams was flying upward two yards ahead of me through that shadowy space inside the ice asteroid. She swung on the D-grip to look back. Dimly lit from below, her face seemed gaunt and lovely and hurt.

"Captain Ulnar, you've got to do something." Her low voice was queerly, coldly calm. "We've got to help Commander Star."

"We're doing all we can," I told her. "After all, the station is not a battleship. We can't run away. With only two obsolete proton guns, we can't put up much of a fight. With all communication out, we can't even call for aid.

"If Commander Star is really under attack from an enemy machine—"

A quavering wail came from old Habibula. His hands

484

had slipped off the D-grip. Jerking convulsively in the flame-colored sweater, his body went sailing away through that dim cavern, whirling like a living satellite toward the far silver sphere of a rocket-fuel tank.

"Help him, Captain." The girl's voice tightened with concern. "He isn't used to enemy machines."

I triggered my hand-jet to overhaul him and tow him back to the cable. His pink skin had faded white, and I could feel his body trembling. He clutched the D-grip frantically.

"Don't speak of such machines!" His voice was a shrill, shallow piping. "But never think that I'm afraid. I've met and conquered dangers far more deadly than any space anomaly. It's simply—simply—simply—"

Clinging to the D-grip, he panted and shook.

"It's simply that I'm weak with mortal hunger and a thirst that won't let go! I'm the hapless guinea pig, remember, for this desperate immortality experiment. Lilith's precious serum has been turning back the years, but it gives me a fearful appetite."

"We're on our way to dinner now."

From the cable stage, the elevator lifted us out to the full-G ring. We found the mess hall dark and empty, but old Habibula observed with a sick, pink grin that its faithful machines were ready to serve us. Greedily, he punched the computer for three full meals. While he was busy, Lilith beckoned me aside.

"Captain—" Her hushed voice was gravely hesitant. "Aren't we interfering with more important duty? At a time like this, shouldn't you be in direct command?"

I couldn't tell her that she and old Habibula presented a problem as strange and dangerous as the anomaly itself.

"Perhaps you don't realize just how desperate this crisis is," I told her carefully. "One wrong move could touch off panic. As things stand, the men are still on duty. Ketzler is a fine young officer. He needs a chance to prove himself."

Her tawny eyes looked hard at me.

"Good enough, I guess." She moved toward the table where Habibula sat waiting for his food. "If you're really free, tell us about the anomaly." Her face seemed oddly urgent. "Every fact you can!"

"The first pioneers got here about thirty years ago," I said. "They found this snowball and a little swarm of stranger rocks. Iron masses two or three miles across—a

485

harder alloy than the nickel-iron of common meteors, and richly veined with more valuable metals."

"I've read reports about them." Leaning over the little table, golden lights playing in her reddish hair, Lilith was listening as intently as if those queer asteroids were somehow as supremely important to her as they had become to me. "How many are there?"

"That's part of the puzzle," I told her. "Even the number is anomalous. The Legion survey ship that made the first chart found five iron asteroids and three snowballs like this one. When the miners got here, four years later, they found only two snowballs, but six iron asteroids."

"So the survey team had made a mistake?"

"Not likely. The miners had simply found the anomaly. They didn't stay to watch it. The iron alloys were too tough for their drills—and then something happened to a loaded ore barge."

Giles Habibula started.

"What's that?" His mud-colored eyes rolled toward me. "What happened to the blessed barge?"

"That's part of the problem. It was a powerless ship, launched from one of those rocks with its load of metal and a miner's family aboard. It sent back a queer laserphone message—something about the stars turning red. It never got to port, and no trace was found."

"Mortal me—"

His gasping voice was interrupted by the arrival of three steaming cups of algae broth and three hot brown yeastcakes. He fell to eating, as eagerly as if the machines had served his own costly caviar.

"Captain, please go on." Lilith was oddly intense. "About the number of these asteroids—"

"Five more years had passed before another colony of miners settled here," I said. "They found only one ice asteroid—the one we're on. But, at the time of their arrival, they charted nine iron asteroids."

Giles Habibula peered anxiously up at me, and hungrily back at his food.

"These miners had brought improved atomic drills. They carved into those hard alloys and some of them struck rich pockets of platinum and gold. Space traders came. Even the men on this ice asteroid made fortunes selling water and rocket fuel and synthetic food. They built the original station. A roaring little metropolis—while it lasted."

Giles Habibula had stopped eating. He sat staring at me,

a sick pallor on his round baby-face and a gray glaze dulling his rust-colored eyes.

"So?" Lilith whispered quickly. "And—?"

"They were building an industrial complex on Lodestone —as they called the largest iron asteroid. A barge terminal. A big atomic smelter. Shops for building and repairing mining machinery. A laserphone center for the whole swarm of rocks.

"Then something happened."

"Whup?" Old Habibula spoke thickly around the unchewed yeastcake in his mouth, spraying crumbs. "Gulp?"

"The laser beams were broken. All communication with the asteroid was cut off. An oxygen tanker had been dropping to land at the smelter. Its crew reported that the asteroid had reddened, flickered, and disappeared."

Old Habibula moved convulsively, overturning a bowl of broth. It flooded the end of the table and dripped on his knees.

"That ended the mining," I said. "Half the people and most of the wealth of the colony had been lost. The survivors scattered. Even this ice asteroid was abandoned, until the Legion came. Commander Ken Star set up the beacon—"

"I know Ken Star." A pink, slow smile warmed old Habibula's round baby-face. "John's younger son—I recall how he used to bring me toys to mend, long ago, when I was on guard duty at John's great place on Phobos. My poor flesh freezes when I think of Ken out in the fearful anomaly now, fighting that enemy machine.

"I love Ken Star—"

"Captain, please go on," Lilith's anxious voice broke in. "Tell us every fact you can about the anomaly."

"Reports of the disappearing rocks got back to the Legion," I said. "Ken Star came out with a survey ship to investigate them. A new iron asteroid popped out of Nowhere just ahead of him. He landed on it, and found the wreck of that missing ore barge."

Old Habibula had been mopping at the spilled broth with a fiber napkin. He froze again, his small eyes watching me with the flat bright blankness of two wet pebbles.

"In life's name!" he gasped. "Where had the blessed ore boat been?"

"Nobody knows. Ken Star landed on the asteroid—his report is in the station files, but it doesn't solve any mysteries. He found the bodies of the missing family, emaciated and frozen hard as iron. He found a diary the miner's wife had started, but it makes no sense."

"What did she write?"

"Most of it is commonplace. It begins with a bit of family history—she must have had forebodings of death, and she wanted her children to know who they were. Her son had been crippled in a mining accident; she was trying to get him to a surgeon. There's a brief record of the flight —positions and velocities, tons of load, kilograms of water and food, tanks of oxygen full and used. The nonsense is in the last few entries.

"Something had put out the stars—"

Old Habibula gulped and neighed.

"What mortal horror could put out the stars?"

"The miner's wife didn't know. She was too busy trying to keep her family alive to write much more. But she writes that the barge is lost, drifting in the dark. She writes that they are searching the dark with the radar gear. She writes that they have picked up an object ahead. She writes that it's approaching them, on a collision course. They are trying to signal, but they get no reply.

"That's the end of the diary. The barge had no rockets of its own. In his comments in the files, Ken Star concludes that the object was that iron asteroid. The collision killed the woman and her family. But Star doesn't even guess where it happened—or what had put out the stars.

"His own geodesic space-drive failed, soon after he left the wrecked barge on that iron asteroid. His landing rockets got him back to this snowball. He named it Nowhere Near and stayed here to watch the rocks while his first officer took the damaged ship out to a point where he could signal for relief.

"When the relief ship came, Star went outside to get equipment for the beacons and the observatory. He found it hard to interest anybody—these odd rocks were less than specks of dust in the whole universe, and people had other problems to solve.

"He had to use his friends in the Legion, but he got his equipment. The rock with the wrecked barge on it was gone again when he came back, but two others had appeared to take its place. He nudged this ice asteroid out of the middle of the anomaly—though not far enough to make it very safe. He installed the beacons and stayed here another year to watch Nowhere, before he went on to something else.

"We've been here since—or the station has. This is my own fourth year. We keep the beacon burning. We chart those rocks as they come and go—there are nineteen, now. We monitor the instruments.

"That's the history of Nowhere Near."

Giles Habibula gulped the last bite of the last yeastcake, and blinked at me uneasily.

"What effects do your instruments show?"

"Optical," I said. "Magnetic. Gravitic. All connected with those rocks that come and go. Observing stars at certain angles through the anomaly, we find their images blurred and spectral lines shifted toward the red. Whenever a rock appears or vanishes, our magnetometers record violent magnetic storms. The motions of the rocks themselves—and even of the station—show abnormal gravitic fields far more intense than their masses could create. The gravitic fields keep the swarm of rocks compact.

"But I can't explain any of those effects."

Old Habibula had drained the last drop of algae broth from the last of the bowls. He sat for a moment staring sadly at the greenish smear of spilled broth beyond his empty dishes.

"That's the dreadful shape of nature!" he wheezed abruptly. "That's why I like machines. I don't trust people, but mortal nature is by far the greater enemy. Worse than any faithless woman. Just when you think you know the rules, she amends 'em. Those who say nature's kind are deluded romantic fools. At the very blessed best, she simply doesn't care."

He licked the last brown crumb of yeastcake from the corner of his mouth.

"Living things are in the race against us, for food and space and power." Hopefully, he licked for another crumb. "The nearer they are to us, the crueler the conflict. Life knows our own dear kin are deadly enough. People might be worse than nature—if they possessed the wondrous mystery of that wicked anomaly.

"Anyhow, each of us is trapped between nature and mankind—pitiless nature and pitiless men!"

He shuddered fearfully.

"That's why I choose machines. Their mission is to serve us. They aren't in mortal competition with us for the precious prize of life, as our fellow beings are. They wear no cloak of wicked mystery, as nature does. They do what they are made to do, and that is that."

"Giles, you're dead wrong."

Lilith Adams had been sitting straight and alert at the little table, gazing down at that dull black death's-head on her finger. Her fine head was tilted slightly, and her lean white face wore a look of desperate intentness—almost I felt as if she were listening for Ken Star to call again from his strange battle in the wild heart of the anomaly.

"I love nature." She looked abruptly back at us, her bronze eyes darkly grave. "I love the seas and fields of Earth. I love the cratered dust of Mars and the methane glaciers of Titan. I love the endless wild infinity of space —even as it looks from Nowhere Near.

"I can't believe this anomaly is natural!"

"We've considered that it might be an artifact," I agreed. "But in twenty years of watching we've never found a clue to indicate any kind of cause for it, nautral or not."

"I think you have a clue now," she said. "You have that enemy machine!"

"Mortal—mortal me!" Old Habibula croaked and sputtered. "Let's not speak of that fearful machine!"

"I think we must," Lilith said. "Not all machines were made by men. Or designed to help men. If enemy machines made this anomaly, I think they may be worse than men or nature either—"

We all started when my intercom whined.

"C-c-c-captain, sir!" Ketzler was stammering with tension and fatigue. "We've got another message from Commander Star, sir. S-s-s-s-something you should know. He says he is under a new attack from that enemy machine. The *Quasar Quest* is wrecked. He's attempting to abandon ship. I th-th-th-thought you'd want to know, sir."

"Thank you, Ketzler. Is Star still aboard?"

"I believe so, sir—though his signal was suddenly broken off. Most of his men had left the wreck in an escape capsule. Star and a few others stayed aboard to cover them. But their capsule was shot to pieces."

I heard him draw a ragged, rasping breath.

"Wh-wh-wh-what shall we do, sir?"

"Duty as usual," I told him. "Keep the station going."

He paused a long time, while I shared his agony.

"Y-y-y-y-yes, sir."

More faintly, a confusion of other lifted voices from the control drum came over the open intercom. Though the words were blurred, the tones were sharp with shock and consternation.

"A light, sir!" Ketzler's voice came shrill with excitement, his stammer gone. "A queer light in space! We can see that enemy machine!"

The terror of his words ringing in my brain, I stared at Lilith. Though the rest of us were on our feet by then, she sat rigid and pale, staring down at the dull black skull on her ring as if its glittering ruby eyes had somehow hypnotized her.

6

The Bubble of Darkness

Old Habibula and Lilith came with me down to the north observatory. Though he was acting half paralyzed with fear, she appeared desperately eager to see that strange light and the enemy machine.

I let them come because the riddle of their visit was not yet solved. Perhaps I had sensed a connection I could not understand, between the problem they had brought to the station and the peril outside—between those asteroids vanishing from the dark heart of the anomaly and those able spacemen vanishing from Scabbard's geodesic flyer.

The men on duty in the zero-G dome seemed unnerved when they saw us flying in on the cable, almost as if they had taken us for mechanized invaders.

"Captain, you sort of startled me." The dome chief hushed a harsh, unnatural laugh. "There's the light—whatever it is!"

A gaunt and fearful ghost in the blood-colored glow from the instruments, he pointed a pale crimson arm at the transite dome. In a moment I found the light—it looked like a yellow star hung in the black pit of Nowhere.

"It's going out, sir," he added huskily. "Estimated magnitude two point three when we first observed it. Now about three point six. But still bright enough to show that —thing!"

The fan-jets lifted us into the greenish glow of the projection cell. We hung to the cold chrome rail at the back of the long narrow tube, watching the huge luminous screen that amplified the image from the electronic telescope.

Here that light was a tiny, bright-green disk. The rest of the screen was only a faintly greenish blankness, until the nervous dome chief adjusted the controls. Shadowy shapes flickered and dissolved, and suddenly we saw the enemy machine.

Old Habibula made a low, hollow moan. I felt Lilith start and stiffen. A numbing something tingled at the back of my neck.

The thing covered half of that enormous tube. We saw it in shades of glowing green, outlined by that fading star. I felt stunned by its size, utterly baffled by its shape.

"A machine!" Even now, Lilith's tight and breathless voice seemed curiously calm. "One men never made!"

"A fearful machine!" whispered old Habibula. "A monstrous machine. I'm not sure I like it!"

If its hugeness was dazing, its shape overwhelmed me. Parts projected out of it, but I could not call them masts or tentacles or towers—they fitted no familiar pattern. Their shadows, greenish black upon the screen, veiled whatever they projected from.

"If machines are designed to do things—" Though I was fighting for control, my voice came out hoarse and shaken. "What is this one for?"

"For nothing good," old Habibula whimpered. "You can see its makers mean us fearful evil!"

"How is that, Giles?" Lilith's voice was breathlessly intent. "What can you tell about it?"

"Too mortal much!" Clutching that cold rail, he shuddered apprehensively. "We can tell that it was built to propel itself through space, even in this fearful anomaly. We can tell that it was built to attack and pursue other spacecraft. We can tell that its unknown weapons were too much for poor Ken Star's *Quasar Quest*. We can tell more, as we watch it work.

"For life's sweet sake—look at that!"

His voice sank into a shivering moan.

Watching the screen, we saw the machine dart closer to that dying star. We saw a long projection, neither arm nor crane nor cable, extend itself to seize the star. The star was covered, dimmed, extinguished. The whole screen went greenish-black.

"What happened?" Lilith whispered sharply. "Where did it go?"

492

"Space is mortal dark out here," old Habibula gasped. "With the nearest star thirty trillion miles away. Since the wicked thing put out the light, it's black as space itself. But at least we saw it work."

"What do you make of that, Giles?"

"Trouble!" he moaned. "Fearful trouble."

With nothing more to see, we left the dome. I escorted Lilith and Habibula back to the full-G ring, and then made a careful tour of the duty posts. I found the men dangerously restive.

The unknown light had been put out. The enemy machine had vanished from our instruments. No new message had come from Commander Star. Only the great electronic chart on the end of the control drum showed the anomaly still growing—that black-bellied creature fatter, its purple legs reaching farther, its bright magnetic web spreading around and beyond us.

Without the chart, the anomaly was still invisible—perhaps that was the most dreadful thing about it. Only our computed drift revealed the intense gravitic forces dragging us deeper into that deadly web in spite of the thrust of our rockets.

The whole station was hushed and breathless with a sense of unseen menace closing in, so intangibly strange that we could not shield ourselves against it. The strain of waiting—waiting for a shape of danger that we could not even imagine—was harder to endure even than the seen threat of that dark machine.

My next long watch had come and gone, when Commander Star reached the station. He came in the smaller escape capsule from the *Quasar Quest,* with only two men of his crew. To avoid detection, they had drifted all the way with dead rockets, keeping radio and laser silence. We had no notice of their coming until their retrorockets fired, fifteen minutes away.

I hurried down to meet Ken Star in the lock. He came out of the capsule with a sling for his right arm and a bandage around his head. His gray face was streaked with grime. Yet I thought he bore himself well.

One of his men had both legs broken, and the other was dying of what seemed to be radiation sickness. At the station hospital, he made the medics do all they could for the injured men before he let them touch him.

Though the medics tried to insist, he refused to go to bed. His wounds were superficial, and he insisted that he had slept in the capsule. Dressed in a uniform of Ketzler's, with clean sling and bandages, he let me take him up to eat in the mess hall.

A slight, quiet man, somewhat stooped, he looked more scholar than soldier. Though the medics had washed off the blood and dirt, his face was still seamed with fatigue. At first I had been vaguely disappointed to find that a son of the legendary John Star could be so small and frail and vulnerable, but I soon began to admire him.

"The rest of the crew left first," he was saying as we left the elevator. "They took the larger capsule, with my executive officer in charge. The three of us tried to keep our attacker entertained, while they got away."

He shook his head slightly, then froze himself, as if the movement hurt.

"That scheme failed," he said. "The capsule was knocked out with what must have been a micro-missile—a tiny projectile fired at a fantastic velocity."

He was limping a little, and he let me catch his arm to help him board the moving rim walk.

"The same sort of micro-missile made scrap metal of the *Quasar Quest*." His voice was harsh and tired and bitter. "We had no chance at all—the finest cruiser in the Legion would have had no better chance.

"Not against those missiles!

"We'd see a faint flash many thousand miles away. The shot would hit us instantly—so hard it excited gamma radiation. I suppose those projectiles would be weighed in milligrams, but they are unbeatable. No possible shield could stop them. No possible ship could evade them.

"If you had seen that machine—"

"We did," I told him. "By the light of—something."

"That something was the *Quasar Quest*." His worn face twitched with pain. "We had just got out of the wreck when they hit it with something else. Nothing that we could detect. But the hulk turned incandescent. Perhaps they were sterilizing it, before they came to pick it up! Another unbeatable weapon!"

"Commander—" I had to stop and steady my own voice. "What is this invader?"

Sagging wearily in the borrowed uniform, his worn body shrugged.

"If you saw it, Captain, you know as much as I do."

At the mess hall, he got off the rim-strip with no help. Though we were early for dinner, we found old Habibula

494

and Lilith already there. Habibula had an open tin of caviar and two bottles of his precious wine on the table before him. When the commander saw them, he stopped with a gasp.

"Lil! Giles!" He seemed delighted, yet somehow disturbed to see them. "I thought you'd be waiting for me, back at sector base."

They were gaping wtih the same astonishment.

"Ken Star!" old Habibula bellowed. "We thought you were dead in space, killed by that enemy machine!"

Flushed and lovely with pleasure, bronze eyes glowing, Lilith came running to throw her arms around him so vigorously that he flinched with pain. I felt a sharper pang of puzzled jealousy. A very remarkable nurse, I thought, to be on kissing terms with Bob Star's brother!

"Ken, we were afraid to wait," she told him. "There was no way of communication, to you or Nowhere Near. We didn't know what had happened. We got passage out here on a chartered ship—and finally persuaded Captain Ulnar to take us aboard."

She gave me a dazzling, half-malicious smile.

Old Habibula came lumbering after the girl. With a hearty warmth, he wrung Ken Star's hand—and then stepped back, his wine-colored eyes squinted fearfully.

"Where have you been?" he gasped. "What mortal peril have you uncovered, to chase you out of Nowhere—"

The shrill whine of my lapel intercom cut him off.

"Captain Ulnar!" Ketzler was on duty, his voice hoarse and breathless with alarm. "We've just observed something I think you ought to know about."

"What is that, Ketzler?"

"We don't know what it is." His voice rose uncertainly. "Something out in the middle of the anomaly. Nothing you can see, sir—except that it's blotting out the stars behind it. It looks like a bubble, sir. A bubble of darkness!"

"Thank you, Ketzler."

"Any—any orders, sir?"

"Watch it," I said. "Report any change."

"It's growing, sir. It's already more than one degree across. And—" His shaken voice hesitated, and rushed on suddenly. "You know we're drifting toward it, sir!"

"I know," I said. "Keep me informed."

"Yes, sir. I'll do that, sir."

The intercom clicked off.

Feeling more deeply shaken than I had wanted Ketzler

and the station crew to know, I looked at Ken Star. He had limped across to the table and sunk into a chair. He sat staring up at Lilith, a gray pallor of dismay on his pinched and haggard face.

"I'm afraid I know what that bubble is," he whispered huskily. "I have a theory, anyhow—a theory that frightens me!"

He extended a bloodless, trembling hand to take the girl's.

"I'm glad you and Giles aren't still waiting back at sector base. I suspect that the Legion is going to need your special skills right here—soon and desperately!"

7

"Older Than the Universe"

Four of us in the drab little mess hall, we gathered at the table. I leaned to punch the computer for our meals, but Ken Star shook his bandaged head.

"Later," he murmured huskily. "Let it wait."

Old Habibula, with a generosity unusual in him, punched for four glasses and shared a bottle of his wine. It was a pale dry vintage half a century old, but nobody commented on its bouquet—or even on the remarkable fact that the sunlight which passed old Earth on its vintage year had not reached Nowhere Near.

Lean and clear and lovely in her white, Lilith sat looking sometimes at Star and Habibula and me, sometimes at the dull black skull on her hand, and sometimes far away. Again I had the sense that she was listening, as if she feared to hear the coming of something dreadful from that bubble of featureless darkness that was growing out in Nowhere.

"Tell us, Ken!" old Habibula croaked. "What is this fearful theory that alarms you so?"

Star took an absent sip of wine. I saw the glass trembling in his frail hand. Settling carefully back into the chair, as

496

if he had suffered more injuries than he reported to the medics, he spoke to Lilith, almost ignoring old Habibula and me.

"I'm tired." His voice was weak, but steady and clear. "Shaken up. But I'll try to give you the facts you're going to need, in some intelligible order. You know I've spent my life digging into the riddle of this anomaly. I led the first survey and helped set up this station. Most of the time since I've been at the big cosmological observatory on Contra-Saturn. That's where I worked out the theory."

He paused as if to rest.

"What's so mortal alarming in a theory?" old Habibula croaked. "Why did you have to send for us?"

"The theory led me to expect something like that enemy machine—some further display of an alien technology advanced far beyond our own. I was prepared for hostility—but I wasn't expecting it quite so soon."

Star's bandaged head shook painfully.

"Our purpose on this first flight of the *Quasar Quest* was only to make a preliminary test. I was not expecting you to follow me here, though now it's fortunate you did. I was intending to return to sector base to pick you up—if we found that your singular skills were needed."

I sat staring at old Habibula's rosy, hairless baby-head and Lilith's lean and desperate loveliness, wondering blankly what possible skills they might possess that would be of any use against the monstrous threat of Nowhere.

"To test the theory," Star went on, "we measured the age of those rocks in the anomaly—"

"How's that?" Old Habibula gave him a fishy stare. "How can you measure the age of a mortal rock?"

"In this case, by spectrographic analysis." Star's worn voice was carefully precise. "Because matter does age. New planetary matter—its elements created perhaps in an exploding supernova—does have a pretty specific atomic composition. It contains a rather definite proportion of the radioactive elements which decay with time."

"A dismal universe," muttered old Habibula. "Where matter itself grows old!"

"For the initial tests," Star went on, "we used the thorium series. The element thorium has a half-life somewhat more than thirteen billion years—which means that in thirteen billion years about half of any given sample of Thorium-232 will decay into the isotope, Lead-208."

Star paused, as if to recover voice and strength.

"Take wine, Ken!" old Habibula urged him. "It's like precious new blood in your veins." With a rare hospitality, he overflowed Star's scarcely tasted glass. "How old are the rocks?"

"Old. . . ." Star's voice faded to a papery whisper. He waved away the wine, with a grateful nod at old Habibula. His haggard eyes darted a sharp glance at me. As if we didn't matter, he spoke again to Lilith. "Unbelievably old . . ."

Nervously, old Habibula gulped his own wine.

Star straightened his bandaged head. He drew a long uneven breath, as if struggling to recover himself. Lilith reached quickly across the table to grasp his hand. For a few seconds he sat silent, smiling at her fondly. Then he spoke again more vigorously.

"Our known universe has an age that we can ascertain," he said. "Our native sun and its planets are about four billion years old. The oldest stars in our galaxy are only a billion years older. Computations show that the expansion of our universe began no more than six billion years ago. Nothing older exists anywhere—except these anomalous rocks!"

That slow smile gone, he sat staring bleakly at Lilith.

"Nobody wanted to believe our results," he said. "We repeated the thorium tests. We ran a control experiment with Uranium-238—which normally decays to another lead isotope, Lead-207, after a half-life of four and a half billion years. Always our answers supported the disquieting theory that we had come to check."

His bloodshot eyes looked haunted.

"Our test results show that these anomalous asteroids now contain less than one percent of the original Uranium-238 and no more than twenty-five percent of the original Thorium-232. That means that the indicated age of these rocks is at least twenty-five billion years.

"They are four times older than our universe!"

Old Habibula's pink moon-face turned pale. He flinched back apprehensively, almost as if the age of those ancient rocks had been a contagious disease that he was afraid of catching from Star.

"Commander," I broke in, "may I ask one question?"

He inclined his bandaged head.

"I've been watching these rocks too, for several years," I said. "They seem peculiar in many ways. How do you know that they are a representative sample of the original

498

matter—wherever they come from! Couldn't the thorium and uranium have been removed by some other process than age?"

"Thank you, Captain." He answered with a methodic, painful care. "I know these rocks are anomalous in other ways than age—in size and shape and composition. But I think we took account of every possible source of error. What we measured was not the total amount of thorium or uranium, but the ratio of each to its own peculiar isotope of lead. What we analyzed was not just the various alloys of the asteroids themselves, but also collected samples of adhering surface dust."

As if he had forgotten me and my objection, he turned stiffly back to Lilith. His frail hand was clutching hers on the tabletop, as if in desperate anxiety.

"Even that dust is four times older than the oldest things known outside of the anomaly," he told her. "Even the dust speaks for the theory that brought me here."

Her lean face looked pale and taut as his.

"What is that theory, Ken?"

Pausing as if to organize his thoughts, he took an absent sip of old Habibula's wine.

"It developed from my work on Contra-Saturn," he said. "I was studying the objects once called quasars—the quasistellar objects which looked like stars but turned out to be exploding galaxies. The biggest bombs in the universe! A single quasar explosion has the force of one hundred millions suns turned into raw energy."

"A fearful thing!" Old Habibula blinked his dull-colored eyes. "Such monstrous bombs make our best weapons seem like mortal foolish toys. I hope you don't expect Lil and me to face such wicked weapons as that!"

"I hope we can keep our battles on a somewhat smaller scale." Star grinned bleakly. "But the enemy is deadly enough."

"Ken, I don't understand." Lilith's eyes had darkened with dread. "What have exploding galaxies to do with the age of these anomalous rocks—or with that enemy machine?"

Moving stiffly in his chair, Star raised his hands to rub at his temples under the edge of that white bandage, as if to ease an ache in his head.

"One possible source exists for such an explosion." His voice was weaker and more weary, yet still painfully precise. "A hundred million supernovas, all touched off at

499

once, would not be enough. The only possible source is a blowout of space itself."

Shivering, old Habibula gulped another glass of wine.

"You know mass curves space," Ken Star said. "When the curvature reaches what is called the Schwarzschild radius, space is bent back until it meets itself. The closed space, with the mass that made it close, is separated from our space-time. But energy enough to explode a galaxy is left behind—the released energy is equal to half the product when the mass ejected is multiplied by the square of the velocity of light."

"Do you mean those rocks were thrown from another universe?"

"That might follow." Star nodded carefully, as if motion hurt his head. "My theory is a new view of the universe. It suggests that all of our own visible world of space and time has grown from the expansion of a Schwarzschild space that was ejected from the older space-time some six billion years ago. It suggests that we are witnessing the birth of a new space-time universe, each time we observe a galaxy exploding."

"Dear mortal me!" panted old Habibula. "The world I thought I lived in was big and giddy enough. I'm not sure I care for your improvement. If nature is that complex, I know I prefer machines—machines, that is, of human make!"

"This new cosmogony staggered me at first, but I'm afraid it has to be accepted." A strange awe glowed in Star's hollowed eyes. "If every exploding galaxy represents a new space-time universe budding out of our own, then the total universe must be truly infinite, not only in space and time but also in multiplicity!"

He glanced sharply at me, as if to answer a skeptical question I had not asked.

"Captain, I've spent years on the math," he said. "My analysis shows that each ejected space-time system will become unstable and expand again. The degenerate matter in its nuclear core will explode into dispersing fragments. Expansion will generate hydrogen atoms, which will ultimately gather into galactic clouds around the separating fragments. As these new galaxies mature, they will in turn contract and explode and so create new space-time universes. The cycles of creation never cease."

"A novel idea of the universe!" I sat staring at him. "I

wasn't meaning to object—it's just too big to grasp at once."

"It makes me giddy." Lilith gave me a quick little smile. She turned back to Ken Star, her bronze eyes darkly solemn. "But I still don't understand the anomaly."

"At first I thought it was simply the scar—the navel, if you like, of our universe. I suspected that our own space-time system had not been completely detached from the old mother world from which ours was born. I believed that those ancient rocks had somehow wandered through a wound in space that was not entirely healed."

"Would your math account for that, sir?" I asked. "Could such a rupture stay open for billions of years? Or would it be closed instantly?"

"Frankly, I don't know." Star paused to press his bandaged temples. "You must consider the fact that each subuniverse would have its own coordinate systems of space and time. Time here may be space there—so that our own six billion years might be only an instant in the older mother world those rocks came from."

"I hadn't thought of that."

"There are other factors, too," he added. "Besides the mass-effects predicted by the Einstein-Schwarzschild equations, there are magnetic and radiation effects that are harder to analyze—the same effects that you have been observing, here at Nowhere Near."

Lilith's darkened eyes were staring at the wall beyond Star, as if she saw something far off and dreadful.

"Ken, does your theory mean that the anomaly is natural?"

"At first I thought so—I desperately hoped so," he said. "Now I doubt that it is entirely natural. The theory implies that the anomaly should shrink, if it changes at all. I'm very much afraid that the expansion we are observing is an artificial effect."

Old Habibula had been about to pour himself another glass of wine. He set the bottle back with a clatter, blinking fearfully at Star.

"For sweet life's sake," he moaned, "what does that mean?"

"I'm afraid that the anomaly is a kind of gate that still connects us with our mother world," Star said huskily. "I still believe that it was nautral in origin, but I'm afraid that it has been enlarged or opened by some application of intelligent technology."

"You mean—" Old Habibula stopped to shudder, clutching at his bottle as if it had been some talisman of safety. "You mean that wicked machine—and that bubble of dreadful darkness—"

"I'm very much afraid that the machine is an invader." Star's voice was faint and bleak. "I'm afraid that the bubble is the visible aspect of the opening interspatial gate through which it came. I'm afraid we must face a hostile technology that has been evolving four times longer than our space-time universe—"

The mess hall door burst open. Ketzler came tottering in. His face was white beneath a long smear of blood. His right hand was clutched against his side, and blood oozed between his fingers.

"Mutiny, sir—" His voice was a bubbling sob, and bright blood trickled down his chin. "Most of the crew— even Gina Lorth. They've got—control drum—docks. I guess—guess they just couldn't take Nowhere—not any more!"

Swaying, he clutched at a table.

"Something—worse, sir!" His voice thickened and broke. "That black bubble—more fighting machines—I was just going to call you, when they hit me—"

He blinked and peered as if his sight were fading.

"Wha—what can we do, sir?"

He crumpled to the floor.

8

The Absolute—Zero!

Resistance to the mutineers, such as it was, had ceased by the time Ketzler reached the mess hall. The leaders were the disgruntled veterans who had wanted to leave with Captain Scabbard. Their only real opposition, apaprently, came from Ketzler and the lock sergeant, Vralik. Vralik died defending the locks.

The attack on Ketzler in the control center had been made only to cover the flight of the mutineers. By the time I reached the ice asteroid from the full-G ring, they were gone. They had blown up our position rockets, wrecked the fire-control gear of our old proton guns, and looted the station safe. They smashed the pilot computer in one of our two emergency rockets, and took off in the other.

The outbreak must have been set off by news of the invaders, because it showed more panic than plan. The mutineers took too many persons aboard a rocket built for only twelve. They left crates of supplies and drums of reserve fuel stacked in the dock. They killed Vralik needlessly—a letter I found in his pocket showed that he had meant to join the plot.

Though I saw no hope for them, I couldn't help wishing them well. The name of Gina Lorth brought me a painful throb of regret. I had been fond of her once. We had come out to the station on the same relief ship, both very young, devoted to the Legion and eager for adventure. A native-born mutineer, even then Gina had what she called a thing against authority. The raw cadet, I had been a fellow rebel until my first promotion began to turn her against me. Sadly, I had watched time dim her bright vitality and the dark spell of Nowhere put out her daring gaiety.

I felt sorry Gina was gone.

Seven of us were left on Nowhere Near—seven counting Ketzler and the two injured men from the *Quasar Quest*. Cool and deft and still alluring, Lilith helped us care for Ketzler. She gave him efficient first aid. Later, in the station hospital, she dressed his wounds and administered a tiny jet-injection.

"A drop of Giles' serum," she said. "It cost the Legion five million. It ought to heal his wounds—and add a good ten years to his normal life."

Nothing had been damaged in the north observatory. I found Ken Star ahead of me there, a gaunt slight ghost moving unsteadily about the red loom and gleam of the electron telescope. No telescope was needed to tell me how fast that bubble of blackness had been growing. A neat round blot against the silver mist of stars, it was now fully two degrees across.

At first it seemed featureless, but a dull orange spark came against it as I looked, creeping toward its center. The orange point grew brighter, yellower, whiter. Suddenly the bubble changed—I suppose because of some optical or psychological effect.

503

No longer a bubble, it was suddenly a wide black funnel. That white star fell fast down its midnight pit, down into Nowhere. We dropped after it. Turning giddy with my sense of that wild and helpless fall, I clutched a hand-rail desperately.

"See that, Captain!"

Ken Star's husky voice seemed at first to come from far away. I had to close my eyes and catch my breath before I could release my sweaty grasp on that cold rail and follow him to the electronic telescope.

"See that light?" he was calling. "That's your mutineers. They've been shot to junk and caught in that sterilizing field—I saw the puff of gas when their fuel exploded. Now the wreck is trapped in a more intense gravitic field—"

Breathlessly, he interrupted himself.

"Here! Come take a look!"

I joined him in front of the green-glowing screen. That black circle filled half of it—still a monstrous funnel to my eyes, so dark and deep that I shrank away from it, dizzy and shivering. The wreckage of the rocket was a hot bright point, toppling down its bottomless throat. Now I found something else—four fainter points, spaced outside the circle.

"Those objects—"

"Can you get the 'scope on one of them, with a higher power?"

Breathing even and hard to still the tremor of my hands, I brought one of those four points to the center of the screen. I turned up the power. The point swelled. It became a greenish blur. Out of the blur emerged another invader machine, the dark twin of Ken Star's attacker.

"Four invaders," Star rasped. "Spaced in tetrahedral pattern around the bubble. Guarding that gateway— perhaps helping create it. I believe they have come from that more ancient space-time universe, to hold a bridge-head against us—"

"Huh!" My exclamation interrupted him. "It's gone!"

The screen was blankly greenish-black again. Turning to the transite dome, I saw that the moving star was gone from that shadow-disk.

"The glowing wreck just went through the gate into— somewhere," Star said. "Without its light, we can't see the invaders. But they're still there."

"And Nowhere Near is still dropping toward them," I said. "That spot covered one degree when we first saw it, five hours ago. Now it covers two—which means we've come halfway. Without the position rockets, we're falling faster. I suppose we have three hours, maybe four."

As helpless as Ketzler, I stared at his gaunt face.

"Commander, what can we do?"

Jetting nearer, he loomed tall in the crimson gloom.

"We do have a weapon," he whispered at last. "Humanity's ultimate defense. A top secret thing— but you will have to know about it now. Because I think we may be forced to use it. Where is Lilith?"

"Still in the hospital," I said. "Doing what she can for those injured men."

I clung to a chrome rail in that zero-G space, still shaken from my giddiness. The riddle of the soldier and the girl spun crazily in my mind.

"Is she—?" I gasped. "Who is she?"

"My niece," he said. "Bob's youngest daughter. Her real name is Lilian Star—Lilith Adams is her own invention. She and her two sisters are keepers of the peace. Chosen guardians of the absolute weapon."

Awe struck me, cold as the black space beyond the transite dome.

"I guess that explains a queer detached aloofness I felt about her—a feeling that almost frightened me. So she isn't a nurse at all?"

"She is a nurse," Star told me. "She says she needs some humane interest, just to balance her power to destroy. She has done original medical work. She led the research team that developed the longevity serum she's testing on Giles Habibula."

Hot humiliation flashed over me.

"And I'm the one who turned them away," I breathed bitterly. "When they came with Scabbard, I wouldn't let them aboard—because I couldn't believe Habibula's tale about how he loved machines!"

"A cover story," Star said. "But Giles does have a feeling for machines."

"Why didn't they tell me? Scabbard's men could have murdered them!"

"They're both more competent than they look." Star grinned faintly in the dim red dark. "Their scheme to get aboard Nowhere Near worked well enough, without compromising anything."

"What is the weapon, sir?"

"Its code designation is the letters AKKA. That's about all you'll need to know about it."

Floating behind that cold chrome rail, I glanced out through the dome at the round black shadow growing in in the core of Nowhere. Something alien as space breathed on my spine.

"Is it—good enough?"

"It's absolute—at least in ordinary space. Just the threat of it, three hundred years ago, was enough to overthrow the Ulnar Emperors and their Purple Hall. With one stroke, in the last century, it destroyed Earth's old satellite and the invading Medusae there. I don't know what will happen when it hits the anomaly."

He peered uneasily at the dome.

"Can you call Lilith from here?"

I tried to call, but the mutineers had evidently wrecked the intercom.

"Let's get her here," he said. "Though the Green Hall has forbidden any needless or premature use of her weapon, I think the time has come to set it up."

The station hospital spun in a half-G ring section, almost grazing the crust of the ice asteroid. Breathless with haste, I burst out of the elevator there. Old Habibula challenged me with a proton-pistol I hadn't known he carried.

"Sorry, Captain." His murky eyes searched me. "What do you want?"

"Commander Star wants Nurse Adams in the north dome," I blurted. "He says it's time to set her weapon up."

"So Ken has told you?" His pink baby-grin was warily friendly. "Now we can stop playing silly games. I've been telling Lil that we've been waiting too mortal long for those fearful invaders to make a gesture of friendship. Wait. I'll bring her."

He waddled into the hospital and returned with Lilith. She turned to smile back toward her patients.

"They're all sleeping," she whispered. "I think they'll recover—"

"If those monstrous machines give 'em time!" old Habibula panted. "Ken says it's time for us to strike. For life's sweet sake, don't waste time!"

Gravely unhurried, she waited for me to lead the way into the elevator. As we dropped, I turned to look at her. Her lean proud loveliness pounded in my veins and ached in my throat—yet now she was a goddess, moving to the seat of cosmic judgment, serenely untouchable.

506

"Please—please forgive me," I stammered. "For sending you away with Scabbard. I—I didn't know."

Her bronze eyes fell to me, aloofly amused.

"You were not to know."

"Couldn't you—couldn't you have trusted me?"

"I asked your name." The dance of light died in her eyes. "I learned you are Lars Ulnar. I remembered that twice keepers of the peace have been kidnapped by Ulnar traitors. I didn't want to be the third."

I said nothing, but she must have seen me flinch.

"Sorry, Lars." A softer smile warmed her gaunt face. "We trust you now."

We left the elevator at the cable stage. I clipped her D-grip to the moving cable and we soared toward the dome through the shadowy heart of the hollowed asteroid.

"Scabbard's mate and those two spacemen?" I twisted around to look at Lilith. She floated behind me, staring toward the dome as if she could already see our unknown antagonists waiting out in Nowhere. "Was it your secret weapon that—disposed of them?"

She nodded silently.

"And mortal well it did!" puffed old Habibula, flying behind her. "Lil's got a precious obligation to protect herself. Even now, when both her sisters share it, the duty of the keeper of the peace is a fearful thing for any being!"

In the dull red dusk of the zero-G dome, I found fanjets for Lilith and old Habibula. She had stopped at the entrance, gazing at that black funnel in the heart of the anomaly, her face gaunt and grave and white. Ken Star came soaring toward us from the red-glinting mass of the electronic telescope.

"Are you quite certain, Ken?" Her solemn question greeted him. "It's an awful decision—the future of worlds at stake. Do you know that they are able and acting to destroy us? Are you sure that no truce is possible? Are you quite certain that they or we must die?"

"You can assure the Green Hall Council that we have made every effort," he answered huskily. "Our signals have got no reply—except unprovoked attacks from weapons we can't counter with anything short of AKKA."

"But radio and laserphones don't work reliably in the anomaly," she said. "How can you be sure that they knew we were trying to signal?"

"We can't." He caught a rasping breath. "But I believe

we have shown forbearance enough. After all, we want to survive—"

An alarm bell interrupted him, chiming from the computer.

"Mortal me!" old Habibula puffed. "What's that?"

Glancing out at that bubble of darkness, I saw another dull spark creeping out across it, the way the mutineers had gone. We soared across to the electron telescope, and I got its image on the screen—a jagged irregular mass, its projecting points and edges glowing faintly though most of it was dark. I recognized its angular coffin-shape.

"It's one of those queer iron asteroids," I said. "The last one to appear. The electronic chart had showed it between us and the bubble. I suppose it has been sucked in ahead of us."

Clinging to the chrome rail, Ken Star spoke urgently to Lilith.

"It's giving light we need," he said. "We can see four of those fighting machines, spaced at the points of a tetrahedron around the bubble—which I think is the gate through which they came. I suggest you pick 'em off."

"Not yet." Moving with a confident skill in that null-G space, she turned to measure that dark blot through the dome again, with her own unfrightened eyes. "I'm not yet certain. The station is an obvious artifact. The fate of the mutineers shows that we are within range of their weapons. Yet they have not attacked us."

"Life's sake, Lil!" old Habibula gasped. "They're dragging us into that tunnel of wicked night—perhaps into another universe! They've left us just a few precious hours. Isn't that attack enough? Can't you see that we're all in fearful danger?"

"You knew this job was risky, Giles." Her smile was a flash of kindly malice. "Yet you accepted it!"

"To save my mortal life!" he wheezed. "Old age was killing me."

She turned to me.

"Captain, we'll try one more signal." Her air of absolute command made her again the goddess judging worlds. "Train the strongest laser beam you can on one of those machines. Transmit the simplest signals possible. Begin with the series of squares. One flash. Four. Nine. And so on.

"Monitor everything you can, for their reply."

508

"Lil, don't!" old Habibula gasped. "You're asking for a dreadful death!"

But her air of power left me no choice. In the increasing light of that asteroid falling into the bubble, I chose the machine that hung northward from it. I set all our search and reception gear to tracking, and trained the main laser beam. Using the computer for a manual key, I tapped one flash.

Watching the angular shadow of that invader, I saw a pale, greenish flicker. Then the screen went blank. The red instrument lights went out. That chrome rail shuddered under my hand. A dull reverberation boomed through No-where Near.

"Well, Lil?" old Habibula croaked faintly. "That's your answer!"

"Answer enough." Her voice was calm in the dark. "We have no choice."

That shot—a few milligrams of matter fired perhaps at one tenth the speed of light—had pierced the armored hollow of the ice asteroid and wrecked our main power plant. For a few seconds, Nowhere Never was dead. The only light was the cold blaze of the stars beyond the transite dome. The only sound was the far roar of our air escaping.

But then the emergency reactors came on. Automatic valves began to thud, sealing off that deadly rush of air. The instrument lights shone again. The green image of that terrible machine swam into the screen again.

"Hurry, Lil!" old Habibula was puffing. "They may fire again! What you promised me was precious immortality —not that I'd be shot like a trapped rat!"

"Quiet, Giles!" Ken Star whispered. "Don't bother her."

But Lilith seemed unaware of any of us. Working very deftly and quickly, she was assembling her weapon. The parts of it were oddly small and simple. She used a worn iron nail and a twist of wire that old Habibula produced, two or three pins from her hair, and her platinum ring —the red-eyed grin of that dull black skull gave me an unpleasant start, but now at last I thought I understood what it meant.

In a few seconds, the thing was done.

Holding it in one steady hand, she pointed it toward that bolt on the stars. She moved her thumb, pressing the end of a bent hairpin against that platinum band. The death's-head leered redly at me. Shivering, I turned from her to watch that iron asteroid, which was brighter now, a tiny

509

yellow star. Waiting for I didn't know exactly what—perhaps for some spectacular explosion—I swung again to the electron telescope. The greenish shadow of the invader was brighter now, but otherwise unchanged.

A low, wordless moan came from old Habibula.

"It doesn't work—"

Lilith's voice was broken, quivering. Her aloof serenity had been shattered. The air of power was gone. She was sobbing like a hurt child.

"I—I don't—know why—"

9

Back Door to Nowhere

Cold fear caught me. For one sick instant I thought the transite dome had somehow turned transparent to heat, draining off our warmth of life. In the ghastly glow of the instruments, old Habibula and Lilith and Ken Star were faint frozen ghosts, floating motionless around me.

Implacable hostility glared down through the dome. The natural universe, the mist and frost and dust of stars, was suddenly as dreadful as that unnatural midnight funnel in the anomaly. Hanging to the hard chrome rail, I shrank from the pitiless, bottomless mystery of infinite space.

We were terribly alone.

"Oh!" Beside me, Lilith made a small, frightened gasp. "No—"

Working with both hands to aim and try her absurd little weapon, she had let herself drift away into that null-G space. Now, flailing out in a sudden unthinking panic, she snatched at the railing. She couldn't reach it.

With a gentle thrust of my fan-jet, I overtook her. Her hand quivered in mine. She stared at me as we flew back together, her eyes black and strange and stricken in that deathly light. She gave me a faint, pale smile.

"Thank you, Lars!" Her cold hand clung to me. "I need you now!"

For a moment we clutched the cold rail, staring at the green and monstrous image of that enemy machine. I still hoped somehow to see her weapon take effect, still feared some grim retaliation. But nothing changed that glowing shadow.

"They aren't even shooting back!" Lilith swung in the air to face Ken Star. "I can't understand it," she whispered bitterly. "Why did my weapon fail?"

"Because of the anomaly, I suppose." His voice was dull and dry, broken with defeat. "Space is different there. The difference affects the transmission of light and radio and gravity. Perhaps it also affects your weapon."

"That might be." She nodded helplessly, her icy hand limp in mine. "AKKA works by producing a peculiar distortion of space, in which matter cannot exist. If the anomaly creates a conflicting distortion—"

Her voice trailed off into desolate silence. Moving like a stiff machine, she took her useless weapon apart and slipped the ring back on her finger. That ugly skull caught the red light, with a mocking wink of evil.

I felt her shiver.

We hung to the rail, watching that funnel of darkness swallowing the northward stars. Though I could not quite see it grow, at every glance it looked larger. The white point of the incandescent iron asteroid was drifting slowly but visibly toward the center of it, moving in the way we would go.

Old Habibula uttered a wordless, tragic moan.

"Giles, you know machines." Ken Star's sudden voice was strained, hoarse, somehow startling. "Tell us how to stop those machines."

"My precious life!" Old Habibula shuddered in the blood-red gloom. "Maybe I do know machines—I know these are wicked. I respect machines because they have a purpose I can understand. These have made their fearful purpose clear.

"Their unknown makers mean no mortal good for us!"

The girl's cold hand shuddered in mine.

"No hope!" she breathed huskily. "Nothing we can do—"

"Perhaps—I think there is!" A quick excitement caught me. "Commander—Commander Star!" I stopped to smooth my shaking voice. "I think there's something we can try. A pretty grim and hopeless thing—but better than waiting to follow that burning boulder into Nowhere!"

His haggard eyes peered through the red dusk at me.

"What's that, Ulnar?"

"I ran a computer analysis on the motions of those rocks," I said "Months ago. The results didn't make much sense till just now. But now I think your theory explains them. I think I know a back door into—into Nowhere!"

Shifting his grip on the cold chrome, he hauled himself toward me.

"Let's hear about it!"

"We'd observed the way those rocks were moving," I said. "At the instant of appearance. At the instant of disappearance. I fed the data into the computer, to search for common elements. In the appearing rocks, I found none—they seem to come out with random directions and velocities. But the rocks that vanished had all been moving up a cone less than one degree across, at nearly the same velocity."

Lilith's hand squeezed mine, alive again.

"What I want to do is take a rocket up that cone," I said. "If your theory is correct, I think it might come through into the world beyond that bubble—without being sterilized! I think it might give us a chance for some sort of surprise attack on whatever is beyond. Not a good chance—but any is better than none!"

He hung gazing at me. His hollowed eyes caught the instrument lights, and his gaunt head looked shockingly like the skull on Lilith's ring. I had to turn away.

"I see no chance at all," his dull voice rasped. "Didn't the mutineers sabotage your spare emergency rocket?"

"I'll take the escape capsule that Lilith and Habibula got here in."

"What will keep the invaders from picking you off like they did the mutineers?"

"I'll maneuver behind the ice asteroid," I said. "Get up velocity and cut the rockets before I come out. I'll coast down the cone. With the rockets dead, they may not detect me."

"Or, again, they may!" He gave me a mirthless, red-eyed grin. "What weapons will you carry?"

"That's a problem," I said. "The mutineers wrecked our big proton-guns—which might be useless anyhow. The best chance I can think of is a couple of tons of cathode plates from the atomic power plant, with an improvised detonator—"

"To turn the capsule into a nuclear missile?" He nodded slowly in that blood-colored dusk. "You're willing to pilot such a missile—on such a desperate strike?"

"I'm going to try." I turned to the dome again, to study that fearful funnel swelling at the heart of the anomaly, the captured asteroid burning brighter now and nearer the center. "We've no more than three hours to try anything."

"Lars!" Lilith's hand clung to mine. "Lars—"

I squeezed her hand, let her go.

"Come along, Habibula." I started out of the dome. "If you're so clever with machines, you can help me rig a detonator for those uranium plates—"

"Wait a moment, Ulnar!" Ken Star's lifted voice interrupted me. "I approve the general outline of your plan—just because it looks better than no plan at all. But I'm going to revise a few details."

"Yes, sir." I stopped obediently, hovering in the dark above the cherry-glinting instruments. "I welcome your suggestions, sir."

"I'm making two changes in your plan," Star said. "First, I'll pilot the capsule by myself—"

"Sir!"

"Listen, Captain!" Ken Star barked sternly at me. "Remember your duty here. Nowhere Near may be a wreck, but it's still your command. You haven't been relieved—"

"Sir, you could relieve me—"

"I could, but I won't."

"But, sir, you aren't fit for such a desperate strike. You're already exhausted—"

"Lilith has given me a shot. Considering the nature of the mission, I'm more fit than you are for it. I've spent most of my life studying this anomaly. I welcome—gladly welcome the bare possibility that I may live to see it from the other side."

"Sir, it's—suicide!"

"It was your own idea, Captain—and I rank you in the Legion!" His low chuckle rippled through the gloom. "I'll pilot the capsule. And I'm making one other change in your plan."

"Yes, sir," I muttered. "What's that, sir?"

"I'm not sure that any homemade nuclear bomb would be very useful against the technology that opened that gate. I'm going to take a more flexible weapon. I'm going to take Giles Habibula—"

"Wa-a-a-a-a-ah!" Old Habibula's broken cry echoed dolefully from the transite dome. "I ain't no mortal weapon. I ain't even in the Legion now. I'm just a peace-

513

loving veteran. I came to Nowhere Near to find immortal youth—not to die in a foreign universe!"

"Giles, I've heard you tell of your own exploits." Ken Star grinned like that small black skull. "I'll take your own word that you are more formidable than any machine— and I'll hear no more about it. I want you aboard in fifteen minutes."

"For life's precious sake, I—I—" Old Habibula floated unsteadily, blinking his rust-colored eyes at Ken Star. "Yes, sir," he wheezed. "I'll be aboard."

Lilith caught Ken Star's arm.

"Shouldn't I come?" she whispered. "Don't you think there might be a different space beyond the anomaly, where my weapon might work again?"

His dull-eyed skull shook bleakly.

"Wait here," he said. "We've yet to find a target on the other side, and we have no assurance that AKKA would function there. Your duty is to guard it faithfully."

I heard the hurt gasp of her breath.

"I'll guard it." I caught a faint flash of red and black and platinum, as she glanced at her deadly ring. "I'll guard it faithfully."

Ken Star swung urgently to me.

"Captain, is the capsule ready?"

"It will be ready, sir," I promised. "In fifteen minutes."

The cable-way was closed now, since that shot from the invader had punctured the air-space we had dug out and sealed off inside the ice asteroid. We had to leave the dome through emergency tubes—and we found that the automatic valves had closed most of them.

Nowhere Near was badly crippled. That micro-missile had exploded against it like a tiny supernova. The blast had torn an enormous crater in the asteroid. The shock wave had shattered equipment everywhere. Debris had carried away half of the full-G ring. Hard radiation from the initial impact had poisoned one whole quadrant of the asteroid.

But we found the capsule intact. Two broken lines from the supply pumps had to be patched, but within that desperate quarter-hour it was filled with fuel and air and water, loaded with space rations, stocked with survival gear. Old Habibula came rolling dolefully aboard, stumbling under a load of wine and caviar that would have buried him at full gravity.

Lilith came with Ken Star to the lock. Standing ready at the lock monitor, I watched their farewell. He kissed

514

her briefly. She murmured something. He started into the lock and stopped to call back sharply:

"Guard your secret well. Trying to use it, we may have compromised it. Avoid capture."

"Trust me, Ken." The smile on her gaunt and bloodless face looked almost gay. "I won't fail!"

"Guard her, Captain," he snapped brusquely at me. "Keepers of the peace have been lost in the past. That must not happen again. The security of AKKA is your first duty now."

"Yes, sir." I gave him a quick salute. "I understand, sir."

Moving with a brisk and almost jaunty haste, as if he felt more eagerness than fear, he slid into the capsule and sealed the hatch. A pang of envy stabbed me as I thumbed the launching-cycle button.

"I wish—" Lilith whispered besides me. "I wish we were going."

I said nothing. They had at least a chance to find what was beyond the anomaly. I thought we had no chance at all—but I saw no need to speak of that. Silently, I caught Lilith's hand. It lay cold and lifeless in my grasp.

The inner valve thudded shut. The pumps roared briefly. The outer valve opened less than halfway—and stuck fast.

"Wait for me," I told Lilith. "I'll see what I can do."

I scrambled into an emergency suit and cycled through the manlock. Inside the main chamber, I slid around the capsule and found room to slip through the jammed valve. Outside, I discovered that it had been fouled by a deflated plastic shaft—a spoke from the broken full-G wheel—blown across the lock.

Working in frantic haste, with emergency tools designed for smaller and more delicate tasks of repair, I slashed away the crumpled plastic tube. The embedded steel cables still fouled the valve. They were too tough for my cutter, almost too heavy for my torch. Precious minutes were gone before I could part them.

Then I found the valve still jammed, the servo-motor dead. Sweating in the suit, I toiled at the hand-wheel to widen the opening far enough so that I could guide the capsule past the knife-edge of the valve.

Outside, we found that we were screened from the invaders only by the flimsy wreckage of the full-G ring. With laserphone dark, for fear of another shot, I jammed my helmet against the capsule to carry sound and shouted a warning to Ken Star that the invaders could see his rockets here.

He let me push the capsule safely beyond the ice asteroid before he fired. That effort drained too much mass from my own pack. When he used his laserphone, in the shadow of the asteroid, to warn me to drive clear, my thrusters were too sluggish.

The roaring jets of the capsule caught me, flung me spinning back toward the station. Flying through the dark, thrusters dead, I caught a frightening glimpse of the anomaly.

The invading machines were still too far for me to see, but that terrible funnel of darkness had swallowed more of the reddened and distorted stars around it. The trapped iron asteroid was brighter now, closer to its black throat, still falling ahead of the station.

Though that giddy glimpse of Nowhere left me cold and shaken, the more normal space around me was deadly enough. Helpless to control my flight, I missed the gray starlit bulk of the ice asteroid. Flying past it, I had time to wonder whether the direction and velocity of my unplanned flight lay within the critical cone that would take me into Nowhere.

Then a whipping metal tentacle struck me savagely.

10

Anomaly in Time

Bruised and dazed, I seized that flailing tentacle. After one stunned instant, I knew what it was—a loose cable from the broken full-G wheel. Though half the ring had been blown away by that exploding micro-missile, wreckage of the rest still spun around the ice asteroid.

The cable twisted away, slipping in my gloves. I held on grimly, for I clung to life itself. Desperately, I kept my grip until my unguided flight was checked. Laboriously then, fighting the centrifugal force that was like inverted gravity, I started climbing toward the axle of the broken wheel.

That took a long time.

Though I had been able to stop that first terrifying slide not far beyond the half-G point, the suit itself, even with empty mass-tanks, was still as heavy as my body. The gloves gave me only a precarious grip on the whirling cable. I climbed and had to rest, climbed and had to rest.

For all my years in space, I could not escape a terrifying illusion. The asteroid seemed suspended overhead, a shadowy starlit bulk. The whirling cable seemed to hang straight down into an insane black pit. The stars themselves seemed to spin crazily around and around and around me, until I had to fight a giddy nausea.

Northward, the anomaly was near one statioanry pole of that whirling universe. The black funnel of the guarded gateway was larger every time I looked, the yellow neck of the trapped asteroid always brighter in its bottomless throat.

Somewhere southward, Ken Star was maneuvering the capsule under cover of the ice asteroid. Once or twice I saw the pale blue jet receding into starry distance. For a time I lost it. Then I saw it coming back—a faint blue flare with the capsule itself a tiny black point at its heart.

It passed while I clung to that slippery cable. The blue flare winked out. A shadow flickered across the whirling stars, just below me. It went on, rockets dead, invisible.

Twisting anxiously on the cable, I looked after it into the anomaly. Dizzy and shivering, I watched the rim of the funnel for the flash of a weapon. I waited for the small new star that would be the capsule, sterilized.

The dark universe kept whirling around me. The funnel kept growing. The point of yellow-white light in its throat was suddenly gone as that remote asteroid went through, into Nowhere.

Nothing else happened.

Muscles knotted and quivering, I climbed up through a cruel agony of sick exhaustion. Though my strength was failing, that savage force decreased as I drew toward the axis of rotation. Without thrusters, I had to make a reckless leap from that broken wheel to the nearly stationary hub that held the locks.

I caught the edge of the collapsed plastic shaft that lay across the lock and hauled myself along it until at last I could drag myself through the fouled valve and fall inside the lock.

For a time I simply lay there, trembling with exhaustion,

517

until I found strength and purpose to cycle myself through the man-lock and clamber out of the suit and look for Lilith. She was gone from the lock deck. Calling her name, I got no answer.

A dreadful stillness hung inside the ruined station. Listening desperately, I heard only the thudding blood in my own ears. Cold alarm clutched at me. Snatching a hand-jet, I soared wildly around the hub, hoarsely shouting her name.

Still she didn't answer, but a muffled sob drew me to the deck of the next lock, the one from which the mutineers had fled. I found her there, lying face down on a pile of space gear which the fugitives had left abandoned on the deck.

"Lilith!"

Whimpering and quivering, she didn't seem to hear. But I saw a darting, furtive movement, caught a flash of black and red and platinum. For one dazed instant I thought she was trying her weapon on me. Then dreadful understanding stunned me.

"Lilith—don't!"

Scrambling for traction in the nearly null gravity of the slowly turning hub, I launched myself across the deck. I came down sprawling on her, caught her arm, twisted her hand away from her teeth.

Fighting back with tigerish fury, she nearly won. I was still reeling from my ordeal in space, and her Legion teachers had trained her well. Feinting, kicking, jabbing with a deadly expertness, she twisted her hand free. She got it nearly back to her lips. To stop her mouth, I kissed her.

"Lars?"

She spoke my name with an unbelieving gasp. Suddenly she was limp, sobbing in my arms. I snatched her hand again, stripped off the poison ring. Her teeth had not reached that ugly skull. Its red wink mocked me, deadly still.

"Lilith—" Panting for breath and strength and courage, I fought a wild impulse to throw the ring down the air duct. "It's just me! And the time hasn't come to—"

I couldn't say it.

"You were gone so long!" Wide and glazed and dark, her bronze eyes stared at me. "I thought you'd been lost in space. When I heard something moving, I was afraid—afraid it was an invader—come to capture me—"

518

She clung to me, shuddering and sobbing.

"Lars! Lars! I'm so terribly glad it's you!"

I kissed her again, this time not to stop her mouth.

After a while she laughed softly in my arms.

"Captain Ulnar, your first duty is the security of AKKA." Her breathless voice mocked Ken Star's brusque command. "I like the way you're attending to it. You've saved my life—and made me human again!"

I held her alive and wonderful in my arms.

"Never—destroy yourself!" The words even were so painful that I could scarcely whisper them. "The invaders will be taking care of that," I told her bleakly. "Too soon now—unless Ken Star and Giles do better than I expect."

"Don't speak of that!" she breathed. "Let's forget!"

We tried to forget. For a little time, we almost did forget. But the stillness of the station was a montrous voice of warning, and our thudding hearts were tramping feet of terror. Imperative dread drove us back to the laser dome.

We were deep in the anomaly. That black funnel had covered half the northward stars. With the electron telescope I searched its long rim for the invading machines hanging there. I found nothing. They were nearer now, I knew, but we had no light to see them by. When they sterilized our asteroid, I thought bleakly, its glow would make them visible again, but not to us.

"Lars—it's the shot!"

Crouching back against me in the chill red gloom of that null-G space, Lilith pointed at the dome. Beyond it, against that vast and featureless pit of blackness, I saw a sudden pale blue flare.

"It's the sterilizing shot!"

"I don't—don't think so." An unbelieving relief took away my voice. "I think it's the retro-rockets of that capsule."

"Giles and Ken?" She hung peering at me, a pink and adorable ghost in that lifeless night. "Can they really be coming back?" She caught a sobbing breath. "Can you call them? Find out what they've found?"

"I'm afraid to risk a call," I said. "Any signal might draw another shot. But it is the capsule—in braking flight toward the station hub."

We were waiting in the hub when the capsule nudged its way back into the lock. The drive motor for the hull valve was still dead, but I stood ready to cycle through the man-lock and seal the valve by hand.

Air roared into the chamber. Shucking off the space suit, I stumbled around the capsule to help with the hatch. It stuck at first, groaned open rustily. A man's head thrust out—shrunken, white-bearded, old. Sunken eyes peered out at me, warily alert.

"Lars Ulnar?" Ken Star's voice was rasping at me, queerly thin, queerly aged, queerly unbelieving. "You are still waiting here?"

"Of course we are." I caught his parchment hand. "Let me help you, sir."

Queerly dwindled, queerly bent, he let me help him through the hatch. Old Habibula followed. Even he was thinner, though his skin still looked smooth and pink as Lilith's. His pebble-colored eyes rolled wildly at her and me.

"Lars!" His voice was a wheezy, unbelieving croak. "Lil! We're mortal glad to find you here—and still alive! When we saw the station not repaired we thought it must have been abandoned."

Squinting strangely at us, he shook his hairless head.

"Did they maroon you here?" he gasped. "Alone in this wicked wreck? Or did the relief ship never come? Have you been trapped out here all this mortal time?"

Leaning on Lilith's arm, as if he needed support even here where gravity was nearly null, Ken Star stood peering with those bright, sunken eyes at her and me.

"How long—" His old voice quavered and broke. "By your time, how long have we been away?"

"Two hours." I studied my watch. "Perhaps a little longer—"

"Two mortal hours!" old Habibula bleated unbelievingly. "You're joking with us—when we've suffered too much and toiled too long and endured too many mortal disasters to be met with silly jokes."

Flushed with indignation, he sobbed for his breath.

"We've just got back from beyond the anomaly. We've fought through perils that would freeze the precious brain in your skull. We've existed for desperate years on synthetic gruel and iron determination. We've set our precious wits against the grimmest riddles of a foreign universe."

He wheezed again, as if gasping for life itself.

"And now you greet us with a silly joke!"

"I don't understand—but it's no joke, Giles." I looked from him to the bent old man who had been Ken Star. "We've been watching the time, because we have so little

520

left. The station is still falling into the anomaly. I don't think we have an hour left."

The old man nodded with a birdlike alertness. The bandage was gone that Ken Star had worn, but I saw the thin blue line of a zig-zag scar across his yellow parchment forehead—an old scar, healed long ago.

"Time is different where we've been," he said. "I hadn't realized just how different—though my theory does explain it. With the shift in space-time coordinates, instants here can be ages there. Most of the time we had no better clocks than our own bodies, but since we left here we have experienced months of time—"

"Mortal years!" old Habibula wailed. "So long I can't recall the precious taste of caviar or wine!"

"If you got through the anomaly—" Stark urgency caught my voice. "Did you find a defense? Did you find any way to stop the invaders?"

"We learned tremendous things!" The old man nodded solemnly. "What we learned points a way to safety—possibly even for us. But I'd expected that dark gateway to be closed long ago."

Dread shadowed his haggard eyes.

"So long as it is open, we're in desperate danger!" He caught my arm with a quick yellow claw. "Let's get to the control center—fast. I want another look—if there is time! I'm afraid that we have been betrayed by that anomaly in time!"

11

"The Mother of Machines!"

We retreated to the control drum, shielded in the core of the ice asteroid. I helped Star from the cable stage into the slowly spinning rim—and stopped with a gasp of dismay when I saw the projected electronic chart on the round south wall.

That monstrous creature had devoured nearly all the

chart. Its ragged purple legs reached down to us and up to the curve of the drum overhead. The bright green circle was deep inside its swollen belly.

"It looks—dreadful!" Lilith's tense fingers clutched my arm. "What does it mean?"

"The computer integrates our instrument readings into that picture of the anomaly," I told her. "The web's the magnetic field. The legs are gravitic vortices—like the one that caught us. The belly is the region where the anomalous effects are so intense we get no readings. That's where the invaders have opened their gateway—"

"Captain," Ken Star broke in sharply, "let's try the telescope. Our flight was blind—it's more luck than astrogation that got us back to Nowhere Near. I'd like to see what's going on behind us."

"We can try," I said. "But our radar and laser gear are dead now, and the telescope requires a source of light—"

"Try it." Urgency crackled in his thin old voice. "I think there'll be light."

One soaring bound carried me across the drum to the console that controlled the telescope. We all stood watching the north wall. The huge round screen was suddenly fringed with wavering points of light—the dimmed and shifting images of stars beyond the anomaly. All the center remained black, empty, ominous.

"There's the funnel, sir," I told Ken Star. "Without a light, we can't pick up the machines."

"Wait!" Ken Star was breathless with expectance. "There'll be light."

Light came. A thin pale feather floated from the rim of the funnel, flowed toward its center. Another streaked to meet it. Slow meteors grew, converging there.

"Debris their micro-missile blasted off this asteroid," Star said. "On the flight here we came through the cloud. It should give us light enough to locate those machines."

For a moment I stood numb. My imagination was too vivid. Those converging points and plumes were the stuff of our own asteroid, falling ahead of us into that unimaginable chasm. We were too close behind.

"Captain!" Star raised his voice. "Before the light is gone—"

Though my fingers were stiff and clumsy at the console, I found the greenish image of the invader stationed north of the anomaly. It was moving, drifting southward. As the light increased, we picked up three other faint greenish shadows, the other invaders, all converging in that black abyss.

"That object!" Star's voice lifted sharply. "Coming to meet them—can you get a better image?"

"Not without a better light."

With the low power we had to use in that poor light, those enormous fighting machines were tiny greenish flecks. At first I could see nothing else. Then I made out a vague blur emerging from the dark ahead of them. In the glow of a new plume of fire, it was suddenly clear.

I heard Lilith gasp.

"A machine?" she breathed. "A ship!"

"The mother of all machines!" old Habibula croaked from the doorway. "It has followed us back from that foreign universe!"

The thing was made of seven unequal spheres, partly fused together. Roughly spindle-shaped, thick at the center, it tapered toward both pointed ends. Three curved rods or tubes made a tight cage that bound the spheres. I shivered with awe at its strangeness—and its enormous size.

"It must be big!"

Dazed, I was trying to imagine just how big it must be. If those gray-green motes flying to meet it were machines a hundred times the size of a Legion cruiser, I thought it must be another hundred times larger.

"Mortal big!" croaked old Habibula. "It's the monstrous mother ship!"

Unbelievingly, I turned to Ken Star.

"Is it really—a ship?"

"Space fort might be a better term," Star said. "It's a good ten miles along those—let's call 'em decks—from nose to tail. The middle globe must be two miles through —and it's filled with things you can't imagine."

"Do you mean—?"

He nodded a brisk answer to that half-spoken question.

"We were aboard." He tugged at his neat white beard. "Long enough at least for this to grow."

"Years!" puffed old Habibula. "Mortal years of fear and famine!"

He had left us on the way from the lock to the drum, and now I saw that he had slipped away to raid his private hoard. His tattered pockets bulged, and he clutched an open bottle of the rare wine of Earth in each baby-hand.

"What does it mean?" Staring at the growing image of that enormous, alien spindle-shape, I felt a chill of puzzled dread. Nothing about it told me anything. I swung blankly back to Ken Star. "What did you discover?"

"Wait, Captain." He lifted a thin yellow claw. "I want to see what it does."

Moving with an old spaceman's cautious rhythm, Habibula waddled across the curve of the drum to a table. Carefully, he planted the bottles of wine. From his bulging pockets he unloaded clinking tins of caviar. The rest of us stood watching the green electronic shadow of that titanic thing.

We saw a port open in the largest central globe—a faint dark dot. We saw the four drifting sparks converge and wheel outside it. We saw them enter and vanish one by one. We saw the dot disappear.

"That valve is fifteen hundred feet across," Star said. "Among the instruments around it is a tube which I suppose is a wave-guide for signals from an outside antenna. That's the entrance Giles found for us."

A new respect drew my eyes to old Habibula. He had opened a can of caviar. Using a small pocket tool that combined opener and spoon, he was stuffing the little black eggs into his mouth. He belched.

"A desperate adventure!" His rust-colored eyes blinked across the table. "I've risked my precious life ten thousand times in faithful service to the Legion. But I've never endured such a dreadful time as this!"

"Giles does possess special skills," Star agreed briskly. "Without them, we should certainly have failed."

"But never did my genius face such a fearful trial!" old Habibula moaned. "You know my hard-earned arts have helped me solve some frightful problems for mankind. I entered the black city of the evil Medusae! I unlocked the inner world of the monstrous Cometeers! I solved the deadly riddle of the Basilisk! But never was a time so mortal black as this!"

He paused to gulp from a tilted bottle.

"Beyond the anomaly, we came into a fearful universe you'd never imagine. A black and dreadful world where human life has no right to be. But for my precious genius, we should both have died there."

"Even with all Giles' peculiar aptitudes, we very nearly did."

Ken Star stood watching the shadowy image of that appalling machine. When I began asking, a little wildly, what they had found beyond the anomaly, his withered hand lifted impatiently to cut me off.

"We've been gone too long," he muttered rustily. "I'm too tired—and too much has happened. When we found the station here, I was hoping we were safe. But now, since we've run into an anomaly in time, I'm afraid we've no leisure for any connected narrative."

"But—Ken!" Lilith's voice was dry with dread. "Can't we do—anything?"

"Nothing." His old voice was slow with dull despair. "Nothing we haven't done."

"Your theory did prove out?" I insisted. "You did come through into another space and time?"

"I'll tell you what I can." He nodded stiffly. "In whatever time there is."

"Come." Old Habibula waved a bottle of his precious wine. "Sit. If we are doomed to die like vermin in a blessed sterilizer—let's not die famished!"

We joined him at the table, where once I had presided at meetings of the station staff. Habibula handed around his bottle of wine, his flat shallow eyes watching jealously. Lilith and I let it go by. We all looked at Ken Star.

"Captain, we followed your proposed path into the anomaly." Ken Star took the bottle and sipped lightly. "With the rockets dead, we let the capsule drift at the angle and velocity you had computed. Ten minutes from the station, the invaders picked us up.

"Our forward ports began flashing with an intermittent blue fluorescence. We knew they were tracking us with some kind of black radiation—something that worked in the anomaly. We kept waiting for a micro-missile or a heat beam.

"I don't know yet why they didn't fire. Maybe they did —maybe our course had already carried us into a space where their missiles couldn't reach us. Anyhow, before we were halfway to the center of the anomaly, the stars went out."

Startled, I recalled the strange last words that miner's wife had written on the ore-barge which drifted into Nowhere.

"We didn't feel anything." Ken Star's dry old voice was papery and faint, but firmly controlled and carefully intelligent. "None of the shock or jolt or pain you might expect. But suddenly we were in another space-time universe—"

525

"A wicked space!" old Habibula wheezed. "A dark and fearful universe!"

A glaze of dread had dulled Ken Star's eyes.

"At first it seemed absolutely dark," he said. "Black and empty everywhere. But then, with the glasses, we did pick up two or three distant galaxies—the nearest must have been a dozen times as far from us as Andromeda is from here. I thought we had dropped into an empty universe—"

"What did you find there?"

"Mortal danger!" Old Habibula's cold-colored eyes peered at me over another open can of caviar. "Fearful things to freeze the precious breath of life. Monstrous evil older than the universe. Ah, it was worse than the worlds of the fearful Cometeers!"

Ken Star had stopped to stare at the telescope screen. It was darker now. The infall of debris from the station must have ceased, because we saw no new sparks or plumes of flame drifting ahead of us into that dreadful chasm. As the last wisps and flecks of incandescence faded, the illuminated image of that unbelievable space fortress faded into darkness. The screen looked empty, dead.

"But the fearful thing is still out there!" old Habibula croaked hoarsely. "Waiting for us in the dark."

Even in the bright-lit drum, I felt a cold tingle at the back of my neck.

"In that other space—" I swung anxiously back to Ken Star. "What did you find?"

"Nothing, for a long time," he said. "In that universal darkness, we couldn't see a thing. Our radar and laser gear didn't work at first. Later, when we had drifted away from the other end of the anomaly, we began to pick up objects—"

"My weapon!" Lilith interrupted him, her face white and desperate. "Would it work there?"

"I don't know." The droop of Ken Star's thin shoulders expressed a dull futility. "Anyhow, they're on this side now. We'll have no chance to try it."

"What were those objects?" Anxiously I urged him on.

"Iron asteroids," he said. "Like those you have been observing, Captain, drifting in and out through the anomaly. A great swarm of them. When we got the laser going we charted eleven hundred.

"Later, we landed on several of them. They're the same queer rocks you have seen. The same tough alloy. The same size—a few miles long. Covered with the same adhering cosmic dust. Old dust. Dust of matter born thirty billion years ago."

His haunted eyes looked blindly up at me.

"Queer rocks!" he muttered. "But one of them you know about. Years ago—even in your time here—it came through the anomaly. Miners have built a town on it. Then it drifted back again."

"You don't mean—Lodestone?"

"That's what they called it."

"Did you find the miners—the people?"

His face turned bleak.

"We landed there," he said. "We spent weeks—maybe months—of that other time, looking for clues. We found empty structures. Abandoned machines. Even frozen supplies that helped us keep alive. But no people. In the time of that other universe, you see, that colony must have been marooned many thousand years ago."

I heard the sharp intake of Lilith's breath.

"The people did survive for several generations," Ken Star continued. "We found notes and diaries, even a graveyard. A pretty grim story. They were trying to find where they were and how to get back. They explored some of the other rocks. Though they were spinning theories, they never cracked the secret. They had no Habibula."

"In life's name, Ken!" Old Habibula blinked uncomfortably. "Don't poke jokes at me!"

"I'm not joking," Ken Star said. "The death of Lodestone is certainly no joke. It died of energy-famine. It had no sun. Its radium and thorium had long ago decayed. Most of the desperate survivors left it at last to look for our universe. What they found was that mother machine. It picked them off with micro-missiles. The last few men left fragmentary records on the rock."

He fell silent, his haggard eyes peering at the blank, greenish screen.

"What are those rocks?" I tried to smooth the hoarseness from my voice. "They seem as queer as the anomaly, as strange as that machine. Did you find out—"

"We learned what they had been." His bright, sunken eyes flashed at me and back at the screen, like the eyes of something hunted. "At one time—I think before our space and time were born—they had been ships!"

12

Multiplex Universe

A shocked stillness filled the drum and vibrated through the whirling ruin of Nowhere Near. Turning blankly to peer at the charted creature that had swallowed us, I heard the stifled catch of Lilith's breath. I started at the click of old Habibula's bottle on the table.

"They couldn't be ships!" I swung to stare at Ken Star. "What makes you think they are?"

"We explored a number of them," Ken Star said. "We found records on Lodestone—narratives written by desperate men who had explored others. Some of them are visibly artifacts. A few still have the shape of ships—queer, enormous ships—even after time we can't calculate."

"But—ships?" A stubborn unbelief shook my voice. "They're miles long!"

His gaunt head nodded at the blank screen.

"So is that thing."

"What—" I had to get my breath. "What happened to them?"

"Time." In the vibrant silence of the drum, his precise old voice echoed like a gong of doom. "Time and catastrophe. I think their last voyage was begun before our own space and time were born."

"You know where they came from?"

About to speak, he stopped to watch that blank screen again. Old Habibula dropped an empty caviar can, which made a shocking clatter. Glancing at Lilith, I found her staring into the mocking ruby eyes of that small skull. Her face was bloodless and desperate. I caught her hand, covering the poison ring. She turned slowly to watch Ken Star, her cold hand limp in mine.

"I think we know," he said at last. "I believe I told you long ago about my theory that our own space-time universe has grown from the space and mass ejected from an exploding galaxy in that mother universe? Well, I think the fleet carried refugees from that galaxy.

"A tremendous, tragic saga! Its heroes, I imagine, were creatures a little like ourselves. We found doorways, anyhow, not much too large for men, and dust of phosphorous and calcium where one of them must have died. Their biochemistry is lost beyond reconstruction, but those ships prove a high technology.

"Only old galaxies explode. Their race must have been ancient and powerful. They have left the traces of an awesome struggle to survive. They must have fled first to the fringes of their galaxy, ahead of the explosion.

"There, with the whole galaxy behind them exploding like a hundred million supernovas, they built their fleet. Apparently the expansion of their old universe had left their galaxy isolated, with no other near enough to reach. Anyhow, they took the dangerous path that the galactic explosion had revealed. They attempted interspatial flight."

He paused again to watch that black circle of greenish darkness, with its dim fringe of shifted stars.

"That one surviving ship is manned with robots," he said. "Its survival is ironic, because it was built to take the greatest danger. The refugees built it to open a way from space to space, for their escape. When the way was open, it was to come through first, to survey the new space and secure a bridgehead for their invasion."

Lilith's cold hand clenched hard on mine.

"I'm not sure what all went wrong," Ken Star said. "We found no records we could read—none except those old machines. But I believe part of the fleet was trapped in that galactic explosion. Nothing less could have fused and battered those magnificent ships into the things we took for natural asteroids.

"I think more of them were mauled when they came into the new universe too soon—while its expanding mass was still as deadly as the exploding galaxy. Perhaps there were other fatal excursions—we can only speculate. But the deadliest surprise of all must have been the anomaly of time."

"And that's a fearful thing!" gasped old Habibula. "But for Lil's precious serum I'd be frozen and dead a thousand years ago in that foreign universe!"

Shivering, he drained his wine.

"The crippled fleet must have been left to wait while the robots came through to prepare for their invasion," Ken Star said. "At the different rates of time, a million years

—or a hundred million—may have passed for the fleet before the robots could send the signal for it to follow.

"By that time, the invading race was dead—"

"So we've just machines to fight?" I whispered. "No living things at all?"

"Just machines." Ken Star nodded. "Such machines as those four robots we saw."

"Mortal great machines!" gasped old Habibula. "On their fearful scale of time and size, we're less than any insect!"

"But still they are machines." Ken Star smiled bleakly at him. "They are excellent machines. They do what they were built to do, and that is all—I am quoting Giles. He observed them. He saw their function in their form. That's how we escaped alive—"

"I thought we had escaped." Old Habibula sat staring sadly at the empty bottle. "Until we found we were still caught in this old game the robots play."

"A game?" Squeezing Lilith's hand, I tried not to shiver. "With robots?"

"I suppose they've been playing it, in different times and spaces, since our universe was born. They make a crossing. They prepare a base. They signal for the fleet. Of course it cannot come—except for those few hulks that are caught and drawn through by the forces of the nexus itself."

"What happens then?"

Sitting hunched and tense and old, Ken Star peered at the screen.

"We're waiting to find out," he said. "I hope the robots conclude that the invasion point was somehow unsuitable. I hope they retreat, to try some other point—perhaps in some other universe."

"Do you think they will?"

"The evidence hints that in the past they have." His gaunt head nodded. "Hundreds of thousands of times, I imagine. The mother machine is old enough itself—though time is almost stopped in the anomaly and those wrecked ships have been exposed to perhaps a billion-fold the time—

"Look at that!" His voice lifted sharply. "Another spray of debris, I suppose, from the shot that hit this asteroid."

The screen glowed again, with sparks and plumes of pale green fire. Born among the dim stars around that circle of darkness, they flowed into it, spilling over the lip of that dreadful funnel, flowing before us in a giddy torrent toward that midnight universe. They lit the mother machine.

It looked bright and near, terribly huge and terribly strange. Parts of it sprang out at me—jutting things that were not booms or planes or antennas or jets. It was swiftly turning—swinging so that its seven fused spheres merged into one, so that their enclosing cage became three projecting tabs.

"It's pointing straight at us!" Alarmed, I turned to Ken Star. "What does that mean?"

"We'll soon know."

Desperately, I swung to the chart on the opposite wall. The green point of Nowhere Near was deep in the creature's belly. The machine was a bright red point. They were creeping together.

"A collision course!" I gasped. "That's what the computer shows. We're going to hit it!"

"I don't think so." Ken Star's old voice seemed oddly calm. "They won't let that happen—whatever they do." His hollowed eyes flashed at old Habibula. "Giles, what do you think?"

"They're machines." Habibula's pebble-colored eyes blinked uneasily. "They're doing what they were built to do. They hold us no malice at all. They aren't wicked like nature or men. But if they read the movement of the asteroid as a threat to their task, they'll destroy us instantly."

"Shall we abandon Nowhere Near?" I looked anxiously at Ken Star. "We might get away in your escape rocket, under cover of the station—"

"Too late to think of that." His haggard head shook grimly. "The station wouldn't give us cover long enough. The robots would pick up the flare of our rockets, and they're programmed to shoot any unidentified craft."

His haunted eyes went back to the dark funnel about to swallow us, to that enormous alien ship waiting in its throat. Now the ship looked like a single globe, ring-marked and greenish, bright in the fall of fire around it.

"We'll have to wait," he muttered huskily. "We'll have to see—"

Old Habibula sat staring at the screen, clutching his empty bottle as if it held some promise of escape.

"Tell 'em how we found that fearful ship," he gasped. "Tell 'em how the laser signal flamed out of it, burning red as blood, to call their fleet—that couldn't answer. Tell 'em how we came to the signal, clinging in the precious shadow of a dead and drifting ship."

Haggard eyes fixed on that black, unthinkable passage before us, on the bright-green image of that monster machine in the ring of falling fire, Ken Star said nothing.

"Tell 'em how we got aboard," croaked old Habibula. "Tell 'em how I found the wave-guide duct. Tell 'em how I opened it. Tell 'em how we had to leave the rocket and climb through that cold steel gut."

The fall of fire that rimmed that dreadful funnel was spreading out to take us in. The bright globe of the robot ship was swelling fast ahead.

"Tell 'em how we hid and schemed and fought to learn the mortal secret of the ship," old Habibula whined forlornly. "Tell 'em how we got into the quarters of the vanished master-creatures. Tell 'em how the wicked robots hunted us. Tell 'em how we got inside that fearful main computer."

Lit by that circular torrent of toppling greenish fire, every part of the alien ship looked bright and cold, unbelievably enormous, chillingly strange. I saw things in motion. Clutching Lilith's icy hand, I braced myself—for precisely what, I could not guess.

"Tell 'em how we got away," whimpered old Habibula. "Tell 'em how we worked it out. Tell 'em how we got back inside our own precious rocket. Tell 'em how we waited till the mortal robot ship had brought us halfway back from that fearful universe. Tell 'em how we pushed off beneath that fan of falling fire."

Watching the bright-green disk of the alien ship growing wider on the screen, I made a quick computation. Its apparent diameter had doubled in the last forty seconds. That meant our falling station had covered half the distance to it in the same forty seconds. We had forty seconds to live—unless something happened.

"Tell 'em how we got back," old Habibula rasped. "Tell 'em how you computed the angle of the sterilizing ray. Tell 'em how we gained our velocity in the shadow of the mortal ship itself, and slipped beneath the fan of fire with all rockets dead, and coasted on to the precious station—"

His rusty voice sobbed and stopped.

"Lars!" Lilith's hand squeezed mine desperately, vibrant and alive again. "Oh, Lars!"

The anomaly was gone.

Black funnel and green machine had flickered off the telescreen. The northward stars shone clear where they had been, no longer dimmed or reddened. Nowhere was nowhere—with a small letter now.

Unbelievingly, I looked at the other end of the drum. That devouring creature had become a thin gray ghost fading from the electronic chart. The bright magnetic web dissolved. In a moment all the chart was blank, except the bright green dot of Nowhere Near.

"They've closed the gate." Ken Star's voice was faint and shaken. "I knew—I nearly knew they would. Giles said they wouldn't let us strike them."

"They're machines," old Habibula wheezed. "They do what they must. When the fleet didn't follow, they had to go back."

"I thought—" I had to catch my breath. "I thought they'd fire on us."

"We got inside their main computer," old Habibula puffed. "We smashed a hatful of transistors to take care of that."

"Giles!" Lilith threw her arms around him, gay malice glinting in her wide bronze eyes and breathless laughter ringing in her voice. "I never quite believed the yarns you used to tell—"

"But now you know I'm an immortal hero!" He kissed her on the mouth. "A mortal hungry hero! We found wonder and danger and secrets enough in that dead universe, but precious little to eat and drink. Let's find my caviar and wine!"

"Come along, Ken." She slipped away from old Habibula to catch Ken Star's time-shrunken arm. "Let's go by the station hospital. I want to look at our patients there—and you need a shot of Giles' serum."

I stood alone in the drum as they all turned to go, the taste of triumph strangely flat. Nowhere Near was safe again and still my own command—though now our task was done. Interstellar communication would be open now. We could report to sector base and request relief.

Heavy at heart, I stood watching Lilith. Here in our own native space and time, her weapon would work again. She was once more a goddess, no longer afraid of the dull cold skull on her finger. With life and death to give, serene in absolute authority, she was leaving me.

I took a step to follow her, but I couldn't chase a goddess. I stopped and let her go, trying not to envy her laughing joke for old Habibula, her thoughtful hand on Ken Star's arm. Woodenly, I turned back to the computer.

After all, I had enough to keep me busy. Nowhere Near had lost air and suffered damage. The blast area had to be decontaminated. The wrecked atomic plant had to be inspected. Interstellar communication had to be restored. I had to keep us all still alive, while we waited for relief.

"Lars—" I heard Lilith's voice, choked and high. "Did you think—did you think I didn't need you now?"

I turned and saw her coming back to me, flying across that low-G space like a white and graceful bird. I caught her in my trembling arms, warm and quick and wonderful. Tears shining in her wide bronze eyes, she clung to me desperately, more girl now than goddess. I held her hard, and kissed the white distress from her face, knowing now that she needed me.